The Collected
Max Carrados Investigations

The Collected
Max Carrados Investigations
The Cases of the Renowned Blind
Edwardian Detective

Ernest Bramah

LEONAUR

The Collected Max Carrados Investigations
The Cases of the Renowned Blind Edwardian Detective
by Ernest Bramah

FIRST EDITION

Leonaur is an imprint
of Oakpast Ltd

ISBN: 978-1-78282-209-7 (hardcover)
ISBN: 978-1-78282-210-3 (softcover)

http://www.leonaur.com

Publisher's Notes

Contents

Introduction

In offering a series of stories which continue the adventures of a group of characters already introduced to the reading public, a writer is inevitably at a certain disadvantage. In contriving their first appearance he has been able to select both the occasion and the moment which lend themselves most effectively to his plan. He has begun at the beginning—or, at least, at what, so far as you and he and the tale he has to tell are concerned, must be accepted as the beginning. Buttonholing you at the intersection of these three lines of destiny he has, in effect, exclaimed: My dear Reader! the very man I wished to see. I want to introduce rather a remarkable character to you—Max Carrados, whom you see approaching. You will notice that he is blind—quite blind; but so far from that crippling his interests in life or his energies, it has merely impelled him to develop those senses which in most of us lie half dormant and practically unused. Thus you will understand that while he may be at a disadvantage when you are at an advantage, he is at an advantage when you are at a disadvantage. The alert, slightly spoffish gentleman with the knowing look, who accompanies him, is his friend Carlyle. He has a private inquiry business now; formerly he was a solicitor, but... (here the voice becomes discreetly inaudible). . . . and having run up across Carrados again. . . . And so on.

This is well enough once, but it should not be repeated. One cannot begin at the beginning twice. In any case, it does not dispose of an obvious dilemma: those among prospective readers who are acquainted with the first book do not need to be informed of the how, when and wherefore of Carrados and his associates; those who are not so acquainted (possibly even a larger class) do need to be informed, and may resent the omission. In the circumstances a word of explanation where it can conveniently be avoided seems to offer the least harmful course.

Max Carrados was published in the spring of 1914. It consisted of eight tales, each separate and complete in itself, but connected (as are the nine of the present volume) by the central figure of Carrados. The first story, *The Coin of Dionysius*, cleared the necessary ground. Carlyle, a private inquiry agent, who has descended in the social scale owing to an irregularity—an indiscretion rather than a crime—is very desirous one evening of testing the genuineness of a certain rare and valuable Sicilian *tetradrachm*, for upon its authenticity an immediate arrest depends. It is too late at night for him to get in touch with expert professional opinion, but finally he is referred to a certain gifted amateur, a Mr Max Carrados, who lives at Richmond. To Richmond he accordingly proceeds, and is at once recognised by Carrados as a former friend, Calling by name. The recognition is not at first mutual, for Carrados has also changed his name—he was formerly Max Wynn— in order to qualify for a considerable fortune, and he, like Carlyle, has altered in appearance with passing years. More to the point, he has become blind: "Literally. . . I was riding along a bridle-path through a wood about a dozen years ago with a friend.

He was in front. At one point a twig sprang back— you know how easily a thing like that happens. It just flicked my eye—nothing to think twice about. . . . . It is called *amaurosis*."

Carlyle fails to recognise Carrados because the latter is an altered personality, with a different name, and living in unexpected circumstances, but to the blind man the change in Carlyle is negligible against the identity of a remembered voice. They talk of old times and of present times. Carlyle explains his business, and Carrados confesses that the idea of criminal investigation has always attracted him. Even yet, he thinks, he might not be entirely out at it, for blindness has unexpected compensations: "A new world to explore, new experiences, new powers awakening; strange new perceptions; life in the fourth dimension."

Not regarding the suggestion of co-operation seriously, Carlyle puts the offer aside, but, later, Carrados returns to it again. Then the private detective remembers the object of his visit, the meanwhile forgotten coin, and to settle the matter, and to demonstrate to Carrados his helplessness (for the idea of the blind man being an expert must, of course, have been someone's blunder), he slyly offers to put his friend on the track of a mystery. "Yes," he accordingly replied, with crisp deliberation, as he recrossed the room; "yes, I will, Max. Here is the clue to what seems to be a rather remarkable fraud." He put the *tetradrachm* into his host's hand. "What do you make of it?" For a few seconds Carrados handled the piece with the delicate manipulation of his finger-tips, while Carlyle looked on with a self-appreciative grin. Then with equal gravity the blind man weighed the coin in the balance of his hand. Finally he touched it with his tongue.

"Well?" demanded the other.

"Of course I have not much to go on, and if I was more fully in your confidence I might come to another conclusion "

"Yes, yes," interposed Carlyle, with amused encouragement.

"Then I should advise you to arrest the parlour-maid, Nina Brun, communicate with the police authorities of Padua for particulars of the career of Helene Brunesi, and suggest to Lord Seastoke that he should return to London to see what further depredations have been made in his cabinet."

Mr Carlyle's groping hand sought and found a chair, on which he dropped blankly. His eyes were unable to detach themselves for a single moment from the very ordinary spectacle of Mr Carrados's mildly benevolent face, while the sterilised ghost of his now forgotten amusement still lingered about his features.

"Good heavens!" he managed to articulate, "how do you know?"

"Isn't that what you wanted of me?" asked Carrados suavely.

"Don't humbug, Max," said Carlyle severely. "This is no joke." An undefined mistrust of his own powers suddenly possessed him in the presence of this mystery. "How do you come to know of Nina Brun and Lord Seastoke?"

"You are a detective, Louis," replied Carrados. "How does one know these things?"

The bottom having been thus knocked out of his objection, Carlyle has no option but to promise Carrados the reversion of "the next murder" that comes his way. Actually, it is a case involving thirty-five murders that redeems this pledge.

But in spite of every device of Carrados's perspicuity there is still the cardinal deficiency that he cannot see. Whatever remains outside the range of four supertrained senses, aided by that subtle and elusive perception (every man in odd moments has surprised his own mind in the act of throwing out faint-spun and wholly forgotten tentacles of search towards it) called in vague ignorance the "sixth sense"—all beyond these must be for ever a *terra incognita* to his knowledge. To remedy this he has a personal attendant called Parkinson. Carlyle ingenuously falls into a proposed test that Carrados suggests—his powers of observation against those of Parkinson. When it comes to actual specified details the visitor finds that he only has a loose and general idea of the appearance of the man who has admitted him. On the other hand, when Parkinson is called up he is able to run off a precise and categorical description of Mr Carlyle—although his period of observation had certainly not been the more favourable—from the size and material of the caller's boots, with a button missing from the left foot, to the fashion and fabric of his watch-chain. A very ordinary man of strictly limited ability, he has, in fact, trained this one faculty of detailed observation and retention to supply his master's need.

These three men—Carrados, Carlyle and Parkinson—are the only characters of any prominence who are carried over from the first book to the second. An Inspector Beedel makes an occasional and unimportant appearance in both. In the story called *The Mystery of the Poisoned Dish of Mushrooms* a Mrs Bellmark (niece to Carlyle) will be met; she is the lady whose acquaintance Carrados formed in "The Comedy at Fountain Cottage," when a very opportune buried treasure was unearthed in her suburban garden. Every generation not unnaturally "fancies itself," and whatever is happening is therefore somewhat more wonderful than anything that has ever happened before.

But for this present age there is, of course, a special reason why the exploits of the sightless obtain prominence, and why every inch won in the narrowing of the gulf between the seeing and the blind is hailed almost with the satisfaction of a martial victory. That the general condition of the blind is being raised, that they are, in the mass, more capable and infinitely less dependent than at any period of the past, is undeniable, and these things are plainly to the good; but when we think that blind men individually do more surprising feats and carry themselves more confidently in their blindness than has ever been done before, we deceive ourselves, in the superficiality that is common to the times. The higher capacity under blindness is a form of genius and, like other kinds of genius, it is not the prerogative of any century or of any system.

Judged by this standard, Max Carrados is by no means a superblind man, and although for convenience the qualities of more than one blind prototype may have been collected within a single frame, on the other hand literary licence must be judged to have its limits, and many of the realities of fact have been deemed too improbable to be transferred to fiction. Carrados's opening exploit, that of accurately deciding an antique coin to be a forgery, by the sense of touch, is far from being unprecedented.

The curious and the incredulous may be referred to a little book, first published in 1820. This is entitled *Biography of the Blind*, or the *Lives of such as have distinguished themselves as Poets, Philosophers, Artists, &c.*, and it is by James Wilson, "Who has been Blind from his Infancy." From the authorities given (they are stated in every case), it is obvious that these lives and anecdotes are available elsewhere, but probably in no other single volume is so much that is informing and entertaining on this one subject brought together. The coin incident finds its warrant in the biography of Nicholas Saunderson, LL.D., F.R.S., who was born in Yorkshire in the year 1682. When about twelve months old he lost not only his sight but the eyes themselves from an attack of smallpox.

In 1707 he proceeded to Cambridge, where he appears to have made some stir; at all events he was given his M.A. in 1711 by a special process and immediately afterwards elected Lucasian Professor of Mathematics. Of his lighter qualities Wilson says: "He could with great nicety and exactness perceive the smallest degree of roughness, or defect of polish, on a surface; thus, in a set of Roman medals he distinguished the genuine from the false, though they had been counterfeited with such exactness as to deceive a connoisseur who had judged from the eye. By the sense of touch also, he distinguished the least variation; and he has been seen in a garden, when observations were making on the sun, to take notice of every cloud that interrupted the observation, almost as justly as others could see it. He could also tell when anything was held near his face, or when he passed by a tree at no great distance, merely from the different impulse of the air on his face.

His ear was also equally exact; he could readily distinguish the fourth part of a note by the quickness of this sense; and could judge of the size of a room, and of his distance from the wall. And if he ever walked over a pavement in courts or *piazzas* which reflected sound, and was afterwards conducted thither again, he could tell in what part of the walk he had stood, merely by the note it sounded."

The Coin of Dionysius
A.k.a. *The Master Coiner Unmasked*

It was eight o'clock at night and raining, scarcely a time when a business so limited in its clientele as that of a coin dealer could hope to attract any customer, but a light was still showing in the small shop that bore over its window the name of Baxter, and in the even smaller office at the back the proprietor himself sat reading the latest *Pall Mall*. His enterprise seemed to be justified, for presently the door bell gave its announcement, and throwing down his paper Mr Baxter went forward.

As a matter of fact the dealer had been expecting someone and his manner as he passed into the shop was unmistakably suggestive of a caller of importance. But at the first glance towards his visitor the excess of deference melted out of his bearing, leaving the urbane, self-possessed shopman in the presence of the casual customer.

"Mr Baxter, I think?" said the latter. He had laid aside his dripping umbrella and was unbuttoning overcoat and coat to reach an inner pocket. "You hardly remember me, I suppose? Mr Carlyle—two years ago I took up a case for you——"

"To be sure. Mr Carlyle, the private detective——"

"Inquiry agent," corrected Mr Carlyle precisely.

"Well," smiled Mr Baxter, "for that matter I am a coin dealer and not an antiquarian or a numismatist. Is there anything in that way that I can do for you?"

"Yes," replied his visitor; "it is my turn to consult you." He had taken a small wash-leather bag from the inner pocket and now turned something carefully out upon the counter. "What can you tell me about that?"

The dealer gave the coin a moment's scrutiny.

"There is no question about this," he replied. "It is a Sicilian *tet-*

13

radrachm of Dionysius."

"Yes, I know that—I have it on the label out of the cabinet. I can tell you further that it's supposed to be one that Lord Seastoke gave two hundred and fifty pounds for at the Brice sale in '94."

"It seems to me that you can tell me more about it than I can tell you," remarked Mr Baxter. "What is it that you really want to know?"

"I want to know," replied Mr Carlyle, "whether it is genuine or not."

"Has any doubt been cast upon it?"

"Certain circumstances raised a suspicion—that is all."

The dealer took another look at the *tetradrachm* through his magnifying glass, holding it by the edge with the careful touch of an expert. Then he shook his head slowly in a confession of ignorance.

"Of course I could make a guess——"

"No, don't," interrupted Mr Carlyle hastily. "An arrest hangs on it and nothing short of certainty is any good to me."

"Is that so, Mr Carlyle?" said Mr Baxter, with increased interest. "Well, to be quite candid, the thing is out of my line. Now if it was a rare Saxon penny or a doubtful noble I'd stake my reputation on my opinion, but I do very little in the classical series."

Mr Carlyle did not attempt to conceal his disappointment as he returned the coin to the bag and replaced the bag in the inner pocket.

"I had been relying on you," he grumbled reproachfully. "Where on earth am I to go now?"

"There is always the British Museum."

"Ah, to be sure, thanks. But will anyone who can tell me be there now?"

"Now? No fear!" replied Mr Baxter. "Go round in the morning——"

"But I must know tonight," explained the visitor, reduced to despair again. "Tomorrow will be too late for the purpose."

Mr Baxter did not hold out much encouragement in the circumstances.

"You can scarcely expect to find anyone at business now," he remarked. "I should have been gone these two hours myself only I happened to have an appointment with an American millionaire who fixed his own time." Something indistinguishable from a wink slid off Mr Baxter's right eye. "Offmunson he's called, and a bright young pedigree-hunter has traced his descent from Offa, King of Mercia.

14

So he—quite naturally—wants a set of Offas as a sort of collateral proof."

"Very interesting," murmured Mr Carlyle, fidgeting with his watch. "I should love an hour's chat with you about your millionaire customers—some other time. Just now—look here, Baxter, can't you give me a line of introduction to some dealer in this sort of thing who happens to live in town? You must know dozens of experts."

"Why, bless my soul, Mr Carlyle, I don't know a man of them away from his business," said Mr Baxter, staring. "They may live in Park Lane or they may live in Petticoat Lane for all I know. Besides, there aren't so many experts as you seem to imagine. And the two best will very likely quarrel over it. You've had to do with 'expert witnesses,' I suppose?"

"I don't want a witness; there will be no need to give evidence. All I want is an absolutely authoritative pronouncement that I can act on. Is there no one who can really say whether the thing is genuine or not?"

Mr Baxter's meaning silence became cynical in its implication as he continued to look at his visitor across the counter. Then he relaxed.

"Stay a bit; there is a man—an amateur—I remember hearing wonderful things about some time ago. They say he really does know."

"There you are," exclaimed Mr Carlyle, much relieved. "There always is someone. Who is he?"

"Funny name," replied Baxter. "Something Wynn or Wynn something." He craned his neck to catch sight of an important motor car that was drawing to the kerb before his window. "Wynn Carrados! You'll excuse me now, Mr Carlyle, won't you? This looks like Mr Offmunson."

Mr Carlyle hastily scribbled the name down on his cuff.

"Wynn Carrados, right. Where does he live?"

"Haven't the remotest idea," replied Baxter, referring the arrangement of his tie to the judgment of the wall mirror. "I have never seen the man myself. Now, Mr Carlyle, I'm sorry I can't do any more for you. You won't mind, will you?"

Mr Carlyle could not pretend to misunderstand. He enjoyed the distinction of holding open the door for the transatlantic representative of the line of Offa as he went out, and then made his way through the muddy streets back to his office. There was only one way of tracing a private individual at such short notice—through the pages of the directories, and the gentleman did not flatter himself by a very high estimate of his chances.

Fortune favoured him, however. He very soon discovered a Wynn Carrados living at Richmond, and, better still, further search failed to unearth another. There was, apparently, only one householder at all events of that name in the neighbourhood of London. He jotted down the address and set out for Richmond.

The house was some distance from the station, Mr Carlyle learned. He took a taxicab and drove, dismissing the vehicle at the gate. He prided himself on his power of observation and the accuracy of the deductions which resulted from it—a detail of his business. "It's nothing more than using one's eyes and putting two and two together," he would modestly declare, when he wished to be deprecatory rather than impressive, and by the time he had reached the front door of "The Turrets" he had formed some opinion of the position and tastes of the man who lived there.

A man-servant admitted Mr Carlyle and took in his card—his private card with the bare request for an interview that would not detain Mr Carrados for ten minutes. Luck still favoured him; Mr Carrados was at home and would see him at once. The servant, the hall through which they passed, and the room into which he was shown, all contributed something to the deductions which the quietly observant gentleman was half unconsciously recording.

"Mr Carlyle," announced the servant.

The room was a library or study. The only occupant, a man of about Carlyle's own age, had been using a typewriter up to the moment of his visitor's entrance. He now turned and stood up with an expression of formal courtesy.

"It's very good of you to see me at this hour," apologised the caller.

The conventional expression of Mr Carrados's face changed a little.

"Surely my man has got your name wrong?" he exclaimed. "Isn't it Louis Calling?"

The visitor stopped short and his agreeable smile gave place to a sudden flash of anger or annoyance.

"No, sir," he replied stiffly. "My name is on the card which you have before you."

"I beg your pardon," said Mr Carrados, with perfect good-humour. "I hadn't seen it. But I used to know a Calling some years ago—at St Michael's."

"St Michael's!" Mr Carlyle's features underwent another change, no less instant and sweeping than before. "St Michael's! Wynn Carrados? Good heavens! it isn't Max Wynn—old 'Winning' Wynn?"

"A little older and a little fatter—yes," replied Carrados. "I *have* changed my name, you see."

"Extraordinary thing meeting like this," said his visitor, dropping into a chair and staring hard at Mr Carrados. "I have changed more than my name. How did you recognise me?"

"The voice," replied Carrados. "It took me back to that little smoke-dried attic den of yours where we——"

"My God!" exclaimed Carlyle bitterly, "don't remind me of what we were going to do in those days." He looked round the well-furnished, handsome room and recalled the other signs of wealth that he had noticed. "At all events, you seem fairly comfortable, Wynn."

"I am alternately envied and pitied," replied Carrados, with a placid tolerance of circumstance that seemed characteristic of him. "Still, as you say, I am fairly comfortable."

"Envied, I can understand. But why are you pitied?"

"Because I am blind," was the tranquil reply.

"Blind!" exclaimed Mr Carlyle, using his own eyes superlatively. "Do you mean—literally blind?"

"Literally. . . . I was riding along a bridle-path through a wood about a dozen years ago with a friend. He was in front. At one point a twig sprang back—you know how easily a thing like that happens. It just flicked my eye—nothing to think twice about."

"And that blinded you?"

"Yes, ultimately. It's called *amaurosis*."

"I can scarcely believe it. You seem so sure and self-reliant. Your eyes are full of expression—only a little quieter than they used to be. I believe you were typing when I came. . . . Aren't you having me?"

"You miss the dog and the stick?" smiled Carrados. "No; it's a fact."

"What an awful infliction for you, Max. You were always such an impulsive, reckless sort of fellow—never quiet. You must miss such a fearful lot."

"Has anyone else recognised you?" asked Carrados quietly.

"Ah, that was the voice, you said," replied Carlyle.

"Yes; but other people heard the voice as well. Only I had no blundering, self-confident eyes to be hoodwinked."

"That's a rum way of putting it," said Carlyle. "Are your ears never hoodwinked, may I ask?"

"Not now. Nor my fingers. Nor any of my other senses that have to look out for themselves."

"Well, well," murmured Mr Carlyle, cut short in his sympathetic emotions. "I'm glad you take it so well. Of course, if you find it an advantage to be blind, old man——" He stopped and reddened. "I beg your pardon," he concluded stiffly.

"Not an advantage perhaps," replied the other thoughtfully. "Still it has compensations that one might not think of. A new world to explore, new experiences, new powers awakening; strange new perceptions; life in the fourth dimension. But why do you beg my pardon, Louis?"

"I am an ex-solicitor, struck off in connexion with the falsifying of a trust account, Mr Carrados," replied Carlyle, rising.

"Sit down, Louis," said Carrados suavely. His face, even his incredibly living eyes, beamed placid good-nature. "The chair on which you will sit, the roof above you, all the comfortable surroundings to which you have so amiably alluded, are the direct result of falsifying a trust account. But do I call you 'Mr Carlyle' in consequence? Certainly not, Louis."

"I did not falsify the account," cried Carlyle hotly. He sat down, however, and added more quietly: "But why do I tell you all this? I have never spoken of it before."

"Blindness invites confidence," replied Carrados. "We are out of the running—human rivalry ceases to exist. Besides, why shouldn't you? In my case the account *was* falsified."

"Of course that's all bunkum, Max," commented Carlyle. "Still, I appreciate your motive."

"Practically everything I possess was left to me by an American cousin, on the condition that I took the name of Carrados. He made his fortune by an ingenious conspiracy of doctoring the crop reports and unloading favourably in consequence. And I need hardly remind you that the receiver is equally guilty with the thief."

"But twice as safe. I know something of that, Max. . . . Have you any idea what my business is?"

"You shall tell me," replied Carrados.

"I run a private inquiry agency. When I lost my profession I had to do something for a living. This occurred. I dropped my name, changed my appearance and opened an office. I knew the legal side down to the ground and I got a retired Scotland Yard man to organise the outside work."

"Excellent!" cried Carrados. "Do you unearth many murders?"

"No," admitted Mr Carlyle; "our business lies mostly on the conventional lines among divorce and defalcation."

"That's a pity," remarked Carrados. "Do you know, Louis, I always had a secret ambition to be a detective myself. I have even thought lately that I might still be able to do something at it if the chance came my way. That makes you smile?"

"Well, certainly, the idea——"

"Yes, the idea of a blind detective—the blind tracking the alert——"

"Of course, as you say, certain faculties are no doubt quickened," Mr Carlyle hastened to add considerately, "but, seriously, with the exception of an artist, I don't suppose there is any man who is more utterly dependent on his eyes."

Whatever opinion Carrados might have held privately, his genial exterior did not betray a shadow of dissent. For a full minute he continued to smoke as though he derived an actual visual enjoyment from the blue sprays that travelled and dispersed across the room. He had already placed before his visitor a box containing cigars of a brand which that gentleman keenly appreciated but generally regarded as unattainable, and the matter-of-fact ease and certainty with which the blind man had brought the box and put it before him had sent a questioning flicker through Carlyle's mind.

"You used to be rather fond of art yourself, Louis," he remarked presently. "Give me your opinion of my latest purchase—the bronze lion on the cabinet there." Then, as Carlyle's gaze went about the room, he added quickly: "No, not that cabinet—the one on your left."

Carlyle shot a sharp glance at his host as he got up, but Carrados's expression was merely benignly complacent. Then he strolled across to the figure.

"Very nice," he admitted. "Late Flemish, isn't it?"

"No. It is a copy of Vidal's 'Roaring lion.'"

"Vidal?"

"A French artist." The voice became indescribably flat. "He, also, had the misfortune to be blind, by the way."

"You old humbug, Max!" shrieked Carlyle, "you've been thinking that out for the last five minutes." Then the unfortunate man bit his lip and turned his back towards his host.

"Do you remember how we used to pile it up on that obtuse

19

ass Sanders and then roast him?" asked Carrados, ignoring the half-smothered exclamation with which the other man had recalled himself.

"Yes," replied Carlyle quietly. "This is very good," he continued, addressing himself to the bronze again. "How ever did he do it?"

"With his hands."

"Naturally. But, I mean, how did he study his model?"

"Also with his hands. He called it 'seeing near.'"

"Even with a lion—handled it?"

"In such cases he required the services of a keeper, who brought the animal to bay while Vidal exercised his own particular gifts....You don't feel inclined to put me on the track of a mystery, Louis?"

Unable to regard this request as anything but one of old Max's unquenchable pleasantries, Mr Carlyle was on the point of making a suitable reply when a sudden thought caused him to smile knowingly. Up to that point he had, indeed, completely forgotten the object of his visit. Now that he remembered the doubtful Dionysius and Mr Baxter's recommendation he immediately assumed that some mistake had been made. Either Max was not the Wynn Carrados he had been seeking or else the dealer had been misinformed; for although his host was wonderfully expert in the face of his misfortune, it was inconceivable that he could decide the genuineness of a coin without seeing it. The opportunity seemed a good one of getting even with Carrados by taking him at his word.

"Yes," he accordingly replied, with crisp deliberation, as he re-crossed the room; "yes, I will, Max. Here is the clue to what seems to be a rather remarkable fraud." He put the *tetradrachm* into his host's hand. "What do you make of it?"

For a few seconds Carrados handled the piece with the delicate manipulation of his finger-tips while Carlyle looked on with a self-appreciative grin. Then with equal gravity the blind man weighed the coin in the balance of his hand. Finally he touched it with his tongue.

"Well?" demanded the other.

"Of course I have not much to go on, and if I was more fully in your confidence I might come to another conclusion——"

"Yes, yes," interposed Carlyle, with amused encouragement.

"Then I should advise you to arrest the parlour-maid, Nina Brun, communicate with the police authorities of Padua for particulars of the career of Helene Brunesi, and suggest to Lord Seastoke that he should return to London to see what further depredations have been made in his cabinet."

Mr Carlyle's groping hand sought and found a chair, on to which he dropped blankly. His eyes were unable to detach themselves for a single moment from the very ordinary spectacle of Mr Carrados's mildly benevolent face, while the sterilised ghost of his now forgotten amusement still lingered about his features.

"Good heavens!" he managed to articulate, "how do you know?"

"Isn't that what you wanted of me?" asked Carrados suavely.

"Don't humbug, Max," said Carlyle severely. "This is no joke." An undefined mistrust of his own powers suddenly possessed him in the presence of this mystery. "How do you come to know of Nina Brun and Lord Seastoke?"

"You are a detective, Louis," replied Carrados. "How does one know these things? By using one's eyes and putting two and two together."

Carlyle groaned and flung out an arm petulantly.

"Is it all bunkum, Max? Do you really see all the time—though that doesn't go very far towards explaining it."

"Like Vidal, I see very well—at close quarters," replied Carrados, lightly running a forefinger along the inscription on the *tetradrachm*. "For longer range I keep another pair of eyes. Would you like to test them?"

Mr Carlyle's assent was not very gracious; it was, in fact, faintly sulky. He was suffering the annoyance of feeling distinctly unimpressive in his own department; but he was also curious.

"The bell is just behind you, if you don't mind," said his host. "Parkinson will appear. You might take note of him while he is in."

The man who had admitted Mr Carlyle proved to be Parkinson.

"This gentleman is Mr Carlyle, Parkinson," explained Carrados the moment the man entered. "You will remember him for the future?"

Parkinson's apologetic eye swept the visitor from head to foot, but so lightly and swiftly that it conveyed to that gentleman the comparison of being very deftly dusted.

"I will endeavour to do so, sir," replied Parkinson, turning again to his master.

"I shall be at home to Mr Carlyle whenever he calls. That is all."

"Very well, sir."

"Now, Louis," remarked Mr Carrados briskly, when the door had closed again, "you have had a good opportunity of studying Parkinson.

What is he like?"

"In what way?"

"I mean as a matter of description. I am a blind man—I haven't seen my servant for twelve years—what idea can you give me of him? I asked you to notice."

"I know you did, but your Parkinson is the sort of man who has very little about him to describe. He is the embodiment of the ordinary. His height is about average——"

"Five feet nine," murmured Carrados. "Slightly above the mean."

"Scarcely noticeably so. Clean-shaven. Medium brown hair. No particularly marked features. Dark eyes. Good teeth."

"False," interposed Carrados. "The teeth—not the statement."

"Possibly," admitted Mr Carlyle. "I am not a dental expert and I had no opportunity of examining Mr Parkinson's mouth in detail. But what is the drift of all this?"

"His clothes?"

"Oh, just the ordinary evening dress of a valet. There is not much room for variety in that."

"You noticed, in fact, nothing special by which Parkinson could be identified?"

"Well, he wore an unusually broad gold ring on the little finger of the left hand."

"But that is removable. And yet Parkinson has an ineradicable mole—a small one, I admit—on his chin. And you a human sleuth-hound. Oh, Louis!"

"At all events," retorted Carlyle, writhing a little under this good-humoured satire, although it was easy enough to see in it Carrados's affectionate intention—"at all events, I dare say I can give as good a description of Parkinson as he can give of me."

"That is what we are going to test. Ring the bell again."

"Seriously?"

"Quite. I am trying my eyes against yours. If I can't give you fifty out of a hundred I'll renounce my private detectorial ambition for ever."

"It isn't quite the same," objected Carlyle, but he rang the bell.

"Come in and close the door, Parkinson," said Carrados when the man appeared. "Don't look at Mr Carlyle again—in fact, you had better stand with your back towards him, he won't mind. Now describe to me his appearance as you observed it."

Parkinson tendered his respectful apologies to Mr Carlyle for the liberty he was compelled to take, by the deferential quality of his voice.

"Mr Carlyle, sir, wears patent leather boots of about size seven and very little used. There are five buttons, but on the left boot one button—the third up—is missing, leaving loose threads and not the more usual metal fastener. Mr Carlyle's trousers, sir, are of a dark material, a dark grey line of about a quarter of an inch width on a darker ground. The bottoms are turned permanently up and are, just now, a little muddy, if I may say so."

"Very muddy," interposed Mr Carlyle generously. "It is a wet night, Parkinson."

"Yes, sir; very unpleasant weather. If you will allow me, sir, I will brush you in the hall. The mud is dry now, I notice. Then, sir," continued Parkinson, reverting to the business in hand, "there are dark green cashmere hose. A curb-pattern key-chain passes into the left-hand trouser pocket."

From the visitor's nether garments the photographic-eyed Parkinson proceeded to higher ground, and with increasing wonder Mr Carlyle listened to the faithful catalogue of his possessions. His fetter-and-link albert of gold and platinum was minutely described. His spotted blue ascot, with its gentlemanly pearl scarf-pin, was set forth, and the fact that the buttonhole in the left lapel of his morning coat showed signs of use was duly noted. What Parkinson saw he recorded but he made no deductions. A handkerchief carried in the cuff of the right sleeve was simply that to him and not an indication that Mr Carlyle was, indeed, left-handed.

But a more delicate part of Parkinson's undertaking remained. He approached it with a double cough.

"As regards Mr Carlyle's personal appearance; sir——"

"No, enough!" cried the gentleman concerned hastily. "I am more than satisfied. You are a keen observer, Parkinson."

"I have trained myself to suit my master's requirements, sir," replied the man. He looked towards Mr Carrados, received a nod and withdrew.

Mr Carlyle was the first to speak.

"That man of yours would be worth five pounds a week to me, Max," he remarked thoughtfully. "But, of course——"

"I don't think that he would take it," replied Carrados, in a voice of equally detached speculation. "He suits me very well. But you have the chance of using his services—indirectly."

"You still mean that—seriously?"

"I notice in you a chronic disinclination to take me seriously, Louis. It is really—to an Englishman—almost painful. Is there something inherently comic about me or the atmosphere of The Turrets?"

"No, my friend," replied Mr Carlyle, "but there is something essentially prosperous. That is what points to the improbable. Now what is it?"

"It might be merely a whim, but it is more than that," replied Carrados. "It is, well, partly vanity, partly *ennui*, partly"—certainly there was something more nearly tragic in his voice than comic now—"partly hope."

Mr Carlyle was too tactful to pursue the subject.

"Those are three tolerable motives," he acquiesced. "I'll do anything you want, Max, on one condition."

"Agreed. And it is?"

"That you tell me how you knew so much of this affair." He tapped the silver coin which lay on the table near them. "I am not easily flabbergasted," he added.

"You won't believe that there is nothing to explain—that it was purely second-sight?"

"No," replied Carlyle tersely; "I won't."

"You are quite right. And yet the thing is very simple."

"They always are—when you know," soliloquised the other. "That's what makes them so confoundedly difficult when you don't."

"Here is this one then. In Padua, which seems to be regaining its old reputation as the birthplace of spurious antiques, by the way, there lives an ingenious craftsman named Pietro Stelli. This simple soul, who possesses a talent not inferior to that of Cavino at his best, has for many years turned his hand to the not unprofitable occupation of forging rare Greek and Roman coins. As a collector and student of certain Greek colonials and a specialist in forgeries I have been familiar with Stelli's workmanship for years. Latterly he seems to have come under the influence of an international crook called—at the moment—Dompierre, who soon saw a way of utilizing Stelli's genius on a royal scale. Helene Brunesi, who in private life is—and really is, I believe—Madame Dompierre, readily lent her services to the enterprise."

"Quite so," nodded Mr Carlyle, as his host paused.

"You see the whole sequence, of course?"

"Not exactly—not in detail," confessed Mr Carlyle.

"Dompierre's idea was to gain access to some of the most celebrated cabinets of Europe and substitute Stelli's fabrications for the genuine coins. The princely collection of rarities that he would thus amass might be difficult to dispose of safely but I have no doubt that he had matured his plans. Helene, in the person of Nina Bran, an Anglicised French parlour-maid—a part which she fills to perfection—was to obtain wax impressions of the most valuable pieces and to make the exchange when the counterfeits reached her. In this way it was obviously hoped that the fraud would not come to light until long after the real coins had been sold, and I gather that she has already done her work successfully in several houses. Then, impressed by her excellent references and capable manner, my housekeeper engaged her, and for a few weeks she went about her duties here. It was fatal to this detail of the scheme, however, that I have the misfortune to be blind. I am told that Helene has so innocently angelic a face as to disarm suspicion, but I was incapable of being impressed and that good material was thrown away.

"But one morning my material fingers—which, of course, knew nothing of Helene's angelic face—discovered an unfamiliar touch about the surface of my favourite Euclideas, and, although there was doubtless nothing to be seen, my critical sense of smell reported that wax had been recently pressed against it. I began to make discreet inquiries and in the meantime my cabinets went to the local bank for safety. Helene countered by receiving a telegram from Angiers, calling her to the death-bed of her aged mother. The aged mother succumbed; duty compelled Helene to remain at the side of her stricken patriarchal father, and doubtless The Turrets was written off the syndicate's operations as a bad debt."

"Very interesting," admitted Mr Carlyle; "but at the risk of seeming obtuse"—his manner had become delicately chastened—"I must say that I fail to trace the inevitable connexion between Nina Brun and this particular forgery—assuming that it is a forgery."

"Set your mind at rest about that, Louis," replied Carrados. "It is a forgery, and it is a forgery that none but Pietro Stelli could have achieved. That is the essential connexion. Of course, there are accessories. A private detective coming urgently to see me with a notable *tetradrachm* in his pocket, which he announces to be the clue to a remarkable fraud—well, really, Louis, one scarcely needs to be blind to see through that."

"And Lord Seastoke? I suppose you happened to discover that

Nina Brun had gone there?"

"No, I cannot claim to have discovered that, or I should certainly have warned him at once when I found out—only recently—about the gang. As a matter of fact, the last information I had of Lord Seastoke was a line in yesterday's *Morning Post* to the effect that he was still at Cairo. But many of these pieces——" He brushed his finger almost lovingly across the vivid chariot race that embellished the reverse of the coin, and broke off to remark: "You really ought to take up the subject, Louis. You have no idea how useful it might prove to you some day."

"I really think I must," replied Carlyle grimly. "Two hundred and fifty pounds the original of this cost, I believe."

"Cheap, too; it would make five hundred pounds in New York today. As I was saying, many are literally unique. This gem by Kimon is—here is his signature, you see; Peter is particularly good at lettering—and as I handled the genuine *tetradrachm* about two years ago, when Lord Seastoke exhibited it at a meeting of our society in Albemarle Street, there is nothing at all wonderful in my being able to fix the locale of your mystery. Indeed, I feel that I ought to apologize for it all being so simple."

"I think," remarked Mr Carlyle, critically examining the loose threads on his left boot, "that the apology on that head would be more appropriate from me."

The Knight's Cross Signal Problem

A.k.a *The Mystery of the Signals*

"Louis," exclaimed Mr Carrados, with the air of genial gaiety that Carlyle had found so incongruous to his conception of a blind man, "you have a mystery somewhere about you! I know it by your step."

Nearly a month had passed since the incident of the false Dionysius had led to the two men meeting. It was now December. Whatever Mr Carlyle's step might indicate to the inner eye it betokened to the casual observer the manner of a crisp, alert, self-possessed man of business. Carlyle, in truth, betrayed nothing of the pessimism and despondency that had marked him on the earlier occasion.

"You have only yourself to thank that it is a very poor one," he retorted. "If you hadn't held me to a hasty promise——"

"To give me an option on the next case that baffled you, no matter what it was——"

"Just so. The consequence is that you get a very unsatisfactory affair that has no special interest to an amateur and is only baffling because it is—well——"

"Well, baffling?"

"Exactly, Max. Your would-be jest has discovered the proverbial truth. I need hardly tell you that it is only the insoluble that is finally baffling and this is very probably insoluble. You remember the awful smash on the Central and Suburban at Knight's Cross Station a few weeks ago?"

"Yes," replied Carrados, with interest. "I read the whole ghastly details at the time."

"You read?" exclaimed his friend suspiciously.

"I still use the familiar phrases," explained Carrados, with a smile. "As a matter of fact, my secretary reads to me. I mark what I want to hear and when he comes at ten o'clock we clear off the morning

27

papers in no time."

"And how do you know what to mark?" demanded Mr Carlyle cunningly.

Carrados's right hand, lying idly on the table, moved to a news-paper near. He ran his finger along a column heading, his eyes still turned towards his visitor.

"'The Money Market. Continued from page 2. British Railways,'" he announced.

"Extraordinary," murmured Carlyle.

"Not very," said Carrados. "If someone dipped a stick in treacle and wrote 'Rats' across a marble slab you would probably be able to distinguish what was there, blindfold."

"Probably," admitted Mr Carlyle. "At all events we will not test the experiment."

"The difference to you of treacle on a marble background is scarce-ly greater than that of printers' ink on newspaper to me. But anything smaller than *pica* I do not read with comfort, and below long primer I cannot read at all. Hence the secretary. Now the accident, Louis."

"The accident: well, you remember all about that. An ordinary Central and Suburban passenger train, non-stop at Knight's Cross, ran past the signal and crashed into a crowded electric train that was just beginning to move out. It was like sending a garden roller down a row of hand-lights. Two carriages of the electric train were flattened out of existence; the next two were broken up. For the first time on an English railway there was a good stand-up smash between a heavy steam-engine and a train of light cars, and it was 'bad for the Co.'"

"Twenty-seven killed, forty something injured, eight died since," commented Carrados.

"That was bad for the Co.," said Carlyle. "Well, the main fact was plain enough. The heavy train was in the wrong. But was the engine-driver responsible? He claimed, and he claimed vehemently from the first and he never varied one iota, that he had a 'clear' signal—that is to say, the green light, it being dark. The signalman concerned was equally dogged that he never pulled off the signal—that it was at 'dan-ger' when the accident happened and that it had been for five minutes before. Obviously, they could not both be right."

"Why, Louis?" asked Mr Carrados smoothly.

"The signal must either have been up or down—red or green."

"Did you ever notice the signals on the Great Northern Railway, Louis?"

"Not particularly. Why?"

"One winterly day, about the year when you and I were concerned in being born, the engine-driver of a Scotch express received the 'clear' from a signal near a little Huntingdon station called Abbots Ripton. He went on and crashed into a goods train and into the thick of the smash a down express mowed its way. Thirteen killed and the usual tale of injured. He was positive that the signal gave him a 'clear'; the signalman was equally confident that he had never pulled it off the 'danger.' Both were right, and yet the signal was in working order. As I said, it was a winterly day; it had been snowing hard and the snow froze and accumulated on the upper edge of the signal arm until its weight bore it down. That is a fact that no fiction writer dare have invented, but to this day every signal on the Great Northern pivots from the centre of the arm instead of from the end, in memory of that snowstorm."

"That came out at the inquest, I presume?" said Mr Carlyle. "We have had the Board of Trade inquiry and the inquest here and no explanation is forthcoming. Everything was in perfect order. It rests between the word of the signalman and the word of the engine-driver—not a jot of direct evidence either way. Which is right?"

"That is what you are going to find out, Louis?" suggested Carrados.

"It is what I am being paid for finding out," admitted Mr Carlyle frankly. "But so far we are just where the inquest left it, and, between ourselves, I candidly can't see an inch in front of my face in the matter."

"Nor can I," said the blind man, with a rather wry smile. "Never mind. The engine-driver is your client, of course?"

"Yes," admitted Carlyle. "But how the deuce did you know?"

"Let us say that your sympathies are enlisted on his behalf. The jury were inclined to exonerate the signalman, weren't they? What has the company done with your man?"

"Both are suspended. Hutchins, the driver, hears that he may probably be given charge of a lavatory at one of the stations. He is a decent, bluff, short-spoken old chap, with his heart in his work. Just now you'll find him at his worst—bitter and suspicious. The thought of swabbing down a lavatory and taking pennies all day is poisoning him."

"Naturally. Well, there we have honest Hutchins: taciturn, a little touchy perhaps, grown grey in the service of the company, and manifesting quite a bulldog-like devotion to his favourite 538."

"Why, that actually was the number of his engine—how do you know it?" demanded Carlyle sharply.

"It was mentioned two or three times at the inquest, Louis," replied Carrados mildly.

"And you remembered—with no reason to?"

"You can generally trust a blind man's memory, especially if he has taken the trouble to develop it."

"Then you will remember that Hutchins did not make a very good impression at the time. He was surly and irritable under the ordeal. I want you to see the case from all sides."

"He called the signalman—Mead—a 'lying young dog,' across the room, I believe. Now, Mead, what is he like? You have seen him, of course?"

"Yes. He does not impress me favourably. He is glib, ingratiating, and distinctly 'greasy.' He has a ready answer for everything almost before the question is out of your mouth. He has thought of everything."

"And now you are going to tell me something, Louis," said Carrados encouragingly.

Mr Carlyle laughed a little to cover an involuntary movement of surprise.

"There is a suggestive line that was not touched at the inquiries," he admitted. "Hutchins has been a saving man all his life, and he has received good wages. Among his class he is regarded as wealthy. I daresay that he has five hundred pounds in the bank. He is a widower with one daughter, a very nice-mannered girl of about twenty. Mead is a young man, and he and the girl are sweethearts—have been informally engaged for some time. But old Hutchins would not hear of it; he seems to have taken a dislike to the signalman from the first and latterly he had forbidden him to come to his house or his daughter to speak to him."

"Excellent, Louis," cried Carrados in great delight. "We shall clear your man in a blaze of red and green lights yet and hang the glib, 'greasy' signalman from his own signal-post."

"It is a significant fact, seriously?"

"It is absolutely convincing."

"It may have been a slip, a mental lapse on Mead's part which he discovered the moment it was too late, and then, being too cowardly to admit his fault, and having so much at stake, he took care to make detection impossible. It may have been that, but my idea is rather that probably it was neither quite pure accident nor pure design. I can imagine Mead meanly pluming himself over the fact that the life of this man who stands in his way, and whom he must cordially dislike, lies in his power. I can imagine the idea becoming an obsession as he dwells on it. A dozen times with his hand on the lever he lets his mind explore the possibilities of a moment's defection. Then one day he pulls the signal off in sheer bravado—and hastily puts it at danger again. He may have done it once or he may have done it oftener before he was caught in a fatal moment of irresolution. The chances are about even that the engine-driver would be killed. In any case he would be disgraced, for it is easier on the face of it to believe that a man might run past a danger signal in absentmindedness, without noticing it, than that a man should pull off a signal and replace it without being conscious of his actions."

"The fireman was killed. Does your theory involve the certainty of the fireman being killed, Louis?"

"No," said Carlyle. "The fireman is a difficulty, but looking at it from Mead's point of view—whether he has been guilty of an error or a crime—it resolves itself into this: First, the fireman may be killed. Second, he may not notice the signal at all. Third, in any case he will loyally corroborate his driver and the good old jury will discount that."

Carrados smoked thoughtfully, his open, sightless eyes merely appearing to be set in a tranquil gaze across the room.

"It would not be an improbable explanation," he said presently. "Ninety-nine men out of a hundred would say: 'People do not do these things.' But you and I, who have in our different ways studied criminology, know that they sometimes do, or else there would be no curious crimes. What have you done on that line?"

To anyone who could see, Mr Carlyle's expression conveyed an answer.

"You are behind the scenes, Max. What was there for me to do? Still I must do something for my money. Well, I have had a very close inquiry made confidentially among the men. There might be a whisper of one of them knowing more than had come out—a man restrained by friendship, or enmity, or even grade jealousy. Nothing came of that. Then there was the remote chance that some private person had noticed the signal without attaching any importance to it then, one who would be able to identify it still by something associated with the time. I went over the line myself. Opposite the signal the line on one side is shut in by a high blank wall; on the other side are houses, but coming below the butt-end of a scullery the signal does not happen to be visible from any road or from any window."

"My poor Louis!" said Carrados, in friendly ridicule. "You were at the end of your tether?"

"I was," admitted Carlyle. "And now that you know the sort of job it is I don't suppose that you are keen on wasting your time over it."

"That would hardly be fair, would it?" said Carrados reasonably. "No, Louis, I will take over your honest old driver and your greasy young signalman and your fatal signal that cannot be seen from anywhere."

"But it is an important point for you to remember, Max, that although the signal cannot be seen from the box, if the mechanism had gone wrong, or anyone tampered with the arm, the automatic indicator would at once have told Mead that the green light was showing. Oh, I have gone very thoroughly into the technical points, I assure you."

"I must do so too," commented Mr Carrados gravely.

"For that matter, if there is anything you want to know, I dare say that I can tell you," suggested his visitor. "It might save your time."

"True," acquiesced Carrados. "I should like to know whether anyone belonging to the houses that bound the line there came of age or got married on the twenty-sixth of November."

Mr Carlyle looked across curiously at his host.

"I really do not know, Max," he replied, in his crisp, precise way. "What on earth has that got to do with it, may I inquire?"

"The only explanation of the Pont St Lin swing-bridge disaster of '75 was the reflection of a green bengal light on a cottage window."

Mr Carlyle smiled his indulgence privately.

"My dear chap, you mustn't let your retentive memory of obscure happenings run away with you," he remarked wisely. "In nine cases out of ten the obvious explanation is the true one. The difficulty, as here, lies in proving it. Now, you would like to see these men?"

"I expect so; in any case, I will see Hutchins first."

"Both live in Holloway. Shall I ask Hutchins to come here to see you—say tomorrow? He is doing nothing."

"No," replied Carrados. "Tomorrow I must call on my brokers and my time may be filled up."

"Quite right; you mustn't neglect your own affairs for this—experiment," assented Carlyle.

"Besides, I should prefer to drop in on Hutchins at his own home. Now, Louis, enough of the honest old man for one night. I have a lovely thing by Eumenes that I want to show you. Today is—Tuesday. Come to dinner on Sunday and pour the vials of your ridicule on my want of success."

"That's an amiable way of putting it," replied Carlyle. "All right, I will."

Two hours later Carrados was again in his study, apparently, for a wonder, sitting idle. Sometimes he smiled to himself, and once or twice he laughed a little, but for the most part his pleasant, impassive face reflected no emotion and he sat with his useless eyes tranquilly fixed on an unseen distance. It was a fantastic caprice of the man to mock his sightlessness by a parade of light, and under the soft brilliance of a dozen electric brackets the room was as bright as day. At length he stood up and rang the bell.

"I suppose Mr Greatorex isn't still here by any chance, Parkinson?" he asked, referring to his secretary.

"I think not, sir, but I will ascertain," replied the man.

"Never mind. Go to his room and bring me the last two files of *The Times*. Now"—when he returned—"turn to the earliest you have there. The date?"

"November the second."

"That will do. Find the Money Market; it will be in the Supplement. Now look down the columns until you come to British Railways."

"I have it, sir."

"Central and Suburban. Read the closing price and the change."

"Central and Suburban Ordinary, 66½ - 67½, fall 1/8. Preferred Ordinary, 81 - 81½, no change. Deferred Ordinary, 27½ - 27¾, fall ¼. That is all, sir."

"Now take a paper about a week on. Read the Deferred only."

"27 - 27¼, no change."

"Another week."

"29½ - 30, rise 5/8."

"Another."

"31½ - 32½, rise 1."

"Very good. Now on Tuesday the twenty-seventh November."

"31 7/8 - 32¾, rise ½."

"Yes. The next day."

"24½ - 23½, fall 9."

33

"Quite so, Parkinson. There had been an accident, you see."

"Yes, sir. Very unpleasant accident. Jane knows a person whose sister's young man has a cousin who had his arm torn off in it—torn off at the socket, she says, sir. It seems to bring it home to one, sir."

"That is all. Stay—in the paper you have, look down the first money column and see if there is any reference to the Central and Suburban."

"Yes, sir. 'City and Suburbans, which after their late depression on the projected extension of the motor bus service, had been steadily creeping up on the abandonment of the scheme, and as a result of their own excellent traffic returns, suffered a heavy slump through the lamentable accident of Thursday night. The Deferred in particular at one time fell eleven points as it was felt that the possible dividend, with which rumour has of late been busy, was now out of the question.'"

"Yes; that is all. Now you can take the papers back. And let it be a warning to you, Parkinson, not to invest your savings in speculative railway deferreds."

"Yes, sir. Thank you, sir, I will endeavour to remember." He lingered for a moment as he shook the file of papers level. "I may say, sir, that I have my eye on a small block of cottage property at Acton. But even cottage property scarcely seems safe from legislative depredation now, sir."

The next day Mr Carrados called on his brokers in the city. It is to be presumed that he got through his private business quicker than he expected, for after leaving Austin Friars he continued his journey to Holloway, where he found Hutchins at home and sitting morosely before his kitchen fire. Rightly assuming that his luxuriant car would involve him in a certain amount of public attention in Klondyke Street, the blind man dismissed it some distance from the house, and walked the rest of the way, guided by the almost imperceptible touch of Parkinson's arm.

"Here is a gentleman to see you, father," explained Miss Hutchins, who had come to the door. She divined the relative positions of the two visitors at a glance.

"Then why don't you take him into the parlour?" grumbled the ex-driver. His face was a testimonial of hard work and general sobriety but at the moment one might hazard from his voice and manner that he had been drinking earlier in the day.

"I don't think that the gentleman would be impressed by the difference between our parlour and our kitchen," replied the girl quaintly, "and it is warmer here."

"What's the matter with the parlour now?" demanded her father sourly. "It was good enough for your mother and me. It used to be good enough for you."

"There is nothing the matter with it, nor with the kitchen either." She turned impassively to the two who had followed her along the narrow passage. "Will you go in, sir?"

"I don't want to see no gentleman," cried Hutchins noisily. "Unless"—his manner suddenly changed to one of pitiable anxiety—"unless you're from the Company, sir, to—to——"

"No; I have come on Mr Carlyle's behalf," replied Carrados, walking to a chair as though he moved by a kind of instinct.

Hutchins laughed his wry contempt.

"Mr Carlyle!" he reiterated; "Mr Carlyle! Fat lot of good he's been. Why don't he *do* something for his money?"

"He has," replied Carrados, with imperturbable good-humour; "he has sent me. Now, I want to ask you a few questions."

"A few questions!" roared the irate man. "Why, blast it, I have done nothing else but answer questions for a month. I didn't pay Mr Carlyle to ask me questions; I can get enough of that for nixes. Why don't you go and ask Mr Herbert Ananias Mead your few questions—then you might find out something."

There was a slight movement by the door and Carrados knew that the girl had quietly left the room.

"You saw that, sir?" demanded the father, diverted to a new line of bitterness. "You saw that girl—my own daughter, that I've worked for all her life?"

"No," replied Carrados.

"The girl that's just gone out—she's my daughter," explained Hutchins.

"I know, but I did not see her. I see nothing. I am blind."

"Blind!" exclaimed the old fellow, sitting up in startled wonderment. "You mean it, sir? You walk all right and you look at me as if you saw me. You're kidding surely."

"No," smiled Carrados. "It's quite right."

"Then it's a funny business, sir—you what are blind expecting to find something that those with their eyes couldn't," ruminated Hutchins sagely.

"There are things that you can't see with your eyes, Hutchins."

"Perhaps you are right, sir. Well, what is it you want to know?"

"Light a cigar first," said the blind man, holding out his case and waiting until the various sounds told him that his host was smoking contentedly. "The train you were driving at the time of the accident was the six-twenty-seven from Notcliff. It stopped everywhere until it reached Lambeth Bridge, the chief London station of your line. There it became something of an express, and leaving Lambeth Bridge at seven-eleven, should not stop again until it fetched Swanstead on Thames, eleven miles out, at seven-thirty-four. Then it stopped on and off from Swanstead to Ingerfield, the terminus of that branch, which it reached at eight-five."

Hutchins nodded, and then, remembering, said: "That's right, sir."

"That was your business all day—running between Notcliff and Ingerfield?"

"Yes, sir. Three journeys up and three down mostly."

"With the same stops on all the down journeys?"

"No. The seven-eleven is the only one that does a run from the Bridge to Swanstead. You see, it is just on the close of the evening rush, as they call it. A good many late business gentlemen living at Swanstead use the seven-eleven regular. The other journeys we stop at every station to Lambeth Bridge, and then here and there beyond."

"There are, of course, other trains doing exactly the same journey—a service, in fact?"

"Yes, sir. About six."

"And do any of those—say, during the rush—do any of those run non-stop from Lambeth to Swanstead?"

Hutchins reflected a moment. All the choler and restlessness had melted out of the man's face. He was again the excellent artisan, slow but capable and self-reliant.

"That I couldn't definitely say, sir. Very few short-distance trains pass the junction, but some of those may. A guide would show us in a minute but I haven't got one."

"Never mind. You said at the inquest that it was no uncommon thing for you to be pulled up at the 'stop' signal east of Knight's Cross Station. How often would that happen—only with the seven-eleven, mind."

"Perhaps three times a week; perhaps twice."

"The accident was on a Thursday. Have you noticed that you were pulled up oftener on a Thursday than on any other day?"

A smile crossed the driver's face at the question.

"You don't happen to live at Swanstead yourself, sir?" he asked in reply.

"No," admitted Carrados. "Why?"

"Well, sir, we were *always* pulled up on Thursday; practically always, you may say. It got to be quite a saying among those who used the train regular; they used to look out for it."

Carrados's sightless eyes had the one quality of concealing emotion supremely. "Oh," he commented softly, "always; and it was quite a saying, was it? And *why* was it always so on Thursday?"

"It had to do with the early closing, I'm told. The suburban traffic was a bit different. By rights we ought to have been set back two minutes for that day, but I suppose it wasn't thought worth while to alter us in the time-table, so we most always had to wait outside Three Deep tunnel for a west-bound electric to make good."

"You were prepared for it then?"

"Yes, sir, I was," said Hutchins, reddening at some recollection, "and very down about it was one of the jury over that. But, mayhap once in three months, I did get through even on a Thursday, and it's not for me to question whether things are right or wrong just because they are not what I may expect. The signals are my orders, sir—stop! go on! and it's for me to obey, as you would a general on the field of battle. What would happen otherwise! It was nonsense what they said about going cautious; and the man who started it was a barber who didn't know the difference between a 'distance' and a 'stop' signal down to the minute they gave their verdict. My orders, sir, given me by that signal, was 'Go right ahead and keep to your running time!'"

Carrados nodded a soothing assent. "That is all, I think," he remarked.

"All!" exclaimed Hutchins in surprise. "Why, sir, you can't have got much idea of it yet."

"Quite enough. And I know it isn't pleasant for you to be taken along the same ground over and over again."

The man moved awkwardly in his chair and pulled nervously at his grizzled beard.

"You mustn't take any notice of what I said just now, sir," he apologised. "You somehow make me feel that something may come of it; but I've been badgered about and accused and cross-examined from one to another of them these weeks till it's fairly made me bitter against everything. And now they talk of putting me in a lavatory— me that has been with the company for five and forty years and on

37

the foot-plate thirty-two—a man suspected of running past a danger signal."

"You have had a rough time, Hutchins; you will have to exercise your patience a little longer yet," said Carrados sympathetically.

"You think something may come of it, sir? You think you will be able to clear me? Believe me, sir, if you could give me something to look forward to it might save me from——" He pulled himself up and shook his head sorrowfully. "I've been near it," he added simply.

Carrados reflected and took his resolution.

"To-day is Wednesday. I think you may hope to hear something from your general manager towards the middle of next week."

"Good God, sir! You really mean that?"

"In the interval show your good sense by behaving reasonably. Keep civilly to yourself and don't talk. Above all"—he nodded towards a quart jug that stood on the table between them, an incident that filled the simple-minded engineer with boundless wonder when he recalled it afterwards—"above all, leave that alone."

Hutchins snatched up the vessel and brought it crashing down on the hearthstone, his face shining with a set resolution.

"I've done with it, sir. It was the bitterness and despair that drove me to that. Now I can do without it."

The door was hastily opened and Miss Hutchins looked anxiously from her father to the visitors and back again.

"Oh, whatever is the matter?" she exclaimed. "I heard a great crash."

"This gentleman is going to clear me, Meg, my dear," blurted out the old man irrepressibly. "And I've done with the drink for ever."

"Hutchins! Hutchins!" said Carrados warningly.

"My daughter, sir; you wouldn't have her not know?" pleaded Hutchins, rather crest-fallen. "It won't go any further."

Carrados laughed quietly to himself as he felt Margaret Hutchins's startled and questioning eyes attempting to read his mind. He shook hands with the engine-driver without further comment, however, and walked out into the commonplace little street under Parkinson's unobtrusive guidance.

"Very nice of Miss Hutchins to go into half-mourning, Parkinson," he remarked as they went along. "Thoughtful, and yet not ostentatious."

"Yes, sir," agreed Parkinson, who had long ceased to wonder at his master's perceptions.

"The Romans, Parkinson, had a saying to the effect that gold carries no smell. That is a pity sometimes. What jewellery did Miss Hutchins wear?"

"Very little, sir. A plain gold brooch representing a merry-thought—the merry-thought of a sparrow, I should say, sir. The only other article was a smooth-backed gun-metal watch, suspended from a gun-metal bow."

"Nothing showy or expensive, eh?"

"Oh dear no, sir. Quite appropriate for a young person of her position."

"Just what I should have expected." He slackened his pace. "We are passing a hoarding, are we not?"

"Yes, sir."

"We will stand here a moment. Read me the letterpress of the poster before us."

"This 'Oxo' one, sir?"

"Yes."

"'Oxo,' sir."

Carrados was convulsed with silent laughter. Parkinson had infinitely more dignity and conceded merely a tolerant recognition of the ludicrous.

"That was a bad shot, Parkinson," remarked his master when he could speak. "We will try another."

For three minutes, with scrupulous conscientiousness on the part of the reader and every appearance of keen interest on the part of the hearer, there were set forth the particulars of a sale by auction of superfluous timber and builders' material.

"That will do," said Carrados, when the last detail had been reached. "We can be seen from the door of No. 107 still?"

"Yes, sir."

"No indication of anyone coming to us from there?"

"No, sir."

Carrados walked thoughtfully on again. In the Holloway Road they rejoined the waiting motor car. "Lambeth Bridge Station," was the order the driver received.

From the station the car was sent on home and Parkinson was instructed to take two first-class singles for Richmond, which could be reached by changing at Stafford Road. The "evening rush" had not yet commenced and they had no difficulty in finding an empty carriage when the train came in.

Parkinson was kept busy that journey describing what he saw at various points between Lambeth Bridge and Knight's Cross. For a quarter of a mile Carrados's demands on the eyes and the memory of his remarkable servant were wide and incessant. Then his questions ceased. They had passed the "stop" signal, east of Knight's Cross Station.

The following afternoon they made the return journey as far as Knight's Cross. This time, however, the surroundings failed to interest Carrados. "We are going to look at some rooms," was the information he offered on the subject, and an imperturbable "Yes, sir" had been the extent of Parkinson's comment on the unusual proceeding. After leaving the station they turned sharply along a road that ran parallel with the line, a dull thoroughfare of substantial, elderly houses that were beginning to sink into decrepitude. Here and there a corner residence displayed the brass plate of a professional occupant, but for the most part they were given up to the various branches of second-rate apartment letting.

"The third house after the one with the flagstaff," said Carrados.

Parkinson rang the bell, which was answered by a young servant, who took an early opportunity of assuring them that she was not tidy as it was rather early in the afternoon. She informed Carrados, in reply to his inquiry, that Miss Chubb was at home, and showed them into a melancholy little sitting-room to await her appearance.

"I shall be 'almost' blind here, Parkinson," remarked Carrados, walking about the room. "It saves explanation."

"Very good, sir," replied Parkinson.

Five minutes later, an interval suggesting that Miss Chubb also found it rather early in the afternoon, Carrados was arranging to take rooms for his attendant and himself for the short time that he would be in London, seeing an oculist.

"One bedroom, mine, must face north," he stipulated. "It has to do with the light."

Miss Chubb replied that she quite understood. Some gentlemen, she added, had their requirements, others their fancies. She endeavoured to suit all. The bedroom she had in view from the first *did* face north. She would not have known, only the last gentleman, curiously enough, had made the same request.

"A sufferer like myself?" inquired Carrados affably.

Miss Chubb did not think so. In his case she regarded it merely as a fancy. He had said that he could not sleep on any other side. She had

had to turn out of her own room to accommodate him, but if one kept an apartment-house one had to be adaptable; and Mr Ghoosh was certainly very liberal in his ideas.

"Ghoosh? An Indian gentleman, I presume?" hazarded Carrados.

It appeared that Mr Ghoosh was an Indian. Miss Chubb confided that at first she had been rather perturbed at the idea of taking in "a black man," as she confessed to regarding him. She reiterated, however, that Mr Ghoosh proved to be "quite the gentleman." Five minutes of affability put Carrados in full possession of Mr Ghoosh's manner of life and movements—the dates of his arrival and departure, his solitariness and his daily habits.

"This would be the best bedroom," said Miss Chubb.

It was a fair-sized room on the first floor. The window looked out on to the roof of an outbuilding; beyond, the deep cutting of the railway line. Opposite stood the dead wall that Mr Carlyle had spoken of.

Carrados "looked" round the room with the discriminating glance that sometimes proved so embarrassing to those who knew him.

"I have to take a little daily exercise," he remarked, walking to the window and running his hand up the woodwork. "You will not mind my fixing a 'developer' here, Miss Chubb—a few small screws?"

Miss Chubb thought not. Then she was sure not. Finally she ridiculed the idea of minding with scorn.

"If there is width enough," mused Carrados, spanning the upright critically. "Do you happen to have a wooden foot-rule convenient?"

"Well, to be sure!" exclaimed Miss Chubb, opening a rapid succession of drawers until she produced the required article. "When we did out this room after Mr Ghoosh, there was this very ruler among the things that he hadn't thought worth taking. This is what you require, sir?"

"Yes," replied Carrados, accepting it, "I think this is exactly what I require." It was a common new white-wood rule, such as one might buy at any small stationer's for a penny. He carelessly took off the width of the upright, reading the figures with a touch; and then continued to run a finger-tip delicately up and down the edges of the instrument.

"Four and seven-eighths," was his unspoken conclusion.

"I hope it will do, sir."

"Admirably," replied Carrados. "But I haven't reached the end of my requirements yet, Miss Chubb."

"No, sir?" said the landlady, feeling that it would be a pleasure to oblige so agreeable a gentleman, "what else might there be?"

"Although I can see very little I like to have a light, but not any kind of light. Gas I cannot do with. Do you think that you would be able to find me an oil lamp?"

"Certainly, sir. I got out a very nice brass lamp that I have specially for Mr Ghoosh. He read a good deal of an evening and he preferred a lamp."

"That is very convenient. I suppose it is large enough to burn for a whole evening?"

"Yes, indeed. And very particular he was always to have it filled every day."

"A lamp without oil is not very useful," smiled Carrados, following her towards another room, and absentmindedly slipping the foot-rule into his pocket.

Whatever Parkinson thought of the arrangement of going into second-rate apartments in an obscure street it is to be inferred that his devotion to his master was sufficient to overcome his private emotions as a self-respecting "man." At all events, as they were approaching the station he asked, and without a trace of feeling, whether there were any orders for him with reference to the proposed migration.

"None, Parkinson," replied his master. "We must be satisfied with our present quarters."

"I beg your pardon, sir," said Parkinson, with some constraint. "I understood that you had taken the rooms for a week certain."

"I am afraid that Miss Chubb will be under the same impression. Unforeseen circumstances will prevent our going, however. Mr Greatorex must write to-morrow, enclosing a cheque, with my regrets, and adding a penny for this ruler which I seem to have brought away with me. It, at least, is something for the money."

Parkinson may be excused for not attempting to understand the course of events.

"Here is your train coming in, sir," he merely said.

"We will let it go and wait for another. Is there a signal at either end of the platform?"

"Yes, sir; at the further end."

"Let us walk towards it. Are there any of the porters or officials about here?"

"No, sir; none."

"Take this ruler. I want you to go up the steps—there are steps up the signal, by the way?"

"Yes, sir."

"I want you to measure the glass of the lamp. Do not go up any higher than is necessary, but if you have to stretch be careful not to mark on the measurement with your nail, although the impulse is a natural one. That has been done already."

Parkinson looked apprehensively around and about. Fortunately the part was a dark and unfrequented spot and everyone else was moving towards the exit at the other end of the platform. Fortunately, also, the signal was not a high one.

"As near as I can judge on the rounded surface, the glass is four and seven-eighths across," reported Parkinson.

"Thank you," replied Carrados, returning the measure to his pocket, "four and seven-eighths is quite near enough. Now we will take the next train back."

Sunday evening came, and with it Mr Carlyle to The Turrets at the appointed hour. He brought to the situation a mind poised for any eventuality and a trenchant eye. As the time went on and the impenetrable Carrados made no allusion to the case, Carlyle's manner inclined to a waggish commiseration of his host's position. Actually, he said little, but the crisp precision of his voice when the path lay open to a remark of any significance left little to be said.

It was not until they had finished dinner and returned to the library that Carrados gave the slightest hint of anything unusual being in the air. His first indication of coming events was to remove the key from the outside to the inside of the door.

"What are you doing, Max?" demanded Mr Carlyle, his curiosity overcoming the indirect attitude.

"You have been very entertaining, Louis," replied his friend, "but Parkinson should be back very soon now and it is as well to be prepared. Do you happen to carry a revolver?"

"Not when I come to dine with you, Max," replied Carlyle, with all the aplomb he could muster. "Is it usual?"

Carrados smiled affectionately at his guest's agile recovery and touched the secret spring of a drawer in an antique bureau by his side. The little hidden receptacle shot smoothly out, disclosing a pair of dull-blued pistols.

"Tonight, at all events, it might be prudent," he replied, handing one to Carlyle and putting the other into his own pocket. "Our man may be here at any minute, and we do not know in what temper he will come."

"Our man!" exclaimed Carlyle, craning forward in excitement. "Max! you don't mean to say that you have got Mead to admit it?"

"No one has admitted it," said Carrados. "And it is not Mead."

"Not Mead. . . . Do you mean that Hutchins——?"

"Neither Mead nor Hutchins. The man who tampered with the signal—for Hutchins was right and a green light *was* exhibited—is a young Indian from Bengal. His name is Drishna and he lives at Swanstead."

Mr Carlyle stared at his friend between sheer surprise and blank incredulity.

"You really mean this, Carrados?" he said.

"My fatal reputation for humour!" smiled Carrados. "If I am wrong, Louis, the next hour will expose it."

"But why—why—why? The colossal villainy, the unparalleled audacity!" Mr Carlyle lost himself among incredulous superlatives and could only stare.

"Chiefly to get himself out of a disastrous speculation," replied Carrados, answering the question. "If there was another motive—or at least an incentive—which I suspect, doubtless we shall hear of it."

"All the same, Max, I don't think that you have treated me quite fairly," protested Carlyle, getting over his first surprise and passing to a sense of injury. "Here we are and I know nothing, absolutely nothing, of the whole affair."

"We both have our ideas of pleasantry, Louis," replied Carrados genially. "But I dare say you are right and perhaps there is still time to atone." In the fewest possible words he outlined the course of his investigations. "And now you know all that is to be known until Drishna arrives."

"But will he come?" questioned Carlyle doubtfully. "He may be suspicious."

"Yes, he will be suspicious."

"Then he will not come."

"On the contrary, Louis, he will come because my letter will make him suspicious. He *is* coming; otherwise Parkinson would have telephoned me at once and we should have had to take other measures."

"What did you say, Max?" asked Carlyle curiously.

"I wrote that I was anxious to discuss an Indo-Scythian inscription with him, and sent my car in the hope that he would be able to oblige me."

"But is he interested in Indo-Scythian inscriptions?"

"I haven't the faintest idea," admitted Carrados, and Mr Carlyle was throwing up his hands in despair when the sound of a motor car wheels softly kissing the gravel surface of the drive outside brought him to his feet.

"By gad, you are right, Max!" he exclaimed, peeping through the curtains. "There is a man inside."

"Mr Drishna," announced Parkinson, a minute later.

The visitor came into the room with leisurely self-possession that might have been real or a desperate assumption. He was a slightly built young man of about twenty-five, with black hair and eyes, a small, carefully trained moustache, and a dark olive skin. His physiognomy was not displeasing, but his expression had a harsh and supercilious tinge. In attire he erred towards the immaculately spruce.

"Mr Carrados?" he said inquiringly.

Carrados, who had risen, bowed slightly without offering his hand.

"This gentleman," he said, indicating his friend, "is Mr Carlyle, the celebrated private detective."

The Indian shot a very sharp glance at the object of this description. Then he sat down.

"You wrote me a letter, Mr Carrados," he remarked, in English that scarcely betrayed any foreign origin, "a rather curious letter, I may say. You asked me about an ancient inscription. I know nothing of antiquities; but I thought, as you had sent, that it would be more courteous if I came and explained this to you."

"That was the object of my letter," replied Carrados.

"You wished to see me?" said Drishna, unable to stand the ordeal of the silence that Carrados imposed after his remark.

"When you left Miss Chubb's house you left a ruler behind." One lay on the desk by Carrados and he took it up as he spoke.

"I don't understand what you are talking about," said Drishna guardedly. "You are making some mistake."

"The ruler was marked at four and seven-eighths inches—the measure of the glass of the signal lamp outside."

The unfortunate young man was unable to repress a start. His face lost its healthy tone. Then, with a sudden impulse, he made a step forward and snatched the object from Carrados's hand.

"If it is mine I have a right to it," he exclaimed, snapping the ruler in two and throwing it on to the back of the blazing fire. "It is noth-

45

ing."

"Pardon me, I did not say that the one you have so impetuously disposed of was yours. As a matter of fact, it was mine. Yours is—elsewhere."

"Wherever it is you have no right to it if it is mine," panted Drishna, with rising excitement. "You are a thief, Mr Carrados. I will not stay any longer here."

He jumped up and turned towards the door. Carlyle made a step forward, but the precaution was unnecessary.

"One moment, Mr Drishna," interposed Carrados, in his smoothest tones. "It is a pity, after you have come so far, to leave without hearing of my investigations in the neighbourhood of Shaftesbury Avenue."

Drishna sat down again.

"As you like," he muttered. "It does not interest me."

"I wanted to obtain a lamp of a certain pattern," continued Carrados. "It seemed to me that the simplest explanation would be to say that I wanted it for a motor car. Naturally I went to Long Acre. At the first shop I said: 'Wasn't it here that a friend of mine, an Indian gentleman, recently had a lamp made with a green glass that was nearly five inches across?' No, it was not there but they could make me one. At the next shop the same; at the third, and fourth, and so on. Finally my persistence was rewarded. I found the place where the lamp had been made, and at the cost of ordering another I obtained all the details I wanted. It was news to them, the shopman informed me, that in some parts of India green was the danger colour and therefore tail lamps had to show a green light. The incident made some impression on him and he would be able to identify their customer—who paid in advance and gave no address—among a thousand of his countrymen. Do I succeed in interesting you, Mr Drishna?"

"Do you?" replied Drishna, with a languid yawn. "Do I look interested?"

"You must make allowance for my unfortunate blindness," apologised Carrados, with grim irony.

"Blindness!" exclaimed Drishna, dropping his affectation of unconcern as though electrified by the word, "do you mean—really blind—that you do not see me?"

"Alas, no," admitted Carrados.

The Indian withdrew his right hand from his coat pocket and with a tragic gesture flung a heavy revolver down on the table between them.

"I have had you covered all the time, Mr Carrados, and if I had wished to go and you or your friend had raised a hand to stop me, it would have been at the peril of your lives," he said, in a voice of melancholy triumph. "But what is the use of defying fate, and who successfully evades his destiny? A month ago I went to see one of our people who reads the future and sought to know the course of certain events. 'You need fear no human eye,' was the message given to me. Then she added: 'But when the sightless sees the unseen, make your peace with Yama.' And I thought she spoke of the Great Hereafter!"

"This amounts to an admission of your guilt," exclaimed Mr Carlyle practically.

"I bow to the decree of fate," replied Drishna. "And it is fitting to the universal irony of existence that a blind man should be the instrument. I don't imagine, Mr Carlyle," he added maliciously, "that you, with your eyes, would ever have brought that result about."

"You are a very cold-blooded young scoundrel, sir!" retorted Mr Carlyle. "Good heavens! do you realize that you are responsible for the death of scores of innocent men and women?"

"Do *you* realise, Mr Carlyle, that you and your government and your soldiers are responsible for the death of thousands of innocent men and women in my country every day? If England was occupied by the Germans who quartered an army and an administration with their wives and their families and all their expensive paraphernalia on the unfortunate country until the whole nation was reduced to the verge of famine, and the appointment of every new official meant the callous death sentence on a thousand men and women to pay his salary, then if you went to Berlin and wrecked a train you would be hailed a patriot. What Boadicea did and—and Samson, so have I. If they were heroes, so am I."

"Well, upon my word!" cried the highly scandalised Carlyle, "what next! Boadicea was a—er—semi-legendary person, whom we may possibly admire at a distance. Personally, I do not profess to express an opinion. But Samson, I would remind you, is a Biblical character. Samson was mocked as an enemy. You, I do not doubt, have been entertained as a friend."

"And haven't I been mocked and despised and sneered at every day of my life here by your supercilious, superior, empty-headed men?" flashed back Drishna, his eyes leaping into malignity and his voice trembling with sudden passion. "Oh! how I hated them as I passed them in the street and recognised by a thousand petty insults their lordly English contempt for me as an inferior being—a nigger. How I longed with Caligula that a nation had a single neck that I might destroy it at one blow. I loathe you in your complacent hypocrisy, Mr Carlyle, despise and utterly abominate you from an eminence of superiority that you can never even understand."

"I think we are getting rather away from the point, Mr Drishna," interposed Carrados, with the impartiality of a judge. "Unless I am misinformed, you are not so ungallant as to include everyone you have met here in your execration?"

"Ah, no," admitted Drishna, descending into a quite ingenuous frankness. "Much as I hate your men I love your women. How is it possible that a nation should be so divided—its men so dull-witted and offensive, its women so quick, sympathetic and capable of appreciating?"

"But a little expensive, too, at times?" suggested Carrados.

Drishna sighed heavily.

"Yes; it is incredible. It is the generosity of their large nature. My allowance, though what most of you would call noble, has proved quite inadequate. I was compelled to borrow money and the interest became overwhelming. Bankruptcy was impracticable because I should have then been recalled by my people, and much as I detest England a certain reason made the thought of leaving it unbearable."

"Connected with the Arcady Theatre?"

"You know? Well, do not let us introduce the lady's name. In order to restore myself I speculated on the Stock Exchange. My credit was good through my father's position and the standing of the firm to which I am attached. I heard on reliable authority, and very early, that the Central and Suburban, and the Deferred especially, was safe to fall heavily, through a motor bus amalgamation that was then a secret. I opened a bear account and sold largely. The shares fell, but only fractionally, and I waited. Then, unfortunately, they began to go up. Adverse forces were at work and rumours were put about. I could not stand the settlement, and in order to carry over an account I was literally compelled to deal temporarily with some securities that were not technically my own property."

"Embezzlement, sir," commented Mr Carlyle icily. "But what is embezzlement on the top of wholesale murder!"

"That is what it is called. In my case, however, it was only to be temporary. Unfortunately, the rise continued. Then, at the height of my despair, I chanced to be returning to Swanstead rather earlier than

48

usual one evening, and the train was stopped at a certain signal to let another pass. There was conversation in the carriage and I learned certain details. One said that there would be an accident some day, and so forth. In a flash—as by an inspiration—I saw how the circumstance might be turned to account. A bad accident and the shares would certainly fall and my position would be retrieved. I think Mr Carrados has somehow learned the rest."

"Max," said Mr Carlyle, with emotion, "is there any reason why you should not send your man for a police officer and have this monster arrested on his own confession without further delay?"

"Pray do so, Mr Carrados," acquiesced Drishna. "I shall certainly be hanged, but the speech I shall prepare will ring from one end of India to the other; my memory will be venerated as that of a martyr; and the emancipation of my motherland will be hastened by my sacrifice."

"In other words," commented Carrados, "there will be disturbances at half-a-dozen disaffected places, a few unfortunate police will be clubbed to death, and possibly worse things may happen. That does not suit us, Mr Drishna."

"And how do you propose to prevent it?" asked Drishna, with cool assurance.

"It is very unpleasant being hanged on a dark winter morning; very cold, very friendless, very inhuman. The long trial, the solitude and the confinement, the thoughts of the long sleepless night before, the hangman and the pinioning and the noosing of the rope, are apt to prey on the imagination. Only a very stupid man can take hanging easily."

"What do you want me to do instead, Mr Carrados?" asked Drishna shrewdly.

Carrados's hand closed on the weapon that still lay on the table between them. Without a word he pushed it across.

"I see," commented Drishna, with a short laugh and a gleaming eye. "Shoot myself and hush it up to suit your purpose. Withhold my message to save the exposures of a trial, and keep the flame from the torch of insurrectionary freedom."

"Also," interposed Carrados mildly, "to save your worthy people a good deal of shame, and to save the lady who is nameless the unpleasant necessity of relinquishing the house and the income which you have just settled on her. She certainly would not then venerate your memory."

"What is that?"

"The transaction which you carried through was based on a felony and could not be upheld. The firm you dealt with will go to the courts, and the money, being directly traceable, will be held forfeit as no good consideration passed."

"Max!" cried Mr Carlyle hotly, "you are not going to let this scoundrel cheat the gallows after all?"

"The best use you can make of the gallows is to cheat it, Louis," replied Carrados. "Have you ever reflected what human beings will think of us a hundred years hence?"

"Oh, of course I'm not really in favour of hanging," admitted Mr Carlyle.

"Nobody really is. But we go on hanging. Mr Drishna is a dangerous animal who for the sake of pacific animals must cease to exist. Let his barbarous exploit pass into oblivion with him. The disadvantages of spreading it broadcast immeasurably outweigh the benefits."

"I have considered," announced Drishna. "I will do as you wish."

"Very well," said Carrados. "Here is some plain notepaper. You had better write a letter to someone saying that the financial difficulties in which you are involved make life unbearable."

"But there are no financial difficulties—now."

"That does not matter in the least. It will be put down to an hallucination and taken as showing the state of your mind."

"But what guarantee have we that he will not escape?" whispered Mr Carlyle.

"He cannot escape," replied Carrados tranquilly. "His identity is too clear."

"I have no intention of trying to escape," put in Drishna, as he wrote. "You hardly imagine that I have not considered this eventuality, do you?"

"All the same," murmured the ex-lawyer, "I should like to have a jury behind me. It is one thing to execute a man morally; it is another to do it almost literally."

"Is that all right?" asked Drishna, passing across the letter he had written.

Carrados smiled at this tribute to his perception.

"Quite excellent," he replied courteously. "There is a train at nine-forty. Will that suit you?"

Drishna nodded and stood up. Mr Carlyle had a very uneasy feeling that he ought to do something but could not suggest to himself what.

The next moment he heard his friend heartily thanking the visitor for the assistance he had been in the matter of the Indo-Scythian inscription, as they walked across the hall together. Then a door closed.

"I believe that there is something positively uncanny about Max at times," murmured the perturbed gentleman to himself.

The Tragedy at Brookbend Cottage

"Max," said Mr Carlyle, when Parkinson had closed the door behind him, "this is Lieutenant Hollyer, whom you consented to see."

"To hear," corrected Carrados, smiling straight into the healthy and rather embarrassed face of the stranger before him. "Mr Hollyer knows of my disability?"

"Mr Carlyle told me," said the young man, "but, as a matter of fact, I had heard of you before, Mr Carrados, from one of our men. It was in connexion with the foundering of the *Ivan Saratov*."

Carrados wagged his head in good-humoured resignation.

"And the owners were sworn to inviolable secrecy!" he exclaimed. "Well, it is inevitable, I suppose. Not another scuttling case, Mr Hollyer?"

"No, mine is quite a private matter," replied the lieutenant. "My sister, Mrs Creake—but Mr Carlyle would tell you better than I can. He knows all about it."

"No, no; Carlyle is a professional. Let me have it in the rough, Mr Hollyer. My ears are my eyes, you know."

"Very well, sir. I can tell you what there is to tell, right enough, but I feel that when all's said and done it must sound very little to another, although it seems important enough to me."

"We have occasionally found trifles of significance ourselves," said Carrados encouragingly. "Don't let that deter you."

This was the essence of Lieutenant Hollyer's narrative:

"I have a sister, Millicent, who is married to a man called Creake. She is about twenty-eight now and he is at least fifteen years older. Neither my mother (who has since died), nor I, cared very much about Creake. We had nothing particular against him, except, perhaps, the moderate disparity of age, but none of us appeared to have anything in common. He was a dark, taciturn man, and his moody silence

52

froze up conversation. As a result, of course, we didn't see much of each other."

"This, you must understand, was four or five years ago, Max," interposed Mr Carlyle officiously.

Carrados maintained an uncompromising silence. Mr Carlyle blew his nose and contrived to impart a hurt significance into the operation. Then Lieutenant Hollyer continued:

"Millicent married Creake after a very short engagement. It was a frightfully subdued wedding—more like a funeral to me. The man professed to have no relations and apparently he had scarcely any friends or business acquaintances. He was an agent for something or other and had an office off Holborn. I suppose he made a living out of it then, although we knew practically nothing of his private affairs, but I gather that it has been going down since, and I suspect that for the past few years they have been getting along almost entirely on Millicent's little income. You would like the particulars of that?"

"Please," assented Carrados.

"When our father died about seven years ago, he left three thousand pounds. It was invested in Canadian stock and brought in a little over a hundred a year. By his will my mother was to have the income of that for life and on her death it was to pass to Millicent, subject to the payment of a lump sum of five hundred pounds to me. But my father privately suggested to me that if I should have no particular use for the money at the time, he would propose my letting Millicent have the income of it until I did want it, as she would not be particularly well off. You see, Mr Carrados, a great deal more had been spent on my education and advancement than on her; I had my pay, and, of course, I could look out for myself better than a girl could."

"Quite so," agreed Carrados.

"Therefore I did nothing about that," continued the lieutenant. "Three years ago I was over again but I did not see much of them. They were living in lodgings. That was the only time since the marriage that I have seen them until last week. In the meanwhile our mother had died and Millicent had been receiving her income. She wrote me several letters at the time. Otherwise we did not correspond much, but about a year ago she sent me their new address—Brookbend Cottage, Mulling Common—a house that they had taken. When I got two months' leave I invited myself there as a matter of course, fully expecting to stay most of my time with them, but I made an excuse to get away after a week. The place was dismal and unendurable, the whole life and atmosphere indescribably depressing." He looked round with an instinct of caution, leaned forward earnestly, and dropped his voice. "Mr Carrados, it is my absolute conviction that Creake is only waiting for a favourable opportunity to murder Millicent."

"Go on," said Carrados quietly. "A week of the depressing surroundings of Brookbend Cottage would not alone convince you of that, Mr Hollyer."

"I am not so sure," declared Hollyer doubtfully. "There was a feeling of suspicion and—before me—polite hatred that would have gone a good way towards it. All the same there *was* something more definite. Millicent told me this the day after I went there. There is no doubt that a few months ago Creake deliberately planned to poison her with some weed-killer. She told me the circumstances in a rather distressed moment, but afterwards she refused to speak of it again—even weakly denied it—and, as a matter of fact, it was with the greatest difficulty that I could get her at any time to talk about her husband or his affairs. The gist of it was that she had the strongest suspicion that Creake doctored a bottle of stout which he expected she would drink for her supper when she was alone. The weed-killer, properly labelled, but also in a beer bottle, was kept with other miscellaneous liquids in the same cupboard as the beer but on a high shelf. When he found that it had miscarried he poured away the mixture, washed out the bottle and put in the dregs from another. There is no doubt in my mind that if he had come back and found Millicent dead or dying he would have contrived it to appear that she had made a mistake in the dark and drunk some of the poison before she found out."

"Yes," assented Carrados. "The open way; the safe way."

"You must understand that they live in a very small style, Mr Carrados, and Millicent is almost entirely in the man's power. The only servant they have is a woman who comes in for a few hours every day. The house is lonely and secluded. Creake is sometimes away for days and nights at a time, and Millicent, either through pride or indifference, seems to have dropped off all her old friends and to have made no others. He might poison her, bury the body in the garden, and be a thousand miles away before anyone began even to inquire about her. What am I to do, Mr Carrados?"

"He is less likely to try poison than some other means now," pondered Carrados. "That having failed, his wife will always be on her guard. He may know, or at least suspect, that others know. No. . . . The commonsense precaution would be for your sister to leave the man,

Mr Hollyer. She will not?"

"No," admitted Hollyer, "she will not. I at once urged that." The young man struggled with some hesitation for a moment and then blurted out: "The fact is, Mr Carrados, I don't understand Millicent. She is not the girl she was. She hates Creake and treats him with a silent contempt that eats into their lives like acid, and yet she is so jealous of him that she will let nothing short of death part them. It is a horrible life they lead. I stood it for a week and I must say, much as I dislike my brother-in-law, that he has something to put up with. If only he got into a passion like a man and killed her it wouldn't be altogether incomprehensible."

"That does not concern us," said Carrados. "In a game of this kind one has to take sides and we have taken ours. It remains for us to see that our side wins. You mentioned jealousy, Mr Hollyer. Have you any idea whether Mrs Creake has real ground for it?"

"I should have told you that," replied Lieutenant Hollyer. "I happened to strike up with a newspaper man whose office is in the same block as Creake's. When I mentioned the name he grinned. 'Creake,' he said, 'oh, he's the man with the romantic typist, isn't he?' 'Well, he's my brother-in-law,' I replied. 'What about the typist?' Then the chap shut up like a knife. 'No, no,' he said, 'I didn't know he was married. I don't want to get mixed up in anything of that sort. I only said that he had a typist. Well, what of that? So have we; so has everyone.' There was nothing more to be got out of him, but the remark and the grin meant—well, about as usual, Mr Carrados."

Carrados turned to his friend.

"I suppose you know all about the typist by now, Louis?"

"We have had her under efficient observation, Max," replied Mr Carlyle, with severe dignity.

"Is she unmarried?"

"Yes; so far as ordinary repute goes, she is."

"That is all that is essential for the moment. Mr Hollyer opens up three excellent reasons why this man might wish to dispose of his wife. If we accept the suggestion of poisoning—though we have only a jealous woman's suspicion for it—we add to the wish the determination. Well, we will go forward on that. Have you got a photograph of Mr Creake?"

The lieutenant took out his pocket-book.

"Mr Carlyle asked me for one. Here is the best I could get."

Carrados rang the bell.

"This, Parkinson," he said, when the man appeared, "is a photograph of a Mr——What first name, by the way?"

"Austin," put in Hollyer, who was following everything with a boyish mixture of excitement and subdued importance.

"——of a Mr Austin Creake. I may require you to recognise him."

Parkinson glanced at the print and returned it to his master's hand.

"May I inquire if it is a recent photograph of the gentleman, sir?" he asked.

"About six years ago," said the lieutenant, taking in this new actor in the drama with frank curiosity. "But he is very little changed."

"Thank you, sir. I will endeavour to remember Mr Creake, sir."

Lieutenant Hollyer stood up as Parkinson left the room. The interview seemed to be at an end.

"Oh, there's one other matter," he remarked. "I am afraid that I did rather an unfortunate thing while I was at Brookbend. It seemed to me that as all Millicent's money would probably pass into Creake's hands sooner or later I might as well have my five hundred pounds, if only to help her with afterwards. So I broached the subject and said that I should like to have it now as I had an opportunity for investing."

"And you think?"

"It may possibly influence Creake to act sooner than he otherwise might have done. He may have got possession of the principal even and find it very awkward to replace it."

"So much the better. If your sister is going to be murdered it may as well be done next week as next year so far as I am concerned. Excuse my brutality, Mr Hollyer, but this is simply a case to me and I regard it strategically. Now Mr Carlyle's organisation can look after Mrs Creake for a few weeks but it cannot look after her for ever. By increasing the immediate risk we diminish the permanent risk."

"I see," agreed Hollyer. "I'm awfully uneasy but I'm entirely in your hands."

"Then we will give Mr Creake every inducement and every opportunity to get to work. Where are you staying now?"

"Just now with some friends at St Albans."

"That is too far." The inscrutable eyes retained their tranquil depth but a new quality of quickening interest in the voice made Mr Carlyle forget the weight and burden of his ruffled dignity. "Give me a few minutes, please. The cigarettes are behind you, Mr Hollyer." The blind man walked to the window and seemed to look out over the cypress-shaded lawn. The lieutenant lit a cigarette and Mr Carlyle picked up *Punch*. Then Carrados turned round again.

"You are prepared to put your own arrangements aside?" he demanded of his visitor.

"Certainly."

"Very well. I want you to go down now—straight from here—to Brookbend Cottage. Tell your sister that your leave is unexpectedly cut short and that you sail tomorrow."

"The *Martian*?"

"No, no; the *Martian* doesn't sail. Look up the movements on your way there and pick out a boat that does. Say you are transferred. Add that you expect to be away only two or three months and that you really want the five hundred pounds by the time of your return. Don't stay in the house long, please."

"I understand, sir."

"St Albans is too far. Make your excuse and get away from there today. Put up somewhere in town, where you will be in reach of the telephone. Let Mr Carlyle and myself know where you are. Keep out of Creake's way. I don't want actually to tie you down to the house, but we may require your services. We will let you know at the first sign of anything doing and if there is nothing to be done we must release you."

"I don't mind that. Is there nothing more that I can do now?"

"Nothing. In going to Mr Carlyle you have done the best thing possible; you have put your sister into the care of the shrewdest man in London." Whereat the object of this quite unexpected eulogy found himself becoming covered with modest confusion.

"Well, Max?" remarked Mr Carlyle tentatively when they were alone.

"Well, Louis?"

"Of course it wasn't worth while rubbing it in before young Hollyer, but, as a matter of fact, every single man carries the life of any other man—only one, mind you—in his hands, do what you will."

"Provided he doesn't bungle," acquiesced Carrados.

"Quite so."

"And also that he is absolutely reckless of the consequences."

"Of course."

"Two rather large provisos. Creake is obviously susceptible to both. Have you seen him?"

"No. As I told you, I put a man on to report his habits in town. Then, two days ago, as the case seemed to promise some interest—for he certainly is deeply involved with the typist, Max, and the thing might take a sensational turn any time—I went down to Mulling Common myself. Although the house is lonely it is on the electric tram route. You know the sort of market garden rurality that about a dozen miles out of London offers—alternate bricks and cabbages. It was easy enough to get to know about Creake locally. He mixes with no one there, goes into town at irregular times but generally every day, and is reputed to be devilish hard to get money out of. Finally I made the acquaintance of an old fellow who used to do a day's gardening at Brookbend occasionally. He has a cottage and a garden of his own with a greenhouse, and the business cost me the price of a pound of tomatoes."

"Was it—a profitable investment?"

"As tomatoes, yes; as information, no. The old fellow had the fatal disadvantage from our point of view of labouring under a grievance. A few weeks ago Creake told him that he would not require him again as he was going to do his own gardening in future."

"That is something, Louis."

"If only Creake was going to poison his wife with *hyoscyamine* and bury her, instead of blowing her up with a dynamite cartridge and claiming that it came in among the coal."

"True, true. Still——"

"However, the chatty old soul had a simple explanation for everything that Creake did. Creake was mad. He had even seen him flying a kite in his garden where it was bound to get wrecked among the trees. 'A lad of ten would have known better,' he declared. And certainly the kite did get wrecked, for I saw it hanging over the road myself. But that a sane man should spend his time 'playing with a toy' was beyond him."

"A good many men have been flying kites of various kinds lately," said Carrados. "Is he interested in aviation?"

"I dare say. He appears to have some knowledge of scientific subjects. Now what do you want me to do, Max?"

"Will you do it?"

"Implicitly—subject to the usual reservations."

"Keep your man on Creake in town and let me have his reports after you have seen them. Lunch with me here now. 'Phone up to your office that you are detained on unpleasant business and then give the deserving Parkinson an afternoon off by looking after me while we take a motor run round Mulling Common. If we have time we might go on to Brighton, feed at the 'Ship,' and come back in the cool."

"Amiable and thrice lucky mortal," sighed Mr Carlyle, his glance wandering round the room.

But, as it happened, Brighton did not figure in that day's itinerary. It had been Carrados's intention merely to pass Brookbend Cottage on this occasion, relying on his highly developed faculties, aided by Mr Carlyle's description, to inform him of the surroundings. A hundred yards before they reached the house he had given an order to his chauffeur to drop into the lowest speed and they were leisurely drawing past when a discovery by Mr Carlyle modified their plans.

"By Jupiter!" that gentleman suddenly exclaimed, "there's a board up, Max. The place is to be let."

Carrados picked up the tube again. A couple of sentences passed and the car stopped by the roadside, a score of paces past the limit of the garden. Mr Carlyle took out his notebook and wrote down the address of a firm of house agents.

"You might raise the bonnet and have a look at the engines, Harris," said Carrados. "We want to be occupied here for a few minutes."

"This is sudden; Hollyer knew nothing of their leaving," remarked Mr Carlyle.

"Probably not for three months yet. All the same, Louis, we will go on to the agents and get a card to view, whether we use it today or not."

A thick hedge, in its summer dress effectively screening the house beyond from public view, lay between the garden and the road. Above the hedge showed an occasional shrub; at the corner nearest to the car a chestnut flourished. The wooden gate, once white; which they had passed, was grimed and rickety. The road itself was still the unpretentious country lane that the advent of the electric car had found it. When Carrados had taken in these details there seemed little else to notice. He was on the point of giving Harris the order to go on when his ear caught a trivial sound.

"Someone is coming out of the house, Louis," he warned his friend. "It may be Hollyer, but he ought to have gone by this time."

"I don't hear anyone," replied the other, but as he spoke a door banged noisily and Mr Carlyle slipped into another seat and ensconced himself behind a copy of *The Globe*.

"Creake himself," he whispered across the car, as a man appeared at the gate. "Hollyer was right; he is hardly changed. Waiting for a car, I suppose."

But a car very soon swung past them from the direction in which Mr Creake was looking and it did not interest him. For a minute or two longer he continued to look expectantly along the road. Then he walked slowly up the drive back to the house.

"We will give him five or ten minutes," decided Carrados. "Harris is behaving very naturally."

Before even the shorter period had run out they were repaid. A telegraph-boy cycled leisurely along the road, and, leaving his machine at the gate, went up to the cottage. Evidently there was no reply, for in less than a minute he was trundling past them back again. Round the bend an approaching tram clanged its bell noisily, and, quickened by the warning sound, Mr Creake again appeared, this time with a small portmanteau in his hand. With a backward glance he hurried on towards the next stopping-place, and, boarding the car as it slackened down, he was carried out of their knowledge.

"Very convenient of Mr Creake," remarked Carrados, with quiet satisfaction. "We will now get the order and go over the house in his absence. It might be useful to have a look at the wire as well."

"It might, Max," acquiesced Mr Carlyle a little dryly. "But if it is, as it probably is, in Creake's pocket, how do you propose to get it?"

"By going to the post office, Louis."

"Quite so. Have you ever tried to see a copy of a telegram addressed to someone else?"

"I don't think I have ever had occasion yet," admitted Carrados. "Have you?"

"In one or two cases I have perhaps been an accessory to the act. It is generally a matter either of extreme delicacy or considerable expenditure."

"Then for Hollyer's sake we will hope for the former here." And Mr Carlyle smiled darkly and hinted that he was content to wait for a friendly revenge.

A little later, having left the car at the beginning of the straggling High Street, the two men called at the village post office. They had already visited the house agent and obtained an order to view Brookbend Cottage, declining, with some difficulty, the clerk's persistent offer to accompany them. The reason was soon forthcoming. "As a matter of fact," explained the young man, "the present tenant is under *our* notice to leave."

"Unsatisfactory, eh?" said Carrados encouragingly.

"He's a corker," admitted the clerk, responding to the friendly tone. "Fifteen months and not a doit of rent have we had. That's why I should have liked——"

"We will make every allowance," replied Carrados.

The post office occupied one side of a stationer's shop. It was not without some inward trepidation that Mr Carlyle found himself committed to the adventure. Carrados, on the other hand, was the personification of bland unconcern.

"You have just sent a telegram to Brookbend Cottage," he said to the young lady behind the brasswork lattice. "We think it may have come inaccurately and should like a repeat." He took out his purse. "What is the fee?"

The request was evidently not a common one. "Oh," said the girl uncertainly, "wait a minute, please." She turned to a pile of telegram duplicates behind the desk and ran a doubtful finger along the upper sheets. "I think this is all right. You want it repeated?"

"Please." Just a tinge of questioning surprise gave point to the courteous tone.

"It will be four pence. If there is an error the amount will be refunded."

Carrados put down a coin and received his change.

"Will it take long?" he inquired carelessly, as he pulled on his glove.

"You will most likely get it within a quarter of an hour," she replied.

"Now you've done it," commented Mr Carlyle, as they walked back to their car. "How do you propose to get that telegram, Max?"

"Ask for it," was the laconic explanation.

And, stripping the artifice of any elaboration, he simply asked for it and got it. The car, posted at a convenient bend in the road, gave him a warning note as the telegraph-boy approached. Then Carrados took up a convincing attitude with his hand on the gate while Mr Carlyle lent himself to the semblance of a departing friend. That was the inevitable impression when the boy rode up.

"Creake, Brookbend Cottage?" inquired Carrados, holding out his hand, and without a second thought the boy gave him the envelope and rode away on the assurance that there would be no reply.

"Some day, my friend," remarked Mr Carlyle, looking nervously towards the unseen house, "your ingenuity will get you into a tight corner."

"Then my ingenuity must get me out again," was the retort. "Let us have our 'view' now. The telegram can wait."

An untidy workwoman took their order and left them standing at the door. Presently a lady whom they both knew to be Mrs Creake appeared.

"You wish to see over the house?" she said, in a voice that was utterly devoid of any interest. Then, without waiting for a reply, she turned to the nearest door and threw it open.

"This is the drawing-room," she said, standing aside.

They walked into a sparsely furnished, damp-smelling room and made a pretence of looking round, while Mrs Creake remained silent and aloof.

"The dining-room," she continued, crossing the narrow hall and opening another door.

Mr Carlyle ventured a genial commonplace in the hope of inducing conversation. The result was not encouraging. Doubtless they would have gone through the house under the same frigid guidance had not Carrados been at fault in a way that Mr Carlyle had never known him fail before. In crossing the hall he stumbled over a mat and almost fell.

"Pardon my clumsiness," he said to the lady. "I am, unfortunately, quite blind. But," he added, with a smile, to turn off the mishap, "even a blind man must have a house."

The man who had eyes was surprised to see a flood of colour rush into Mrs Creake's face.

"Blind!" she exclaimed, "oh, I beg your pardon. Why did you not tell me? You might have fallen."

"I generally manage fairly well," he replied. "But, of course, in a strange house——"

She put her hand on his arm very lightly.

"You must let me guide you, just a little," she said.

The house, without being large, was full of passages and inconvenient turnings. Carrados asked an occasional question and found Mrs Creake quite amiable without effusion. Mr Carlyle followed them from room to room in the hope, though scarcely the expectation, of learning something that might be useful.

"This is the last one. It is the largest bedroom," said their guide. Only two of the upper rooms were fully furnished and Mr Carlyle at once saw, as Carrados knew without seeing, that this was the one which the Creakes occupied.

"A very pleasant outlook," declared Mr Carlyle.

"Oh, I suppose so," admitted the lady vaguely. The room, in fact, looked over the leafy garden and the road beyond. It had a French window opening on to a small balcony, and to this, under the strange influence that always attracted him to light, Carrados walked.

"I expect that there is a certain amount of repair needed?" he said, after standing there a moment.

"I am afraid there would be," she confessed.

"I ask because there is a sheet of metal on the floor here," he continued. "Now that, in an old house, spells dry rot to the wary observer."

"My husband said that the rain, which comes in a little under the window, was rotting the boards there," she replied. "He put that down recently. I had not noticed anything myself."

It was the first time she had mentioned her husband; Mr Carlyle pricked up his ears.

"Ah, that is a less serious matter," said Carrados. "May I step out on to the balcony?"

"Oh yes, if you like to." Then, as he appeared to be fumbling at the catch, "Let me open it for you."

But the window was already open, and Carrados, facing the various points of the compass, took in the bearings.

"A sunny, sheltered corner," he remarked. "An ideal spot for a deckchair and a book."

She shrugged her shoulders half contemptuously.

"I dare say," she replied, "but I never use it."

"Sometimes, surely," he persisted mildly. "It would be my favourite retreat. But then——"

"I was going to say that I had never even been out on it, but that would not be quite true. It has two uses for me, both equally romantic; I occasionally shake a duster from it, and when my husband returns late without his latchkey he wakes me up and I come out here and drop him mine."

Further revelation of Mr Creake's nocturnal habits was cut off, greatly to Mr Carlyle's annoyance, by a cough of unmistakable significance from the foot of the stairs. They had heard a trade cart drive up to the gate, a knock at the door, and the heavy-footed woman tramp along the hall.

"Excuse me a minute, please," said Mrs Creake.

"Louis," said Carrados, in a sharp whisper, the moment they were alone, "stand against the door."

With extreme plausibility Mr Carlyle began to admire a picture so situated that while he was there it was impossible to open the door more than a few inches. From that position he observed his confederate go through the curious procedure of kneeling down on the bedroom floor and for a full minute pressing his ear to the sheet of metal that had already engaged his attention. Then he rose to his feet, nodded, dusted his trousers, and Mr Carlyle moved to a less equivocal position.

"What a beautiful rose-tree grows up your balcony," remarked Carrados, stepping into the room as Mrs Creake returned. "I suppose you are very fond of gardening?"

"I detest it," she replied.

"But this *Glorie*, so carefully trained——?"

"Is it?" she replied. "I think my husband was nailing it up recently." By some strange fatality Carrados's most aimless remarks seemed to involve the absent Mr Creake. "Do you care to see the garden?"

The garden proved to be extensive and neglected. Behind the house was chiefly orchard. In front, some semblance of order had been kept up; here it was lawn and shrubbery, and the drive they had walked along. Two things interested Carrados: the soil at the foot of the balcony, which he declared on examination to be particularly suitable for roses, and the fine chestnut-tree in the corner by the road.

As they walked back to the car Mr Carlyle lamented that they had learned so little of Creake's movements.

"Perhaps the telegram will tell us something," suggested Carrados. "Read it, Louis."

Mr Carlyle cut open the envelope, glanced at the enclosure, and in spite of his disappointment could not restrain a chuckle.

"My poor Max," he explained, "you have put yourself to an amount of ingenious trouble for nothing. Creake is evidently taking a few days' holiday and prudently availed himself of the Meteorological Office forecast before going. Listen:

Immediate prospect for London warm and settled. Further outlook cooler but fine.

Well, well; I did get a pound of tomatoes for *my* four pence."

"You certainly scored there, Louis," admitted Carrados, with humorous appreciation. "I wonder," he added speculatively, "whether it is Creake's peculiar taste usually to spend his week-end holiday in London."

"Eh?" exclaimed Mr Carlyle, looking at the words again, "by gad, that's rum, Max. They go to Weston-super-Mare. Why on earth should he want to know about London?"

"I can make a guess, but before we are satisfied I must come here again. Take another look at that kite, Louis. Are there a few yards of string hanging loose from it?"

"Yes, there are."

"Rather thick string—unusually thick for the purpose?"

"Yes; but how do you know?"

As they drove home again Carrados explained, and Mr Carlyle sat aghast, saying incredulously: "Good God, Max, is it possible?"

An hour later he was satisfied that it was possible. In reply to his inquiry someone in his office telephoned him the information that "they" had left Paddington by the four-thirty for Weston.

It was more than a week after his introduction to Carrados that Lieutenant Hollyer had a summons to present himself at The Turrets again. He found Mr Carlyle already there and the two friends awaiting his arrival.

"I stayed in all day after hearing from you this morning, Mr Carrados," he said, shaking hands. "When I got your second message I was all ready to walk straight out of the house. That's how I did it in the time. I hope everything is all right?"

"Excellent," replied Carrados. "You'd better have something before we start. We probably have a long and perhaps an exciting night before us."

"And certainly a wet one," assented the lieutenant. "It was thundering over Mulling way as I came along."

"That is why you are here," said his host. "We are waiting for a certain message before we start, and in the meantime you may as well understand what we expect to happen. As you saw, there is a thunderstorm coming on. The Meteorological Office morning forecast predicted it for the whole of London if the conditions remained. That was why I kept you in readiness. Within an hour it is now inevitable that we shall experience a deluge. Here and there damage will be done to trees and buildings; here and there a person will probably be struck and killed."

"Yes."

"It is Mr Creake's intention that his wife should be among the victims."

"I don't exactly follow," said Hollyer, looking from one man to the other. "I quite admit that Creake would be immensely relieved if such a thing did happen, but the chance is surely an absurdly remote one."

"Yet unless we intervene it is precisely what a coroner's jury will decide has happened. Do you know whether your brother-in-law has any practical knowledge of electricity, Mr Hollyer?"

"I cannot say. He was so reserved, and we really knew so little of him——"

"Yet in 1896 an Austin Creake contributed an article on 'Alternating Currents' to the American *Scientific World*. That would argue a fairly intimate acquaintanceship."

"But do you mean that he is going to direct a flash of lightning?"

"Only into the minds of the doctor who conducts the post-mortem, and the coroner. This storm, the opportunity for which he has been waiting for weeks, is merely the cloak to his act. The weapon which he has planned to use—scarcely less powerful than lightning but much more tractable—is the high voltage current of electricity that flows along the tram wire at his gate."

"Oh!" exclaimed Lieutenant Hollyer, as the sudden revelation struck him.

"Some time between eleven o'clock tonight—about the hour when your sister goes to bed—and one-thirty in the morning—the time up to which he can rely on the current—Creake will throw a stone up at the balcony window. Most of his preparation has long been made; it only remains for him to connect up a short length to the window handle and a longer one at the other end to tap the live wire. That done, he will wake his wife in the way I have said. The moment she moves the catch of the window—and he has carefully filed its parts to ensure perfect contact—she will be electrocuted as effectually as if she sat in the executioner's chair in Sing Sing prison."

"But what are we doing here!" exclaimed Hollyer, starting to his feet, pale and horrified. "It is past ten now and anything may happen."

"Quite natural, Mr Hollyer," said Carrados reassuringly, "but you need have no anxiety. Creake is being watched, the house is being watched, and your sister is as safe as if she slept tonight in Windsor Castle. Be assured that whatever happens he will not be allowed to complete his scheme; but it is desirable to let him implicate himself to the fullest limit. Your brother-in-law, Mr Hollyer, is a man with a peculiar capacity for taking pains."

"He is a damned cold-blooded scoundrel!" exclaimed the young officer fiercely. "When I think of Millicent five years ago——"

"Well, for that matter, an enlightened nation has decided that electrocution is the most humane way of removing its superfluous citizens," suggested Carrados mildly. "He is certainly an ingenious-minded gentleman. It is his misfortune that in Mr Carlyle he was fated to be opposed by an even subtler brain——"

"No, no! Really, Max!" protested the embarrassed gentleman.

"Mr Hollyer will be able to judge for himself when I tell him that it was Mr Carlyle who first drew attention to the significance of the abandoned kite," insisted Carrados firmly. "Then, of course, its object became plain to me—as indeed to anyone. For ten minutes, perhaps, a wire must be carried from the overhead line to the chestnut-tree. Creake has everything in his favour, but it is just within possibility that the driver of an inopportune tram might notice the appendage. What of that? Why, for more than a week he has seen a derelict kite with its yards of trailing string hanging in the tree. A very calculating mind, Mr Hollyer. It would be interesting to know what line of action Mr Creake has mapped out for himself afterwards. I expect he has half-a-dozen artistic little touches up his sleeve.

"Possibly he would merely singe his wife's hair, burn her feet with a red-hot poker, shiver the glass of the French window, and be content with that to let well alone. You see, lightning is so varied in its effects that whatever he did or did not do would be right. He is in the impregnable position of the body showing all the symptoms of death by lightning shock and nothing else but lightning to account for it—a dilated eye, heart contracted in systole, bloodless lungs shrunk to a third the normal weight, and all the rest of it. When he has removed a few outward traces of his work Creake might quite safely 'discover' his dead wife and rush off for the nearest doctor. Or he may have decided to arrange a convincing alibi, and creep away, leaving the discovery to another. We shall never know; he will make no confession."

"I wish it was well over," admitted Hollyer. "I'm not particularly jumpy, but this gives me a touch of the creeps."

"Three more hours at the worst, lieutenant," said Carrados cheerfully. "Ah-ha, something is coming through now."

He went to the telephone and received a message from one quarter; then made another connection and talked for a few minutes with someone else.

"Everything working smoothly," he remarked between times over his shoulder. "Your sister has gone to bed, Mr Hollyer."

Then he turned to the house telephone and distributed his orders.

"So we," he concluded, "must get up."

By the time they were ready a large closed motor car was waiting. The lieutenant thought he recognised Parkinson in the well-swathed form beside the driver, but there was no temptation to linger for a second on the steps. Already the stinging rain had lashed the drive into the semblance of a frothy estuary; all round the lightning jagged its course through the incessant tremulous glow of more distant lightning, while the thunder only ceased its muttering to turn at close quarters and crackle viciously.

"One of the few things I regret missing," remarked Carrados tranquilly; "but I hear a good deal of colour in it."

The car slushed its way down to the gate, lurched a little heavily across the dip into the road, and, steadying as it came upon the straight, began to hum contentedly along the deserted highway.

"We are not going direct?" suddenly inquired Hollyer, after they had travelled perhaps half-a-dozen miles. The night was bewildering enough but he had the sailor's gift for location.

"No; through Hunscott Green and then by a field-path to the orchard at the back," replied Carrados. "Keep a sharp look out for the man with the lantern about here, Harris," he called through the tube.

"Something flashing just ahead, sir," came the reply, and the car slowed down and stopped.

Carrados dropped the near window as a man in glistening waterproof stepped from the shelter of a lich-gate and approached.

"Inspector Beedel, sir," said the stranger, looking into the car.

"Quite right, Inspector," said Carrados. "Get in."

"I have a man with me, sir."

"We can find room for him as well."

"We are very wet."

"So shall we all be soon."

The lieutenant changed his seat and the two burly forms took places side by side. In less than five minutes the car stopped again, this time in a grassy country lane.

"Now we have to face it," announced Carrados. "The inspector will show us the way."

The car slid round and disappeared into the night, while Beedel led the party to a stile in the hedge. A couple of fields brought them to the Brookbend boundary. There a figure stood out of the black foliage, exchanged a few words with their guide and piloted them along the shadows of the orchard to the back door of the house.

"You will find a broken pane near the catch of the scullery window," said the blind man.

"Right, sir," replied the inspector. "I have it. Now who goes through?"

"Mr Hollyer will open the door for us. I'm afraid you must take off your boots and all wet things, lieutenant. We cannot risk a single spot inside."

They waited until the back door opened, then each one divested himself in a similar manner and passed into the kitchen, where the remains of a fire still burned. The man from the orchard gathered together the discarded garments and disappeared again.

Carrados turned to the lieutenant.

"A rather delicate job for you now, Mr Hollyer. I want you to go up to your sister, wake her, and get her into another room with as little fuss as possible. Tell her as much as you think fit and let her understand that her very life depends on absolute stillness when she is alone. Don't be unduly hurried, but not a glimmer of a light, please."

Ten minutes passed by the measure of the battered old alarum on the dresser shelf before the young man returned.

"I've had rather a time of it," he reported, with a nervous laugh, "but I think it will be all right now. She is in the spare room."

"Then we will take our places. You and Parkinson come with me to the bedroom. Inspector, you have your own arrangements. Mr Carlyle will be with you."

They dispersed silently about the house. Hollyer glanced apprehensively at the door of the spare room as they passed it but within was as quiet as the grave. Their room lay at the other end of the passage.

"You may as well take your place in the bed now, Hollyer," directed Carrados when they were inside and the door closed. "Keep well down among the clothes. Creake has to get up on the balcony, you know, and he will probably peep through the window, but he dare come no farther. Then when he begins to throw up stones slip on this dressing-gown of your sister's. I'll tell you what to do after."

The next sixty minutes drew out into the longest hour that the lieutenant had ever known. Occasionally he heard a whisper pass between the two men who stood behind the window curtains, but he could see nothing. Then Carrados threw a guarded remark in his direction.

"He is in the garden now."

Something scraped slightly against the outer wall. But the night was full of wilder sounds, and in the house the furniture and the boards creaked and sprung between the yawling of the wind among the chimneys, the rattle of the thunder and the pelting of the rain. It was a time to quicken the steadiest pulse, and when the crucial moment came, when a pebble suddenly rang against the pane with a sound that the tense waiting magnified into a shivering crash, Hollyer leapt from the bed on the instant.

"Easy, easy," warned Carrados feelingly. "We will wait for another knock." He passed something across. "Here is a rubber glove. I have cut the wire but you had better put it on. Stand just for a moment at the window, move the catch so that it can blow open a little, and drop immediately. Now."

Another stone had rattled against the glass. For Hollyer to go through his part was the work merely of seconds, and with a few touches Carrados spread the dressing-gown to more effective disguise about the extended form. But an unforeseen and in the circumstances rather horrible interval followed, for Creake, in accordance with some detail of his never-revealed plan, continued to shower missile after missile against the panes until even the unimpressionable Parkinson shivered.

"The last act," whispered Carrados, a moment after the throwing had ceased. "He has gone round to the back. Keep as you are. We take cover now." He pressed behind the arras of an extemporised wardrobe, and the spirit of emptiness and desolation seemed once more to reign over the lonely house.

From half-a-dozen places of concealment ears were straining to catch the first guiding sound. He moved very stealthily, burdened, perhaps, by some strange scruple in the presence of the tragedy that he had not feared to contrive, paused for a moment at the bedroom door, then opened it very quietly, and in the fickle light read the consummation of his hopes.

"At last!" they heard the sharp whisper drawn from his relief. "At last!"

He took another step and two shadows seemed to fall upon him from behind, one on either side. With primitive instinct a cry of terror and surprise escaped him as he made a desperate movement to wrench himself free, and for a short second he almost succeeded in dragging one hand into a pocket. Then his wrists slowly came together and the handcuffs closed.

"I am Inspector Beedel," said the man on his right side. "You are charged with the attempted murder of your wife, Millicent Creake."

"You are mad," retorted the miserable creature, falling into a desperate calmness. "She has been struck by lightning."

"No, you blackguard, she hasn't," wrathfully exclaimed his brother-in-law, jumping up. "Would you like to see her?"

"I also have to warn you," continued the inspector impassively, "that anything you say may be used as evidence against you."

A startled cry from the farther end of the passage arrested their attention.

"Mr Carrados," called Hollyer, "oh, come at once."

At the open door of the other bedroom stood the lieutenant, his eyes still turned towards something in the room beyond, a little empty bottle in his hand.

"Dead!" he exclaimed tragically, with a sob, "with this beside her. Dead just when she would have been free of the brute."

The blind man passed into the room, sniffed the air, and laid a gentle hand on the pulseless heart.

"Yes," he replied. "That, Hollyer, does not always appeal to the woman, strange to say."

The Clever Mrs. Straithwaite

Mr Carlyle had arrived at The Turrets in the very best possible spirits. Everything about him, from his immaculate white spats to the choice gardenia in his buttonhole, from the brisk decision with which he took the front-door steps to the bustling importance with which he had positively brushed Parkinson aside at the door of the library, proclaimed consequence and the extremely good terms on which he stood with himself.

"Prepare yourself, Max," he exclaimed. "If I hinted at a case of exceptional delicacy that will certainly interest you by its romantic possibilities——?"

"I should have the liveliest misgivings. Ten to one it would be a jewel mystery," hazarded Carrados, as his friend paused with the point of his communication withheld, after the manner of a quizzical youngster with a promised *bon-bon* held behind his back. "If you made any more of it I should reluctantly be forced to the conclusion that the case involved a society scandal connected with a priceless pearl necklace."

Mr Carlyle's face fell.

"Then it *is* in the papers, after all?" he said, with an air of disappointment.

"What is in the papers, Louis?"

"Some hint of the fraudulent insurance of the Hon. Mrs Straithwaite's pearl necklace," replied Carlyle.

"Possibly," admitted Carrados. "But so far I have not come across it."

Mr Carlyle stared at his friend, and marching up to the table brought his hand down on it with an arresting slap.

"Then what in the name of goodness are you talking about, may I ask?" he demanded caustically. "If you know nothing of the Straithwaite affair, Max, what other pearl necklace case are you referring to?"

Carrados assumed the air of mild deprecation with which he frequently apologised for a blind man venturing to make a discovery.

"A philosopher once made the remark——"

"Had it anything to do with Mrs Straithwaite's—the Hon. Mrs Straithwaite's—pearl necklace? And let me warn you, Max, that I have read a good deal both of Mill and Spencer at odd times."

"It was neither Mill nor Spencer. He had a German name, so I will not mention it. He made the observation, which, of course, we recognise as an obvious commonplace when once it has been expressed, that in order to have an accurate knowledge of what a man will do on any occasion it is only necessary to study a single characteristic action of his."

"Utterly impracticable," declared Mr Carlyle.

"I therefore knew that when you spoke of a case of exceptional interest to *me*, what you really meant, Louis, was a case of exceptional interest to *you*."

Mr Carlyle's sudden thoughtful silence seemed to admit that possibly there might be something in the point.

"By applying, almost unconsciously, the same useful rule, I became aware that a mystery connected with a valuable pearl necklace and a beautiful young society *belle* would appeal the most strongly to your romantic imagination."

"Romantic! I, romantic? Thirty-five and a private inquiry agent! You are—positively feverish, Max."

"Incurably romantic—or you would have got over it by now: the worst kind."

"Max, this may prove a most important and interesting case. Will you be serious and discuss it?"

"Jewel cases are rarely either important or interesting. Pearl necklace mysteries, in nine cases out of ten, spring from the miasma of social pretence and vapid competition and only concern people who do not matter in the least. The only attractive thing about them is the name. They are so barren of originality that a criminological Linnæus could classify them with absolute nicety. I'll tell you what, we'll draw up a set of tables giving the solution to every possible pearl necklace case for the next twenty-one years."

"We will do any mortal thing you like, Max, if you will allow Parkinson to administer a bromo-seltzer and then enable me to meet the officials of the Direct Insurance without a blush."

For three minutes Carrados picked his unerring way among the furniture as he paced the room silently but with irresolution in his face. Twice his hand went to a paper-covered book lying on his desk, and twice he left it untouched.

"Have you ever been in the lion-house at feeding-time, Louis?" he demanded abruptly.

"In the very remote past, possibly," admitted Mr Carlyle guardedly.

"As the hour approaches it is impossible to interest the creatures with any other suggestion than that of raw meat. You came a day too late, Louis." He picked up the book and skimmed it adroitly into Mr Carlyle's hands. "I have already scented the gore, and tasted in imagination the joy of tearing choice morsels from other similarly obsessed animals."

"'*Catalogue des monnaies grecques et romaines*,'" read the gentleman. "'To be sold by auction at the Hotel Drouet, Paris, salle 8, April the 24th, 25th, etc.' H'm." He turned to the plates of photogravure illustration which gave an air to the volume. "This is an event, I suppose?"

"It is the sort of dispersal we get about once in three years," replied Carrados. "I seldom attend the little sales, but I save up and then have a week's orgy."

"And when do you go?"

"Today. By the afternoon boat—Folkestone. I have already taken rooms at Mascot's. I'm sorry it has fallen so inopportunely, Louis."

Mr Carlyle rose to the occasion with a display of extremely gentlemanly feeling—which had the added merit of being quite genuine.

"My dear chap, your regrets only serve to remind me how much I owe to you already. *Bon voyage*, and the most desirable of Eu—Eu—well, perhaps it would be safer to say, of Kimons, for your collection."

"I suppose," pondered Carrados, "this insurance business might have led to other profitable connexions?"

"That is quite true," admitted his friend. "I have been trying for some time—but do not think any more of it, Max."

"What time is it?" demanded Carrados suddenly.

"Eleven-twenty-five."

"Good. Has any officious idiot had anyone arrested?"

"No, it is only——"

"Never mind. Do you know much of the case?"

"Practically nothing as yet, unfortunately. I came——"

"Excellent. Everything is on our side. Louis, I won't go this afternoon—I will put off till the night boat from Dover. That will give us nine hours."

"Nine hours?" repeated the mystified Carlyle, scarcely daring to put into thought the scandalous inference that Carrados's words conveyed.

"Nine full hours. A pearl necklace case that cannot at least be left straight after nine hours' work will require a column to itself in our chart. Now, Louis, where does this Direct Insurance live?"

Carlyle had allowed his blind friend to persuade him into—as they had seemed at the beginning—many mad enterprises. But none had ever, in the light of his own experience, seemed so foredoomed to failure as when, at eleven-thirty, Carrados ordered his luggage to be on the platform of Charing Cross Station at eight-fifty and then turned light-heartedly to the task of elucidating the mystery of Mrs Straithwaite's pearl necklace in the interval.

The head office of the Direct and Intermediate Insurance Company proved to be in Victoria Street. Thanks to Carrados's speediest car, they entered the building as the clocks of Westminster were striking twelve, but for the next twenty minutes they were consigned to the general office while Mr Carlyle fumed and displayed his watch ostentatiously. At last a clerk slid off his stool by the speaking-tube and approached them.

"Mr Carlyle?" he said. "The general manager will see you now, but as he has another appointment in ten minutes he will be glad if you will make your business as short as possible. This way, please."

Mr Carlyle bit his lip at the pompous formality of the message but he was too experienced to waste any words about it and with a mere nod he followed, guiding his friend until they reached the Manager's room. But, though subservient to circumstance, he was far from being negligible when he wished to create an impression.

"Mr Carrados has been good enough to give us a consultation over this small affair," he said, with just the necessary touches of deference and condescension that it was impossible either to miss or to resent. "Unfortunately he can do little more as he has to leave almost at once to direct an important case in Paris."

The general manager conveyed little, either in his person or his manner, of the brisk precision that his message seemed to promise. The name of Carrados struck him as being somewhat familiar—something a little removed from the routine of his business and a matter therefore that he could unbend over. He continued to stand comfortably before his office fire, making up by a tolerant benignity of his hard and bulbous eye for the physical deprivation that his attitude entailed on his visitors.

"Paris, egad?" he grunted. "Something in your line that France can take from us since the days of—what's-his-name—Vidocq, eh? Clever fellow, that, what? Wasn't it about him and the Purloined Letter?"

Carrados smiled discreetly.

"Capital, wasn't it?" he replied. "But there is something else that Paris can learn from London, more in your way, sir. Often when I drop in to see the principal of one of their chief houses or the head of a government department, we fall into an entertaining discussion of this or that subject that may be on the *tapis*. 'Ah, *monsieur*,' I say, after perhaps half-an-hour's conversation, 'it is very amiable of you and sometimes I regret our insular methods, but it is not thus that great businesses are formed. At home, if I call upon one of our princes of industry—a railway director, a merchant, or the head of one of our leading insurance companies—nothing will tempt him for a moment from the stern outline of the business in hand. You are too complaisant; the merest gossip takes advantage of you.'"

"That's quite true," admitted the general manager, occupying the revolving chair at his desk and assuming a serious and very determined expression. "Slackers, I call them. Now, Mr Carlyle, where are we in this business?"

"I have your letter of yesterday. We should naturally like all the particulars you can give us."

The manager threw open a formidable-looking volume with an immense display of energy, sharply flattened some typewritten pages that had ventured to raise their heads, and lifted an impressive finger.

"We start here, the 27th of January. On that day Karsfeld, the Princess Street jeweller, y'know, who acted as our jewellery assessor, forwards a proposal of the Hon. Mrs Straithwaite to insure a pearl necklace against theft. Says that he has had an opportunity of examining it and passes it at five thousand pounds. That business goes through in the ordinary way; the premium is paid and the policy taken out.

"A couple of months later Karsfeld has a little unpleasantness with us and resigns. Resignation accepted. We have nothing against him, you understand. At the same time there is an impression among the directors that he has been perhaps a little too easy in his ways, a little too—let us say, expansive, in some of his valuations and too accommodating to his own clients in recommending to us business of a—

well—speculative basis; business that we do not care about and which we now feel is foreign to our traditions as a firm. However"—the general manager threw apart his stubby hands as though he would shatter any fabric of criminal intention that he might be supposed to be insidiously constructing—"that is the extent of our animadversion against Karsfeld. There are no irregularities and you may take it from me that the man is all right."

"You would propose accepting the fact that a five-thousand-pound necklace was submitted to him?" suggested Mr Carlyle.

"I should," acquiesced the manager, with a weighty nod. "Still— this brings us to April the third—this break, so to speak, occurring in our routine, it seemed a good opportunity for us to assure ourselves on one or two points. Mr Bellitzer—you know Bellitzer, of course; know *of* him, I should say—was appointed *vice* Karsfeld and we wrote to certain of our clients, asking them—as our policies entitled us to do—as a matter of form to allow Mr Bellitzer to confirm the assessment of his predecessor. Wrapped it up in silver paper, of course; said it would certify the present value and be a guarantee that would save them some formalities in case of ensuing claim, and so on. Among others, wrote to the Hon. Mrs Straithwaite to that effect—April fourth. Here is her reply of three days later. Sorry to disappoint us, but the necklace has just been sent to her bank for custody as she is on the point of leaving town. Also scarcely sees that it is necessary in her case as the insurance was only taken so recently."

"That is dated April the seventh?" inquired Mr Carlyle, busy with pencil and pocket-book.

"April seventh," repeated the manager, noting this conscientiousness with an approving glance and then turning to regard questioningly the indifferent attitude of his other visitor. "That put us on our guard—naturally. Wrote by return regretting the necessity and suggesting that a line to her bankers, authorizing them to show us the necklace, would meet the case and save her any personal trouble. Interval of a week. Her reply, April sixteenth. Thursday last. Circumstances have altered her plans and she has returned to London sooner than she expected. Her jewel-case has been returned from the bank, and will we send our man round—'our man,' Mr Carlyle!—on Saturday morning not later than twelve, please."

The manager closed the record book, with a sweep of his hand cleared his desk for revelations, and leaning forward in his chair fixed Mr Carlyle with a pragmatic eye.

"On Saturday Mr Bellitzer goes to Luneburg Mansions and the Hon. Mrs Straithwaite shows him the necklace. He examines it carefully, assesses its insurable value up to five thousand, two hundred and fifty pounds, and reports us to that effect. But he reports something else, Mr Carlyle. It is not the necklace that the lady had insured."

"Not the necklace?" echoed Mr Carlyle.

"No. In spite of the number of pearls and a general similarity there are certain technical differences, well known to experts, that made the fact indisputable. The Hon. Mrs Straithwaite has been guilty of misrepresentation. Possibly she has no fraudulent intention. We are willing to pay to find out. That's your business."

Mr Carlyle made a final note and put away his book with an air of decision that could not fail to inspire confidence.

"Tomorrow," he said, "we shall perhaps be able to report something."

"Hope so," vouchsafed the manager. "'Morning."

From his position near the window, Carrados appeared to wake up to the fact that the interview was over.

"But so far," he remarked blandly, with his eyes towards the great man in the chair, "you have told us nothing of the theft."

The manager regarded the speaker dumbly for a moment and then turned to Mr Carlyle.

"What does he mean?" he demanded pungently.

But for once Mr Carlyle's self-possession had forsaken him. He recognised that somehow Carrados had been guilty of an appalling lapse, by which his reputation for prescience was wrecked in that quarter for ever, and at the catastrophe his very ears began to exude embarrassment.

In the awkward silence Carrados himself seemed to recognise that something was amiss.

"We appear to be at cross-purposes," he observed. "I inferred that the disappearance of the necklace would be the essence of our investigation."

"Have I said a word about it disappearing?" demanded the manager, with a contempt-laden raucity that he made no pretence of softening. "You don't seem to have grasped the simple facts about the case, Mr Carrados. Really, I hardly think——Oh, come in!"

There had been a knock at the door, then another. A clerk now entered with an open telegram.

"Mr Longworth wished you to see this at once, sir."

"We may as well go," whispered Mr Carlyle with polite depression to his colleague.

"Here, wait a minute," said the manager, who had been biting his thumb-nail over the telegram. "No, not you"—to the lingering clerk—"you clear." Much of the embarrassment that had troubled Mr Carlyle a minute before seemed to have got into the manager's system. "I don't understand this," he confessed awkwardly. "It's from Bellitzer. He wires:

Have just heard alleged robbery Straithwaite pearls. Advise strictest investigation.

Mr Carlyle suddenly found it necessary to turn to the wall and consult a highly coloured lithographic inducement to insure. Mr Carrados alone remained to meet the manager's constrained glance.

"Still, *he* tells us really nothing about the theft," he remarked sociably.

"No," admitted the manager, experiencing some little difficulty with his breathing, "he does not."

"Well, we still hope to be able to report something tomorrow. Goodbye."

It was with an effort that Mr Carlyle straightened himself sufficiently to take leave of the manager. Several times in the corridor he stopped to wipe his eyes.

"Max, you unholy fraud," he said, when they were outside, "you knew all the time."

"No; I told you that I knew nothing of it," replied Carrados frankly. "I am absolutely sincere."

"Then all I can say is, that I see a good many things happen that I don't believe in."

Carrados's reply was to hold out a coin to a passing newsboy and to hand the purchase to his friend who was already in the car.

"There is a slang injunction to 'keep your eyes skinned.' That being out of my power, I habitually 'keep my ears skinned.' You would be surprised to know how very little you hear, Louis, and how much you miss. In the last five minutes up there I have had three different newsboys' account of this development."

"By Jupiter, she hasn't waited long!" exclaimed Mr Carlyle, referring eagerly to the headlines. "'*Pearl Necklace Sensation. Society Lady's £5000 Trinket Disappears.*' Things are moving. Where next, Max?"

"It is now a quarter to one," replied Carrados, touching the fingers of his watch. "We may as well lunch on the strength of this new turn. Parkinson will have finished packing; I can telephone him to come to us at Merrick's in case I require him. Buy all the papers, Louis, and we will collate the points."

The undoubted facts that survived a comparison were few and meagre, for in each case a conscientious journalist had touched up a few vague or doubtful details according to his own ideas of probability. All agreed that on Tuesday evening—it was now Thursday—Mrs Straithwaite had formed one of a party that had occupied a box at the new Metropolitan Opera House to witness the performance of *La Pucella*, and that she had been robbed of a set of pearls valued in round figures at five thousand pounds. There agreement ended. One version represented the theft as taking place at the theatre. Another asserted that at the last moment the lady had decided not to wear the necklace that evening and that its abstraction had been cleverly effected from the flat during her absence. Into a third account came an ambiguous reference to Markhams, the well-known jewellers, and a conjecture that their loss would certainly be covered by insurance.

Mr Carlyle, who had been picking out the salient points of the narratives, threw down the last paper with an impatient shrug.

"Why in heaven's name have we Markhams coming into it now?" he demanded. "What have they to lose by it, Max? What do you make of the thing?"

"There is the second genuine string—the one Bellitzer saw. That belongs to someone."

"By gad, that's true—only five days ago, too. But what does our lady stand to make by that being stolen?"

Carrados was staring into obscurity between an occasional moment of attention to his cigarette or coffee.

"By this time the lady probably stands to wish she was well out of it," he replied thoughtfully. "Once you have set this sort of stone rolling and it has got beyond you——" He shook his head.

"It has become more intricate than you expected?" suggested Carlyle, in order to afford his friend an opportunity of withdrawing.

Carrados pierced the intention and smiled affectionately.

"My dear Louis," he said, "one-fifth of the mystery is already solved."

"One-fifth? How do you arrive at that?"

"Because it is one-twenty-five and we started at eleven-thirty."

He nodded to their waiter, who was standing three tables away, and paid the bill. Then with perfect gravity he permitted Mr Carlyle to lead him by the arm into the street, where their car was waiting, Parkinson already there in attendance.

"Sure I can be of no further use?" asked Carlyle. Carrados had previously indicated that after lunch he would go on alone, but, because he was largely sceptical of the outcome, the professional man felt guiltily that he was deserting. "Say the word?"

Carrados smiled and shook his head. Then he leaned across.

"I am going to the opera house now; then, possibly, to talk to Markham a little. If I have time I must find a man who knows the Straithwaites, and after that I may look up Inspector Beedel if he is at the Yard. That is as far as I can see yet, until I call at Luneburg Mansions. Come round on the third anyway."

"Dear old chap," murmured Mr Carlyle, as the car edged its way ahead among the traffic. "Marvellous shots he makes!"

In the meanwhile, at Luneburg Mansions, Mrs Straithwaite had been passing anything but a pleasant day. She had awakened with a headache and an overnight feeling that there was some unpleasantness to be gone on with. That it did not amount to actual fear was due to the enormous self-importance and the incredible ignorance which ruled the butterfly brain of the young society beauty—for in spite of three years' experience of married life Stephanie Straithwaite was as yet on the enviable side of two and twenty.

Anticipating an early visit from a particularly obnoxious sister-in-law, she had remained in bed until after lunch in order to be able to deny herself with the more conviction. Three journalists who would have afforded her the mild excitement of being interviewed had called and been in turn put off with polite regrets by her husband. The objectionable sister-in-law postponed her visit until the afternoon and for more than an hour Stephanie "suffered agonies." When the visitor had left and the martyred hostess announced her intention of flying immediately to the consoling society of her own bridge circle, Straithwaite had advised her, with some significance, to wait for a lead. The unhappy lady cast herself bodily down upon a couch and asked whether she was to become a nun. Straithwaite merely shrugged his shoulders and remembered a club engagement. Evidently there was no need for him to become a monk: Stephanie followed him down the hall, arguing and protesting. That was how they came jointly to encounter Carrados at the door.

"I have come from the Direct Insurance in the hope of being able to see Mrs Straithwaite," he explained, when the door opened rather suddenly before he had knocked. "My name is Carrados—Max Carrados."

There was a moment of hesitation all round. Then Stephanie read difficulties in the straightening lines of her husband's face and rose joyfully to the occasion.

"Oh yes; come in, Mr Carrados," she exclaimed graciously. "We are not quite strangers, you know. You found out something for Aunt Pigs; I forget what, but she was most frantically impressed."

"Lady Poges," enlarged Straithwaite, who had stepped aside and was watching the development with slow, calculating eyes. "But, I say, you are blind, aren't you?"

Carrados's smiling admission turned the edge of Mrs Straithwaite's impulsive, "Teddy!"

"But I get along all right," he added. "I left my man down in the car and I found your door first shot, you see."

The references reminded the velvet-eyed little mercenary that the man before her had the reputation of being quite desirably rich, his queer taste merely an eccentric hobby. The consideration made her resolve to be quite her nicest possible, as she led the way to the drawing-room. Then Teddy, too, had been horrid beyond words and must be made to suffer in the readiest way that offered.

"Teddy is just going out and I was to be left in solitary bereavement if you had not appeared," she explained airily. "It wasn't very compy only to come to see me on business by the way, Mr Carrados, but if those are your only terms I must agree."

Straithwaite, however, did not seem to have the least intention of going. He had left his hat and stick in the hall and he now threw his yellow gloves down on a table and took up a negligent position on the arm of an easy-chair.

"The thing is, where do we stand?" he remarked tentatively.

"That is the attitude of the insurance company, I imagine," replied Carrados.

"I don't see that the company has any standing in the matter. We haven't reported any loss to them and we are not making any claim, so far. That ought to be enough."

"I assume that they act on general inference," explained Carrados. "A limited liability company is not subtle, Mrs Straithwaite. This one knows that you have insured a five-thousand-pound pearl necklace with it, and when it becomes a matter of common knowledge that you have had one answering to that description stolen, it jumps to the conclusion that they are one and the same."

"But they aren't—worse luck," explained the hostess. "This was a string that I let Markhams send me to see if I would keep."

"The one that Bellitzer saw last Saturday?"

"Yes," admitted Mrs Straithwaite quite simply.

Straithwaite glanced sharply at Carrados and then turned his eyes with lazy indifference to his wife.

"My dear Stephanie, what are you thinking of?" he drawled. "Of course those could not have been Markhams' pearls. Not knowing that you are much too clever to do such a foolish thing, Mr Carrados will begin to think that you have had fraudulent designs upon his company."

Whether the tone was designed to exasperate or merely fell upon a fertile soil, Stephanie threw a hateful little glance in his direction.

"I don't care," she exclaimed recklessly; "I haven't the least little objection in the world to Mr Carrados knowing exactly how it happened."

Carrados put in an instinctive word of warning, even raised an arresting hand, but the lady was much too excited, too voluble, to be denied.

"It doesn't really matter in the least, Mr Carrados, because nothing came of it," she explained. "There never were any real pearls to be insured. It would have made no difference to the company, because I did not regard this as an ordinary insurance from the first. It was to be a loan."

"A loan?" repeated Carrados.

"Yes. I shall come into heaps and heaps of money in a few years' time under Prin-Prin's will. Then I should pay back whatever had been advanced."

"But would it not have been better—simpler—to have borrowed purely on the anticipation?"

"We have," explained the lady eagerly. "We have borrowed from all sorts of people, and both Teddy and I have signed heaps and heaps of papers, until now no one will lend any more."

The thing was too tragically grotesque to be laughed at. Carrados turned his face from one to the other and by ear, and by even finer perceptions, he focussed them in his mind—the delicate, feather-headed beauty, with the heart of a cat and the irresponsibility of a kitten, eye and mouth already hardening under the stress of her frantic life, and, across the room, her debonair consort, whose lank pose and nonchalant attitude towards the situation Carrados had not yet categorised.

Straithwaite's dry voice, with its habitual drawl, broke into his reflection.

"I don't suppose for a moment that you either know or care what this means, my dear girl, but I will proceed to enlighten you. It means the extreme probability that unless you can persuade Mr Carrados to hold his tongue, you, and—without prejudice—I also, will get two years' hard. And yet, with unconscious but consummate artistry, it seems to me that you have perhaps done the trick; for, unless I am mistaken, Mr Carrados will find himself unable to take advantage of your guileless confidence, whereas he would otherwise have quite easily found out all he wanted."

"That is the most utter nonsense, Teddy," cried Stephanie, with petulant indignation. She turned to Carrados with the assurance of meeting understanding. "We know Mr Justice Enderleigh very well indeed, and if there was any bother I should not have the least difficulty in getting him to take the case privately and in explaining everything to him. But why should there be? Why indeed?" A brilliant little new idea possessed her. "Do you know any of these insurance people at all intimately, Mr Carrados?"

"The general manager and I are on terms that almost justify us in addressing each other as 'silly ass,'" admitted Carrados.

"There you see, Teddy, you needn't have been in a funk. Mr Carrados would put everything right. Let me tell you exactly how I had arranged it. I dare say you know that insurances are only too pleased to pay for losses: it gives them an advertisement. Freddy Tantroy told me so, and his father is a director of hundreds of companies. Only, of course, it must be done quite regularly. Well, for months and months we had both been most frightfully hard up, and, unfortunately, everyone else—at least all our friends—seemed just as stony. I had been absolutely racking my poor brain for an idea when I remembered papa's wedding present. It was a string of pearls that he sent me from Vienna, only a month before he died; not real, of course, because poor papa was always quite utterly on the verge himself, but very good imitation and in perfect taste. Otherwise I am sure papa would rather have sent a silver pen-wiper, for although he had to live abroad because of what people said, his taste was simply exquisite and he was most romantic in his ideas. What do you say, Teddy?"

"Nothing, dear; it was only my throat ticking."

"I wore the pearls often and millions of people had seen them. Of course our own people knew about them, but others took it for granted that they were genuine for me to be wearing them. Teddy will tell you that I was almost babbling in delirium, things were becoming so ghastly, when an idea occurred. Tweety—she's a cousin of Teddy's, but quite an aged person—has a whole coffer full of jewels that she never wears and I knew that there was a necklace very like mine among them. She was going almost immediately to Africa for some shooting, so I literally flew into the wilds of Surrey and begged her on my knees to lend me her pearls for the Lycester House dance. When I got back with them I stamped on the clasp and took it at once to Karsfeld in Princess Street. I told him they were only paste but I thought they were rather good and I wanted them by the next day. And of course he looked at them, and then looked again, and then asked me if I was certain they were imitation, and I said, Well, we had never thought twice about it, because poor papa was always rather chronic, only certainly he did occasionally have fabulous streaks at the tables, and finally, like a great owl, Karsfeld said:

"'I am happy to be able to congratulate you, madam. They are undoubtedly Bombay pearls of very fine orient. They are certainly worth five thousand pounds.'"

From this point Mrs Straithwaite's narrative ran its slangy, obvious course. The insurance effected—on the strict understanding of the lady with herself that it was merely a novel form of loan, and after satisfying her mind on Freddy Tantroy's authority that the Direct and Intermediate could stand a temporary loss of five thousand pounds—the genuine pearls were returned to the cousin in the wilds of Surrey and Stephanie continued to wear the counterfeit. A decent interval was allowed to intervene and the plot was on the point of maturity when the company's request for a scrutiny fell like a thunderbolt. With many touching appeals to Mr Carrados to picture her frantic distraction, with appropriate little gestures of agony and despair, Stephanie described her absolute prostration, her subsequent wild scramble through the jewel stocks of London to find a substitute. The danger over, it became increasingly necessary to act without delay, not only to anticipate possible further curiosity on the part of the insurance, but in order to secure the means with which to meet an impending obligation held over them by an inflexibly obdurate Hebrew.

The evening of the previous Tuesday was to be the time; the opera house, during the performance of *La Pucella*, the place. Straithwaite, who was not interested in that precise form of drama, would not be expected to be present, but with a false moustache and a few other touches which his experience as an amateur placed within his easy reach, he was to occupy a stall, an end stall somewhere beneath his wife's box. At an agreed signal Stephanie would jerk open the catch of the necklace, and as she leaned forward the ornament would trickle off her neck and disappear into the arena beneath. Straithwaite, the only one prepared for anything happening, would have no difficulty in securing it. He would look up quickly as if to identify the box, and with the jewels in his hand walk deliberately out into the passage. Before anyone had quite realised what was happening he would have left the house.

Carrados turned his face from the woman to the man.

"This scheme commended itself to you, Mr Straithwaite?"

"Well, you see, Stephanie is so awfully clever that I took it for granted that the thing would go all right."

"And three days before, Bellitzer had already reported misrepresentation and that two necklaces had been used!"

"Yes," admitted Straithwaite, with an air of reluctant candour, "I had a suspicion that Stephanie's native ingenuity rather fizzled there. You know, Stephanie dear, there *is* a difference, it seems, between Bombay and Californian pearls."

"The wretch!" exclaimed the girl, grinding her little teeth vengefully. "And we gave him champagne!"

"But nothing came of it; so it doesn't matter?" prompted Straithwaite.

"Except that now Markhams' pearls have gone and they are hinting at all manner of diabolical things," she wrathfully reminded him.

"True," he confessed. "That is by way of a sequel, Mr Carrados. I will endeavour to explain that part of the incident, for even yet Stephanie seems unable to do me justice."

He detached himself from the arm of the chair and lounged across the room to another chair, where he took up exactly the same position.

"On the fatal evening I duly made my way to the theatre—a little late, so as to take my seat unobserved. After I had got the general hang I glanced up occasionally until I caught Stephanie's eye, by which I knew that she was there all right and concluded that everything was going along quite jollily. According to arrangement, I was to cross the theatre immediately the first curtain fell and standing opposite

Stephanie's box twist my watch chain until it was certain that she had seen me. Then Stephanie was to fan herself three times with her programme. Both, you will see, perfectly innocent operations, and yet conveying to each other the intimation that all was well. Stephanie's idea, of course. After that, I would return to my seat and Stephanie would do her part at the first opportunity in Act II.

"However, we never reached that. Towards the end of the first act something white and noiseless slipped down and fell at my feet. For the moment I thought they were the pearls gone wrong. Then I saw that it was a glove—a lady's glove. Intuition whispered that it was Stephanie's before I touched it. I picked it up and quietly got out. Down among the fingers was a scrap of paper—the corner torn off a programme. On it were pencilled words to this effect:

"'Something quite unexpected. Can do nothing tonight. Go back at once and wait. May return early. Frightfully worried.—S.'"

"You kept the paper, of course?"

"Yes. It is in my desk in the next room. Do you care to see it?"

"Please."

Straithwaite left the room and Stephanie flung herself into a charming attitude of entreaty.

"Mr Carrados, you will get them back for us, won't you? It would not really matter, only I seem to have signed something and now Markhams threaten to bring an action against us for culpable negligence in leaving them in an empty flat."

"You see," explained Straithwaite, coming back in time to catch the drift of his wife's words, "except to a personal friend like yourself, it is quite impossible to submit these clues. The first one alone would raise embarrassing inquiries; the other is beyond explanation. Consequently I have been obliged to concoct an imaginary burglary in our absence and to drop the necklace case among the rhododendrons in the garden at the back, for the police to find."

"Deeper and deeper," commented Carrados.

"Why, yes. Stephanie and I are finding that out, aren't we, dear? However, here is the first note; also the glove. Of course I returned immediately. It was Stephanie's strategy and I was under her orders. In something less than half-an-hour I heard a motor car stop outside. Then the bell here rang.

"I think I have said that I was alone. I went to the door and found a man who might have been anything standing there. He merely said: 'Mr Straithwaite?' and on my nodding handed me a letter. I tore it open in the hall and read it. Then I went into my room and read it again. This is it:

Dear T.,—Absolutely ghastly. We simply must put off tonight. Will explain that later. Now what do you think? Bellitzer is here in the stalls and young K. D. has asked him to join us at supper at the Savoy. It appears that the creature is Something and I suppose the D.'s want to borrow off him. I can't get out of it and I am literally quaking. Don't you see, he will spot something? Send me the M. string at once and I will change somehow before supper. I am scribbling this in the dark. I have got the Willoughby's man to take it. Don't, don't fail.—S.

"It is ridiculous, preposterous," snapped Stephanie. "I never wrote a word of it—or the other. There was I, sitting the whole evening. And Teddy—oh, it is maddening!"

"I took it into my room and looked at it closely," continued the unruffled Straithwaite. "Even if I had any reason to doubt, the internal evidence was convincing, but how could I doubt? It read like a continuation of the previous message. The writing was reasonably like Stephanie's under the circumstances, the envelope had obviously been obtained from the box-office of the theatre and the paper itself was a sheet of the programme. A corner was torn off; I put against it the previous scrap and they exactly fitted." The gentleman shrugged his shoulders, stretched his legs with deliberation and walked across the room to look out of the window. "I made them up into a neat little parcel and handed it over," he concluded.

Carrados put down the two pieces of paper which he had been minutely examining with his finger-tips and still holding the glove addressed his small audience collectively.

"The first and most obvious point is that whoever carried out the scheme had more than a vague knowledge of your affairs, not only in general but also relating to this—well, loan, Mrs Straithwaite."

"Just what I have insisted," agreed Straithwaite. "You hear that, Stephanie?"

"But who is there?" pleaded Stephanie, with weary intonation. "Absolutely no one in the wide world. Not a soul."

"So one is liable to think offhand. Let us go further, however, merely accounting for those who are in a position to have information. There are the officials of the insurance company who suspect something; there is Bellitzer, who perhaps knows a little more. There is the lady in Surrey from whom the pearls were borrowed, a Mr Tantroy who seems to have been consulted, and, finally, your own servants. All these people have friends, or underlings, or observers. Suppose Mr Bellitzer's confidential clerk happens to be the sweetheart of your maid?"

"They would still know very little."

"The arc of a circle may be very little, but, given that, it is possible to construct the entire figure. Now your servants, Mrs Straithwaite? We are accusing no one, of course."

"There is the cook, Mullins. She displayed alarming influenza on Tuesday morning, and although it was most frightfully inconvenient I packed her off home without a moment's delay. I have a horror of the influenza. Then Fraser, the parlour-maid. She does my hair—I haven't really got a maid, you know."

"Beta," prompted Straithwaite.

"Oh yes, Beta. She's a daily girl and helps in the kitchen. I have no doubt she is capable of any villainy."

"And all were out on Tuesday evening?"

"Yes. Mullins gone home. Beta left early as there was no dinner, and I told Fraser to take the evening after she had dressed me so that Teddy could make up and get out without being seen."

Carrados turned to his other witness.

"The papers and the glove have been with you ever since?"

"Yes, in my desk."

"Locked?"

"Yes."

"And this glove, Mrs Straithwaite? There is no doubt that it is yours?"

"I suppose not," she replied. "I never thought. I know that when I came to leave the theatre one had vanished and Teddy had it here."

"That was the first time you missed it?"

"Yes."

"But it might have gone earlier in the evening—mislaid or lost or stolen?"

"I remember taking them off in the box. I sat in the corner farthest from the stage—the front row, of course—and I placed them on the support."

"Where anyone in the next box could abstract one without much difficulty at a favourable moment."

"That is quite likely. But we didn't see anyone in the next box."

"I have half an idea that I caught sight of someone hanging back," volunteered Straithwaite.

"Thank you," said Carrados, turning towards him almost gratefully. "That is most important—that you think you saw someone hanging back. Now the other glove, Mrs Straithwaite; what became of that?"

"An odd glove is not very much good, is it?" said Stephanie. "Certainly I wore it coming back. I think I threw it down somewhere in here. Probably it is still about. We are in a frantic muddle and nothing is being done."

The second glove was found on the floor in a corner. Carrados received it and laid it with the other.

"You use a very faint and characteristic scent, I notice, Mrs Straithwaite," he observed.

"Yes; it is rather sweet, isn't it? I don't know the name because it is in Russian. A friend in the Embassy sent me some bottles from Petersburg."

"But on Tuesday you supplemented it with something stronger," he continued, raising the gloves delicately one after the other to his face.

"Oh, eucalyptus; rather," she admitted. "I simply drenched my handkerchief with it."

"You have other gloves of the same pattern?"

"Have I? Now let me think! Did you give them to me, Teddy?"

"No," replied Straithwaite from the other end of the room. He had lounged across to the window and his attitude detached him from the discussion. "Didn't Whitstable?" he added shortly.

"Of course. Then there are three pairs, Mr Carrados, because I never let Bimbi lose more than that to me at once, poor boy."

"I think you are rather tiring yourself out, Stephanie," warned her husband.

Carrados's attention seemed to leap to the voice; then he turned courteously to his hostess.

"I appreciate that you have had a trying time lately, Mrs Straithwaite," he said. "Every moment I have been hoping to let you out of the witness-box——"

"Perhaps tomorrow——" began Straithwaite, recrossing the room.

"Impossible; I leave town tonight," replied Carrados firmly. "You have three pairs of these gloves, Mrs Straithwaite. Here is one. The other two——?"

"One pair I have not worn yet. The other—good gracious, I haven't been out since Tuesday! I suppose it is in my glove-box."

"I must see it, please."

Straithwaite opened his mouth, but as his wife obediently rose to her feet to comply he turned sharply away with the word unspoken.

"These are they," she said, returning.

"Mr Carrados and I will finish our investigation in my room," interposed Straithwaite, with quiet assertiveness. "I should advise you to lie down for half-an-hour, Stephanie, if you don't want to be a nervous wreck tomorrow."

"You must allow the culprit to endorse that good advice, Mrs Straithwaite," added Carrados. He had been examining the second pair of gloves as they spoke and he now handed them back again. "They are undoubtedly of the same set," he admitted, with extinguished interest, "and so our clue runs out."

"I hope you don't mind," apologised Straithwaite, as he led his guest to his own smoking-room. "Stephanie," he confided, becoming more cordial as two doors separated them from the lady, "is a creature of nerves and indiscretions. She forgets. Tonight she will not sleep. Tomorrow she will suffer." Carrados divined the grin. "So shall I!"

"On the contrary, pray accept my regrets," said the visitor. "Besides," he continued, "there is nothing more for me to do here, I suppose. . . ."

"It is a mystery," admitted Straithwaite, with polite agreement. "Will you try a cigarette?"

"Thanks. Can you see if my car is below?" They exchanged cigarettes and stood at the window lighting them.

"There is one point, by the way, that may have some significance." Carrados had begun to recross the room and stopped to pick up the two fictitious messages. "You will have noticed that this is the outside sheet of a programme. It is not the most suitable for the purpose; the first inner sheet is more convenient to write on, but there the date appears. You see the inference? The programme was obtained before——"

"Perhaps. Well——?" for Carrados had broken off abruptly and was listening.

"You hear someone coming up the steps?"

"It is the general stairway."

"Mr Straithwaite, I don't know how far this has gone in other quarters. We may only have a few seconds before we are interrupted."

"What do you mean?"

"I mean that the man who is now on the stairs is a policeman or has worn the uniform. If he stops at your door——"

The heavy tread ceased. Then came the authoritative knock.

"Wait," muttered Carrados, laying his hand impressively on Straithwaite's tremulous arm. "I may recognise the voice."

They heard the servant pass along the hall and the door unlatched; then caught the jumble of a gruff inquiry.

"Inspector Beedel of Scotland Yard!" The servant repassed their door on her way to the drawing-room. "It is no good disguising the fact from you, Mr Straithwaite, that you may no longer be at liberty. But I am. Is there anything you wish done?"

There was no time for deliberation. Straithwaite was indeed between the unenviable alternatives of the familiar proverb, but, to do him justice, his voice had lost scarcely a ripple of its usual *sang-froid*.

"Thanks," he replied, taking a small stamped and addressed parcel from his pocket, "you might drop this into some obscure pillar-box, if you will."

"The Markham necklace?"

"Exactly. I was going out to post it when you came."

"I am sure you were."

"And if you could spare five minutes later—if I am here——"

Carrados slid his cigarette-case under some papers on the desk.

"I will call for that," he assented. "Let us say about half-past eight."

★★★★★★

"I am still at large, you see, Mr Carrados; though after reflecting on the studied formality of the inspector's business here, I imagine that you will scarcely be surprised."

"I have made it a habit," admitted Carrados, "never to be surprised."

"However, I still want to cut a rather different figure in your eyes. You regard me, Mr Carrados, either as a detected rogue or a repentant ass?"

"Another excellent rule is never to form deductions from uncertainties."

Straithwaite made a gesture of mild impatience.

"You only give me ten minutes. If I am to put my case before you, Mr Carrados, we cannot fence with phrases. . . . Today you have had an exceptional opportunity of penetrating into our mode of life. You will, I do not doubt, have summed up our perpetual indebtedness and the easy credit that our connexion procures; Stephanie's social ambitions and expensive popularity; her utterly extravagant incapacity to see any other possible existence; and my tacit acquiescence. You will, I know, have correctly gauged her irresponsible, neurotic temperament, and judged the result of it in conflict with my own. What possibly has escaped you, for in society one has to disguise these things, is that I still love my wife.

"When you dare not trust the soundness of your reins you do not try to pull up a bolting horse. For three years I have endeavoured to guide Stephanie round awkward corners with as little visible restraint as possible. When we differ over any project upon which she has set her heart Stephanie has one strong argument."

"That you no longer love her?"

"Well, perhaps; but more forcibly expressed. She rushes to the top of the building—there are six floors, Mr Carrados, and we are on the second—and climbing on to the banister she announces her intention of throwing herself down into the basement. In the meanwhile I have followed her and drag her back again. One day I shall stay where I am and let her do as she intends."

"I hope not," said Carrados gravely.

"Oh, don't be concerned. She will then climb back herself. But it will mark an epoch. It was by that threat that she obtained my acquiescence to this scheme—that and the certainty that she would otherwise go on without me. But I had no intention of allowing her to land herself—to say nothing of us both—behind the bars of a prison if I could help it. And, above all, I wished to cure her of her fatuous delusion that she is clever, in the hope that she may then give up being foolish.

"To fail her on the occasion was merely to postpone the attempt. I conceived the idea of seeming to cooperate and at the same time involving us in what appeared to be a clever counter-fraud. The thought of the real loss will perhaps have a good effect; the publicity will certainly prevent her from daring a second 'theft.' A sordid story, Mr Carrados," he concluded. "Do not forget your cigarette-case in reality."

The paternal shake of Carrados's head over the recital was neutralised by his benevolent smile.

"Yes, yes," he said. "I think we can classify you, Mr Straithwaite. One point—the glove?"

"That was an afterthought. I had arranged the whole story and the first note was to be brought to me by an attendant. Then, on my way, in my overcoat pocket I discovered a pair of Stephanie's gloves which she had asked me to carry the day before. The suggestion flashed— how much more convincing if I could arrange for her to seem to drop the writing in that way. As she said, the next box *was* empty; I merely took possession of it for a few minutes and quietly drew across one of her gloves. And that reminds me—of course there was nothing in it, but your interest in them made me rather nervous."

Carrados laughed outright. Then he stood up and held out his hand.

"Goodnight, Mr Straithwaite," he said, with real friendliness. "Let me give you the Quaker's advice: Don't attempt another conspiracy— but if you do, don't produce a 'pair' of gloves of which one is still suggestive of scent, and the other identifiable with eucalyptus!"

"Oh——!" said Straithwaite.

"Quite so. But at all hazard suppress a second pair that has the same peculiarity. Think over what it must mean. Goodbye."

Twelve minutes later Mr Carlyle was called to the telephone.

"It is eight-fifty-five and I am at Charing Cross," said a voice he knew. "If you want local colour contrive an excuse to be with Markham when the first post arrives tomorrow." A few more words followed, and an affectionate valediction.

"One moment, my dear Max, one moment. Do I understand you to say that you will post me on the report of the case from Dover?"

"No, Louis," replied Carrados, with cryptic discrimination. "I only said that I will post you on *a* report of the case from Dover."

94

The Last Exploit of Harry the Actor
A.k.a. *The Great Safe Deposit Coup*

The one insignificant fact upon which turned the following incident in the joint experiences of Mr Carlyle and Max Carrados was merely this: that having called upon his friend just at the moment when the private detective was on the point of leaving his office to go to the safe deposit in Lucas Street, Piccadilly, the blind amateur accompanied him, and for ten minutes amused himself by sitting quite quietly among the palms in the centre of the circular hall while Mr Carlyle was occupied with his deed-box in one of the little compartments provided for the purpose.

The Lucas Street depository was then (it has since been converted into a picture palace) generally accepted as being one of the strongest places in London. The front of the building was constructed to represent a gigantic safe door, and under the colloquial designation of "The Safe" the place had passed into a synonym for all that was secure and impregnable. Half of the marketable securities in the west of London were popularly reported to have seen the inside of its coffers at one time or another, together with the same generous proportion of family jewels. However exaggerated an estimate this might be, the substratum of truth was solid and auriferous enough to dazzle the imagination. When ordinary safes were being carried bodily away with impunity or ingeniously fused open by the scientifically equipped cracksman, nervous bond-holders turned with relief to the attractions of an establishment whose modest claim was summed up in its telegraphic address: "Impregnable."

To it went also the jewel-case between the lady's social engagements, and when in due course "the family" journeyed north—or south, east or west—whenever, in short, the London house was closed, its capacious storerooms received the plate-chest as an established custom. Not a few traders also—jewellers, financiers, dealers in pictures, antiques and costly *bijouterie*, for instance—constantly used its facilities for any stock that they did not requite immediately to hand.

There was only one entrance to the place, an exaggerated keyhole, to carry out the similitude of the safe-door alluded to. The ground floor was occupied by the ordinary offices of the company; all the strong-rooms and safes lay in the steel-cased basement. This was reached both by a lift and by a flight of steps. In either case the visitor found before him a grille of massive proportions. Behind its bars stood a formidable commissionaire who never left his post, his sole duty being to open and close the grille to arriving and departing clients. Beyond this, a short passage led into the round central hall where Carrados was waiting. From this part, other passages radiated off to the vaults and strong-rooms, each one barred from the hall by a grille scarcely less ponderous than the first one. The doors of the various private rooms put at the disposal of the company's clients, and that of the manager's office, filled the wall-space between the radiating passages. Everything was very quiet, everything looked very bright, and everything seemed hopelessly impregnable.

"But I wonder?" ran Carrados's dubious reflection; as he reached this point.

"Sorry to have kept you so long, my dear Max," broke in Mr Carlyle's crisp voice. He had emerged from his compartment and was crossing the hall, deed-box in hand. "Another minute and I will be with you."

Carrados smiled and nodded and resumed his former expression, which was merely that of an uninterested gentleman waiting patiently for another. It is something of an attainment to watch closely without betraying undue curiosity, but others of the senses—hearing and smelling, for instance—can be keenly engaged while the observer possibly has the appearance of falling asleep.

"Now," announced Mr Carlyle, returning briskly to his friend's chair, and drawing on his grey suede gloves.

"You are in no particular hurry?"

"No," admitted the professional man, with the slowness of mild surprise. "Not at all. What do you propose?"

"It is very pleasant here," replied Carrados tranquilly. "Very cool and restful with this armoured steel between us and the dust and scurry of the hot July afternoon above. I propose remaining here for a few minutes longer."

"Certainly," agreed Mr Carlyle, taking the nearest chair and eyeing Carrados as though he had a shrewd suspicion of something more than met the ear. "I believe some very interesting people rent safes here. We may encounter a bishop, or a winning jockey, or even a musical comedy actress. Unfortunately it seems to be rather a slack time."

"Two men came down while you were in your cubicle," remarked Carrados casually. "The first took the lift. I imagine that he was a middle-aged, rather portly man. He carried a stick, wore a silk hat, and used spectacles for close sight. The other came by the stairway. I infer that he arrived at the top immediately after the lift had gone. He ran down the steps, so that the two were admitted at the same time, but the second man, though the more active of the pair, hung back for a moment in the passage and the portly one was the first to go to his safe."

Mr Carlyle's knowing look expressed: "Go on, my friend; you are coming to something." But he merely contributed an encouraging "Yes?"

"When you emerged just now our second man quietly opened the door of his pen a fraction. Doubtless he looked out. Then he closed it as quietly again. You were not his man, Louis."

"I am grateful," said Mr Carlyle expressively. "What next, Louis?"

"That is all; they are still closeted."

Both were silent for a moment. Mr Carlyle's feeling was one of unconfessed perplexity. So far the incident was utterly trivial in his eyes; but he knew that the trifles which appeared significant to Max had a way of standing out like signposts when the time came to look back over an episode. Carrados's sightless faculties seemed indeed to keep him just a move ahead as the game progressed.

"Is there really anything in it, Max?" he asked at length.

"Who can say?" replied Carrados. "At least we may wait to see them go. Those tin deed-boxes now. There is one to each safe, I think?"

"Yes, so I imagine. The practice is to carry the box to your private lair and there unlock it and do your business. Then you lock it up again and take it back to your safe."

"Steady! our first man," whispered Carrados hurriedly. "Here, look at this with me." He opened a paper—a prospectus—which he pulled from his pocket, and they affected to study its contents together.

"You were about right, my friend," muttered Mr Carlyle, pointing to a paragraph of assumed interest. "Hat, stick and spectacles. He is a clean-shaven, pink-faced old boy. I believe—yes, I know the man by sight. He is a bookmaker in a large way, I am told."

"Here comes the other," whispered Carrados.

The bookmaker passed across the hall, joined on his way by the manager whose duty it was to counterlock the safe, and disappeared along one of the passages. The second man sauntered up and down, waiting his turn. Mr Carlyle reported his movements in an undertone and described him. He was a younger man than the other, of medium height, and passably well dressed in a quiet lounge suit, green Alpine hat and brown shoes. By the time the detective had reached his wavy chestnut hair, large and rather ragged moustache, and sandy, freckled complexion, the first man had completed his business and was leaving the place.

"It isn't an exchange lay, at all events," said Mr Carlyle. "His inner case is only half the size of the other and couldn't possibly be substituted."

"Come up now," said Carrados, rising. "There is nothing more to be learned down here."

They requisitioned the lift and on the steps outside the gigantic keyhole stood for a few minutes discussing an investment as a couple of trustees or a lawyer and a client who were parting there might do. Fifty yards away, a very large silk hat with a very curly brim marked the progress of the bookmaker towards Piccadilly.

The lift in the hall behind them swirled up again and the gate clashed. The second man walked leisurely out and sauntered away without a backward glance.

"He has gone in the opposite direction," exclaimed Mr Carlyle, rather blankly. "It isn't the 'lame goat' nor the 'follow-me-on,' nor even the homely but efficacious sand-bag."

"What colour were his eyes?" asked Carrados.

"Upon my word, I never noticed," admitted the other.

"Parkinson would have noticed," was the severe comment.

"I am not Parkinson," retorted Mr Carlyle, with asperity, "and, strictly as one dear friend to another, Max, permit me to add, that while cherishing an unbounded admiration for your remarkable gifts, I have the strongest suspicion that the whole incident is a ridiculous mare's nest, bred in the fantastic imagination of an enthusiastic criminologist."

Mr Carrados received this outburst with the utmost benignity. "Come and have a coffee, Louis," he suggested. "Mehmed's is only a street away."

Mehmed proved to be a cosmopolitan gentleman from Mocha whose shop resembled a house from the outside and an Oriental divan when one was within. A turbaned Arab placed cigarettes and cups of coffee spiced with saffron before the customers, gave *salaam* and withdrew.

"You know, my dear chap," continued Mr Carlyle, sipping his black coffee and wondering privately whether it was really very good or very bad, "speaking quite seriously, the one fishy detail—our ginger friend's watching for the other to leave—may be open to a dozen very innocent explanations."

"So innocent that tomorrow I intend taking a safe myself."

"You think that everything is all right?"

"On the contrary, I am convinced that something is very wrong."

"Then why——?"

"I shall keep nothing there, but it will give me the *entrée*. I should advise you, Louis, in the first place to empty your safe with all possible speed, and in the second to leave your business card on the manager."

Mr Carlyle pushed his cup away, convinced now that the coffee was really very bad.

"But, my dear Max, the place—'The Safe'—is impregnable!"

"When I was in the States, three years ago, the head porter at one hotel took pains to impress on me that the building was absolutely fireproof. I at once had my things taken off to another hotel. Two weeks later the first place was burnt out. It *was* fireproof, I believe, but of course the furniture and the fittings were not and the walls gave way."

"Very ingenious," admitted Mr Carlyle, "but why did you really go? You know you can't humbug me with your superhuman sixth sense, my friend."

Carrados smiled pleasantly, thereby encouraging the watchful attendant to draw near and replenish their tiny cups.

"Perhaps," replied the blind man, "because so many careless people were satisfied that it was fireproof."

"Ah-ha, there you are—the greater the confidence the greater the risk. But only if your self-confidence results in carelessness. Now do you know how this place is secured, Max?"

"I am told that they lock the door at night," replied Carrados, with bland malice.

"And hide the key under the mat to be ready for the first arrival in the morning," crowed Mr Carlyle, in the same playful spirit. "Dear old chap! Well, let me tell you———"

"That force is out of the question. Quite so," admitted his friend.

"That simplifies the argument. Let us consider fraud. There again the precautions are so rigid that many people pronounce the forms a nuisance. I confess that I do not. I regard them as a means of protecting my own property and I cheerfully sign my name and give my password, which the manager compares with his record-book before he releases the first lock of my safe. The signature is burned before my eyes in a sort of crucible there, the password is of my own choosing and is written only in a book that no one but the manager ever sees, and my key is the sole one in existence."

"No duplicate or master-key?"

"Neither. If a key is lost it takes a skilful mechanic half-a-day to cut his way in. Then you must remember that clients of a safe-deposit are not multitudinous. All are known more or less by sight to the officials there, and a stranger would receive close attention. Now, Max, by what combination of circumstances is a rogue to know my password, to be able to forge my signature, to possess himself of my key, and to resemble me personally? And, finally, how is he possibly to determine beforehand whether there is anything in my safe to repay so elaborate a plant?" Mr Carlyle concluded in triumph and was so carried away by the strength of his position that he drank off the contents of his second cup before he realised what he was doing.

"At the hotel I just spoke of," replied Carrados, "there was an attendant whose one duty in case of alarm was to secure three iron doors. On the night of the fire he had a bad attack of toothache and slipped away for just a quarter of an hour to have the thing out. There was a most up-to-date system of automatic fire alarm; it had been tested only the day before and the electrician, finding some part not absolutely to his satisfaction, had taken it away and not had time to replace it. The night watchman, it turned out, had received leave to present himself a couple of hours later on that particular night, and the hotel fireman, whose duties he took over, had missed being notified. Lastly, there was a big riverside blaze at the same time and all the engines were down at the other end of the city."

Mr Carlyle committed himself to a dubious monosyllable. Carrados leaned forward a little.

"All these circumstances formed a coincidence of pure chance. Is it not conceivable, Louis, that an even more remarkable series might be brought about by design?"

"Our tawny friend?"

"Possibly. Only he was not really tawny." Mr Carlyle's easy attitude suddenly stiffened into rigid attention. "He wore a false moustache."

"He wore a false moustache!" repeated the amazed gentleman. "And you cannot see! No, really, Max, this is beyond the limit!"

"If only you would not trust your dear, blundering old eyes so implicitly you would get nearer that limit yourself," retorted Carrados. "The man carried a five-yard aura of spirit gum, emphasised by a warm, perspiring skin. That inevitably suggested one thing. I looked for further evidence of making-up and found it—these preparations all smell. The hair you described was characteristically that of a wig—worn long to hide the joining and made wavy to minimize the length. All these things are trifles. As yet we have not gone beyond the initial stage of suspicion. I will tell you another trifle. When this man retired to a compartment with his deed-box, he never even opened it. Possibly it contains a brick and a newspaper. He is only watching."

"Watching the bookmaker."

"True, but it may go far wider than that. Everything points to a plot of careful elaboration. Still, if you are satisfied——"

"I am quite satisfied," replied Mr Carlyle gallantly. "I regard 'The Safe' almost as a national institution, and as such I have an implicit faith in its precautions against every kind of force or fraud." So far Mr Carlyle's attitude had been suggestive of a rock, but at this point he took out his watch, hummed a little to pass the time, consulted his watch again, and continued: "I am afraid that there were one or two papers which I overlooked. It would perhaps save me coming again tomorrow if I went back now——"

"Quite so," acquiesced Carrados, with perfect gravity. "I will wait for you."

For twenty minutes he sat there, drinking an occasional tiny cup of boiled coffee and to all appearance placidly enjoying the quaint atmosphere which Mr Mehmed had contrived to transplant from the shore of the Persian Gulf.

At the end of that period Carlyle returned, politely effusive about the time he had kept his friend waiting but otherwise bland and unassailable. Anyone with eyes might have noticed that he carried a parcel of about the same size and dimensions as the deed-box that fitted his safe.

The next day Carrados presented himself at the safe-deposit as an intending renter. The manager showed him over the vaults and strong-rooms, explaining the various precautions taken to render the guile or force of man impotent: the strength of the chilled-steel walls, the casing of electricity-resisting concrete, the stupendous isolation of the whole inner fabric on metal pillars so that the watchman, while inside the building, could walk above, below, and all round the outer walls of what was really—although it bore no actual relationship to the advertising device of the front—a monstrous safe; and, finally, the arrangement which would enable the basement to be flooded with steam within three minutes of an alarm. These details were public property. "The Safe" was a showplace and its directors held that no harm could come of displaying a strong hand.

Accompanied by the observant eyes of Parkinson, Carrados gave an adventurous but not a hopeful attention to these particulars. Submitting the problem of the tawny man to his own ingenuity, he was constantly putting before himself the question: How shall I set about robbing this place? and he had already dismissed force as impracticable. Nor, when it came to the consideration of fraud, did the simple but effective safeguards which Mr Carlyle had specified seem to offer any loophole.

"As I am blind I may as well sign in the book," he suggested, when the manager passed to him a gummed slip for the purpose. The precaution against one acquiring particulars of another client might well be deemed superfluous in his case.

But the manager did not fall into the trap.

"It is our invariable rule in all cases, sir," he replied courteously. "What word will you take?" Parkinson, it may be said, had been left in the hall.

"Suppose I happen to forget it? How do we proceed?"

"In that case I am afraid that I might have to trouble you to establish your identity," the manager explained. "It rarely happens."

"Then we will say 'Conspiracy.'"

The word was written down and the book closed.

"Here is your key, sir. If you will allow me—your keyring——"

A week went by and Carrados was no nearer the absolute solution of the problem he had set himself. He had, indeed, evolved several ways by which the contents of the safes might be reached, some simple and desperate, hanging on the razor-edge of chance to fall this way or that; others more elaborate, safer on the whole, but more liable to break down at some point of their ingenious intricacy. And setting aside complicity on the part of the manager—a condition that

Carrados had satisfied himself did not exist—they all depended on a relaxation of the forms by which security was assured. Carrados continued to have several occasions to visit the safe during the week, and he "watched" with a quiet persistence that was deadly in its scope. But from beginning to end there was no indication of slackness in the business-like methods of the place; nor during any of his visits did the "tawny man" appear in that or any other disguise. Another week passed; Mr Carlyle was becoming inexpressibly waggish, and Carrados himself, although he did not abate a jot of his conviction, was compelled to bend to the realities of the situation. The manager, with the obstinacy of a conscientious man who had become obsessed with the pervading note of security, excused himself from discussing abstract methods of fraud. Carrados was not in a position to formulate a detailed charge; he withdrew from active investigation, content to await his time.

It came, to be precise, on a certain Friday morning, seventeen days after his first visit to "The Safe." Returning late on the Thursday night, he was informed that a man giving the name of Draycott had called to see him. Apparently the matter had been of some importance to the visitor for he had returned three hours later on the chance of finding Mr Carrados in. Disappointed in this, he had left a note. Carrados cut open the envelope and ran a finger along the following words:—

Dear Sir,—I have today consulted Mr Louis Carlyle, who thinks that you would like to see me. I will call again in the morning, say at nine o'clock. If this is too soon or otherwise inconvenient I entreat you to leave a message fixing as early an hour as possible.

Yours faithfully, Herbert Draycott.
P.S.—I should add that I am the renter of a safe at the Lucas Street depository. H.D.

A description of Mr Draycott made it clear that he was not the West-End bookmaker. The caller, the servant explained, was a thin, wiry, keen-faced man. Carrados felt agreeably interested in this development, which seemed to justify his suspicion of a plot.

At five minutes to nine the next morning Mr Draycott again presented himself.

"Very good of you to see me so soon, sir," he apologised, on Carrados at once receiving him. "I don't know much of English ways—I'm an Australian—and I was afraid it might be too early."

"You could have made it a couple of hours earlier as far as I am concerned," replied Carrados. "Or you either for that matter, I imagine," he added, "for I don't think that you slept much last night."

"I didn't sleep at all last night," corrected Mr Draycott. "But it's strange that you should have seen that. I understood from Mr Carlyle that you—excuse me if I am mistaken, sir—but I understood that you were blind."

Carrados laughed his admission lightly.

"Oh yes," he said. "But never mind that. What is the trouble?"

"I'm afraid it means more than just trouble for me, Mr Carrados." The man had steady, half-closed eyes, with the suggestion of depth which one notices in the eyes of those whose business it is to look out over great expanses of land or water; they were turned towards Carrados's face with quiet resignation in their frankness now. "I'm afraid it spells disaster. I am a working engineer from the Mount Magdalena district of Coolgardie. I don't want to take up your time with outside details so I will only say that about two years ago I had an opportunity of acquiring a share in a very promising claim—gold, you understand, both reef and alluvial. As the work went on I put more and more into the undertaking—you couldn't call it a venture by that time. The results were good, better than we had dared to expect, but from one cause and another the expenses were terrible. We saw that it was a bigger thing than we had bargained for and we admitted that we must get outside help."

So far Mr Draycott's narrative had proceeded smoothly enough under the influence of the quiet despair that had come over the man. But at this point a sudden recollection of his position swept him into a frenzy of bitterness.

"Oh, what the blazes is the good of going over all this again!" he broke out. "What can you or anyone else do anyhow? I've been robbed, rooked, cleared out of everything I possess," and tormented by recollections and by the impotence of his rage the unfortunate engineer beat the oak table with the back of his hand until his knuckles bled.

Carrados waited until the fury had passed.

"Continue, if you please, Mr Draycott," he said. "Just what you thought it best to tell me is just what I want to know."

"I'm sorry, sir," apologised the man, colouring under his tanned skin. "I ought to be able to control myself better. But this business has shaken me. Three times last night I looked down the barrel of my revolver, and three times I threw it away. . . . Well, we arranged that I should come to London to interest some financiers in the property. We might have done it locally or in Perth, to be sure, but then, don't you see, they would have wanted to get control. Six weeks ago I landed here. I brought with me specimens of the quartz and good samples of extracted gold, dust and nuggets, the clearing up of several weeks' working, about two hundred and forty ounces in all. That includes the Magdalena Lodestar, our lucky nugget, a lump weighing just under seven pounds of pure gold.

"I had seen an advertisement of this Lucas Street safe-deposit and it seemed just the thing I wanted. Besides the gold, I had all the papers to do with the claims—plans, reports, receipts, licences and so on. Then when I cashed my letter of credit I had about one hundred and fifty pounds in notes. Of course I could have left everything at a bank but it was more convenient to have it, as it were, in my own safe, to get at any time, and to have a private room that I could take any gentlemen to. I hadn't a suspicion that anything could be wrong. Negotiations hung on in several quarters—it's a bad time to do business here, I find. Then, yesterday, I wanted something. I went to Lucas Street, as I had done half-a-dozen times before, opened my safe, and had the inner case carried to a room. . . . Mr Carrados, it was empty!"

"Quite empty?"

"No." He laughed bitterly. "At the bottom was a sheet of wrapper paper. I recognised it as a piece I had left there in case I wanted to make up a parcel. But for that I should have been convinced that I had somehow opened the wrong safe. That was my first idea."

"It cannot be done."

"So I understand, sir. And, then, there was the paper with my name written on it in the empty tin. I was dazed; it seemed impossible. I think I stood there without moving for minutes—it was more like hours. Then I closed the tin box again, took it back, locked up the safe and came out."

"Without notifying anything wrong?"

"Yes, Mr Carrados." The steady blue eyes regarded him with pained thoughtfulness. "You see, I reckoned it out in that time that it must be someone about the place who had done it."

"You were wrong," said Carrados.

"So Mr Carlyle seemed to think. I only knew that the key had never been out of my possession and I had told no one of the password. Well, it did come over me rather like cold water down the neck, that there was I alone in the strongest dungeon in London and not a living soul knew where I was."

"Possibly a sort of up-to-date Sweeney Todd's?"

"I'd heard of such things in London," admitted Draycott. "Anyway, I got out. It was a mistake; I see it now. Who is to believe me as it is—it sounds a sort of unlikely tale. And how do they come to pick on me? to know what I had? I don't drink, or open my mouth, or hell round. It beats me."

"They didn't pick on you—you picked on them," replied Carrados. "Never mind how; you'll be believed all right. But as for getting anything back——"The unfinished sentence confirmed Mr Draycott in his gloomiest anticipations.

"I have the numbers of the notes," he suggested, with an attempt at hopefulness. "They can be stopped, I take it?"

"Stopped? Yes," admitted Carrados. "And what does that amount to? The banks and the police stations will be notified and every little public-house between here and Land's End will change one for the scribbling of 'John Jones' across the back. No, Mr Draycott, it's awkward, I dare say, but you must make up your mind to wait until you can get fresh supplies from home. Where are you staying?"

Draycott hesitated.

"I have been at the Abbotsford, in Bloomsbury, up to now," he said, with some embarrassment. "The fact is, Mr Carrados, I think I ought to have told you how I was placed before consulting you, because I—I see no prospect of being able to pay my way. Knowing that I had plenty in the safe, I had run it rather close. I went chiefly yesterday to get some notes. I have a week's hotel bill in my pocket, and"—he glanced down at his trousers—"I've ordered one or two other things unfortunately."

"That will be a matter of time, doubtless," suggested the other encouragingly.

Instead of replying Draycott suddenly dropped his arms on to the table and buried his face between them. A minute passed in silence.

"It's no good, Mr Carrados," he said, when he was able to speak; "I can't meet it. Say what you like, I simply can't tell those chaps that I've lost everything we had and ask them to send me more. They couldn't do it if I did. Understand, sir. The mine is a valuable one; we have the greatest faith in it, but it has gone beyond our depth. The three of us have put everything we own into it. While I am here they are doing labourers' work for a wage, just to keep going ... waiting, oh, my God!

waiting for good news from me!"

Carrados walked round the table to his desk and wrote. Then, without a word, he held out a paper to his visitor.

"What's this?" demanded Draycott, in bewilderment. "It's—it's a cheque for a hundred pounds."

"It will carry you on," explained Carrados imperturbably. "A man like you isn't going to throw up the sponge for this set-back. Cable to your partners that you require copies of all the papers at once. They'll manage it, never fear. The gold . . . must go. Write fully by the next mail. Tell them everything and add that in spite of all you feel that you are nearer success than ever."

Mr Draycott folded the cheque with thoughtful deliberation and put it carefully away in his pocket-book.

"I don't know whether you've guessed as much, sir," he said in a queer voice, "but I think that you've saved a man's life to-day. It's not the money, it's the encouragement . . . and faith. If you could see you'd know better than I can say how I feel about it."

Carrados laughed quietly. It always amused him to have people explain how much more he would learn if he had eyes.

"Then we'll go on to Lucas Street and give the manager the shock of his life," was all he said. "Come, Mr Draycott, I have already rung up the car."

But, as it happened, another instrument had been destined to apply that stimulating experience to the manager. As they stepped out of the car opposite "The Safe" a taxicab drew up and Mr Carlyle's alert and cheery voice hailed them.

"A moment, Max," he called, turning to settle with his driver, a transaction that he invested with an air of dignified urbanity which almost made up for any small pecuniary disappointment that may have accompanied it. "This is indeed fortunate. Let us compare notes for a moment. I have just received an almost imploring message from the manager to come at once. I assumed that it was the affair of our colonial friend here, but he went on to mention Professor Holmfast Bulge. Can it really be possible that he also has made a similar discovery?"

"What did the manager say?" asked Carrados.

"He was practically incoherent, but I really think it must be so. What have you done?"

"Nothing," replied Carrados. He turned his back on "The Safe" and appeared to be regarding the other side of the street. "There is a tobacconist's shop directly opposite?"

"There is."

"What do they sell on the first floor?"

"Possibly they sell 'Rubbo.' I hazard the suggestion from the legend 'Rub in Rubbo for Everything' which embellishes each window."

"The windows are frosted?"

"They are, to halfway up, mysterious man."

Carrados walked back to his motor car.

"While we are away, Parkinson, go across and buy a tin, bottle, box or packet of 'Rubbo.'"

"What is 'Rubbo,' Max?" chirped Mr Carlyle with insatiable curiosity.

"So far we do not know. When Parkinson gets some, Louis, you shall be the one to try it."

They descended into the basement and were passed in by the grille-keeper, whose manner betrayed a discreet consciousness of something in the air. It was unnecessary to speculate why. In the distance, muffled by the armoured passages, an authoritative voice boomed like a sonorous bell heard under water.

"What, however, are the facts?" it was demanding, with the causticity of baffled helplessness. "I am assured that there is no other key in existence; yet my safe has been unlocked. I am given to understand that without the password it would be impossible for an unauthorised person to tamper with my property. My password, deliberately chosen, is 'anthropophaginian,' sir. Is it one that is familiarly on the lips of the criminal classes? But my safe is empty! What is the explanation? Who are the guilty persons? What is being done? Where are the police?"

"If you consider that the proper course to adopt is to stand on the doorstep and beckon in the first constable who happens to pass, permit me to say, sir, that I differ from you," retorted the distracted manager. "You may rely on everything possible being done to clear up the mystery. As I told you, I have already telephoned for a capable private detective and for one of my directors."

"But that is not enough," insisted the professor angrily. "Will one mere private detective restore my £6000 Japanese 4½ *per cent*. bearer bonds? Is the return of my irreplaceable notes on 'Polyphyletic Bridal Customs among the mid-Pleistocene Cave Men' to depend on a solitary director? I demand that the police shall be called in—as many as are available. Let Scotland Yard be set in motion. A searching inquiry must be made. I have only been a user of your precious establishment for six months, and this is the result."

"There you hold the key of the mystery, Professor Bulge," interposed Carrados quietly.

"Who is this, sir?" demanded the exasperated professor at large.

"Permit me," explained Mr Carlyle, with bland assurance. "I am Louis Carlyle, of Bampton Street. This gentleman is Mr Max Carrados, the eminent amateur specialist in crime."

"I shall be thankful for any assistance towards elucidating this appalling business," condescended the professor sonorously. "Let me put you in possession of the facts——"

"Perhaps if we went into your room," suggested Carrados to the manager, "we should be less liable to interruption."

"Quite so; quite so," boomed the professor, accepting the proposal on everyone else's behalf. "The facts, sir, are these: I am the unfortunate possessor of a safe here, in which, a few months ago, I deposited—among less important matter—sixty bearer bonds of the Japanese Imperial Loan—the bulk of my small fortune—and the manuscript of an important projected work on 'Polyphyletic Bridal Customs among the mid-Pleistocene Cave Men.' Today I came to detach the coupons which fall due on the fifteenth, to pay them into my bank a week in advance, in accordance with my custom. What do I find? I find the safe locked and apparently intact, as when I last saw it a month ago. But it is far from being intact, sir. It has been opened; ransacked, cleared out. Not a single bond; not a scrap of paper remains."

It was obvious that the manager's temperature had been rising during the latter part of this speech and now he boiled over.

"Pardon my flatly contradicting you, Professor Bulge. You have again referred to your visit here a month ago as your last. You will bear witness of that, gentlemen. When I inform you that the professor had access to his safe as recently as on Monday last you will recognise the importance that the statement may assume."

The professor glared across the room like an infuriated animal, a comparison heightened by his notoriously hircine appearance.

"How dare you contradict me, sir!" he cried, slapping the table sharply with his open hand. "I was not here on Monday."

The manager shrugged his shoulders coldly.

"You forget that the attendants also saw you," he remarked. "Cannot we trust our own eyes?"

"A common assumption, yet not always a strictly reliable one," insinuated Carrados softly.

"I cannot be mistaken."

"Then can you tell me, without looking, what colour Professor Bulge's eyes are?"

There was a curious and expectant silence for a minute. The professor turned his back on the manager and the manager passed from thoughtfulness to embarrassment.

"I really do not know, Mr Carrados," he declared loftily at last. "I do not refer to mere trifles like that."

"Then you can be mistaken," replied Carrados mildly yet with decision.

"But the ample hair, the venerable flowing beard, the prominent nose and heavy eyebrows——"

"These are just the striking points that are most easily counterfeited. They 'take the eye.' If you would ensure yourself against deception, learn rather to observe the eye itself, and particularly the spots on it, the shape of the fingernails, the set of the ears. These things cannot be simulated."

"You seriously suggest that the man was not Professor Bulge—that he was an impostor?"

"The conclusion is inevitable. Where were you on Monday, Professor?"

"I was on a short lecturing tour in the Midlands. On Saturday I was in Nottingham. On Monday in Birmingham. I did not return to London until yesterday."

Carrados turned to the manager again and indicated Draycott, who so far had remained in the background.

"And this gentleman? Did he by any chance come here on Monday?"

"He did not, Mr Carrados. But I gave him access to his safe on Tuesday afternoon and again yesterday."

Draycott shook his head sadly.

"Yesterday I found it empty," he said. "And all Tuesday afternoon I was at Brighton, trying to see a gentleman on business."

The manager sat down very suddenly.

"Good God, another!" he exclaimed faintly.

"I am afraid the list is only beginning," said Carrados. "We must go through your renters' book."

The manager roused himself to protest.

"That cannot be done. No one but myself or my deputy ever sees the book. It would be—unprecedented."

"The circumstances are unprecedented," replied Carrados.

"If any difficulties are placed in the way of these gentlemen's investigations, I shall make it my duty to bring the facts before the Home Secretary," announced the professor; speaking up to the ceiling with the voice of a brazen trumpet.

Carrados raised a deprecating hand.

"May I make a suggestion?" he remarked. "Now; I am blind. If, therefore——?"

"Very well," acquiesced the manager. "But I must request the others to withdraw."

For five minutes Carrados followed the list of safe-renters as the manager read them to him. Sometimes he stopped the catalogue to reflect a moment; now and then he brushed a finger-tip over a written signature and compared it with another. Occasionally a password interested him. But when the list came to an end he continued to look into space without any sign of enlightenment.

"So much is perfectly clear and yet so much is incredible," he mused. "You insist that you alone have been in charge for the last six months?"

"I have not been away a day this year."

"Meals?"

"I have my lunch sent in."

"And this room could not be entered without your knowledge while you were about the place?"

"It is impossible. The door is fitted with a powerful spring and a feather-touch self-acting lock. It cannot be left unlocked unless you deliberately prop it open."

"And, with your knowledge, no one has had an opportunity of having access to this book?"

"No," was the reply.

Carrados stood up and began to put on his gloves.

"Then I must decline to pursue my investigation any further," he said icily.

"Why?" stammered the manager.

"Because I have positive reason for believing that you are deceiving me."

"Pray sit down, Mr Carrados. It is quite true that when you put the last question to me a circumstance rushed into my mind which—so far as the strict letter was concerned—might seem to demand 'Yes' instead of 'No.' But not in the spirit of your inquiry. It would be absurd to attach any importance to the incident I refer to."

"That would be for me to judge."

"You shall do so, Mr Carrados. I live at Windermere Mansions with my sister. A few months ago she got to know a married couple who had recently come to the opposite flat. The husband was a middle-aged, scholarly man who spent most of his time in the British Museum. His wife's tastes were different; she was much younger, brighter, gayer; a mere girl in fact, one of the most charming and unaffected I have ever met. My sister Amelia does not readily——"

"Stop!" exclaimed Carrados. "A studious middle-aged man and a charming young wife! Be as brief as possible. If there is any chance it may turn on a matter of minutes at the ports. She came here, of course?"

"Accompanied by her husband," replied the manager stiffly. "Mrs Scott had travelled and she had a hobby of taking photographs wherever she went. When my position accidentally came out one evening she was carried away by the novel idea of adding views of a safe-deposit to her collection—as enthusiastic as a child. There was no reason why she should not; the place has often been taken for advertising purposes."

"She came, and brought her camera—under your very nose!"

"I do not know what you mean by 'under my very nose.' She came with her husband one evening just about our closing time. She brought her camera, of course—quite a small affair."

"And contrived to be in here alone?"

"I take exception to the word 'contrived.' It—it happened. I sent out for some tea, and in the course——"

"How long was she alone in here?"

"Two or three minutes at the most. When I returned she was seated at my desk. That was what I referred to. The little rogue had put on my glasses and had got hold of a big book. We were great chums, and she delighted to mock me. I confess that I was startled—merely instinctively—to see that she had taken up this book, but the next moment I saw that she had it upside down."

"Clever! She couldn't get it away in time. And the camera, with half-a-dozen of its specially sensitised films already snapped over the last few pages, by her side!"

"That child!"

"Yes. She is twenty-seven and has kicked hats off tall men's heads in every capital from Petersburg to Buenos Aires! Get through to Scotland Yard and ask if Inspector Beedel can come up."

The manager breathed heavily through his nose.

"To call in the police and publish everything would ruin this establishment—confidence would be gone. I cannot do it without further authority."

"Then the professor certainly will."

"Before you came I rang up the only director who is at present in town and gave him the facts as they then stood. Possibly he has arrived by this. If you will accompany me to the boardroom we will see."

They went up to the floor above, Mr Carlyle joining them on the way.

"Excuse me a moment," said the manager.

Parkinson, who had been having an improving conversation with the hall porter on the subject of land values, approached.

"I am sorry, sir," he reported, "but I was unable to procure any 'Rubbo.' The place appears to be shut up."

"That is a pity; Mr Carlyle had set his heart on it."

"Will you come this way, please?" said the manager, reappearing.

In the boardroom they found a white-haired old gentleman who had obeyed the manager's behest from a sense of duty, and then remained in a distant corner of the empty room in the hope that he might be overlooked. He was amiably helpless and appeared to be deeply aware of it.

"This is a very sad business, gentlemen," he said, in a whispering, confiding voice. "I am informed that you recommend calling in the Scotland Yard authorities. That would be a disastrous course for an institution that depends on the implicit confidence of the public."

"It is the only course," replied Carrados.

"The name of Mr Carrados is well known to us in connexion with a delicate case. Could you not carry this one through?"

"It is impossible. A wide inquiry must be made. Every port will have to be watched. The police alone can do that." He threw a little significance into the next sentence. "I alone can put the police in the right way of doing it."

"And you will do that, Mr Carrados?"

Carrados smiled engagingly. He knew exactly what constituted the great attraction of his services.

"My position is this," he explained. "So far my work has been entirely amateur. In that capacity I have averted one or two crimes, remedied an occasional injustice, and now and then been of service to my professional friend, Louis Carlyle. But there is no reason at all why

I should serve a commercial firm in an ordinary affair of business for nothing. For any information I should require a fee, a quite nominal fee of, say, one hundred pounds."

The director looked as though his faith in human nature had received a rude blow.

"A hundred pounds would be a very large initial fee for a small firm like this, Mr Carrados," he remarked in a pained voice.

"And that, of course, would be independent of Mr Carlyle's professional charges," added Carrados.

"Is that sum contingent on any specific performance?" inquired the manager.

"I do not mind making it conditional on my procuring for you, for the police to act on, a photograph and a description of the thief."

The two officials conferred apart for a moment. Then the manager returned.

"We will agree, Mr Carrados, on the understanding that these things are to be in our hands within two days. Failing that——"

"No, no!" cried Mr Carlyle indignantly, but Carrados good-humouredly put him aside.

"I will accept the condition in the same sporting spirit that inspires it. Within forty-eight hours or no pay. The cheque, of course, to be given immediately the goods are delivered?"

"You may rely on that."

Carrados took out his pocket-book, produced an envelope bearing an American stamp, and from it extracted an unmounted print.

"Here is the photograph," he announced. "The man is called Ulysses K. Groom, but he is better known as 'Harry the Actor.' You will find the description written on the back."

Five minutes later, when they were alone, Mr Carlyle expressed his opinion of the transaction.

"You are an unmitigated humbug, Max," he said, "though an amiable one, I admit. But purely for your own private amusement you spring these things on people."

"On the contrary," replied Carrados, "people spring these things on me."

"Now this photograph. Why have I heard nothing of it before?"

Carrados took out his watch and touched the fingers.

"It is now three minutes to eleven. I received the photograph at twenty past eight."

"Even then, an hour ago you assured me that you had done nothing."

"Nor had I—so far as result went. Until the keystone of the edifice was wrung from the manager in his room, I was as far away from demonstrable certainty as ever."

"So am I—as yet," hinted Mr Carlyle.

"I am coming to that, Louis. I turn over the whole thing to you. The man has got two clear days' start and the chances are nine to one against catching him. We know everything, and the case has no further interest for me. But it is your business. Here is your material.

"On that one occasion when the 'tawny' man crossed our path, I took from the first a rather more serious view of his scope and intention than you did. That same day I sent a cipher cable to Pierson of the New York service. I asked for news of any man of such and such a description—merely negative—who was known to have left the States; an educated man, expert in the use of disguises, audacious in his operations, and a specialist in 'dry' work among banks and strong-rooms."

"Why the States, Max?"

"That was a sighting shot on my part. I argued that he must be an English-speaking man. The smart and inventive turn of the modern Yank has made him a specialist in ingenious devices, straight or crooked. Unpickable locks and invincible lock-pickers, burglar-proof safes and safe-specializing burglars, come equally from the States. So I tried a very simple test. As we talked that day and the man walked past us, I dropped the words 'New York'—or, rather, 'Noo Y'rk'—in his hearing."

"I know you did. He neither turned nor stopped."

"He was that much on his guard; but into his step there came—though your poor old eyes could not see it, Louis—the 'psychological pause,' an absolute arrest of perhaps a fifth of a second; just as it would have done with you if the word 'London' had fallen on your ear in a distant land. However, the whys and the wherefores don't matter. Here is the essential story.

"Eighteen months ago 'Harry the Actor' successfully looted the office safe of M'Kenkie, J. F. Higgs & Co.; of Cleveland, Ohio. He had just married a smart but very facile third-rate vaudeville actress—English by origin—and wanted money for the honeymoon. He got about five hundred pounds, and with that they came to Europe and stayed in London for some months. That period is marked by the Congreave Square post office burglary, you may remember. While studying such of the British institutions as most appealed to him, the 'Actor's' attention became fixed on this safe-deposit. Possibly the implied challenge contained in its telegraphic address grew on him until it became a point of professional honour with him to despoil it; at all events he was presumedly attracted by an undertaking that promised not only glory but very solid profit.

"The first part of the plot was, to the most skilful criminal 'impersonator' in the States, mere skittles. Spreading over those months he appeared at 'The Safe' in twelve different characters and rented twelve safes of different sizes. At the same time he made a thorough study of the methods of the place. As soon as possible he got the keys back again into legitimate use, having made duplicates for his own private ends, of course. Five he seems to have returned during his first stay; one was received later, with profuse apologies, by registered post; one was returned through a leading Berlin bank. Six months ago he made a flying visit here, purely to work off two more. One he kept from first to last, and the remaining couple he got in at the beginning of his second long residence here, three or four months ago.

"This brings us to the serious part of the cool enterprise. He had funds from the Atlantic and South-Central Mail-car coup when he arrived here last April. He appears to have set up three establishments; a home, in the guise of an elderly scholar with a young wife, which, of course, was next door to our friend the manager; an observation point, over which he plastered the inscription 'Rub in Rubbo for Everything' as a reason for being; and, somewhere else, a dressing-room with essential conditions of two doors into different streets.

"About six weeks ago he entered the last stage. Mrs Harry, with quite ridiculous ease, got photographs of the necessary page or two of the record-book. I don't doubt that for weeks before then everyone who entered the place had been observed, but the photographs linked them up with the actual men into whose hands the 'Actor's' old keys had passed—gave their names and addresses, the numbers of their safes, their passwords and signatures. The rest was easy."

"Yes, by Jupiter; mere play for a man like that," agreed Mr Carlyle, with professional admiration. "He could contrive a dozen different occasions for studying the voice and manner and appearance of his victims. How much has he cleared?"

"We can only speculate as yet. I have put my hand on seven doubtful callers on Monday and Tuesday last. Two others he had ignored for some reason; the remaining two safes had not been allotted. There is one point that raises an interesting speculation."

"What is that, Max?"

"The 'Actor' has one associate, a man known as 'Billy the Fondant,' but beyond that—with the exception of his wife, of course—he does not usually trust anyone. It is plain, however, that at least seven men must latterly have been kept under close observation. It has occurred to me——"

"Yes, Max?"

"I have wondered whether Harry has enlisted the innocent services of one or other of our clever private inquiry offices."

"Scarcely," smiled the professional. "It would hardly pass muster."

"Oh, I don't know. Mrs Harry, in the character of a jealous wife or a suspicious sweetheart, might reasonably——"

Mr Carlyle's smile suddenly faded.

"By Jupiter!" he exclaimed. "I remember——"

"Yes, Louis?" prompted Carrados, with laughter in his voice.

"I remember that I must telephone to a client before Beedel comes," concluded Mr Carlyle, rising in some haste.

At the door he almost ran into the subdued director, who was wringing his hands in helpless protest at a new stroke of calamity.

"Mr Carrados," wailed the poor old gentleman in a tremulous bleat, "Mr Carrados, there is another now—Sir Benjamin Gump. He insists on seeing me. You will not—you will not desert us?"

"I should have to stay a week," replied Carrados briskly, "and I'm just off now. There will be a procession. Mr Carlyle will support you, I am sure."

He nodded "Good-morning" straight into the eyes of each and found his way out with the astonishing certainty of movement that made so many forget his infirmity. Possibly he was not desirous of encountering Draycott's embarrassed gratitude again, for in less than a minute they heard the swirl of his departing car.

"Never mind, my dear sir," Mr Carlyle assured his client, with impenetrable complacency. "Never mind. *I* will remain instead. Perhaps I had better make myself known to Sir Benjamin at once."

The director turned on him the pleading, trustful look of a cornered dormouse.

"He is in the basement," he whispered. "I shall be in the boardroom—if necessary."

Mr Carlyle had no difficulty in discovering the centre of interest in the basement. Sir Benjamin was expansive and reserved, bewildered and decisive, long-winded and short-tempered, each in turn and more or less all at once. He had already demanded the attention of the manager, Professor Bulge, Draycott and two underlings to his case and they were now involved in a babel of inutile reiteration. The inquiry agent was at once drawn into a circle of interrogation that he did his best to satisfy impressively while himself learning the new facts.

The latest development was sufficiently astonishing. Less than an hour before Sir Benjamin had received a parcel by district messenger. It contained a jewel-case which ought at that moment to have been securely reposing in one of the deposit safes. Hastily snatching it open, the recipient's incredible forebodings were realised. It was empty— empty of jewels, that is to say, for, as if to add a sting to the blow, a neatly inscribed card had been placed inside, and on it the agitated baronet read the appropriate but at the moment rather gratuitous maxim: "*Lay not up for yourselves treasures upon earth——*"

The card was passed round and all eyes demanded the expert's pronouncement.

"'*—where moth and rust doth corrupt and where thieves break through and steal.*' H'm," read Mr Carlyle with weight. "This is a most important clue, Sir Benjamin——"

"Hey, what? What's that?" exclaimed a voice from the other side of the hall. "Why, damme if I don't believe you've got another! Look at that, gentlemen; look at that. What's on, I say? Here now, come; give me my safe. I want to know where I am."

It was the bookmaker who strode tempestuously in among them, flourishing before their faces a replica of the card that was in Mr Carlyle's hand.

"Well, upon my soul this is most extraordinary," exclaimed that gentleman, comparing the two. "You have just received this, Mr—Mr Berge, isn't it?"

"That's right, Berge—'Iceberg' on the course. Thank the Lord Harry, I can take my losses coolly enough, but this—this is a facer. Put into my hand half-an-hour ago inside an envelope that ought to be here and as safe as in the Bank of England. What's the game, I say? Here, Johnny, hurry and let me into my safe."

Discipline and method had for the moment gone by the board. There was no suggestion of the boasted safeguards of the establishment. The manager added his voice to that of the client, and when the attendant did not at once appear he called again.

"John, come and give Mr Berge access to his safe at once."

"All right, sir," pleaded the harassed key-attendant; hurrying up with the burden of his own distraction. "There's a silly fathead got in what thinks this is a left-luggage office, so far as I can make out—a foreigner."

"Never mind that now," replied the manager severely. "Mr Berge's safe: No. 01724."

The attendant and Mr Berge went off together down one of the brilliant colonnaded vistas. One or two of the others who had caught the words glanced across and became aware of a strange figure that was drifting indecisively towards them. He was obviously an elderly German tourist of pronounced type—long-haired, spectacled, outrageously garbed and involved in the mental abstraction of his philosophical race. One hand was occupied with the manipulation of a pipe, as markedly Teutonic as its owner; the other grasped a carpet-bag that would have ensured an opening laugh to any low comedian.

Quite impervious to the preoccupation of the group, the German made his way up to them and picked out the manager.

"This was a safety deposit, *nicht wahr?*"

"Quite so," acquiesced the manager loftily, "but just now———"

"Your fellow was dense of gomprehension." The eyes behind the clumsy glasses wrinkled to a ponderous humour. "He forgot his own business. Now this goot bag———"

Brought into fuller prominence, the carpet-bag revealed further details of its overburdened proportions. At one end a flannel shirt cuff protruded in limp dejection; at the other an ancient collar, with the grotesque attachment known as a "dickey," asserted its presence. No wonder the manager frowned his annoyance. "The Safe" was in low enough repute among its patrons at that moment without any burlesque interlude to its tragic hour.

"Yes, yes," he whispered, attempting to lead the would-be depositor away, "but you are under a mistake. This is not———"

"It was a safety deposit? Goot. Mine bag—I would deposit him in safety till the time of mine train. *Ja?*"

"*Nein, nein!*" almost hissed the agonised official. "Go away, sir, go away! It isn't a cloakroom. John, let this gentleman out."

The attendant and Mr Berge were returning from their quest. The inner box had been opened and there was no need to ask the result. The bookmaker was shaking his head like a baffled bull.

"Gone, no effects," he shouted across the hall. "Lifted from 'The Safe,' by crumb!"

To those who knew nothing of the method and operation of the fraud it seemed as if the financial security of the Capital was tottering. An amazed silence fell, and in it they heard the great grille door of the basement clang on the inopportune foreigner's departure. But, as if it was impossible to stand still on that morning of dire happenings, he was immediately succeeded by a dapper, keen-faced man in severe clerical attire who had been let in as the intruder passed out.

"Canon Petersham!" exclaimed the professor, going forward to greet him.

"My dear Professor Bulge!" reciprocated the canon. "You here! A most disquieting thing has happened to me. I must have my safe at once." He divided his attention between the manager and the professor as he monopolised them both. "A most disquieting and—and outrageous circumstance. My safe, please—yes, yes, Rev. Henry Noakes Petersham. I have just received by hand a box, a small box of no value but one that I *thought*, yes, I am convinced that it was the one, a box that was used to contain certain valuables of family interest which should at this moment be in my safe here. No. 7436? Very likely, very likely. Yes, here is my key. But not content with the disconcerting effect of that, professor, the box contained—and I protest that it's a most unseemly thing to quote *any* text from the Bible in this way to a clergyman of my position—well, here it is. *Lay not up for yourselves treasures upon earth*——Why, I have a dozen sermons of my own in my desk now on that very verse. I'm particularly partial to the very needful lesson that it teaches. And to apply it to *me*! It's monstrous!"

"No. 7436, John," ordered the manager, with weary resignation.

The attendant again led the way towards another armour-plated aisle. Smartly turning a corner, he stumbled over something, bit a profane exclamation in two, and looked back.

"It's that bloomin' foreigner's old bag again," he explained across the place in aggrieved apology. "He left it here after all."

"Take it upstairs and throw it out when you've finished," said the manager shortly.

"Here, wait a minute," pondered John, in absent-minded familiarity. "Wait a minute. This is a funny go. There's a label on that wasn't here before. 'Why not look inside?'"

"'Why not look inside?'" repeated someone.

"That's what it says."

There was another puzzled silence. All were arrested by some intangible suggestion of a deeper mystery than they had yet touched.

One by one they began to cross the hall with the conscious air of men who were not curious but thought that they might as well see.

"Why, curse my crumpet," suddenly exploded Mr Berge, "if that ain't the same writing as these texts!"

"By gad, but I believe you are right," assented Mr Carlyle. "Well, why not look inside?"

The attendant, from his stooping posture, took the verdict of the ring of faces and in a trice tugged open the two buckles. The central fastening was not locked, and yielded to a touch. The flannel shirt, the weird collar and a few other garments in the nature of a "top-dressing" were flung out and John's hand plunged deeper....

Harry the Actor had lived up to his dramatic instinct. Nothing was wrapped up; nay, the rich booty had been deliberately opened out and displayed, as it were, so that the overturning of the bag, when John the keybearer in an access of riotous extravagance lifted it up and strewed its contents broadcast on the floor, was like the looting of a smuggler's den, or the realization of a speculator's dream, or the bursting of an Aladdin's cave, or something incredibly lavish and bizarre. Bank-notes fluttered down and lay about in all directions, relays of sovereigns rolled away like so much dross, bonds and scrip for thousands and tens of thousands clogged the downpouring stream of jewellery and unset gems.

A yellow stone the size of a four-pound weight and twice as heavy dropped plump upon the canon's toes and sent him hopping and grimacing to the wall. A ruby-hilted *kris* cut across the manager's wrist as he strove to arrest the splendid rout. Still the miraculous cornucopia deluged the ground, with its pattering, ringing, bumping, crinkling, rolling, fluttering produce until, like the final tableau of some spec-tacular ballet, it ended with a golden rain that masked the details of the heap beneath a glittering veil of yellow sand.

"My dust!" gasped Draycott.

"My fivers, by golly!" ejaculated the bookmaker, initiating a plunge among the spoil.

"My Japanese bonds, coupons and all, and—yes, even the manu-script of my work on 'Polyphyletic Bridal Customs among the mid-Pleistocene Cave Men.' Hah!" Something approaching a cachinnation of delight closed the professor's contribution to the pandemonium, and eyewitnesses afterwards declared that for a moment the dignified scientist stood on one foot in the opening movement of a can-can.

"My wife's diamonds, thank heaven!" cried Sir Benjamin, with the air of a schoolboy who was very well out of a swishing.

"But what does it mean?" demanded the bewildered canon. "Here are my family heirlooms—a few decent pearls, my grandfather's collection of *camei* and other trifles—but who———?"

"Perhaps this offers some explanation," suggested Mr Carlyle, unpinning an envelope that had been secured to the lining of the bag. "It is addressed 'To Seven Rich Sinners.' Shall I read it for you?"

For some reason the response was not unanimous, but it was sufficient. Mr Carlyle cut open the envelope.

My Dear Friends,—Aren't you glad? Aren't you happy at this moment? Ah yes; but not with the true joy of regeneration that alone can bring lightness to the afflicted soul. Pause while there is yet time. *Cast off the burden of your sinful lusts, for what shall it profit a man if he shall gain the whole world and lose his own soul?* (Mark, chap. viii., v. 36.)

Oh, my friends, you have had an all-fired narrow squeak. Up till the Friday in last week I held your wealth in the hollow of my ungodly hand and rejoiced in my nefarious cunning, but on that day as I with my guilty female accomplice stood listening with worldly amusement to the testimony of a converted brother at a meeting of the Salvation Army on Clapham Common, the gospel light suddenly shone into our rebellious souls and then and there we found salvation. Hallelujah!

What we have done to complete the unrighteous scheme upon which we had laboured for months has only been for your own good, dear friends that you are, though as yet divided from us by your carnal lusts.

Let this be a lesson to you. Sell all you have and give it to the poor—through the organisation of the Salvation Army by preference—*and thereby lay up for yourselves treasures where neither moth nor rust doth corrupt and where thieves do not break through and steal.* (Matthew, chap, vi., v. 20.)

    Yours in good works,

                    Private Henry, the Salvationist.

P.S. (in haste).—I may as well inform you that no crib is really uncrackable, though the Cyrus J. Coy Co.'s Safe Deposit on West 24th Street, N.Y., comes nearest the kernel. And even that I could work to the bare rock if I took hold of the job with both hands—that is to say I could have done in my sinful days.

As for you, I should recommend you to change your T.A. to Peanut.'

U.K.G.

"There sounds a streak of the old Adam in that postscript, Mr Carlyle," whispered Inspector Beedel, who had just arrived in time to hear the letter read.

The Tilling Shaw Mystery

"I will see Miss George now," assented Carrados. Parkinson retired and Greatorex looked round from his chair. The morning "clearing-up" was still in progress.

"Shall I go?" he inquired.

"Not unless the lady desires it. I don't know her at all."

The secretary was not unobservant and he had profited from his association with Mr Carrados. Without more ado, he began to get his papers quietly together.

The door opened and a girl of about twenty came eagerly yet half timorously into the room. Her eyes for a moment swept Carrados with an anxious scrutiny. Then, with a slight shade of disappointment, she noticed that they were not alone.

"I have come direct from Oakshire to see you, Mr Carrados," she announced, in a quick, nervous voice that was evidently the outcome of a desperate resolution to be brave and explicit. "The matter is a dreadfully important one to me and I should very much prefer to tell it to you alone."

There was no need for Carrados to turn towards his secretary; that discriminating young gentleman was already on his way. Miss George flashed him a shy look of thanks and filled in the moment with a timid survey of the room.

"Is it something that you think I can help you with?"

"I had hoped so. I had heard in a roundabout way of your wonderful power—ought I to tell you how—does it matter?"

"Not in the least if it has nothing to do with the case," replied Carrados.

"When this dreadful thing happened I instinctively thought of you. I felt sure that I ought to come and get you to help me at once. But I—I have very little money, Mr Carrados, only a few pounds,

124

and I am not so childish as not to know that very clever men require large fees. Then when I got here my heart sank, for I saw at once from your house and position that what seemed little even to me would be ridiculous to you—that if you did help me it would be purely out of kindness of heart and generosity."

"Suppose you tell me what the circumstances are," suggested Carrados cautiously. Then, to afford an opening, he added: "You have recently gone into mourning, I see."

"See!" exclaimed the girl almost sharply. "Then you are not blind?"

"Oh yes," he replied; "only I use the familiar expression, partly from custom, partly because it sounds unnecessarily pedantic to say, 'I deduce from certain observations.'"

"I beg your pardon. I suppose I was startled not so much by the expression as by your knowledge. I ought to have been prepared. But I am already wasting your time and I came so determined to be business-like. I got a copy of the local paper on the way, because I thought that the account in it would be clearer to you than I could tell it. Shall I read it?"

"Please; if that was your intention."

"It is *The Stinbridge Herald*," explained the girl, taking a closely folded newspaper from the handbag which she carried. "Stinbridge is our nearest town—about six miles from Tilling Shaw, where we live. This is the account:

MYSTERIOUS TRAGEDY AT TILLING
WELL-KNOWN AGRICULTURALIST ATTEMPTS MURDER
AND COMMITS SUICIDE

The districts of Great Tilling, Tilling Shaw and the immediate neighbourhood were thrown into a state of unusual excitement on Thursday last by the report of a tragedy in their midst such as has rarely marked the annals of our law-abiding countryside. A *Herald* representative was early on the scene, and his inquiries elucidated the fact that it was only too true that in this case rumour had not exaggerated the circumstances, rather the reverse indeed. On the afternoon of the day in question, Mr Frank Whitmarsh, of High Barn, presented himself at Barony, the residence of his uncle, Mr William Whitmarsh, with the intention of seeing him in reference to a dispute that was pending between them. This is understood to be connected with an alleged trespass in pursuit of game, each relative claiming exclusive sporting rights over a piece of water known as Hunstan Mere.

On this occasion the elder gentleman was not at home and Mr Frank Whitmarsh, after waiting for some time, departed, leaving a message to the effect that he would return, and, according to one report, "have it out with Uncle William," later in the evening.

This resolution he unfortunately kept. Returning about eight-forty-five p.m. he found his uncle in and for some time the two men remained together in the dining-room. What actually passed between them has not yet transpired, but it is said that for half-an-hour there had been nothing to indicate to the other occupants of the house that anything unusual was in progress when suddenly two shots rang out in rapid succession. Mrs Lawrence, the housekeeper at Barony, and a servant were the soonest on the spot, and, conquering the natural terror that for a moment held them outside the now silent room, they summoned up courage to throw open the door and to enter. The first thing that met their eyes was the body of Mr Frank Whitmarsh lying on the floor almost at their feet.

In their distressed state it was immediately assumed by the horrified women that he was dead, or at least seriously wounded, but a closer examination revealed the fact that the gentleman had experienced an almost miraculous escape. At the time of the tragedy he was wearing a large old-fashioned silver watch; and in this the bullet intended for his heart was found, literally embedded deep in the works. The second shot had, however, effected its purpose, for at the other side of the room, still seated at the table, was Mr William Whitmarsh, already quite dead, with a terrible wound in his head and the weapon, a large-bore revolver of obsolete pattern, lying at his feet.

Mr Frank Whitmarsh subsequently explained that the shock of the attack, and the dreadful appearance presented by his uncle when, immediately afterwards, he turned his hand against himself, must have caused him to faint.

Readers of *The Herald* will join in our expression of sympathy for all members of the Whitmarsh family, and in our congratulations to Mr Frank Whitmarsh on his providential escape.

The inquest is fixed for Monday and it is anticipated that the funeral will take place on the following day.'

"That is all," concluded Miss George.

"All that is in the paper," amended Carrados.

"It is the same everywhere—'attempted murder and suicide'—that is what everyone accepts as a matter of course," went on the girl quickly. "How do they know that my father tried to kill Frank, or that he killed himself? How can they know, Mr Carrados?"

"Your father, Miss George?"

"Yes. My name is Madeline Whitmarsh. At home everyone looks at me as if I was an object of mingled pity and reproach. I thought that they might know the name here, so I gave the first that came into my head. I think it is a street I was directed along. Besides, I don't want it to be known that I came to see you in any case."

"Why?"

Much of the girl's conscious nervousness had stiffened into an attitude of unconscious hardness. Grief takes many forms, and whatever she had been before, the tragic episode had left Miss Whitmarsh a little hurt and cynical.

"You are a man living in a town and can do as you like. I am a girl living in the country and have therefore to do largely as my neighbours like. For me to set up my opinion against popular feeling would constitute no small offence; to question its justice would be held to be adding outrageous insult to enormous injury."

"So far I am unable to go beyond the newspaper account. On the face of it, your father—with what provocation of course I do not know—did attempt this Mr Frank Whitmarsh's life and then take his own. You imply another version. What reason have you?"

"That is the terrible part of it," exclaimed the girl, with rising distress. "It was that which made me so afraid of coming to you, although I felt that I must, for I dreaded that when you asked me for proofs and I could give you none you would refuse to help me. We were not even in time to hear him speak, and yet I know, *know* with absolute conviction, that my father would not have done this. There are things that you cannot explain, Mr Carrados, and—well, there is an end of it."

Her voice sank to an absent-minded whisper.

"Everyone will condemn him now that he cannot defend himself, and yet he could not even have had the revolver that was found at his feet."

"What is that?" demanded Carrados sharply. "Do you mean that?"

"Mean what?" she asked, with the blankness of one who has lost the thread of her own thoughts.

"What you said about the revolver—that your father could not have had it?"

"The revolver?" she repeated half wearily; "oh yes. It was a heavy, old-fashioned affair. It had been lying in a drawer of his desk for more than ten years because once a dog came into the orchard in broad daylight light and worried half-a-dozen lambs before anyone could do anything."

"Yes, but why could he not have it on Thursday?"

"I noticed that it was gone. After Frank had left in the afternoon I went into the room where he had been waiting, to finish dusting. The paper says the dining-room, but it was really papa's business-room and no one else used it. Then when I was dusting the desk I saw that the revolver was no longer there."

"You had occasion to open the drawer?"

"It is really a very old bureau and none of the drawers fit closely. Dust lies on the ledges and you always have to open them a little to dust properly. They were never kept locked."

"Possibly your father had taken the revolver with him."

"No. I had seen it there after he had gone. He rode to Stinbridge immediately after lunch and did not return until nearly eight. After he left I went to dust his room. It was then that I saw it. I was doing the desk when Frank knocked and interrupted me. That is how I came to be there twice."

"But you said that you had no proof, Miss Whitmarsh," Carrados reminded her, with deep seriousness. "Do you not recognise the importance—the deadly importance—that this one shred of evidence may assume?"

"Does it?" she replied simply. "I am afraid that I am rather dull just now. All yesterday I was absolutely dazed; I could not do the most ordinary things. I found myself looking at the clock for minutes together, yet absolutely incapable of grasping what time it was. In the same way I know that it struck me as being funny about the revolver but I always had to give it up. It was as though everything was there but things would not fit in."

"You are sure, absolutely sure, that you saw the revolver there after your father had left, and missed it before he returned?"

"Oh yes," said the girl quickly; "I remember realizing how curious it was at the time. Besides there is something else. I so often had things to ask papa about when he was out of the house that I got into the way of making little notes to remind me later. This morning I found on my dressing-table one that I had written on Thursday afternoon."

"About this weapon?"

"Yes; to ask him what could have become of it."

Carrados made a further inquiry, and this was Madeline Whitmarsh's account of affairs existing between the two branches of the family:

Until the time of William Whitmarsh, father of the William Whitmarsh just deceased, the properties of Barony and High Barn had formed one estate, descending from a William senior to a William junior down a moderately long line of yeomen Whitmarshes. Through the influence of his second wife this William senior divided the property, leaving Barony with its four hundred acres of good land to William junior, and High Barn, with which went three hundred acres of poor land, to his other son, father of the Frank implicated in the recent tragedy. But though divided, the two farms still had one common link. Beneath their growing corn and varied pasturage lay, it was generally admitted, a seam of coal at a depth and of a thickness that would render its working a paying venture. Even in William the Divider's time, when the idea was new, money in plenty would have been forthcoming, but he would have none of it, and when he died his will contained a provision restraining either son from mining or exploiting his land for mineral without the consent and co-operation of the other.

This restriction became a legacy of hate. The brothers were only half-brothers and William having suffered unforgettably at the hands of his stepmother had old scores to pay off. Quite comfortably prosperous on his own rich farm, and quite satisfied with the excellent shooting and the congenial life, he had not the slightest desire to increase his wealth. He had the old dour, peasant-like instinct to cling to the house and the land of his forefathers. From this position no argument moved him.

In the meanwhile, on the other side of the new boundary fence, Frank senior was growing poorer year by year. To his periodical entreaties that William would agree to shafts being sunk on High Barn he received an emphatic "Never in my time!" The poor man argued, besought, threatened and swore; the prosperous one shook his head and grinned. Carrados did not need to hear the local saying: "Half brothers: whole haters; like the Whitmarshes," to read the situation.

"Of course I do not really understand the business part of it," said Madeline, "and many people blamed poor papa, especially when Uncle Frank drank himself to death. But I know that it was not mere obstinacy. He loved the undisturbed, peaceful land just as it was, and his father had wished it to remain the same. Collieries would bring swarms of strange men into the neighbourhood, poachers and trespassers, he said. The smoke and dust would ruin the land for miles round and drive away the game, and in the end, if the work did not turn out profitable, we should all be much worse off than before."

"Does the restriction lapse now; will Mr Frank junior be able to mine?"

"It will now lie with Frank and my brother William, just as it did before with their fathers. I should expect Willie to be quite favourable. He is more—modern."

"You have not spoken of your brother."

"I have two. Bob, the younger, is in Mexico," she explained; "and Willie in Canada with an engineering firm. They did not get on very well with papa and they went away."

It did not require preternatural observation to deduce that the late William Whitmarsh had been "a little difficult."

"When Uncle Frank died, less than six months ago, Frank came back to High Barn from South Africa. He had been away about two years."

"Possibly he did not get on well with his father?"

Madeline smiled sadly.

"I am afraid that no two Whitmarsh men ever did get on together," she admitted.

"Your father and young Frank, for instance?"

"Their lands adjoin; there were always quarrels and disputes," she replied. "Then Frank had his father's grievance over again."

"He wished to mine?"

"Yes. He told me that he had had experience of coal in Natal."

"There was no absolute ostracism between you then? You were to some extent friends?"

"Scarcely." She appeared to reflect. "Acquaintances. . . . We met occasionally, of course, at people's houses."

"You did not visit High Barn?"

"Oh no."

"But there was no particular reason why you should not?"

"Why do you ask me that?" she demanded quickly, and in a tone that was quite incompatible with the simple inquiry. Then, recognising the fact, she added, with shamefaced penitence: "I beg your pardon, Mr Carrados. I am afraid that my nerves have gone to pieces since Thursday. The most ordinary things affect me inexplicably."

"That is a common experience in such circumstances," said Carrados reassuringly. "Where were you at the time of the tragedy?"

"I was in my bedroom, which is rather high up, changing. I had driven down to the village, to give an order, and had just returned. Mrs Lawrence told me that she had been afraid there might be quarrelling, but no one would ever have dreamed of this, and then came a loud shot and then, after a few seconds, another not so loud, and we rushed to the door—she and Mary first—and everything was absolutely still."

"A loud shot and then another not so loud?"

"Yes; I noticed that even at the time. I happened to speak to Mrs Lawrence of it afterwards and then she also remembered that it had been like that."

Afterwards Carrados often recalled with grim pleasantry that the two absolutely vital points in the fabric of circumstantial evidence that was to exonerate her father and fasten the guilt upon another had dropped from the girl's lips utterly by chance. But at the moment the facts themselves monopolised his attention.

"You are not disappointed that I can tell you so little?" she asked timidly.

"Scarcely," he replied. "A suicide who could not have had the weapon he dies by, a victim who is miraculously preserved by an opportune watch, and two shots from the same pistol that differ materially in volume, all taken together do not admit of disappointment."

"I am very stupid," she said. "I do not seem able to follow things. But you will come and clear my father's name?"

"I will come," he replied. "Beyond that who shall prophesy?"

It had been arranged between them that the girl should return at once, while Carrados would travel down to Great Tilling late that same afternoon and put up at the local fishing inn. In the evening he would call at Barony, where Madeline would accept him as a distant connexion of the family. The arrangement was only for the benefit of the domestics and any casual visitor who might be present, for there was no possibility of a near relation being in attendance. Nor was there any appreciable danger of either his name or person being recognised in those parts, a consideration that seemed to have some weight with the girl, for, more than once, she entreated him not to disclose to anyone his real business there until he had arrived at a definite conclusion.

It was nine o'clock, but still just light enough to distinguish the prominent features of the landscape, when Carrados, accompanied by Parkinson, reached Barony. The house, as described by the man-servant, was a substantial grey stone building, very plain, very square, very exposed to the four winds. It had not even a porch to break the flat surface, and here and there in the line of its three solid storeys a window had been built up by some frugal, tax-evading Whitmarsh of a hundred years ago.

"Sombre enough," commented Carrados, "but the connexion be-tween environment and crime is not yet capable of analysis. We get murders in brand-new suburban villas and the virtues, light-hearted-ness and good-fellowship, in moated granges. What should you say about it, eh, Parkinson?"

"I should say it was damp, sir," observed Parkinson, with his wisest air.

Madeline Whitmarsh herself opened the door. She took them down the long flagged hall to the dining-room, a cheerful enough apartment whatever its exterior might forebode.

"I am glad you have come now, Mr Carrados," she said hurriedly, when the door was closed. "Sergeant Brewster is here from Stinbridge police station to make some arrangements for the inquest. It is to be held at the schools here on Monday. He says that he must take the re-volver with him to produce. Do you want to see it before he goes?"

"I should like to," replied Carrados.

"Will you come into papa's room then? He is there."

The sergeant was at the table, making notes in his pocket-book, when they entered. An old-fashioned revolver lay before him.

"This gentleman has come a long way on hearing about poor papa," said the girl. "He would like to see the revolver before you take it, Mr Brewster."

"Good-evening, sir," said Brewster. "It's a bad business that brings us here."

Carrados "looked" round the room and returned the policeman's greeting. Madeline hesitated for a moment, and then, picking up the weapon, put it into the blind man's hand.

"A bit out of date, sir," remarked Brewster, with a nod. "But in good order yet, I find."

"An early French make, I should say; one of Lefaucheux's prob-ably," said Carrados. "You have removed the cartridges?"

"Why, yes," admitted the sergeant, producing a matchbox from his pocket. "They're pin-fire, you see, and I'm not too fond of carrying a thing like that loaded in my pocket as I'm riding a young horse."

"Quite so," agreed Carrados, fingering the cartridges. "I wonder if you happened to mark the order of these in the chambers?"

"That was scarcely necessary, sir. Two, together, had been fired; the other four had not."

"I once knew a case—possibly I read of it—where a pack of cards lay on the floor. It was a murder case and the guilt or innocence of an accused man depended on the relative positions of the fifty-first and fifty-second cards."

"I think you must have read of that, sir," replied Brewster, endeavouring to implicate first Miss Whitmarsh and then Parkinson in his meaning smile. "However, this is straightforward enough."

"Then, of course, you have not thought it worth while to look for anything else?"

"I have noted all the facts that have any bearing on the case. Were you referring to any particular point, sir?"

"I was only wondering," suggested Carrados, with apologetic mildness, "whether you, or anyone, had happened to find a wad lying about anywhere."

The sergeant stroked his well-kept moustache to hide the smile that insisted, however, on escaping through his eyes.

"Scarcely, sir," he replied, with fine irony. "Bulleted revolver cartridges contain no wad. You are thinking of a shot-gun, sir."

"Oh," said Carrados, bending over the spent cartridge he was examining, "that settles it, of course."

"I think so, sir," assented the sergeant, courteously but with a quiet enjoyment of the situation. "Well, miss, I'll be getting back now. I think I have everything I want."

"You will excuse me a few minutes?" said Miss Whitmarsh, and the two callers were left alone.

"Parkinson," said Carrados softly, as the door closed, "look round on the floor. There is no wad lying within sight?"

"No, sir."

"Then take the lamp and look behind things. But if you find one don't disturb it."

For a minute strange and gigantic shadows chased one another across the ceiling as Parkinson moved the table-lamp to and fro behind the furniture. The man to whom blazing sunlight and the deepest shade were as one sat with his eyes fixed tranquilly on the unseen wall before him.

"There is a little pellet of paper here behind the couch, sir," announced Parkinson.

"Then put the lamp back."

Together they drew the cumbrous old piece of furniture from the wall and Carrados went behind. On hands and knees, with his face almost to the floor, he appeared to be studying even the dust that lay there. Then with a light, unerring touch he carefully picked up the thing that Parkinson had found. Very gently he unrolled it, using his long, delicate fingers so skilfully that even at the end the particles of dust still clung here and there to the surface of the paper.

"What do you make of it, Parkinson?"

Parkinson submitted it to the judgment of a single sense.

"A cigarette-paper to all appearance, sir. I can't say it's a kind that I've had experience of. It doesn't seem to have any distinct watermark but there is a half-inch of glossy paper along one edge."

"Amber-tipped. Yes?"

"Another edge is a little uneven; it appears to have been cut."

"This edge opposite the mouthpiece. Yes, yes."

"Patches are blackened, and little holes—like pinpricks—burned through. In places it is scorched brown."

"Anything else?"

"I hope there is nothing I have failed to observe, sir," said Parkinson, after a pause.

Carrados's reply was a strangely irrelevant question.

"What is the ceiling made of?" he demanded.

"Oak boards, sir, with a heavy cross-beam."

"Are there any plaster figures about the room?"

"No, sir."

"Or anything at all that is whitewashed?"

"Nothing, sir."

Carrados raised the scrap of tissue paper to his nose again, and for the second time he touched it with his tongue.

"Very interesting, Parkinson," he remarked, and Parkinson's responsive "Yes, sir" was a model of discreet acquiescence.

"I am sorry that I had to leave you," said Miss Whitmarsh, returning, "but Mrs Lawrence is out and my father made a practice of offering everyone refreshment."

"Don't mention it," said Carrados. "We have not been idle. I came from London to pick up a scrap of paper, lying on the floor of this room. Well, here it is." He rolled the tissue into a pellet again and held it before her eyes.

"The wad!" she exclaimed eagerly. "Oh, that proves that I was right?"

"Scarcely 'proves,' Miss Whitmarsh."

"But it shows that one of the shots was a blank charge, as you suggested this morning might have been the case."

"Hardly even that."

"What then?" she demanded, with her large dark eyes fixed in a curious fascination on his inscrutable face.

"That behind the couch we have found this scrap of powder-singed paper."

There was a moment's silence. The girl turned away her head.

"I am afraid that I am a little disappointed," she murmured.

"Perhaps better now than later. I wished to warn you that we must prove every inch of ground. Does your cousin Frank smoke cigarettes?"

"I cannot say, Mr Carrados. You see . . . I knew so little of him."

"Quite so; there was just the chance. And your father?"

"He never did. He despised them."

"That is all I need ask you now. What time tomorrow shall I find you in, Miss Whitmarsh? It is Sunday, you remember."

"At any time. The curiosity I inspire doesn't tempt me to encounter my friends, I can assure you," she replied, her face hardening at the recollection. "But . . . Mr Carrados——"

"Yes?"

"The inquest is on Monday afternoon. . . . I had a sort of desperate faith that you would be able to vindicate papa."

"By the time of the inquest, you mean?"

"Yes. Otherwise——"

"The verdict of a coroner's jury means nothing, Miss Whitmarsh. It is the merest formality."

"It means a very great deal to me. It haunts and oppresses me. If they say—if it goes out—that papa is guilty of the attempt of murder, and of suicide, I shall never raise my head again."

Carrados had no desire to prolong a futile discussion.

"Goodnight," he said, holding out his hand.

"Goodnight, Mr Carrados." She detained him a moment, her voice vibrant with quiet feeling. "I already owe you more than I can ever hope to express. Your wonderful kindness——"

"A strange case," moralised Carrados, as they walked out of the quadrangular yard into the silent lane. "Instructive, but I more than half wish I'd never heard of it."

"The young lady seems grateful, sir," Parkinson ventured to suggest.

"The young lady is the case, Parkinson," replied his master rather grimly.

A few score yards farther on a swing gate gave access to a field-path, cutting off the corner that the high road made with the narrow lane. This was their way, but instead of following the brown line of trodden earth Carrados turned to the left and indicated the line of buildings that formed the back of one side of the quadrangle they had passed through.

"We will investigate here," he said. "Can you see a way in?"

Most of the buildings opened on to the yard, but at one end of the range Parkinson discovered a door, secured only by a wooden latch. The place beyond was impenetrably dark, but the sweet, dusty smell of hay, and, from beyond, the occasional click of a horse's shoe on stone and the rattle of a head-stall chain through the manger ring told them that they were in the chaff-pen at the back of the stable.

Carrados stretched out his hand and touched the wall with a single finger.

"We need go no farther," he remarked, and as they resumed their way across the field he took out a handkerchief to wipe the taste of whitewash off his tongue.

Madeline had spoken of the gradual decay of High Barn, but Carrados was hardly prepared for the poverty-stricken desolation which Parkinson described as they approached the homestead on the following afternoon. He had purposely selected a way that took them across many of young Whitmarsh's ill-stocked fields, fields in which sedge and charlock wrote an indictment of neglected drains and half-hearted tillage. On the land, the gates and hedges had been broken and unkempt; the buildings, as they passed through the farmyard, were empty and showed here and there a skeletonry of bare rafters to the sky.

"Starved," commented the blind man, as he read the signs. "The thirsty owner and the hungry land: they couldn't both be fed."

Although it was afternoon the bolts and locks of the front door had to be unfastened in answer to their knock. When at last the door was opened a shrivelled little old woman, rather wicked-looking in a comic way, and rather begrimed, stood there.

"Mr Frank Whitmarsh?" she replied to Carrados's polite inquiry; "oh yes, he lives here. Frank," she called down the passage, "you're wanted."

"What is it, mother?" responded a man's full, strong voice rather lazily.

"Come and see!" and the old creature ogled Carrados with her beady eyes as though the situation constituted an excellent joke between them.

There was the sound of a chair being moved and at the end of the passage a tall man appeared in his shirt sleeves.

"I am a stranger to you," explained Carrados, "but I am staying at the Bridge Inn and I heard of your wonderful escape on Thursday. I was so interested that I have taken the liberty of coming across to congratulate you on it."

"Oh, come in, come in," said Whitmarsh. "Yes ... it was a sort of miracle, wasn't it?"

He led the way back into the room he had come from, half kitchen, half parlour. It at least had the virtue of an air of rude comfort, and some of the pewter and china that ornamented its mantelpiece and dresser would have rejoiced a collector's heart.

"You find us a bit rough," apologised the young man, with something of contempt towards his surroundings. "We weren't expecting visitors."

"And I was hesitating to come because I thought that you would be surrounded by your friends."

This very ordinary remark seemed to afford Mrs Whitmarsh unbounded entertainment and for quite a number of seconds she was convulsed with silent amusement at the idea.

"Shut up, mother," said her dutiful son. "Don't take any notice of her," he remarked to his visitors, "she often goes on like that. The fact is," he added, "we Whitmarshes aren't popular in these parts. Of course that doesn't trouble me; I've seen too much of things. And, taken as a boiling, the Whitmarshes deserve it."

"Ah, wait till you touch the coal, my boy, then you'll see," put in the old lady, with malicious triumph.

"I reckon we'll show them then, eh, mother?" he responded bumptiously. "Perhaps you've heard of that, Mr——?"

"Carrados—Wynn Carrados. This is my man, Parkinson. I have to be attended because my sight has failed me. Yes, I had heard something about coal. Providence seems to be on your side just now, Mr Whitmarsh. May I offer you a cigarette?"

"Thanks, I don't mind for once in a way."

"They're Turkish; quite innocuous, I believe."

"Oh, it isn't that. I can smoke cutty with any man, I reckon, but the paper affects my lips. I make my own and use a sort of paper with an end that doesn't stick."

"The paper is certainly a drawback sometimes," agreed Carrados. "I've found that. Might I try one of yours?"

They exchanged cigarettes and Whitmarsh returned to the subject of the tragedy.

"This has made a bit of a stir, I can tell you," he remarked, with complacency.

"I am sure it would. Well, it was the chief topic of conversation when I was in London."

"Is that a fact?" Avowedly indifferent to the opinion of his neighbours, even Whitmarsh was not proof against the pronouncement of the metropolis. "What do they say about it up there?"

"I should be inclined to think that the interest centres round the explanation you will give at the inquest of the cause of the quarrel."

"There! What did I tell you?" exclaimed Mrs Whitmarsh.

"Be quiet, mother. That's easily answered, Mr Carrados. There was a bit of duck shooting that lay between our two places. But perhaps you saw that in the papers?"

"Yes," admitted Carrados, "I saw that. Frankly, the reason seemed inadequate to so deadly a climax."

"What did I say?" demanded the irrepressible dame. "They won't believe it."

The young man cast a wrathful look in his mother's direction and turned again to the visitor.

"That's because you don't know Uncle William. *Any* reason was good enough for him to quarrel over. Here, let me give you an instance. When I went in on Thursday he was smoking a pipe. Well, after a bit I took out a cigarette and lit it. I'm damned if he didn't turn round and start on me for that. How does that strike you for one of your own family, Mr Carrados?"

"Unreasonable, I am bound to admit. I am afraid that I should have been inclined to argue the point. What did you do, Mr Whitmarsh?"

"I hadn't gone there to quarrel," replied the young man, half sulky at the recollection. "It was his house. I threw it into the fireplace."

"Very obliging," said Carrados. "But, if I may say so, it isn't so much a matter of speculation why he should shoot you as why he should shoot himself."

"The gentleman seems friendly. Better ask his advice, Frank," put in the old woman in a penetrating whisper.

"Stow it, mother!" said Whitmarsh sharply. "Are you crazy? Her idea of a coroner's inquest," he explained to Carrados, with easy contempt, "is that I am being tried for murder. As a matter of fact, Uncle William was a very passionate man, and, like many of that kind, he frequently went beyond himself. I don't doubt that he was sure he'd killed me, for he was a good shot and the force of the blow sent me backwards. He was a very proud man too, in a way—wouldn't stand correction or any kind of authority, and when he realised what he'd done and saw in a flash that he would be tried and hanged for it, suicide seemed the easiest way out of his difficulties, I suppose."

"Yes; that sounds reasonable enough," admitted Carrados.

"Then you don't think there will be any trouble, sir?" insinuated Mrs Whitmarsh anxiously.

Frank had already professed his indifference to local opinion, but Carrados was conscious that both of them hung rather breathlessly on to his reply.

"Why, no," he declared weightily. "I should see no reason for anticipating any. Unless," he added thoughtfully, "some clever lawyer was instructed to insist that there must be more in the dispute than appears on the surface."

"Oh, them lawyers, them lawyers!" moaned the old lady in a panic. "They can make you say anything."

"They can't make me say anything." A cunning look came into his complacent face. "And, besides, who's going to engage a lawyer?"

"The family of the deceased gentleman might wish to do so."

"Both of the sons are abroad and could not be back in time."

"But is there not a daughter here? I understood so."

Whitmarsh gave a short, unpleasant laugh and turned to look at his mother.

"Madeline won't. You may bet your bottom tikkie it's the last thing she would want."

The little old creature gazed admiringly at her big showy son and responded with an appreciative grimace that made her look more humorously rat-like than ever.

"He! he! Missie won't," she tittered. "That would never do. He! he!" Wink succeeded nod and meaning smile until she relapsed into a state of quietness; and Parkinson, who had been fascinated by her contortions, was unable to decide whether she was still laughing or had gone to sleep.

Carrados stayed a few more minutes and before they left he asked to see the watch.

"A unique memento, Mr Whitmarsh," he remarked, examining it. "I should think this would become a family heirloom."

"It's no good for anything else," said Whitmarsh practically. "A famous time-keeper it was, too."

"The fingers are both gone."

"Yes; the glass was broken, of course, and they must have caught in the cloth of my pocket and ripped off."

"They naturally would; it was ten minutes past nine when the shot was fired."

The young man thought and then nodded.

"About that," he agreed.

"Nearer than 'about,' if your watch was correct. Very interesting, Mr Whitmarsh. I am glad to have seen the watch that saved your life."

Instead of returning to the inn Carrados directed Parkinson to take the road to Barony. Madeline was at home, and from the sound of voices it appeared that she had other visitors, but she came out to Carrados at once, and at his request took him into the empty dining-room while Parkinson stayed in the hall.

"Yes?" she said eagerly.

"I have come to tell you that I must throw up my brief," he said. "There is nothing more to be done and I return to town to-night."

"Oh!" she stammered helplessly. "I thought—I thought——"

"Your cousin did not abstract the revolver when he was here on Thursday, Miss Whitmarsh. He did not at his leisure fire a bullet into his own watch to make it appear, later in the day, as if he had been attacked. He did not reload the cartridge with a blank charge. He did not deliberately shoot your father and then fire off the blank cartridge. He *was* attacked and the newspaper version is substantially correct. The whole fabric so delicately suggested by inference and innuendo falls to pieces."

"Then you desert me, Mr Carrados?" she said, in a low, bitter voice.

"I have seen the watch—the watch that saved Whitmarsh's life," he continued, unmoved. "It would save it again if necessary. It indicates ten minutes past nine—the time to a minute at which it is agreed the shot was fired. By what prescience was he to know at what exact minute his opportunity would occur?"

"When I saw the watch on Thursday night the fingers were not there."

"They are not, but the shaft remains. It is of an old-fashioned pattern and it will only take the fingers in one position. That position indicates ten minutes past nine."

"Surely it would have been an easy matter to have altered that afterwards?"

"In this case fate has been curiously systematic, Miss Whitmarsh. The bullet that shattered the works has so locked the action that it will not move a fraction this way or that."

"There is something more than this—something that I do not understand," she persisted. "I think I have a right to know."

"Since you insist, there is. There is the wad of the blank cartridge that you fired in the outbuilding."

"Oh!" she exclaimed, in the moment of startled undefence, "how do you—how can you——"

"You must leave the conjurer his few tricks for effect. Of course you naturally would fire it where the precious pellet could not get lost—the paper you steamed off the cigarette that Whitmarsh threw into the empty fire-grate; and of course the place must be some distance from the house or even that slight report might occasion remark."

"Yes," she confessed, in a sudden abandonment to weary indifference, "it has been useless. I was a fool to set my cleverness against yours. Now, I suppose, Mr Carrados, you will have to hand me over to justice?

"Well; why don't you say something?" she demanded impatiently, as he offered no comment.

"People frequently put me in this embarrassing position," he explained diffidently, "and throw the responsibility on me. Now a number of years ago a large and stately building was set up in London and it was beautifully called 'The Royal Palace of Justice.' That was its official name and that was what it was to be; but very soon people got into the way of calling it the Law Courts, and to-day, if you asked a Londoner to direct you to the Palace of Justice he would undoubtedly set you down as a religious maniac. You see my difficulty?"

"It is very strange," she said, intent upon her own reflections, "but I do not feel a bit ashamed to you of what I have done. I do not even feel afraid to tell you all about it, although of some of that I must certainly be ashamed. Why is it?"

"Because I am blind?"

"Oh no," she replied very positively.

Carrados smiled at her decision but he did not seek to explain that when he could no longer see the faces of men the power was gradually given to him of looking into their hearts, to which some in their turn—strong, free spirits—instinctively responded.

"There is such a thing as friendship at first sight," he suggested.

"Why, yes; like quite old friends," she agreed. "It is a pity that I had no very trusty friend, since my mother died when I was quite little. Even my father has been—it is queer to think of it now—well, almost a stranger to me really."

She looked at Carrados's serene and kindly face and smiled.

"It is a great relief to be able to talk like this, without the necessity for lying," she remarked. "Did you know that I was engaged?"

"No; you had not told me that."

"Oh no, but you might have heard of it. He is a clergyman whom I met last summer. But, of course, that is all over now."

"You have broken it off?"

"Circumstances have broken it off. The daughter of a man who had the misfortune to be murdered might just possibly be tolerated as a vicar's wife, but the daughter of a murderer and suicide—it is unthinkable! You see, the requirements for the office are largely social, Mr Carrados."

"Possibly your vicar may have other views."

"Oh, he isn't a vicar yet, but he is rather well-connected, so it is quite assured. And he would be dreadfully torn if the choice lay with him. As it is, he will perhaps rather soon get over my absence. But, you see, if we married he could never get over my presence; it would always stand in the way of his preferment. I worked very hard to make it possible, but it could not be."

"You were even prepared to send an innocent man to the gallows?"

"I think so, at one time," she admitted frankly. "But I scarcely thought it would come to that. There are so many well-meaning people who always get up petitions. . . . No, as I stand here looking at myself over there, I feel that I couldn't quite have hanged Frank, no matter how much he deserved it. . . . You are very shocked, Mr Carrados?"

"Well," admitted Carrados, with pleasant impartiality, "I have seen the young man, but the penalty, even with a reprieve, still seems to me a little severe."

"Yet how do you know, even now, that he is, as you say, an innocent man?"

"I don't," was the prompt admission. "I only know, in this astonishing case, that so far as my investigation goes, he did not murder your father by the act of his hand."

"Not according to your Law Courts?" she suggested. "But in the great Palace of Justice?. . . Well, you shall judge."

She left his side, crossed the room, and stood by the square, ugly window, looking out, but as blind as Carrados to the details of the somnolent landscape.

"I met Frank for the first time after I was at all grown-up about three years ago, when I returned from boarding-school. I had not seen him since I was a child, and I thought him very tall and manly. It seemed a frightfully romantic thing in the circumstances to meet him secretly—of course my thoughts flew to Romeo and Juliet. We put impassioned letters for one another in a hollow tree that stood on the boundary hedge. But presently I found out—gradually and incredulously at first and then one night with a sudden terrible certainty—that my ideas of romance were not his. . . . I had what is called, I believe, a narrow escape. I was glad when he went abroad, for it was only my self-conceit that had suffered. I was never in love with him: only in love with the idea of being in love with him.

"A few months ago Frank came back to High Barn. I tried never to meet him anywhere, but one day he overtook me in the lanes. He said that he had thought a lot about me while he was away, and would I marry him. I told him that it was impossible in any case, and, besides, I was engaged. He coolly replied that he knew. I was dumbfounded and asked him what he meant.

"Then he took out a packet of my letters that he had kept somewhere all the time. He insisted on reading parts of them up and telling me what this and that meant and what everyone would say it proved. I was horrified at the construction that seemed capable of being put on my foolish but innocent gush. I called him a coward and a blackguard and a mean cur and a sneaking cad and everything I could think of in one long breath, until I found myself faint and sick with excitement and the nameless growing terror of it.

"He only laughed and told me to think it over, and then walked on, throwing the letters up into the air and catching them.

"It isn't worth while going into all the times he met and threatened me. I was to marry him or he would expose me. He would never allow me to marry anyone else. And then finally he turned round and said that he didn't really want to marry me at all; he only wanted to force father's consent to start mining and this had seemed the easiest way."

"That is what is called blackmail, Miss Whitmarsh; a word you don't seem to have applied to him. The punishment ranges up to penal servitude for life in extreme cases."

"Yes, that is what it really was. He came on Thursday with the letters in his pocket. That was his last threat when he could not move me. I can guess what happened. He read the letters and proposed a bargain. And my father, who was a very passionate man, and very proud in certain ways, shot him as he thought, and then, in shame and in the madness of despair, took his own life. . . . Now, Mr Carrados, you were to be my judge."

"I think," said the blind man, with a great pity in his voice, "that it will be sufficient for you to come up for Judgment when called upon."

★★★★★★

Three weeks later a registered letter bearing the Liverpool postmark was delivered at The Turrets. After he had read it Carrados put it away in a special drawer of his desk, and once or twice in after years, when his work seemed rather barren, he took it out and read it. This is what it contained:

Dear Mr Carrados,—Some time after you had left me that Sunday afternoon, a man came in the dark to the door and asked for me. I did not see his face for he kept in the shade, but his figure was not very unlike that of your servant Parkinson. A packet was put into my hands and he was gone without a word. From this I imagine that perhaps you did not leave quite as soon as you had intended.

Thank you very much indeed for the letters. I was glad to have the miserable things, to drop them into the fire, and to see them pass utterly out of my own and everybody else's life. I wonder who else in the world would have done so much for a forlorn creature who just flashed across a few days of his busy life? and then I wonder who else could.

But there is something else for which I thank you now far, far more, and that is for saving me from the blindness of my own passionate folly. When I look back on the abyss of meanness, treachery and guilt into which I would have wilfully cast myself, and been condemned to live in all my life, I can scarcely trust myself to write.

I will not say that I do not suffer now. I think I shall for many years to come, but all the bitterness and I think all the hardness have been drawn out.

You will see that I am writing from Liverpool. I have taken a second-class passage to Canada and we sail tonight. Willie, who returned to Barony last week, has lent me all the money I shall need until I find work. Do not be apprehensive. It is not with the vague uncertainty of an indifferent typist or a downtrodden governess that I go, but as an efficient domestic servant—a capable cook, housemaid or 'general,' as need be. It sounds rather incredible at first, does it not, but such things happen, and I shall get on very well.

Goodbye, Mr Carrados; I shall remember you very often and very gratefully.

Madeline Whitmarsh.

P.S.—Yes, there is friendship at first sight.

The Comedy at Fountain Cottage

Carrados had rung up Mr Carlyle soon after the inquiry agent had reached his office in Bampton Street on a certain morning in April. Mr Carlyle's face at once assumed its most amiable expression as he recognised his friend's voice.

"Yes, Max," he replied, in answer to the call, "I am here and at the top of form, thanks. Glad to know that you are back from Trescoe. Is there—anything?"

"I have a couple of men coming in this evening whom you might like to meet," explained Carrados. "Manoel the Zambesia explorer is one and the other an East-End slum doctor who has seen a few things. Do you care to come round to dinner?"

"Delighted," warbled Mr Carlyle, without a moment's consideration. "Charmed. Your usual hour, Max?" Then the smiling complacence of his face suddenly changed and the wire conveyed an exclamation of annoyance. "I am really very sorry, Max, but I have just remembered that I have an engagement. I fear that I must deny myself after all."

"Is it important?"

"No," admitted Mr Carlyle. "Strictly speaking, it is not in the least important; this is why I feel compelled to keep it. It is only to dine with my niece. They have just got into an absurd doll's house of a villa at Groat's Heath and I had promised to go there this evening."

"Are they particular to a day?"

There was a moment's hesitation before Mr Carlyle replied.

"I am afraid so, now it is fixed," he said. "To you, Max, it will be ridiculous or incomprehensible that a third to dinner—and he only a middle-aged uncle—should make a straw of difference. But I know that in their *bijou* way it will be a little domestic event to Elsie—an added anxiety in giving the butcher an order, an extra course for dinner, perhaps; a careful drilling of the one diminutive maid-servant, and she is such a charming little woman—eh? Who, Max? No! No! I did not say the maid-servant; if I did it is the fault of this telephone. Elsie is such a delightful little creature that, upon my soul, it would be too bad to fail her now."

"Of course it would, you old humbug," agreed Carrados, with sympathetic laughter in his voice. "Well, come tomorrow instead. I shall be alone."

"Oh, besides, there is a special reason for going, which for the moment I forgot," explained Mr Carlyle, after accepting the invitation. "Elsie wishes for my advice with regard to her next-door neighbour. He is an elderly man of retiring disposition and he makes a practice of throwing kidneys over into her garden."

"Kittens! Throwing kittens?"

"No, no, Max. Kidneys. Stewed k-i-d-n-e-y-s. It is a little difficult to explain plausibly over a badly vibrating telephone, I admit, but that is what Elsie's letter assured me, and she adds that she is in despair."

"At all events it makes the lady quite independent of the butcher, Louis!"

"I have no further particulars, Max. It may be a solitary diurnal offering, or the sky may at times appear to rain kidneys. If it is a mania the symptoms may even have become more pronounced and the man is possibly showering beef-steaks across by this time. I will make full inquiry and let you know."

"Do," assented Carrados, in the same light-hearted spirit. "Mrs Nickleby's neighbourly admirer expressed his feelings by throwing cucumbers, you remember, but this man puts him completely in the shade."

It had not got beyond the proportions of a jest to either of them when they rang off—one of those whimsical occurrences in real life that sound so fantastic in outline. Carrados did not give the matter another thought until the next evening when his friend's arrival revived the subject.

"And the gentleman next door?" he inquired among his greetings. "Did the customary offering arrive while you were there?"

"No," admitted Mr Carlyle, beaming pleasantly upon all the familiar appointments of the room, "it did not, Max. In fact, so diffident has the mysterious philanthropist become, that no one at Fountain Cottage has been able to catch sight of him lately, although I am told that Scamp—Elsie's terrier—betrays a very self-conscious guilt and suspiciously muddy paws every morning."

"Fountain Cottage?"

"That is the name of the toy villa."

"Yes, but Fountain something, Groat's Heath—Fountain Court: wasn't that where Metrobe——?"

"Yes, yes, to be sure, Max. Metrobe the traveller, the writer and scientist——"

"Scientist!"

"Well, he took up spiritualism or something, didn't he? At any rate, he lived at Fountain Court, an old red-brick house in a large neglected garden there, until his death a couple of years ago. Then, as Groat's Heath had suddenly become a popular suburb with a tube railway, a land company acquired the estate, the house was razed to the ground and in a twinkling a colony of Noah's ark villas took its place. There is Metrobe Road here, and Court Crescent there, and Mansion Drive and what not, and Elsie's little place perpetuates another landmark."

"I have Metrobe's last book there," said Carrados, nodding towards a point on his shelves. "In fact he sent me a copy. 'The Flame beyond the Dome' it is called—the queerest farrago of balderdash and metaphysics imaginable. But what about the neighbour, Louis? Did you settle what we might almost term 'his hash'?"

"Oh, he is mad, of course. I advised her to make as little fuss about it as possible, seeing that the man lives next door and might become objectionable, but I framed a note for her to send which will probably have a good effect."

"Is he mad, Louis?"

"Well, I don't say that he is strictly a lunatic, but there is obviously a screw loose somewhere. He may carry indiscriminate benevolence towards Yorkshire terriers to irrational lengths. Or he may be a food specialist with a grievance. In effect he is mad on at least that one point. How else are we to account for the circumstances?"

"I was wondering," replied Carrados thoughtfully.

"You suggest that he really may have a sane object?"

"I suggest it—for the sake of argument. If he has a sane object, what is it?"

"That I leave to you, Max," retorted Mr Carlyle conclusively. "If he has a sane object, pray what is it?"

"For the sake of the argument I will tell you that in half-a-dozen words, Louis," replied Carrados, with good-humoured tolerance. "If he is not mad in the sense which you have defined, the answer stares

148

us in the face. His object is precisely that which he is achieving."

Mr Carlyle looked inquiringly into the placid, unemotional face of his blind friend, as if to read there whether, incredible as it might seem, Max should be taking the thing seriously after all.

"And what is that?" he asked cautiously.

"In the first place he has produced the impression that he is eccentric or irresponsible. That is sometimes useful in itself. Then what else has he done?"

"What else, Max?" replied Mr Carlyle, with some indignation. "Well, whatever he wishes to achieve by it I can tell you one thing else that he has done. He has so demoralised Scamp with his confounded kidneys that Elsie's neatly arranged flower-beds—and she took Fountain Cottage principally on account of an unusually large garden—are hopelessly devastated. If she keeps the dog up, the garden is invaded night and day by an army of peregrinating feline marauders that scent the booty from afar. He has gained the everlasting annoyance of an otherwise charming neighbour, Max. Can you tell me what he has achieved by that?"

"The everlasting esteem of Scamp probably. Is he a good watchdog, Louis?"

"Good heavens, Max!" exclaimed Mr Carlyle, coming to his feet as though he had the intention of setting out for Groat's Heath then and there, "is it possible that he is planning a burglary?"

"Do they keep much of value about the house?"

"No," admitted Mr Carlyle, sitting down again with considerable relief. "No, they don't. Bellmark is not particularly well endowed with worldly goods—in fact, between ourselves, Max, Elsie could have done very much better from a strictly social point of view, but he is a thoroughly good fellow and idolizes her. They have no silver worth speaking of, and for the rest—well, just the ordinary petty cash of a frugal young couple."

"Then he probably is not planning a burglary. I confess that the idea did not appeal to me. If it is only that, why should he go to the trouble of preparing this particular succulent dish to throw over his neighbour's ground when cold liver would do quite as well?"

"If it is not only that, why should he go to the trouble, Max?"

"Because by that bait he produces the greatest disturbance of your niece's garden."

"And, if sane, why should he wish to do that?"

"Because in those conditions he can the more easily obliterate his own traces if he trespasses there at nights."

"Well, upon my word, that's drawing a bow at a venture, Max. If it isn't burglary, what motive could the man have for any such nocturnal perambulation?"

An expression of suave mischief came into Carrados's usually imperturbable face.

"Many imaginable motives surely, Louis. You are a man of the world. Why not to meet a charming little woman——"

"No, by gad!" exclaimed the scandalised uncle warmly; "I decline to consider the remotest possibility of that explanation. Elsie——"

"Certainly not," interposed Carrados, smothering his quiet laughter. "The maid-servant, of course."

Mr Carlyle reined in his indignation and recovered himself with his usual adroitness.

"But, you know, that is an atrocious libel, Max," he added. "I never said such a thing. However, is it probable?"

"No," admitted Carrados. "I don't think that in the circumstances it is at all probable."

"Then where are we, Max?"

"A little further than we were at the beginning. Very little. . . . Are you willing to give me a roving commission to investigate?"

"Of course, Max, of course," assented Mr Carlyle heartily. "I—well, as far as I was concerned, I regarded the matter as settled."

Carrados turned to his desk and the ghost of a smile might possibly have lurked about his face. He produced some stationery and indicated it to his visitor.

"You don't mind giving me a line of introduction to your niece?"

"Pleasure," murmured Carlyle, taking up a pen. "What shall I say?"

Carrados took the inquiry in its most literal sense and for reply he dictated the following letter:—"'My Dear Elsie,'—If that is the way you usually address her," he parenthesised.

"Quite so," acquiesced Mr Carlyle, writing:—

The bearer of this is Mr Carrados, of whom I have spoken to you.

"You have spoken of me to her, I trust, Louis?" he put in.

"I believe that I have casually referred to you," admitted the writer.

"I felt sure you would have done. It makes the rest easier."

He is not in the least mad although he frequently does things which to the uninitiated appear more or less eccentric at the moment. I think that you would be quite safe in complying with any suggestion he may make.

Your affectionate uncle,

Louis Carlyle.

He accepted the envelope and put it away in a pocket-book that always seemed extraordinarily thin for the amount of papers it contained.

"I may call there tomorrow," he added.

Neither again referred to the subject during the evening, but when Parkinson came to the library a couple of hours after midnight to know whether he would be required again, he found his master rather deeply immersed in a book and a gap on the shelf where "The Flame beyond the Dome" had formerly stood.

It is not impossible that Mr Carlyle supplemented his brief note of introduction with a more detailed communication that reached his niece by the ordinary postal service at an earlier hour than the other. At all events, when Mr Carrados presented himself at the toy villa on the following afternoon he found Elsie Bellmark suspiciously disposed to accept him and his rather gratuitous intervention among her suburban troubles as a matter of course.

When the car drew up at the bright green wooden gate of Fountain Cottage another visitor, apparently a good-class working man, was standing on the path of the trim front garden, lingering over a reluctant departure. Carrados took sufficient time in alighting to allow the man to pass through the gate before he himself entered. The last exchange of sentences reached his ear.

"I'm sure, marm, you won't find anyone to do the work at less."

"I can quite believe that," replied a very fair young lady who stood nearer the house, "but, you see, we do all the gardening ourselves, thank you."

Carrados made himself known and was taken into the daintily pretty drawing-room that opened on to the lawn behind the house.

"I do not need to ask if you are Mrs Bellmark," he had declared.

"I have Uncle Louis's voice?" she divined readily.

"The niece of his voice, so to speak," he admitted. "Voices mean a great deal to me, Mrs Bellmark."

"In recognising and identifying people?" she suggested.

"Oh, very much more than that. In recognising and identifying their moods—their thoughts even. There are subtle lines of trouble and the deep rings of anxious care quite as patent to the ear as to the sharpest eye sometimes."

Elsie Bellmark shot a glance of curiously interested speculation to the face that, in spite of its frank, open bearing, revealed so marvellously little itself.

"If I had any dreadful secret, I think that I should be a little afraid to talk to you, Mr Carrados," she said, with a half-nervous laugh.

"Then please do not have any dreadful secret," he replied, with quite youthful gallantry. "I more than suspect that Louis has given you a very transpontine idea of my tastes. I do not spend all my time tracking murderers to their lairs, Mrs Bellmark, and I have never yet engaged in a hand-to-hand encounter with a band of cut-throats."

"He told us," she declared, the recital lifting her voice into a tone that Carrados vowed to himself was wonderfully thrilling, "about this: He said that you were once in a sort of lonely underground cellar near the river with two desperate men whom you could send to penal servitude. The police, who were to have been there at a certain time, had not arrived, and you were alone. The men had heard that you were blind but they could hardly believe it. They were discussing in whispers which could not be overheard what would be the best thing to do, and they had just agreed that if you really were blind they would risk the attempt to murder you. Then, Louis said, at that very moment you took a pair of scissors from your pocket, and coolly asking them why they did not have a lamp down there, you actually snuffed the candle that stood on the table before you. Is that true?"

Carrados's mind leapt vividly back to the most desperate moment of his existence, but his smile was gently deprecating as he replied:

"I seem to recognise the touch of truth in the inclination to do *anything* rather than fight," he confessed. "But, although he never suspects it, Louis really sees life through rose-coloured opera glasses. Take the case of your quite commonplace neighbour——"

"That is really what you came about?" she interposed shrewdly.

"Frankly, it is," he replied. "I am more attracted by a turn of the odd and grotesque than by the most elaborate tragedy. The fantastic conceit of throwing stewed kidneys over into a neighbour's garden irresistibly appealed to me. Louis, as I was saying, regards the man in the romantic light of a humanitarian monomaniac or a demented food reformer. I take a more subdued view and I think that his action, when rightly understood, will prove to be something quite obviously natural."

"Of course it is very ridiculous, but all the same it has been desperately annoying," she confessed. "Still, it scarcely matters now. I am only sorry that it should have been the cause of wasting your valuable time, Mr Carrados."

"My valuable time," he replied, "only seems valuable to me when I am, as you would say, wasting it. But is the incident closed? Louis told me that he had drafted you a letter of remonstrance. May I ask if it has been effective?"

Instead of replying at once she got up and walked to the long French window and looked out over the garden where the fruit-trees that had been spared from the older cultivation were rejoicing the eye with the promise of their pink and white profusion.

"I did not send it," she said slowly, turning to her visitor again. "There is something that I did not tell Uncle Louis, because it would only have distressed him without doing any good. We may be leaving here very soon."

"Just when you had begun to get it well in hand?" he said, in some surprise.

"It is a pity, is it not, but one cannot foresee these things. There is no reason why you should not know the cause, since you have interested yourself so far, Mr Carrados. In fact," she added, smiling away the seriousness of the manner into which she had fallen, "I am not at all sure that you do not know already."

He shook his head and disclaimed any such prescience.

"At all events you recognised that I was not exactly light-hearted," she insisted. "Oh, you did not say that *I* had dark rings under my eyes, I know, but the cap fitted excellently. . . . It has to do with my husband's business. He is with a firm of architects. It was a little venturesome taking this house—we had been in apartments for two years—but Roy was doing so well with his people and I was so enthusiastic for a garden that we did—scarcely two months ago. Everything seemed quite assured. Then came this thunderbolt. The partners—it is only a small firm, Mr Carrados—required a little more capital in the business. Someone whom they know is willing to put in two thousand pounds, but he stipulates for a post with them as well. He, like my husband, is a draughtsman. There is no need for the services of both and so——"

"Is it settled?"

"In effect, it is. They are as nice as can be about it but that does not alter the facts. They declare that they would rather have Roy than the new man and they have definitely offered to retain him if he can bring in even one thousand pounds. I suppose they have some sort of compunction about turning him adrift, for they have asked him to think it over and let them know on Monday. Of course, that is the end of it. It may be—I don't know—I don't like to think, how long before Roy gets another position equally good. We must endeavour to get this house off our hands and creep back to our three rooms. It is ... luck."

Carrados had been listening to her wonderfully musical voice as another man might have been drawn irresistibly to watch the piquant charm of her delicate face.

"Yes," he assented, almost to himself, "it is that strange, inexplicable grouping of men and things that, under one name or another, we all confess ... just luck."

"Of course you will not mention this to Uncle Louis yet, Mr Carrados?"

"If you do not wish it, certainly not."

"I am sure that it would distress him. He is so soft-hearted, so kind, in everything. Do you know, I found out that he had had an invitation to dine somewhere and meet some quite important people on Tuesday. Yet he came here instead, although most other men would have cried off, just because he knew that we small people would have been disappointed."

"Well, you can't expect me to see any self-denial in that," exclaimed Carrados. "Why, I was one of them myself."

Elsie Bellmark laughed outright at the expressive disgust of his tone.

"I had no idea of that," she said. "Then there is another reason. Uncle is not very well off, yet if he knew how Roy was situated he would make an effort to arrange matters. He would, I am sure, even borrow himself in order to lend us the money. That is a thing Roy and I are quite agreed on. We will go back; we will go under, if it is to be; but we will not borrow money, not even from Uncle Louis."

Once, subsequently, Carrados suddenly asked Mr Carlyle whether he had ever heard a woman's voice roll like a celestial kettle-drum. The professional gentleman was vastly amused by the comparison, but he admitted that he had not.

"So that, you see," concluded Mrs Bellmark, "there is really nothing to be done."

"Oh, quite so; I am sure that you are right," assented her visitor readily. "But in the meanwhile I do not see why the annoyance of your next-door neighbour should be permitted to go on."

"Of course: I have not told you that, and I could not explain it to uncle," she said. "I am anxious not to do anything to put him out because I have a hope—rather a faint one, certainly—that the man may be willing to take over this house."

It would be incorrect to say that Carrados pricked up his ears—if that curious phenomenon has any physical manifestation—for the sympathetic expression of his face did not vary a fraction. But into his mind there came a gleam such as might inspire a patient digger who sees the first speck of gold that justifies his faith in an unlikely claim.

"Oh," he said, quite conversationally, "is there a chance of that?"

"He undoubtedly did want it. It is very curious in a way. A few weeks ago, before we were really settled, he came one afternoon, saying he had heard that this house was to be let. Of course I told him that he was too late, that we had already taken it for three years."

"You were the first tenants?"

"Yes. The house was scarcely ready when we signed the agreement. Then this Mr Johns, or Jones—I am not sure which he said—went on in a rather extraordinary way to persuade me to sublet it to him. He said that the house was dear and I could get plenty, more convenient, at less rent, and it was unhealthy, and the drains were bad, and that we should be pestered by tramps and it was just the sort of house that burglars picked on, only he had taken a sort of fancy to it and he would give me a fifty-pound premium for the term."

"Did he explain the motive for this rather eccentric partiality?"

"I don't imagine that he did. He repeated several times that he was a queer old fellow with his whims and fancies and that they often cost him dear."

"I think we all know that sort of old fellow," said Carrados. "It must have been rather entertaining for you, Mrs Bellmark."

"Yes, I suppose it was," she admitted. "The next thing we knew of him was that he had taken the other house as soon as it was finished."

"Then he would scarcely require this?"

"I am afraid not." It was obvious that the situation was not disposed of. "But he seems to have so little furniture there and to live so solitarily," she explained, "that we have even wondered whether he might not be there merely as a sort of caretaker."

155

"And you have never heard where he came from or who he is?"

"Only what the milkman told my servant—our chief source of local information, Mr Carrados. He declares that the man used to be the butler at a large house that stood here formerly, Fountain Court, and that his name is neither Johns nor Jones. But very likely it is all a mistake."

"If not, he is certainly attached to the soil," was her visitor's rejoinder. "And, apropos of that, will you show me over your garden before I go, Mrs Bellmark?"

"With pleasure," she assented, rising also. "I will ring now and then I can offer you tea when we have been round. That is, if you——?"

"Thank you, I do," he replied. "And would you allow my man to go through into the garden—in case I require him?"

"Oh, certainly. You must tell me just what you want without thinking it necessary to ask permission, Mr Carrados," she said, with a pretty air of protection. "Shall Amy take a message?"

He acquiesced and turned to the servant who had appeared in response to the bell.

"Will you go to the car and tell my man—Parkinson—that I require him here. Say that he can bring his book; he will understand."

"Yes, sir."

They stepped out through the French window and sauntered across the lawn. Before they had reached the other side Parkinson reported himself.

"You had better stay here," said his master, indicating the sward generally. "Mrs Bellmark will allow you to bring out a chair from the drawing-room."

"Thank you, sir; there is a rustic seat already provided," replied Parkinson.

He sat down with his back to the houses and opened the book that he had brought. Let in among its pages was an ingeniously contrived mirror.

When their promenade again brought them near the rustic seat Carrados dropped a few steps behind.

"He is watching you from one of the upper rooms, sir," fell from Parkinson's lips as he sat there without raising his eyes from the page before him.

The blind man caught up to his hostess again.

"You intended this lawn for croquet?" he asked.

"No; not specially. It is too small, isn't it?"

"Not necessarily. I think it is in about the proportion of four by five all right. Given that, size does not really matter for an unsophisticated game."

To settle the point he began to pace the plot of ground, across and then lengthways. Next, apparently dissatisfied with this rough measurement, he applied himself to marking it off more exactly by means of his walking-stick. Elsie Bellmark was by no means dull but the action sprang so naturally from the conversation that it did not occur to her to look for any deeper motive.

"He has got a pair of field-glasses and is now at the window," communicated Parkinson.

"I am going out of sight," was the equally quiet response. "If he becomes more anxious tell me afterwards."

"It is quite all right," he reported, returning to Mrs Bellmark with the satisfaction of bringing agreeable news. "It should make a splendid little ground, but you may have to level up a few dips after the earth has set."

A chance reference to the kitchen garden by the visitor took them to a more distant corner of the enclosure where the rear of Fountain Cottage cut off the view from the next house windows.

"We decided on this part for vegetables because it does not really belong to the garden proper," she explained. "When they build farther on this side we shall have to give it up very soon. And it would be a pity if it was all in flowers."

With the admirable spirit of the ordinary Englishwoman, she spoke of the future as if there was no cloud to obscure its prosperous course. She had frankly declared their position to her uncle's best friend because in the circumstances it had seemed to be the simplest and most straightforward thing to do; beyond that, there was no need to whine about it.

"It is a large garden," remarked Carrados. "And you really do all the work of it yourselves?"

"Yes; I think that is half the fun of a garden. Roy is out here early and late and he does all the hard work. But how did you know? Did uncle tell you?"

"No; you told me yourself."

"I? Really?"

"Indirectly. You were scorning the proffered services of a horticultural mercenary at the moment of my arrival."

"Oh, I remember," she laughed. "It was Irons, of course. He is a great nuisance, he is so stupidly persistent. For some weeks now he has been coming time after time, trying to persuade me to engage him. Once when we were all out he had actually got into the garden and was on the point of beginning work when I returned. He said he saw the milkmen and the grocers leaving samples at the door so he thought that he would too!"

"A practical jester evidently. Is Mr Irons a local character?"

"He said that he knew the ground and the conditions round about here better than anyone else in Groat's Heath," she replied. "Modesty is not among Mr Irons's handicaps. He said that he——How curious!"

"What is, Mrs Bellmark?"

"I never connected the two men before, but he said that he had been gardener at Fountain Court for seven years."

"Another family retainer who is evidently attached to the soil."

"At all events they have not prospered equally, for while Mr Johns seems able to take a nice house, poor Irons is willing to work for half-a-crown a day, and I am told that all the other men charge four shillings."

They had paced the boundaries of the kitchen garden, and as there was nothing more to be shown Elsie Bellmark led the way back to the drawing-room. Parkinson was still engrossed in his book, the only change being that his back was now turned towards the high paling of clinker-built oak that separated the two gardens.

"I will speak to my man," said Carrados, turning aside.

"He hurried down and is looking through the fence, sir," reported the watcher.

"That will do then. You can return to the car."

"I wonder if you would allow me to send you a small hawthorn-tree?" inquired Carrados among his felicitations over the teacups five minutes later. "I think it ought to be in every garden."

"Thank you—but is it worth while?" replied Mrs Bellmark, with a touch of restraint. As far as mere words went she had been willing to ignore the menace of the future, but in the circumstances the offer seemed singularly inept and she began to suspect that outside his peculiar gifts the wonderful Mr Carrados might be a little bit obtuse after all.

"Yes; I think it is," he replied, with quiet assurance.

"In spite of——?"

"I am not forgetting that unless your husband is prepared on

Monday next to invest one thousand pounds you contemplate leaving here."

"Then I do not understand it, Mr Carrados."

"And I am unable to explain as yet. But I brought you a note from Louis Carlyle, Mrs Bellmark. You only glanced at it. Will you do me the favour of reading me the last paragraph?"

She picked up the letter from the table where it lay and complied with cheerful good-humour.

"There is some suggestion that you want me to accede to," she guessed cunningly when she had read the last few words.

"There are some three suggestions which I hope you will accede to," he replied. "In the first place I want you to write to Mr Johns next door—let him get the letter tonight—inquiring whether he is still disposed to take this house."

"I had thought of doing that shortly."

"Then that is all right. Besides, he will ultimately decline."

"Oh," she exclaimed—it would be difficult to say whether with relief or disappointment—"do you think so? Then why——"

"To keep him quiet in the meantime. Next I should like you to send a little note to Mr Irons—your maid could deliver it also to-night, I dare say?"

"Irons! Irons the gardener?"

"Yes," apologetically. "Only a line or two, you know. Just saying that, after all, if he cares to come on Monday you can find him a few days' work."

"But in any circumstances I don't want him."

"No; I can quite believe that you could do better. Still, it doesn't matter, as he won't come, Mrs Bellmark; not for half-a-crown a day, believe me. But the thought will tend to make Mr Irons less restive also. Lastly, will you persuade your husband not to decline his firm's offer until Monday?"

"Very well, Mr Carrados," she said, after a moment's consideration. "You are Uncle Louis's friend and therefore our friend. I will do what you ask."

"Thank you," said Carrados. "I shall endeavour not to disappoint you."

"I shall not be disappointed because I have not dared to hope. And I have nothing to expect because I am still completely in the dark."

"I have been there for nearly twenty years, Mrs Bellmark."

"Oh, I am sorry!" she cried impulsively.

"So am I—occasionally," he replied. "Good-bye, Mrs Bellmark. You will hear from me shortly, I hope. About the hawthorn, you know."

It was, indeed, in something less than forty-eight hours that she heard from him again. When Bellmark returned to his toy villa early on Saturday afternoon Elsie met him almost at the gate with a telegram in her hand.

"I really think, Roy, that everyone we have to do with here goes mad," she exclaimed, in tragi-humorous despair. "First it was Mr Johns or Jones—if he is Johns or Jones—and then Irons who wanted to work here for half of what he could get at heaps of places about, and now just look at this wire that came from Mr Carrados half-an-hour ago."

This was the message that he read:

Please procure sardine tin opener mariner's compass and bottle of champagne. Shall arrive 6.45 bringing Crataegus Coccinea.—Carrados.

"Could anything be more absurd?" she demanded.

"Sounds as though it was in code," speculated her husband. "Who's the foreign gentleman he's bringing?"

"Oh, that's a kind of special hawthorn—I looked it up. But a bottle of champagne, and a compass, and a sardine tin opener! What possible connexion is there between them?"

"A very resourceful man might uncork a bottle of champagne with a sardine tin opener," he suggested.

"And find his way home afterwards by means of a mariner's compass?" she retorted. "No, Roy dear, you are not a sleuth-hound. We had better have our lunch."

They lunched, but if the subject of Carrados had been tabooed the meal would have been a silent one.

"I have a compass on an old watch-chain somewhere," volunteered Bellmark.

"And I have a tin opener in the form of a bull's head," contributed Elsie.

"But we have no champagne, I suppose?"

"How could we have, Roy? We never have had any. Shall you mind going down to the shops for a bottle?"

"You really think that we ought?"

"Of course we must, Roy. We don't know what mightn't happen if we didn't. Uncle Louis said that they once failed to stop a jewel robbery because the jeweller neglected to wipe his shoes on the shop doormat, as Mr Carrados had told him to do. Suppose Johns is a desperate anarchist and he succeeded in blowing up Buckingham Palace because we——"

"All right. A small bottle, eh?"

"No. A large one. Quite a large one. Don't you see how exciting it is becoming?"

"If you are excited already you don't need much champagne," argued her husband.

Nevertheless he strolled down to the leading wine-shop after lunch and returned with his purchase modestly draped in the light summer overcoat that he carried on his arm. Elsie Bellmark, who had quite abandoned her previous unconcern, in the conviction that "something was going to happen," spent the longest afternoon that she could remember, and even Bellmark, in spite of his continual adjurations to her to "look at the matter logically," smoked five cigarettes in place of his usual Saturday afternoon pipe and neglected to do any gardening.

At exactly six-forty-five a motorcar was heard approaching. Elsie made a desperate rally to become the self-possessed hostess again. Bellmark was favourably impressed by such marked punctuality. Then a Regent Street delivery van bowled past their window and Elsie almost wept.

The suspense was not long, however. Less than five minutes later another vehicle raised the dust of the quiet suburban road, and this time a private car stopped at their gate.

"Can you see any policemen inside?" whispered Elsie.

Parkinson got down and opening the door took out a small tree which he carried up to the porch and there deposited. Carrados followed.

"At all events there isn't much wrong," said Bellmark. "He's smiling all the time."

"No, it isn't really a smile," explained Elsie; "it's his normal expression."

She went out into the hall just as the front door was opened.

"It is the 'Scarlet-fruited thorn' of North America," Bellmark heard the visitor remarking. "Both the flowers and the berries are wonderfully good. Do you think that you would permit me to choose the spot for it, Mrs Bellmark?"

Bellmark joined them in the hall and was introduced.

"We mustn't waste any time," he suggested. "There is very little light left."

"True," agreed Carrados. "And Coccinea requires deep digging."

They walked through the house, and turning to the right passed into the region of the vegetable garden. Carrados and Elsie led the way, the blind man carrying the tree, while Bellmark went to his out-house for the required tools.

"We will direct our operations from here," said Carrados, when they were half-way along the walk. "You told me of a thin iron pipe that you had traced to somewhere in the middle of the garden. We must locate the end of it exactly."

"My rosary!" sighed Elsie, with premonition of disaster, when she had determined the spot as exactly as she could. "Oh, Mr Carrados!"

"I am sorry, but it might be worse," said Carrados inflexibly. "We only require to find the elbow-joint. Mr Bellmark will investigate with as little disturbance as possible."

For five minutes Bellmark made trials with a pointed iron. Then he cleared away the soil of a small circle and at about a foot deep exposed a broken inch pipe.

"The fountain," announced Carrados, when he had examined it. "You have the compass, Mr Bellmark?"

"Rather a small one," admitted Bellmark.

"Never mind, you are a mathematician. I want you to strike a line due east."

The reel and cord came into play and an adjustment was finally made from the broken pipe to a position across the vegetable garden.

"Now a point nine yards, nine feet and nine inches along it."

"My onion bed!" cried Elsie tragically.

"Yes; it is really serious this time," agreed Carrados. "I want a hole a yard across, digging here. May we proceed?"

Elsie remembered the words of her uncle's letter—or what she imagined to be his letter—and possibly the preamble of selecting the spot had impressed her.

"Yes, I suppose so. Unless," she added hopefully, "the turnip bed will do instead? They are not sown yet."

"I am afraid that nowhere else in the garden will do," replied Car-rados.

Bellmark delineated the space and began to dig. After clearing to about a foot deep he paused.

"About deep enough, Mr Carrados?" he inquired.

"Oh, dear no," replied the blind man.

"I am two feet down," presently reported the digger.

"Deeper!" was the uncompromising response.

Another six inches were added and Bellmark stopped to rest.

"A little more and it won't matter which way up we plant Coccinea," he remarked.

"That is the depth we are aiming for," replied Carrados.

Elsie and her husband exchanged glances. Then Bellmark drove his spade through another layer of earth.

"Three feet," he announced, when he had cleared it.

Carrados advanced to the very edge of the opening.

"I think that if you would loosen another six inches with the fork we might consider the ground prepared," he decided.

Bellmark changed his tools and began to break up the soil. Presently the steel prongs grated on some obstruction.

"Gently," directed the blind watcher. "I think you will find a half-pound cocoa tin at the end of your fork."

"Well, how on earth you spotted that——!" was wrung from Bellmark admiringly, as he cleared away the encrusting earth. "But I believe you are about right." He threw up the object to his wife, who was risking a catastrophe in her eagerness to miss no detail. "Anything in it besides soil, Elsie?"

"She cannot open it yet," remarked Carrados. "It is soldered down."

"Oh, I say," protested Bellmark.

"It is perfectly correct, Roy. The lid is soldered on."

They looked at each other in varying degrees of wonder and speculation. Only Carrados seemed quite untouched.

"Now we may as well replace the earth," he remarked.

"Fill it all up again?" asked Bellmark.

"Yes; we have provided a thoroughly disintegrated subsoil. That is the great thing. A depth of six inches is sufficient merely for the roots."

There was only one remark passed during the operation.

"I think I should plant the tree just over where the tin was," Carrados suggested. "You might like to mark the exact spot." And there the hawthorn was placed.

Bellmark, usually the most careful and methodical of men, left the tools where they were, in spite of a threatening shower. Strangely silent, Elsie led the way back to the house and taking the men into the drawing-room switched on the light.

"I think you have a tin opener, Mrs Bellmark?"

Elsie, who had been waiting for him to speak, almost jumped at the simple inquiry. Then she went into the next room and returned with the bull-headed utensil.

"Here it is," she said, in a voice that would have amused her at any other time.

"Mr Bellmark will perhaps disclose our find."

Bellmark put the soily tin down on Elsie's best table-cover without eliciting a word of reproach, grasped it firmly with his left hand, and worked the opener round the top.

"Only paper!" he exclaimed, and without touching the contents he passed the tin into Carrados's hands.

The blind man dexterously twirled out a little roll that crinkled pleasantly to the ear, and began counting the leaves with a steady finger.

"They're banknotes!" whispered Elsie in an awestruck voice. She caught sight of a further detail. "Banknotes for a hundred pounds each. And there are dozens of them!"

"Fifty, there should be," dropped Carrados between his figures. "Twenty-five, twenty-six——"

"Good God," murmured Bellmark; "that's five thousand pounds!"

"Fifty," concluded Carrados, straightening the edges of the sheaf. "It is always satisfactory to find that one's calculations are exact." He detached the upper ten notes and held them out. "Mrs Bellmark, will you accept one thousand pounds as a full legal discharge of any claim that you may have on this property?"

"Me—I?" she stammered. "But I have no right to any in any circumstances. It has nothing to do with us."

"You have an unassailable moral right to a fair proportion, because without you the real owners would never have seen a penny of it. As regards your legal right"—he took out the thin pocket-book and extracting a business-looking paper spread it open on the table before them—"here is a document that concedes it. 'In consideration of the valuable services rendered by Elsie Bellmark, etc., etc., in causing to be discovered and voluntarily surrendering the sum of five thousand pounds deposited and not relinquished by Alexis Metrobe, late of, etc., etc., deceased, Messrs Binstead & Polegate, solicitors, of 77a Bedford Row, acting on behalf of the administrator and next-of-kin of the said etc., etc., do hereby'—well, that's what they do. Signed, witnessed and stamped at Somerset House."

"I suppose I shall wake presently," said Elsie dreamily.

"It was for this moment that I ventured to suggest the third requirement necessary to bring our enterprise to a successful end," said Carrados.

"Oh, how thoughtful of you!" cried Elsie. "Roy, the champagne."

Five minutes later Carrados was explaining to a small but enthralled audience.

"The late Alexis Metrobe was a man of peculiar character. After seeing a good deal of the world and being many things, he finally embraced spiritualism, and in common with some of its most pronounced adherents he thenceforward abandoned what we should call 'the commonsense view.'

"A few years ago, by the collation of the *Book of Revelations*, a set of *Zadkiel's Almanacs*, and the complete works of Mrs Mary Baker Eddy, Metrobe discovered that the end of the world would take place on the tenth of October 1910. It therefore became a matter of urgent importance in his mind to ensure pecuniary provision for himself for the time after the catastrophe had taken place."

"I don't understand," interrupted Elsie. "Did he expect to survive it?"

"You cannot understand, Mrs Bellmark, because it is fundamentally incomprehensible. We can only accept the fact by the light of cases which occasionally obtain prominence. Metrobe did not expect to survive, but he was firmly convinced that the currency of this world would be equally useful in the spirit-land into which he expected to pass. This view was encouraged by a lady medium at whose feet he sat. She kindly offered to transmit to his banking account in the Hereafter, without making any charge whatever, any sum that he cared to put into her hands for the purpose. Metrobe accepted the idea but not the offer. His plan was to deposit a considerable amount in a spot of which he alone had knowledge, so that he could come and help himself to it as required."

"But if the world had come to an end——?"

"Only the material world, you must understand, Mrs Bellmark. The spirit world, its exact impalpable counterpart, would continue as before and Metrobe's hoard would be spiritually intact and available. That is the prologue.

"About a month ago there appeared a certain advertisement in a good many papers. I noticed it at the time and three days ago I had only to refer to my files to put my hand on it at once. It reads:

> Alexis Metrobe. Any servant or personal attendant of the late
> Alexis Metrobe of Fountain Court, Groat's Heath, possessing
> special knowledge of his habits and movements may hear of
> something advantageous on applying to Binstead & Polegate,
> 77a Bedford Row, W.C.

"The solicitors had, in fact, discovered that five thousand pounds' worth of securities had been realised early in 1910. They readily ascertained that Metrobe had drawn that amount in gold out of his bank immediately after, and there the trace ended. He died six months later. There was no hoard of gold and not a shred of paper to show where it had gone, yet Metrobe lived very simply within his income. The house had meanwhile been demolished but there was no hint or whisper of any lucky find.

"Two inquirers presented themselves at 77a Bedford Row. They were informed of the circumstances and offered a reward, varying according to the results, for information that would lead to the recovery of the money. They are both described as thoughtful, slow-spoken men. Each heard the story, shook his head, and departed. The first caller proved to be John Foster, the ex-butler. On the following day Mr Irons, formerly gardener at the court, was the applicant.

"I must now divert your attention into a side track. In the summer of 1910 Metrobe published a curious work entitled *The Flame beyond the Dome*. In the main it is an eschatological treatise, but at the end he tacked on an epilogue, which he called 'The Fable of the Chameleon.' It is even more curious than the rest and with reason, for under the guise of a speculative essay he gives a cryptic account of the circumstances of the five thousand pounds and, what is more important, details the exact particulars of its disposal. His reason for so doing is characteristic of the man. He was conscious by experience that he possessed an utterly treacherous memory, and having had occasion to move the treasure from one spot to another he feared that when the time came his bemuddled shade would be unable to locate it. For future reference, therefore, he embodied the details in his book, and to make sure that plenty of copies should be in existence he circulated it by the only means in his power—in other words, he gave a volume to everyone he knew and to a good many people whom he didn't.

"So far I have dealt with actualities. The final details are partly speculative but they are essentially correct. Metrobe conveyed his gold

166

to Fountain Court, obtained a stout oak coffer for it, and selected a spot *west* of the fountain. He chose a favourable occasion for burying it, but by some mischance Irons came on the scene. Metrobe explained the incident by declaring that he was burying a favourite parrot. Irons thought nothing particular about it then, although he related the fact to the butler, and to others, in evidence of the general belief that 'the old cock was quite barmy.' But Metrobe himself was much disturbed by the accident. A few days later he dug up the box. In pursuance of his new plan he carried his gold to the Bank of England and changed it into these notes. Then transferring the venue to one due *east* of the fountain, he buried them in this tin, satisfied that the small space it occupied would baffle the search of anyone not in possession of the exact location."

"But, I say!" exclaimed Mr Bellmark. "Gold might remain gold, but what imaginable use could be made of bank-notes after the end of the world?"

"That is a point of view, no doubt. But Metrobe, in spite of his foreign name, was a thorough Englishman. The world might come to an end, but he was satisfied that somehow the Bank of England would ride through it all right. I only suggest that. There is much that we can only guess."

"That is all there is to know, Mr Carrados?"

"Yes. Everything comes to an end, Mrs Bellmark. I sent my car away to call for me at eight. Eight has struck. That is Harris announcing his arrival."

He stood up, but embarrassment and indecision marked the looks and movements of the other two.

"How can we possibly take all this money, though?" murmured Elsie, in painful uncertainty. "It is entirely your undertaking, Mr Carrados. It is the merest fiction bringing me into it at all."

"Perhaps in the circumstances," suggested Bellmark nervously— "you remember the circumstances, Elsie?—Mr Carrados would be willing to regard it as a loan——"

"No, no!" cried Elsie impulsively. "There must be no half measures. We know that a thousand pounds would be nothing to Mr Carrados, and he knows that a thousand pounds are everything to us." Her voice reminded the blind man of the candle-snuffing recital. "We will take this great gift, Mr Carrados, quite freely, and we will not spoil the generous satisfaction that you must have in doing a wonderful and a splendid service by trying to hedge our obligation."

167

"But what can we ever do to thank Mr Carrados?" faltered Bell-mark mundanely.

"Nothing," said Elsie simply. "That is it."

"But I think that Mrs Bellmark has quite solved that," interposed Carrados.

The Game Played in the Dark

"It's a funny thing, sir," said Inspector Beedel, regarding Mr Carrados with the pensive respect that he always extended towards the blind amateur, "it's a funny thing, but nothing seems to go on abroad now but what you'll find some trace of it here in London if you take the trouble to look."

"In the right quarter," contributed Carrados.

"Why, yes," agreed the inspector. "But nothing comes of it nine times out of ten, because it's no one's particular business to look here or the thing's been taken up and finished from the other end. I don't mean ordinary murders or single-handed burglaries, of course, but"—a modest ring of professional pride betrayed the quiet enthusiast—"real First-Class Crimes."

"The State Antonio Five *per cent*. Bond Coupons?" suggested Carrados.

"Ah, you are right, Mr Carrados." Beedel shook his head sadly, as though perhaps on that occasion someone ought to have looked. "A man has a fit in the inquiry office of the Agent-General for British Equatoria, and two hundred and fifty thousand pounds' worth of faked securities is the result in Mexico. Then look at that jade fylfot charm pawned for one-and-three down at the Basin and the use that could have been made of it in the Kharkov 'ritual murder' trial."

"The West Hampstead Lost Memory puzzle and the Baripur bomb conspiracy that might have been smothered if one had known."

"Quite true, sir. And the three children of that Chicago millionaire—Cyrus V. Bunting, wasn't it?—kidnapped in broad daylight outside the New York Lyric and here, three weeks later, the dumb girl who chalked the wall at Charing Cross. I remember reading once in a financial article that every piece of foreign gold had a string from it leading to Threadneedle Street. A figure of speech, sir, of course, but apt enough, I don't doubt. Well, it seems to me that every big crime done abroad leaves a finger-print here in London—if only, as you say, we look in the right quarter."

"And at the right moment," added Carrados. "The time is often the present; the place the spot beneath our very noses. We take a step and the chance has gone for ever."

The inspector nodded and contributed a weighty monosyllable of sympathetic agreement. The most prosaic of men in the pursuit of his ordinary duties, it nevertheless subtly appealed to some half-dormant streak of vanity to have his profession taken romantically when there was no serious work on hand.

"No; perhaps not 'forever' in one case in a thousand, after all," amended the blind man thoughtfully. "This perpetual duel between the Law and the Criminal has sometimes appeared to me in the terms of a game of cricket, inspector. Law is in the field; the Criminal at the wicket. If Law makes a mistake—sends down a loose ball or drops a catch—the Criminal scores a little or has another lease of life. But if *he* makes a mistake—if he lets a straight ball pass or spoons towards a steady man—he is done for. His mistakes are fatal; those of the Law are only temporary and retrievable."

"Very good, sir," said Mr Beedel, rising—the conversation had taken place in the study at The Turrets, where Beedel had found occasion to present himself—"very apt indeed. I must remember that. Well, sir, I only hope that this 'Guido the Razor' lot will send a catch in our direction."

The 'this' delicately marked Inspector Beedel's instinctive contempt for Guido. As a craftsman he was compelled, on his reputation, to respect him, and he had accordingly availed himself of Carrados's friendship for a confabulation. As a man—he was a foreigner: worse, an Italian, and if left to his own resources the inspector would have opposed to his sinuous flexibility those rigid, essentially Britannia-metal, methods of the Force that strike the impartial observer as so ponderous, so amateurish and conventional, and, it must be admitted, often so curiously and inexplicably successful.

The offence that had circuitously brought "*il Rasojo*" and his "lot" within the cognizance of Scotland Yard outlines the kind of story that is discreetly hinted at by the society paragraphist of the day, politely disbelieved by the astute reader, and then at last laid indiscreetly bare in all its details by the inevitable princessly "Recollections" of a generation later. It centred round an impending royal marriage in Vienna, a certain jealous "Countess X." (here you have the discretion of the paragrapher), and a document or two that might be relied upon (the aristocratic biographer will impartially sum up the contingencies) to play the deuce with the approaching nuptials. To procure the evidence of these papers the countess enlisted the services of Guido, as reliable a scoundrel as she could probably have selected for the commission. To a certain point—to the abstraction of the papers, in fact—he succeeded, but it was with pursuit close upon his heels. There was that disadvantage in employing a rogue to do work that implicated roguery, for whatever moral right the countess had to the property, her accomplice had no legal right whatever to his liberty.

On half-a-dozen charges at least he could be arrested on sight in as many capitals of Europe. He slipped out of Vienna by the Nordbahn with his destination known, resourcefully stopped the express outside Czaslau and got away across to Chrudim. By this time the game and the moves were pretty well understood in more than one keenly interested quarter. Diplomacy supplemented justice and the immediate history of Guido became that of a fox hunted from covert to covert with all the familiar earths stopped against him. From Pardubitz he passed on to Glatz, reached Breslau and went down the Oder to Stettin. Out of the liberality of his employer's advances he had ample funds to keep going, and he dropped and rejoined his accomplices as the occasion ruled.

A week's harrying found him in Copenhagen, still with no time to spare, and he missed his purpose there. He crossed to Malmo by ferry, took the connecting night train to Stockholm and the same morning sailed down the Saltsjon, ostensibly bound for Obo, intending to cross to Revel and so get back to central Europe by the less frequented routes. But in this move again luck was against him and receiving warning just in time, and by the mysterious agency that had so far protected him, he contrived to be dropped from the steamer by boat among the islands of the crowded Archipelago, made his way to Helsingfors and within forty-eight hours was back again on the Frihavnen with pursuit for the moment blinked and a breathing-time to the good.

To appreciate the exact significance of these wanderings it is necessary to recall the conditions. Guido was not zigzagging a course about Europe in an aimless search for the picturesque, still less inspired by any love of the melodramatic. To him every step was vital, each tangent or rebound the necessary outcome of his much-badgered plans.

In his pocket reposed the papers for which he had run grave risks. The price agreed upon for the service was sufficiently lavish to make the risks worth taking time after time; but in order to consummate the transaction it was necessary that the booty should be put into his employer's hand. Halfway across Europe that employer was waiting with such patience as she could maintain, herself watched and shadowed at every step. The Countess X. was sufficiently exalted to be personally immune from the high-handed methods of her country's secret service, but every approach to her was tapped. The problem was for Guido to earn a long enough respite to enable him to communicate his position to the countess and for her to go or to reach him by a trusty hand. Then the whole fabric of intrigue could fall to pieces, but so far Guido had been kept successfully on the run and in the meanwhile time was pressing.

"They lost him after the *Hutola*," Beedel reported, in explaining the circumstances to Max Carrados. "Three days later they found that he'd been back again in Copenhagen but by that time he'd flown. Now they're without a trace except the inference of these 'Orange peach blossom' agonies in *The Times*. But the countess has gone hurriedly to Paris; and Lafayard thinks it all points to London."

"I suppose the Foreign Office is anxious to oblige just now?"

"I expect so, sir," agreed Beedel, "but, of course, my instructions don't come from that quarter. What appeals to *us* is that it would be a feather in our caps—they're still a little sore up at the Yard about Hans the Piper."

"Naturally," assented Carrados. "Well, I'll see what I can do if there is real occasion. Let me know anything, and, if you see your chance yourself, come round for a talk if you like on—today's Wednesday?—I shall be in at any rate on Friday evening."

Without being a precisian, the blind man was usually exact in such matters. There are those who hold that an engagement must be kept at all hazard: men who would miss a death-bed message in order to keep literal faith with a beggar. Carrados took lower, if more substantial, ground. "My word," he sometimes had occasion to remark, "is subject to contingencies, like everything else about me. If I make a promise it is conditional on nothing which seems more important arising to counteract it. That, among men of sense, is understood." And, as it happened, something did occur on this occasion.

He was summoned to the telephone just before dinner on Friday evening to receive a message personally. Greatorex, his secretary, had taken the call, but came in to say that the caller would give him nothing beyond his name—Brebner. The name was unknown to Carrados, but such incidents were not uncommon, and he proceeded to comply.

"Yes," he responded; "I am Max Carrados speaking. What is it?"

"Oh, it is you, sir, is it? Mr Brickwill told me to get to you direct."

"Well, you are all right. Brickwill? Are you the British Museum?"

"Yes. I am Brebner in the Chaldean Art Department. They are in a great stew here. We have just found out that someone has managed to get access to the Second Inner Greek Room and looted some of the cabinets there. It is all a mystery as yet."

"What is missing?" asked Carrados.

"So far we can only definitely speak of about six trays of Greek coins—a hundred to a hundred and twenty, roughly."

"Important?"

The line conveyed a caustic bark of tragic amusement.

"Why, yes, I should say so. The beggar seems to have known his business. All fine specimens of the best period. Syracuse—Messana—Croton—Amphipolis. Eumenes—Evainetos—Kimons. The chief quite wept."

Carrados groaned. There was not a piece among them that he had not handled lovingly.

"What are you doing?" he demanded.

"Mr Brickwill has been to Scotland Yard, and, on advice, we are not making it public as yet. We don't want a hint of it to be dropped anywhere, if you don't mind, sir."

"That will be all right."

"It was for that reason that I was to speak with you personally. We are notifying the chief dealers and likely collectors to whom the coins, or some of them, may be offered at once if it is thought that we haven't found it out yet. Judging from the expertness displayed in the selection, we don't think that there is any danger of the lot being sold to a pawnbroker or a metal-dealer, so that we are running very little real risk in not advertising the loss."

"Yes; probably it is as well," replied Carrados. "Is there anything that Mr Brickwill wishes me to do?"

"Only this, sir; if you are offered a suspicious lot of Greek coins, or hear of them, would you have a look—I mean ascertain whether they are likely to be ours, and if you think they are communicate with us and Scotland Yard at once."

"Certainly," replied the blind man. "Tell Mr Brickwill that he can rely on me if any indication comes my way. Convey my regrets to him and tell him that I feel the loss quite as a personal one. . . . I don't think that you and I have met as yet, Mr Brebner?"

"No, sir," said the voice diffidently, "but I have looked forward to the pleasure. Perhaps this unfortunate business will bring me an introduction."

"You are very kind," was Carrados's acknowledgment of the compliment. "Any time . . . I was going to say that perhaps you don't know my weakness, but I have spent many pleasant hours over your wonderful collection. That ensures the personal element. Goodbye."

Carrados was really disturbed by the loss although his concern was tempered by the reflection that the coins would inevitably in the end find their way back to the Museum. That their restitution might involve ransom to the extent of several thousand pounds was the least poignant detail of the situation. The one harrowing thought was that the booty might, through stress or ignorance, find its way into the melting-pot. That dreadful contingency, remote but insistent, was enough to affect the appetite of the blind enthusiast.

He was expecting Inspector Beedel, who would be full of his own case, but he could not altogether dismiss the aspects of possibility that Brebner's communication opened before his mind. He was still concerned with the chances of destruction and a very indifferent companion for Greatorex, who alone sat with him, when Parkinson presented himself. Dinner was over but Carrados had remained rather longer than his custom, smoking his mild Turkish cigarette in silence.

"A lady wishes to see you, sir. She said you would not know her name, but that her business would interest you."

The form of message was sufficiently unusual to take the attention of both men.

"You don't know her, of course, Parkinson?" inquired his master.

For just a second the immaculate Parkinson seemed tongue-tied. Then he delivered himself in his most ceremonial strain.

"I regret to say that I cannot claim the advantage, sir," he replied.

"Better let me tackle her, sir," suggested Greatorex with easy confidence. "It's probably a sub."

The sportive offer was declined by a smile and a shake of the head. Carrados turned to his attendant.

"I shall be in the study, Parkinson. Show her there in three minutes.

You stay and have another cigarette, Greatorex. By that time she will either have gone or have interested me."

In three minutes' time Parkinson threw open the study door.

"The lady, sir," he announced.

Could he have seen, Carrados would have received the impression of a plainly, almost dowdily, dressed young woman of buxom figure. She wore a light veil, but it was ineffective in concealing the unattraction of the face beneath. The features were swart and the upper lip darkened with the more than incipient moustache of the southern brunette. Worse remained, for a disfiguring rash had assailed patches of her skin. As she entered she swept the room and its occupant with a quiet but comprehensive survey.

"Please take a chair, *Madame*. You wished to see me?"

The ghost of a demure smile flickered about her mouth as she complied, and in that moment her face seemed less uncomely. Her eye lingered for a moment on a cabinet above the desk, and one might have noticed that her eye was very bright. Then she replied.

"You are Signor Carrados, in—in the person?"

Carrados made his smiling admission and changed his position a fraction—possibly to catch her curiously pitched voice the better.

"The great collector of the antiquities?"

"I do collect a little," he admitted guardedly.

"You will forgive me, *Signor*, if my language is not altogether good. When I live at Naples with my mother we let boardings, chiefly to Inglish and Amerigans. I pick up the words, but since I marry and go to live in Calabria my Inglish has gone all red—no, no, you say, rusty. Yes, that is it; quite rusty."

"It is excellent," said Carrados. "I am sure that we shall understand one another perfectly."

The lady shot a penetrating glance but the blind man's expression was merely suave and courteous. Then she continued:

"My husband is of name Ferraja—Michele Ferraja. We have a vineyard and a little property near Forenzana." She paused to examine the tips of her gloves for quite an appreciable moment. "*Signor*," she burst out, with some vehemence, "the laws of my country are not good at all."

"From what I hear on all sides," said Carrados, "I am afraid that your country is not alone."

"There is at Forenzana a poor labourer, Gian Verde of name," continued the visitor, dashing volubly into her narrative. "He is one day

175

digging in the vineyard, the vineyard of my husband, when his spade strikes itself upon an obstruction. 'Aha,' says Gian, 'what have we here?' and he goes down upon his knees to see. It is an oil jar of red earth, *Signor*, such as was anciently used, and in it is filled with silver money.

"Gian is poor but he is wise. Does he call upon the authorities? No, no; he understands that they are all corrupt. He carries what he has found to my husband for he knows him to be a man of great honour.

"My husband also is of brief decision. His mind is made up. 'Gian,' he says, 'keep your mouth shut. This will be to your ultimate profit.' Gian understands, for he can trust my husband. He makes a sign of mutual implication. Then he goes back to the spade digging.

"My husband understands a little of these things but not enough. We go to the collections of Messina and Naples and even Rome and there we see other pieces of silver money, similar, and learn that they are of great value. They are of different sizes but most would cover a *lira* and of the thickness of two. On the one side imagine the great head of a pagan deity; on the other—oh, so many things I cannot remember what." A gesture of circumferential despair indicated the hopeless variety of design.

"A *biga* or *quadriga* of mules?" suggested Carrados. "An eagle carrying off a hare, a figure flying with a wreath, a trophy of arms? Some of those perhaps?"

"*Si, si bene*," cried Madame Ferraja. "You understand, I perceive, *Signor*. We are very cautious, for on every side is extortion and an unjust law. See, it is even forbidden to take these things out of the country, yet if we try to dispose of them at home they will be seized and we punished, for they are *tesoro trovato*, what you call treasure troven and belonging to the State—these coins which the industry of Gian discovered and which had lain for so long in the ground of my husband's vineyard."

"So you brought them to England?"

"*Si, Signor*. It is spoken of as a land of justice and rich nobility who buy these things at the highest prices. Also my speaking a little of the language would serve us here."

"I suppose you have the coins for disposal then? You can show them to me?"

"My husband retains them. I will take you, but you must first give *parola d'onore* of an English *Signor* not to betray us, or to speak of the circumstance to another."

Carrados had already foreseen this eventuality and decided to accept it. Whether a promise exacted on the plea of treasure trove would bind him to respect the despoilers of the British Museum was a point for subsequent consideration. Prudence demanded that he should investigate the offer at once and to cavil over Madame Ferraja's conditions would be fatal to that object. If the coins were, as there seemed little reason to doubt, the proceeds of the robbery, a modest ransom might be the safest way of preserving irreplaceable treasures, and in that case Carrados could offer his services as the necessary intermediary.

"I give you the promise you require, *Madame*," he accordingly declared.

"It is sufficient," assented *Madame*. "I will now take you to the spot. It is necessary that you alone should accompany me, for my husband is so distraught in this country, where he understands not a word of what is spoken, that his poor spirit would cry 'We are surrounded!' if he saw two strangers approach the house. Oh, he is become most dreadful in his anxiety, my husband. Imagine only, he keeps on the fire a cauldron of molten lead and he would not hesitate to plunge into it this treasure and obliterate its existence if he imagined himself endangered."

"So," speculated Carrados inwardly. "A likely precaution for a simple vine-grower of Calabria! Very well," he assented aloud, "I will go with you alone. Where is the place?"

Madame Ferraja searched in the ancient purse that she discovered in her rusty handbag and produced a scrap of paper.

"People do not understand sometimes my way of saying it," she explained. "*Sette*, Herringbone———"

"May I———?" said Carrados, stretching out his hand. He took the paper and touched the writing with his finger-tips. "Oh yes, 7 Heronsbourne Place. That is on the edge of Heronsbourne Park, is it not?" He transferred the paper casually to his desk as he spoke and stood up. "How did you come, Madame Ferraja?"

Madame Ferraja followed the careless action with a discreet smile that did not touch her voice.

"By motor bus—first one then another, inquiring at every turning. Oh, but it was interminable," sighed the lady.

"My driver is off for the evening—I did not expect to be going out—but I will 'phone up a taxi and it will be at the gate as soon as we are." He despatched the message and then, turning to the house

177

telephone, switched on to Greatorex.

"I'm just going round to Heronsbourne Park," he explained. "Don't stay, Greatorex, but if anyone calls expecting to see me, they can say that I don't anticipate being away more than an hour."

Parkinson was hovering about the hall. With quite novel officiousness he pressed upon his master a succession of articles that were not required. Over this usually complacent attendant the unattractive features of Madame Ferraja appeared to exercise a stealthy fascination, for a dozen times the lady detected his eyes questioning her face and a dozen times he looked guiltily away again. But his incongruities could not delay for more than a few minutes the opening of the door.

"I do not accompany you, sir?" he inquired, with the suggestion plainly tendered in his voice that it would be much better if he did.

"Not this time, Parkinson."

"Very well, sir. Is there any particular address to which we can telephone in case you are required, sir?"

"Mr Greatorex has instructions."

Parkinson stood aside, his resources exhausted. Madame Ferraja laughed a little mockingly as they walked down the drive.

"Your manservant thinks I may eat you, Signor Carrados," she declared vivaciously.

Carrados, who held the key of his usually exact attendant's perturbation—for he himself had recognised in Madame Ferraja the angelic Nina Brun, of the Sicilian *tetradrachm* incident, from the moment she opened her mouth—admitted to himself the humour of her audacity. But it was not until half-an-hour later that enlightenment rewarded Parkinson. Inspector Beedel had just arrived and was speaking with Greatorex when the conscientious valet, who had been winnowing his memory in solitude, broke in upon them, more distressed than either had ever seen him in his life before, and with the breathless introduction: "It was the ears, sir! I have her ears at last!" poured out his tale of suspicion, recognition and his present fears.

In the meanwhile the two objects of his concern had reached the gate as the summoned taxicab drew up.

"Seven Heronsbourne Place," called Carrados to the driver.

"No, no," interposed the lady, with decision, "let him stop at the beginning of the street. It is not far to walk. My husband would be on the verge of distraction if he thought in the dark that it was the arrival of the police;—who knows?"

"Brackedge Road, opposite the end of Heronsbourne Place,"

178

amended Carrados.

Heronsbourne Place had the reputation, among those who were curious in such matters, of being the most reclusive residential spot inside the four-mile circle. To earn that distinction it was, needless to say, a *cul-de-sac*. It bounded one side of Heronsbourne Park but did not at any point of its length give access to that pleasance. It was entirely devoted to unostentatious little houses, something between the villa and the cottage, some detached and some in pairs, but all possessing the endowment of larger, more umbrageous gardens than can generally be secured within the radius. The local house agent described them as "delightfully old-world" or "completely modernised" according to the requirement of the applicant.

The cab was dismissed at the corner and Madame Ferraja guided her companion along the silent and deserted way. She had begun to talk with renewed animation, but her ceaseless chatter only served to emphasize to Carrados the one fact that it was contrived to disguise.

"I am not causing you to miss the house with looking after me— No. 7, Madame Ferraja?" he interposed.

"No, certainly," she replied readily. "It is a little farther. The numbers are from the other end. But we are there. *Ecco!*"

She stopped at a gate and opened it, still guiding him. They passed into a garden, moist and sweet-scented with the distillate odours of a dewy evening. As she turned to relatch the gate the blind man endeavoured politely to anticipate her. Between them his hat fell to the ground.

"My clumsiness," he apologised, recovering it from the step. "My old impulses and my present helplessness, alas, Madame Ferraja!"

"One learns prudence by experience," said *Madame* sagely. She was scarcely to know, poor lady, that even as she uttered this trite aphorism, under cover of darkness and his hat, Mr Carrados had just ruined his signet ring by blazoning a golden "7" upon her garden step to establish its identity if need be. A *cul-de-sac* that numbered from the closed end seemed to demand some investigation.

"Seldom," he replied to her remark. "One goes on taking risks. So we are there?"

Madame Ferraja had opened the front door with a latchkey. She dropped the latch and led Carrados forward along the narrow hall. The room they entered was at the back of the house, and from the position of the road it therefore overlooked the park. Again the door was locked behind them.

"The celebrated Mr Carrados!" announced Madame Ferraja, with a sparkle of triumph in her voice. She waved her hand towards a lean, dark man who had stood beside the door as they entered. "My husband."

"Beneath our poor roof in the most fraternal manner," commented the dark man, in the same derisive spirit. "But it is wonderful."

"The even more celebrated Monsieur Dompierre, unless I am mistaken?" retorted Carrados blandly. "I bow on our first real meeting."

"You knew!" exclaimed the Dompierre of the earlier incident incredulously. "Stoker, you were right and I owe you a hundred *lire*. Who recognised you, Nina?"

"How should I know?" demanded the real Madame Dompierre crossly. "This blind man himself, by chance."

"You pay a poor compliment to your charming wife's personality to imagine that one could forget her so soon," put in Carrados. "And you a Frenchman, Dompierre!"

"You knew, Monsieur Carrados," reiterated Dompierre, "and yet you ventured here. You are either a fool or a hero."

"An enthusiast—it is the same thing as both," interposed the lady. "What did I tell you? What did it matter if he recognised? You see?"

"Surely you exaggerate, Monsieur Dompierre," contributed Carrados. "I may yet pay tribute to your industry. Perhaps I regret the circumstance and the necessity but I am here to make the best of it. Let me see the things *Madame* has spoken of, and then we can consider the detail of their price, either for myself or on behalf of others."

There was no immediate reply. From Dompierre came a saturnine chuckle and from Madame Dompierre a titter that accompanied a grimace. For one of the rare occasions in his life Carrados found himself wholly out of touch with the atmosphere of the situation. Instinctively he turned his face towards the other occupant of the room, the man addressed as "Stoker," whom he knew to be standing near the window.

"This unfortunate business *has* brought me an introduction," said a familiar voice.

For one dreadful moment the universe stood still round Carrados. Then, with the crash and grind of overwhelming mental tumult, the whole strategy revealed itself, like the sections of a gigantic puzzle falling into place before his eyes.

There had been no robbery at the British Museum! That plausible concoction was as fictitious as the intentionally transparent tale of treasure trove. Carrados recognised now how ineffective the one device would have been without the other in drawing him—how convincing the two together—and while smarting at the humiliation of his plight he could not restrain a dash of admiration at the ingenuity—the accurately conjectured line of inference—of the plot. It was again the familiar artifice of the cunning pitfall masked by the clumsily contrived trap just beyond it. And straightway into it he had blundered!

"And this," continued the same voice, "is Carrados, Max Carrados, upon whose perspicuity a government—only the present government, let me in justice say—depends to outwit the undesirable alien! My country; O my country!"

"Is it really Monsieur Carrados?" inquired Dompierre in polite sarcasm. "Are you sure, Nina, that you have not brought a man from Scotland Yard instead?"

"*Basta!* he is here; what more do you want? Do not mock the poor sightless gentleman," answered Madame Dompierre, in doubtful sympathy.

"That is exactly what I was wondering," ventured Carrados mildly. "I am here—what more do you want? Perhaps you, Mr Stoker——?"

"Excuse me. 'Stoker' is a mere colloquial appellation based on a trifling incident of my career in connection with a disabled liner. The title illustrates the childish weakness of the criminal classes for nicknames, together with their pitiable baldness of invention. My real name is Montmorency, Mr Carrados—Eustace Montmorency."

"Thank you, Mr Montmorency," said Carrados gravely. "We are on opposite sides of the table here tonight, but I should be proud to have been with you in the stokehold of the *Benvenuto*."

"That was pleasure," muttered the Englishman. "This is business."

"Oh, quite so," agreed Carrados. "So far I am not exactly complaining. But I think it is high time to be told—and I address myself to you—why I have been decoyed here and what your purpose is."

Mr Montmorency turned to his accomplice.

"Dompierre," he remarked, with great clearness, "why the devil is Mr Carrados kept standing?"

"Ah, oh, heaven!" exclaimed Madame Dompierre with tragic resignation, and flung herself down on a couch.

"*Scusi*," grinned the lean man, and with burlesque grace he placed a chair for their guest's acceptance.

"Your curiosity is natural," continued Mr Montmorency, with a cold eye towards Dompierre's antics, "although I really think that by this time you ought to have guessed the truth. In fact, I don't doubt that you have guessed, Mr Carrados, and that you are only endeavouring to gain time. For that reason—because it will perhaps convince you that we have nothing to fear—I don't mind obliging you."

"Better hasten," murmured Dompierre uneasily.

"Thank you, Bill," said the Englishman, with genial effrontery. "I won't fail to report your intelligence to the Rasojo. Yes, Mr Carrados, as you have already conjectured, it is the affair of the Countess X. to which you owe this inconvenience. You will appreciate the compliment that underlies your temporary seclusion, I am sure. When circumstances favoured our plans and London became the inevitable place of meeting, you and you alone stood in the way. We guessed that you would be consulted and we frankly feared your intervention. You were consulted. We know that Inspector Beedel visited you two days ago and he has no other case in hand. Your quiescence for just three days had to be obtained at any cost. So here you are."

"I see," assented Carrados. "And having got me here, how do you propose to keep me?"

"Of course that detail has received consideration. In fact we secured this furnished house solely with that in view. There are three courses before us. The first, quite pleasant, hangs on your acquiescence. The second, more drastic, comes into operation if you decline. The third—but really, Mr Carrados, I hope you won't oblige me even to discuss the third. You will understand that it is rather objectionable for me to contemplate the necessity of two able-bodied men having to use even the smallest amount of physical compulsion towards one who is blind and helpless. I hope you will be reasonable and accept the inevitable."

"The inevitable is the one thing that I invariably accept," replied Carrados. "What does it involve?"

"You will write a note to your secretary explaining that what you have learned at 7 Heronsbourne Place makes it necessary for you to go immediately abroad for a few days. By the way, Mr Carrados, although this is Heronsbourne Place it is *not* No. 7."

"Dear, dear me," sighed the prisoner. "You seem to have had me at every turn, Mr Montmorency."

"An obvious precaution. The wider course of giving you a different street altogether we rejected as being too risky in getting you here. To continue: To give conviction to the message you will direct your man Parkinson to follow by the first boat-train to-morrow, with all the requirements for a short stay, and put up at Mascot's, as usual, awaiting your arrival there."

"Very convincing," agreed Carrados. "Where shall I be in reality?"

"In a charming though rather isolated bungalow on the south coast. Your wants will be attended to. There is a boat. You can row or fish. You will be run down by motor car and brought back to your own gate. It's really very pleasant for a few days. I've often stayed there myself."

"Your recommendation carries weight. Suppose, for the sake of curiosity, that I decline?"

"You will still go there but your treatment will be commensurate with your behaviour. The car to take you is at this moment waiting in a convenient spot on the other side of the park. We shall go down the garden at the back, cross the park, and put you into the car—anyway."

"And if I resist?"

The man whose pleasantry it had been to call himself Eustace Montmorency shrugged his shoulders.

"Don't be a fool," he said tolerantly. "You know who you are dealing with and the kind of risks we run. If you call out or endanger us at a critical point we shall not hesitate to silence you effectively."

The blind man knew that it was no idle threat. In spite of the cloak of humour and fantasy thrown over the proceedings, he was in the power of coolly desperate men. The window was curtained and shuttered against sight and sound, the door behind him locked. Possibly at that moment a revolver threatened him; certainly weapons lay within reach of both his keepers.

"Tell me what to write," he asked, with capitulation in his voice.

Dompierre twirled his *mustachios* in relieved approval. Madame laughed from her place on the couch and picked up a book, watching Montmorency over the cover of its pages. As for that gentleman, he masked his satisfaction by the practical business of placing on the table before Carrados the accessories of the letter.

"Put into your own words the message that I outlined just now."

"Perhaps to make it altogether natural I had better write on a page of the notebook that I always use," suggested Carrados.

"Do you wish to make it natural?" demanded Montmorency, with latent suspicion.

183

"If the miscarriage of your plan is to result in my head being knocked—yes, I do," was the reply.

"Good!" chuckled Dompierre, and sought to avoid Mr Montmorency's cold glance by turning on the electric table-lamp for the blind man's benefit. Madame Dompierre laughed shrilly.

"Thank you, *Monsieur*," said Carrados, "you have done quite right. What is light to you is warmth to me—heat, energy, inspiration. Now to business."

He took out the pocket-book he had spoken of and leisurely proceeded to flatten it down upon the table before him. As his tranquil, pleasant eyes ranged the room meanwhile it was hard to believe that the shutters of an impenetrable darkness lay between them and the world. They rested for a moment on the two accomplices who stood beyond the table, picked out Madame Dompierre lolling on the sofa on his right, and measured the proportions of the long, narrow room. They seemed to note the positions of the window at the one end and the door almost at the other, and even to take into account the single pendent electric light which up till then had been the sole illuminant.

"You prefer pencil?" asked Montmorency.

"I generally use it for casual purposes. But not," he added, touching the point critically, "like this."

Alert for any sign of retaliation, they watched him take an insignificant penknife from his pocket and begin to trim the pencil. Was there in his mind any mad impulse to force conclusions with that puny weapon? Dompierre worked his face into a fiercer expression and touched reassuringly the handle of his knife. Montmorency looked on for a moment, then, whistling softly to himself, turned his back on the table and strolled towards the window, avoiding Madame Nina's pursuant eye.

Then, with overwhelming suddenness, it came, and in its form altogether unexpected.

Carrados had been putting the last strokes to the pencil, whittling it down upon the table. There had been no hasty movement, no violent act to give them warning; only the little blade had pushed itself nearer and nearer to the electric light cord lying there . . . and suddenly and instantly the room was plunged into absolute darkness.

"To the door, Dom!" shouted Montmorency in a flash. "I am at the window. Don't let him pass and we are all right."

"I am here," responded Dompierre from the door.

"He will not attempt to pass," came the quiet voice of Carrados from across the room. "You are now all exactly where I want you. You are both covered. If either moves an inch, I fire—and remember that I shoot by sound, not sight."

"But—but what does it mean?" stammered Montmorency, above the despairing wail of Madame Dompierre.

"It means that we are now on equal terms—three blind men in a dark room. The numerical advantage that you possess is counterbalanced by the fact that you are out of your element—I am in mine."

"Dom," whispered Montmorency across the dark space, "strike a match. I have none."

"I would not, Dompierre, if I were you," advised Carrados, with a short laugh. "It might be dangerous." At once his voice seemed to leap into a passion. "Drop that matchbox," he cried. "You are standing on the brink of your grave, you fool! Drop it, I say; let me hear it fall."

A breath of thought—almost too short to call a pause—then a little thud of surrender sounded from the carpet by the door. The two conspirators seemed to hold their breath.

"That is right." The placid voice once more resumed its sway. "Why cannot things be agreeable? I hate to have to shout, but you seem far from grasping the situation yet. Remember that I do not take the slightest risk. Also please remember, Mr Montmorency, that the action even of a hair-trigger automatic scrapes slightly as it comes up. I remind you of that for your own good, because if you are so ill-advised as to think of trying to pot me in the dark, that noise gives me a fifth of a second start of you. Do you by any chance know Zinghi's in Mercer Street?"

"The shooting gallery?" asked Mr Montmorency a little sulkily.

"The same. If you happen to come through this alive and are interested you might ask Zinghi to show you a target of mine that he keeps. Seven shots at twenty yards, the target indicated by four watches, none of them so loud as the one you are wearing. He keeps it as a curiosity."

"I wear no watch," muttered Dompierre, expressing his thought aloud.

"No, Monsieur Dompierre, but you wear a heart, and that not on your sleeve," said Carrados. "Just now it is quite as loud as Mr Montmorency's watch. It is more central too—I shall not have to allow any margin. That is right; breathe naturally"—for the unhappy Dompierre had given a gasp of apprehension. "It does not make any difference to me, and after a time holding one's breath becomes really painful."

"*Monsieur*," declared Dompierre earnestly, "there was no intention of submitting you to injury, I swear. This Englishman did but speak within his hat. At the most extreme you would have been but bound and gagged. Take care: killing is a dangerous game."

"For you—not for me," was the bland rejoinder. "If you kill me you will be hanged for it. If I kill you I shall be honourably acquitted. You can imagine the scene—the sympathetic court—the recital of your villainies—the story of my indignities. Then with stumbling feet and groping hands the helpless blind man is led forward to give evidence. Sensation! No, no, it isn't really fair but I can kill you both with absolute certainty and Providence will be saddled with all the responsibility. Please don't fidget with your feet, Monsieur Dompierre. I know that you aren't moving but one is liable to make mistakes."

"Before I die," said Montmorency—and for some reason laughed unconvincingly in the dark—"before I die, Mr Carrados, I should really like to know what has happened to the light. That, surely, isn't Providence?"

"Would it be ungenerous to suggest that you are trying to gain time? You ought to know what has happened. But as it may satisfy you that I have nothing to fear from delay, I don't mind telling you. In my hand was a sharp knife—contemptible, you were satisfied, as a weapon; beneath my nose the 'flex' of the electric lamp. It was only necessary for me to draw the one across the other and the system was short-circuited. Every lamp on that fuse is cut off and in the distributing-box in the hall you will find a burned-out wire. You, perhaps—but Monsieur Dompierre's experience in plating ought to have put him up to simple electricity."

"How did you know that there is a distributing-box in the hall?" asked Dompierre, with dull resentment.

"My dear Dompierre, why beat the air with futile questions?" replied Max Carrados. "What does it matter? Have it in the cellar if you like."

"True," interposed Montmorency. "The only thing that need concern us now——"

"But it is in the hall—nine feet high," muttered Dompierre in bitterness. "Yet he, this blind man——"

"The only thing that need concern us," repeated the Englishman, severely ignoring the interruption, "is what you intend doing in the end, Mr Carrados?"

"The end is a little difficult to foresee," was the admission. "So far, I am all for maintaining the *status quo*. Will the first grey light of morning find us still in this *impasse?* No, for between us we have condemned the room to eternal darkness. Probably about daybreak Dompierre will drop off to sleep and roll against the door. I, unfortunately mistaking his intention, will send a bullet through—— Pardon, *Madame*, I should have remembered—but pray don't move."

"I protest, *Monsieur*——"

"Don't protest; just sit still. Very likely it will be Mr Montmorency who will fall off to sleep the first after all."

"Then we will anticipate that difficulty," said the one in question, speaking with renewed decision. "We will play the last hand with our cards upon the table if you like. Nina, Mr Carrados will not injure you whatever happens—be sure of that. When the moment comes you will rise——"

"One word," put in Carrados with determination. "My position is precarious and I take no risks. As you say, I cannot injure Madame Dompierre, and you two men are therefore my hostages for her good behaviour. If she rises from the couch you, Dompierre, fall. If she advances another step Mr Montmorency follows you."

"Do nothing rash, *carissima*," urged her husband, with passionate solicitude. "You might get hit in place of me. We will yet find a better way."

"You dare not, Mr Carrados!" flung out Montmorency, for the first time beginning to show signs of wear in this duel of the temper. "He dare not, Dompierre. In cold blood and unprovoked! No jury would acquit you!"

"Another who fails to do you justice, Madame Nina," said the blind man, with ironic gallantry. "The action might be a little high-handed, one admits, but when you, appropriately clothed and in your right complexion, stepped into the witness-box and I said: 'Gentlemen of the jury, what is my crime? That I made Madame Dompierre a widow!' can you doubt their gratitude and my acquittal? Truly my countrymen are not all bats or monks, *Madame*." Dompierre was breathing with perfect freedom now, while from the couch came the sounds of stifled emotion, but whether the lady was involved in a paroxysm of sobs or of laughter it might be difficult to swear.

★★★★★★

It was perhaps an hour after the flourish of the introduction with which Madame Dompierre had closed the door of the trap upon the blind man's entrance.

The minutes had passed but the situation remained unchanged, though the ingenuity of certainly two of the occupants of the room had been tormented into shreds to discover a means of turning it to their advantage. So far the terrible omniscience of the blind man in the dark and the respect for his markmanship with which his coolness had inspired them, dominated the group. But one strong card yet remained to be played, and at last the moment came upon which the conspirators had pinned their despairing hopes.

There was the sound of movement in the hall outside, not the first about the house, but towards the new complication Carrados had been strangely unobservant. True, Montmorency had talked rather loudly, to carry over the dangerous moments. But now there came an unmistakable step and to the accomplices it could only mean one thing. Montmorency was ready on the instant.

"Down, Dom!" he cried, "throw yourself down! Break in, Guido. Break in the door. We are held up!"

There was an immediate response. The door, under the pressure of a human battering-ram, burst open with a crash. On the threshold the intruders—four or five in number—stopped starkly for a moment, held in astonishment by the extraordinary scene that the light from the hall, and of their own bull's-eyes, revealed.

Flat on their faces, to present the least possible surface to Carrados's aim, Dompierre and Montmorency lay extended beside the window and behind the door. On the couch, with her head buried beneath the cushions, Madame Dompierre sought to shut out the sight and sound of violence. Carrados—Carrados had not moved, but with arms resting on the table and fingers placidly locked together he smiled benignly on the new arrivals. His attitude, compared with the extravagance of those around him, gave the impression of a complacent modern deity presiding over some grotesque ceremonial of pagan worship.

"So, Inspector, you could not wait for me, after all?" was his greeting.

The Bunch of Violets
An episode in the war-time activities of Max Carrados

When Mr. J. Beringer Hulse, in the course of one of his periodical calls at the War Office, had been introduced to Max Carrados he attached no particular significance to the meeting. His own business there lay with Mr. Flinders, one of the quite inconspicuous departmental powers so lavishly produced by a few years of intensive warfare: business that was more confidential than exacting at that stage and hitherto carried on *à deux*. The presence on this occasion of a third, this quiet, suave, personable stranger, was not out of line with Mr. Hulse's open-minded generalities on British methods: "A little singular, perhaps, but not remarkable," would have been the extent of his private comment. He favoured Max with a hard, entirely friendly, American stare, said, "Vurry pleased to make your acquaintance, Mr. Carrados," as they shook hands, and went on with his own affair.

Of course Hulse was not to know that Carrados had been brought in especially to genialise with him. Most of the blind man's activities during that period came within the "Q-class" order. No one ever heard of them, very often they would have seemed quite meaningless under description, and generally they were things that he alone could do—or do as effectively at all events. In the obsolete phraseology of the day, they were his "bit."

"There's this man Hulse," Flinders had proceeded, when it came to the business on which Carrados had been asked to call at Whitehall. "Needless to say, he's no fool or Jonathan wouldn't have sent him on the ticket he carries. If anything, he's too keen—wants to see everything, do anything and go everywhere. In the meanwhile he's kicking up his heels here in London with endless time on his hands and the Lord only knows who mayn't have a go at him."

"You mean for information—or does he carry papers?" asked Carrados.

"Well, at present, information chiefly. He necessarily knows a lot of things that would be priceless to the Huns, and a clever man or woman might find it profitable to nurse him."

"Still, he must be on his guard if, as you say, he is

No one imagines that London in 1917 is a snakeless Eden or expects that German agents today are elderly professors who say, 'How vos you?' and '*Ja, ja!*'"

"My dear fellow," said Flinders sapiently, "every American who came to London before the war was on his guard against a pleasant-spoken gentleman who would accost him with, 'Say, stranger, does this happen to be your wallet lying around here on the sidewalk?' and yet an unending procession of astute, long-headed citizens met him, exactly as described, year after year, and handed over their five hundred or five thousand pounds on a tale that would have made a common or Michaelmas goose blush to be caught listening to."

"It's a curious fact," admitted Carrados thoughtfully. "And this Hulse?"

"Oh, he's quite an agreeable chap, you'll find. He may know a trifle more than you and be a little wider awake and see further through a brick wall and so on, but he won't hurt your feelings about it. Well, will you do it for us?"

"Certainly," replied Carrados. "What is it, by the way?"

Flinders laughed his apologies and explained more precisely.

"Hulse has been over here a month now, and it may be another month before the details come through which he will take on to Paris. Then he will certainly have documents of very special importance that he must carry about with him. Well, in the meanwhile, of course, he is entertained and may pal up with anyone or get himself into Lord knows what. We can't keep him here under lock and key or expect him to make a report of every fellow he has a drink with or every girl he meets."

"Quite so," nodded the blind man.

"Actually, we have been asked to take precautions. It isn't quite a case for the C.I.D.—not at this stage, that is to say. So if I introduce him to you and you fix up an evening for him or something of the sort and find out where his tastes lie, and—and, in fact, keep a general shepherding eye upon him " He broke off abruptly, and Carrados divined that he had reddened furiously and was kicking himself in spirit. The blind man raised a deprecating hand.

"Why should you think that so neat a compliment would pain me, Flinders?" he asked quietly. "Now if you had questioned the genuineness of some of my favourite *tetradrachms* I might have had reason to be annoyed. As it is, yes, I will gladly keep a general shepherding ear on J. Beringer as long as may be needful."

"That's curious," said Flinders, looking up quickly. "I didn't think that I had mentioned his front name."

"I don't think that you have," agreed Carrados.

"Then how had you heard of him before?"

"You don't give an amateur conjurer much chance," replied the other whimsically. "When you brought me to this chair I found a table by me, and happening to rest a hand on it my fingers had 'read' a line of writing before I realised it—just as your glance might as unconsciously do," and he held up an envelope addressed to Hulse.

"That is about the limit," exclaimed Flinders with some emphasis. "Do you know, Carrados, if I hadn't always led a very blameless life I should be afraid to have you around the place."

Thus it came about that the introduction was made and in due course the two callers left together.

"You'll see Mr. Carrados down, won't you?" Flinders had asked, and, slightly puzzled but not disposed to question English ways, Hulse had assented. In the passage Carrados laid a light hand on his companion's arm. Through some subtle perception he read Hulse's mild surprise.

"By the way, I don't think that Flinders mentioned my infirmity," he remarked. "This part of the building is new to me and I happen to be quite blind."

"You astonish me," declared Hulse, and he had to be assured that the statement was literally exact. "You don't seem to miss much by it, Mr. Carrados. Ever happen to hear of Laura Bridgman?"

"Oh, yes," replied Carrados. "She was one of your star cases. But Laura Bridgman's attainments really were wonderful. She was also deaf and dumb, if you remember."

"That is so," assented Hulse. "My people come from New Hampshire not far from Laura's home, and my mother had some of her needlework framed as though it was a picture. That's how I come to know of her, I reckon."

They had reached the street meanwhile and Carrados heard the door of his waiting car opened to receive him.

"I'm going on to my club now to lunch," he remarked with his hand still on his companion's arm. "Of course we only have a wartime menu, but if you would keep me company you would be acting the Good Samaritan," and Beringer Hulse, who was out to see as much as possible of England, France and Berlin within the time—perhaps, also, not uninfluenced by the appearance of the rather sumptuous vehicle—did not refuse.

"Vurry kind of you to put it in that way, Mr. Carrados," he said, in his slightly business-like, easy style. "Why, certainly I will."

During the following weeks Carrados continued to make himself very useful to the visitor, and Hulse did not find his stay in London any less agreeably varied thereby. He had a few other friends—acquaintances rather—he had occasion now and then to mention, but they, one might infer, were either not quite so expansive in their range of hospitality or so pressing for his company. The only one for whom he had ever to excuse himself was a Mr. Darragh, who appeared to have a house in Densham Gardens (he was a little shrewdly curious as to what might be inferred of the status of a man who lived in Densham Gardens), and, well, yes, there was Darragh's sister, Violet. Carrados began to take a private interest in the Darragh household, but there was little to be learned beyond the fact that the house was let furnished to the occupant from month to month. Even during the complexities of war that fact alone could not be regarded as particularly incriminating.

There came an evening when Hulse, having an appointment to dine with Carrados and to escort him to a theatre afterwards, presented himself in a mixed state of elation and remorse. His number had come through at last, he explained, and he was to leave for Paris in the morning. Carrados had been most awfully, most frightfully—Hulse became quite touchingly incoherent in his anxiety to impress upon the blind man the fullness of the gratitude he felt, but, all the same, he had come to ask whether he might cry off for the evening. There was no need to inquire the cause. Carrados raised an accusing finger and pointed to the little bunch of violets with which the impressionable young man had adorned his button-hole.

"Why, yes, to some extent," admitted Hulse, with a facile return to his ingenuous, easy way. "I happened to see Miss Darragh down town this afternoon. There's a man they know whom I've been crazy to meet for weeks, a Jap who has the whole *ju-jitsu* business at his finger-ends. Best *ju-jitsuist* out of Japan, Darragh says. Mighty useful thing, *ju-jitsu*, nowadays, Carrados."

"At any time, indeed," conceded Carrados. "And he will be there tonight?"

"Certain. They've tried to fix it up for me half-a-dozen times before, but this Kuromi could never fit it in. Of course this will be the only chance."

"True," agreed the blind man, rather absent-mindedly. "Your last night here."

"I don't say that in any case I should not have liked to see Violet—Miss Darragh—again before I went, but I wouldn't have gone back on an arranged thing for that," continued Hulse virtuously. "Now this *ju-jitsu* I look on more in the light of business."

"Rather a rough-and-tumble business one would think," suggested Carrados. "Nothing likely to drop out of your pockets in the process and get lost?"

Hulse's face displayed a rather more superior smile than he would have permitted himself had his friend been liable to see it and be snubbed thereby.

"I know what you mean, of course," he replied, getting up and going to the blind man's chair, "but don't you worry about me, Father William. Just put your hand to my breast pocket."

"Sewn up," commented Carrados, touching the indicated spot on his guest's jacket.

"Sewn up: that's it; and since I've had any important papers on me it always has been sewn up, no matter how often I change. No fear of anything dropping out now—or being lifted out, eh? No, *sir*, if what I carry there chanced to vanish, I guess no excuses would be taken and J. B. H. would automatically drop down to the very bottom of the class. As it is, if it's missing I shall be missing too, so that won't trouble me."

"What time do you want to get there?"

"Darragh's? Well, I left that open. Of course I couldn't promise until I had seen you. Anyway, not until after dinner, I said."

"That makes it quite simple, then," declared Carrados. "Stay and have dinner here, and afterwards we will go on to Darragh's together instead of going to the theatre."

"That's most terribly kind of you," replied Hulse. "But won't it be rather a pity—the tickets, I mean, and so forth?"

"There are no tickets as it happens," said Carrados. "I left that over until tonight. And I have always wanted to meet a *ju-jitsu* champion. Quite providential, isn't it?"

★★★★★★

It was nearly nine o'clock, and seated in the drawing-room of his furnished house in Densham Gardens, affecting to read an evening paper, Mr. Darragh was plainly ill at ease. The strokes of the hour, sounded by the little gilt clock on the mantelpiece, seemed to mark the limit of his patience. A muttered word escaped him and he looked up with a frown.

"It was nine that Hulse was to be here by, wasn't it, Violet?" he asked.

Miss Darragh, who had been regarding him for some time in furtive anxiety, almost jumped at the simple question.

"Oh, yes, Hugh—about nine, that is. Of course he had to—"

"Yes, yes," interrupted Darragh irritably; "we've heard all that. And Sims," he continued, more for the satisfaction of voicing his annoyance than to engage in conversation, "swore by everything that we should have that coat by eight at the very latest. My God! what rotten tools one has to depend on!"

"Perhaps—" began Violet timidly, and stopped at his deepening scowl.

"Yes?" said Darragh, with a deadly smoothness in his voice. "Yes, Violet; pray continue. You were about to say—"

"It was really nothing, Hugh," she pleaded. "Nothing at all."

"Oh, yes, Violet, I am sure that you have some helpful little suggestion to make," he went on in the same silky, deliberate way. Even when he was silent his unspoken thoughts seemed to be lashing her with bitterness, and she turned painfully away to pick up the paper he had flung aside. "The situation, Kato," resumed Darragh, addressing himself to the third occupant of the room, "is bluntly this: If Sims isn't here with that coat before young Hulse arrives, all our carefully-thought-out plan, a month's patient work, and about the last both of our cash and credit, simply go to the devil! . . . and Violet wants to say that perhaps Mr. Sims forgot to wind his watch last night or poor Mrs. Sims's cough is worse. . . . Proceed, Violet; don't be diffident."

The man addressed as "Kato" knocked a piece off the chessboard he was studying and stooped to pick it up again before he replied. Then he looked from one to the other with a face singularly devoid of expression.

"Perhaps. Who says?" he replied in his quaintly-ordered phrases. "If it is to be, my friend, it will be."

"Besides, Hugh," put in Violet, with a faint dash of spirit, "it isn't

194

really quite so touch-and-go as that. If Sims comes before Hulse has left, Kato can easily slip out and change coats then."

Darragh was already on his restless way towards the door. Apparently he did not think it worth while to reply to either of the speakers, but his expression, especially when his eyes turned to Violet, was one of active contempt. As the door closed after him, Kato sprang to his feet and his impassive look gave place to one almost of menace. His hands clenched unconsciously and with slow footsteps he seemed to be drawn on in pursuit. A little laugh, mirthless and bitter, from the couch, where Violet had seated herself, recalled him.

"Is it true, Kato," she asked idly, "that you are really the greatest *ju-jitsuist* outside Japan?"

"Polite other people say so," replied the Japanese, his voice at once gentle and deprecating.

"And yet you cannot keep down even your little temper!"

Kato thought this over for a moment; then he crossed to the couch and stood regarding the girl with his usual impenetrable gravity.

"On contrary, I can keep down my temper very well," he said seriously. "I can keep it so admirably that I, whose ancestors were Samurai and very high nobles, have been able to become thief and swindler and"—his moving hand seemed to beat the air for a phrase—"and lowdown dog and still to live. What does anything it matter that is connected with me alone? But there are three things that do matter—three that I do not allow myself to be insulted and still to live: my emperor, my country, and—you. And so," concluded Kato Kuromi, in a somewhat lighter vein, "now and then, as you say, my temper gets the better of me slightly."

"Poor Kato," said Violet, by no means disconcerted at this delicate avowal. "I really think that I am sorrier for you than I am for Hugh, or even for myself. But it's no good becoming romantic at this time of day, my dear man." The lines of her still quite young and attractive face hardened in keeping with her thoughts. "I suppose I've had my chance. We're all of a pattern and I'm as crooked as any of you now."

"No, no," protested Kato loyally; "not you of yourself. It is we bad fellows round you. Darragh ought never to have brought you into these things, and then to despise you for your troubles—that is why my temper now and then *ju-jitsues* me. This time it is the worst of all—the young man Hulse, for whose benefit you pass yourself as the sister of your husband. How any mortal man possessing you—"

"Another cigarette, Kato, please," interrupted Violet, for the monotonous voice had become slightly more penetrating than was prudent. "That's all in the way of business, my friend. We aren't a firm of family solicitors. Jack Hulse had to be fascinated and I—well, if there is any hitch I don't think that it can be called my fault," and she demonstrated for his benefit the bewitching smile that had so effectually enslaved the ardent Beringer.

"Fascinated!" retorted Kato, fixing on the word jealously, and refusing to be pacified by the bribery of the smile. "Yes, so infatuated has become this very susceptible young man that you lead him about like pet lamb at the end of blue ribbon. Business? Perhaps. But how have you been able to do this, Violet? And you husband—Darragh—to him simply business, very good business—and he forces you to do this full of shame thing and mocks at you for reward."

"Kato, Kato—" urged Violet, breaking through his scornful laughter.

"I am what your people call yellow man," continued Kato relentlessly, and you are the one white woman of my dreams—dreams that I would not lift finger to spoil by trying to make real. But if I should have been Darragh not ten thousand times the ten thousand pounds that Hulse carries would tempt me to lend you to another man's arms."

"Oh, Kato, how horrid you can be!"

"Horrid for me to say, but 'business' for you to do! How have you discovered so much, Violet—what Hulse carries, where he carries it, the size and shape the packet makes, even the way he so securely keeps it? 'Business' eh? Your husband cares not so long as we succeed. But I, Kato Kuromi, care." He went nearer so that his mere attitude was menacing as he stood over her, and his usually smooth voice changed to a tone she had never heard there before. "*How* have you learned all this? How, unless you and Hulse—"

"'Sssh!" she exclaimed in sharp dismay as her ear caught a sound beyond.

"—oh yes," continued Kato easily, his voice instantly as soft and unconcerned as ever, "it will be there, you mean. The views in the valley of Kedu are considered very fine and the river itself"

It was Darragh whom Violet had heard approaching, and he entered the room in a much better temper than he had left it. At the door he paused a moment to encourage someone forward—a seedy, diffident man of more than middle age, who carried a brown-paper parcel.

"Come on, Sims hurry up, man!" urged Darragh impatiently, but without the sting of contempt that had poisoned his speech before. "And, oh, Phillips"—looking back and dropping his voice—"when Mr. Hulse arrives show him into the morning-room at first. Not up here, you understand? Now, Sims."

After a rather helpless look round for something suitable on which to lay his parcel, the woebegone-looking individual was attempting to untie it on an upraised knee.

"Yes, sir," he replied, endeavouring to impart a modicum of briskness into his manner. "I'm sorry to be a bit late, sir; I was delayed."

"Oh, well, never mind that now," said Darragh magnanimously. "Thing quite all right?"

"Mrs. Sims isn't worse?" asked Violet kindly.

Mr. Sims managed to get his back to the group before he ventured to reply.

"No, miss," he said huskily; "she's better now. She's dead: died an hour ago. That's why I wasn't quite able to get here by eight."

From each of his hearers this tragedy drew a characteristic response. Violet gave a little moan of sympathy and turned away. Kato regarded Sims, and continued to regard him, with the tranquil incuriosity of the unpitying East. Darragh—Darragh alone spoke, and his tone was almost genial.

"Devilish lucky that you were able to get here by now in the circumstances, Sims," he said.

"Well, sir," replied Sims practically, "you see, I shall need the money just as much now—though not quite for the same purpose as I had planned." He took the garment from the paper and shook it out before displaying it for Darragh's approval. "I think you will find that quite satisfactory, sir."

"Exactly the same as the one your people made for Mr. Hulse a week ago?" asked Darragh, glancing at the jacket and then passing it on to Violet for her verdict.

"To a stitch, sir. A friend of mine up at the shop got the measurements and the cloth is a length from the same piece."

"But the cut, Sims," persisted his patron keenly; "the cut is the most important thing about it. It makes all the difference in the world."

"Yes, sir," acquiesced Sims dispassionately; "you can rely on that. I used to be a first-class cutter myself before I took to drink. I am yet, when I'm steady. And I machined both coats myself."

"That should do then," said Darragh complacently. "Now you

were to have—"

"Ten guineas and the cost of the cloth you promised, sir. Of course it's a very big price, and I won't deny that I've been a bit uneasy about it from time to time when I—"

"That's all right." Darragh had no wish to keep Mr. Sims in evidence a minute longer than was necessary.

"I shouldn't like to be doing anything wrong, sir," persisted the poor creature; "and when you stipulated that it wasn't to be mentioned—"

"Well, well, man; it's a bet, didn't I tell you? I stand to win a clear hundred if I can fool Hulse over this coat. That's the long and short of it."

"I'm sure I hope it is, sir. I've never been in trouble for anything yet, and it would break my wife's 'art—"

He stopped suddenly and his weak face changed to a recollection of his loss; then without another word he turned and made shakily for the door.

"See him safely away, Katty, and pay him down below," said Darragh. "I'll settle with you later," and the Japanese, with a careless "All right-o," followed.

"Now, Violet, slip into it," continued her husband briskly. "We don't want to keep Hulse waiting when he comes." From a drawer in a cabinet near at hand he took a paper packet, prepared in readiness, and passed it to her. "You have the right cotton?"

"Yes, Hugh," said Violet, opening a little work-basket. She had already satisfied herself that the coat was a replica of the one the young American would wear, and she now transferred the dummy package to the corresponding pocket and with a few deft stitches secured it in the same way as she had already learned that the real contents were safeguarded. "And, Hugh—"

"Well, well?" responded Darragh, with a return of his old impatience.

"I don't wish to know all your plans, Hugh," continued Violet meekly, "but I do want to warn you. You are running a most tremendous risk with Kato."

"Oh, Kato!"

"It is really serious, Hugh. You don't believe in patriotism, I know, but Kato happens to. When he learns that it isn't ten thousand pounds at all, but confidential war plans, that this scoop consists of, something terrible may happen."

"It might, Violet. Therefore I haven't told him, and I am so arranging things that he will never know. Cheer up, my girl, there will be no tragedy. All the same, thanks for the hint. It shows a proper regard for your husband's welfare."

"Oh, Hugh, Hugh," murmured Violet, "if only you were more often—"

Whatever might have been the result—if indeed there was yet hope in an appeal to another and a better nature that he might once have possessed— it came too late. The words were interrupted by the sudden reappearance of Kato, his business with Sims completed. He opened and closed the door quietly but very quickly, and at a glance both the Darraghs saw that something unforeseen had happened.

"Here's pretty go," reported the Japanese. "Hulse just come and brought someone with him!"

For a moment all the conspirators stood aghast at the unexpected complication. Hugh Darragh was the first to speak.

"Damnation!" he exclaimed, with a terrible look in his wife's direction; "that may upset everything. What ghastly muddle have you made now?"

"I—I don't know," pleaded Violet weakly. "I never dreamt of such a thing. Are you sure?"

"Slow man," amplified Kato with a nod. "Fellow who walk " He made a few steps with studied deliberation.

"Blind! It's Max Carrados," exclaimed Violet, in a flash of enlightenment. "They have been great friends lately and Jack has often spoken of him. He's most awfully clever in his way, but stone blind. Hugh, Kato, don't you see? It's rather unfortunate his being here, but it can't really make any difference."

"True, if he is quite blind," admitted Kato.

"I'll look into it," said Darragh briskly. "Coat's all ready for you, Kato."

"I think no, yet," soliloquised the Japanese, critically examining it. "Keep door, 'alf-a-mo', Violet, if please." His own contribution to the coat's appearance was simple but practical—a gentle tension here and there, a general rumple, a dust on the floor and a final shake. "One week wear," he announced gravely as he changed into it and hid his own away.

"Take your time, Mr. Carrados," Darragh's voice was heard insisting on the stairs outside, and the next moment he stood just inside the room, and before Hulse had quite guided Carrados into view, drew

Violet's attention to the necessity of removing the button-hole that the Americans still wore by a significant movement to the lapel of his own coat. It required no great *finesse* on the girl's part to effect the transfer of the little bunch of flowers to her own person within five minutes of the guests' arrival.

"A new friend to see you, Violet—Mr. Carrados," announced Darragh most graciously. "Mr. Carrados, my sister."

"Not to see you exactly, Miss Darragh," qualified Carrados. "But none the less to know you as well as if I did, I hope."

"I wanted you to meet Max before I went, Miss Darragh," explained Hulse; "so I took the liberty of bringing him round."

"You really *are* going then?" she asked.

"Yes. There seems no doubt about it this time. Twelve hours from now I hope to be in Paris. I should say," amended the ingenuous young man, "I *dread* to be in Paris, for it may mean a long absence. That's where I rely on Carrados to become what is called a 'connecting file' between us—to cheer my solitude by letting me know when he has met you, or heard of you, or, well, anything in fact."

"Take care, Mr. Hulse," she said. "Gallantry by proxy is a dangerous game."

"That's just it," retorted Hulse. "Max is the only man I shouldn't be jealous of—because he can't see you!"

While these amiable exchanges were being carried on between the two young people, with Max Carrados standing benignly by, Darragh found an opportunity to lower his voice for Kato's benefit.

"It's all right about him," he declared. "We carry on."

"As we arranged?" asked Kato.

"Yes; exactly. Come across now." He raised his voice as he led Kato towards the other group. "I don't think that either of you has met Mr. Kuromi yet—Mr. Hulse, Mr. Carrados."

"I have been pining to meet you for weeks, sir," responded Hulse with enthusiasm. "Mr. Darragh tells me what a wonderful master of *ju-jitsu* you are."

"Oh, well; little knack, you know," replied Kato modestly. "You are interested?"

"Yes, indeed. I regard it as a most useful accomplishment at any time and particularly now. I only wish I'd taken it up when I had the leisure."

"Let me find you an easy-chair, Mr. Carrados," said Violet attentively. "I am sure that you won't be interested in so strenuous a subject

200

as *ju-jitsu.*"

"Oh, yes, I am, though," protested the blind man. "I am interested in everything."

"But surely—"

"I can't actually see the *ju-jitsuing,* you would say? Quite true, but do you know, Miss Darragh, that makes a great deal less difference than you might imagine. I have my sense of touch, my sense of taste, my hearing—even my unromantic nose—and you would hardly believe how they have rallied to my assistance since sight went. For instance—"

They had reached the chair to which Miss Darragh had piloted him. To guide him into it she had taken both his hands, but now Carrados had gently disengaged himself and was lightly holding her left hand between both of his.

"For instance, Hulse and I were speaking of you the other day—forgive our impertinence—and he happened to mention that you disliked rings of any sort and had never worn one. His eyes, you see, and perhaps a careless remark on your part. Now I *know* that until quite recently you continually wore a ring upon this finger."

Silence had fallen upon the other men as they followed Carrados's exposition. Into the moment of embarrassment that succeeded this definite pronouncement Mr. Hulse threw a cheerful note.

"Oh ho, Max, you've come a cropper this time," he exclaimed. "Miss Darragh has never worn a ring. Have you?"

"N-o," replied Violet, a little uncertain of her ground, as the blind man continued to smile benevolently upon her.

"A smooth and rather broad one," he continued persuasively. "Possibly a wedding ring?"

"Wait a minute, Violet, wait a minute," interposed Darragh, endeavouring to look judicially wise with head bent to one side. He was doubtful if Violet could carry the point without incurring some suspicion, and he decided to give her a lead out of it. "Didn't I see you wearing some sort of plain ring a little time ago? You have forgotten, but I really believe Mr. Carrados may be right. Think again."

"Of course!" responded Violet readily; "how stupid of me! It was my mother's wedding ring. I found it in an old desk and wore it to keep it safe. That was really how I found out that I could not bear the feel of one and I soon gave it up."

"What did I say?" claimed Darragh genially. "I thought that we should be right."

"This is really much interesting," said Kato. "I very greatly like your system, Mr. Carrados."

"Oh, it's scarcely a system," deprecated Max good-naturedly; "it's almost second nature with me now. I don't have to consider, say, 'Where is the window?' if I want it. I know with certainty that the window lies over here." He had not yet taken the chair provided, and suiting the action to the word he now took a few steps towards the wall where the windows were. "Am I not right?" And to assure himself he stretched out a hand and encountered the heavy curtains.

"Yes, yes," admitted Violet hurriedly, "but, oh, please do be careful, Mr. Carrados. They are most awfully particular about the light here since the last raid. We go in fear and trembling lest a glimmer should escape."

Carrados smiled and nodded and withdrew from the dangerous area. He faced the room again.

"Then there is the electric light—heat at a certain height of course."

"True," assented Kato, "but why *electric* light?"

"Because no other is noiseless and entirely without smell; think—gas, oil, candles, all betray their composition yards away. Then"—indicating the fireplace—"I suppose you can only smell soot in damp weather? The mantelpiece"—touching it—"inlaid marble. The wallpaper"—brushing his hand over its surface—"arrangement of pansies on a criss-cross background"; lifting one finger to his lips—"colour scheme largely green and gold."

Possibly Mr. Hulse thought that his friend had demonstrated his qualities quite enough. Possibly—it any rate he now created a diversion:

"Engraving of Mrs. Siddons as the Tragic Muse, suspended two feet seven inches from the ceiling on a brass-headed nail supplied by a one-legged ironmonger whose Aunt Jane—"

All contributed a sufficiently appreciative laugh—Carrados's not the least hearty—except Kato, whose Asiatic dignity was proof against the form of jesting.

"You see what contempt familiarity breeds, Miss Darragh," remarked the blind man. "I look to you, Mr. Kuromi, to avenge me by putting Hulse in a variety of undignified attitudes on the floor."

"Oh, I shan't mind that if at the same time you put me up to a trick or two," said Hulse, turning to the Japanese.

"You wish?"

202

"Indeed I do. I've seen the use of it. It's good; it's scientific. When I was crossing, one of the passengers held up a bully twice his weight in the neatest way possible. It looked quite simple, something like this, if I may?" Kato nodded his grave assent and submitted himself to Mr. Hulse's vigorous grasp. "'Now,' said the man I'm speaking of, 'struggle and your right arm's broken.' But I expect you know the grip?"

"Oh, yes," replied Kato, veiling his private amusement, "and therefore foolish to struggle. Expert does not struggle; gives way." He appeared to do so, to be falling helplessly in fact, but the assailant found himself compelled to follow, and the next moment he was lying on his back with Kato politely extending a hand to assist him up again.

"I must remember that," said Hulse thoughtfully. "Let me see, it goes—do you mind putting me wise on that again, Mr. Kuromi? The motion picture just one *iota* slower this time, please."

For the next ten or twenty minutes the demonstration went on in admirable good humour, and could Max Carrados have seen he would certainly have witnessed his revenge. At the end of the lesson both men were warm and dusty—so dusty that Miss Darragh felt called upon to apologise laughingly for the condition of the rug. But if clothes were dusty, hands were positively dirty—there was no other word for it.

"No, really, the poor mat can't be so awful as that," declared the girl. "Wherever have you been, Mr. Kuromi? and, oh, Mr. Hulse you are just as bad."

"I do not know," declared Kato, regarding his grimy fingers seriously. "Nowhere of myself. Yes, I think it must be your London atmosphere among the rug after all."

"At all events you can't Oh, Hugh, take them to the bathroom, will you? And I'll try to entertain Mr. Carrados meanwhile—only he will entertain me instead, I know."

It was well and simply done throughout—nothing forced, and the sequence of development quite natural. Indeed, it was not until Hulse saw Kuromi take off his coat in the bathroom that he even thought of what he carried. "Well, Carrados," he afterwards pleaded to his friend, "now could I wash my hands before those fellows like a guy who isn't used to washing? It isn't natural. It isn't human." So for those few minutes the two coats hung side by side, and Darragh kindly brushed them. When Hulse put on his own again his hand instinctively felt for the hidden packet; his fingers reassured themselves among the familiar objects of his pockets, and his mind was perfectly at ease.

"You old scoundrel, Max," he said, when he returned to the drawing room. "You told Kuromi to wipe the floor with me and, by crumbs, he did! Have a cigarette all the same."

Miss Darragh laughed pleasantly and took the opportunity to move away to learn from her accomplices if all had gone well. Carrados was on the point of passing over the proffered olive branch when he changed his mind. He leaned forward and with slow deliberation chose a cigarette from the American's case. Exactly when the first subtle monition of treachery reached him—by what sense it was conveyed—Hulse never learned, for there were experiences among the finer perceptions that the blind man did not willingly discuss. Not by voice or outward manner in that arresting moment did he betray an inkling of his suspicion, yet by some responsive telephony Hulse at once, though scarcely conscious of it then, grew uneasy and alert.

"Thanks; I'll take a light from yours," remarked Carrados, ignoring the lit match, and he rose to avail himself. His back was towards the others, who still had a word of instruction to exchange. With cool precision he handled the cloth on Hulse's outstretched arm, critically touched the pocket he was already familiar with, and then deliberately drew the lapel to his face.

"You wore some violets?" he said beneath his breath.

"Yes," replied Hulse, "but I— Miss Darragh——"

"But there never have been any *here!* By heavens, Hulse, we're in it! You had your coat off just now?"

"Yes, for a minute—"

"Quietly. Keep your cigarette going. You'll have to leave this to me. Back me up—discreetly—whatever I do."

"Can't we challenge it and insist—"

"Not in this world. They have at least one other man downstairs—in Cairo, a Turk by the way, before I was blind, of course. Not up to Mr. Kuromi, I expect—"

"Cool again?" asked Miss Darragh sociably. It was her approach that had sent Carrados off into irrelevancies. "Was the experience up to anticipation?"

"Yes, I think I may say it was," admitted Hulse guardedly. "There is certainly a lot to learn here. I expect you've seen it all before?"

"Oh, no. It is a great honour to get Mr. Kuromi to 'show it off,' as he quaintly calls it."

"Yes, I should say so," replied the disillusioned young man with deadly simplicity. "I quite feel that."

"J. B. H. is getting strung up," thought Carrados. "He may say something unfortunate presently." So he deftly insinuated himself into the conversation and for a few minutes the commonplaces of the topic were rigidly maintained.

"Care for a hand at auction?" suggested Darragh, joining the group. He had no desire to keep his guests a minute longer than he need, but at the same time it was his line to behave quite naturally until they left. "Oh, but I forgot—Mr. Carrados—"

"I am well content to sit and listen " Carrados assured him. "Consider how often I have to do that without the entertainment of a game to listen to! And you are four without me."

"It really hardly seems—" began Violet.

"I'm sure Max will feel it if he thinks that he is depriving us," put in Hulse loyally, so with some more polite protestation it was arranged and the game began, Carrados remaining where he was. In the circumstances a very high standard of bridge could not be looked for; the calling was a little wild; the play more than a little loose; the laughter rather shrill or rather flat; the conversation between the hands forced and spasmodic. All were playing for time in their several interpretations of it; the blind man alone was thinking beyond the immediate moment.

Presently there was a more genuine burst of laughter than any hitherto. Kato had revoked, and, confronted with it, had made a naive excuse. Carrados rose with the intention of going nearer when a distressing thing occurred. Halfway across the room he seemed to slip, plunged forward helplessly, and came to the floor, involved in a light table as he fell. All the players were on their feet in an instant. Darragh assisted his guest to rise; Violet took an arm; Kato looked about the floor curiously, and Hulse—Hulse stared hard at Max and wondered what the thunder this portended.

"Clumsy, clumsy," murmured Carrados beneath his breath. "Forgive me, Miss Darragh."

"Oh, Mr. Carrados!" she exclaimed in genuine distress. "Aren't you really hurt?"

"Not a bit of it," he declared lightly. "Or at all events," he amended, bearing rather more heavily upon her support as he took a step, "nothing to speak of."

"Here is pencil," said Kuromi, picking one up from the polished floor. "You must have slipped on this."

"Stepping on a pencil is like that," contributed Hulse wisely. "It acts as a kind of roller-skate."

"Please don't interrupt the game any more," pleaded the victim. "At the most, at the very worst, it is only—oh!—a negligible strain."

"I don't know that any strain, especially of the ankle, is negligible, Mr. Carrados," said Darragh with cunning foresight. "I think it perhaps ought to be seen to."

"A compress when I get back will be all that is required," maintained Carrados. "I should hate to break up the evening."

"Don't consider that for a moment," urged the host hospitably. "If you really think that it would be wiser in the end—"

"Well, perhaps—" assented the other, weakening in his resolution.

"Shall I 'phone up a taxi?" asked Violet.

"Thank you, if you would be so kind—or, no; perhaps my own car would be rather easier in the circumstances. My man will be about, so that it will take very little longer."

"I'll get through for you," volunteered Darragh. "What's your number?"

The telephone was in a corner of the room. The connection was soon obtained and Darragh turned to his guest for the message.

"I'd better speak," said Carrados—he had limped across on Hulse's arm—taking over the receiver. "Excellent fellow, but he'd probably conclude that I'd been killed. . . . That you, Parkinson? . . . Yes, at 155 Densham Gardens. I'm held up here by a slight accident. . . . No, no, nothing serious, but I might have some difficulty in getting back without assistance. Tell Harris I shall need him after all, as soon as he can get here—the car that's handiest. That's—oh, and, Parkinson, bring along a couple of substantial walking-sticks with you. Any time now. That's all. . . . Yes . . . yes." He put up the receiver with a thrill of satisfaction that he had got his message safely through. "Held up"—a phrase at once harmless and significant—was the arranged shift-key into code. It was easy for a blind man to receive some hurt that held him up. Once or twice Carrados's investigations had got him into tight places, but in one way or another he had invariably got out again.

"How far is your place away?" someone asked, and out of the reply a time-marking conversation on the subject of getting about London's darkened streets and locomotion in general arose. Under cover of this Kato drew Darragh aside to the deserted card-table.

"Not your pencil, Darragh?" he said quietly, displaying the one he had picked up.

"No; why?"

"I not altogether like this, is why," replied the Japanese. "I think it Carrados own pencil. That man have too many ways of doing things, Darragh. It was mistake to let him 'phone."

"Oh, nonsense; you heard what he said. Don't get jumpy, man. The thing has gone like clockwork."

"So far, yes. But I think I better go now and come back in one hour or so, safer for all much."

Darragh, for very good reasons, had the strongest objections to allowing his accomplice an opportunity of examining the spoil alone. "Look here, Katty," he said with decision, "I must have you in case there does come a scrimmage. I'll tell Phillips to fasten the front door well, and then we can see that it's all right before anyone comes in. If it is, there's no need for you to run away; if there's the least doubt we can knock these two out and have plenty of time to clear by the back way we've got." Without giving Kato any chance of raising further objection he turned to his guests again.

"I think I remember your tastes, Hulse," he said suavely. "I hope that you have no objection to Scotch whisky, Mr. Carrados? We still have a few bottles left. Or perhaps you prefer champagne?"

Carrados had very little intention of drinking anything in that house, nor did he think that with ordinary procrastination it would be necessary.

"You are very kind," he replied tentatively. "Should you permit the invalid either, Miss Darragh?"

"Oh, yes, in moderation," she smiled. "I think I hear your car," she added, and stepping to the window ventured to peep out.

It was true. Mr. Darragh had run it a shade too fine for once. For a moment he hesitated which course to take—to see who was arriving or to convey a warning to his henchman down below. He had turned towards the door when Violet's startled voice recalled him to the window.

"Hugh!" she called sharply. "Here, Hugh;" and as he reached her, in a breathless whisper, "There are men inside the car—two more at least."

Darragh had to decide very quickly this time. His choice was not without its element of fineness. "Go down and see about it, Katty," he said, looking Kato straight in the eyes. "And tell Phillips about the whisky."

"Door locked," said the Japanese tersely. "Key other side."

"The key was on this side," exclaimed Darragh fiercely. "Hulse—"

"Hell!" retorted Beringer expressively. "That jacket doesn't go out of the room without me this journey."

Darragh had him covered before he had finished speaking.

"Quick," he rapped out. "I'll give you up to three, and if the key isn't out then, by God, I'll plug you, Hulse! One, two—"

The little "*ping!*" that followed was not the automatic speaking, but the release of the electric light switch as Carrados, unmarked among this climax, pressed it up. In the absolute blackness that followed Darragh spun round to face the direction of this new opponent.

"Shoot by all means, Mr. Darragh, if you are used to firing in the dark," said Carrados's imperturbable voice. "But in any case remember that I am. As I am a dead shot by sound, perhaps everyone had better remain exactly where he—or she, I regret to have to add, Miss Darragh—now is."

"You dog!" spat out Darragh.

"I should not even talk," advised the blind man. "I am listening for my friends and I might easily mistake your motive among the hum of conversation."

He had not long to wait. In all innocence Phillips had opened the door to Parkinson, and immeasurably to his surprise two formidable-looking men of official type had followed in from somewhere. By a sort of instinct—or possibly a momentary ray of light had been their guide— they came direct to the locked door.

"Parkinson," called Carrados.

"Yes, sir," replied that model attendant.

"We are all in here; Mr. Hulse and myself, and three—I am afraid that I can make no exception—three unfriendlies. At the moment the electric light is out of action, the key of the locked door has been mislaid, and firearms are being promiscuously flourished in the dark. That is the position. Now if you have the key, Hulse—"

"I have," replied Hulse grimly, "but for a fact I dropped it down my neck out of harm's way and where the plague it's got to—"

As it happened the key was not required. The heavier of the officers outside, believing in the element of surprise, stood upon one foot and shot the other forward with the force and action of an engine piston-rod. The shattered door swung inward and the three men rushed into the room.

Darragh had made up his mind, and as the door crashed he raised his hand to fire into the thick. But at that moment the light flashed on again and almost instantly was gone. Before his dazzled eyes and startled mind could adjust themselves to this he was borne down. When he rose again his hands were manacled.

"So," he breathed laboriously, bending a vindictive eye upon his outwitter. "When next we meet it will be my turn, I think."

"We shall never meet again," replied Carrados impassively. "There is no other turn for you, Darragh."

"But where the blazes has Kuromi got to?" demanded Hulse with sharp concern. "He can't have quit?"

One of the policemen walked to a table in the farthest corner of the room, looked down beyond it, and silently raised a beckoning hand. They joined him there.

"Rum way these foreigners have of doing things," remarked the other disapprovingly. "Now who the Hanover would ever think of a job like that?"

"I suppose," mused the blind man, as he waited for the official arrangements to go through, "that presently I shall have to live up to Hulse's overwhelming bewonderment. And yet if I pointed out to him that the button-hole of the coat he is now wearing still has a stitch in it to keep it in shape and could not by any possibility . . . Well, well, perhaps better not. It is a mistake for the conjurer to explain."

The Virginiola Fraud

If there was one thing more than another about Max Carrados that came as a continual surprise, even a mild shock, to his acquaintances, it was the wide and unrestricted scope of his amusements. Had the blind man displayed a pensive interest in chamber music, starred by an occasional visit to the opera, taken a daily walk in the park on his attendant's arm, and found his normal recreation in chess or in being read to, the routine would have seemed an eminently fit and proper one. But to call at The Turrets and learn that Carrados was out on the river punting, or to find him in his gymnasium, probably with the gloves on, outraged one's sense of values.

The only extraordinary thing in fact about his recreations was their ordinariness. He frequently spent an afternoon at Lord's when there was the prospect of a good game being put up; he played golf, bowls, croquet and cards; fished in all waters, and admitted that he had never missed the University Boat Race since the great finish of '91. When he walked about the streets anywhere within two miles of his house he was quite independent of any guidance, and on one occasion he had saved a mesmerised girl's life on Richmond Bridge by dragging her into one of the recesses just in time to escape an uncontrollable dray that had jumped the kerb.

This prelude is by way of explaining the attitude of a certain Mr Marrable whom Carrados knew, as he knew a hundred strange and useful people. Marrable had chambers in the neighbourhood of Piccadilly which he furnished and decorated on a lavish and expensive scale. His *bric-à-brac*, pictures, books and appointments, indeed, constituted the man's means of living, for he was one of the best all-round judges of art and the antique in London, and with a nonchalant air of indifference he very pleasantly and profitably lounged his way through life on the honey extracted from one facile transaction after another. Living on his wits in a strictly legitimate sense, he enjoyed all the advantages of being a dealer without the necessity of maintaining a place of business. It was not even necessary for him to find "bargains" in the general sense, for buying in the ordinary market and selling in a very special and restricted one disclosed a substantial margin. This commercial system, less rare than one might imagine, involved no misrepresentation: his wealthy and exclusive clients were quite willing to pay the difference for the *cachet* of Mr Marrable's connoisseurship and also, perhaps, for the amiable reluctance with which he carried on his operations.

The business that took Carrados to the amateur dealer's rooms one day in April has nothing to do with this particular incident. It was quite friendly and satisfactory on both sides, but it was not until Carrados rose to leave that the tangent of the visit touched the circle of the *Virginiola*.

"I am due at Gurnard's at about three-thirty," remarked Marrable, glancing at a Louis XVI. *ormolu* clock for which he had marked off a certain musical comedy countess at two hundred and fifty guineas. "Your way at all?"

"Gurnard & Lane's—the auctioneers?"

"Yes. They have a book sale on this afternoon."

"I hope I haven't been keeping you," apologised Carrados.

"Oh, not at all. There is nothing I want among the earlier lots." He picked up a catalogue from a satinwood desk in which Mademoiselle Mars had once kept her play-bills and glanced down the pages. "No. 191 is the first I have marked: *An Account of the Newly Discovered Islands of Sir George Sommers, called 'Virginiola.'* You aren't a competitor, by the way?"

"No," replied Carrados; "but if you don't mind I should like to go with you."

Marrable looked at him with slightly suspicious curiosity.

"You'd find it uncommonly dull, surely, seeing nothing," he remarked.

"I generally contrive to extract some interest from what is going on," said Carrados modestly. "And as I have never yet been at a book sale—"

"Oh, come, by all means," interposed the other. "I shall be very glad of your company. Only I was surprised for the moment at the idea. I should warn you, however, that it isn't anything great in the way of a dispersal—no Caxtons or first-folio Shakespeares. Consequently there will be an absence of ducal bibliophiles and literary Cabinet ministers, and we shall have a crowd of more or less frowsy dealers."

They had walked down into the street as they conversed. Marrable held up a finger to the nearest taxicab on an adjacent rank, opened the door for Carrados, and gave the driver the address of the auction rooms of which he had spoken.

"I don't expect to get very much," he speculated, turning over the later pages of the catalogue, which he still carried in his hand. "I've marked a dozen lots, but I'm not particularly keen on half of them. But I should certainly like to land the *Virginiola*."

"It is rare, I suppose?" inquired Carrados. Indifferent to books from the bibliophile's standpoint, he was able to feel the interest that one collector is generally willing to extend to the tastes of another.

"Yes," assented Marrable with weighty consideration. "Yes. In a way it is extremely rare. But this copy is faulty—the Dedication and Address pages are missing. That will bring down the bidding enormously, and yet it is just the defect that makes it attractive to me."

For a moment he was torn between the secretiveness bred of his position and a human desire to expound his shrewdness. The weakness triumphed.

"A few months ago," he continued, "I came across another copy of the *Virginiola* among the lumber of a Bristol second-hand book-dealer's stock. It was altogether a rotten specimen—both covers gone, scores of pages ripped away, and most of those that remained appallingly torn and dirty. It was a fragment in fact, and I was not tempted even at the nominal guinea that was put upon it. But now—"

"Quite so," agreed Carrados.

"The first few pages were just the scrap that was presentable. I have a wonderful memory for details like that. The pages I want were discoloured, but they were sound. Sunshine or a chloride of lime bath will restore them to condition. If I get this *Virginiola* I shall run down to Bristol to-morrow."

"I congratulate you," said Carrados. "Unless, of course, your Bristol friend runs up to London today!" Mr. Marrable started rather violently. Then he shook his head with a knowing look.

"No; he won't do that. He is only a little backstreet huckster. True, if he found out that a *Virginiola* short of the pages he possesses was being sold he might have written to a London dealer, but he won't find out. For some reason they have overlooked the defect in cataloguing. Of course every expert will spot the omission at once, as I did this morning, and the book will be sold as faulty, but if my Bristol friend, as you call him, did happen to see a catalogue there would be nothing to suggest any profitable opening to him."

"Splendid," admitted the blind man. "What would a perfect *Virginiola* be worth?"

"Auction price? Oh, about five hundred guineas."

"And today's copy?"

"Ah, that's more difficult ground. You see, every perfect copy is alike, but every imperfect copy is different. Well, say anything from a hundred and fifty to three hundred, according to who wants it. I shall be very content to take it halfway."

"Two hundred and twenty-five? Yes, I suppose so.

Five hundred, less two twenty-five plus one leaves two hundred and seventy-four guineas to the good. You shall certainly pay for the taxi!"

"Oh, I don't mind standing the taxi," declared Mr Marrable magniloquently; "but don't pin me down to five hundred—that's the auction price. I should want a trifle above—if I decided to let the book go out of my own library, that is to say. Probably I should keep it. Well, here we are."

The cab had drawn to the kerb opposite the door of Messrs Gurnard's unpretentious frontage. Mr Marrable piloted his friend into the sale-room and to a vacant chair by the wall, and then went off to watch the fray at closer quarters. Carrados heard the smooth-tongued auctioneer referring to an item as No. 142, and for the next fifty lots he followed the strangely unexciting progress of the sale with his own peculiar speculative interest.

"Lot 191," announced the easy, untiring voice. "*An Account of the Newly Discovered Islands, etc.*" At last the atmosphere pulsed to a faint thrill of expectation. "Unfortunately we had not the book before us when the catalogue was drawn up. Lot 191 is imperfect and is sold not subject to return; a very desirable volume all the same. What may I say for Lot 191, please? *An Account, etc.*, in original leather, faulty, and not subject to return."

As Mr Marrable had indicated, the defective *Virginiola* occupied a rather special position. Did anyone else want it? was in several minds; and if so, how much did he want it? Everyone waited until at last the question seemed to fine down into: Did anyone want it?

"May I say two hundred guineas?" suggested the auctioneer persuasively.

A large, heavy-faced man, who might have been a cattle-dealer from the North by every indication that his appearance gave, opened the bidding. He, at any rate, could have dissipated the uncertainty and saved the room the waiting. Holding, as he did, two commissions, he was bound to make the price a point above the lower of the orders.

"A hundred and twenty-one pounds."

"Guineas," came back like a slap from across the tables.

"A hundred and twenty-eight pounds."

"Guineas."

"A hundred and thirty-five."

"Guineas."

"A hundred and fifty."

"Guineas."

The duel began to resemble the efforts of some unwieldy pachyderm to shake off the attack of a nimble carnivore by fruitless twists and plunges. But now other voices, nods and uplifted eyebrows joined in, complicating a direct issue, and the forked arithmetic played in among pounds and guineas with bewildering iteration. Then, as suddenly as it had grown, the fusillade shrivelled away, leaving the two original antagonists like two doughty champions emerging from a melee.

"Two hundred and thirty."

"Guineas."

"Two hundred and fifty."

"Guineas."

"Two hundred and seventy."

There was no response. The large man in the heavy ulster and pot-hat was to survive the attack after all, apparently: the elephant to outlast the jaguar.

"Two hundred and seventy pounds?" The auctioneer swept a comprehensive inquiry at every participant in the fray and raised his hammer., "It's against you, sir. No advance? At two hundred and seventy pounds ... ?"

The hammer began to fall. A score of pencils wrote

"£270" against Lot 191.

"And eighty!"

The voice of the new bidder cut in crisp and businesslike. Without ostentation it conveyed the cheerful message: "Now we are just beginning. I feel uncommonly fit." It caught the hammer in mid-air and arrested it. It made the large man feel tired and discouraged. He pushed back his hat, shook his head slowly, with his eyes fixed on his catalogue, and remained in stolid meditation. Carrados smiled inwardly at the restraint and strategy of his friend.

"Two hundred and eighty. Thank you, sir. Two hundred and eighty pounds . . . ?" He knew by intuition that the price was final and the hammer fell decisively. "Mr. Marrable. . . . Lot 192, *History and Antiquities of the County, etc.* Put it in the bidding, please. One pound . . . ?"

After the sale Mr Marrable came round to Carrados's chair in very good spirits. Certainly he had had to give a not insignificant price for the *Virginiola*, but the attendant circumstances had elated him. Then he had secured the greater part of the other lots he wanted, and at quite moderate valuations.

"I've paid my cheque and got my delivery note," he explained. "I shall send my men round for the books when I get back. What do you think of the business?"

"Vastly entertaining," replied Carrados. "I have enjoyed myself thoroughly."

"Oh, well . . . But they were out for the *Virginiola*, weren't they?"

"Yes," admitted Carrados. "I feel that it is my turn to stand a taxi. Can I drop you?"

Mr Marrable assented graciously and they set out again.

"Look here," said that gentleman as they approached his door, "I think that I can put my hand on the Rimini cameo I told you about, if you don't mind coming up again. Do you care to, now that you are here?"

"Certainly," replied Carrados. "I should like to handle it."

"May as well turn off the taxi then. There is a stand quite near."

The cameo proved interesting and led to the display of one or two other articles of *bijouterie*. The host rang for tea and easily prevailed on Carrados—who could be entertained by anyone except the rare individual who had no special knowledge on any subject whatever—to remain. Thus it came about that the blind man was still there when the servant arrived with the books.

"I say, Carrados," called out Mr Marrable. He had crossed the room to speak with his man, who had come up immediately on his return. The servant continued to explain, and it was evident that something annoying had happened. "Here's a devilish fine thing," continued Mr Marrable, dividing his attention between the two. "Felix has just been to Gurnard's and they tell him that the *Virginiola* cannot be found!"

"'Mislaid for the moment,' the gentleman said," amplified Felix.

"They send me back my cheque pending the book's recovery, but did you ever hear of such a thing? I was going down to Bristol by an early train tomorrow. Now I don't know what the deuce to do."

"Why not go back and find out what has really happened?" suggested Carrados. "They will tell you more than they would tell your man. If the book is stolen you may as well put off your journey. If it is mislaid—taken off by someone else in mistake, I expect they mean—it may be on its way back by now."

"Yes; I suppose I'd better go. You've had enough of it, I suppose?"

"On the contrary I was going to ask you to let me accompany you. It may be getting interesting."

"I hope not," retorted Marrable. "Come if you can spare the time, but the very tamest ending will suit me the best."

Felix had called up another cab by the time they reached the door, and for the second time that afternoon they spun through the West End streets with the auction rooms for their destination.

"Your turn to pay again, I think," proposed Carrados when they arrived. "You take the odd numbers and I'll take the even!"

Inside, most of the staff were obviously distracted by the strain of the untoward event and it was very evident that barbed words had been on the wing. In the private office to which Mr Marrable's card gained them immediate admittance they found all those actually concerned in the loss engaged in saying the same things over to each other for the hundredth time.

"The book isn't on the shelves now and there's the number in the delivery note; that's all I know about it," a sale-room porter was reiterating with the air of an extremely reasonable martyr.

"Yes, yes," admitted the auctioneer who had conducted the sale, "no one Oh, I'm glad you are here, Mr Marrable. You've heard of our—er—eh—"

"My man came back with something about the book —the *Virginiola*—being mislaid," replied Mr Marrable.

"That is all I know so far."

"Well, it's very regrettable, of course, and we must ask your indulgence; but what has happened is simple enough and I hope it isn't serious."

"What concerns me," interposed Mr Marrable, "is merely this: Am I to have the book, and when?"

"We hope to deliver it into your hands—well, in a very short time. As I was saying, what has happened is this: Another purchaser bought certain lots. Among them was Lot 91. My sale clerk, in the stress of his duties, inadvertently filled in the delivery note as Lot 191." A gesture of despairing protest from the unfortunate young man referred to passed unheeded.

"Consequently, as this gentleman took away his purchases at the end of the sale, he carried off the *Virginiola* among them. When he comes to look into the parcel he will at once discover the substitution and—er—of course return the volume."

"I see," assented Mr Marrable. "That seems straightforward enough, but the delay is unfortunate for me. Have you sent after the purchaser, by the way?"

"We haven't sent after the purchaser because he happens to live in Derbyshire," was the reply. "Here is his card. We are writing at once, but the probability is that he is staying in London overnight at least."

"You might wire."

"We will, of course, wire if you ask us to do so, Mr Marrable, but it seems to indicate an attitude of distrust towards Mr—er—Mr Dillworthy of Cullington Grange that I see no reason to entertain."

"Assuming the whole incident to be accidental, I think you are doing quite right. But in order to save time mayn't it perhaps be worth while anticipating that something else may have been at work?" They all looked at Mr Carrados, who advanced this suggestion diffidently. The young man in the background breathed an involuntary "Ah!" of agreement and came a little more to the front.

"Do you suggest that Mr Dillworthy of Cullington Grange would actually deny possession of the book?" inquired the auctioneer a little cuttingly.

"Pardon me," replied Carrados blandly, "but do you know Mr Dillworthy of Cullington Grange?"

"No, certainly, I—"

"Nor, of course, the purchaser of Lot 91? That naturally follows. Then for the purpose of our hypothesis I would suggest that we eliminate Mr Dillworthy, who quite reasonably may not have been within a hundred miles of Charing Cross today. What remains? His visiting-card, that would cost about a crown at the outside to reproduce, or might much more cheaply be picked up from a hundred halls or office tables."

The auctioneer smiled.

"An elaborate plant, eh? Have you any practical knowledge, sir, of the difficulty, the impossibility, that would attend the disposal of this imperfect copy the moment our loss is notified?"

"But suppose it should become a perfect copy in the meantime? That might throw dust in their eyes. Eh, Marrable?"

"I say!" exclaimed the *virtuoso*, with his ideas forcibly directed into a new channel. "Yes, there is that, you know, Mr Trenchard."

"Even in that very unlikely event the *Virginiola* remains a white elephant. It cannot be got off to-day nor yet tomorrow. Any bookseller would require time in which to collate the volume; it dare not be offered by auction. It is like a Gainsborough or a Leonardo illegally come by—so much unprofitable lumber after it is stolen."

"Then," hazarded Carrados, "there is the alternative, which might suggest itself to a really intelligent artist, of selling it before it is stolen." The conditions were getting a little beyond Mr Trenchard's easy access. "Sell it before it is stolen?" he repeated. "Why?"

"Because of the extreme difficulty, as you have proved, of selling it after."

"But how, I mean?"

"I think," interposed a quiet voice from the doorway, "that we had better accept Mr Carrados's advice, if he does us the great service of offering it, without discussion, Leonard. I have the pleasure of speaking to Mr Max Carrados, have I not?" continued a white-haired old gentleman, advancing into the room. "My young friend Trenchard, in his jealousy for the firm's reputation, starts with the conviction that it is impossible for us to be victimised. You and I know better, Mr Carrados. Now will you tell me—I am Mr Ing, by the way—will you tell me what has really happened?"

"I wish I could," admitted Carrados frankly. "Unfortunately I know less of the circumstances than you do, and although I was certainly present during a part of the sale, I never even 'saw' the book"—he spread out the fingers of a hand to illustrate—"and probably I was not within several yards of it or its present holder."

"But you have some idea of the method adopted—some theory," persisted Mr Ing. "You can tell us what to do."

"Even there I can only put two and two together and suggest investigation on commonsense lines."

"It is necessary to go to an expert even for that sometimes," submitted the old gentleman with a very comical look. "Now, Mr Carrados, pray enlighten us."

"May I put a few questions then?"

"By all means."

"Do you require me, sir?" inquired Mr Trenchard distantly.

"Not if you will kindly leave the sale-book and papers, I think, thank you," replied Carrados. "This young gentleman, though." The sale clerk came forward eagerly. "You have the delivery note there? No, I don't want it. This gentleman, whom we will refer to as Mr Dillworthy—91 is the first thing he bought?"

"Yes, sir."

"The price?"

"Three pounds fifteen."

"Is that a good price or a bargain?"

The clerk looked towards Mr Ing.

"It's Coulthorp's *Marvellous Recoveries*, sir; the edition of 1674," he explained.

"A fair price," commented the old gentleman. "Yes, quite a good auction figure."

"The *Virginiola* is folio, I believe. What size is *Marvellous Recoveries*?"

"It is folio also."

"What was the next lot that Dr Dillworthy bought?"

"Lot 198."

"Any others?"

"Yes, sir. Lots 211, 217 and 234."

"And the prices of these four lots?"

"Lot 198, a guinea; 211, twelve-and-six; 217, fifteen shillings; 234, twenty-three shillings."

"Those must be very low prices?"

"They are books in no great demand. At every sale from mixed sources there are a certain number of make-weight lots."

"We find, then, that Mr Dillworthy bought 91 at a good price. After that he did nothing until 191 had passed. Then he at once secured four lots of cheap books. This gives a certain colour to suspicion, but it may be pure coincidence. Now," he continued, addressing himself to the clerk again, "after the delivery slip had been made out, did Mr Dillworthy borrow a pen from you?"

The youth's ingenuous face suddenly flashed to a recollection.

"Suffering Moses!" he exclaimed irrepressibly.

"Well—"

"Then he did?" demanded Mr Ing, too keenly interested to stop to reprove the manner.

"Not exactly, sir. He didn't borrow a pen, but I lent him one."

"Ah!" remarked Carrados, "that sounds even better. How did it come about?"

"His bill was six pounds twelve and six. He gave me seven pounds and I made out the delivery form and gave it to him with the change. Then he said: 'Could you do with a fiver instead of five ones, by the way? I may run short of change,' and he held out a banknote. 'Certainly, if you will kindly write your name and address on the back,' I replied, and I gave him a pen."

"The one you had been using?"

"Yes; it was in my hand. He turned away and I thought that he was doing what I asked, but before he would have had time to do that he handed me the pen back and said: 'Thanks; after all, I'll leave it as it is.'"

"Who sent in the book for sale?"

"Described as 'the property of a gentleman,'" contributed Mr Marrable. "I wondered."

"If you will excuse me for a moment," said Mr Ing, "I will find out."

He returned from another office smiling amiably but shaking his head.

"'The property of a gentleman,'" he repeated with senile deliberateness. "I find that the owner expressed a definite wish for the transaction to be treated confidentially. It is no unusual thing for a client to desire that. On certain points of etiquette, Mr Carrados, I am just as jealous for the firm as Trenchard could be, so that until we can obtain consent I am afraid that the gentleman must remain anonymous."

"The question is," volunteered Mr Marrable, "where has the volume got to, rather than where has it come from?"

"Sometimes," remarked the blind man, "after looking in many unlikely places one finds the key in the lock itself. At all events we seem to have come to the end of our usefulness here. Unless one of your people happens to come forward with a real clue, Mr Ing, I venture to predict that you will find more profit in investigating farther afield."

"But what are we to do?" exclaimed the old gentleman rather blankly, when he saw that Carrados was preparing to go. "We are absolute babes at this sort of thing—at least I know that I am."

"The remedy for that is quite simple. Put the case into the hands of the police."

"True, true; but it is not so absolutely simple to us. We have various interests and, yes, let us say, old-fashioned prejudices to consider. I suppose"—he became quite touchingly wistful—"I suppose that you could not be persuaded, Mr Carrados?"

"I'm afraid not," replied Carrados. "I have other irons in the fire just now. But before you do call in the police, by the way, there is Mr Trenchard's view to be considered."

"You mean?"

"I mean that it would be as well to make sure that the *Virginiola* has been stolen."

"By wiring to Cullington Grange?"

"Assuming that there is a Cullington Grange. Then there is a harmless experiment in collateral proof that you might like to make in the meantime if the reply is delayed, as it reasonably may be through a dozen causes."

"And what is that, Mr Carrados?"

"Send up Charing Cross Road and find out among the second-hand shops whether the other books Mr Dillworthy took away with him were sold there immediately after the sale. They were only bought to round off the operation. They would be a dangerous incubus to keep, but if our man is a cool hand he may contrive to realise a pound or so for them before anything is known. You might even learn something else in the process."

"Aye, aye, to be sure," acquiesced Mr Ing. "We'll do that at once. And then, Mr Carrados, just a parting hint. If you were taking up the case what would you do then?"

The temptation to be oracular was irresistible. Carrados smiled inwardly.

"I should try to find a tall, short-sighted, Welsh book-dealer who smokes perique tobacco, suffers from a weak chest, wears thick-soled boots and always carries an umbrella," he replied with impressive gravity. Mr Ing, the saleroom porter, the young clerk and Mr Marrable all looked at each other and then began to repeat the varied attributes of the required individual.

"There's that—what's his name?—old chap with a red waistcoat who's always here," hopefully suggested the porter in an aside. "He wears specs, and I've never seen him without an umbrella."

"He's a Scotchman and stands about five feet three, fathead!" whispered the clerk. "Isn't Mr Powis Welsh, sir?"

"To be sure. Powis of Redmayne Street is the man," assented Mr Ing. "Isn't that correct, Mr Carrados?"

"I don't know," replied Carrados, "but if he answers to the description it probably is."

"And then?"

"Then I think I should call and encourage him to talk to me—about Shakespeare."

"Why, dash it, Carrados," cried Mr Marrable, "you said that you knew nothing of book-collecting and yet you seem to be aware that Powis specialises Shakespeariana and to know that the *Virginiola* would interest him. I wonder how much you have been getting at me!"

"Oh, I suppose that I'm beginning to pick up a thing or two," admitted the blind man diffidently.

In the course of his experience of crime, fragments of many mysteries had been brought to Carrados's notice —detached chapters of chequered human lives to which the opening and the finis had never been supplied. Some had fascinated him and yet remained impenetrable to the end, yet the theft of the *Virginiola*, a mere coup of cool effrontery in which he felt no great interest after he had pierced the method, was destined to unfold itself before his mind without an effort on his part.

The sale at Gurnard's had taken place on a Wednesday. Friday brought Carrados a reminder of the stone that he had set rolling in the appearance of a visiting-card bearing the name and address of Mr Powis of Redmayne Street. Mr Powis was shown in and proved to be a tall, mild-looking man with a chronic cough. He carried a moderate parcel in one hand and, despite the bright, settled condition of the weather, an umbrella in the other.

"I'm an antiquarian bookseller, Mr Carrados," he remarked by way of introduction. "I haven't the honour of your custom that I know of, but I dare say you can guess what brings me here."

"You might tell me," replied Carrados.

"Oh yes, Mr Carrados, I will tell you. Certainly I will tell you," retorted Mr Powis, in a rather louder voice than was absolutely necessary. "Mr Ing looked in at my place of pizzness yesterday. He said that he was 'just passing'—'just passing,' you understand."

Mr Powis emphasised the futility of the subterfuge by laughing sardonically.

"A charming old gentleman," remarked Carrados pleasantly. "I don't suppose that he would deceive a rabbit."

"I don't suppose that he could," asserted Mr Powis. "'By the way,' he said, 'did you see the *Virginiola* we sold yesterday?' 'By the way!' Yes, that was it."

Carrados nodded his smiling appreciation.

"'Oh-ho,' I thought, 'the *Virginiola!*' 'Yes, Mr Ing,' I said, 'it was a nice copy parring the defect, but a week ago I could have shown you a nicer and a perfect one to poot.'

"'You've got one too, have you?' he asked.

"'Certainly I have,' I replied, 'or I should not say so. At least I had, but it may be sold now. It has gone to a gentleman in Rutland.'

"'Rutland; that's a little place,' he remarked thoughtfully. 'Have you any objection to mentioning your customer's name?'

"'Not in the least, Mr Ing,' I told him. 'Why should I have? It has taken me five and twenty years to make my connection, but let all the trade have it. Sir Roland Chargrave of Densmore Hall is the gentleman.'

"Now, look you, Mr Carrados, I could see by the way Mr Ing gasped when I told him that things are not all right. It seems to be your doing that I am brought into it and I want to know where I stand."

"Have you any misgivings as to where you stand?" inquired Carrados.

"No, Mr Carrados, I have not," exclaimed the visitor indignantly. "I pought my *Virginiola* three or four weeks ago and I paid a goot price for it."

"Then you certainly have nothing to trouble about."

"Put I have a goot deal to trouble about," vociferated Mr Powis. "I have a copy of the *Virginiola* to dispose of—"

"Oh, you still have it, then?"

"Yes, Mr Carrados, I have. Thanks to what is peing said pehind my pack, the pook was returned to me this morning. My name has been connected with a stolen copy and puyers are very shy, look you, when they hear that. And word, it travels; oh yes. You may not know how, but today they will be saying in Wales: 'Have you heard what is peing said of Mr Powis of London?' And tomorrow in Scotland it will be: 'That old tamn rascal Powis has been caught at last!'"

In spite of Mr Powis's desperate seriousness Carrados could not restrain a laugh at the forcefulness of the recital. "Come, come, Mr Powis," he said soothingly, "it isn't as bad as that, you know. In any case you have only to display your receipt."

"Oh, very goot, very goot indeed!" retorted the Welshman in an extremity of satire. "Show a buyer my receipt! Excellent! That would be a capital way to carry on the antiquarian pook pizzness! Besides," he added, rather lamely, "in this case it happens that I do not possess a receipt."

"Isn't that—rather an oversight?" suggested Carrados.

"No doubt I could easily procure one. Let me tell you the circumstances, Mr Carrados. I only want to convince you that I have nothing to conceal."

With this laudable intention Mr Powis's attitude became more and more amiable and his manner much less Welsh. He had, in fact, used up all the indignation that he had generated in anticipation of a wordy conflict—a species of protective mimicry common to mild-tempered men.

"I bought this book from the Rev. Mr Winch, the vicar of Fordridge, in Leicestershire. A few weeks ago I received a registered parcel from Fordridge containing a fine copy of the *Virginiola*. The same post brought me a letter from Mr Winch. I dare say I have it here. . . . No, never mind; it was to the effect that the book had been in the writer's family for many generations. Being something of a collector, he had never wished to sell it, but an unexpected misfortune now obliged him to raise a sum of money. He had contracted blood-poisoning in his hand and he had to come up to London for an operation. After that he would have to take a long sea voyage. He went on to say that he had heard of me as a likely buyer and would call on me in a day or two. In the meantime he sent the book to give me full opportunity of examining it.

"Nothing could be more straightforward, Mr Carrados. Two days later Mr Winch walked into my place. We discussed the price, and finally we agreed upon—well, a certain figure."

"You can rely upon my discretion, Mr Powis."

"I paid him £260."

"That would be a fair price in the circumstances?"

"I thought so, Mr Carrados. I don't say that it wasn't a bargain, but it wasn't an outrageous bargain."

"You have occasionally done better?" smiled Carrados.

"Frequently. If I buy a book for threepence and sell it again for a shilling I do better, although it doesn't sound so well. Of course I am a dealer and I have to live on my profits and to pay for my bad bargains with my good bargains. Now if I had had an immediate customer in view the book might have been worth a good deal more to me. I may say that Wednesday's price at Gurnard's surprised me. Prices have certainly been going up, but only five years ago it would have required a practically perfect copy to make that."

"At all events, Mr Winch accepted?"

"I think I may say that he was perfectly satisfied," amended Mr Powis. "You see, Mr Carrados, he wanted the money at once, and, apart from the uncertainty and expense, he could not have waited for an auction. I was making out a cheque when he reminded me that his right hand was useless and asked me to initial it to 'bearer.' That is why I come to have no receipt."

"Yes," assented Carrados. "Yes, that is it. How was the letter signed?"

"It was typewritten, like the rest of it. You remember that his hand was bad when he wrote."

"True. Did you notice the postmark—was it Fordridge?"

"Yes; you should understand that Mr Winch posted on the book before he left Fordridge for London." It seemed to the visitor that Mr Carrados was rather slow even for a blind man.

"I think I am beginning to grasp the position," said Carrados mildly. "Of course you had no occasion to write to him at Fordridge?"

"Nothing whatever. Besides, he was coming to London almost immediately. If I wrote it was to be to the Fitzalan Hotel, off the Strand. Now here is the book, Mr Carrados. You saw—you examined, that is, the auction *Virginiola*?"

"No, unfortunately I did not."

"I am sorry. You would now have recognised how immeasurably superior my copy is, even apart from the missing pages."

"I can quite believe it." He was turning over the leaves of the book, which Mr Powis had passed to him.

"But this writing on the dedication page?"

"Oh, that," said the dealer carelessly. "Some former owner has written his name there."

"I suppose it constitutes a blot?"

"Why, yes, in a small way it does," admitted Mr Powis. "Had it been 'Wm. Shakespeare,' it would have added a thousand guineas; as it's only 'Wm. Shoelack,' it knocks two or three off."

"Possibly," suggested Carrados, "it was this blemish that decided Sir Roland Chargrave against the book?"

"No, no," insisted Mr Powis. "Someone has hinted something to him. I don't say that you are to blame, Mr Carrados, but a suspicion has been created; it has got about."

"But Sir Roland is the one man whom it could not affect," pointed out Carrados. "He, at any rate, would know that this copy is unimpeachable, because when the other was being stolen this was actually in his hands and had been for—for how long?"

"Five or six days; he kept it for about a week. And that no doubt is true as a specific case; but a malicious rumour is wide, Mr Carrados. So-and-so is unreliable; he deals in questionable property; better be careful. It is enough. No, no; Mr Chatton said nothing about any objection to the book, merely that Sir Roland had decided not to retain it."

"Mr Chatton?"

"He is the secretary or the librarian there. I have frequently done business with him in the old baronet's time. This man is a nephew who succeeded only a few months ago. Well, Mr Carrados, I hope I have convinced you that I came by this *Virginiola* in a legitimate manner?"

"Scarcely that."

"I haven't!" exclaimed Mr Powis in blank astonishment.

"I never doubted it. At the sale I happened to hear you remark to a friend that you had recently bought a copy. My suggestion to Mr Ing was merely to hint that, with your exceptional knowledge, your unique experience, you would probably be able to put them on the right line as to the disposal of the stolen copy and so on. An unfortunate misunderstanding."

Mr Powis stared and then nodded several times with an expression of acute resignation.

"That old man is past work," he remarked feelingly. "I might have saved myself a journey. Well, I'll go now, Mr Carrados."

"Not yet," declared Carrados hospitably; "I am going to persuade you to stay and lunch with me, Mr Powis. I want"—he was still fingering the early pages of the *Virginiola* with curious persistence—"I want you to explain to me the way in which these interesting old books were bound."

With the departure of Mr Powis a few hours later Carrados might reasonably conclude that he had heard the last of the *Virginiola* theft, for he was now satisfied that it would never reach publicity as a police court case. But, willy-nilly, the thing pursued him. Mr Carlyle was to have dined with him one evening in the following week. It was a definite engagement, but during the day the inquiry agent telephoned his friend to know what he should do. A young gentleman who had been giving him some assistance in a case was thrown on his hands for the evening.

"You are the most amiable of men, Max," chirruped Mr Carlyle; "but, really, I don't like to ask—"

"Bring him by all means," assented the most amiable of men. "I expect two or three others to turn up tonight." So Mr Carlyle brought him.

"Mr Chatton, Max."

An unobtrusive young man, whose face wore a perpetual expression of docile willingness, shook hands with Carrados. Anything less like the sleek, competent self-assurance of the conventional private secretary it would be difficult to imagine. Mr Chatton's manner was that of a well-meaning man who habitually blundered from a too conscientious sense of duty, knew it all along, and was pained at the inevitableness of the recurring catastrophe.

"I have just taken up a case that might interest you, Max," said Mr Carlyle, as the three of them stood together. "Simple enough, but it involves a valuable old book that has been stolen. Gurnard's called me in"—and he proceeded to outline the particulars of the missing *Virginiola*.

"And you went down yourself to Gurnard's to look into it, Mr Chatton?" said Carrados, masking the species of admiration that he felt for his new acquaintance.

"Well, I don't know about looking into it," confessed Mr Chatton. "You see, it doesn't really concern Sir Roland at all now. But I thought that I ought to offer them any information—a description or something of that sort might be wanted—when I heard of their loss. Of course," he added, with a deepening of his habitual look of rueful perturbation, "we can't help it, but it's very distressing to think of them losing so much money over our affair."

"Not a bit of it, not a bit of it," cried Mr Carlyle heartily. "It's all in the way of business and Gurnard's won't feel a touch like that. Very good of you to take all the trouble you have, I say." He turned his beaming, self-confident eye towards his host to explain. "I happened to meet Mr Chatton there this morning and ever since he has been helping me to put about inquiries in likely quarters and so on. I haven't any doubt of pulling our man up in a week or two, unless it's the work of a secret bibliomaniac, and Gurnard's don't entertain that."

"Wednesday last, you say," pondered Carrados.

"Aren't they rather late in turning it over to you?"

"Just what I complained of. Then it came out that they had been pinning their faith to the advice of some officious idiot who happened to be present at the sale. Nothing came of it, of course."

"They did not happen to mention the idiot's name?" inquired Max tentatively.

"No. The old gentleman—Mr Ing—said that he had already got into hot water once through doing that." Mr Carlyle began to laugh in his hearty way over a recollection of the incident. "Do you know what this genius's brilliant idea was? He put them on the track of a copy of this book that had been recently sold to a dealer, assuming that it must necessarily be the stolen copy. And so it had been recently sold, Max, but it happened to be before the other was stolen!"

"Very amusing," agreed Carrados.

"Do you know, I can't help thinking that I was somehow to blame for that," confessed Mr Chatton in a troubled voice. "You remember, I told you—"

"No, no," protested Mr Carlyle encouragingly.

"How could it be your fault?"

"Well, it's very good of you to reassure me," continued the young man, relieved but not convinced. "But I really think I may have introduced a confusing element. I should like Mr Carrados to judge. . . . When I learned from Sir Roland that he intended sending this *Virginiola* to Gurnard's, knowing that it was a valuable book, I saw the necessity of going over it carefully with another copy—'collating' it is called—to find out whether anything was missing. The British Museum doesn't possess an example, and in any case I could not well spare a day just then to come to London for the purpose. So I wrote to a few dealers, rather, I am afraid, giving them the impression that we wished to buy a copy. In this way I got what I wanted sent up on approval and I was able to go through the two thoroughly. At the moment I argued that my duty to my employer justified the subterfuge, but I don't know, I don't know; I really question whether it was quite legitimate."

"Oh, nonsense," remonstrated Mr Carlyle, to whom the subtleties did not appeal. "Rather a smart way of getting what you wanted in the circumstances, don't you think, Max?"

Carrados paid a willing if equivocal tribute to the wider problem of Mr Chatton's brooding conscientiousness.

"Very ingenious altogether," he admitted.

★★★★★★

Mr. Carlyle did not pull his man up in a few weeks; in fact he never reached him at all. For the key to the disappearance of the *Virginiola* he had to wait two years. He was at The Turrets one day when his host was called away for a short time to see a man who had come on business.

Carlyle had picked up a newspaper, when Carrados came back from the door and opening one of the inner drawers of his desk threw out a long envelope.

"There," he remarked as he went on again, "is something that may interest you more."

He was quite right. The inquiry agent cut open the envelope that was addressed to himself and read the following narrative:—

In the year 1609 a seafaring gentleman called Somers—Sir George Somers—was wrecked on an island in the Atlantic. This island—one of a group—although destitute of human inhabitants, was overrun by pigs. During the first part of their enforced residence there the ship-wrecked mariners were much concerned by unearthly shrieks and wailings that filled the night. With the simple piety of the time these were attributed to the activity of witches, imps and demons. In fact, in addition to the varied appellations of *Virginiola*, Bermoothes, Somers Islands, etc., the place was enticingly called "The Ile of Divels."

In due course the castaways were rescued and returned to England. In due course, also, there appeared a variety of printed accounts of their adventures. (We are prone to think that the tendency is modern, Louis, but it is not.) One of these coming into the hands of a cynical, middle-aged playwright on the look-out for a new plot to annex, was at once pressed into his scheme. Doubtless he saw behind the shadowy "divels" the substantial outlines of the noisy "hogges." However, the idea was good enough for a background. He wrote his play and called it *The Tempest*. This is the explanation offered to me of the high and increasing value of rare early works on Bermuda. They can be classed among the Shakespeariana. There is also another reason: they can be classed among the Americana.

About three hundred years later a certain young gentleman who combined fairly expensive tastes with good commercial ability suc-ceeded to a title and its appendages. Among the latter were a mansion in Rutlandshire, which he determined was too expensive, a library in which he was not vastly interested, and a private secretary whose services he continued to retain. One day about six months after his succession Sir Roland Chargrave called in his secretary to receive instructions.

"Look here, Chatton," he said, "I have decided to let this place furnished for a time. See Turvey about the value and then advertise it for something more than he advises. It ought to bring in a decent rental. Then there are some valuable things here that are no earthly good to me. I'll start with the library."

"You intend to dispose of the library, Sir Roland?" faltered the secretary.

"No. The library gives a certain distinction to a fellow and the Chargraves have always had one. I'll keep the library, but I'll weed out all the old stuff that will make high prices. Uncle Vernon left a valuation list which appears to have been made out about ten years ago. One book alone—*An Account of Virginiola*—he puts down at £300. Then there are a dozen others that ought to bring another £200 among them. I require £500 just now. Here is a list of the books I have picked out. Send them off to Gurnard's to be sold as soon as possible. Don't have my name catalogued. I don't want it to be known that I'm selling anything. That's all."

The secretary withdrew with an accentuation of his unhappy manner. It was very distressing to him, this dispersal of the family heirlooms. It was also extremely inconvenient personally, because he had already sold the *Virginiola* himself only a week before. For he also had expenses. Perhaps he had fallen into the hands of the Jews; perhaps it was the Jewesses. At all events, like Sir Roland, he required money, and again like Sir Roland, the *Virginiola* had seemed the most suitable method. He had quietly withdrawn the book about the time of his former master's death, and thus saved the new baronet quite an item in duty. He had secured Sir Vernon's valuation list and after six months had concluded that he was safe. He had taken extraordinary pains to cover his identity in selling the book and the old dotard appeared to have made two lists and to have deposited one elsewhere!

Like a wise man Mr Chatton set about discovering how he could retrieve himself. He had had charge of the library and he knew that it was too late to report the book as lost. In any case he would be dismissed; if inquiry was made at that stage he would be prosecuted. From the depths of his brooding melancholy Mr Chatton evolved a scheme.

The first thing was to get back the *Virginiola* a little before the sale. By that time he had sent in the list, but not the books. Doubtless he still had some of the illicit funds in hand. Now the *Virginiola* had been valued at £300 by old Sir Vernon, but if at the sale it was discovered to be imperfect in an important detail then it might realise only a fraction of that sum. There was also another consideration. A name had been indelibly written on one of the early pages, and if Mr Powis was not to recognise his property that page must be temporarily removed.

I think it was Chatton's undoubted intention to buy back the book if possible and run no further risk with it. What he had not taken into account was the enormous rise in the value of this class of work. What had been reasonably worth £300 ten years before, the market now apprised at nearly double. Even the imperfect copy reached nearly the original estimate and thereby Chatton's first string failed.

But this painstakingly conscientious young man had not been content to risk all on a single chance. What form his second venture took it will be unnecessary to recall to you. He calculated on the chances of the saleroom, and he succeeded. The *Virginiola* was recovered; the abstracted sheet was cunningly replaced, probably certain erasable marks that had been put in for fuller disguise were removed, and Mr Powis received back his property with formal regrets.

I anticipate an indignant question rising to your lips. I did not tell you this before, Louis, because of one curious fact. The story is entirely speculative on my part so far as demonstrable proof is concerned. Chatton, who is rather a remarkable young man, did not leave behind him one solitary shred of evidence that would stand before a jury. Time and Mr Chatton's future career can alone bring my justification, but some day if we have the opportunity (I am committing this to paper in case we should not) we will go over the evidence together. In the meanwhile Gurnard's can, as you said, stand the loss.

Here the typewritten account ended, but at the foot of the last page Carrados had pasted a newspaper cutting. From it Mr Carlyle learned that "Vernon Howard, *alias* Digby Skeffington, etc., etc., whose real name was said to be Chatton, well connected," had, the week before, been convicted, chiefly on the king's evidence of a female accomplice, of obtaining valuable jewellery under false pretences. Sentence had been deferred, pending further inquiries.

The Disappearance of Marie Severe

"I wonder if you might happen to be interested in this case of Marie Severe, Mr. Carrados?"

If Carrados's eyes had been in the habit of expressing emotion they would doubtless have twinkled as Inspector Beedel thus casually introduced the subject of the Swanstead on Thames schoolgirl whose inexplicable disappearance two weeks earlier had filled column upon column of every newspaper with excited speculation until the sheer impossibility of keeping the sensation going without a shred of actual fact had relegated Marie Severe to the obscurity of an occasional paragraph.

"If you are concerned with it, I am sure that I shall be interested, Inspector," said the blind man encouragingly. "It is still being followed, then?"

"Why, yes, sir, I have it in hand, but as for following it—well, 'following' is perhaps scarcely the word now."

"Ah," commented Carrados. "There was very little to follow; I remember."

"I don't think that I've ever known a case of the kind with less, sir. For all the trace she left, the girl might have melted out of existence, and from that day to this, with the exception of that printed communication received by her mother—you remember that, Mr. Carrados?—there hasn't been a clue worth wasting so much as shoe leather on."

"You have had plenty of hints all the same, I suppose?"

Inspector Beedel threw out a gesture of mild despair. It conveyed the patient exasperation of the conscientious and long-suffering man.

"I should say that the case 'took on' remarkably, Mr. Carrados. I doubt if there has been a more popular sensation of its kind for years. Mind you, I'm all in favour of publicity in the circumstances the photographs and description may bring important facts to light, but sometimes it's a bit trying for those who have to do the work at our end. 'Seen in Northampton,' 'seen in Ealing,' 'heard of in West Croydon,' 'girl answering to the description observed in the waiting-room at Charing Cross,' 'suspicious-looking man with likely girl noticed about the Victoria Dock, Hull,' 'seen and spoken to near Chorley, Lancs,' 'caught sight of apparently struggling in a luxurious motor car on the Portsmouth Road,' 'believed to have visited a Watford picture palace'—they've all been gone into as carefully as though we believed that each one was the real thing at last."

"And you haven't, eh?"

The Inspector looked round. He knew well enough that they were alone in the study at The Turrets, but the action had become something of a mannerism with him.

"I don't mind admitting to you, sir, that I've never had any other opinion than that the father of the little girl went down that day and got her away. Where she is now, and whether dead or alive, I can't pretend to say, but that he's at the bottom of it I'm firmly convinced. And what's more," he added with slow significance, "I *hope* so."

"Why in particular?" inquired the other.

Beedel felt in his breast—pocket, took out a formidable wallet, and from among its multitudinous contents selected a cabinet photograph sheathed in its protecting envelope of glazed transparent paper.

"If you could make out anything of what this portrait shows, you'd understand better what I mean, Mr. Carrados," he replied delicately.

Carrados shook his head but nevertheless held out his hand for the photograph.

"No good, I'm afraid," he confessed before he took it. "A print of this sort is one of the few things that afford no graduation to the sense of touch. No, no"—as he passed his finger-tips over the paper—"a gelatino-chloride surface of mathematical uniformity, Inspector, and nothing more. Now had it been the negative—"

"I am sure that that could be procured if you wished to have it, Mr. Carrados. Anyway, I dare say that you've seen in some of the papers what this young girl is like. She is ten years old and big—at least tall—for her age. This picture is the last taken—some time this year—and I am told that it is just like her."

"How should you describe it, Inspector?"

"I am not much good at that sort of thing," said the large man with a shy awkwardness, "but it makes as sweet a picture as ever I've seen. She is very straight-set, and yet with a sort of gracefulness such as a young wild animal might have. It's a full-faced position, and she is looking straight out at you with an expression that is partly serious and partly amused, and as noble and gracious with it all as a young princess might be. I have children of my own, Mr. Carrados, and of course I think they're very nice and pretty, but this—this is quite a different thing. Her hair is curly without being in separate curls, and the description calls it black. Eyes dark brown with straight eyebrows, complexion a sort of glowing brown, small regular teeth. Of course we have a full description of what she was wearing and so forth."

"Yes, yes," assented Carrados idly. "The Van Brown Studio, Photographers, eh? These people are quite well off, then?"

"Oh yes; very nice house and good position—Mrs. Severe, that is to say. You will remember that she obtained a divorce from her husband four or five years ago. I've turned up the particulars and it wasn't what you'd call a bad case as things go, but the lady seemed determined, and in the end Severe didn't defend. She had five or six hundred a year of her own, but he had nothing beyond his salary, and he threw his position up then, and ever since he has been going steadily down. He's almost on the last rung now and picks up his living casual."

"What's the case against him?"

"Well, it scarcely amounts to a case as yet because there is no evidence of his being seen with the child, nor is there anything to connect him with her after the disappearance. Still, it is a working hypothesis. If it was the act of a tramp or a maniac, experience goes to show that we should have found her, dead or alive, by now. Mrs. Severe is all for it being her husband. Of course the decree gave her the custody of Marie. Severe asked to be allowed to see her occasionally, and at first a servant took the child to have tea with him once a month. That was at his rooms. Then he asked to be met in one of the parks or at a gallery. He hadn't got so much as a room then, you see, sir. At last the servant reported that he had grown so shabby as to shame her that the child should be seen with him, though she did say that he was always sober and very kind to Marie, bringing her a little toy or something even when he didn't seem to have sixpence for himself.

"After that the visits were stopped altogether. Then about a month ago these two, husband and wife, met accidentally in the street. Severe said that he hoped to be doing a bit better soon, and asked for the visits to be continued. How it would have gone I cannot say, but Mrs.

Severe happened to have a friend with her, an American lady called Miss Julp, who seems to be living with her now, and the middle-aged female—she's a hard sister, that Cornelia Julp, I should say—pushed her way into the conversation and gave her views on his conduct until Severe must have had some trouble with his hands. Finally Mrs. Severe had an unfortunate impulse to end the discussion by giving her husband a banknote. She says she got the most awful look she ever saw on any face. Then Severe very deliberately tore up the note, dropped the pieces down a gutter grid that they were standing near, dusted his fingers on his handkerchief, raised his hat and walked away without another word. That was the last she saw of him, but she professes to have been afraid of something happening ever since."

"Then something happens, and so, of course, it must be Severe?" suggested Carrados.

"It does look a bit like that so far, I must admit, sir," assented the inspector. "Still, Mrs. Severe's opinions aren't quite all. Severe's account of his movements on the afternoon in question—say between twelve-thirty and four in particular—are not satisfactory. Latterly he has been occupying a miserable room off Red Lion Street. He went out at twelve and returned about five—that he doesn't deny. Says he spent the time walking about the streets and in the Holborn news-room, but can mention no one who saw him during those five hours. On the other hand, a porter at Swanstead station identifies him as a passenger who alighted there from the 1.17 that afternoon."

"From a newspaper likeness?"

"In the first instance, Mr. Carrados. Afterwards in person."

"Did they speak, or is it merely visual?"

"Only from what he saw of him."

"Struck, I suppose, by the remarkable fact that the passenger wore a hat and a tie—as shown in the picture, or inspired to notice him closely by something indescribably suggestive in the passenger's way of giving up his ticket? It may be all right, Beedel, I admit, but I heartily distrust the weight of importance that these casual identifications are being given on vital points nowadays. Are you satisfied with this yourself?"

"Only as corroborative, sir. Until we find the girl or some trace of her we're bound to make casts in the hope of picking up a line. Well, then there's the letter Mrs. Severe received."

"Have you that with you?"

The Inspector took up the wallet that he had not yet returned to his pocket and selected another enclosure.

"It's a very unusual form," he commented as he handed the envelope to Mr. Carrados and waited for his opinion.

The blind man passed his finger-tips across the paper and at once understood the point of singularity. The lines were printed, but not in consecutive form, every letter being on a little separate square of paper. It was evident that they had been cut out from some other sheet and then pasted on the envelope to form the address.

"London, E. C., 5.30 p.m., 15th May," read Carrados from the postmark.

"The day of the kidnapping. There is a train from Swanstead arriving at Lambeth Bridge at 4.47," remarked Beedel.

"What was your porter doing when that left?"

"He was off duty, sir."

Carrados took out the enclosure and read it off as he had already done the envelope, but with a more deliberative touch, for the print was smaller. The type and the paper were suggestive of a newspaper origin. In most cases whole words had been found available.

"Do not be alarmed," ran the patchwork message. "The girl is in good hands. Only risk lies in pressing search. Wait and she will return uninjured."

"You have identified the newspaper?"

"Yes; it is all cut from *The Times* of May the 13th. The printing on the back of the words fixes it absolutely. Premeditated, Mr. Carrados."

"The whole incident points to that. The date of the newspaper means little, but the deliberate selection of words, the careful way they have been cut out and aligned, taken in conjunction with the time the child disappeared and the time that this was posted—yes, I think you may assume premeditation, Inspector."

"Stationery of the commonest description; immediate return to London, and the method of a man who used this print because he feared that under any disguise his handwriting might be recognised."

Carrados nodded.

"Severe cannot hope to retain the child, of course," he remarked casually. "What motive do you infer?"

"Mrs. Severe is convinced that it is to distress her, out of revenge."

"And this letter is to reassure her?"

The Inspector bit his lip as he smiled at the quiet thrust.

"It might also be to influence her towards suspending search," he suggested.

"At all events I dare say that it has reassured her?"

"In a certain way, yes, it has. It has enabled us to establish that the act is not one of casual lust or vagabondage. There is an alternative that we naturally did not suggest to her."

"And that is?"

"Another Thelby Wood case, Mr. Carrados. The maniacal infatuation of someone who would be the last to be suspected. Some man of good position, a friend and neighbour possibly, who sees this beautiful young creature—the schoolfriend of his own daughters or sitting before him in church it may be—and becomes the slave of his diseased imagination until he is prepared to risk everything for that one overpowering object. A primitive man for the time, one may say, or, even worse, a satyr or a gorilla."

"I wonder," observed Carrados thoughtfully, "if you also have ever felt that you would like to drop it and become a monk, Inspector. Or a Stylites on a pole."

Beedel laughed softly and then rubbed his chin in the same contemplative spirit.

"I think I know what you mean, sir," he admitted. "It's a black page. But," he added with wholesome philosophy, "after all, it is only a page in a longish book. And if I was in a monastery there'd be one or two more things done that I've helped to keep undone."

"Including the cracking of my head, Inspector? Very true. We must take the world as we find it and ourselves as we are. And I wish that I could agree with you about Severe. It would be a more endurable outlook: spite and revenge are at least decent human motives. Unfortunately, the only hint I can offer is a negative one." He indicated the printed cuttings on the sheet that Beedel had submitted to him. "This photo-mountant costs about sixpence a pot, but you can buy a bottle of gum for a penny.

"Well, sir," said Beedel, "I did think of having that examined, but I waited for you to see the letter as it stood. After all, it didn't strike me as a point one could put much reliance on."

"Quite right," assented Mr. Carrados, "there is nothing personal or definite in it. It may suggest a photographer, amateur or professional, but it would be preposterous to assume so much from this alone. Severe, even, may have—. There are hundreds of chances. I should disregard it for the moment."

"There is nothing more to be got from the letter?"

"There may be, but it is rather elusive at present. What has been done with it?"

"I received it from Mrs. Severe and it has been in my possession ever since."

"You haven't submitted it to a chemist for any purpose?"

"No, sir. I gave a copy of the wording to some newspaper gentlemen, but no one but myself has handled it."

"Very good. Now if you care to leave it with me for a few days."

Inspector Beedel expressed his immediate willingness and would have added his tribute of obligation for Mr. Carrados's service, but the blind man cut him short.

"Don't rely on anything, Inspector," he warned him. "I am afraid that this resolves itself into a game of chance. Just one touch of luck may give us a winning point, or it may go the other way. In any case there is no reason why I should not motor round by Swanstead one of these days when I am out. If anything fresh turns up before you hear from me you had better telephone me. Now exactly where did this happen?"

The actual facts surrounding the disappearance of Marie Severe constituted the real mystery of the case. Arling Avenue, Swanstead, was one of those leisurely suburban roads where it is impossible to imagine anything happening hurriedly from the delivery of an occasional telegram to the activity of the local builder. Houses, detached houses each surrounded by its rood or more of garden, had been built here and there along its length at one time or another, but even the most modern one had now become matured, and the vacant plots between them had reverted from the condition of "eligible sites" into very passable fields of buttercups and daisies again, so that Arling Avenue remained a pleasant and exclusive thoroughfare.

One side of the road was entirely unbuilt on and afforded the prospect of a level meadow where hay was made and real animals grazed in due season. The inhabitants of Arling Avenue never failed to point out to visitors this evidence of undeniable rurality. It even figured in the prospectus of Homewood, the Arling Avenue day school for girls and little boys which the Misses Chibwell had carried on with equal success and inconspicuousness until the Severe affair suddenly brought them into the glare of a terrifying publicity.

Mrs. Severe's house, The Hollies, was the first in the road, as the road was generally regarded—that is to say, from the direction of the station. Beedel picked up a loose sheet of paper and scored it heav-

238

ily with a plan of the neighbourhood as he explained the position with some minuteness. Next to The Hollies came Arling Lodge. After Arling Lodge there was one of the vacant plots of ground before the next house was reached, but between the Lodge and the vacant plot was a broad grassy opening, unfenced towards the road, and here the inspector's pencil underlined the deepest significance, culminating in an ominous X about the centre of the space. Originally the opening had doubtless marked the projection of another road, but the scheme had come to nothing.

Occasionally a little band of exploring children with the fictitious optimism of youth pecked among its rank and tangled growth in the affectation of hoping to find blackberries there; once in a while a passing chair-mender or travelling tinker regarded it favourably for the scene of his midday siesta, but its only legitimate use seemed to be that of affording access to the side door of Arling Lodge garden. The inspector pencilled in the garden door as an afterthought, with the parenthesis that it was seldom used and always kept locked. Then he followed out the avenue as far as the school, indicating all the houses and other features. The whole distance traversed did not exceed two hundred yards.

A few minutes before two o'clock on the afternoon of her disappearance Marie Severe set out as usual for Miss Chibwell's school. Since the incident of the unfortunate encounter with her former husband Mrs. Severe had considered it necessary to exercise a peculiar vigilance over her only child. Thenceforward Marie never went out alone; never, with the exception of the short walk to school and back, that is to say, for in that quiet straight road, in the full light of day, it was ridiculous to imagine that anything could happen. It was ridiculous, but all the same the vaguely uneasy woman generally walked to the garden gate with the little girl and watched her until the diminished figure passed, with a last gay wave of hand or satchel, out of her sight into the school yard.

"That's how it would have been on this occasion," narrated Beedel, "only just as they got to the garden gate a tradesman whom Mrs. Severe wanted to speak with drove up and passed in by the back way. The lady looked along the avenue, and as it happened at that moment Miss Chibwell was standing in the road by her gate. No one else was in sight, so it isn't to be wondered at that Mrs. Severe went back to the house immediately without another thought.

"That was the last that has been seen of Marie. As a matter of fact,

Miss Chibwell turned back into her garden almost as soon as Mrs. Severe did. When the child did not appear for the afternoon school the mistress thought nothing of it. She is a little short-sighted and although she had seen the two at their gate she concluded that they were going out together somewhere. Consequently it was not until four o'clock, when Marie did not return home, that the alarm was raised."

Continuous narration was not congenial to Inspector Beedel's mental attitude. He made frequent pauses as though to invite cross-examination. Sometimes Carrados ignored the opening, at others he found it more convenient to comply.

"The inference is that someone was waiting in this space just beyond Arling Lodge?" he now contributed.

"I think it is reasonable to assume that, sir. Premeditated, we both admit. Doubtless a favourable opportunity was being looked for and there it was. At all events there"—he tapped the X as the paper lay beneath Carrados's hand—"there is the very last trace that we can rely on."

"The scent, you mean?"

"Yes, Mr. Carrados. We got one of our dogs down the next morning and put him on the trail. We gave him the scent of a boot and from the gate he brought us without a pause to where I have marked this X. There the line ended. There can be no doubt that from that point the girl had been picked up and carried. That is a very remarkable thing. It could scarcely have been done openly past the houses. The fences on all sides are of such a nature that it is incredible for any man to have got an unwilling or insensible burden of that sort over without at least laying it down in the process. If our dog is to be trusted, it wasn't laid down. Some sort of a vehicle remains. We find no recent wheel-marks and no one seems to have seen anything that would answer about at that time.

"You are determined to mystify me, Inspector," smiled Carrados.

"I'm that way myself, sir," said the detective.

"And I know you too well to ask if you have done this and that—"

"I've done everything," admitted Beedel modestly.

"Is this X spot commanded by any of the houses? Here is Arling Lodge There is one window overlooking, but now the trees are too much out for anything to be seen. Besides, it's only a passage window. Dr. Ellerslie took me up there himself to settle the point."

"Ellerslie—Dr. Ellerslie?"

"The gentleman who lives there. At least he doesn't live altogether there, as I understand that he has it for a weekend place. Boating, I believe, sir. His regular practice is in town."

"Harley Street? Prescott Ellerslie, do you know?"

"That is the same, Mr. Carrados."

"Oh, a very well-known man. He has a great reputation as an operator for peritonitis. Nothing less than fifty guineas a time, inspector." Perhaps the fee did not greatly impress Mr. Carrados, but doubtless he judged that it would interest Inspector Beedel. "And this house on the other side—Lyncote?"

"A retired Indian army colonel lives there—Colonel Doige."

"I mean as regards overlooking the spot."

"No; it is quite cut off from there. It cannot be seen."

Carrados's interpreting finger stopped lightly over a detail of the plan that it was again exploring. The inspector's pencil had now added a line of dots leading from The Hollies gate to the X.

"The line the dog took," Beedel explained, following the other's movement. "You notice that the girl turned sharply out of the avenue into this opening at right angles."

"I was just considering that."

"Something took her attention suddenly or someone called her there—I wonder what, Mr. Carrados."

"I wonder," echoed the blind man, raising the anonymous letter to his face again.

Mr. Carrados frequently professed to find inspiration in the surroundings of light and brilliance to which his physical sense was dead, but when he wished to go about his work with everyone else at a notable disadvantage he not unnaturally chose the dark. It was therefore night when, in accordance with his promise to Beedel, he motored round by Swanstead, or, more exactly, it was morning, for the clock in the square ivied tower of the parish church struck two as the car switch-backed over the humped bridge from Middlesex into Surrey.

"This will do, Harris; wait here," he said a little later. He knew that there were trees above and wide open spaces on both sides. The station lay just beyond, and from the station to Arling Avenue was a negligible step. Even at that hour Arling Avenue might have been awake to the intrusion of an alien car of rather noticeable proportions. The adaptable Harris picked out Mr. Carrados's most substantial rug and went to sleep, to dream of a wayside cycle shop and tea-rooms where he could devote himself to pedigree Wyandottes. With Parkinson at his elbow Carrados walked slowly on to Arling Avenue. What was lacking on Beedel's plan Parkinson's eyes supplied; on a subtler plane, in the moist, warm night, full of quiet sounds and earthy odours, other details were filled in like the work of a lightning cartoonist before the blind man's understanding.

They walked the length of the avenue once and then returned to the grassy opening where the last trace of Marie Severe had evaporated.

"I will stay here. You walk on back to the highroad and wait for me. I may be some time. If I want you, you will hear the whistle."

"Very good, sir." Parkinson knew of old that there were times when his master would have no human eye upon him as he went about his work, and with a magnificent stolidity the man had not a particle of curiosity. It did not even occur to him to wonder. But for nearly half-an-hour the more inquiring creatures of the night looked down—or up, according to their natures—to observe the strange attitudes and quiet persistence of the disturber of the solitude as he crossed and re-crossed their little domain, studied its boundaries, and explored every corner of its miniature thickets.

A single petal picked up near the locked door to the garden of Arling Lodge seemed a small return for such perseverance, but it is to be presumed that the patient search had not been in vain, for it was immediately after the discovery that Carrados left the opening, and with the cool effrontery that marked his methods he opened the front gate of Dr. Ellerslie's garden and made his way with slow but unerring insight along the boundary wall.

"A blind man," he had once replied to Mr. Carlyle's nervous remonstrance—"a blind man carries on his face a sufficient excuse for every indiscretion."

It was nearly three o'clock when, by the light of the street lamp at the corner of the avenue and the highroad, Parkinson saw his master approaching. But to the patient and excellent servitor's disappointment Carrados at that moment turned back and retraced his steps in the same leisurely manner. As a matter of fact, a new consideration had occurred to the blind man and he continued to pace up and down the footpath as he considered it.

"Oh, sir!"

He stopped at once, but betraying no surprise, without the start which few can restrain when addressed suddenly in the dark. It was always dark to him, but was it ever sudden? Was he indeed ignorant of the obscure figure that had appeared at the gate during his perambulation?

"I have seen you walking up and down at this hour and I wondered—I wondered whether you had any news."

"Who are you?" he asked.

"I am Mrs. Severe. My little girl Marie disappeared from here two weeks ago. You must surely know about it; everybody does."

"Yes, I know," he admitted. "Inspector Beedel told me."

"Oh, Inspector Beedel!" There was obvious disappointment in her voice. "He is very kind and promises—but nothing comes of it, and the days go on, the days go on," she repeated tragically.

"Ida! Ida!" Someone was calling from one of the upper windows, but Carrados was speaking also and Mrs. Severe merely waved her hand back towards the house without responding.

"Your little girl was very fond of flowers?"

"Oh yes, indeed." The pleasant recollection dwarfed the poor lady's present sense of calamity and for a moment she was quite bright. "She loved them. She would bury her face in a bunch of flowers and drink their scent. She almost lived in the garden. They were more to her than toys or dolls, I am sure. But how do you know?"

"I only guessed."

"Ida! Ida!" The rather insistent, nasally querulous voice was raised again and this time Mrs. Severe replied.

"Yes, dear, immediately," she called back, still lingering, however, to discover whether she had anything to hope from this outlandish visitant.

"Had Marie been ill recently?" Carrados detained her with the question.

"Ill! Oh no." The reply was instant and emphatic. It was almost—if one could credit a mother's pride in her child's health being carried to such a length—it was almost resentful.

"Nothing that required the services of a doctor?"

"Marie never requires the services of a doctor." The tone, distant and constrained, made it clear that Mrs. Severe had given up any expectations in this quarter. "My child, I am glad to say, does not know what illness means," she added deliberately.

"Ida! Oh, here you are." The very unromantically accoutred form of a keen-visaged, middle-aged female, padding heavily in bedroom slippers along the garden walk, gave its quietus to the situation.

"What a scare you gave me, dearie. Why, whoever—"

"Goodnight," said Mrs. Severe, turning from the gate.

Carrados raised his hat and resumed his interrupted stroll. He had not sought the interview and he made no effort to prolong it, for there was little to be got from that source.

"A strange flare of maternal pride," he remarked in his usual detached fashion as he rejoined Parkinson.

About five o'clock on the same day—five o'clock in the afternoon, let it be understood—Inspector Beedel was called to the telephone.

"Oh, nothing fresh so far, Mr. Carrados," he reported when he identified his caller. "I shan't forget to let you know whenever there—"

"But I think that possibly there is," replied Mr. Carrados. "Or at least there might be if you went down to Arling Lodge and insisted on seeing the child who slept there last night."

"Arling Lodge? Dr. Ellerslie's? You don't mean to say, sir—"

"That is for you to satisfy yourself. Dr. Ellerslie is a widower with no children. Marie Severe was drugged by *phronolal* on some flowers which she was given. *Phronolal* is a new anaesthetic which is practically unknown outside medical circles. She was carried into the garden of Arling Lodge and into the house. The bunch of flowers was thrown down temporarily inside the wall, probably while the door was re-locked. The girl's hair caught on a raspberry cane six yards from the back door along the path leading there. Ellerslie had previously sent away the two people who look after the place—a housekeeper and her husband who sees to the garden. That letter, by the way, was associable with *phronolal*. Now you have all that I know, inspector, and I hope to goodness that I am clear of it."

"But, good heavens, Mr. Carrados, this is really terrible!" protested Beedel, moved to emotion in spite of his rich experience of questionable humanity. "A man in his position! Is he a maniac?"

"I don't know. To tell you frankly, inspector, I haven't gone an inch further than I was compelled to go in order to be sure. Make use of the information as you like, but I don't want to have anything more to do with the case. It isn't a pleasant thing to have pulled down a man like Ellerslie—a callous, exacting machine in the operating-room, one hears, but a man who was doing fine work—saving useful lives every day. I'm sick of it, Beedel, that's all."

"I understand, sir. Still, there's the other side, isn't there, after all? Of course I'll keep your name out of it as you wish, but I shall be given a good deal of credit that I oughtn't to accept. If you don't do anything for a few weeks the papers are always more complimentary when you do do it."

"I'm afraid that you will have to put up with that," replied Carrados drily.

There was an acquiescent laugh from the other end and a reference to the speaker's indebtedness. Then: "Well, I'll get the necessary authority and go down at once, sir."

"Yes. Goodbye," said Carrados. He hung up the receiver with the only satisfaction that he had experienced since he had fixed on Ellerslie—satisfaction to have done with it. The thing was unpalatable enough in itself, and to add another element of distaste, through one or two circumstances that had come his way in the past, he had an actual regard for the surgeon whom some called brutal, but who was universally admitted to be splendidly efficient. It would have been a much more congenial business to the blind man to clear him than to implicate. He betook himself to a tray of Sicilian coins of the autonomous period to get the taste out of his mouth and swore that he would not read a word of any stage of the proceedings.

"A Mr. Severe wishes to see you, sir."

So it happened that about an hour after he had definitely shelved his interest in the case Max Carrados was again drawn into its complications. Had Severe been merely a well-to-do suppliant, perhaps . . . but the blind man had enough of the vagabond spirit to ensure his sympathy towards one whom he knew, on the contrary, to be extremely ill-to-do. In a flash of imagination he saw the outcast walking from Red Lion Street to Richmond, and, denied admission, from Richmond back to Red Lion Street again, because he hadn't sixpence to squander, the man who always bought a little toy. . .

"It is nearly seven, isn't it, Parkinson? Mr. Severe will stay and dine with me," were almost the first words the visitor heard.

"Very well, sir."

"I? Dine?" interposed Severe quickly. "No, no. I really—"

"If you will be so good as to keep me company," said Carrados with suave determination. Parkinson retired, knowing that the thing was settled. "I am quite alone, Mr. Severe, and my selfishness takes that form. If a man calls on me about breakfast-time he must stay to breakfast, at lunch-time to lunch, and so on."

"Your friends, doubtless," suggested Severe with latent bitterness.

"Well, I am inclined to describe anyone who will lighten my darkness for an hour as a friend. You would yourself in the circumstances, you know." And then, quite unconsciously, under this treatment the years of degradation slipped from Severe and he found himself accepting the invitation in the conventional phrases and talking to his host just as though they were two men of the same world in the old times. Guessing what had brought him, and knowing that it mattered little or nothing then, Carrados kept his guest clear of the subject of the disappearance until they were alone again after dinner. Then, to be denied no longer, Severe tackled it with a blunt inquiry:

"Scotland Yard has been consulting you about Marie, Mr. Carrados?"

"Surely that is not in the papers?"

"I don't know," replied Severe, "but they aren't my authority. Among the people I have mostly to do with many shrewd bits of information circulate that never get into the Press. Sometimes they are mere headwork, of course, but quite often they have ground. Just at present I am something of a celebrity in my usual haunts—I am 'Jones' in town, by the way, but my identity has come out—and everything to do with the notorious Severe affair comes round to me. I hear that Inspector Beedel, who has the case in hand, has just been to see you. Your co-operation is inferred."

"And if so?" queried Carrados.

"If so," continued his visitor, "I have a word to say. Beedel got it into his thick, unimaginative skull that I must be the kidnapper because, on the orthodox 'motive' lines, he couldn't fix on anyone else. As a matter of fact, Mr. Carrados, I have rather too much affection for my little daughter to have taken her out of a comfortable home. My unfortunate wife may have her faults—I don't mind admitting that she has—serious faults and a great many of them, but she would at least give Marie decent surroundings. When I heard of the child's disappearance—it was in the early evening papers the next morning—I was distracted. I dreaded every edition to see a placard announcing that the body had been found and to read the usual horrible details of insane or bestial outrage. I searched my pockets and found a shilling and a few coppers. Without any clear idea of what I expected to do, I tore off to the station and spent my money on a third single to Swanstead."

"Oh," interposed Carrados, "the 1.17 arrival?"

Severe laughed contemptuously.

"The station porter, you mean?" he said. "Yes; that bright youth merely predated his experience by twenty-four hours when he saw that there was bunce in it a few days later. Oh, I dare say he really thought it then. As for me, before I had got to Swanstead I had realised my mistake. What could I do in any case? Nothing that the least efficient local bobby could not do much better. Least of all did I wish to meet Ida—Mrs. Severe. No I walked out of the station, turned to the right instead of the left and padded back to town."

"And you have come now, a fortnight or more later, to tell me this, Mr. Severe?"

"Well, I have come to have small hopes of Beedel. At first I didn't care two straws what they thought, expecting every hour to hear the worst. But that may not have happened. Two weeks have passed without anything being found, so that the child may be alive somewhere. If you are taking it up there is a chance—provided only that you don't let them obsess you with the idea that I have had anything to do with it."

"I don't imagine that you have had anything to do with it, Mr. Severe, and I believe that Marie is still alive."

"Thank God for that," said Severe with sudden intensity. "I am very, very glad to hear you express that opinion, Mr. Carrados. I don't suppose that I shall see much of the girl as time goes on or that she will be taught to regard the Fifth Commandment very seriously. All the same, the relief of hearing that makes me your debtor for ever... Anxious as I am, I will be content with that. I won't worry you for your clues or your ideas...but I will tell you one thing. It may amuse you. *My* notion, a few days ago, of what might have happened—"

"Yes?" encouraged his host.

"It shows you the wild ideas one gets in such circumstances. My former wife is, if I may be permitted to say so, the most amiable and devoted creature in the world. Subject to that, I will readily concede that a more self-opinionated, credulous, dogmatically wrong-headed and crank-ridden woman does not exist. There isn't a silly fad that she hasn't taken up—and what's more tragic, absolutely believed in for the time—from ozonised milk to rhythmic yawning. Some time ago she was swept into Christian Science. An atrocious harpy called Julp—a professional 'healer'—fastened on her and has dominated her ever since. Well, fantastic as it seems now, I was actually prepared to believe that Marie had been ill and under their really sincere but grotesque 'healing' had died. Then to hide the failure of their creed or because they got panic-stricken—"

Then Carrados interrupted, an incivility he rarely committed.

"Yes, yes, I see," he said quickly. "But your daughter never is ill?"

"Never ill? Marie? Oh, isn't she! In the past six months I've—"

"But Mrs. Severe deliberately said—her words—that Marie 'does not know what illness means.'"

"That's their jargon. They hold that illness does not exist and so it has no meaning. But I should describe Marie as a delicate child on the whole—bilious attacks and so on."

"Christian Scientists. . . gastric trouble. . .Prescott Ellerslie? Good heavens! This comes of half doing a thing," muttered Carrados.

"Nothing wrong, I hope?" ventured the visitor.

"Wait." Severe wondered what the deuce turn the business was taking, but there being no incentive to do anything else, he waited. Coffee, rather more fragrant that that purveyed at the nocturnal stall, and fat Egyptian cigarettes of a subtle aroma somehow failed nevertheless to make the time pass quickly. Yet five minutes would have covered Carrados's absence.

"Nothing wrong, but an unfortunate oversight," he remarked when he returned. "I was too late to catch Beedel, so we must try to mend matters at the other end if we can. I shall have to ask you to go with me. I have ordered the car and I can tell you how we stand on the way."

"I shall be glad if you can make any use of me," said Severe.

"I hope that I may. And as for anything being wrong," added Carrados with deliberation, "so far as Marie is concerned I think we may find that the one thing necessary for her future welfare has been achieved."

"That's all I ask," said Severe.

"But it isn't all that I ask," retorted the blind man almost sharply; This time there was nothing clandestine about the visit to Arling Avenue. On the contrary, the pace they kept up made it necessary that the horn should give pretty continuous notice of their presence.

If it was a race, however, they had the satisfaction of being successful.

The manner—more suggestive of the trained nurse than the domestic servant—of the maid who came to the door of Arling Lodge made it clear to Carrados, apart from any other indication, that the catastrophe of Beedel's arrival had not yet been launched. When the young person at the door began conscientiously, but with obvious inexperience, to prevaricate with the truth, the caller merely accepted her statements and wrote a few words on his card.

"When Dr. Ellerslie does return, will you please give him this at once?" he said. "I will wait."

It is to be inferred that the great specialist's return had been providentially timed, for Carrados was scarcely seated when Prescott Ellerslie hurried into the room with the visiting-card in his hand.

"Mr. Carrados?" he postulated. "Will you please explain this rather unusually worded request for an interview?"

"Certainly I will," replied Carrados. "The wording is prompted by the necessity of compelling your immediate attention. The interview is the outcome of my desire to be of use to you."

"Thank you," said Ellerslie with non-committal courtesy. "And the occasion?"

"The occasion is the impending visit of Inspector Beedel from Scotland Yard, not, this time, to look out of your landing window, but to demand the surrender of the missing Marie Severe and, if you deny any knowledge of her, armed with authority to search your house."

"Oh," replied the doctor with astonishing composure. "And if the situation develops on the lines which you have so pointedly indicated, how do you propose to help me?"

"That depends a little on your explanation of the circumstances."

"Surely between Mr. Carrados and Scotland Yard there is nothing that remains to be explained!"

"Mr. Carrados can only speak for himself," replied the blind man with unmoved good humour. "And in his case there are several things to be explained. There is probably not a great deal of time before the inspector's arrival, but there may be enough if you are disposed—"

"Very well," acquiesced Ellerslie. "You are quite right in assuming Marie Severe to be in this house. I had her brought here...out of revenge, to redress an old and very grievous injury. Perhaps you had guessed that?"

"Not in those terms," said Carrados mildly.

"Yet so it was. Ten years ago a very sweet and precious little child, my only daughter, was wantonly done to death by an ignorant and credulous woman who had charge of her, in the tenets of her faith. It is called Christian Science. The opportunity was put before me and to-day I stand convicted of having outraged every social and legal form by snatching Marie Severe from just that same fate."

Carrados nodded gravely.

"Yes," he assented. "That is the thing I missed."

"I used to see her on her way to school, whenever I was here," went on the doctor wistfully, "and soon I came to watch for her and to know the times at which she ought to pass. She was of all living creatures the gayest and the most vivid, glowing and vibrant with the compelling joy of life, a little being of wonderful grace, delicacy and charm. She has, I found when I came to know her somewhat, that distinction of manner which one is prone to associate unreasonably only with the children of the great and wealthy—a young nobility. In much the reminded me constantly of my own lost child; in other ways she attracted me by her diversity. Such, Mr. Carrados, was the nature of my interest in Marie Severe.

"I don't know the Severes and I have never even spoken to the mother. I believe that she has only lived here about a year, and in any case I have no concern in the social life of Swanstead. But a few months ago my worthy old housekeeper struck up an acquaintance with one of Mrs. Severe's servants, a staid, middle-aged person who had gone into the family as Marie's nurse. The friendship begun down our respective gardens—they adjoin—developed to the stage of these two dames taking tea occasionally with one another. My Mrs. Glass is a garrulous old woman. Hitherto my difficulty had often been to keep her quiet. Now I let her talk and deftly steered the conversation. I learned that my neighbours were Christian Scientists and had a so—called 'healer' living with them. The information struck me with a sudden dread."

'I suppose they are never ill, then?' I inquired carelessly.

"Mrs. Severe had not been ill since she had embraced Christian Science, and Miss Julp was described in a phrase obviously of her own importing as being 'all selvage.' The servants were allowed to see a doctor if they wished, although they were strongly pressed to have done with such 'trickery' in dispelling a mere 'illusion.'"

'And isn't there a child?' I asked.

"Marie, it appeared, had from time to time suffered from the 'illusion' that she had not felt well—had suffered pain. Under Miss Julp's spiritual treatment the 'hallucination' had been dispelled. Mrs. Glass had laughed, looked very knowing and then given her friend away in her appreciation of the joke. The faithful nurse had accepted the situation and as soon as her mistress's back was turned had doctored Marie according to her own simple notions. Under this double influence the child had always picked up again, but the two women had ominously speculated what would happen if she fell 'really ill.' I led her on to details of the sicknesses—their symptoms, frequency and so on. It was a

250

congenial topic between the motherly old creature and the nurse and I could not have had a better medium. I learned a good deal from her chatter. It did not reassure me.

"From that time, without allowing my interest to appear, I sought better opportunities to see the child. I inspired Mrs. Glass to suggest to the nurse that Miss Marie might come and explore the garden here— it is a large and tangled place, such as an adventuring child would love to roam in, and this one, as I found, was passionately fond of flowers and growing things and birds and little animals. I got a pair of tame squirrels and turned them loose here. You can guess her enchantment when she discovered them. I went out with nuts for her to give them and we were friends at once. All the time I was examining her without her knowledge. I don't suppose it ever occurred to her that I might be a doctor. The result practically confirmed the growing suspicion that everything I had heard pointed to. And the tragic irony of the situation was that it had been appendicitis that my child—my child—had perished from!"

"Oh, so this was appendicitis, then?"

"Yes. It was appendicitis of that insidious and misleading type to which children are particularly liable. These apparently negligible turns at intervals of weeks were really inflammation of the appendix and the condition was inevitably passing into one of general suppurative peritonitis. Very soon there would come another 'illusion' according to the mother and Miss Julp, another 'bilious turn' according to the nurse, similar to those already experienced, but apparently more obstinate. The Christian Scientists would argue with it, Hannah would surreptitiously dose it. This time, however, it would hang on. Still there would be no really very alarming symptoms to wring the natural affection of the mother, nothing severe enough to have the nurse into mutiny. The pulse running at about 140 would be the last thing they would notice."

"And then?" Ellerslie was pacing the room in savage indignation, but Carrados had Beedel's impending visit continually before him.

"Then she would be dead. Quite suddenly and unceremoniously this fair young life, which in ten minutes I could render immune from this danger for all the future, would go clean out—extinguished to demonstrate that appendicitis does not exist and that Mind is All in All. If my diagnosis was correct there could be no appeal, no shockful realisation of the true position to give the mother a chance. It would be inevitable, but it would be quite unlooked for.

"What was I to do, should you say, Mr. Carrados, in this emergency? I had dealt with these fanatics before and I knew that if I took so unusual a course as to go to Mrs. Severe I should at the best be met by polite incredulity and a text from Mrs. Mary Baker Eddy's immortal work. And by doing that I should have made any other line of action risky, if not impossible. You, I believe, are a humane man. What was I to do?"

"What you did do," said his visitor, "was about the most dangerous thing that a doctor could be mixed up in."

"Oh; no," replied Ellerslie, "he does a much more dangerous thing whenever he operates on a septiferous subject, whenever he enters a fever-stricken house. To career and reputation, you would say; but believe me, Mr. Carrados, life is quite as important as livelihood, and every doctor does that sort of thing every day. Well, like many very ordinary men whom you may meet, I am something of a maniac and something of a mystic. Incredible as it will doubtless seem to the world tomorrow, I found that, at the risk of my professional career, at the risk, possibly, of a criminal conviction, the greatest thing that I should ever do would be to save this one exquisite young life. Elsewhere other men just as good could take my place, but here it was I and I alone."

"Well, you did it?" prompted Carrados. "I must remind you that the time presses and I want to know the facts."

"Yes I did it. I won't delay with the precautions I had taken in securing the child or with the scheme that I had worked out for returning her. I believed that I had a very good chance of coming through undiscovered and I infer that I have to thank you that I did not. Marie has not the slightest idea where she is and when I go into the room I am sufficiently disguised. She thinks that she has had an accident."

"Of course you must have had assistance?"

"I have had the devoted help of an assistant and two nurses, but the whole responsibility is mine. I managed to send off Mrs. Glass and her husband for a holiday so as to keep them out of it. That was after I had decided upon the operation. To justify what I was about to do there had to be no mistake about the necessity. I contrived a final test.

"Less than three weeks ago I saw Hannah and the little girl come to the house one afternoon. Shortly afterwards Mrs. Glass knocked at my door. Could she ask Hannah to tea and, as Mrs. Severe and her friend were being out until late, might Miss Marie also stay? There was, as she knew, no need for her to ask me, but my housekeeper is primitive in her ideas of duty. Of course I readily assented, but I suggested that Marie should have tea with me; and so it was arranged.

"Before tea she amused herself about the garden. I told her to gather me a bunch of flowers and when she came in with them I noticed that she had scratched her arm with a thorn. I hurried through the meal, for I had then determined what to do. When we had finished, without ringing the bell, I gave her a chair in front of the fire and sat down opposite her. There was a true story about a clever goose that I had promised her.

"'But you are going to sleep, Marie,' I said, looking at her fixedly. 'It is the heat of the fire.'

"'I think I must be,' she admitted drowsily. 'Oh, how silly. I can scarcely keep my eyes open.'

"'You are going to sleep,' I repeated. 'You are very, very tired.' I raised my hand and moved it slowly before her face. 'You can hardly see my hand now. Your eyes are closed. When I stop speaking you will be asleep.' I dropped my hand and she was fast asleep.

"I had made my arrangements and had everything ready. From her arm, where the puncture of the needle was masked by the scratch, I secured a few drops of blood. Then I applied a simple styptic to the place and verified by a more leisurely examination some of the symptoms I had already looked for. When I woke her, a few minutes later, she had no inkling of what had passed.

"'Why,' I was saying as she awakened, 'I don't believe that you have heard a word about old Solomon!'

"I applied the various laboratory tests to the blood which I had obtained without delay. The result, taken in conjunction with the other symptoms, was conclusive. I was resolved upon my course from that moment. The operation itself was simple and completely successful. The condition demonstrated the pressing necessity for what I did. Marie Severe will probably outlive her mother now—especially if the lady remains faithful to Christian Science. As for the sequel . . . I am sorry, but I don't regret."

★★★★★★

"A surprise, eh, inspector?"

Inspector Beedel, accompanied by Mrs. Severe and—if the comparative degree may be used to indicate her relative importance—even more accompanied by Miss Julp, had arrived at Arling Lodge and been given immediate admission. It was Carrados who thus greeted him.

Beedel looked at his friend and then at Dr. Ellerslie. With unconscious habit he even noticed the proportions of the room, the position of the door and window, and the chief articles of furniture. His mind moved rather slowly, but always logically, and in cases where "sound intelligence" sufficed he was rarely unsuccessful. He had brought Mrs. Severe to identify Marie, whom he had never seen, and his men remained outside within whistle-call in case of any emergency. He now saw that he might have to shift his ground and he at once proceeded cautiously.

"Well, sir," he admitted, "I did not expect to see you here."

"Nor did I anticipate coming. Mrs. Severe"—he bowed to her—"I think that we have already met informally. Your friend, Miss Julp, unless I am mistaken? It is a good thing that we are all here."

"That is my name, sir," struck in the recalcitrant Cornelia, "but I am not aware—"

"At the gate early—very early—this morning, Miss Julp. I recognise your step. But accept my assurance, my dear lady"—for Miss Julp had given a start of maidenly confusion at the recollection—"that although I heard, I did not see you. Well, inspector, I have since found that I misled you. The mistake was mine—a fundamental error. You were right. Mrs. Severe was right. Dr. Ellerslie is unassailably right. I speak for him because it was I who fastened an unsupportable motive on his actions. Marie Severe is in this house, but she was received here by Dr. Ellerslie in his professional capacity and strictly in the relation of doctor and patient...Mr. Severe has at length admitted that he alone is to blame. You see, you were right after all."

"Arthur! Oh!" exclaimed Mrs. Severe, deeply moved.

"But why," demanded the other lady hostilely, "why should the man want her here?"

"Mr. Severe was apprehensive on account of his daughter's health," replied Carrados gravely. "His story is that, fearing something serious, he submitted her to this eminent specialist, who found a dangerous—a critical—condition that could only be removed by immediate operation. Dr. Ellerslie has saved your daughter's life, Mrs. Severe."

"Fiddlesticks!" shouted Miss Julp excitedly. "It's an outrage—a criminal outrage. An operation! There was no danger—there couldn't be with me at hand. You've done it this time, Doctor Ellerslie. My gosh, but this will be a case!"

Mrs. Severe sank into a chair, pale and trembling.

"I can scarcely believe it," she managed to say. "It is a crime. Dr. Ellerslie—no doctor had the right. Mr. Severe has no authority whatever. The court gave me sole control of Marie."

"Excuse me," put in Carrados with the blandness of perfect self-control and cognisance of his point, "excuse me, but have you ever informed Dr. Ellerslie of that ruling?"

"No," admitted Mrs. Severe with faint surprise. "No. Why should I?"

"Quite so. Why should you? But have you any knowledge that Dr. Ellerslie is acquainted with the details of your unhappy domestic differences?"

"I do not know at all. What do these things matter?"

"Only this: Why should Dr. Ellerslie question the authority of a parent who brings his child? It shows at least that he is the one who is concerned about her welfare. For all Dr. Ellerslie knew, you might be the unauthorised one, Mrs. Severe. A doctor can scarcely be expected to withhold a critical operation while he investigates the family affairs of his patients."

"But all this time—this dreadful suspense. He must have known." Carrados shrugged his shoulders and seemed to glance across the room to where their host had so far stood immovable.

"I did know, Mrs. Severe. I could not help knowing. But I knew something else, and to a doctor the interests of his patient must over-rule every ordinary consideration. Should the occasion arise, I shall be prepared at any time to justify my silence."

"Oh, the occasion will arise and pretty sharp, don't you fear," chimed in the irrepressible Miss Julp. "There's a sight more in this business, Ida, than we've got at yet. A mighty cute idea putting up Severe now. I never did believe that he was in it. He's a piece too mean-spirited to have the nerve. And where is Arthur Severe now? Gone, of course; quit the country and at someone else's expense."

"Not at all," said Carrados very obligingly. "Since you ask, Miss Julp"—he raised his voice—"Mr. Severe!"

The door opened and Severe strolled into the room with great *sang-froid*. He bowed distantly to his wife and nodded familiarly to the police official.

"Well, inspector," he remarked, "you've cornered me at last, you see."

"I'm not so sure of that," retorted Beedel shortly.

"Oh, come now; you are too modest. My unconvincing alibi that you broke down. The printed letter so conclusively from my hand. And Grigson—your irrefutable, steadfast witness from the station here, inspector. There's no getting round Grigson now, you know."

Beedel rubbed his chin helpfully but made no answer. Things seemed to have reached a momentary *impasse*.

"Perhaps we may at least all sit down," suggested Ellerslie, to break the silence. "There are rather a lot of us, but I think the chairs will go round."

"If I wasn't just dead tired I would sooner drop than sit down in the house of a man calling himself a doctor," declared Miss Julp. Then she sat down rather heavily. Sharp on the action came a piercing yell, a deep—wrung "Yag!" of pain and alarm, and the lady was seen bounding to her feet, to turn and look suspiciously at the place she had just vacated.

"It was a needle, Cornelia," said Mrs. Severe, who sat next to her. "See, here it is;"

"Dear me, how unfortunate," exclaimed Ellerslie, following the action; "one of my surgical needles. I do hope that it has been properly sterilised since the last operation."

"What's that?" demanded Miss Julp sharply.

"Well," explained the doctor slowly, "I mean that there is such a thing as bloodpoisoning. At least," he amended, "for me there is such a thing as bloodpoisoning. For you, fortunately, it does not exist. Any more than pain does," he added thoughtfully.

"Do you mean," demanded Miss Julp with slow precision, "that through your carelessness, your criminal carelessness, I run any risk of blood-poisoning?"

"Cornelia!" exclaimed Mrs. Severe in pale incredulity.

"Of course not," retorted the surgeon. "How can you if such a thing does not exist?"

"I don't care whether it exists or not—"

"Cornelia !" repeated her faithful disciple in horror.

"Be quiet, Ida. This is my business. It isn't like an ordinary illness. I've always had a horror of bloodpoisoning. I have nightmares about it. My father died of it. He had to have glass tubes put in his veins, and the night he died. Oh, I tell you I can't stand the thought of it. There's nothing else I believe in, but bloodpoisoning—"

She shuddered. "I tell you, doctor," she declared with a sudden descent to the practical, "if I get laid up from this you'll have to stand the racket, and pretty considerable damages as well."

"But at the worst this is a very simple matter," protested Ellerslie. "If you will let me dress the place—"

Miss Julp went as red as a swarthy-complexioned lady of forty-five could be expected to go.

"How can I let you dress the place?" she snapped. "It is—"

"Oh, Cornelia, Cornelia!" exclaimed Mrs. Severe reproachfully, through her disillusioned tears, "would you really be so false to the great principles which you have taught me?"

"I have a trained nurse here," suggested the doctor. "She would do it as well as I could."

"Are you really going?" demanded Mrs. Severe, for there was no doubt that Miss Julp was going and going with alacrity.

"I don't abate one *iota* of my principles, Ida," she remarked. "But one has to discriminate. There are natural illnesses and there are unnatural illnesses. We say with truth that there can be no death, but no one will deny that Christian Scientists do, as a matter of fact, in the ordinary sense, die. Perhaps this is rather beyond you yet, dear, but I hope that some day you will see it in the light of its deeper mystery."

"Do you?" replied Mrs. Severe with cold disdain. "At present I only see that there is one law of indulgence for yourself and another for your dupes."

"After all," interposed Ellerslie, "this embarrassing discussion need never have arisen. I now see that the offending implement is only one of Mrs. Glass's darning needles. How careless of her! You need have no fear, Miss Julp."

"Oh, you coward!" exclaimed Miss Julp breathlessly. "You coward! I won't stay here a moment longer. I will go home."

"I won't detain you," said Mrs. Severe as Cornelia passed her. "Your home is in Chicago, I believe? Ann will help you to pack."

Carrados rose and touched Beedel on the arm.

"You and I are not wanted here, inspector," he whispered. "The bottom's dropped out of the case," and they slipped away together.

Mrs. Severe looked across the room towards her late husband, hesitated and then slowly walked up to him.

"There is a great deal here that I do not understand," she said, "but is not this so, that you were willing to go to prison to shield this man who has been good to Marie?"

Severe flushed a little. Then he dropped his deliberate reply.

"I am willing to go to hell for this man for his goodness to Marie," he said curtly.

"Oh!" exclaimed Mrs. Severe with a little cry. "I wish you never said that you would go to hell for me!"

The outcast stared. Then a curious look, a twisted smile of tenderness and half-mocking humour crossed his features.

"My dear," he responded gravely, "perhaps not. But I often thought it!"

Dr. Ellerslie, who had followed out the last two of his departing guests, looked in at the door.

"Marie is awake, I hear," he said. "Will you go up now, Mrs. Severe?"

With a shy smile the lady held out her hand towards the shabby man.

"You must go with me, Arthur," she stipulated.

The Secret of Dunstan's Tower

It was a peculiarity of Mr Carrados that he could drop the most absorbing occupation of his daily life at a moment's notice if need be, apply himself exclusively to the solution of some criminological problem, possibly a matter of several days, and at the end of the time return and take up the thread of his private business exactly where he had left it.

On the morning of the 3rd of September he was dictating to his secretary a monograph to which he had given the attractive title, "The Portrait of Alexander the Great, as Jupiter Ammon, on an unedited octadrachm of Macedonia," when a telegram was brought in. Greatorex, the secretary, dealt with such communications as a matter of course, and, taking the envelope from Parkinson's salver, he cut it open in the pause between a couple of sentences.

"This is a private matter of yours, sir," he remarked, after glancing at the message. "Handed in at Netherhempsfield, 10.48 a.m. Repeated. One step higher. Quite baffled. Tulloch."

"Oh yes; that's all right," said Carrados. "No reply, Parkinson. Have you got down 'the Roman supremacy'?"

"'... the type of workmanship that still enshrined the memory of Spartan influence down to the era of Roman supremacy,'" read the secretary.

"That will do. How are the trains for Netherhempsfield?"

Greatorex put down the notebook and took up an "ABC."

"Waterloo departure 11—" He cocked an eye towards the desk clock. "Oh, that's no good. 12.17, 2.11, 5.9, 7.25."

"The 5.9 should do," interposed Carrados. "Arrival?"

"6.48."

"Now what has the gazetteer to say about the place?"

The yellow railway guide gave place to a weightier volume, and the secretary read out the following details:

Netherhempsfield, parish and village, pop. 732, South Down-shire. 2728 acres land and 27 water; soil rich loam, occupied as arable, pasture, orchard and woodland; subsoil various. The church of St Dunstan (restored 1740) is Saxon and Early English. It possesses an oak roof with curious grotesque bosses, and contains brasses and other memorials (earliest 13th century) of the Aynosforde family. In the 'Swinefield,' 1½ miles south-west of the village, are 15 large stones, known locally as the Judge and Jury, which constitute the remains of a Druidical circle and temple. Dunstan's Tower, a moated residence built in the baronial style, and probably dating from the 14th century, is the seat of the Aynosfordes."

"I can give three days easily," mused Carrados.

"Yes, I'll go down by the 5.9."

"Do I accompany you, sir?" inquired Greatorex.

"Not this time, I think. Have three days off yourself. Just pick up the correspondence and take things easy. Send on anything to me, care of Dr Tulloch. If I don't write, expect me back on Friday."

"Very well, Mr Carrados. What books shall I put out for Parkinson to pack?"

"Say . . . Gessner's *Thesaurus* and—yes, you may as well add Hilarion's *Celtic Mythology*."

Six hours later Carrados was on his way to Netherhempsfield. In his pocket was the following letter, which may be taken as offering the only explanation why he should suddenly decide to visit a place of which he had never even heard until that morning:—

Dear Mr Carrados ('Old Wynn,' it used to be),—Do you remember a fellow at St Michael's who used to own insects and the name of Tulloch—'Earwigs,' they called him? Well, you will find it at the end of this epistle, if you have the patience to get there. I ran across Jarvis about six months ago on Euston platform —you'll recall him by his red hair and great feet—and we had a rapid and comprehensive *powwow*. He told me who you were, having heard of you from Lessing, who seems to be editing a high-class review. He always was a trifle eccentric, Lessing.

As for yours truly, well, at the moment I'm local demon in a G—f—s— little place that you'd hardly find on anything less than a 4-inch ordnance. But I won't altogether say it mightn't be worse, for there's trout in the stream, and after half-a-decade of Cinder Moor, in the Black Country, a great and holy peace broods on the smiling land.

But you will guess that I wouldn't be taking up the time of a busy man of importance unless I had something to say, and you'd be right. It may interest you, or it may not, but here it is. Living about two miles out of the village, at a sort of mediaeval stronghold known as Dunstan's Tower, there is an ancient county family called Aynosforde. And, for the matter of that, they are about all there is here, for the whole place seems to belong to them, and their authority runs from the power to charge you two-pence if you sell a pig between Friday night and Monday morning to the right to demand an exchange of scabbards with the reigning sovereign whenever he comes within seven bowshot flights of the highest battlement of Dunstan's Tower. (I don't gather that any reigning sovereign ever has come, but that isn't the Aynosfordes' fault.) But, levity apart, these Aynosfordes, without being particularly rich, or having any title, are accorded an extraordinary position. I am told that scarcely a living duchess could hold out against the moral influence old dame Aynosforde could bring to bear on social matters, and yet she scarcely ever goes beyond Netherhempsfield now.

My connection with these high-and-mighties ought to be purely professional, and so, in a manner, it is, but on the top of it I find myself drawn into a full-blooded, old haunted house mystery that takes me clean out of my depth.

Darrish, the man whose place I'm taking for three months, had a sort of arrangement that once a week he should go up to the Tower and amuse old Mrs Aynosforde for a couple of hours under the pretence of feeling her pulse. I found that I was let in for continuing this. Fortunately the old dame was quite amiable at close quarters. I have no social qualifications whatever, and we got on very well together on those terms. I have heard that she considers me 'thoroughly responsible.'

For five or six weeks everything went on swimmingly. I had just enough to do to keep me from doing nothing; people have a delightful habit of not being taken ill in the night, and there is a comfortable cob to trot round on.

Tuesday is my Dunstan's Tower day. Last Tuesday I went as usual.

I recall now that the servants about the place seemed rather wild and the old lady did not keep me quite as long as usual, but these things were not sufficiently noticeable to make any impression on me at the time. On Friday a groom rode over with a note from Swarbrick, the butler. Would I go up that afternoon and see Mrs Aynosforde? He had taken the liberty of asking me on his own responsibility as he thought that she ought to be seen. Deuced queer it struck me, but of course I went.

Swarbrick was evidently on the look-out. He is a regular family retainer, taciturn and morose rather than bland. I saw at once that the old fellow had something on his mind, and I told him that I should like a word with him. We went into the morning-room.

'Now, Swarbrick,' I said, 'you sent for me. What is the matter with your mistress since Tuesday?'

He looked at me dourly, as though he was still in two minds about opening his mouth. Then he said slowly:

'It isn't since Tuesday, sir. It was on that morning.'

'What was?' I asked.

'The beginning of it, Dr Tulloch. Mrs Aynosforde slipped at the foot of the stairs on coming down to breakfast.'

'She did?' I said. 'Well, it couldn't have been very serious at the time. She never mentioned it to me.'

'No, sir,' the old monument assented, with an appalling surface of sublime pride, 'she would not.'

'Why wouldn't she if she was hurt?' I demanded. 'People do mention these things to their medical men, in strict confidence.'

'The circumstances are unusual, sir,' he replied, without a ruffle of his imperturbable respect. 'Mrs Aynosforde was not hurt, sir. She did not actually fall, but she slipped—on a pool of blood.'

'That's unpleasant,' I admitted, looking at him sharply, for an owl could have seen that there was something behind all this. 'How did it come there? Whose was it?'

'Sir Philip Bellmont's, sir.'

I did not know the name. 'Is he a visitor here?' I asked.

'Not at present, sir. He stayed with us in 1662. He died here, sir, under rather unpleasant circumstances.'

There you have it, Wynn. That is the keystone of the whole business. But if I keep to my conversation with the still reluctant Swarbrick I shall run out of foolscap and into midnight. Briefly, then, the 'unpleasant circumstances' were as follows:— Just about two and a half centuries ago, when Charles II. was back, and things in England were rather gay, a certain Sir Philip Bellmont was a guest at Dunstan's Tower. There were dice, and there was a lady—probably a dozen, but the particular one was the Aynosforde's young wife. One night there was a flare-up. Bellmont was run through with a rapier, and an ugly doubt turned on whether the point came out under the shoulder-blade, or went in there. Dripping on to every stair, the unfortunate man was carried up to his room.

He died within a few hours, convinced, from the circumstances, of treachery all round, and with his last breath he left an anathema on every male and female Aynosforde as the day of their death approached. There are fourteen steps in the flight that Bellmont was carried up, and when the pool appears in the hall some Aynosforde has just two weeks to live. Each succeeding morning the stain may be found one stair higher. When it reaches the top there is a death in the family.

This was the gist of the story. As far as you and I are concerned, it is, of course, merely a matter as to what form our scepticism takes, but my attitude is complicated by the fact that my nominal patient has become a real one. She is seventy-two and built to be a nonagenarian, but she has gone to bed with the intention of dying on Tuesday week. And I firmly believe she will.

'How does she know that she is the one?' I asked. There aren't many Aynosfordes, but I knew that there were some others.

To this Swarbrick maintained a discreet ambiguity. It was not for him to say, he replied, but I can see that he, like most of the natives round here, is obsessed with Aynosfordism.

'And for that matter,' I objected, 'your mistress is scarcely entitled to the distinction. She will not really be an Aynosforde at all—only one by marriage.'

'No, sir,' he replied readily, 'Mrs Aynosforde was also a Miss Aynosforde, sir—one of the Dorset Aynosfordes. Mr Aynosforde married his cousin.'

'Oh,' I said, ' do the Aynosfordes often marry cousins?'

'Very frequently, sir. You see, it is difficult otherwise for them to find eligible partners.'

Well, I saw the lady, explaining that I had not been altogether satisfied with her condition on the Tuesday. It passed, but I was not able to allude to the real business. Swarbrick, in his respectful, cast-iron way, had impressed on me that Sir Philip Bellmont must not be mentioned, assuring me that even Darrish would not venture to do so. Mrs Aynosforde was certainly a little feverish, but there was nothing the matter with her. I left, arranging to call again on the Sunday.

When I came to think it over, the first form it took was: Now who is playing a silly practical joke, or working a deliberate piece of mischief? But I could not get any further on those lines, because I do not know enough of the circumstances. Darrish might know, but Darrish is cruising off Spitsbergen, suffering from a nervous breakdown. The people here are amiable enough superficially, but they plainly regard me as an outsider. It was then that I thought of you. From what Jarvis had told me I gathered that you were keen on a mystery for its own sake. Furthermore, though I understand that you are now something of a dook, you might not be averse to a quiet week in the country, jogging along the lanes, smoking a peaceful pipe of an evening and yarning over old times. But I was not going to lure you down and then have the thing turn out to be a ridiculous and transparent hoax, no matter how serious its consequences. I owed it to you to make some reasonable investigation myself. This I have now done.

On Sunday when I went there Swarbrick, with a very long face, reported that on each morning he had found the stain one step higher. The patient, needless to say, was appreciably worse. When I came down I had made up my mind.

'Look here, Swarbrick,' I said, 'there is only one thing for it. I must sit up here tonight and see what happens.'

He was very dubious at first, but I believe the fellow is genuine in his attachment to the house. His final scruple melted when he learned that I should not require him to sit up with me. I enjoined absolute secrecy, and this, in a large rambling place like the Tower, is not difficult to maintain. All the maidservants had fled. The only people sleeping within the walls now, beyond those I have mentioned, are two of Mrs Aynosforde's grandchildren (a girl and a young man whom I merely know by sight), the housekeeper and a footman. All these had retired long before the butler admitted me by an obscure little door, about half-an-hour after midnight.

The staircase with which we are concerned goes up from the dining hall. A much finer, more modern way ascends from the entrance hall. This earlier one, however, only gives access now to three rooms, a lovely oak-panelled chamber occupied by my patient and two small rooms, turned nowadays into a *boudoir* and a bathroom. When Swarbrick had left me in an easy-chair, wrapped in a couple of rugs, in a corner of the dark dining hall, I waited for half-an-hour and then proceeded to make my own preparations. Moving very quietly, I crept up the stairs, and at the top drove one drawing-pin into the lintel about a foot up, another at the same height into the baluster opposite, and across the stairs fastened a black thread, with a small bell hanging over the edge. A touch and the bell would ring, whether the thread broke or not. At the foot of the stairs I made another attachment and hung another bell.

'I think, my unknown friend,' I said, as I went back to the chair, 'you are cut off above and below now.'

I won't say that I didn't close my eyes for a minute through the whole night, but if I did sleep it was only as a watchdog sleeps. A whisper or a creak of a board would have found me alert. As it was, however, nothing happened. At six o'clock Swarbrick appeared, respectfully solicitous about my vigil.

'We've done it this time, Swarbrick,' I said in modest elation. 'Not the ghost of a ghost has appeared. The spell is broken.'

He had crossed the hall and was looking rather strangely at the stairs. With a very queer foreboding I joined him and followed his glance. By heavens, Wynn, there, on the sixth step up, was a bright red patch! I am not squeamish; I cleared four steps at a stride, and stooping down I dipped my finger into the stuff and felt its slippery viscidity against my thumb. There could be no doubt about it; it was the genuine thing. In my baffled amazement I looked in every direction for a possible clue to human agency. Above, more than twenty feet above, were the massive rafters and boarding of the roof itself. By my side reared a solid stone wall, and beneath was simply the room we stood in, for the space below the stairway was not enclosed.

I pointed to my arrangement of bells.

'Nobody has gone up or down, I'll swear,' I said a little warmly. Between ourselves, I felt a bit of an ass for my pains, before the monumental Swarbrick.

'No, sir,' he agreed. 'I had a similar experience myself on Saturday night.'

'The deuce you did,' I exclaimed. 'Did you sit up then?'

'Not exactly, sir,' he replied, 'but after making all secure at night I hung a pair of irreplaceable Dresden china cups in a similar way. They were both still intact in the morning, sir.'

Well, there you are. I have nothing more to say on the subject. 'Hope not,' you'll be muttering. If the thing doesn't tempt you, say no more about it. If it does, just wire a time and I'll be at the station. Welcome isn't the word.—Yours as of yore,

Jim Tulloch.

P.S.—Can put your man up all right. J.T.

Carrados had "wired a time," and he was seized on the platform by the awaiting and exuberant Tulloch and guided with elaborate carefulness to the doctor's cart, which was, as its temporary owner explained, "knocking about somewhere in the lane outside."

"Splendid little horse," he declared. "Give him a hedge to nibble at and you can leave him to look after himself for hours. Motors? He laughs at them, Wynn, merely laughs."

Parkinson and the luggage found room behind, and the splendid little horse shook his shaggy head and launched out for home. For a mile the conversation was a string of, "Do you ever come across Brown now?" "You know Sugden was killed flying?" "Heard of Marling only last week; he's gone on the stage." "By the way, that appalling ass Sanders married a girl with a pot of money and runs horses now," and doubtless it would have continued in a similar strain to the end of the journey if an encounter with a farmer's country trap had not interrupted its tenor. The lane was very narrow at that point and the driver of the trap drew into the hedge and stopped to allow the doctor to pass. There was a mutual greeting, and Tulloch pulled up also when their hubs were clear.

"No more sheep killed, I hope?" he called back.

"No, sir; I can't complain that we have," said the driver cheerfully. "But I do hear that Mr Stone, over at Daneswood, lost one last night."

"In the same way, do you mean?"

"So I heard. It's a queer business, doctor."

"It's a blackguardly business. It's a marvel what the fellow thinks

266

he's doing."

"He'll get nabbed, never fear, sir. He'll do it once too often."

"Hope so," said the doctor. "Good-day." He shook the reins and turned to his visitor. "One of our local 'Farmer Jarges.' It's part of the business to pass the time o' day with them all and ask after the cow or the pig, if no other member of the family happens to be on the sick list."

"What is the blackguardly business?" asked Carrados.

"Well, that is a bit out of the common, I'll admit. About a week ago this man, Bailey, found one of his sheep dead in the field. It had been deliberately killed —head cut half off. It hadn't been done for meat, because none was taken. But, curiously enough, something else had been taken. The animal had been opened and the heart and intestines were gone. What do you think of that, Wynn?"

"Revenge, possibly."

"Bailey declares that he hasn't got the shadow of an enemy in the world. His three or four labourers are quite content. Of course a thing like that makes a tremendous sensation in a place like this. You may see as many as five men talking together almost any day now. And here, on the top if it, comes another case at Stone's. It looks like one of those outbreaks that crop up from time to time for no obvious reason and then die out again."

"No reason, Jim?"

"Well, if it isn't revenge, and if it isn't food, what is there to be got by it?"

"What is there to be got when an animal is killed?" Tulloch stared without enlightenment.

"What is there that I am here to trace?"

"Godfrey Dan'l, Wynn! You don't mean to say that there is any connection between ?"

"I don't say it," declared Carrados promptly. "But there is very strong reason why we should consider it. It solves a very obvious question that faces us. A pricked thumb does not produce a pool. Did you microscope it?"

"Yes, I did. I can only say that it's mammalian. My limited experience doesn't carry me beyond that. Then what about the entrails, Wynn? Why take those?"

"That raises a variety of interesting speculations certainly."

"It may to you. The only thing that occurs to me is that it might be a blind."

"A very unfortunate one, if so. A blind is intended to allay curiosity—to suggest an obvious but fictitious motive. This, on the contrary, arouses curiosity. The abstraction of a haunch of mutton would be an excellent blind. Whereas now, as you say, what about the entrails?"

Tulloch shook his head.

"I've had my shot," he answered. "Can you suggest anything?"

"Frankly, I can't," admitted Carrados.

"On the face of it, I don't suppose anyone short of an oracle could. Pity our local shrine has got rusty in the joints." He levelled his whip and pointed to a distant silhouette that showed against the last few red streaks in the western sky a mile away. "You see that solitary old outpost of paganism—"

The splendid little horse leapt forward in indignant surprise as the extended whip fell sharply across his shoulders. Tulloch's ingenuous face seemed to have caught the rubicundity of the distant sunset.

"I'm beastly sorry, Wynn, old man," he muttered. "I ought to have remembered."

"My blindness?" contributed Carrados. "My dear chap, everyone makes a point of forgetting that. It's quite a recognised form of compliment among friends. If it were baldness I probably should be touchy on the subject; as it's only blindness I'm not."

"I'm very glad you take it so well," said Tulloch.

"I was referring to a stone circle that we have here. Perhaps you have heard of it?"

"The Druids' altar!" exclaimed Carrados with an inspiration. "Jim, to my everlasting shame, I had forgotten it."

"Oh, well, it isn't much to look at," confessed the practical doctor. "Now in the church there are a few decent monuments—all Aynosfordes, of course."

"Aynosfordes—naturally. Do you know how far that remarkable race goes back?"

"A bit beyond Adam I should fancy," laughed Tulloch. "Well, Darrish told me that they really can trace to somewhere before the Conquest. Some antiquarian Johnny has claimed that the foundations of Dunstan's Tower cover a Celtic stronghold. Are you interested in that sort of thing?"

"Intensely," replied Carrados; "but we must not neglect other things. This gentleman who owned the unfortunate sheep, the second victim, now? How far is Daneswood away?"

"About a mile—mile and a half at the most." Carrados turned

towards the back seat.

"Do you think that in seven minutes' time you would be able to distinguish the details of a red mark on the grass, Parkinson?"

Parkinson took the effect of three objects, the sky above, the herbage by the roadside, and the back of his hand, and then spoke regretfully.

"I'm afraid not, sir; not with any certainty," he replied.

"Then we need not trouble Mr Stone tonight," said Carrados philosophically.

After dinner there was the peaceful pipe that Tulloch had forecast, and mutual reminiscences until the long clock in the corner, striking the smallest hour of the morning, prompted Tulloch to suggest retirement.

"I hope you have everything," he remarked tentatively, when he had escorted the guest to his bedroom. "Mrs Jones does for me very well, but you are an unknown quantity to her as yet."

"I shall be quite all right, you may be sure," replied Carrados, with his engagingly grateful smile. "Parkinson will already have seen to everything. We have a complete system, and I know exactly where to find anything I require."

Tulloch gave a final glance round.

"Perhaps you would prefer the window closed?" he suggested.

"Indeed I should not. It is south-west, isn't it?"

"Yes."

"And a south-westerly breeze to bring the news. I shall sit here for a little time." He put his hand on the top rail of a chair with unhesitating precision and drew it to the open casement. "There are a thousand sounds that you in your arrogance of sight ignore, a thousand individual scents of hedge and orchard that come to me up here. I suppose it is quite dark to you now, Jim? What a lot you seeing people must miss!"

Tulloch guffawed, with his hand on the door knob. "Well, don't let your passion for nocturnal nature study lead you to miss breakfast at eight. My eyes won't, I promise you. Ta-ta."

He jigged off to his own room and in ten minutes was soundly asleep. But the oak clock in the room beneath marked the quarters one by one until the next hour struck, and then round the face again until the little finger stood at three, and still the blind man sat by the open window that looked out over the south-west, interpreting the multitudinous signs of the quiet life that still went on under the dark cover of the warm summer night.

"The word lies with you, Wynn," remarked Tulloch at breakfast the next morning—he was twelve minutes late, by the way, and found his guest interested in the titles of Dr Darrish's excellent working library. "I am supposed to be on view here from nine to ten, and after that I am due at Abbot's Farm somewhere about noon. With those reservations, I am at your disposal for the day."

"Do you happen to go anywhere near the 'Swinefield' on your way to Abbot's Farm?" asked Carrados.

"The 'Swinefield'? Oh, the Druids' circle. Yes, one way—and it's as good as any other—passes the wheel-track that leads up to it."

"Then I should certainly like to inspect the site."

"There's really nothing to see, you know," apologised the doctor. "Only a few big rocks on end. They aren't even chiselled smooth."

"I am curious," volunteered Carrados, "to discover why fifteen stones should be called 'The Judge and Jury.'"

"Oh, I can explain that for you," declared Tulloch. "Two of them are near together with a third block across the tops. That's the Judge. The twelve jurymen are scattered here and there. But we'll go, by all means."

"There is a public right of way, I suppose?" asked Carrados, when, in due course, the trap turned from the highway into a field track.

"I don't know about a right," said Tulloch, "but I imagine that any-one goes across who wants to. Of course it's not a Stonehenge, and we have very few visitors, or the Aynosfordes might put some restrictions. As for the natives, there isn't a man who wouldn't sooner walk ten miles to see a five-legged calf than cross the road to look at a Phidias. And for that matter," he added thoughtfully, "this is the first time I've been really up to the place myself."

"It's on Aynosforde property, then?"

"Oh yes. Most of the parish is, I believe. But this 'Swinefield' is part of the park. There is an oak plantation across there or Dunstan's Tower would be in sight."

They had reached the gate of the enclosure. The doctor got down to open it, as he had done the former ones.

"This is locked," he said, coming back to the step, "but we can climb over easy enough. You can get down all right?"

"Thanks," replied Carrados. He descended and followed Tulloch, stopping to pat the little horse's neck.

"He'll be all right," remarked the doctor with a backward nod. "I fancy Tommy's impressionable years must have been spent between the shafts of a butcher's cart. Now, Wynn, how do we proceed?"

"I should like to have your arm over this rough ground. Then if you will take me from stone to stone—"

They paced the broken circle leisurely, Carrados judging the appearance of the remains by touch and by the answers to the innumerable questions that he put. They were approaching the most important monument the Judge—when Tulloch gave a shout of delight.

"Oh, the beauty!" he cried with enthusiasm. "I must see you closer. Wynn, do you mind—a minute—"

"Lady, Jim?" murmured Carrados. "Certainly not. I'll stand like Tommy."

Tulloch shot off with a laugh and Carrados heard him racing across the grass in the direction of the trilithon. He was still amused when he returned, after a very short interval.

"No, Wynn, not a lady, but it occurred to me that you might have been farther off. A beautiful airy creature very brightly clad. A Purple Emperor, in fact. I haven't netted a butterfly for years, but the sight gave me all the old excitement of the chase."

"Tolerably rare, too, aren't they?"

"Generally speaking, they are. I remember waiting in an oak grove with a twenty-foot net for a whole day once, and not a solitary Emperor crossed my path."

"An oak grove; yes, you said there was an oak plantation here."

"I didn't know the trick then. You needn't go to that trouble. His Majesty has rather peculiar tastes for so elegant a being. You just hang a piece of decidedly ripe meat anywhere near."

"Yes, Jim?"

"Do you notice anything?" demanded the doctor, with his face up to the wind.

"Several things," replied Carrados.

"Apropos of high meat? Do you know, Wynn, I lost that Purple Emperor here, round the blocks. I thought it must have soared, as I couldn't quite fathom its disappearance. This used to be the Druids' altar, they say. I don't know if you follow me, but it would be a devilish rum go if—eh?"

Carrados accepted the suggestion of following Jim's idea with impenetrable gravity.

"I haven't the least doubt that you are right," he assented. "Can you get up?"

"It's about ten feet high," reported Tulloch, "and not an inch of crevice to get a foothold on. If only we could bring the trap in here—"

"I'll give you a back," said Carrados, taking a position against one of the pillars. "You can manage with that?"

"Sure you can stand it?"

"Only be as quick as you can."

"Wait a minute," said Tulloch with indecision. "I think someone is coming."

"I know there is," admitted Carrados, "but it is only a matter of seconds. Make a dash for it."

"No," decided Tulloch. "One looks ridiculous. I believe it is Miss Aynosforde. We'd better wait."

A young girl with a long thin face, light hair and the palest blue eyes that it would be possible to imagine had come from the wood and was approaching them hurriedly. She might have been eighteen, but she was "dressed young," and when she spoke she expressed the ideas of a child.

"You ought not to come in here," was her greeting. "It belongs to us."

"I am sorry if we are trespassing," apologised Tulloch, colouring with chagrin and surprise. "I was under the impression that Mrs Aynosforde allowed visitors to inspect these ruins. I am Dr Tulloch." "I don't know anything about that," said the girl vaguely. "But Dunstan will be very cross if he sees you here. He is always cross if he finds that anyone has been here. He will scold me afterwards. And he makes faces in the night."

"We will go," said Tulloch quietly. "I am sorry that we should have unconsciously intruded." He raised his hat and turned to walk away, but Miss Aynosforde detained him.

"You must not let Dunstan know that I spoke to you about it," she implored him. "That would be as bad. Indeed," she added plaintively, "whatever I do always makes him cruel to me."

"We will not mention it, you may be sure," replied the doctor. "Good-morning."

"Oh, it is no good!" suddenly screamed the girl. "He has seen us; he is coming!"

Tulloch looked round in the direction that Miss Aynosforde's frightened gaze indicated. A young man whom he knew by sight as her brother had left the cover of the wood and was strolling leisurely towards them. Without waiting to encounter him the girl turned and fled, to hide herself behind the farthest pillar, running with ungainly movements of her long, wispish arms and uttering a low cry as she went. As young Aynosforde approached he courteously raised his hat to the two elder men. He appeared to be a few years older than his sister, and in him her colourless ovine features were moulded to a firmer cast.

"I am afraid that we are trespassing," said the doctor, awkward between his promise to the girl and the necessity of glossing over the situation. "My friend is interested in antiquities—"

"My unfortunate sister!" broke in Aynosforde quietly, with a sad smile. "I can guess what she has been saying. You are Dr Tulloch, are you not?"

"Yes."

"Our grandmother has a foolish but amiable weakness that she can keep poor Edith's infirmity dark. I cannot pretend to maintain that appearance before a doctor ... and I am sure that we can rely on the discretion of your friend?"

"Oh, certainly," volunteered Tulloch. "He is—"

"Merely an amateur," put in Carrados, suavely, but with the incisiveness of a scalpel.

"You must, of course, have seen that Edith is a little unusual in her conversation," continued the young man. "Fortunately, it is nothing worse than that. She is not helpless, and she is never violent. I have some hope, indeed, that she will outgrow her delusions. I suppose"— he laughed a little as he suggested it—"I suppose she warned you of my displeasure if I saw you here?"

"There was something of the sort," admitted Tulloch, judging that the circumstances nullified his promise. Aynosforde shook his head slowly.

"I am sorry that you have had the experience," he remarked. "Let me assure you that you are welcome to stay as long as you like under the shadows of these obsolete fossils, and to come as often as you please. It is a very small courtesy; the place has always been accessible to visitors."

"I am relieved to find that I was not mistaken," said the doctor.

"When I have read up the subject I should like to come again," interposed Carrados. "For the present we have gone all over the ground." He took Tulloch's arm, and under the insistent pressure the doctor turned towards the gate. "Good-morning, Mr Aynosforde."

"What a thing to come across!" murmured Tulloch when they were out of earshot. "I remember Darrish making the remark that the girl was simple for her years or something of that sort, but I only took it that she was backward. I wonder if the old ass knew more than he told me!"

They were walking without concern across the turf and had almost reached the gate when Carrados gave a sharp, involuntary cry of pain and wrenched his arm free. As he did so a stone of dangerous edge and size fell to the ground between them.

"Damnation!" cried Tulloch, his face darkening with resentment. "Are you hurt, old man?"

"Come on," curtly replied Carrados between his set teeth.

"Not until I've given that young cub something to remember," cried the outraged doctor truculently. "It was Aynosforde, Wynn. I wouldn't have believed it, but I just caught sight of him in time. He laughed and ran behind a pillar when you were hit."

"Come on," reiterated Carrados, seizing his friend's arm and compelling him towards the gate. "It was only the funny bone, fortunately. Would you stop to box the village idiot's ears because he puts out his tongue at you?"

"Village idiot!" exclaimed Tulloch. "I may only be a thick-skulled, third-rate general practitioner of no social pretension whatever, but I'm blistered if I'll have my guests insulted by a long-eared pedigree blighter without putting up a few plain words about it. An Aynosforde or not, he must take the consequences; he's no village idiot."

"No," was Carrados's grim retort; "he is something much more dangerous—the castle maniac."

Tulloch would have stopped in sheer amazement, but the recovered arm dragged him relentlessly on.

"Aynosforde! Mad!"

"The girl is on the borderline of imbecility; the man has passed beyond the limit of a more serious phase. The ground has been preparing for generations; doubtless in him the seed has quietly germinated for years. Now his time has come."

"I heard that he was a nice, quiet young fellow, studious and interested in science. He has a workshop and a laboratory."

"Yes, anything to occupy his mind. Well, in future he will have a padded room and a keeper."

"But the sheep killed by night and the parts exposed on the Druids' altar? What does it mean, Wynn?"

"It means madness, nothing more and nothing less. He is the receptacle for the last dregs of a rotten and decrepit stock that has dwindled down to mental atrophy. I don't believe that there is any method in his midnight orgies. The Aynosfordes are certainly a venerable line, and it is faintly possible that its remote ancestors were Druid priests who sacrificed and practised haruspicy on the very spot that we have left. I have no doubt that on that questionable foundation you would find advocates of a more romantic theory."

"Moral atavism?" suggested the doctor shrewdly.

"Yes—reincarnation. I prefer the simpler alternative. Aynosforde has been so fed up with pride of family and traditions of his ancient race that his mania takes this natural trend. You know what became of his father and mother?"

"No, I have never heard them mentioned."

"The father is in a private madhouse. The mother —another cousin, by the way—died at twenty-five."

"And the blood stains on the stairs? Is that his work?"

"Short of actual proof, I should say yes. It is the realisation of another family legend, you see. Aynosforde may have an insane grudge against his grandmother, or it may be simply apeish malignity, put into his mind by the sight of blood."

"What do you propose doing, then? We can't leave the man at large."

"We have nothing yet to commit him on. You would not sign for a reception order on the strength of seeing him throw a stone? We must contrive to catch him in the act tonight, if possible." Tulloch woke up the little horse with a sympathetic touch—they were ambling along the highroad again by this time—and permitted himself to smile.

"And how do you propose to do that, Excellency?" he asked.

"By sprinkling the ninth step with iodide of nitrogen. A warm night ... it will dry in half-an-hour."

"Well, do you know, I never thought of that," admitted the doctor. "Certainly that would give us the alarm if a feather brushed it. But we don't possess a chemist's shop, and I very much doubt if I can put my hand on any iodine."

"I brought a couple of ounces," said Carrados with diffidence. "Also a bottle of 4880 ammonia to be on the safe side."

"You really are a bit of a *sine qua non*, Wynn," declared Tulloch expressively.

"It was such an obvious thing," apologised the blind man. "I suppose Brook Ashfield is too far for one of us to get over to this afternoon?"

"In Dorset?"

"Yes. Colonel Eustace Aynosforde is the responsible head of the family now, and he should be en the spot if possible. Then we ought to get a couple of men from the county lunatic asylum. We don't know what may be before us."

"If it can't be done by train we must wire or perhaps Colonel Aynosforde is on the telephone. We can go into that as soon as we get back. We are almost at Abbot's Farm now. I will cut it down to fifteen minutes at the outside. You don't mind waiting here?"

"Don't hurry," replied Carrados. "Few cases are matters of minutes. Besides, I told Parkinson to come on here from Daneswood on the chance of our picking him up."

"Oh, it's Parkinson, to be sure," said the doctor. "Thought I knew the figure crossing the field. Well, I'll leave you to him."

He hastened along the rutty approach to the farmhouse, and Tommy, under the pretext of being driven there by certain pertinacious flies, imperceptibly edged his way towards the long grass by the roadside. In a few minutes Parkinson announced his presence at the step of the vehicle.

"I found what you described, sir," he reported. "These are the shapes."

Tulloch kept to his time. In less than a quarter of an hour he was back again and gathering up the reins.

"That little job is soon worked off," he remarked with mild satisfaction. "Home now, I suppose, Wynn?"

"Yes," assented Carrados. "And I think that the other little job is morally worked off." He held up a small piece of note-paper, cut to a neat octagon, with two long sides and six short ones. "What familiar object would just about cover that plan, Jim?"

"If it isn't implicating myself in any devilment, I should say that one of our four-ounce bottles would be about the ticket," replied Tulloch.

"It very likely does implicate you to the extent of being one of your four-ounce bottles, then," said Carrados. "The man who killed Stone's sheep had occasion to use what we will infer to be a four-ounce bottle. It does not tax the imagination to suggest the use he put it to, nor need we wonder that he found it desirable to wash it afterwards—this small, flat bottle that goes conveniently into a waistcoat pocket. On one side of the field—the side remote from the road, Jim, but in the direct line for Dunstan's Tower—there is a stream. There he first washed his hands, carefully placing the little bottle on the grass while he did so. That indiscretion has put us in possession of a ground plan, so to speak, of the vessel."

"Pity it wasn't of the man instead."

"Of the man also. In the field the earth is baked and unimpressionable, but down by the water-side the conditions are quite favourable, and Parkinson got perfect reproductions of the footprints. Soon, perhaps, we may have an opportunity of making a comparison." The doctor glanced at the neat lines to which the papers Carrados held out had been cut.

"It's a moral," he admitted. "There's nothing of the hobnailed about those boots, Wynn."

★★★★★★

Swarbrick had been duly warned and obedience to his instructions had been ensured by the note that conveyed them bearing the signature of Colonel Aynosforde. Between eleven and twelve o'clock a light in a certain position gave the intelligence that Dunstan Aynosforde was in his bedroom and the coast quite clear. A little group of silent men approached the Tower, and four, crossing one of the two bridges that spanned the moat, melted spectrally away in a dark angle of the walls.

Every detail had been arranged. There was no occasion for whispered colloquies about the passages, and with the exception of the butler's sad and respectful greeting of an Aynosforde, scarcely a word was spoken. Carrados, the colonel and Parkinson took up their positions in the great dining hall, where Dr Tulloch had waited on the occasion of his vigil. A screen concealed them from the stairs and the chairs on which they sat did not creak—all the blind man asked for. The doctor, who had carried a small quantity of some damp powder wrapped in a saturated sheet of blotting-paper, occupied himself for five minutes distributing it minutely over the surface of the ninth stair. When this was accomplished he disappeared and the silence of a sleeping house settled upon the ancient Tower.

A party, however, is only as quiet as its most restless member, and the colonel soon discovered a growing inability to do nothing at all and to do it in absolute silence. After an exemplary hour he began to breathe whispered comments on the situation into his neighbour's ear, and it required all Carrados's tact and good humour to repress his impatience. Two o'clock passed and still nothing had happened.

"I began to feel uncommonly dubious, you know," whispered the colonel, after listening to the third clock strike the hour. "We stand to get devilishly chaffed if this gets about. Suppose nothing happens?"

"Then your aunt will probably get up again," replied Carrados.

"True, true. We shall have broken the continuity. But, you know, Mr Carrados, there are some things about this portent, visitation—call it what you will— that even I don't fully understand down to this day. There is no doubt that my grandfather, Oscar Aynosforde, who died in 1817, did receive a similar omen, or summons, or whatever it may be. We have it on the authority—"

Carrados clicked an almost inaudible sound of warning and laid an admonishing hand on the colonel's arm. "Something going on," he breathed.

The soldier came to the alert like a terrier at a word, but his straining ears could not distinguish a sound beyond the laboured ticking of the hall clock beyond.

"I hear nothing," he muttered to himself. He had not long to wait. Halfway up the stairs something snapped off like the miniature report of a toy pistol. Before the sound could translate itself to the human brain another louder discharge had swallowed it up and out of its echo a crackling fusillade again marked the dying effects of the scattered explosive.

At the first crack Carrados had swept aside the screen. "Light, Parkinson!" he cried.

An electric lantern flashed out and centred its circle of brilliance on the stairs opposite. Its radiance pierced the nebulous balloon of violet smoke that was rising to the roof and brought out every detail of the wall beyond.

"Good heavens!" exclaimed Colonel Aynosforde, "there is a stone out. I knew nothing of this." As he spoke the solid block of masonry slid back into its place and the wall became as blankly impenetrable as before.

"Colonel Aynosforde," said Carrados, after a hurried word with Parkinson, "you know the house. Will you take my man and get round to Dunstan's work-room at once? A good deal depends upon securing him immediately."

"Am I to leave you here without any protection, sir?" inquired Parkinson in mild rebellion.

"Not without any protection, thank you, Parkinson. I shall be in the dark, remember."

They had scarcely gone when Dr Tulloch came stumbling in from the hall and the main stairs beyond, calling on Carrados as he bumped his way past a succession of inopportune pieces of furniture.

"Are you there, Wynn?" he demanded, in high-strung irritation. "What the devil's happening? Aynosforde hasn't left his room, we'll swear, but hasn't the iodide gone off?"

"The iodide has gone off and Aynosforde has left his room, though not by the door. Possibly he is back in it by now."

"The deuce!" exclaimed Tulloch blankly. "What am I to do?"

"Return—" began Carrados, but before he could say more there was a confused noise and a shout outside the window.

"We are saved further uncertainty," said the blind man. "He has thrown himself down into the moat."

"He will be drowned!"

"Not if Swarbrick put the drag-rake where he was instructed, and if those keepers are even passably expert," replied Carrados imperturbably. "After all, drowning . . . But perhaps you had better go and see, Jim."

In a few minutes men began to return to the dining hall as though where the blind man was constituted their headquarters. Colonel Aynosforde and Parkinson were the first, and immediately afterwards Swarbrick entered from the opposite side, bringing a light.

"They've got him out," exclaimed the colonel. "Upon my word, I don't know whether it's for the best or the worst, Mr Carrados." He turned to the butler, who was lighting one after another of the candles of the great hanging centre-pieces. "Did you know anything of a secret passage giving access to these stairs, Swarbrick?" he inquired.

"Not personally, sir," replied Swarbrick, "but we always understood that formerly there was a passage and hiding chamber somewhere, though the positions had been lost. We last had occasion to use it when we were defeated at Naseby, sir."

Carrados had walked to the stairs and was examining the wall.

"This would be the principal stairway, then?" he asked.

"Yes, sir, until we removed the Elizabethan gallery when we restored in 1712."

"It is on the same plan as the 'Priest's Chamber' at Lapwood. If you investigate in the daylight, Colonel Aynosforde, you will find that you command a view of both bridges when the stone is open. Very convenient sometimes, I dare say."

"Very, very," assented the colonel absently. "Every moment," he explained, "I am dreading that Aunt Eleanor will make her appearance. She must have been disturbed."

"Oh, I took that into account," said Tulloch, catching the remark as he put his head in at the door and looked round. "I recommended a sleeping draught when I was here last—no, this evening. We have got our man in all right now," he continued, "and if we can have a dry suit—"

"I will accompany you, sir," said Swarbrick.

"Is he—violent?" asked the colonel, dropping his voice.

"Violent? Well," admitted Tulloch, holding out two dripping objects that he had been carrying, "we thought it just as well to cut his boots off." He threw them down in a corner and followed the butler out of the room.

Carrados took two pieces of shaped white paper from his pocket and ran his fingers round the outlines. Then he picked up Dunstan Aynosforde's boots and submitted them to a similar scrutiny.

"Very exact, Parkinson," he remarked approvingly.

"Thank you, sir," replied Parkinson with modest pride.

The Mystery of the Poisoned Dish of Mushrooms

Sometime during November of a recent year, newspaper readers who are in the habit of being attracted by curious items of quite negligible importance might have followed the account of the tragedy of a St. Abbots schoolboy which appeared in the Press under the headings, "Fatal Dish of Mushrooms," "Are Toadstools Distinguishable?" or some similarly alluring title.

The facts relating to the death of Charlie Winpole were simple and straightforward and the jury sworn to the business of investigating the cause had no hesitation in bringing in a verdict in accordance with the medical evidence. The witnesses who had anything really material to contribute were only two in number, Mrs. Dupreen and Robert Wilberforce Slark, M.D. A couple of hours would easily have disposed of every detail of an inquiry that was generally admitted to have been a pure formality, had not the contention of an interested person delayed the inevitable conclusion by forcing the necessity of an adjournment.

Irene Dupreen testified that she was the widow of a physician and lived at Hazlehurst, Chesset Avenue, St. Abbots, with her brother. The deceased was their nephew, an only child and an orphan, and was aged twelve. He was a ward of Chancery and the Court had appointed her as guardian, with an adequate provision for the expenses of his bringing up and education. That allowance would, of course, cease with her nephew's death.

Coming to the particulars of the case, Mrs. Dupreen explained that for a few days the boy had been suffering from a rather severe cold. She had not thought it necessary to call in a doctor, recognising it as a mild form of influenza. She had kept him from school and restricted him to his bedroom. On the previous Wednesday, the day before his death, he was quite convalescent, with a good pulse and a normal temperature, but as the weather was cold she decided still to keep him in bed as a measure of precaution. He had a fair appetite, but did not care for the lunch they had, and so she had asked him, before going out in the afternoon, if there was anything that he would especially fancy for his dinner. He had thereupon expressed a partiality for mushrooms, of which he was always very fond.

"I laughed and pulled his ear," continued the witness, much affected at her recollection, "and asked him if that was his idea of a suitable dish for an invalid. But I didn't think that it really mattered in the least then, so I went to several shops about them. They all said that mushrooms were over, but finally I found a few at Lackington's, the greengrocer in Park Road. I bought only half-a-pound; no one but Charlie among us cared for them and I thought that they were already very dry and rather dear."

The connection between the mushrooms and the unfortunate boy's death seemed inevitable. When Mrs. Dupreen went upstairs after dinner she found Charlie apparently asleep and breathing soundly. She quietly removed the tray and without disturbing him turned out the gas and closed the door. In the middle of the night she was suddenly and startlingly awakened by something. For a moment she remained confused, listening. Then a curious sound coming from the direction of the boy's bedroom drew her there. On opening the door she was horrified to see her nephew lying on the floor in a convulsed attitude. His eyes were open and widely dilated; one hand clutched some bedclothes which he had dragged down with him, and the other still grasped the empty water-bottle that had been by his side. She called loudly for help and her brother and then the servant appeared. She sent the latter to a medicine cabinet for mustard leaves and told her brother to get in the nearest available doctor. She had already lifted Charlie on to the bed again. Before the doctor arrived, which was in about half-an-hour, the boy was dead.

In answer to a question the witness stated that she had not seen her nephew between the time she removed the tray and when she found him ill. The only other person who had seen him within a few hours of his death had been her brother, Philip Loudham, who had taken up Charlie's dinner. When he came down again he had made the remark: "The youngster seems lively enough now."

Dr. Slark was the next witness. His evidence was to the effect that about three-fifteen on the Thursday morning he was hurriedly called to Hazlehurst by a gentleman whom he now knew to be Mr. Philip Loudham. He understood that the case was one of convulsions and went provided for that contingency, but on his arrival he found the patient already dead. From his own examination and from what he was told he had no hesitation in diagnosing the case as one of agaric poisoning. He saw no reason to suspect any of the food except the mushrooms, and all the symptoms pointed to *bhurine,* the deadly principle of *Amanita Bhuroides,* or the Black Cap, as it was popularly called, from its fancied resemblance to the head-dress assumed by a judge in passing death sentence, coupled with its sinister and well-merited reputation. It was always fatal.

Continuing his evidence, Dr. Slark explained that only after maturity did the Black Cap develop its distinctive appearance. Up to that stage it had many of the characteristics of *Agaricus campestris,* or common mushroom. It was true that the gills were paler than one would expect to find, and there were other slight differences of a technical kind, but all might easily be overlooked in the superficial glance of the gatherer. The whole subject of edible and noxious fungi was a difficult one and at present very imperfectly understood. He, personally, very much doubted if true mushrooms were ever responsible for the cases of poisoning which one occasionally saw attributed to them. Under scientific examination he was satisfied that all would resolve themselves into poisoning by one or other of the many noxious fungi that could easily be mistaken for the edible varieties.

It was possible to prepare an artificial bed, plant it with proper spawn and be rewarded by a crop of mushroom-like growth of undoubted virulence. On the other hand, the injurious constituents of many poisonous fungi passed off in the process of cooking. There was no handy way of discriminating between the good and the bad except by the absolute identification of species. The salt test and the silver-spoon test were all nonsense and the sooner they were forgotten the better. Apparent mushrooms that were found in woods or growing in the vicinity of trees or hedges should always be regarded with the utmost suspicion.

Dr. Slark's evidence concluded the case so far as the subpoenaed witnesses were concerned, but before addressing the jury the coroner announced that another person had expressed a desire to be heard. There was no reason why they should not accept any evidence that was tendered, and as the applicant's name had been mentioned in the case it was only right that he should have the opportunity of replying publicly.

Mr. Lackington thereupon entered the witness-box and was sworn. He stated that he was a fruiterer and greengrocer, carrying on a business in Park Road, St. Abbots. He remembered Mrs. Dupreen coming to his shop two days before. The basket of mushrooms from which she was supplied consisted of a small lot of about six pounds, brought in by a farmer from a neighbouring village, with whom he had frequent dealings. All had been disposed of and in no other case had illness resulted. It was a serious matter to him as a tradesman to have his name associated with a case of this kind. That was why he had come forward. Not only with regard to mushrooms, but as a general result, people would become shy of dealing with him if it was stated that he sold unwholesome goods.

The coroner, intervening at this point, remarked that he might as well say that he would direct the jury that, in the event of their finding the deceased to have died from the effects of the mushrooms or anything contained among them, there was no evidence other than that the occurrence was one of pure mischance.

Mr. Lackington expressed his thanks for the assurance, but said that a bad impression would still remain. He had been in business in St. Abbots for twenty-seven years and during that time he had handled some tons of mushrooms without a single complaint before. He admitted, in answer to the interrogation, that he had not actually examined every mushroom of the half-pound sold to Mrs. Dupreen, but he weighed them, and he was confident that if a toadstool had been among them he would have detected it. Might it not be a cooking utensil that was the cause?

Dr. Slark shook his head and was understood to say that he could not accept the suggestion.

Continuing, Mr. Lackington then asked whether it was not possible that the deceased, doubtless an inquiring, adventurous boy and as mischievous as most of his kind, feeling quite well again and being confined to the house, had got up in his aunt's absence and taken something that would explain this sad affair? They had heard of a medicine cabinet. What about tablets of *trional* or *veronal* or something of that sort that might perhaps look like sweets? It was all very well for Dr. Slark to laugh, but this matter was a serious one for the witness.

Dr. Slark apologised for smiling—he had not laughed—and gravely remarked that the matter was a serious one for all concerned in the inquiry. He admitted that the reference to *trional* and *veronal* in this connection had, for the moment, caused him to forget the surroundings. He would suggest that in the circumstances perhaps the coroner would think it desirable to order a more detailed examination of the body to be made.

After some further discussion the coroner, while remarking that in most cases an analysis was quite unnecessary, decided that in view of what had transpired it would be more satisfactory to have a complete autopsy carried out. The inquest was accordingly adjourned.

A week later most of those who had taken part in the first inquiry assembled again in the room of the St. Abbots Town Hall which did duty for the Coroner's Court. Only one witness was heard and his evidence was brief and conclusive.

Dr. Herbert Ingpenny, consulting pathologist to St. Martin's Hospital, stated that he had made an examination of the contents of the stomach and viscera of the deceased. He found evidence of the presence of the poison *bhurine* in sufficient quantity to account for the boy's death, and the symptoms, as described by Dr. Slark and Mrs. Dupreen in the course of the previous hearing, were consistent with *bhurine* poisoning. *Bhurine* did not occur naturally except as a constituent of *Amanita Bhuroides*. One-fifth of a grain would be fatal to an adult; in other words, a single fungus in the dish might poison three people. A child, especially if experiencing the effects of a weakening illness, would be even more susceptible. No other harmful substance was present.

Dr. Ingpenny concluded by saying that he endorsed his colleague's general remarks on the subject of mushrooms and other fungi, and the jury, after a plain direction from the coroner, forthwith brought in a verdict in accordance with the medical evidence.

It was a foregone conclusion with anyone who knew the facts or had followed the evidence. Yet five days later Philip Loudham was arrested suddenly and charged with the astounding crime of having murdered his nephew.

It is at this point that Max Carrados makes his first appearance in the Winpole tragedy.

A few days after the arrest, being in a particularly urbane frame of mind himself, and having several hours with no demands on them that could not be fitly transferred to his subordinates, Mr. Carlyle looked round for some social entertainment and with a benevolent condescension very opportunely remembered the existence of his niece living at Groat's Heath.

"Elsie will be delighted," he assented to the suggestion. "She is rather out of the world up there, I imagine. Now if I get there at four, put in a couple of hours."

Mrs. Bellmark was certainly pleased, but she appeared to be still more surprised, and behind that lay an effervescence of excitement that even to Mr. Carlyle's complacent self-esteem seemed out of proportion to the occasion. The reason could not be long withheld.

"Did you meet anyone, Uncle Louis?" was almost her first inquiry.

"Did I meet anyone?" repeated Mr. Carlyle with his usual precision. "Um, no, I cannot say that I met anyone particular. Of course—"

"I've had a visitor and he's coming back again for tea. Guess who it is? But you never will. Mr. Carrados."

"Max Carrados!" exclaimed her uncle in astonishment. "You don't say so. Why, bless my soul, Elsie, I'd almost forgotten that you knew him. It seems years ago What on earth is Max doing in Groat's Heath?"

"That is the extraordinary thing about it," replied Mrs. Bellmark. "He said that he had come up here to look for mushrooms."

"Mushrooms?"

"Yes; that was what he said. He asked me if I knew of any woods about here that he could go into and I told him of the one down Stonecut Lane."

"But don't you know, my dear child," exclaimed Mr. Carlyle, "that mushrooms growing in woods or even near trees are always to be regarded with suspicion? They may look like mushrooms, but they are probably poisonous."

"I didn't know," admitted Mrs. Bellmark; "but if they are, I imagine Mr. Carrados will know."

"It scarcely sounds like it—going to a wood, you know. As it happens, I have been looking up the subject lately. But, in any case, you say that he is coming back here?"

"He asked me if he might call on his way home for a cup of tea, and of course I said, 'Of course.'"

"Of course," also said Mr. Carlyle. "Motoring, I suppose."

"Yes, a big grey car. He had Mr. Parkinson with him."

Mr. Caryle was slightly puzzled, as he frequently was by his friend's proceedings, but it was not his custom to dwell on any topic that involved an admission of inadequacy. The subject of Carrados and

his eccentric quest was therefore dismissed until the sound of a formidable motor car dominating the atmosphere of the quiet suburban
road was almost immediately followed by the entrance of the blind
amateur. With a knowing look towards his niece Carlyle had taken up
a position at the farther end of the room, where he remained in almost
breathless silence.

Carrados acknowledged the hostess's smiling greeting and then
nodded familiarly in the direction of the playful guest.

"Well, Louis," he remarked, "we've caught each other."

Mrs. Bellmark was perceptibly startled, but rippled musically at the
failure of the conspiracy.

"Extraordinary," admitted Mr. Carlyle, coming forward.

"Not so very," was the dry reply. "Your friendly little maid"—to
Mrs. Bellmark—"mentioned your visitor as she brought me in."

"Is it a fact, Max," demanded Mr. Carlyle, "that you have been to—
er—Stonecut Wood to get mushrooms?"

"Mrs. Bellmark told you?"

"Yes. And did you succeed?"

"Parkinson found something that he assured me looked just like
mushrooms."

Mr. Carlyle bestowed a triumphant glance on his niece.

"I should very much like to see these so-called mushrooms. Do
you know, it may be rather a good thing for you that I met you."

"It is always a good thing for me to meet you," replied Carrados.
"You shall see them. They are in the car. Perhaps I shall be able to take
you back to town?"

"If you are going very soon. No, no, Elsie"—in response to Mrs.
Bellmark's protesting "Oh!"—"I don't want to influence Max, but I
really must tear myself away the moment after tea. I still have to clear
up some work on a rather important case I am just completing. It is
quite appropriate to the occasion, too. Do you know all about the
Winpole business, Max?"

"No," admitted Carrados, without any appreciable show of interest. "Do you, Louis?"

"Yes," responded Mr. Carlyle with crisp assurance, "yes, I think
that I may claim I do. In fact it was I who obtained the evidence that
induced the authorities to take up the case against Loudham."

"Oh, do tell us all about it," exclaimed Elsie. "I have only seen
something in the *Indicator*."

Mr. Carlyle shook his head, hemmed and looked wise, and then gave in.

"But not a word of this outside, Elsie," he stipulated. "Some of the evidence won't be given until next week and it might be serious."

"Not a syllable," assented the lady. "How exciting! Go on."

"Well, you know, of course, that the coroner's jury—very rightly, according to the evidence before them—brought in a verdict of accidental death. In the circumstances it was a reflection on the business methods or the care or the knowledge or whatever one may decide of the man who sold the mushrooms, a greengrocer called Lackington. I have seen Lackington, and with a rather remarkable pertinacity in the face of the evidence he insists that he could not have made this fatal blunder—that in weighing so small a quantity as half-a-pound, at any rate, he would at once have spotted anything that wasn't quite all right."

"But the doctor said, Uncle Louis—"

"Yes, my dear Elsie, we know what the doctor said, but, rightly or wrongly, Lackington backs his experience and practical knowledge against theoretical generalities. In ordinary circumstances nothing more would have come of it, but it happens that Lackington has for a lodger a young man on the staff of the local paper, and for a neighbour a pharmaceutical chemist. These three men talked things over more than once—Lackington restive under the damage that had been done to his reputation, the journalist stimulating and keen for a newspaper sensation, the chemist contributing his quota of practical knowledge. At the end of a few days a fabric of circumstance had been woven which might be serious or innocent according to the further development of the suggestion and the manner in which it could be met. These were the chief points of the attack:

"Mrs. Dupreen's allowance for the care and maintenance of Charlie Winpole ceased with his death, as she had told the jury. What she did not mention was that the deceased boy would have come into an inheritance of some fifteen thousand pounds at age and that this fortune now fell in equal shares to the lot of his two nearest relatives—Mrs. Dupreen and her brother, Philip.

"Mrs. Dupreen was by no means in easy circumstances. Philip Loudham was equally poor and had no assured income. He had tried several forms of business and now, at about thirty-five, was spending his time chiefly in writing poems and painting watercolours, none of which brought him any money so far as one could learn.

"Philip Loudham, it was admitted, took up the food round which the tragedy centred.

"Philip Loudham was shown to be in debt and urgently in need of money. There was supposed to be a lady in the case—I hope I need say no more, Elsie."

"Who is she?" asked Mrs. Bellmark with poignant interest.

"We do not know yet. A married woman, it is rumoured, I regret to say. It scarcely matters—certainly not to you, Elsie. To continue:

"Mrs. Dupreen got back from her shopping in the afternoon before her nephew's death at about three o'clock. In less than half-an-hour Loudham left the house and going to the station took a return ticket to Euston. He went by the 3:41 and was back in St. Abbots at 5:43. That would give him barely an hour in town for whatever business he transacted. What was that business?

"The chemist next door supplied the information that although bhurine only occurs in nature in this one form, it can be isolated from the other constituents of the fungus and dealt with like any other liquid poison. But it was a very exceptional commodity, having no commercial uses and probably not half-a-dozen retail chemists in London had it on their shelves. He himself had never stocked it and never been asked for it.

"With this suggestive but by no means convincing evidence," continued Mr. Carlyle, "the young journalist went to the editor of *The Morning Indicator*, to which he acted as St. Abbots correspondent, and asked him whether he cared to take up the inquiry as a 'scoop.' The local trio had carried it as far as they were able. The editor of the *Indicator* decided to look into it and asked me to go on with the case. This is how my connection with it arose."

"Oh, that's how newspapers get to know things?" commented Mrs. Bellmark. "I often wondered."

"It is one way," assented her uncle.

"An American development," contributed Carrados. "It is a little overdone there."

"It must be awful," said the hostess. "And the police methods! In the plays that come from the States—" The entrance of the friendly handmaiden, bringing tea, was responsible for the platitudinous wave. The conversation, in deference to Mr. Carlyle's scruples, marked time until the door closed on her departure.

"My first business," continued the inquiry agent, after making himself useful at the table, "was naturally to discover among the chemists in London whether a sale of *bhurine* coincided with Philip Loudham's

289

hasty visit. If this line failed, the very foundation of the edifice of hypothetical guilt gave way; if it succeeded...Well, it did succeed. In a street off Caistor Square, Tottenham Court Road—Trenion Street—we found a man called Lightcraft, who at once remembered making such a sale. As *bhurine* is a specified poison, the transaction would have to be entered, and Lightcraft's book contained this unassailable piece of evidence. On Wednesday, the sixth of this month, a man signing his name as 'J. D. Williams,' and giving '25 Chalcott Place' as the address, purchased four *drachms* of *bhurine*. Lightcraft fixed the time as about half-past four. I went to 25 Chalcott Place and found it to be a small boarding-house. No one of the name of Williams was known there."

If Mr. Caryle's tone of finality went for anything, Philip Loudham was as good as pinioned. Mrs. Bellmark supplied the expected note of admiration.

"Just fancy!" was the form it took.

"Under the Act the purchaser must be known to the chemist?" suggested Carrados.

"Yes," agreed Mr. Carlyle; "and there our friend Lightcraft may have let himself in for a little trouble. But, as he says—and we must admit that there is something in it—who is to define what 'known to' actually means? A hundred people are known to him as regular or occasional customers and he has never heard their names; a score of names and addresses represent to him regular or occasional customers whom he has never seen. This 'J. D. Williams' came in with an easy air and appeared at all events to know Lightcraft. The face seemed not unfamiliar and Lightcraft was perhaps a little too facile in assuming that he did know him. Well, well, Max, I can understand the circumstances. Competition is keen—especially against the private chemist—and one may give offence and lose a customer. We must all live."

"Except Charlie Winpole," occurred to Max Carrados, but he left the retort unspoken. "Did you happen to come across any inquiry for *bhurine* at other shops?" he asked instead.

"No," replied Carlyle, "no, I did not. It would have been an indication then, of course, but after finding the actual place the others would have no significance. Why do you ask?"

"Oh, nothing. Only don't you think that he was rather lucky to get it first shot if our St. Abbots authority was right?"

"Yes, yes; perhaps he was. But that is of no interest to us now. The great thing is that a peculiarly sinister and deliberate murder is brought home to its perpetrator. When you consider the circumstances, upon my soul, I don't know that I have ever unmasked a more ingenious and cold-blooded ruffian."

"Then he has confessed, uncle?"

"Confessed, my dear Elsie," said Mr. Carlyle, with a tolerant smile, "no, he has not confessed—men of that type never do. On the contrary, he asserted his outraged innocence with a considerable show of indignation. What else was he to do? Then he was asked to account for his movements between 4.15 and 5 o'clock on that afternoon. Egad, the fellow was so cocksure of the safety of his plans that he hadn't even taken the trouble to think that out. First he denied that he had been away from St. Abbots at all. Then he remembered. He had run down to town in the afternoon for a few things.—What things?—Well, chiefly stationery.—Where had he bought it?—At a shop in Oxford Street; he did not know the name.—Would he be able to point it out?—He thought so.—Could he identify the attendant?—No, he could not remember him in the least.

"Had he the bill?—No, he never kept small bills.—How much was the amount?—About three or four shillings.—And the return fare to Euston was three-and-eightpence. Was it not rather an extravagant journey?—He could only say that he did so.—Three or four shillings' worth of stationery would be a moderate parcel. Did he have it sent?—No, he took it with him.—Three or four shillings' worth of stationery in his pocket?—No, it was in a parcel.—Too large to go in his pocket?—Yes.—Two independent witnesses would testify that he carried no parcel. They were townsmen of St. Abbots who had travelled. down in the same carriage with him. Did he still persist that he had been engaged in buying stationery? Then he declined to say anything further—about the best thing he could do."

"And Lightcraft identifies him?"

"Um, well, not quite so positively as we might wish. You see, a fortnight has elapsed. The man who bought the poison wore a moustache—put on, of course—but Lightcraft will say that there is a resemblance and the type of the two men the same."

"I foresee that Mr. Lightcraft's accommodating memory for faces will come in for rather severe handling in cross-examination," said Carrados, as though he rather enjoyed the prospect.

"It will balance Mr. Philip Loudham's unfortunate forgetfulness for localities, Max," rejoined Mr. Carlyle, delivering the thrust with his own inimitable aplomb.

Carrados rose with smiling acquiescence to the shrewdness of the riposte.

"I will be quite generous, Mrs. Bellmark," he observed. "I will take him away now, with the memory of that lingering in your ears—all my crushing retorts unspoken."

"Five-thirty, egad!" exclaimed Mr. Carlyle, displaying his imposing gold watch. "We must—or, at all events, I must. You can think of them in the car, Max."

"I do hope you won't come to blows," murmured the lady. Then she added: "When will the real trial come on, Uncle Louis?"

"The Sessions? Oh, early in January."

"I must remember to look out for it." Possibly she had some faint idea of Uncle Louis taking a leading part in the proceedings. At any rate Mr. Carlyle looked pleased, but when *adieux* had been taken and the door was closed Mrs. Bellmark was left wondering what the enigma of Max Carrados's departing smile had been.

Before they had covered many furlongs Mr. Carlyle suddenly remembered the suspected mushrooms and demanded to see them. A very moderate collection was produced for his inspection. He turned them over sceptically.

"The gills are too pale for true mushrooms, Max," he declared sapiently. "Don't take any risk. Let me drop them out of the window?"

"No." Carrados's hand quietly arrested the threatened action. "No; I have a use for them, Louis, but it is not culinary. You are quite right; they are rank poison. I only want to study them for—a case I am interested in."

"A case! You don't mean to say that there is another mushroom poisoner going?"

"No; it is the same."

"But—but you said—"

"That I did not know all about it? Quite true. Nor do I yet. But I know rather more than I did then."

"Do you mean that Scotland Yard—"

"No, Louis." Mr. Carrados appeared to find something rather amusing in the situation. "I am for the other side."

"The other side! And you let me babble out the whole case for the prosecution! Well, really, Max!"

"But you are out of it now? The public prosecutor has taken it up?"

"True, true. But, for all that, I feel devilishly bad."

"Then I will give you all the whole case for the defence and so we shall be quits. In fact I am relying on you to help me with it."

"With the defence? I—after supplying the evidence that the Public Prosecutor is acting on?"

"Why not? You don't want to hang Philip Loudham—specially if he happens to be innocent—do you?"

"I don't want to hang anyone," protested Mr. Carlyle. "At least—not—as a private individual."

"Quite so. Well, suppose you and I between ourselves find out the actual facts of the case and decide what is to be done. The more usual course is for the prosecution to exaggerate all that tells against the accused and to contradict everything in his favour; for the defence to advance fictitious evidence of innocence and to lie roundly on everything that endangers his client; while on both sides witnesses are piled up to bemuse the jury into accepting the desired version. That does not always make for impartiality or for justice....Now you and I are two reasonable men, Louis—"

"I hope so," admitted Mr. Carlyle. "I hope so."

"You can give away the case for the prosecution and I will expose the weakness of the defence, so, between us, we may arrive at the truth."

"It strikes me as a deuced irregular proceeding. But I am curious to hear the defence all the same."

"You are welcome to all of it that there yet is. An alibi, of course."

"Ah!" commented Mr. Carlyle with expression.

"So recently as yesterday a lady came hurriedly, and with a certain amount of secrecy, to see me. She came on the strength of the introduction afforded by a mutual acquaintanceship with Fromow, the Greek professor. When we were alone she asked me, besought me, in fact, to tell her what to do. A few hours before Mrs. Dupreen had rushed across London to her with the tale of young Loudham's arrest. Then out came the whole story. This woman—well, her name is Guestling, Louis—lives a little way down in Surrey and is married. Her husband, according to her own account—and I have certainly heard a hint about it elsewhere—leads her a studiedly outrageous existence; an admired silken-mannered gentleman in society, a tolerable polecat at home, one infers.

"About a year ago Mrs. Guestling made the acquaintance of Loudham, who was staying in that neighbourhood painting his pretty unsaleable country lanes and golden sunsets. The inevitable, or, to accept the lady's protestations, half the inevitable, followed. Guestling, who adds an insatiable jealousy to his other domestic virtues, vetoed the new acquaintance and thenceforward the two met hurriedly and furtively in town. Had either of them any money they might have snatched their destinies from the hands of Fate and gone off together, but she has nothing and he has nothing and both, I suppose, are poor weak mortals when it comes to doing anything courageous and outright in this censorious world. So they drifted, drifting but not yet wholly wrecked."

"A formidable incentive for a weak and desperate man to secure a fortune by hook or crook, Max," said Carlyle drily.

"That is the motive that I wish to make you a present of. But, as you will insist on your side, it is also a motive for a weak and foolish couple to steal every brief opportunity of a secret meeting. On Wednesday, the sixth, the lady was returning home from a visit to some friends in the Midlands. She saw in the occasion an opportunity and on the morning of the sixth a message appeared in the personal column of *The Daily Telegraph*—their usual channel of communication—making an assignation. That much can be established by the irrefutable evidence of the newspaper. Philip Loudham kept the appointment and for half-an-hour this miserably happy pair sat holding each other's hands in a dreary deserted waiting-room of Bishop's Road Station. That half-hour was from 4.14 to 4.45. Then Loudham saw Mrs. Guestling into Praed Street Station for Victoria, returned to Euston and just caught the 5.7 St. Abbots."

"Can this be corroborated—especially as regards the precise time they were together?"

"Not a word of it. They chose the waiting-room at Bishop's Road for seclusion and apparently they got it. Not a soul even looked in while they were there."

"Then, by Jupiter, Max," exclaimed Mr. Carlyle with emotion, "you have hanged your client!"

Carrados could not restrain a smile at his friend's tragic note of triumph.

"Well, let us examine the rope," he said with his usual imperturbability.

"Here it is." It was a trivial enough shred of evidence that the inquiry agent took from his pocket-book and put into the expectant hand; in point of fact, the salmon-coloured ticket of a "London General" motor omnibus.

"Royal Oak—the stage nearest Paddington—to Tottenham Court

Road—the point nearest Trenion Street," he added significantly.

"Yes," acquiesced Carrados, taking it.

"The man who bought the *bhurine* dropped that ticket on the floor of the shop. He left the door open and Lightcraft followed him to close it. That is how he came to pick the ticket up, and he remembers that it was not there before. Then he threw it into a wastepaper basket underneath the counter, and that is where we found it when I called on him."

"Mr. Lightcraft's memory fascinates me, Louis;" was the blind man's unruffled comment. "Let us drop in and have a chat with him?"

"Do you really think that there is anything more to be got in that quarter?" queried Carlyle dubiously. "I have turned him inside out, you may be sure."

"True; but we approach Mr. Lightcraft from different angles. You were looking for evidence to prove young Loudham guilty. I am looking for evidence to prove him innocent."

"Very well, Max," acquiesced his companion. "Only don't blame me if it turns out as deuced awkward for your man as Mrs. G. has done. Shall I tell you what a counsel may be expected to put to the jury as the explanation of that lady's evidence?"

"No, thanks," said Carrados half sleepily from his corner. "I know. I told her so."

"Oh, very well. I needn't inform you, then," and debarred of that satisfaction Mr. Carlyle withdrew himself into his own corner, where he nursed an indulgent annoyance against the occasional perversity of Max Carrados until the stopping of the car and the variegated attractions displayed in a shop window told him where they were.

Mr. Lightcraft made no pretence of being glad to see his visitors. For some time he declined to open his mouth at all on the subject that had brought them there, repeating with parrot-like obstinacy to every remark on their part, "The matter is sub judice. I am unable to say anything further," until Mr. Carlyle longed to box his ears and bring him to his senses. The ears happened to be rather prominent, for they glowed with sensitiveness, and the chemist was otherwise a lank and pallid man, whose transparent ivory skin and well-defined moustache gave him something of the appearance of a waxwork.

"At all events," interposed Carrados, when his friend turned from the maddening reiteration in despair, "you don't mind telling me a few things about *bhurine*—apart from this particular connection?"

"I am very busy," and Mr. Lightcraft, with his back towards the shop, did something superfluous among the bottles on a shelf.

"I imagine that the time of Mr. Max Carrados, of whom even you may possibly have heard, is as valuable as yours, my good friend," put in Mr. Carlyle with scandalised dignity.

"Mr. Carrados?" Lightcraft turned and regarded the blind man with interest. "I did not know. But you must recognise the unenviable position in which I am put by this gentleman's interference."

"It is his profession, you know," said Carrados mildly, "and, in any case, it would certainly have been someone. Why not help me to get you out of the position?"

"How is that possible?"

"If the case against Philip Loudham breaks down and he is discharged at the next hearing you would not be called upon further."

"That would certainly be a mitigation. But why should it break down?"

"Suppose you let me try the taste of *bhurine*," suggested Carrados. "You have some left?"

"Max, Max!" cried Mr. Carlyle's warning voice, "aren't you aware that the stuff is a deadly poison? One-fifth of a grain—"

"Mr. Lightcraft will know how to administer it." Apparently Mr. Lightcraft did. He filled a graduated measure with cold water, dipped a slender glass rod into a bottle that was not kept on the shelves, and with it stirred the water. Then into another vessel of water he dropped a single spot of the dilution.

"One in a hundred and twenty-five thousand, Mr. Carrados," he said, offering him the mixture.

Carrados just touched the liquid with his lips, considered the impression and then wiped his mouth.

"Now for the smell."

The unstoppered bottle was handed to him and he took in its exhalation.

"Stewed mushrooms!" was his comment. "What is it used for, Mr. Lightcraft?"

"Nothing that I know of."

"But your customer must have stated an application."

The pallid chemist flushed a little at the recollection of that incident.

"Yes," he conceded. "There is a good deal about the whole business that is still a mystery to me. The man came in shortly after I had lit up and nodded familiarly as he said: 'Good-evening, Mr. Lightcraft.' I naturally assumed that he was someone whom I could not quite place. 'I want another half-pound of *nitre*,' he said, and I served him. Had he bought *nitre* before, I have since tried to recall and I cannot. It is a common enough article and I sell it every day. I have a poor memory for faces I am willing to admit. It has hampered me in business many a time. We chatted about nothing in particular as I did up the parcel. After he had paid and turned to go he looked back again. 'By the way, do you happen to have any *bhurine?*' he inquired. Unfortunately I had a few ounces. 'Of course you know its nature?' I cautioned him. 'May I ask what you require it for?' He nodded and held up the parcel of *nitre* he had in his hand. 'The same thing,' he replied, 'taxidermy.' Then I supplied him with half-an-ounce."

"As a matter of fact, is it used in taxidermy?"

"It does not seem to be. I have made inquiry and no one knows of it. *Nitre* is largely used, and some of the dangerous poisons—arsenic and mercuric chloride, for instance—but not this. No, it was a subterfuge."

"Now the poison book, if you please."

Mr. Lightcraft produced it without demur and the blind man ran his finger along the indicated line.

"Yes; this is quite satisfactory. Is it a fact, Mr. Lightcraft, that not half-a-dozen chemists in London stock this particular substance? We are told that"

"I can quite believe it. I certainly don't know of another."

"Strangely enough, your customer of the sixth seems to have come straight here. Do you issue a price-list?"

"Only a localised one of certain photographic goods. *Bhurine* is not included."

"You can suggest no reason why Mr. Phillip Laudham should be inspired to presume that he would be able to procure this unusual drug from you? You have never corresponded with him nor come across his name or address before?"

"No. As far as I can recollect, I know nothing whatever of him."

"Then as yet you must assume that it was pure chance. By the way, Mr. Lightcraft, how does it come that you stock this rare poison, which has no commercial use and for which there is no demand?"

The chemist permitted himself to smile at the blunt terms of the inquiry.

"In the ordinary way I don't stock it," he replied. "This is a small quantity which I had over from my own use."

"Your own use? Oh, then it has a use after all?"

"No, scarcely that. Some time ago it leaked out in a corner of the photographic world that a great revolution in colour photography was on the point of realisation by the use of *bhurine* in one of the processes. I, among others, at once took it up. Unfortunately it was another instance of a discovery that is correct in theory breaking down in practice. Nothing came of it."

"Dear, dear me," said Carrados softly, with sympathetic understanding in his voice; "what a pity. You are interested in photography, Mr. Lightcraft?"

"It is the hobby of my life, sir. Of course most chemists dabble in it as a part of their business, but I devote all my spare time to experimenting. Colour photography in particular."

"Colour photography; yes. It has a great future. This *bhurine* process—I suppose it would have been of considerable financial value if it had worked?"

Mr. Lightcraft laughed quietly and rubbed his hands together. For the moment he had forgotten Loudham and the annoying case and lived in his enthusiasm.

"I should rather say it would, Mr. Carrados," he replied. "It would have been the most epoch-marking thing since Gaudin produced the first dry plate in '54. Consider it—the elaborate processes of Dyndale, Eiloff and Jupp reduced to the simplicity of a single contact print giving the entire range of chromatic variation. Financially it will scarcely bear thinking about by artificial light."

"Was it widely taken up?" asked Carrados.

"The *bhurine* idea?"

"Yes. You spoke of the secret leaking out. Were many in the know?"

"Not at all. The group of initiates was only a small one and I should imagine that, on reflection, every man kept it to himself. It certainly never became public. Then when the theory was definitely exploded, of course no one took any further interest in it."

"Were all who were working on the same lines known to you, Mr. Lightcraft?"

"Well, yes; more or less I suppose they would be," said the chemist thoughtfully. "You see, the man who stumbled on the formula was a member of the Iris—a society of those interested in this subject, of which I was the secretary—and I don't think it ever got beyond the committee."

"How long ago was this?"

"A year—eighteen months. It led to unpleasantness and broke up the society."

"Suppose it happened to come to your knowledge that one of the original circle was quietly pursuing his experiments on the same lines with *bhurine*—what should you infer from it?"

Mr. Lightcraft considered. Then he regarded Carrados with a sharp, almost a startled, glance and then he fell to biting his nails in perplexed uncertainty.

"It would depend on who it was," he replied.

"Was there by any chance one who was unknown to you by sight but whose address you were familiar with?"

"Paulden!" exclaimed Mr. Lightcraft. "Paulden, by heaven! I do believe you're right. He was the ablest of the lot and he never came to the meetings—a corresponding member. Southem, the original man who struck the idea, knew Paulden and told him of it. Southem was an impractical genius who would never be able to make anything work. Paulden—yes, Paulden it was who finally persuaded Southem that there was nothing in it. He sent a report to the same effect to be read at one of the meetings. So Paulden is taking up *bhurine* again—"

"Where does he live?" inquired Carrados.

"Ivor House, Wilmington Lane, Enstead. As secretary I have written there a score of times."

"It is on the Great Western—Paddington," commented the blind man. "Still, can you get out the addresses of the others in the know, Mr. Lightcraft?"

"Certainly, certainly. I have the book of membership. But I am convinced now that Paulden was the man. I believe that I did actually see him once some years ago, but he has grown a moustache since."

"If you had been convinced of that a few days ago it would have saved us some awkwardness," volunteered Mr. Carlyle with a little dignified asperity.

"When you came before, Mr. Carlyle, you were so convinced yourself of it being Mr. Loudham that you wouldn't hear of me thinking of anyone else," retorted the chemist. "You will bear me out so that I never positively identified him as my customer. Now here is the book. Southem, Potter's Bar. Voynich, Islington. Crawford, Streatham Hill. Brown, Southampton Row. Vickers, Clapham Common. Tidey, Fulham. All those I knew quite well—associated with them week after week. Williams I didn't know so closely. He is dead. Bigwood has gone to Canada. I don't think anyone else was in the *bhurine* craze—as we called it afterwards."

"But now? What would you call it now?" queried Carrados.

"Now? Well, I hope that you will get me out of having to turn up at court and that sort of thing, Mr. Carrados. If Paulden is going on experimenting with *bhurine* again on the sly, I shall want all my spare time to do the same myself!"

A few hours later the two investigators rang the bell of a substantial detached house in Enstead, the little country town twenty miles out in Berkshire, and asked to see Mr. Paulden.

"It is no good taking Lightcraft to identify the man," Carrados had decided. "If Paulden denied it, our friend's obliging record in that line would put him out of court."

"I maintain an open mind on the subject," Carlyle had replied. "Lightcraft is admittedly a very bending reed, but there is no reason why he should not have been right before and wrong today."

They were shown into a ceremonial reception-room to wait. Mr. Carlyle diagnosed snug circumstances and the tastes of an indoors, comfort-loving man in the surroundings.

The door opened, but it was to admit a middle-aged matronly lady with good-humour and domestic capability proclaimed by every detail of her smiling face and easy manner.

"You wished to see my husband?" she asked with friendly courtesy.

"Mr. Paulden? Yes, we should like to," replied Carlyle, with his most responsive urbanity. "It is a matter that need not occupy more than a few minutes."

"He is very busy just now. If it has to do with the election"—a local contest was at its height—"he is not interested in politics and scarcely ever votes." Her manner was not curious, but merely reflected a business-like desire to save trouble all round.

"Very sensible too, very sensible indeed," almost warbled Mr. Carlyle with instinctive cajolery. "After all," he continued, mendaciously appropriating as his own an aphorism at which he had laughed heartily a few days before in the theatre, "after all, what does an election do but change the colour of the necktie of the man who picks our pockets? No, no, Mrs. Paulden, it is merely a—um—quite personal matter."

The lady looked from one to the other with smiling amiability.

"Some little mystery," her expression seemed to say. "All right; I don't mind, only perhaps I could help you if I knew."

"Mr. Paulden is in his dark-room now," was what she actually did say. "I am afraid, I am really afraid that I shan't be able to persuade him to come out unless I can take a definite message."

"One understands the difficulty of tempting an enthusiast from his work," suggested Carrados, speaking for the first time. "Would it be permissible to take us to the door of the dark-room, Mrs. Paulden, and let us speak to your husband through it?"

"We can try that way," she acquiesced readily, "if it is really so important."

"I think so," he replied.

The dark-room lay across the hall. Mrs. Paulden conducted them to the door, waited a moment and then knocked quietly.

"Yes?" sang out a voice, rather irritably one might judge, from inside.

"Two gentlemen have called to see you about something, Lance—"

"I cannot see anyone when I am in here," interrupted the voice with rising sharpness. "You know that, Clara—"

"Yes, dear," she said soothingly; "but listen. They are at the door here and if you can spare the time just to come and speak you will know without much trouble if their business is as important as they think."

"Wait a minute," came the reply after a moment's pause, and then they heard someone approach the door from the other side.

It was a little difficult to know exactly how it happened in the obscure light of the corner of the hall. Carrados had stepped nearer to the door to speak. Possibly he trod on Mr. Carlyle's toe, for there was a confused movement; certainly he put out his hand hastily to recover himself. The next moment the door of the dark-room jerked open, the light was let in and the warm odours of a mixed and vitiated atmosphere rolled out. Secure in the well-ordered discipline of his excellent household, Mr. Paulden had neglected the precaution of locking himself in.

"Confound it all," shouted the incensed experimenter in a towering rage, "confound it all, you've spoiled the whole thing now!"

"Dear me," apologised Carrados penitently, "I am so sorry. I think it must have been my fault, do you know. Does it really matter?"

"Matter!" stormed Mr. Paulden, recklessly flinging open the door fully now to come face to face with his disturbers—"matter letting a flood of light into a darkroom in the middle of a delicate experiment!"

"Surely it was very little," persisted Carrados.

"Pshaw," snarled the angry gentleman; "it was enough. You know the difference between light and dark, I suppose?" Mr. Carlyle suddenly found himself holding his breath, wondering how on earth Max had conjured that opportune challenge to the surface.

"No," was the mild and deprecating reply—the appeal *ad misericordiam* that had never failed him yet—"no, unfortunately I don't, for I am blind. That is why I am so awkward."

Out of the shocked silence Mrs. Paulden gave a little croon of pity. The moment before she had been speechless with indignation on her husband's behalf. Paulden felt as though he had struck a suffering animal. He stammered an apology and turned away to close the unfortunate door. Then he began to walk slowly down the hall.

"You wished to see me about something?" he remarked, with matter-of-fact civility. "Perhaps we had better go in here." He indicated the reception-room where they had waited and followed them in. The admirable Mrs. Paulden gave no indication of wishing to join the party.

Carrados came to the point at once.

"Mr. Carlyle," he said, indicating his friend, "has recently been acting for the prosecution in a case of alleged poisoning that the Public Prosecutor has now taken up. I am interested in the defence. Both sides are thus before you, Mr. Paulden."

"How does this concern me?" asked Paulden with obvious surprise.

"You are experimenting with *bhurine*. The victim of this alleged crime undoubtedly lost his life by *bhurine* poisoning. Do you mind telling us when and where you acquired your stock of this scarce substance?"

"I have had—"

"No—a moment, Mr. Paulden, before you reply," struck in Carrados with arresting hand. "You must understand that nothing so grotesque as to connect you with a crime is contemplated. But a man is under arrest and the chief point against him is the half-ounce of *bhurine* that Lightcraft of Trenion Street sold to someone at half-past five last Wednesday fortnight. Before you commit yourself to any statement that it may possibly be difficult to recede from, you should realise that this inquiry will be pushed to the very end."

"How do you know that I am using *bhurine*?"

"That," parried Carrados, "is a blind man's secret."

"Oh, well. And you say that someone has been arrested through this fact?"

"Yes. Possibly you have read something of the St. Abbots mushroom poisoning case?"

"I have no interest in the sensational ephemera of the Press. Very well; it was I who bought the *bhurine* from Lightcraft that Wednesday afternoon. I gave a false name and address, I must admit. I had a sufficient private reason for so doing."

"This knocks what is vulgarly termed 'the stuffing' out of the case for the prosecution," observed Carlyle, who had been taking a note. "It may also involve you in some trouble yourself, Mr. Paulden."

"I don't think that you need regard that very seriously in the circumstances," said Carrados reassuringly.

"They must find some scapegoat, you know," persisted Mr. Carlyle. "Loudham will raise Cain over it."

"I don't think so. Loudham, as the prosecution will roundly tell him, has only himself to thank for not giving a satisfactory account of his movements. Loudham will be lectured, Lightcraft will be fined the minimum, and Mr. Paulden will, I imagine, be told not to do it again."

The man before them laughed bitterly.

"There will be no occasion to do it again," he remarked. "Do you know anything of the circumstances?"

"Lightcraft told us something connected with colour photography. You distrust Mr. Lightcraft, I infer?"

Mr. Paulden came down to the heart-easing medium of the street.

"I've had some once, thanks," was what he said with terse expression. "Let me tell you. About eighteen months ago I was on the edge of a great discovery in colour photography. It was my discovery, whatever you may have heard. *Bhurine* was the medium, and not being then so cautious or suspicious as I have reason to be now, and finding it difficult—really impossible—to procure this substance casually, I sent in an order to Lightcraft to procure me a stock. Unfortunately, in a moment of enthusiasm I had hinted at the anticipated results to a man who was then my friend—a weakling called Southem. Comparing notes with Lightcraft they put two and two together and in a trice most of the secret boiled over.

"If you have ever been within an ace of a monumental discovery you will understand the torment of anxiety and self-reproach that possessed me. For months the result must have trembled in the balance, but even as it evaded me, so it evaded the others. And at last I was able to spread conviction that the *bhurine* process was a failure. I breathed again.

"You don't want to hear of the various things that conspired to baffle me. I proceeded with extreme caution and therefore slowly. About two weeks ago I had another foretaste of success and immediately on it a veritable disaster. By some diabolical mischance I contrived to upset my stock bottle of *bhurine*. It rolled down, smashed to atoms on a developing dish filled with another chemical, and the precious lot was irretrievably lost. To arrest the experiments at that stage for a day was to lose a month. In one place and one alone could I hope to replenish the stock temporarily at such short notice and to do it openly after my last experience filled me with dismay. Well, you know what happened, and now, I suppose, it will all come out."

★★★★★★

A week after his arrest Philip Loudham and his sister were sitting together in the drawing-room at Hazlehurst, nervous and expectant. Loudham had been discharged scarcely six hours before, with such vindication of his character as the frigid intimation that there was no evidence against him afforded. On his arrival home he had found a letter from Max Carrados—a name with which he was now familiar—awaiting him. There had been other notes and telegrams—messages of sympathy and congratulation, but the man who had brought about his liberation did not include these conventionalities. He merely stated that he proposed calling upon Mr. Loudham at nine o'clock that evening and that he hoped it would be convenient for him and all other members of the household to be at home.

"He can scarcely be coming to be thanked," speculated Loudham, breaking the silence that had fallen on them as the hour approached. "I should have called on him myself tomorrow."

Mrs. Dupreen assented absent-mindedly. Both were dressed in black, and both at that moment had the same thought: that they were dreaming this.

"I suppose you won't go on living here, Irene?" continued the brother, speaking to make the minutes seem tolerable.

This at least had the effect of bringing Mrs. Dupreen back into the present with a rush.

"Of course not," she replied almost sharply and looking at him direct. "Why should I, now?"

"Oh, all right," he agreed. "I didn't suppose you would." Then, as the front-door bell was heard to ring: "Thank heaven!"

"Won't you go to meet him in the hall and bring him in?" suggested Mrs. Dupreen. "He is blind, you know."

Carrados was carrying a small leather case which he allowed Loudham to relieve him of, together with his hat and gloves. The introduction to Mrs. Dupreen was made, the blind man put in touch with a chair, and then Philip Loudham began to rattle off the acknowledgment of gratitude of which he had been framing and rejecting openings for the last half-hour.

"I'm afraid it's no good attempting to thank you for the extraordinary service that you've rendered me, Mr. Carrados," he began, "and, above all, I appreciate the fact that, owing to you, it has been possible to keep Mrs. Guestling's name entirely out of the case. Of course you know all about that, and my sister knows, so it isn't worth while beating about the bush. Well, now that I shall have something like a decent income of my own, I shall urge Kitty—Mrs. Guestling—to apply for the divorce that she is richly entitled to, and when that is all settled we shall marry at once and try to forget the experiences on both sides that have led up to it. I hope," he added tamely, "that you don't consider us really much to blame?"

Carrados shook his head in mild deprecation.

"That is an ethical point that has lain outside the scope of my inquiry," he replied. "You would hardly imagine that I should disturb you at such a time merely to claim your thanks. Has it occurred to you why I should have come?"

Brother and sister exchanged looks and by their silence gave reply.

"We have still to find who poisoned Charlie Winpole."

Loudham stared at their guest in frank bewilderment. Mrs. Dupreen almost closed her eyes. When she spoke it was in a pained whisper.

"Is there anything more to be gained by pursuing that idea, Mr. Carrados?" she asked pleadingly. "We have passed through a week of anguish, coming upon a week of grief and great distress. Surely all has been done that can be done?"

"But you would have justice for your nephew if there has been foul play?" Mrs. Dupreen made a weary gesture of resignation. It was

305

Loudham who took up the question.

"Do you really mean, Mr. Carrados, that there is any doubt about the cause?"

"Will you give me my case, please? Thank you." He opened it and produced a small paper bag. "Now a newspaper, if you will." He opened the bag and poured out the contents. "You remember stating at the inquest, Mrs. Dupreen, that the mushrooms you bought looked rather dry? They were dry, there is no doubt, for they had then been gathered four days. Here are some more under precisely the same conditions. They looked, in point of fact, like these?"

"Yes," admitted the lady, beginning to regard Carrados with a new and curious interest.

"Dr. Slark further stated that the only fungus containing the poison *bhurine*—the Amanita called the Black Cap, and also by the country folk the Devil's Scent Bottle—did not assume its forbidding appearance until maturity. He was wrong in one sense there, for experiment proved that if the Black Cap is gathered in its young and deceptive stage and kept, it assumes precisely the same appearance as it withers as if it was ripening naturally. You observe." He opened a second bag and, shaking out the contents, displayed another little heap by the side of the first. "Gathered four days ago," he explained.

"Why, they are as black as ink," commented Loudham. "And the, phew! aroma!"

"One would hardly have got through without you seeing it, Mrs. Dupreen?"

"I certainly hardly think so," she admitted.

"With due allowance for Lackington's biased opinion I also think that his claim might be allowed. Finally, it is incredible that whoever peeled the mushrooms should have passed one of these. Who was the cook on that occasion, Mrs. Dupreen?"

"My maid Hilda. She does all the cooking."

"The one who admitted me?"

"Yes; she is the only servant I have, Mr. Carrados."

"I should like to have her in, if you don't mind."

"Certainly, if you wish it. She is"—Mrs. Dupreen felt that she must put in a favourable word before this inexorable man pronounced judgment—"she is a very good, straightforward girl."

"So much the better."

"I will—" Mrs. Dupreen rose and began to cross the room. "Ring for her? Thank you," and whatever her intention had been the lady rang the bell.

"Yes, ma'am?"

A neat, modest-mannered girl, simple and nervous, with a face as full, as clear and as honest as an English apple. "A pity," thought Mrs. Dupreen, "that this confident, suspicious man cannot see her now."

"Come in, Hilda. This gentleman wants to ask you something."

"Yes, ma' am." The round, blue eyes went appealingly to Carrados, fell upon the fungi spread out before her, and then circled the room with an instinct of escape.

"You remember the night poor Charlie died, Hilda," said Carrados in his suavest tones, "you cooked some mushrooms for his supper, didn't you?"

"No, sir," came the glib reply.

"'No,' Hilda!" exclaimed Mrs. Dupreen in wonderment. "You mean 'yes,' surely, child. Of course you cooked them. Don't you re-member?"

"Yes, ma'am," dutifully replied Hilda.

"That is all right," said the blind man reassuringly. "Nervous wit-nesses very often answer at random at first. You have nothing to be afraid of, my good girl, if you will tell the truth. I suppose you know a mushroom when you see it?"

"Yes, sir," was the rather hesitating reply.

"There was nothing like this among them?" He held up one of the poisonous sort.

"No, sir; indeed there wasn't, sir. I should have known then."

"You would have known then? You were not called at the inquest, Hilda?"

"No, sir."

"If you had been, what would you have told them about these mushrooms that you cooked?"

"I—I don't know, sir."

"Come, come, Hilda. What could you have told them—something that we do not know? The truth, girl, if you want to save yourself?" Then with a sudden, terrible directness the question cleft her trem-bling, guilt-stricken little brain: "Where did you get the other mush-rooms from that you put with those that your mistress brought?"

The eyes that had been mostly riveted to the floor leapt to Car-rados for a single frightened glance, from Carrados to her mistress, to Philip Loudham, and to the floor again. In a moment her face changed and she was in a burst of sobbing.

"Oho, oho, oho!" she wailed. "I didn't know; I didn't know. I meant no harm; indeed I didn't, ma'am."

"Hilda! Hilda!" exclaimed Mrs. Dupreen in bewilderment. "What is it you're saying? What have you done?"

"It was his own fault. Oho, oho, oho!" Every word was punctuated by a gasp. "He always was a little pig and making himself ill with food. You know he was, ma'am, although you were so fond of him. I'm sure I'm not to blame."

"But what was it? What have you done?" besought her mistress. "It was after you went out on that afternoon. He put on his things and slipped down into the kitchen without the master knowing. He said what you were getting for his dinner, ma'am, and that you never got enough of them. Then he told me not to tell about his being down, because he'd seen some white things from his bedroom window growing by the hedge at the bottom of the garden and he was going to get them. He brought in four or five and said they were mushrooms and asked me to cook them with the others and not say anything because you'd say too many were not good for him. And I didn't know any difference. Indeed I'm telling you the truth, ma'am."

"Oh, Hilda, Hilda!" was torn reproachfully from Mrs. Dupreen. "You know what we've gone through. Why didn't you tell us this before?"

"I was afraid. I was afraid of what they'd do. And no one ever guessed until I thought I was safe. Indeed I meant no harm to anyone, but I was afraid that they'd punish me instead." Carrados had risen and was picking up his things.

"Yes," he said, half musing to himself, "I knew it must exist: the one explanation that accounts for everything and cannot be assailed. We have reached the bed-rock of truth at last."

The Ghost at Massingham Mansions

"Do you believe in ghosts, Max?" inquired Mr. Carlyle.

"Only as ghosts," replied Carrados with decision.

"Quite so," assented the private detective with the air of acquiescence with which he was wont to cloak his moments of obfuscation. Then he added cautiously: "And how don't you believe in them, pray?"

"As public nuisances—or private ones for that matter," replied his friend. "So long as they are content to behave as ghosts I am with them. When they begin to meddle with a state of existence that is outside their province—to interfere in business matters and depreciate property—to rattle chains, bang doors, ring bells, predict winners and to edit magazines and to attract attention instead of shunning it, I cease to believe. My sympathies are entirely with the sensible old fellow who was awakened in the middle of the night to find a shadowy form standing by the side of his bed and silently regarding him. For a few minutes the disturbed man waited patiently, expecting some awful communication, but the same profound silence was maintained. 'Well,' he remarked at length, 'if you have nothing to do, I have,' and turning over went to sleep again."

"I have been asked to take up a ghost," Carlyle began to explain.

"Then I don't believe in it," declared Carrados.

"Why not?"

"Because it is a pushful, notoriety-loving ghost, or it would not have gone so far. Probably it wants to get into *The Daily Mail*. The other people, whoever they are, don't believe in it either, Louis, or they wouldn't have called you in. They would have gone to Sir Oliver Lodge for an explanation, or to the nearest priest for a stoup of holy water."

"I admit that I shall direct my researches towards the forces of this world before I begin to investigate any other," conceded Louis Carlyle. "And I don't doubt," he added, with his usual bland complacence, "that I shall hale up some mischievous or aggrieved individual before the ghost is many days older. Now that you have brought me so far, do you care to go on round to the place with me, Max, to hear what they have to say about it?"

Carrados agreed with his usual good nature. He rarely met his friend without hearing the details of some new case, for Carlyle's practice had increased vastly since the night when chance had led him into the blind man's study. They discussed the cases according to their interest, and there the matter generally ended so far as Max Carrados was concerned, until he casually heard the result subsequently from Carlyle's lips or learned the sequel from the newspaper. But these pages are primarily a record of the methods of the one man whose name they bear and therefore for the occasional case that Carrados completed for his friend there must be assumed the unchronicled scores which the inquiry agent dealt capably with himself.

This reminder is perhaps necessary to dissipate the impression that Louis Carlyle was a pretentious humbug. He was, as a matter of fact, in spite of his amiable foibles and the self-assurance that was, after all, merely an asset of his trade, a shrewd and capable business man of his world, and behind his office manner nothing concerned him more than to pocket fees for which he felt that he had failed to render value.

Massingham Mansions proved to be a single block of residential flats overlooking a recreation ground. It was, as they afterwards found, an adjunct to a larger estate of similar property situated down another road. A porter, residing in the basement, looked after the interests of Massingham Mansions; the business office was placed among the other flats. On that morning it presented the appearance of a well-kept, prosperous enough place, a little dull, a little unfurnished, a little depressing perhaps; in fact faintly reminiscent of the superfluous mansions that stand among broad, weedy roads on the outskirts of overgrown seaside resorts; but it was persistently raining at the time when Mr. Carlyle had his first view of it.

"It is early to judge," he remarked, after stopping the car in order to verify the name on the brass plate, "but, upon my word, Max, I really think that our ghost might have discovered more appropriate quarters."

At the office, to which the porter had directed them, they found a managing clerk and two coltish youths in charge. Mr. Carlyle's name produced an appreciable flutter.

"The governor isn't here just now, but I have this matter in hand," said the clerk with an easy air of responsibility—an effect unfortunately marred by a sudden irrepressible giggle from the least overawed of the colts. "Will you kindly step into our private room?" He turned at the door of the inner office and dropped a freezing eye on the offender. "Get those letters copied before you go out to lunch, Binns," he remarked in a sufficiently loud voice. Then he closed the door quickly, before Binns could find a suitable retort.

So far it had been plain sailing, but now, brought face to face with the necessity of explaining, the clerk began to develop some hesitancy in beginning.

"It's a funny sort of business," he remarked, skirting the difficulty.

"Perhaps," admitted Mr. Carlyle; "but that will not embarrass us. Many of the cases that pass through my hands are what you would call 'funny sorts of business.'"

"I suppose so," responded the young man, "but not through ours. Well, this is at No. 11 Massingham. A few nights ago—I suppose it must be more than a week now—Willett, the estate porter, was taking up some luggage to No. 75 Northanger for the people there when he noticed a light in one of the rooms at 11 Massingham. The backs face, though about twenty or thirty yards away. It struck him as curious, because 11 Massingham is empty and locked up. Naturally he thought at first that the porter at Massingham or one of us from the office had gone up for something. Still it was so unusual—being late at night—that it was his business to look into it. On his way round—you know where Massingham Mansions are?—he had to pass here. It was dark, for we'd all been gone hours, but Willett has duplicate keys and he let himself in.

"Then he began to think that something must be wrong, for here, hanging up against their number on the board, were the only two keys of 11 Massingham that there are supposed to be. He put the keys in his pocket and went on to Massingham. Green, the resident porter there, told him that he hadn't been into No. 11 for a week. What was more, no one had passed the outer door, in or out, for a good half—hour. He knew that, because the door 'springs' with a noise when it is opened, no matter how carefully. So the two of them went up. The door of No. 11 was locked and inside everything was as it should be. There was no light then, and after looking well round with the lanterns that they carried they were satisfied that no one was concealed there."

"You say lanterns," interrupted Mr. Carlyle. "I suppose they lit the gas, or whatever it is there, as well?"

"It is gas, but they could not light it because it was cut off at the meter. We always cut it off when a flat becomes vacant."

"What sort of a light was it, then, that Willett saw?"

"It was gas, Mr. Carlyle. It is possible to see the bracket in that room from 75 Northanger. He saw it burning."

"Then the meter had been put on again?"

"It is in a locked cupboard in the basement. Only the office and the porters have keys. They tried the gas in the room and it was dead out; they looked at the meter in the basement afterwards and it was dead off."

"Very good," observed Mr. Carlyle, noting the facts in his pocket-book. "What next?"

"The next," continued the clerk, "was something that had really happened before. When they got down again—Green and Willett—Green was rather chipping Willett about seeing the light, you know, when he stopped suddenly. He'd remembered something. The day before the servant at 12 Massingham had asked him who it was that was using the bathroom at No. 11—she of course knowing that it was empty. He told her that no one used the bathroom. 'Well,' she said, 'we hear the water running and splashing almost every night and it's funny with no one there.' He had thought nothing of it at the time, concluding—as he told her—that it must be the water in the bathroom of one of the underneath flats that they heard. Of course he told Willett then and they went up again and examined the bathroom more closely. Water had certainly been run there, for the sides of the bath were still wet. They tried the taps and not a drop came. When a flat is empty we cut off the water like the gas."

"At the same place—the cupboard in the basement?" inquired Carlyle.

"No; at the cistern in the roof. The trap is at the top of the stairs and you need a longish ladder to get there. The next morning Willett reported what he'd seen and the governor told me to look into it. We didn't think much of it so far. That night I happened to be seeing some friends to the station here—I live not so far off—and I thought I might as well take a turn round here on my way home. I knew that if a light was burning I should be able to see the window lit up from the yard at the back, although the gas itself would be out of sight. And, sure enough, there was the light blazing out of one of the windows of No. 11. I won't say that I didn't feel a bit homesick then, but I'd made up my mind to go up."

"Good man," murmured Mr. Carlyle approvingly.

"Wait a bit," recommended the clerk, with a shame-faced laugh. "So far I had only had to make my mind up. It was then close on midnight and not a soul about. I came here for the keys, and I also had the luck to remember an old revolver that had been lying about in a drawer of the office for years. It wasn't loaded, but it didn't seem quite so lonely with it. I put it in my pocket and went on to Massingham, taking another turn into the yard to see that the light was still on. Then I went up the stairs as quietly as I could and let myself into No. 11."

"You didn't take Willett or Green with you?"

The clerk gave Mr. Carlyle a knowing look, as of one smart man who will be appreciated by another.

"Willett's a very trustworthy chap," he replied, "and we have every confidence in him. Green also, although he has not been with us so long. But I thought it just as well to do it on my own, you understand, Mr. Carlyle. You didn't look in at Massingham on your way? Well, if you had you would have seen that there is a pane of glass above every door, frosted glass to the hall doors and plain over each of those inside. It's to light the halls and passages, you know. Each flat has a small square hall and a longish passage leading off it. As soon as I opened the door I could tell that one of the rooms down the passage was lit up, though I could not see the door of it from there. Then I crept very quietly through the hall into the passage. A regular stream of light was shining from above the end door on the left. The room, I knew, was the smallest in the flat—it's generally used for a servant's bedroom or sometimes for a box-room. It was a bit thick, you'll admit—right at the end of a long passage and midnight, and after what the others had said."

"Yes, yes," assented the inquiry agent. "But you went on?"

"I went on, tiptoeing without a sound. I got to the door, took out my pistol, put my hand almost on the handle and then—"

"Well, well," prompted Mr. Carlyle, as the narrator paused provokingly, with the dramatic instinct of an expert raconteur, "what then?"

"Then the light went out. While my hand was within an inch of the handle the light went out, as clean as if I had been watched all along and the thing timed. It went out all at once, without any warning and without the slightest sound from the beastly room beyond. And then it was as black as hell in the passage and something seemed to be going to happen."

"What did you do?"

"I did a slope," acknowledged the clerk frankly. "I broke all the records down that passage, I bet you. You'll laugh, I dare say, and think you would have stood, but you don't know what it was like. I'd been screwing myself up, wondering what I should see in that lighted room when I opened the door, and then the light went out like a knife, and for all I knew the next second the door would open on me in the dark and Christ only knows what come out."

"Probably I should have run also," conceded Mr. Carlyle tactfully. "And you, Max?"

"You see, I always feel at home in the dark," apologised the blind man. "At all events, you got safely away, Mr.——?"

"My name's Elliott," responded the clerk. "Yes, you may bet I did. Whether the door opened and anybody or anything came out or not I can't say. I didn't look. I certainly did get an idea that I heard the bath water running and swishing as I snatched at the hall door, but I didn't stop to consider that either, and if it was, the noise was lost in the slam of the door and my clatter as I took about twelve flights of stairs six steps at a time. Then when I was safely out I did venture to go round to look up again, and there was that damned light full on again."

"Really?" commented Mr. Carlyle. "That was very audacious of him."

"Him? Oh, well, yes, I suppose so. That's what the governor insists, but he hasn't been up there himself in the dark."

"Is that as far as you have got?"

"It's as far as we can get. The bally thing goes on just as it likes. The very next day we tied up the taps of the gas—meter and the water cistern and sealed the string. Bless you, it didn't make a ha'peth of difference. Scarcely a night passes without the light showing, and there's no doubt that the water runs. We've put copying ink on the door handles and the taps and got into it ourselves until there isn't a man about the place that you couldn't implicate."

"Has anyone watched up there?"

"Willett and Green together did one night. They shut themselves up in the room opposite from ten till twelve and nothing happened. I was watching the window with a pair of opera-glasses from an empty flat here—85 Northanger. Then they chucked it, and before they could have been down the steps the light was there—I could see the gas as plain as I can see this ink-stand. I ran down and met them coming to tell me that nothing had happened. The three of us sprinted up again and the light was out and the flat as deserted as a churchyard. What do you make of that?"

"It certainly requires looking into," replied Mr. Carlyle diplomatically.

"Looking into! Well, you're welcome to look all day and all night too, Mr. Carlyle. It isn't as though it was an old baronial mansion, you see, with sliding panels and secret passages. The place has the date over the front door, 1882—1882 and haunted, by gosh! It was built for what it is, and there isn't an inch unaccounted for between the slates and the foundation."

"These two things—the light and the water running—are the only indications there have been?" asked Mr. Carlyle.

"So far as we ourselves have seen or heard. I ought perhaps to tell you of something else, however. When this business first started I made a few casual inquiries here and there among the tenants. Among others I saw Mr. Belting, who occupies No. 9 Massingham—the flat directly beneath No. 11. It didn't seem any good making up a cock-and-bull story, so I put it to him plainly—had he been annoyed by anything unusual going on at the empty flat above?

"'If you mean your confounded ghost up there, I have not been particularly annoyed,' he said at once, 'but Mrs. Belting has, and I should advise you to keep out of her way, at least until she gets another servant.' Then he told me that their girl, who slept in the bedroom underneath the little one at No. 11, had been going on about noises in the room above—footsteps and tramping and a bump on the floor—for some time before we heard anything of it. Then one day she suddenly said that she'd had enough of it and bolted. That was just before Willett first saw the light."

"It is being talked about, then—among the tenants?"

"You bet!" assented Mr. Elliott pungently. "That's what gets the governor. He wouldn't give a continental if no one knew, but you can't tell where it will end. The people at Northanger don't half like it either. All the children are scared out of their little wits and none of the slaveys will run errands after dark. It'll give the estate a bad name for the next three years if it isn't stopped."

"It shall be stopped," declared Mr. Carlyle impressively. "Of course we have our methods for dealing with this sort of thing, but in order to make a clean sweep it is desirable to put our hands on the offender *in flagranti delicto*. Tell your—er—principal not to have any further concern in the matter. One of my people will call here for any further details that he may require during the day. Just leave everything as it is in the meanwhile. Good-morning, Mr. Elliott, good-morning..."

"A fairly obvious game, I imagine, Max," he commented as they got into the car, "although the details are original and the motive not disclosed as yet. I wonder how many of them are in it?"

"Let me know when you find out," said Carrados, and Mr. Carlyle promised.

Nearly a week passed and the expected revelation failed to make its appearance. Then, instead, quite a different note arrived:

My dear Max—I wonder if you formed any conclusion of that Massingham Mansions affair from Mr. Elliott's refined narrative of the circumstances?

I begin to suspect that Trigget, whom I put on, is somewhat of an ass, though a very remarkable circumstance has come to light which might—if it wasn't a matter of business—offer an explanation of the whole business by stamping it as inexplicable.

You know how I value your suggestions. If you happen to be in the neighbourhood—not otherwise, Max, I protest—I should be glad if you would drop in for a chat.

Yours sincerely,

Louis Carlyle.

Carrados smiled at the ingenuous transparency of the note. He had thought several times of the case since the interview with Elliott, chiefly because he was struck by certain details of the manifestation that divided it from the ordinary methods of the bogy-raiser, an aspect that had apparently made no particular impression on his friend. He was sufficiently interested not to let the day pass without "happening" to be in the neighbourhood of Bampton Street.

"Max," exclaimed Mr. Carlyle, raising an accusing forefinger, "you have come on purpose."

"If I have," replied the visitor, "you can reward me with a cup of that excellent beverage that you were able to conjure up from somewhere down in the basement on a former occasion. As a matter of fact, I have."

Mr. Carlyle transmitted the order and then demanded his friend's serious attention.

"That ghost at Massingham Mansions—"

"I still don't believe in that particular ghost, Louis," commented Carrados in mild speculation.

"I never did, of course," replied Carlyle, "but, upon my word, Max, I shall have to very soon as a precautionary measure. Trigget has been able to do nothing and now he has as good as gone on strike."

"Downed—now what on earth can an inquiry man down to go on strike, Louis? Notebooks? So Trigget has got a chill, like our candid friend Eliott, Eh?"

"He started all right—said that he didn't mind spending a night or a week in a haunted flat, and, to do him justice, I don't believe he did at first. Then he came across a very curious piece of forgotten local history, a very remarkable—er—coincidence in the circumstances, Max."

"I was wondering," said Carrados, "when we should come up against that story, Louis."

"Then you know of it?" exclaimed the inquiry agent in surprise.

"Not at all. Only I guessed it must exist. Here you have the manifestation associated with two things which in themselves are neither usual nor awe-inspiring—the gas and the water. It requires some association to connect them up, to give them point and force. That is the story."

"Yes," assented his friend, "that is the story, and, upon my soul, in the circumstances—well, you shall hear it. It comes partly from the newspapers of many years ago, but only partly, for the circumstances were successfully hushed up in a large measure and it required the stimulated memories of ancient scandal-mongers to fill in the details. Oh yes, it was a scandal, Max, and would have been a great sensation too, I do not doubt, only they had no proper pictorial press in those days, poor beggars. It was very soon after Massingham Mansions had been erected—they were called Enderby House in those days, by the way, for the name was changed on account of this very business. The household at No. 11 consisted of a comfortable, middle-aged married couple and one servant, a quiet and attractive young creature, one is led to understand. As a matter of fact, I think they were the first tenants of that flat."

"The first occupants give the soul to a new house," remarked the blind man gravely. "That is why empty houses have their different characters."

"I don't doubt it for a moment," assented Mr. Carlyle in his incisive way, "but none of our authorities on this case made any reference to the fact. They did say, however, that the man held a good and responsible position—a position for which high personal character and strict morality were essential. He was also well known and regarded in quiet but substantial local circles where serious views prevailed. He was, in short, a man of notorious 'respectability.'

"The first chapter of the tragedy opened with the painful death of the prepossessing handmaiden—suicide, poor creature. She didn't appear one morning and the flat was full of the reek of gas. With great promptitude the master threw all the windows open and called up the porter. They burst open the door of the little bedroom at the end of the passage, and there was the thing as clear as daylight for any coroner's jury to see. The door was locked on the inside and the extinguished gas was turned full on. It was only a tiny room, with no fireplace, and the ventilation of a closed well—fitting door and window was negligible in the circumstances. At all events the girl was proved to have been dead for several hours when they reached her, and the doctor who conducted the autopsy crowned the convincing fabric of circumstances when he mentioned as delicately as possible that the girl had a very pressing reason for dreading an inevitable misfortune that would shortly overtake her. The jury returned the obvious verdict.

"There have been a great many undiscovered crimes in the history of mankind, Max, but it is by no means every ingenious plot that carries. After the inquest, at which our gentleman doubtless cut a very proper and impressive figure, the barbed whisper began to insinuate and to grow in freedom. It is sheerly impossible to judge how these things start, but we know that when once they have been begun they gather material like an avalanche. It was remembered by someone at the flat underneath that late on the fatal night a window in the principal bedroom above had been heard to open, top and bottom, very quietly. Certain other sounds of movement in the night did not tally with the tale of sleep-wrapped innocence.

"Sceptical busybodies were anxious to demonstrate practically to those who differed from them on this question that it was quite easy to extinguish a gas-jet in one room by blowing down the gas-pipe in another; and in this connection there was evidence that the lady of the flat had spoken to her friends more than once of her sentimental young servant's extravagant habit of reading herself to sleep occasionally with the light full on. Why was nothing heard at the inquest, they demanded, of the curious fact that an open novelette lay on the counterpane when the room was broken into? A hundred trifling circumstances were adduced—arrangements that the girl had been making for the future down to the last evening of her life—interpretable hints that she had dropped to her acquaintances—her views on suicide and the best means to that end: a favourite topic, it would seem, among her class—her possession of certain comparatively expensive trinkets on a salary of a very few shillings a week, and so on.

"Finally, some rather more definite and important piece of evidence must have been conveyed to the authorities, for we know now that one fine day a warrant was issued. Somehow rumour preceded its execution. The eminently respectable gentleman with whom it was concerned did not wait to argue out the merits of the case. He locked himself in the bathroom, and when the police arrived they found that instead of an arrest they had to arrange the details for another inquest."

"A very convincing episode," conceded Carrados in response to his friend's expectant air. "And now her spirit passes the long winter evenings turning the gas on and off, and the one amusement of his consists in doing the same with the bath-water—or the other way, the other way about, Louis. Truly, one half the world knows not how the other half lives!"

"All your cheap humour won't induce Trigget to spend another night in that flat, Max," retorted Mr. Carlyle. "Nor, I am afraid, will it help me through this business in any other way."

"Then I'll give you a hint that may," said Carrados. "Try your respectable gentleman's way of settling difficulties."

"What is that?" demanded his friend.

"Blow down the pipes, Louis."

"Blow down the pipes?" repeated Carlyle.

"At all events try it. I infer that Mr. Trigget has not experimented in that direction."

"But what will it do, Max?"

"Possibly it will demonstrate where the other end goes to."

"But the other end goes to the meter."

"I suggest not—not without some interference with its progress. I have already met your Mr. Trigget, you know, Louis. An excellent and reliable man within his limits, but he is at his best posted outside the door of a hotel waiting to see the co-respondent go in. He hasn't enough imagination for this case—not enough to carry him away from what would be his own obvious method of doing it to what is someone else's equally obvious but quite different method. Unless I am doing him an injustice, he will have spent most of his time trying to catch someone getting into the flat to turn the gas and water on and off, whereas I conjecture that no one does go into the flat because it is perfectly simple—ingenious but simple—to produce these phenomena without. Then when Mr. Trigget has satisfied himself that it is physically impossible for anyone to be going in and out, and when, on the top of it, he comes across this romantic tragedy—a tale that might psychologically explain the ghost, simply because the ghost is moulded on the tragedy—then, of course, Mr. Trigget's mental process is swept away from its moorings and his feet begin to get cold."

"This is very curious and suggestive," said Mr. Carlyle. "I certainly assumed—But shall we have Trigget up and question him on the point? I think he ought to be here now—if he isn't detained at the Bull."

Carrados assented, and in a few minutes Mr. Trigget presented himself at the door of the private office. He was a melancholy-looking middle-aged little man, with an ineradicable air of being exactly what he was, and the searcher for deeper or subtler indications of character would only be rewarded by a latent pessimism grounded on the depressing probability that he would never be anything else.

"Come in, Trigget," called out Mr. Carlyle when his employee diffidently appeared. "Come in. Mr. Carrados would like to hear some of the details of the Massingham Mansions case."

"Not the first time I have availed myself of the benefit of your inquiries, Mr. Trigget," nodded the blind man. "Good-afternoon."

"Good-afternoon, sir," replied Trigget with gloomy deference. "It's very handsome of you to put it in that way, Mr. Carrados, sir. But this isn't another Tarporley-Templeton case, if I may say so, sir. That was as plain as a pikestaff after all, sir."

"When we saw the pikestaff, Mr. Trigget; yes, it was," admitted Carrados, with a smile. "But this is insoluble? Ah, well. When I was a boy I used to be extraordinarily fond of ghost stories, I remember, but even while reading them I always had an uneasy suspicion that when it came to the necessary detail of explaining the mystery I should be defrauded with some subterfuge as 'by an ingenious arrangement of hidden wires the artful Muggles had contrived,' etc., or 'an optical illusion effected by means of concealed mirrors revealed the *modus operandi* of the apparition.' I thought that I had been swindled. I think so still. I hope there are no ingenious wires or concealed mirrors here, Mr. Trigget?"

Mr. Trigget looked mildly sagacious but hopelessly puzzled. It was his misfortune that in him the necessities of his business and the proclivities of his nature were at variance, so that he ordinarily presented the curious anomaly of looking equally alert and tired.

"Wires, sir?" he began, with faint amusement.

"Not only wires, but anything that might account for what is going on," interposed Mr. Carlyle. "Mr. Carrados means this, Trigget: you have reported that it is impossible for anyone to be concealed in the flat or to have secret access to it—"

"I have tested every inch of space in all the rooms, Mr. Carrados, sir," protested the hurt Trigget. "I have examined every board and, you may say, every nail in the floor, the skirting-boards, the window frames and in fact wherever a board or a nail exists. There are no secret ways in or out. Then I have taken the most elaborate precautions against the doors and windows being used for surreptitious ingress and egress. They have not been used, sir. For the past week I am the only person who has been in and out of the flat, Mr. Carrados, and yet night after night the gas that is cut off at the meter is lit and turned out again, and the water that is cut off at the cistern splashes about in the bath up to the second I let myself in. Then it's as quiet as the grave and everything is exactly as I left it. It isn't human, Mr. Carrados, sir, and flesh and blood can't stand it—not in the middle of the night, that is to say."

"You see nothing further, Mr. Trigget?"

"I don't indeed, Mr. Carrados. I would suggest doing away with the gas in that room altogether. As a box-room it wouldn't need one."

"And the bathroom?"

"That might be turned into a small bedroom and all the water fittings removed. Then to provide a bathroom—"

"Yes, yes," interrupted Mr. Carlyle impatiently, "but we are retained to discover who in causing this annoyance and to detect the means, not to suggest structural alterations in the flat, Trigget. The fact is that after having put in a week on this job you have failed to bring us an inch nearer its solution. Now Mr. Carrados has suggested"—Mr. Carlyle was not usually detained among the finer shades of humour, but some appreciation of the grotesqueness of the advice required him to control his voice as he put the matter in its baldest form—"Mr. Carrados has suggested that instead of spending the time measuring the chimneys and listening to the wall-paper, if you had simply blown down the gas-pipe—"

Carrados was inclined to laugh, although he thought it rather too bad of Louis.

"Not quite in those terms, Mr. Trigget," he interposed.

"Blow down the gas-pipe, sir?" repeated the amazed man. "What for?"

"To ascertain where the other end comes out," replied Carlyle.

"But don't you see, sir, that that is a detail until you ascertain how it is being done? The pipe may be tapped between the bath and the cistern. Naturally, I considered that. As a matter of fact, the water-pipe isn't tapped. It goes straight up from the bath to the cistern in the attic above, a distance of only a few feet, and I have examined it The gas-pipe, it is true, passes through a number of flats, and without pulling up all the floors it isn't practicable to trace it. But how does that help us, Mr. Carrados? The gas-tap has to be turned on and off; you can't do that with these hidden wires. It has to be lit. I've never heard of lighting gas by optical illusions, sir. Somebody must get in and out of the flat or else it isn't human. I've spent a week, a very trying week, sir, in endeavouring to ascertain how it could be done. I haven't shirked cold and wet and solitude, sir, in the discharge of my duty. I've freely placed my poor gifts of observation and intelligence, such as they are, at the service—"

"Not 'freely,' Trigget," interposed his employer with decision.

"I am speaking under a deep sense of injury, Mr. Carlyle," retorted Mr. Trigget, who, having had time to think it over, had now come to the conclusion that he was not appreciated. "I am alluding to a moral attitude such as we all possess. I am very grieved by what has been suggested. I didn't expect it of you, Mr. Carlyle, sir; indeed I did not. For a week I have done everything that it has been possible to do, everything that a long experience could suggest, and now, as I understand it, sir, you complain that I didn't blow down the gas-pipe, sir. It's hard, sir; it's very hard."

"Oh, well, for heaven's sake don't cry about it, Trigget," exclaimed Mr. Carlyle. "You're always sobbing about the place over something or other. We know you did your best—God help you!" he added aside.

"I did, Mr. Carlyle; indeed I did, sir. And I thank you for that appreciative tribute to my services. I value it highly, very highly indeed, sir." A tremulous note in the rather impassioned delivery made it increasingly plain that Mr. Trigget's regimen had not been confined entirely to solid food that day. His wrongs were forgotten and he approached Mr. Carrados with an engaging air of secrecy.

"What is this tip about blowing down the gas-pipe, sir?" he whispered confidentially. "The old dog's always willing to learn something new."

"Max," said Mr. Carlyle curtly, "is there anything more that we need detain Trigget for?"

"Just this," replied Carrados after a moment's thought. "The gas-bracket—it has a mantle attachment on?"

"Oh no, Mr. Carrados," confided the old dog with the affectation of imparting rather valuable information, "not a mantle on. Oh, certainly no mantle. Indeed—indeed, not a mantle at all."

Mr. Carlyle looked at his friend curiously. It was half evident that something might have miscarried. Furthermore, it was obvious that the warmth of the room and the stress of emotion were beginning to have a disastrous effect on the level of Mr. Trigget's ideas and speech.

"A globe?" suggested Carrados.

"A globe? No sir, not even a globe, in the strict sense of the word. No globe, that is to say, Mr. Carrados. In fact nothing like a globe."

"What is there, then?" demanded the blind man without any break in his unruffled patience. "There may be another way—but surely—surely there must be some attachment?"

"No," said Mr. Trigget with precision, "no attachment at all; nothing at all; nothing whatsoever. Just the ordinary or common or penny plain gas-jet, and above it the what you may call it thingamabob."

"The shade—gas consumer—of course!" exclaimed Carrados. "That is it."

"The tin thingamabob," insisted Mr. Trigget with slow dignity. "Call it what you will. Its purpose is self-evident. It acts as a dispirator—a distributor, that is to say—"

"Louis," struck in Carrados joyously, "are you good for settling it tonight?"

"Certainly, my dear fellow, if you can really give the time."

"Good; it's years since I last tackled a ghost. What about?" His look indicated the other member of the council.

"Would he be of any assistance?"

"Perhaps—then."

"What time?"

"Say eleven-thirty."

"Trigget," rapped out his employer sharply, "meet us at the corner of Middlewood and Enderby Roads at half-past eleven sharp tonight.

If you can't manage it I shall not require your services again."

"Certainly, sir; I shall not fail to be punctual," replied Trigget without a tremor. The appearance of an almost incredible sobriety had possessed him in the face of warning, and both in speech and manner he was again exactly the man as he had entered the room. "I regard it as a great honour, Mr. Carrados, to be associated with you in this business, sir."

"In the meanwhile," remarked Carrados, "if you find the time hang heavy on your hands you might look up the subject of 'platinum black.' It may be the new tip you want."

"Certainly, sir. But do you mind giving me a hint as to what 'platinum black' is?"

"It is a chemical that has the remarkable property of igniting hydrogen or coal gas by mere contact," replied Carrados. "Think how useful that may be if you haven't got a match!"

To mark the happy occasion Mr. Carlyle had insisted on taking his friend off to witness a popular musical comedy. Carrados had a few preparations to make, a few accessories to procure for the night's work, but the whole business had come within the compass of an hour and the theatre spanned the interval between dinner at the Palm Tree and the time when they left the car at the appointed meeting-place. Mr. Trigget was already there, in an irreproachable state of normal dejection. Parkinson accompanied the party, bringing with him the baggage of the expedition.

"Anything going on, Trigget?" inquired Mr. Carlyle.

"I've made a turn round the place, sir, and the light was on," was the reply. "I didn't go up for fear of disturbing the conditions before you saw them. That was about ten minutes ago. Are you going into the yard to look again? I have all the keys, of course."

"Do we, Max?" queried Mr. Carlyle.

"Mr. Trigget might. We need not all go. He can catch us up again."

He caught them up again before they had reached the outer door.

"It's still on, sir," he reported.

"Do we use any special caution, Max?" asked Carlyle.

"Oh no. Just as though we were friends of the ghost, calling in the ordinary way."

Trigget, who retained the keys, preceded the party up the stairs till the top was reached. He stood a moment at the door of No. 11 examining, by the light of the electric lamp he carried, his private marks there and pointing out to the others in a whisper that they had not been tampered with. All at once a most dismal wail, lingering, piercing and ending in something like a sob that died away because the life that gave it utterance had died with it, drawled forebodingly through the echoing emptiness of the deserted flat. Trigget had just snapped off his light and in the darkness a startled exclamation sprang from Mr. Carlyle's lips.

"It's all right, sir," said the little man, with a private satisfaction that he had the diplomacy to conceal. "Bit creepy, isn't it? especially when you hear it by yourself up here for the first time. It's only the end of the bath-water running out."

He had opened the door and was conducting them to the room at the end of the passage. A faint aurora had been visible from that direction when they first entered the hall, but it was cut off before they could identify its source.

"That's what happens," muttered Trigget.

He threw open the bedroom door without waiting to examine his marks there and they crowded into the tiny chamber. Under the beams of the lamps they carried it was brilliantly though erratically illuminated. All turned towards the central object of their quest, a tarnished gas-bracket of the plainest description. A few inches above it hung the metal disc that Trigget had alluded to, for the ceiling was low and at that point it was brought even nearer to the gas by corresponding with the slant of the roof outside.

With the prescience so habitual with him that it had ceased to cause remark among his associates Carrados walked straight to the gas-bracket and touched the burner.

"Still warm," he remarked. "And so are we getting now. A thoroughly material ghost, you perceive, Louis."

"But still turned off, don't you see, Mr. Carrados, sir," put in Trigget eagerly. "And yet no one's passed out."

"Still turned off—and still turned on," commented the blind man.

"What do you mean, Max?"

"The small screwdriver, Parkinson," requested Carrados.

"Well, upon my word!" dropped Mr. Carlyle expressively. For in no longer time than it takes to record the fact Max Carrados had removed a screw and then knocked out the tap. He held it up towards them and they all at once saw that so much of the metal had been filed away that the gas passed through no matter how the tap stood. "How on earth did you know of that?"

"Because it wasn't practicable to do the thing in any other way. Now unhook the shade, Parkinson—carefully."

The warning was not altogether unnecessary, for the man had to stand on tiptoes before he could comply. Carrados received the dingy metal cone and lightly touched its inner surface.

"Ah, here, at the apex, to be sure," he remarked. "The gas is bound to get there. And there, Louis, you have an ever-lit and yet a truly 'safety' match—so far as gas is concerned. You can buy the thing for a shilling, I believe."

Mr. Carlyle was examining the tiny apparatus with interest. So small that it might have passed for the mummy of a midget hanging from a cobweb, it appeared to consist of an insignificant black pellet and an inch of the finest wire.

"Um, I've never heard of it. And this will really light the gas?"

"As often as you like. That is the whole bag of tricks."

Mr. Carlyle turned a censorious eye upon his lieutenant, but Trigget was equal to the occasion and met it without embarrassment.

"I hadn't heard of it either, sir," he remarked conversationally. "Gracious, what won't they be getting out next, Mr. Carlyle!"

"Now for the mystery of the water." Carrados was finding his way to the bathroom and they followed him down the passage and across the hall. "In its way I think that this is really more ingenious than the gas, for, as Mr. Trigget has proved for us, the water does not come from the cistern. The taps, you perceive, are absolutely dry."

"It is forced up?" suggested Mr. Carlyle, nodding towards the outlet.

"That is the obvious alternative. We will test it presently." The blind man was down on his hands and knees following the lines of the different pipes. "Two degrees more cold are not conclusive, because in any case the water had gone out that way. Mr. Trigget, you know the ropes, will you be so obliging as to go up to the cistern and turn the water on."

"I shall need a ladder, sir."

"Parkinson."

"We have a folding ladder out here," said Parkinson, touching Mr. Trigget's arm.

"One moment," interposed Carrados, rising from his investigation among the pipes; "this requires some care. I want you to do it without making a sound or showing a light, if that is possible. Parkinson will help you. Wait until you hear us raising a diversion at the other end of the flat. Come, Louis."

The diversion took the form of tapping the wall and skirting-board in the other haunted room. When Trigget presented himself to report that the water was now on Carrados put him to continue the singular exercise with Mr. Carlyle while he himself slipped back to the bathroom.

"The pump, Parkinson," he commanded in a brisk whisper to his man, who was waiting in the hall.

The appliance was not unlike a powerful tyre pump with some modifications. One tube from it was quickly fitted to the outlet pipe of the bath, another trailed a loose end into the bath itself, ready to take up the water. There were a few other details, the work of moments. Then Carrados turned on the tap, silencing the inflow by the attachment of a short length of rubber tube. When the water had risen a few inches he slipped off to the other room, told his rather mystified confederates there that he wanted a little more noise and bustle put into their performance, and was back again in the bathroom.

"Now, Parkinson," he directed, and turned off the tap. There was about a foot of water in the bath.

Parkinson stood on the broad base of the pump and tried to drive down the handle. It scarcely moved.

"Harder," urged Carrados, interpreting every detail of sound with perfect accuracy.

Parkinson set his teeth and lunged again. Again he seemed to come up against a solid wall of resistance.

"Keep trying; something must give," said his master encouragingly. "Here, let me—" He threw his weight into the balance and for a moment they hung like a group poised before action. Then, somewhere, something did give and the sheathing plunger "drew."

"Now like blazes till the bath is empty. Then you can tell the others to stop hammering." Parkinson, looking round to acquiesce, found himself alone, for with silent step and quickened senses Carrados was already passing down the dark flights of the broad stone stairway.

It was perhaps three minutes later when an excited gentleman in the state of disrobement that is tacitly regarded as falling upon the *punctum caecum* in times of fire, flood and nocturnal emergency shot out of the door of No.7 and bounding up the intervening flights of steps pounded with the knocker on the door of No. 9. As someone did not appear with the instantaneity of a jack-in-the-box, he proceeded to repeat the summons, interspersing it with an occasional "I say!" shouted through the letter-box.

The light above the door made it unconvincing to affect that no one was at home. The gentleman at the door trumpeted the fact through his channel of communication and demanded instant attention. So immersed was he with his own grievance, in fact, that he failed to notice the approach of someone on the other side, and the sudden opening of the door, when it did take place, surprised him on his knees at his neighbour's doorstep, a large and consequential-looking personage as revealed in the light from the hall, wearing the silk hat that he had instinctively snatched up, but with his braces hanging down.

"Mr. Tupworthy of No.7, isn't it?" quickly interposed the new man before his visitor could speak. "But why this—homage? Permit me to raise you, sir."

"Confound it all," snorted Mr. Tupworthy indignantly, "you're flooding my flat. The water's coming through my bathroom ceiling in bucketfuls. The plaster'll fall next. Can't you stop it? Has a pipe burst or something?"

"Something, I imagine," replied No. 9 with serene detachment. "At all events it appears to be over now."

"So I should hope," was the irate retort. "It's bad enough as it is. I shall go round to the office and complain. I'll tell you what it is, Mr. Belting: these mansions are becoming a pandemonium, sir, a veritable pandemonium."

"Capital idea; we'll go together and complain: two will be more effective," suggested Mr. Belting. "But not tonight, Mr. Tupworthy. We should not find anyone there. The office will be closed. Say tomorrow—"

"I had no intention of anything so preposterous as going there tonight. I am in no condition to go. If I don't get my feet into hot water at once I shall be laid up with a severe cold. Doubtless you haven't noticed it, but I am wet through to the skin, saturated, sir." Mr. Belting shook his head sagely.

"Always a mistake to try to stop water coming through the ceiling," he remarked. "It will come, you know. Finds its own level and all that."

"I did not try to stop it—at least not voluntarily. A temporary emergency necessitated a slight rearrangement of our accommodation.

I—I tell you this in confidence—I was sleeping in the bathroom."

At the revelation of so notable a catastrophe Mr. Belting actually seemed to stagger. Possibly his eyes filled with tears; certainly he had to turn and wipe away his emotion before he could proceed.

"Not—not right under it?" he whispered.

"I imagine so," replied Mr. Tupworthy. "I do not conceive that I could have been placed more centrally. I received the full cataract in the region of the ear. Well, if I may rely on you that it has stopped, I will terminate our interview for the present."

"Goodnight," responded the still tremulous Belting. "Goodnight—or good-morning, to be exact." He waited with the door open to light the first flight of stairs for Mr. Tupworthy's descent. Before the door was closed another figure stepped down quietly from the obscurity of the steps leading upwards.

"Mr. Belting, I believe?" said the stranger. "My name is Carrados. I have been looking over the flat above. Can you spare me a few minutes?"

"What, Mr. Max Carrados?"

"The same," smiled the owner of the name.

"Come in, Mr. Carrados," exclaimed Belting, not only without embarrassment, but with positive affection in his voice. "Come in by all means. I've heard of you more than once. Delighted to meet you. This way. I know—I know." He put a hand on his guest's arm and insisted on steering his course until he deposited him in an easy-chair before a fire. "This looks like being a great night. What will you have?"

Carrados put the suggestion aside and raised a corner of the situation.

"I'm afraid that I don't come altogether as a friend," he hinted.

"It's no good," replied his host. "I can't regard you in any other light after this. You heard Tupworthy? But you haven't seen the man, Mr. Carrados. I know—I've heard—but no wealth of the imagination can ever really quite reconstruct Tupworthy, the shoddy magnifico, in his immense porcine complacency, his monumental self-importance. And sleeping right underneath! Gods, but we have lived tonight! Why—why ever did you stop?"

"You associate me with this business?"

"Associate you! My dear Mr. Carrados, I give you the full glorious credit for the one entirely successful piece of low-comedy humour in real life that I have ever encountered. Indeed, in a legal and pecuniary sense, I hold you absolutely responsible."

"Oh!" exclaimed Carrados, beginning to laugh quietly. Then he continued: "I think that I shall come through that all right. I shall refer you to Mr. Carlyle, the private inquiry agent, and he will doubtless pass you on to your landlord, for whom he is acting; and I imagine that he in turn will throw all the responsibility on the ingenious gentleman who has put them to so much trouble. Can you guess the result of my investigation in the flat above?"

"Guess, Mr. Carrados? I don't need to guess: I know. You don't suppose I thought for a moment that such transparent devices as two intercepted pipes and an automatic gas-lighter would impose on a man of intelligence? They were only contrived to mystify the credulous imagination of clerks and porters."

"You admit it, then?"

"Admit! Good gracious, of course I admit it, Mr. Carrados. What's the use of denying it?"

"Precisely. I am glad you see that. And yet you seem far from being a mere practical joker. Does your confidence extend to the length of letting me into your object?"

"Between ourselves," replied Mr. Belting, "I haven't the least objection. But I wish that you would have—say a cup of coffee. Mrs. Belting is still up, I believe. She would be charmed to have the opportunity No? Well, just as you like. Now, my object? You must understand, Mr. Carrados, that I am a man of sufficient leisure and adequate means for the small position we maintain. But I am not unoccupied—not idle. On the contrary, I am always busy. I don't approve of any man passing his time aimlessly. I have a number of interests in life—hobbies, if you like. You should appreciate that, as you are a private criminologist. I am—among other things which don't concern us now—a private retributionist.

"On every side people are becoming far too careless and negligent. An era of irresponsibility has set in. Nobody troubles to keep his word, to carry out literally his undertakings. In my small way I try to set that right by showing them the logical development of their ways. I am, in fact, the sworn enemy of anything approaching sloppiness. You smile at that?"

"It is a point of view," replied Carrados. "I was wondering how the phrase at this moment would convey itself, say, to Mr. Tupworthy's ear."

Mr. Belting doubled up.

"But don't remind me of Tupworthy or I can't get on," he said. "In my method I follow the system of Herbert Spencer towards children. Of course you are familiar with his treatise on 'Education'? If a rough boy persists, after warnings, in tearing or soiling all his clothes, don't scold him for what, after all, is only a natural and healthy instinct overdone. But equally, of course, don't punish yourself by buying him other clothes. When the time comes for the children to be taken to an entertainment little Tommy cannot go with them.

"It would not be seemly, and he is too ashamed, to go in rags. He begins to see the force of practical logic. Very well. If a tradesman promises—promises explicitly—delivery of his goods by a certain time and he fails, he finds that he is then unable to leave them. I pay on delivery, by the way. If a man undertakes to make me an article like another—I am painstaking, Mr. Carrados to point out at the time how exactly like I want it—and it is (as it generally is) on completion something quite different, I decline to be easy-going and to be put off with it. I take the simplest and most obvious instances; I could multiply indefinitely. It is, of course, frequently inconvenient to me, but it establishes a standard."

"I see that you are a dangerous man, Mr. Belting," remarked Carrados. "If most men were like you our national character would be undermined. People would have to behave properly."

"If most men were like me we should constitute an intolerable nuisance," replied Belting seriously. "A necessary reaction towards sloppiness would set in and find me at its head. I am always with minorities."

"And the case in point?"

"The present trouble centres round the kitchen sink. It is cracked and leaks. A trivial cause for so elaborate an outcome, you may say, but you will doubtless remember that two men quarrelling once at a spring as to who should use it first involved half Europe in a war, and the whole tragedy of Lear sprang from a silly business round a word. I hadn't noticed the sink when we took this flat, but the landlord had solemnly sworn to do everything that was necessary. Is a new sink necessary to replace a cracked one? Obviously. Well, you know what landlords are: possibly you are one yourself. They promise you heaven until you have signed the agreement and then they tell you to go to hell. Suggested that we'd probably broken the sink ourselves and would certainly be looked to to replace it.

"An excellent servant caught a cold standing in the drip and left.

Was I to be driven into paying for a new sink myself? Very well, I thought, if the reasonable complaint of one tenant is nothing to you, see how you like the unreasonable complaints of fifty. The method served a useful purpose too. When Mrs. Belting heard that old tale about the tragedy at No. 11 she was terribly upset; vowed that she couldn't stay alone in here at night on any consideration.

"'My dear,' I said, 'don't worry yourself about ghosts. I'll make as good a one as ever lived, and then when you see how it takes other people in, just remember next time you hear of another that some-one's pulling the string.' And I really don't think that she'll ever be afraid of ghosts again."

"Thank you," said Carrados, rising. "Altogether I have spent a very entertaining evening, Mr. Belting. I hope your retaliatory method won't get you into serious trouble this time."

"Why should it?" demanded Belting quickly.

"Oh, well, tenants are complaining, the property is being depreci-ated. The landlord may think that he has legal redress against you."

"But surely I am at liberty to light the gas or use the bath in my own flat when and how I like?"

A curious look had come into Mr. Belting's smiling face; a curious note must have sounded in his voice. Carrados was warned and, being warned, guessed.

"You are a wonderful man," he said with upraised hand. "I capitu-late. Tell me how it is, won't you?"

"I knew the man at 11. His tenancy isn't really up till March, but he got an appointment in the north and had to go. His two unexpired months weren't worth troubling about, so I got him to sublet the flat to me—all quite regularly—for a nominal consideration, and not to mention it."

"But he gave up the keys?"

"No. He left them in the door and the porter took them away. Very unwarrantable of him; surely I can keep my keys where I like? However, as I had another...Really, Mr. Carrados, you hardly imagine that unless I had an absolute right to be there I should penetrate into a flat, tamper with the gas and water, knock the place about, tramp up and down—"

"I go," said Carrados, "to get our people out in haste. Goodnight."

"Goodnight, Mr. Carrados. It's been a great privilege to meet you. Sorry I can't persuade you. . ."

The Missing Actress Sensation

First nights are not what they were, even within the memory of playgoers who would be startled to hear anyone else refer to them as "elderly." But there are yet occasions of exception, and the production of Call a Spade at the Argosy Theatre was marked by at least one feature of note. The play itself was "sound," though not epoch-making. The performance of the leading lady was satisfactory and exactly what was to be expected from her. The leading gentleman was equally effective in a part which —as eight out of twelve dramatic critics happily phrased it on the morrow—"fitted him like a glove"; and on the same preponderance of opinion the character actor "contrived to extract every ounce of humour from the material at his disposal." In other words, Call a Spade might so far be relied upon to run an attenuating course for about fifty nights and then to be discreetly dropped, "pending the continuance of its triumphal progress at another West End house—should a suitable habitation become available."

But a very different note came into the reviews when the writers passed to the achievement of another member of the company—a young actress described on the programme as Miss Una Roscastle. Miss Roscastle was unknown to London critics and London audiences. She had come from Dublin with no very great dramatic reputation, but it is to be presumed that the quite secondary part which she had been given on her first metropolitan appearance was peculiarly suited to her talent. No one was more surprised than the author at the remarkable characterisation that "Mary Ryan" assumed in Miss Roscastle's hands. He was the more surprised because he had failed to notice anything of the kind at rehearsals.

Dimly he suspected that the young lady had got more out of the part than he had ever put into it, and while outwardly loud in his expression of delight, he was secretly uncertain whether to be pleased or annoyed. The leading lady also went out of her way to congratulate the young neophyte effusively on her triumph—and then slapped her unfortunate dresser on very insufficient provocation; but the lessee manager spoke of his latest acquisition with a curious air of restraint. At the end of the second act Miss Roscastle took four calls. After that she was only required for the first few minutes of the last act, and many among the audience noted with surprise that she did not appear with the company at the fall of the curtain—she had, in fact, already left the house.

All the same the success of the piece constituted a personal triumph for herself. Thenceforth, instead of, "Oh yes, you might do worse than book seats at the Argosy," the people who had been, said, "Now don't forget; you positively *must* see Miss Roscastle in *Call a Spade*," and as the Press had said very much the same, the difference to the box-office was something, but to the actress it was everything. Miss Roscastle, indeed, had achieved that rare distinction of "waking to find herself famous." Nothing could have seemed more assured and roseate than her professional future.

About a week later Max Carrados was interrupted one afternoon in the middle of composing an article on Sicilian numismatics by a telephone call from Mr Carlyle. The blind man smiled as he returned his friend's greeting, for Louis Carlyle's voice was wonderfully suggestive in its phases of the varying aspects of the speaker himself, and at that moment it conveyed a portrait of Mr Carlyle in his very best early-morning business manner—spruce and debonair, a little obtuse to things beyond his experience and impervious to criticism, but self-confident, trenchant and within his limits capable. In its crisp yet benign complacency Carrados could almost have sworn to resplendent patent boots, the current shade in suede gloves and a carefully selected *picotee*.

"If you are doing nothing better tonight, Max," continued the inquiry agent, "would you join me at the Argosy Theatre? I have a box, and we might go on to the Savoy afterwards. Now don't say you are engaged, there's a good fellow," he urged. "You haven't given me the chance of playing host for a month or more."

"The fact is," confessed Carrados, "I was there for the first night only a week ago."

"How unfortunate," exclaimed the other. "But don't you think that you could put up with it again?"

"I am sure I can," agreed Carrados. "Yes, I will join you there with pleasure."

"Delightful," crowed Mr Carlyle. "Let us say—"

The essential details were settled in a trice, but the "call" had not yet expired and the sociable gentleman still held the wire. "Were you interested in Miss Roscastle, Max?"

"Decidedly."

"That is fortunate. My choice of a theatre is not unconnected with a case I have on hand. I may be able to tell you something about the lady."

"Possibly we shall not be alone?" suggested Carrados.

"Well, no; not absolutely," admitted Carlyle. "Charming young fellow, though. I'm sure you'll like him, Max. Trevor Enniscorthy, a younger son of old Lord Sleys."

"Conventional rotter, between ourselves?" inquired Max.

"Not a bit of it," declared Mr Carlyle loyally. "A young fellow of five and twenty is none the worse for being enamoured of a fascinating creature who happens to be on the stage. He is Oh, very well. Goodbye, Max. Eight-fifteen, remember."

They were all punctual. In fact, "If Mr Enniscorthy could have got me along we should have been here before the doors opened," declared Mr Carlyle when the blind man joined them. "Now why are there no programmes about here, I wonder?"

"I hardly fancy they anticipate their box-holders arriving twenty minutes before the curtain rises," suggested Carrados.

"There are some," exclaimed Mr Enniscorthy, dashing out as an attendant crossed the circle. He was back in a moment, and standing in the obscurity of the box eagerly tore open the programme. "Still in," he muttered, coming forward and throwing the paper down for the others to refer to. "Oh, excuse my impatience," he apologised, colouring. "I am rather—"

He left them to supply the rest.

"Mr Enniscorthy has given me permission to explain his position, Max," began Mr Carlyle, but the young man abruptly cut short the proposition stated in this vein of deference.

"I'd rather put it that if Mr Carrados would help me with his advice I should be most awfully grateful," he said in a very clear, rather highly pitched voice. "I suppose it's inevitable to feel no end of an ass over this sort of thing, but I'm desperately in earnest and I must go through with it."

"Admirable!" beamed Mr Carlyle's inextinguishable eye, and he murmured: "Very natural, I am sure," in the voice of a man who has just been told to go up higher.

"Perhaps you know that there is a Miss Roscastle put down as appearing in this piece?" went on Enniscorthy. "Well, I knew Miss Roscastle rather well in Ireland. I came to London because I followed her here."

"Engaged?" dropped quietly from Carrados's lips.

"I cannot say that we were actually engaged," was the admission, "but it—well, you know how these things stand. At all events she knew what I felt towards her and she did not discourage my hopes."

"Did your people know of this, Mr Enniscorthy?"

"I had not spoken to my father or to my stepmother, but they might easily have heard something of it," replied the young man. "Miss Roscastle, although she did not go about much, was received by the very best people in Dublin. Of course for many things I did not like her being on the stage; in fact I detested it, but she had taken the step before I knew her, and how could I object? Then she got the offer of this London engagement. She was ambitious to get on in her profession, and took it. In a very short time I found it impossible to exist there without seeing her, so I made an excuse to get away and followed."

"Let me see," put in Mr Carlyle ingenuously; "I forget the exact dates."

"Miss Roscastle came on Monday, October the 4th," said Enniscorthy. "The piece opened on the following Thursday week—the 14th. I left Kingstown by the early boat yesterday. At this end we were nearly an hour late, and after going to my hotel, changing and dining, I had just time to come on here and bag the last stall. I thought that I would send a note round after the first act and ask Una to give me a few minutes afterwards. But it never came to that. Instead I got a very large surprise. 'Mary Ryan' came on, and I looked—and looked again. I didn't need glasses, but I got a pair out of the automatic box in front of me and had another level stare. Well, it wasn't Miss Roscastle. This girl was like her. I suppose to most people they would be wonderfully alike, and her voice—although it wasn't really Irish—yes, her voice was similar. But to me there were miles of difference. I saw at once that she was an understudy, although 'Miss Una Roscastle' was still down in the programme, and I began to quake at the thought of something having happened to her.

"I slipped out into the corridor—I had an end seat— and got hold

336

of a programme girl.

"'Do you know why Miss Roscastle is out of the cast to-night?' I asked her. 'Is she indisposed?'

"She took the programme out of my hand and pointed to a name in it.

"'She's in all right,' she replied—stupidly, I thought. 'There's her name.'

"'Yes, she is on the programme,' I replied, 'but not on the stage. Look through the glass there. That is not Miss Roscastle.'

"She glanced through the glazed door and then turned away as though she suspected me of chaffing her.

"'It's the only Miss Roscastle I've ever seen here,' she said as she went.

"I wandered about and interrogated one or two other attendants. They all gave me the same answer. I began to get frightened.

"'They must be misled by the resemblance,' I assured myself. 'It really is wonderful.' I went back to my seat and then remembered that I had got no further with my original inquiry, which was to find out whether Una was ill or not. I couldn't remain. I kept my eyes fixed on 'Mary Ryan' every time she was on the stage, and every time I became more and more convinced. Finally I got up again and going round sent in my card to the manager."

"Stokesey?" asked Carrados.

"Yes. I didn't know who was technically the right man, but he, at any rate, had engaged Miss Roscastle. He saw me at once.

"'I have come across from Dublin to see Miss Roscastle,' I told him, 'and I am very disappointed to find her out of the cast. Can you tell me why she is away?'

"'Surely you are mistaken,' he replied, opening a programme that lay before him. 'Do you know Miss Roscastle by sight?'

"'Very well indeed,' I retorted. 'Better than your staff do. The "Mary Ryan" tonight is not Miss Roscastle.'

"'I will inquire,' he said, walking to the door. 'Please wait a minute.'

"He was rigidly courteous, but instinct was telling me all the time that it was sheer bluff. He had nothing to inquire. In a moment he was back again.

"'I am informed that the programme is correct,' he said with the same smooth insincerity, standing in the middle of the room for me to leave. 'Miss Roscastle is on the stage at this moment. The make-up must have deceived you, Mr Enniscorthy.'

"I had nothing to reply, because I did not even know what to think. I simply proceeded to walk out.

"'One moment.' I had reached the door when Mr Stokesey spoke. 'You are a friend of Miss Roscastle, I suppose?'

"'Yes,' I replied. 'I think I may claim that.'

"'Then I would merely suggest to you that to start a rumour crediting her with being out of the piece is a service she would fail to appreciate. Good-evening.'

"I left the theatre because I despaired of getting any real information after that, and it occurred to me that I could do better elsewhere. Although Una and I did not correspond, I had begged her, before she left, to let me know that she arrived safely, and she had sent me just half-a-dozen lines. I now took a taxi and drove off to the address she had given—a sort of private hotel or large boarding-house near Holborn.

"'Can you tell me if Miss Roscastle is in?' I asked at the office.

"'Roscastle?' said the fellow there. 'Oh, the young lady from the theatre. Why, she left us more than a week ago—nearer two, I should say.'

"This was another facer.

"'Can you give me the address she went to?' I asked.

"'Couldn't; against our rule,' he replied. 'Any letters for her were to be sent to the theatre.'

"I didn't think it would be successful to offer him a bribe, so I thanked him and walked away. As the hall porter opened the door for me I dropped him a word. In two minutes he came out to where I was waiting.

"'A Miss Roscastle left here a week or two ago,' I said. 'They won't give me her address, but you can get it. Here's a Bradbury. I'll be here again in half-an-hour and if you've got the address—the house, not the theatre—there'll be another for you when I've verified it.'

"He looked a bit doubtful. Evidently a decent fellow, I thought.

"'It's quite all right,' I assured him. 'We are engaged, but I've only just come over.'

"He was waiting for me when I returned. The first thing he did was to tender me the note back again—a a piece of superfluous honesty that prepared me for the worst.

"'I'm sorry, sir, but it's no go,' he explained. 'The young lady left no address beyond the theatre.'

"'You called a cab for her when she went?' I suggested.

"'Yes, sir, but she gave the directions while I was bringing out her things. I never heard where it was to go.'"

"And that is as far as we have got up to this moment, Max," struck in Mr Carlyle briskly.

"I'm afraid it is," corroborated Enniscorthy. "I got round to the stage door here in time to see most of the people leave, but neither Miss Roscastle nor the girl like her were among them."

"She is off half-an-hour before the piece finishes," explained Carrados. "And of course she might not leave by the stage door."

"In any case it is an extraordinary enough business, is it not, Mr Carrados?" said Enniscorthy, rather anxious not to be set down a blundering young idiot for his pains. "What does it mean?"

"So far I would describe it as—curious," admitted Carrados guardedly. "Investigation may justify a stronger term. In the meanwhile we need not miss the play."

By this time the theatre had practically filled and the orchestra was tuning up for the overture. With nothing to occupy his attention, Mr Enniscorthy began to manifest an unhappy restlessness that increased until the play had been proceeding for some few minutes. Then Carrados heard Mr Carlyle murmur, "Charming! Charming!" in a tone of mature connoisseurship; there was a spontaneous round of applause and "Mary Ryan" was on the scene.

"The understudy again," Enniscorthy whispered to his companions.

"Well," remarked Mr Carlyle when the curtain descended for the first interval, "you are still equally convinced, Mr Enniscorthy?"

"There isn't the shadow of a doubt," he replied. Carrados had been writing a few lines on one of his cards. He now summoned an attendant.

"Mr Stokesey is in the house?" he asked. "Then give him this, please—when you next go that way." Before the curtain rose the girl came round to the box again.

"Mr Carrados?" she inquired. "Mr Stokesey told me to say that he would save you the trouble by looking in here during the next interval."

"Shall I remain?" asked Enniscorthy.

"Oh yes. Stokesey is a most amiable man to do with. I know him slightly. His attitude to you was evidently the outcome of the circumstances. We shall all get along very nicely."

339

The second act was the occasion of "Mary Ryan's" great opportunity and again she carried the enthusiasm of the audience. After the curtain the young actress had to respond to an insistent call. In the darkness Mr Stokesey entered the box and stood waiting at the back.

"Glad to see you here again, Mr Carrados," he remarked, shaking hands with the blind man as soon as the lights were up. Then he looked at the other occupants. "My word, I have put my head into the lion's den!" he continued, his smile deepening into a good-natured grin. "Don't shoot, Mr Enniscorthy; I will climb down without. I see that the game is up."

"What are you going to tell us?" asked Carrados.

"Everything I know. The lady who has just gone off is not Miss Roscastle. Mr Enniscorthy was quite right; she wasn't here last night either."

"Then why is her name still in the programme, and why do you and your people keep up the fiction?" demanded Enniscorthy.

"Because I hoped that Miss Roscastle might have returned to the cast tonight, and, failing tonight, I hope that she will return tomorrow. Because we happen to have a substitute in Miss Linknorth so extraordinarily like the original lady in appearance and voice that no one—excluding yourself—will have noticed the difference, and because I have a not unreasonable objection to announcing that the chief attraction of my theatre is out of the cast. Is there anything very unaccountable in that?"

Mr Carlyle nodded acquiescence to this moderate proposition; Enniscorthy seemed to admit it reluctantly; it remained for Carrados to accept the challenge.

"Only one thing," he replied with some reluctance.

"And what is that?"

"That Miss Roscastle will not return to the cast and that you are well aware why she never can return to it."

"I—what?" demanded the astonished manager.

"Miss Roscastle cannot *return* to the cast because she has never been in it."

Stokesey wavered, burst into a roar of laughter and sat down.

"I give in," he exclaimed heartily. "That's my last ditch. Now you really do know everything that I do."

"But why has she not been in?" demanded Enniscorthy.

"Better ask the lady herself. I cannot even guess."

"I will when I can find her." Not for the first time the young man was assailed by a horrid fear that he might have been making a fool of himself. "Where in the meantime is she?"

"The Lord alone knows," retorted Mr Stokesey feelingly. "Don't annihilate me, Mr Enniscorthy; I don't mean a member of the peerage. But, I'll tell you, the lady put me in a very deuced fix."

"Won't you take us into your confidence?" suggested Carrados.

"I will, Mr Carrados, because I want a consideration from you in return. I can put it into a very few words. Twenty minutes before the curtain went up on the first night a note was sent in to Miss Roscastle. She read it, put on her hat and coat and went out hurriedly by the stage door."

"Well?" said Carlyle encouragingly.

"That is all. That is the last we saw of her—heard of her. She never returned."

"But—but—" stammered Enniscorthy, and came up short before the abysmal nature of the prospect confronting him.

"There are a good many 'buts' to be taken into consideration, Mr Enniscorthy," said the manager, with a rather cryptic look. "Fortunately we had Miss Linknorth, and the first costume, as you know, is immaterial. Up to the last possible moment we hung on to Miss Roscastle's return. Then the other had to go on."

"With not very serious consequences to the success of the play, apparently," remarked Carrados.

"That's the devilment of it," exclaimed Stokesey warmly. "Don't you see the hole it has put me into? If 'Mary Ryan' had remained a negligible quantity it wouldn't have mattered two straws. But for her own diabolical vanity Miss Linknorth made a confounded success of the part. Of course it was too late to have any alteration printed on the first night and now Miss Roscastle is the draw of the piece. People come to see Miss Roscastle. Miss Roscastle is the piece."

"But if you explained that Miss Linknorth was really the creator of the part—" suggested Mr Carlyle. Stokesey rattled a provocative laugh at the back of his throat.

"You run a theatre for a few seasons, my dear fellow, and then talk," he retorted. "You can't explain; you can't do anything; you can only just sit there. People cease to be rational beings when they set out for a theatre. If you breathe on a howling success it goes out. If you move a gold mine of a piece from one theatre to another, next door, everyone promptly decides to stay away. Don't ask me the reasons; there are none. It isn't a business; it ought to come under the Gaming Act."

"Mr Stokesey is also faced by the alternative that after he had announced Miss Linknorth, Miss Roscastle might appear any time and claim her place." The manager nodded. "That's another consideration," he said.

"But could she?" inquired Mr Carlyle. "After absenting herself in this way?"

"Oh, goodness knows; I dare say she could—agreements are no good when it comes to anything happening. At any rate here am I with an element of success after a procession of distinct non-stops. If we get well set, whatever happens will matter less. Now I haven't gone to any Machiavellian lengths in arranging this, but I have taken the chance as it came along. I've told you everything I know. Is there any reason why you shouldn't do us all a good turn by keeping it strictly to yourselves?"

"I don't know that I particularly owe you any consideration, Mr Stokesey, or that you owe me any," announced Mr Enniscorthy. "Just now I am only concerned in discovering what has become of Miss Roscastle. You know her address?"

"In Kensington?"

"Well, yes."

"74 Westphalia Mansions."

"You sent there of course?"

"Heavens, yes! The various forms of messages must be six inches deep all over the hall by now. Last Friday I had a man sitting practically all day on her doorstep."

"But she has someone there—a housekeeper or maid?"

"I don't think so. She told me that she was taking a little furnished flat—asked me if the neighbourhood was a suitable one. I imagine there was something about a daily woman until she found how she liked it. We've had no one from there anyway."

"Then it comes to this, that for a week there has been absolutely no trace of Miss Roscastle's existence! Do you quite realise your responsibility, Mr Stokesey?" demanded Enniscorthy with increased misgivings.

The manager, who had turned to go, caught Mr Carlyle's eye over the concerned young man's shoulder.

"I don't think that Miss Roscastle's friends need have any anxiety about her personal safety," he replied with expression. "At all events I've done everything I can for you; I hope that you will not fail to meet my views. If there's anything else that occurs to you, Mr Carrados, I shall be in my office. Goodnight."

"Callous brute!" muttered Mr Enniscorthy. "He ought to have put it in the hands of the police a week ago."

Mr Carlyle glanced at Carrados, who had transferred his interest to the rendering of the last musical item of the interval.

"Possibly Miss Roscastle would prefer a less public investigation if she had a voice in the matter," said the professional man.

"If she happens to be shut up in some beastly underground cellar I imagine she would prefer whatever gets her out the soonest. I dare say it sounds fantastic, but such things really do happen now and then, you know, and why not?"

"You don't know of any threats or blackmailing letters?"

"No," admitted the young man; "but I do know this, that if Una was at liberty she would never allow another actress to take her place and use her name in this way."

"A very significant suggestion," put in Carrados from his detached attitude. "Mr Enniscorthy has given you a really valuable hint, Louis."

"I don't mean that Miss Roscastle is really out-of-the-way jealous," Enniscorthy hastened to add, "but in her profession—"

"Oh, most natural, most natural," agreed the urbane Carlyle. "Everyone has to look after his own interest. Now—"

"I don't suppose that you are particularly keen on this act," interposed the blind man. "Are you, Mr Enniscorthy?"

"I'd much rather be doing something," was the reply.

"I was going to suggest that you might go round to Westphalia Mansions, just to make sure that there is no one there now. Then if you would find your way to our table at the Savoy we could hear your report."

"Yes, certainly. I shall be glad to think that I can be of some assistance by going." Mr Carlyle's optimistic temper was almost incapable of satire, but he could not refrain from, "You can—poor beggar!" on Enniscorthy's departure. "I suppose," he continued, turning to his friend, "I suppose you think that Stokesey may? Eh?"

"I fancy that in the absence of our young friend he may be induced to become more confidential. He may have some good ground for believing that the missing lady will not upset his ingenious plan. He, at all events, discounts the 'underground cellar.'"

"Oh, that!" commented Carlyle with an indulgent smile. "But, after all, what is the answer, Max? Enniscorthy is a thoroughly eligible young fellow and this was the first chance of her career. What is the inducement?"

"That much we can safely emphasise. What, in a word, would induce an ambitious young lady to throw up a good engagement, Louis?"

"A better?" suggested Mr Carlyle.

"Exactly," agreed Carrados; "a better."

It is unnecessary to follow the course of Mr Carlyle's inquiry on the facts already disclosed, for, less than twenty-four hours later, the whole situation was changed and Mr Stokesey's discreet prevarication had been torn into shreds. The manager had calculated in vain—if he had calculated and not just accepted the chance that presented itself. At all events the fiction proved too elaborate to be maintained and late in the afternoon of the following day all the evening papers blazed out with the

Sensational Disappearance of Popular London Actress

The event was particularly suited to the art of the contents bill, for when the news came to be analysed there was little else to be learned beyond the name of the missing actress and the fact that "at the theatre a policy of questionable reticence is being maintained towards all inquiry." That phrase caused two men at least to smile as they realised the embarrassment of Mr Stokesey's dubious position.

The conditions being favourable, the Missing Actress sensation caught on at once and effectually asphyxiated public interest in all the other sensations that up to that moment had been satisfying the mental requirements of the nation—a "Mysterious Submarine," an "Eloping Dean" (three wives), and an "Are We Becoming Too Intellectual?" correspondence. Supply followed demand, and it very soon became difficult to decide, not where Miss Roscastle was, but where she was not. Public opinion wavered between Genoa, on the authority of a retired lime and slate merchant of Hull who had had a presentiment while directing a breathless lady to the docks, when a Wilson liner was on the point of sailing; Leatherhead, the suggestion of a booking-office clerk who had been struck by the peculiar look in a veiled lady's eyes as she asked for a third-class return to Cheam; and Accrington, where a young lady with a marked Irish accent and a theatrical manner had inquired about lodgings at three different houses and then abruptly left, saying that she would come back if she thought any more about it.

Before the novelty was two days old Scotland Yard had been stirred into recognising its existence. A London clue was forthcoming, apparently the wildest and most circumstantial of them all. A plain-clothes constable of the A Division reported that an hour after midnight three days before he had noticed a shabby-genteel man, who seemed to be waiting for someone, loitering on the Embankment near the Boadicea statue. There was nothing in the circumstance to interest him, but when he repassed the spot ten minutes later the man had been joined by a woman. The sharp eyes of the constable told him that the woman was well and even fashionably dressed, although she had made some precaution to conceal it, and the fact quickened his observation.

As he shambled past—an Embankment dead-beat for the occasion—he heard the name "Roscastle" spoken by one of the two. He could not distinguish by which, nor the sense in which the word was used, but his notebook, with the name written down under the correct date, corroborated so much. On neither occasion had he seen the face of the man distinctly—the threadbare individual had sought the shadows—but he was able to describe that of the woman in some detail. He was shown half-a-dozen photographs and at once identified that of Miss Roscastle. The crowning touch requisite to make this story entirely popular was supplied by an inspector of river police.

According to the newspaper account, the patrol boat was off the Embankment near Westminster Bridge between one and a quarter-past on the night in question when a distinct splash was heard. The crew made for the spot, flashed the lights about and drifted up and down several times, but without finding a trace of any human presence. At once the public voice demanded that the river should be dragged from Chelsea to The Pool, and, pending the result, every shabby wastrel who appeared on the Embankment arrested.

In his private office Mr Carlyle threw down the last of his morning papers with an expression that began as a knowing smile but ended rather dubiously. For his own part he would have much preferred that the disappearance of Miss Roscastle had not leaked out—that he had been left to pursue his course unaided, but, in the circumstances, he carefully read everything on the chance of a useful hint. The Embankment story both amused and puzzled him.

He dismissed the subject to its proper mental pigeonhole and had turned to deal with his most confidential correspondence when something very like an altercation breaking the chaste decorum of his outer office caused him to stop and frown. The next moment there was a hurrying step outside, the door was snatched open and

Mr Enniscorthy, pale and distracted, stumbled into the room. Behind him appeared the indignant face of Mr Carlyle's chief clerk. Then the visitor extinguished the outraged vision by flinging back the door as he went forward.

"Have you seen the papers?" he demanded. "Is there anything dreadful in them?"

"I have seen the papers, yes," replied the puzzled agent. "I am not aware—"

"I mean the evening papers—just out. No, I see you haven't. Here, read that and tell me. I haven't—I dare not look."

Mr Carlyle took the journal that Enniscorthy thrust under his eyes—it was the earliest Star—glanced into his visitor's face a little severely and then focussed the column.

"Good heavens!" he exclaimed, "what is this! Missing Actress. Embankment Clue. Body Found!'"

"Ah!" groaned Enniscorthy. "That was on the bills. Is it ?"

"It's all right, it's all right, my dear sir," reported Mr Carlyle, glancing along the lines. "This is the body of a man . . . the man who was seen . . . most extraordinary . . ."

"My God!" was wrung from the distressed young man as he dropped into a chair. "Oh, my God! I thought—" He took out his handkerchief, wiped and fanned his face, and for the next few minutes looked rather languidly on things.

"Very distressing," commiserated Mr Carlyle when he had come to the end of the report. "Can I get you anything—brandy, a glass of water—? The mere act sipping, I am medically informed, has a beneficial effect in case of faintness. I have—"

"Nothing, thanks. I shall be all right now. Sorry to have made an ass of myself. You have heard—anything?"

"Nothing definite so far," was the admission. "But there may be something worth following in this story after all. I shall go down to the mortuary shortly. Do you care to accompany me?"

"No, thanks," replied the visitor. "I have had enough of that particular form of excitement for one morning. . . . Unless, of course, there is anything—"

He was assured that there was nothing to be effected by his presence and half-an-hour later Mr Carlyle made his way alone to the obscure mortuary where the unclaimed dead hold their grim reception.

An inspector of the headquarters investigation staff who had been put on to the case was standing by the side of one of the shells when Carlyle entered. He was a man whom the private agent had more than once good-naturedly obliged in small matters that had come within his reach. He now greeted Mr Carlyle with consideration and stood aside to allow him to approach the body.

"The Embankment case, I suppose, sir?" he remarked. "Not very attractive, but I've seen many worse in here." He jerked off the upper part of the rough coverlet and exposed a visage that caused Mr Carlyle to turn away with a "Tch, tch!" of emotion. Then a sense of duty drew him round again and he proceeded to note the descriptive points of the dead man in his pocket-book.

"No marks of violence, I suppose?" he asked.

"Nothing beyond the usual abrasions that we always find. A clear case of drowning—suicide—it seems to be."

"And the things?"

The inspector nodded towards a seedy suit laid out for identification and an overcoat, once rakish of its fashion and now frayed and mouldering, put with it.

"Fur collar too, Mr Carlyle," pointed out his guide. "'Velvet and rags,' isn't it? 'Where moth and rust doth corrupt.' A sermon could be made out of this."

"Very true; very true indeed," replied Mr Carlyle, who always responded to the sentimentally obvious. "It is a sermon, inspector. But what have we here?"

Beside the garments had been collected together a heap of metal discs—quite a considerable heap, numbering some hundreds. Carlyle took up a few and examined them. They were all alike—flat, perfectly round and somewhat under an inch in diameter. They were quite plain and apparently of lead.

"H'm, curious," he commented. "In his pockets?"

"Yes; both overcoat pockets. Very determined, wasn't he? They would have kept him down till the Day of Judgment. I've counted them—just five hundred."

"Any money?"

The inspector smiled his tragi-comic appreciation— the coin embellished the moral of his unwritten sermon —and pointed.

"A halfpenny!" he replied.

"Poor fellow!" said Mr Carlyle. "Well, well; perhaps it is better as it is. You might pull up the cloth again now, please. . . . There are no letters or papers, I see."

The detective hesitated a moment and then recalled the obligation he was under.

"There is a scrap of paper that I have kept from the Press so far," he admitted. "It was tightly clenched in the man's right hand—so tight that we had to use a screw-driver to get it out, and the water had barely reached it." He was extracting a slip of paper from his notebook as he spoke and he now unfolded it. "You won't put it about, will you, Mr Carlyle? I don't know that there's anything tangible in it, but—well, see for yourself."

"Extraordinary!" admitted the gentleman. He read the words a second time: "'Fool! What does it matter now?' Why, it might almost—"

"It might be addressed to the coroner, or to anyone who tries to find out who he is or what it means, you would say. Well, so it might, sir. Anyhow, that is all."

"By the way, I suppose he is the man your fellow saw?"

"Everything tallies, Mr Carlyle—length of immersion, place, and so on. Our man thinks he is the same, but you may remember that he didn't claim to be very positive on this point."

There seemed nothing else to be learned and Mr Carlyle took his departure. His acquaintance had also finished and their ways lay together as far as Trafalgar Square. Before they parted the inspector had promised to communicate with Mr Carlyle as soon as the dead man was identified.

"And if he has a room anywhere he probably will be, with all this talk about Miss Roscastle. Then we may find something there that will help us," he predicted. "If he is purely casual the chances are we shall never hear."

His experience was justified and he kept his promise.

Two days later Carlyle heard that the unknown had been identified as the occupant of a single room in a Lambeth lodging-house. He had only occupied it for a few weeks and he was known there as Mr Hay. Tenement gossip described him as a foreigner and credited him with having seen better days—an easy enough surmise in the circumstances. Mr Carlyle had been on the point of turning his attention to a Monte Carlo Miss Roscastle when this information reached him. He set off at once for Lambeth, but at Tubb's Grove disappointment met him at the door.

The landlady of the ramshackle establishment—a female with a fluent if rather monotonous delivery—was still smarting from the unappreciated honour of the police officials' visit and the fierce light of publicity that it had thrown upon her house. All Mr Carlyle's bland cajolery was futile and in the end he had to disburse a sum that bore an appreciable relation to a week's rent before he was allowed to inspect the room and to command conversation that was not purely argumentative.

Then the barrenness of the land was revealed. Mr Hay had been irregular with his rent at the best, and when he disappeared he was a week in arrears. After two days' absence, with the easy casuistry of her circumstances, the lady had decided that he was not returning and had proceeded to "do out" the room for the next tenant. The lodger's "few things" she had bundled together into a cupboard, whence they had been retrieved by the police, in spite of her indignant protest. But the lodger's "papers and such-like rubbish" she confessed to burning, to get them out of the way. Mr Carlyle spent a profitless half-hour and then returned, calling at Scotland Yard on his way back. His friend the inspector shook his head; there was nothing among the seized property that afforded any clue.

It was at this point that Mr Carlyle's ingenuous mind suggested looking up Carrados, whom he had not seen since the visit to the theatre.

"Max was interested in this case from the first; I am sure he will be expecting to hear from me about it," was the form in which the proposal conveyed itself to him.

The same evening he ran down to Richmond for an hour, after ascertaining that his friend was at home and disengaged.

"You might have brought Enniscorthy with you," remarked Carrados when the subject had been started.

"Nice, genuine young fellow. Evidently deeply in love with the girl, but he is young enough to take the attack safely. What have you told him?"

"He is back in Ireland just now—got an idea that he might learn something from some people there, and rushed off. What I have told him—well"—experience endowed Mr Carlyle with sudden caution—"what would you have told him, Max?"

Carrados smiled at the innocent guile of the invitation.

"To answer that I should have to know just what you know," he replied. "I suppose you have gone into this Embankment development?"

"Yes." He had come intending to make some show of his progress and to sound Carrados discreetly, but once again in the familiar room and under the sway of the clear-visioned blind man's virile personality he suddenly found himself submitting quite naturally to the suave, dominating influence. "Yes; but I must confess, Max, that I am unable to explain much of that incident. It suggests blackmail at the bottom, and if the plain-clothes man was correct and saw Miss Roscastle there last Thursday—"

"It was blackmail; but the plain-clothes man was not correct, though he had every excuse for making the mistake. There is one quiet, retiring personage in this drama who has been signally overlooked in all the clamour."

"You mean?"

"I suggest that if Miss Linknorth had been subpoenaed for the inquest and asked to account for her movements after leaving the theatre on Thursday last it might have turned public speculation into another channel—though probably a wrong one."

"Miss Linknorth!" The idea certainly turned Mr Carlyle's thoughts into a new channel.

"Has it occurred to you what an extraordinary act of self-effacement it must have been on the part of this young unknown actress to allow her well-earned success to be credited to another? As Enniscorthy reminded us, ladies of the profession are rather keen on their chances."

"Yes; but Stokesey, you remember, insisted on keeping it dark."

"I am not overlooking that. But although it was to Stokesey's interest to keep up the fiction, and also to the interest of everyone else about the theatre—people who were merely concerned in the run of the piece—it would have richly paid the Linknorth to have her identity established while the iron was hot, whatever the outcome. A paragraph to the Press the next day would have done it. There wasn't a hint. I am not overlooking the fact that Miss Linknorth's name now appears on the programme, but that is an unforeseen development so far as she is concerned, and her golden opportunity has gone by. With the exception of the first row of the pit and of the gallery you won't find that one *per cent,* of the house now really knows who created 'Mary Ryan' or regards the Linknorth as anything but a makeshift."

"Then what was the incentive?"

"Suppose it has been made worth Miss Linknorth's while? It is not necessarily a crude question of money. Friendship might make it worth her while, or ambition in some quarter we have not looked for, or a dozen other considerations—anything but the box-office of the

Argosy Theatre, which certainly did not make it worth her while."

"Yes, that is feasible enough, Max, but how does it help us?"

"Do you ever have toothache, Louis?" demanded Carrados inconsequently.

"No, I am glad to say," admitted Mr Carlyle. "Have you got a turn now, old man? Never mind this confounded 'shop.' I'll go and then you can—"

"Not at all," interposed Carrados, smiling benignly at his friend's consideration; "and don't be too ready to condemn toothache indiscriminately. I have sometimes found it very stimulating. The only way to cure it is to concentrate the mind so terrifically that you forget the ache. Then it stops. I imagine that a mathematician could succeed by working out a monumental problem. I have frequently done it by 'discovering' a hoard of Greek coins of the highest art period on one of the islands and classifying the find. On Monday night I thought that I was in for a devil of a time. I at once, set myself to discover a workable theory for everyone's conduct in this affair, one, of course, that would stand the test of every objection based on fact. The correct hypothesis must, indeed, be strengthened by every new circumstance that came out. At twelve o'clock, after two hours' mental sudation, I began to see light— excuse the phrase. By this time the toothache had gone, but I was so taken up with the idea that I called out Harris and drove to Scotland Yard then and there on the chance of finding Beedel or one of the others I know. . . . Why on earth didn't you let me have that 'Fool!' message, Louis?"

"My dear fellow," protested Mr Carlyle, "I can't beat up for advice on every day of my life."

"At all events it might have saved me an hour's strenuous thinking."

"Well, you know, Max, perhaps that would have left you in the middle of the toothache. Now the message ?"

"The message? Oh, that settled it. You may take it as assured, Louis, that although Miss Roscastle's departure from the theatre was hurried, in order to allow her to catch the boat-train from Charing Cross, she had enough time to think out the situation and to secure Miss Linknorth's allegiance. Whether Stokesey knows any more than he admits, we need not inquire. The great thing is that Miss Roscastle had some reason—some fairly strong reason—for not wanting her absence from the cast to become public. We agreed, Louis, that a better engagement would alone satisfactorily explain her defection. What better engagement would you suggest—it could scarcely be a theatrical one?"

"A brilliant marriage?"

"Our minds positively ident, Louis. 'A brilliant marriage'—my exact expression. One, moreover, that suddenly becomes possible and cannot be delayed. One —here we are on difficult ground—one that may be jeopardised if at that early stage Miss Roscastle's identity in it comes to light, or if, possibly, her absence from London is discovered. That sign-post," said Carrados, with his unseeing eyes fixed on the lengthening vistas that rose before his mind, "points in a good many directions."

"The blackmailer?" hazarded Carlyle.

"I gave a good deal of attention to every phase of that gentleman's presence," replied Carrados. "It corroborates, but it does not entirely explain. I would say that he merely intervened. In my view, Miss Roscastle would have acted precisely as she did if there had been no Mr Hay. At all events he did intervene and had to be dealt with."

"It had occurred to me, Max, whether it was Miss Linknorth's job to impersonate the other?"

"It may have been originally. If so, it failed, for Hay proceeded with his demand. His price was five hundred pounds in English or French gold—an interesting phase of your ordinary blackmailer's antipathy to paper—merely an *hors d'oeuvre* to the solid things to come, of course. But he was not dealing with a fool. Whether Miss Roscastle frankly had not five hundred pounds just then, or whether she was better advised, we cannot say. She temporised, the Linknorth being the intermediary. Then the dummy pieces? Hay was a menace and had to be held off. At one point there may well have been the pretence of handing over the cash and then at the last moment some specious difficulty, necessitating a short delay, is raised. That would account for the otherwise unnecessary detail of the lead counterfeits, for there is no need of them on Thursday.

"Then, when the danger is past, when the tricked scoundrel has lost his sting, then there is no attempt at evasion or compromise. Fool! 'What does it matter now?' is the contemptuously unguarded message and the five hundred doits are pressed upon him to complete his humiliation. Why doesn't it matter, Louis? Is there any other answer than that Miss Roscastle is safely married?"

"It certainly looks like it," agreed Mr Carlyle. "But if there was anything so serious as to have compromised the marriage, surely Hay could still have held it over her, as against her husband?"

"If it was as against the husband before—yes, perhaps. But suppose the chink in the armour was the good grace of some third person whose consent was necessary? This brilliant marriage . . . Well, I don't commit myself any further. At any rate, in the lady's estimation she is safe, and if she had deliberately sought to goad Hay into suicide she couldn't have done better. He read the single line that shattered his greedy dreams and its disdainful triumph struck him like a whip. He had spent literally his last penny on pressing his unworthy persecution, and now he stood, beggared and beaten, on the Embankment at midnight—'he, a gentleman.' . . . It doesn't matter how he took it. He went over, and the muddy waters of the Thames closed over the last page of his rotten history."

"Max!" exclaimed Mr Carlyle with feeling. "Remember the poor beggar, with all his failings, is dead now. Not that I should mind," he added cheerfully, "but I saw him afterwards, you know. Enniscorthy had the sense to keep away. And, by Gad! Max, that reminds me that this is rather rough on my confiding young client—running up a bill to have a successful rival sprung upon his hopes. Have you any idea who he is?"

"Yes," admitted Carrados, "I have an idea, but today it is nothing more than that. When does Enniscorthy return?"

"He ought to be back in London on Friday morning."

"By then I should know something definite. If you will make an appointment with him for Friday at half-past eleven I will look in on my way through town."

"Certainly, Max, certainly." There was a note of faithful expectation in Mr Carlyle's voice that caused his friend to smile. He crossed the room to his most-used desk and opened one of the smaller drawers.

"For this simple demonstration, Louis, I require only two appliances, neither of which, as you will see, is a rabbit or a handkerchief. In other and saner words, there are only two exhibits. That is from *The Morning Mail;* this is from the Westminster street refuse tip."

"This" was a small brown canvas bag. Traces of red sealing-wax still marked the neck and across it were stamped the words:

Banque de l'Union
Clairvaux

Mr Carlyle looked inside. It was empty, but a few specks of dull grey metal still lodged among the cloth. He turned to the other object, as Carrados had indicated an extract from the daily Press. It was a mere slip of paper and consisted of the following paragraph:

"From Clairvaux, in the Pas de Calais, France, where he purchased a country estate when he was driven into exile, it is reported that ex-King Constantine of Villalyia has been lying dangerously ill for the past week."

"Quite so, quite so," murmured Carlyle, quietly turning over the cutting to satisfy himself that he was reading the right side.

★★★★★★

"I see that you haven't anything very hopeful to report," said Mr Enniscorthy—he and Max Carrados had entered Mr Carlyle's office within a minute of each other two days later—"but let me have it out."

"It isn't quite a matter of being hopeful or the reverse," replied the blind man. "It is merely final to your ambition. You know Prince Ulric of Villalyia?"

"I have been presented. He hunted in Ireland last season."

"He knew Miss Roscastle?"

"They were acquainted, she has told me."

"It went deeper than you imagined. Miss Roscastle is Princess Ulric of Villalyia today."

"Una! Oh," cried Enniscorthy, "but—but that is impossible! You don't mean that she—"

"I mean exactly what I say. They were married within a week of her disappearance from London."

Enniscorthy's pained gaze went from face to face. The fatal presentiment that had always just robbed him of the heroic—the fear that he might be making an ass of himself—again assailed him.

"But isn't Ulric in the line of succession? They couldn't be really married without the king's consent. Of course Villalyia is a republic now, but—"

"But it may not be tomorrow if the expected war breaks out? Quite true, Mr Enniscorthy. And in the meanwhile the forms and ceremonies are maintained at the exile Court of Clairvaux. Yet the king gave his consent."

"Gave his consent! For his son to marry an actress?"

"Ah, there was a little sleight of hand there. He only knew Miss Roscastle as Miss Eileen O'Rourke, the last representative of a line of Irish kings. She was a Miss O'Rourke?"

"Yes. Roscastle was only her stage name. The O'Rourkes were a very old but impoverished family."

354

"Royal, we may assume. This business was the outcome of one of the interminable domestic squabbles that the Villalyia Petrosteins seemed to wage in order to supply the Continental comic papers with material. Ex-King Constantine recently quarrelled simultaneously and irrevocably with his eldest son Robert and his first cousin Michael. Robert, who lives in Paris, has respectably married a robust minor princess who has presented him with six unattractive daughters and now, by all report, stopped finally. Hating both son and cousin almost equally, old Constantine, who had fumed himself into a fever, sent off for his other son, Ulric, and demanded that he should at once marry and found a prolific line of sons to embitter Robert and cut out the posterity of Michael. Prince Ulric merely replied that there was only one woman whom he wished to marry and she was not of sufficiently exalted station, and as she refused to marry him morganatically—yes, Mr Enniscorthy—there was no prospect of his ever marrying at all.

"The king suddenly found that he was very ill. Ulric was obdurate. The constitution allowed the reigning monarch to sanction such an alliance, provided there were no religious difficulties, and I understand that Miss Roscastle is a Catholic. Constantine recognised that if he was to gratify his whim he must consent, and that at once, as he was certainly dying. As things were, Ulric would probably renounce and marry ignominiously or die unmarried and the hated Michaels would step in, for, once king, the conventional Robert would never give his consent to such an alliance. Besides, it would be a 'damned slap in the face' to half the remaining royalty of Europe, and Constantine had always posed as a democratic sovereign —that was why his people ran him out. He coughed himself faint and then commanded the lady to be sent for."

"If only Una had confided in me I would—yes, I would willingly have flown to serve her."

"I think that Miss Roscastle was well qualified to serve herself," responded Carrados dryly. "Now you can put together the whole story, Mr Enniscorthy. Many pages of it are necessarily obscure. What the man Hay knew and threatened—whether it was with him in view or the emissaries of the hostile Robert and Michael that she took the sudden chance of concealing her absence and cloaking her identity— what other wheels there were, what other influences at work—these are only superfluities. The essential thing is that, in spite of cross-currents, everything went well—for her, and perhaps for you; the lady's married and there's an end of it."

"I hope that she will be as happy as I should have tried to make her," said Enniscorthy rather shakily.

"I shall always think of her. Mr Carrados, I will write to thank you when I am better able to express myself. Mr Carlyle, you know my address. Good-morning."

"A very manly way of taking it and very properly expressed—very well indeed," declared Mr. Carlyle with warm approval as the door closed. "Max, that is the outcome of good blood—blood and breeding."

"Nonsense, you romantic old humbug," said Carrados with affectionate contempt. "I have heard exactly the same words in similar circumstances once before and they were spoken by a Canning Town bricklayer's labourer."

One incident only remains to be added. A month later Mr Carlyle was passing the Kemble Club when he became conscious of someone trying to avoid him. With a not unnatural impulse he made for his acquaintance and insisted on being recognised.

"Ah, Mr Stokesey," he exclaimed, "*Call a Spade* is still going strong, I see."

"Mr Carlyle, to be sure," said the manager. "Bother me if I didn't mistake you for a deadhead who always strikes me for a pass. Good heavens! yes; they come in droves and companies to see the part that the romantic Princess Ulric of Villalyia didn't create! I've had three summonses for my pit queue. Didn't I tell you it was a gamble? When I have to find a successor— when, mind, I say—I'm going to put on *You Never Can Tell*! What?"

The Ingenious Mr. Spinola

"You seem troubled, Parkinson. Have you been reading the Money Article again?"

Parkinson, who had been lingering a little aimlessly about the room, exhibited symptoms of embarrassed guilt. Since an unfortunate day, when it had been convincingly shown to the excellent fellow that to leave his accumulated savings on deposit at the bank was merely an uninviting mode of throwing money away, it is not too much to say that his few hundreds had led Parkinson a sorry life. Inspired by a natural patriotism and an appreciation of the advantage of 4½ over 1¼ *per cent.*, he had at once invested in Consols. A very short time later a terrible line in a financial daily—"Consols weak"—caught his agitated eye. Consols were precipitately abandoned and a "sound industrial" took their place. Then came the rumours of an impending strike and the Conservative press voiced gloomy forebodings for the future of industrial capital. An urgent selling order, bearing Mr. Parkinson's signature, was the immediate outcome.

In the next twelve months Parkinson's few hundreds wandered through many lands and in a modest way went to support monarchies and republics, to carry on municipal enterprise and to spread the benefits of commerce. And, through all, they contrived to exist. They even assisted in establishing a rubber plantation in Madagascar and exploiting an oil discovery in Peru and yet survived. If everything could have been lost by one dire reverse Parkinson would have been content—even relieved; but with her proverbial inconsequence Fortune began by smiling and continued to smile—faintly, it is true, but appreciably—on her timorous votary. In spite of his profound ignorance of finance each of Parkinson's qualms and tremors resulted in a slight pecuniary margin to his credit. At the end of twelve months he had drawn a respectable interest, was somewhat to the good in capital, and as a waste product had acquired an abiding reputation among a small but choice coterie as a very "knowing one."

"Thank you, sir, but I am sorry if I seemed engrossed in my own affairs," he apologised in answer to Mr. Carrados's inquiry. "As a matter of fact," he added, "I hoped that I had finished with Stock Exchange transactions for the future."

"Ah, to be sure," assented Carrados. "A block of cottages Acton way, wasn't it to be?"

"I did at one time consider the investment, but on reflection I decided against property of that description. The association with houses occupied by the artisan class would not have been congenial, sir.

"Still, it might have been profitable."

"Possibly, sir. I have, however, taken up a mortgage on a detached house standing in its own grounds at Highgate. It was strongly recommended by your own estate agents—by Mr. Lethbridge himself, sir."

"I hope it will prove satisfactory, Parkinson."

"I hope so, sir, but I do not feel altogether reassured now, after seeing it."

"After seeing it? But you saw it before you took it up, surely?"

"As a matter of fact, no, sir. It was pointed out to me that the security was ample, and as I had no practical knowledge of house—valuing there was nothing to be gained by inspecting it. At the same time I was given the opportunity, I must admit; but as we were rather busy then—it was just before we went to Rome, sir—I never went there."

"Well, after all," admitted Carrados, "I hold a fair number of mortgage securities on railways and other property that I have never been within a thousand miles of. I am not in a position to criticise you, Parkinson. And this house—I suppose that it does really exist?"

"Oh yes, sir. I spent yesterday afternoon in the neighbourhood. Now that the trees are out there is not a great deal that can be actually seen from the road, but I satisfied myself that in the winter the house must be distinctly visible from several points."

"That is very satisfactory," said Carrados with equal seriousness. "But, after all, the title is the chief thing."

"So I am given to understand. Doubtless it would not be sound business, sir, but I think that if the title had been a little worse, and the appearance of the grounds a little better, I should have felt more secure. But what really concerned me is that the house is being talked about."

"Talked about?"

"Yes. It is in a secluded position, but there are some old-fashioned cottages near and these people notice things, sir. It is not difficult to induce them to talk. Refreshments are procurable at one of the cottages and I had tea there. I have since thought, from a remark made to me on leaving, that the idea may have got about that I was connected with the Scotland Yard authorities. I had no apprehension at the time of creating such an impression, sir, but I wished to make a few casual inquiries."

Carrados nodded. "Quite so," he murmured encouragingly.

"It was then that I discovered what I have alluded to. These people, having become suspicious, watch all that is to be seen at Strathblane Lodge—as it is called—and talk. They do not know what goes on there."

"That must be very disheartening for them."

"Well, sir, they find it trying. Up to less than a year ago the house was occupied by a commercial gentleman and everything was quite regular. But with the new people they don't know which are the family and who are the servants. Two or three men having the appearance of mechanics seem to be there continually, and sometimes, generally in the evening, there are visitors of a class whom one would not associate with the unpretentious nature of the establishment. Gentlemen for the most part, but occasionally ladies, I was told, coming in taxis or private motor cars and generally in evening dress."

"That ought to reassure these neighbours—the private cars and evening dress."

"I cannot say that it does, sir. And what I heard made me a little nervous also."

Something was evidently on the ingenuous creature's mind. The blind man's face wore a faintly amused smile, but he gauged the real measure of his servant's apprehension.

"Nervous of what, Parkinson?" he inquired kindly.

"Some thought that it might be a gambling-house, but others said it looked as if a worse business was carried on there. I should not like there to be any scandal or exposure, sir, and perhaps the mortgage forfeited in consequence."

"But, good heavens, man! you don't imagine that a mortgage is like a public-house licence, to be revoked in consequence of a rowdy tenant, surely?"

Parkinson's dubious silence made it increasingly plain that he had, indeed, associated his security with some such contingency, a conviction based, it appeared, when he admitted his fears, on a settled belief in the predatory intentions of a government with whom he was not in sympathy.

"Don't give the thing another thought," counselled his employer. "If Lethbridge recommended the investment you may be sure that it is all right. As for what goes on there—that doesn't matter two straws to you, and in any case it is probably idle chatter."

"Thank you, sir. It is a relief to have your assurance. I see now that I ought to have paid no attention to such conversation, but being anxious—and seeing Sir Fergus Copling go there "Sir Fergus Copling? You saw him there?"

"Yes, sir. I thought that I remembered a car that was waiting for the gate to be opened. Then I recognised Sir Fergus: it was the small dark blue car that he has come here in. And just after what I had been hearing—"

"But Sir Fergus Copling! He's a testimonial of propriety. Do you know what you are talking about, Parkinson?"

The excellent man looked even more deeply troubled than he had been about his money.

"Not in that sense, sir," he protested. "I only understood that he was a gentleman of position and a very large income, and after just listening to what was being said Carrados's scepticism was intelligible. Copling was the last man to be associated with a scandal of fast life. He had come into his baronetcy quite unexpectedly a few years previously while engaged in the drab but apparently congenial business of teaching arithmetic at a public school. The chief advantage of the change of fortune, as it appeared to the recipient, was that it enabled him to transfer his attention from the lower to the higher mathematics. Without going out of his way to flout the conventions, he set himself a comparatively simple standard of living. He was too old and fixed, he said, to change much—forty and a bachelor—and the most optimistic spinster in town had reluctantly come to acquiesce.

Carrados had not forgotten this conversation when next he encountered Sir Fergus a week or so later. He knew the man well enough to be able to lead up to the subject and when an identifiable footstep fell on his ear in the hall of the Metaphysical (the dullest club in Europe, it was generally admitted) he called across to the baronet, who, as a matter of fact, had been too abstracted to notice him or anyone else.

"You aren't a member, are you?" asked Copling when they had

shaken hands. "I didn't know that you went in for this sort of thing." The motion of his head indicated the monumental library which he had just quitted, but it might possibly be taken as indicating the general atmosphere of profound somnolence that enveloped the Metaphysical.

"I am not a member," admitted Carrados. "I only came to gather some material."

"Statistics?" queried Copling with interest. "We have a very useful range of works." He suddenly remembered his acquaintance's affliction. "By the way, can I be of any use to you?"

"Yes, if you will," said Carrados. "Let me go to lunch with you. There is an appalling bore hanging about and he'll nab me if I don't get past under protection."

Copling assented readily enough and took the blind man's arm.

"Where, though?" he asked at the door. "I generally"—he hesitated, with a shy laugh—"I generally go to an A.B.C. tea-shop myself. It doesn't waste so much time. But, of course—"

"Of course, a tea-shop by all means," assented Carrados.

"You are sure that you don't mind?" persisted the baronet anxiously.

"Mind? Why, I'm a shareholder!" chuckled Carrados.

"This suits me very well," remarked the ex-schoolmaster when they were seated in a remote corner of a seething general room. "Fellows used to do their best to get me into the way of going to swell places, but I always seem to drift back here. I don't mind the prices, Carrados, but hang me if I like to pay the prices simply to be inconvenienced. Yes, hot milk, please."

Carrados endorsed this reasonable philosophy. Carlton or Coffeehouse, the Ritz or the tea-shop, it was all the same to him—life, and very enjoyable life at that. He sat and, like the spider, drew from within himself the fabric of the universe by which he was surrounded. In that inexhaustible faculty he found perfect content: he never required "to be amused."

"No, not statistics," he said presently, returning to the unfinished conversation of the club hall. "Scarcely that. More in the nature of topography, perhaps. Have you considered, Copling, how everything is specialised nowadays? Does anyone read the old-fashioned unpretentious *Guide-book to London* still? One would hardly think so to see how the subject is cut up. We have 'Famous London Blind-alleys,' 'Historical West-Central Door-Knockers,' 'Footsteps of Dr. Johnson between Gough Square and John Street, Adelphi,' 'The Thames from Hungerford Bridge to Charing Cross Pier,' 'Oxford Street Paving Stones on which De Quincey sat,' and so on."

"They are not familiar to me," said Sir Fergus simply.

"Nor to me; yet they sound familiar. Well, I touched journalism myself once, years ago. What do you say to 'Mysterious Double-fronted Houses of the outer Northern Suburbs'? Too comprehensive?"

"I don't know. The subject must be limited. But do you seriously contemplate such a work?"

"If I did," replied Carrados, "what could you tell me about Strathblane Lodge, Highgate?"

"Oh!" A slow smile broke on Copling's face. "That is rather extraordinary, isn't it? Do you know old Spinola? Have you been there?"

"So far I don't know the venerable Mr. Spinola and I have not been there. What is the peculiarity?"

"But you know of the automatic card-player?"

The words brought a certain amount of enlightenment. Carrados had heard more than once casual allusions to a wonderful mechanical contrivance that played cards with discrimination. He had not thought anything more of it, classing it with Kempelen's famous imposture which had for a time mystified and duped the chess world more than a century ago. So far, also, some reticence appeared to be observed about the modern contrivance, as though its inventor had no desire to have it turned into a popular show: at all events not a word about it had appeared in the Press.

"I have heard something, but not much, and I certainly have not seen it. What is it—a fraud, surely?"

Copling replied with measured consideration between the process of investigating his lightly boiled egg. It was plain that the automaton had impressed him.

"I naturally approached the subject with scepticism," he admitted, "but at the end of several demonstrations I am converted to a position of passive acquiescence. Spinola, at all events, is no charlatan. His knowledge of mathematics is profound. As you know, Carrados, the subject is my own and I am not likely to be imposed on in that particular. It was purely the scientific aspect of the invention that attracted me, for I am not a gambler in the ordinary sense. Spinola's explanation of the principles of the contrivance, when he found that I was capable of following them, was lucid and convincing. Of course he does not disclose all the details of the mechanism, but he shows enough."

"It is a gamble, then, not a mere demonstration?"

"He has spent many years on the automaton, and it must have cost thousands of pounds in experiment and construction. He makes no secret of hoping to reimburse his outlay."

"What do you play?"

"Piquet—Rubicon piquet. The figure could, he claims, be set to play any game by changing or elaborating the mechanism. He had to construct it for one definite set of chances and he selected piquet as a suitable medium."

"It wins?"

"Against me invariably in the end."

"Why should it win, Copling? In a game that is nine-tenths chance, why should it win?"

"I am an indifferent player. If the tactics of the game have been reduced to machinery and the combinations are controlled by a dispassionate automaton, the one-tenth would constitute a winning factor."

"And against expert players?"

Sir Fergus admitted that to the best of his knowledge the figure still had the advantage. In answer to Carrados's further inquiry he estimated his losses at two or three hundred pounds. The stakes were whatever the visitor suggested—Spinola was something of a grandee, one inferred—and at half-crown points Sir Fergus had found the game quite expensive enough.

"Why do people go if they invariably lose?" asked the blind man. "My dear fellow, why do they go to Monte Carlo?" was the retort, accompanied by a tolerant shrug. "Besides, I don't positively say that they always lose. One hears of people winning, though I have never seen it happen. Then I fancy that the novelty has taken with a certain set. It is a thing at the moment to go up there and have the rather bizarre experience. There is an element of the creep in it, you know—sitting and playing against that serene and unimpressionable contrivance."

"What do the others do? There is quite a company, I gather."

"Oh yes, sometimes. Occasionally one may find oneself alone. Well, the others often watch the play. Sometimes sets play bridge on their own. Then there is coffee and wine. Nothing formal, I assure you."

"Rowdy ever?"

"Oh no. The old man has a presence; I doubt if anyone would feel encouraged to go too far under Spinola's eye. Yet practically nothing seems to be known of him, not even his nationality. I have heard half-a-dozen different tales from as many cocksure men—he is a South American Spaniard ruined by a revolution; a Jesuit expelled from France through politics; an Irishman of good family settled in Warsaw, where he stole the plans from a broken-down Polish inventor; a Virginia military man, who suddenly found that he was dying from cancer and is doing this to provide a fortune for an only and beautiful daughter, and so on."

"Is there a beautiful daughter?"

"Not that I have ever seen. No, the man just cropped up, as odd people do in great capitals. Nobody really knows anything about him, but his queer salon has caught on to a certain extent."

Now any novel phase of life attracted Carrados. The mixed company that Spinola's enterprise was able to draw to an out-of-the-way suburb—the peculiar blend of science and society—was not much in itself. The various constituents could be met elsewhere to more advantage, but the assemblage might engender piquancy. And the man himself and his machine? In any case they should repay attention.—

"How does one procure the *entree?*" he inquired.

Copling raised a quizzical eyebrow.

"You also?" he replied. "Oh, I see; you think—Well, if you are going to discover any sleight-of-hand about the business I don't mind—"

"Yes?" prompted Carrados, for Sir Fergus had pulled up on an obvious afterthought.

"I did not intend going up again," said Copling slowly. "As a matter of fact, I have seen all that interests me. And—I suppose I may as well tell you, Carrados—I made someone a sort of promise to have nothing to do with gambling. She feels very strongly on the subject."

"She is very wise," commented the blind man.

Elation mingled with something faintly apologetic in the abrupt bestowal of the baronet's unexpected confidence.

"It was really quite a sudden and romantic happening," he continued, led on by the imperceptible encouragement of his companion's attitude. "She is called Mercia. She does not know who I am—not that that's anything," he added modestly. "She is an orphan and earns her own living. I was able to be of some slight service to her in the science galleries at South Kensington, where she was collecting material for her employer. Then we met there again and had lunch together, and so on."

"At tea-shops?"

"Oh yes. Her tastes are very simple. She doesn't like shows and society and all that."

"I congratulate you. When is it to be?"

"It? Oh! Well, we haven't settled anything like that yet. Of course this is all in confidence, Carrados."

"Absolutely—though the lady has done me rather an ill turn."

"How?"

"Well, weren't you going to introduce me to Mr. Spinola?"

"True," assented Sir Fergus. "And I don't see why I shouldn't," he added valiantly. "I need not play, and if there is any bunkum about the thing I should certainly like to see how it is done. What evening will suit you?"

An early date had suited both, and shortly after eight o'clock—an hour at which they were likely to find few guests before them—Carrados's car drew up at Strathbane Lodge. By arrangement he had picked up Copling, who lived—"*of all places in the world*," as people had said when they heard of it—in an unknown street near Euston. Parkinson, out of regard for the worthy man's feelings, had been left behind on the occasion and in ignorance of his master's destination.

The appearance of the place was certainly not calculated to re-assure a nervous investor. The entirely neglected garden seemed to convey a hint that the tenant might be contemplating a short occupation and a hasty flight. Nor did the exterior of the house do much to remove the unfortunate impression. Only a philosopher or an habitual defaulter would live in such a state.

The venerable Mr. Spinola received them in the salon set apart for the display of the automaton and for cards in general. It was a room of fair proportions—doubtless the largest in the house—and quite passably furnished, though in a rather odd and incongruous style. But probably any furniture on earth would have seemed incongruous to the strange, idol-like presence which the inventor had thought fit to adapt to the uses of his mechanism. The figure was placed on a low pedestal, sufficiently raised from the carpet on four plain wooden legs for all the space underneath to be clearly visible. The body was a squat, cross-legged conception, typical of an Indian deity, the head singularly life-like through the heavy gilding with which the face was covered, and behind the merely contemplative expression that dominated the golden mask the carver had by chance or intention lined a faint suggestion of cynical contempt.

"You have come to see my little figure—Aurelius, as we call him among ourselves?" said the bland old gentleman benignly. "That is right; that is right." He shook hands with them both, and received Mr. Carrados, on Sir Fergus's introduction, as though he was a very dear friend from whom he had long been parted. It was difficult indeed for Max to disengage himself from the effusive Spinola's affection without a wrench.

"Mr. Carrados happens to be blind, Mr. Spinola," interposed Copling, seeing that their host was so far in ignorance of the fact.

"Impossible! Impossible!" exclaimed Spinola, riveting his own very bright eyes on his guest's insentient ones. "Yet," he added, "one would not jest "It is quite true," was the matter-of-fact corroboration. "My hands must be my eyes, Mr. Spinola. In place of seeing, will you permit me to touch your wonderful creation?"

The old man's assent was immediate and cordial. They moved across the room towards the figure, the inventor modestly protesting:

"You flatter me, my dear sir. After all, it is but a toy in large; nothing but a toy."

A weary-looking youth, the only other occupant of the room, threw down the illustrated weekly that he had picked up on the new arrivals' entrance and detained Copling.

"Yes, I had been toying a little before you arrived," he remarked flippantly. "I came early to cut Dora Lascelle off from the idle crowd and the silly little rabbit isn't coming, it appears. I didn't want to play, because, for a fact, I have no money, but the old thing bored me to hysterics. Good God! how he can talk so little on anything really entertaining, like *The Giddy Flappers* or Trixie Fluff's divorce, and so much about strange, unearthly things that no other living creature has ever seen even in a dream, baffles my imagination. What's an 'integral calculus,' Copling? No, don't tell me, after all. Let me forget the benumbing episode as soon as possible."

"Do you wish for a game, Sir Fergus?" broke in Spinola's soft voice from across the room. "Doubtless Mr. Carrados might like to follow someone else's play before he makes the experiment."

Copling hesitated. He had not come to play, as he had already told his friend, but Max gave no sign of coming to his assistance.

"Perhaps you, Crediton?" said the mathematician; but young Crediton shook his head and smiled wisely. Copling was too easygoing to stand out. He crossed the room and sat down at the automaton's table.

"And the stake?"

"Suppose we merely have a guinea on the game?" suggested the visitor.

Spinola acquiesced with the air of one to whom a three-penny bit or a kingdom would have been equally indifferent. The deal fell to Copling and the automaton therefore had the first "elder hand," with the advantage of a discard of five cards against its opponent's three.

Carrados had already been shown the theory of the contrivance. He now followed Spinola's operations as the game proceeded. The old man picked up the twelve cards dealt to the automaton and carefully arranged them in their proper places on a square shield that was connected with the front of the figure. As each fell into its slot it registered its presence on the delicate mechanism that the figure contained.

"The discard," remarked Spinola, and moved a small lever. The left hand of the automaton was raised, came over the shield which hid its cards from the opponent, touched one with an extended finger, and affixing it by suction, lifted the selected card from the slot and dropped it face downwards on the table.

"A little slow, a little cumbersome," apologised the inventor as the motions were repeated until five cards had been thrown out. "The left hand is used for the discard alone, as a different movement is necessary." He picked up the five new cards from the stock and arranged them as he had done the hand. "Now we proceed to the play."

Crediton strolled across to watch the game. He stood behind Copling, while Carrados remained near the automaton. Spinola opened the movements.

"Aurelius has no voice, of course," he said, studying the display of cards, "so I—point of five."

"Good," conceded the opponent.

Spinola registered the detail on one of an elaborate set of dials that produced a further development in the machinery.

"Spades," he announced, declaring the suit that he had won the "points" on. "Tierce major."

"Quart to the queen—hearts," claimed Copling, and Spinola moved another dial to register the opponent's advantage.

"Three kings."

"Good," was the reply.

"Three tens," added the senior player, as his three kings, being good against the other hand, enabled him to count the lower trio also. "Five for the point and two trios—eleven." Every detail of the scoring and of the ensuing play was registered as the other things had been.

This finished the preliminaries and the play of the hands began.

The automaton, in response to the release of the machinery, moved its right arm with the same deliberation that had marked its former action and laid a card face upwards on the table. For the blind man's benefit each card was named as it was played. At the end of the hand Copling had won "the cards"—a matter of ten extra points with seven tricks to five and the score stood to his advantage at 27–17.

"Not bad for the junior hand," commented Crediton. "Do you know"—he addressed the inventor—"there is a sort of 'average,' as they call it, that you are supposed to play up to? I forget how it goes, but 27 is jolly high for the minor hand, I know."

"I have heard of it," replied Spinola politely. Crediton could not make out why the other two men smiled broadly.

The succeeding hands developed no particular points of interest. The scoring ruled low and in the end Copling won by 129 to 87. Spinola purred congratulation.

"I am always delighted to see Aurelius lose," he declared, paying out his guinea with a princely air.

"Why?" demanded Crediton.

"Because it shows that I have succeeded beyond expectation, my dear young sir: I have made him almost human. Now, Mr. Carrados."

"With pleasure," assented the blind man. "Though I am afraid that I shall not afford you the delight of losing, Mr. Spinola."

"One never knows, one never knows," beamed the old man. "Shall we say "Half-crown points for variety?"

"Very good. Ah, our deal." He dealt the hands and proceeded to dispose the twelve that fell to the automaton on the shield. There was a moment of indecision. "Pray, Mr. Carrados, do you not arrange your cards?"

"I have done so." He had, in fact, merely spread out his hand in the usual fan formation and run an identifying finger once round the upper edges. The cards remained as they had been dealt, face downwards.

"Wonderful! And that enables you to distinguish them?"

"The ink and the impression on a plain surface—oh yes." He threw out the full discard as he spoke and took in the upper five of the stock.

"You overwhelm us; you accentuate the tiresome deliberation of poor Aurelius." Spinola was hovering about the external fittings of the figure with unusual fussiness. When at length he released the left hand it seemed for an almost perceptible moment that the action hung.

Then the arm descended and carried out the discard.

"Point of five," said Carrados.

"Good."

"In spades. Quint major in spades also, tierce to the knave in clubs, fourteen aces"—*i.e.* four aces; "fourteen" in the language of piquet as they score that number. He did not wait for his opponent to assent to each count, knowing, after the point had passed, that the other calls were good against anything that could possibly be held. "Five, twenty, twenty-three, ninety-seven." Having reached thirty before his opponent scored, and without a card having so far been played, his score automatically advanced by sixty. That is the "repique."

"By Jove!" exclaimed Crediton, "that's the first time I've ever known Aurelius repiqued."

"Oh, it has happened," retorted Spinola almost testily.

The play of the hand was bound to go in Carrados's favour—he held eight certain tricks. He won "the cards" with two tricks to spare and the round closed at 119-5.

"You look like being delighted again, Mr. Spinola," remarked Crediton a little critically.

"Suppose you make yourself useful by dealing for me," interposed Carrados. "Of course," he reminded his host, "it does not do for me to handle any cards but my own."

"I had not thought of that," replied Spinola, looking at him shrewdly. "If you had no conscience you would be a dangerous opponent, Mr. Carrados."

"The same might be said of any man," was the reply. "That is why it is so satisfactory to play an automaton."

"Oh, Aurelius has no conscience, you know," chimed in Crediton sapiently. "Mr. Spinola couldn't find room for it among the wheels."

The second hand was not eventful. Each player had to be content to make about the "average" which Crediton had ingenuously discovered. It raised the scores to 33-30. Two hands followed in the same prudent spirit; the fifth—Carrados's "elder"—found the position 169-67.

"Only two this time," remarked Carrados, taking in.

"Jupiter!" murmured Crediton. It is unusual for the senior hand to leave even one of the five cards to which he is entitled. It indicated an unusually strong hand. The automaton evidently thought so too. It availed itself of all the six alternative cards and, as the play disclosed, completely cut up its own hand to save the repique by beating Carrados on the point. It won the point, to find that its opponent only held a low quart, a tierce and three kings. As a result Carrados won "the cards" and the score stood 199-79. The discard was, in fact, an experiment in bluff. Carrados might have held a quint and fourteen kings for all the opposing hand disclosed.

"What on earth did you do that for?" demanded Copling. He himself played an eminently straightforward game—and generally lost.

"I'll bet I know," put in Crediton. "You are getting rather close, Mr. Spinola—the last hand and you need twenty—one to save the Rubicon." The "Rubicon" means that instead of the loser's score being deducted from the winner's in arriving at the latter's total, it is added to it—a possible difference of nearly 200 points.

"We shall see; we shall see," muttered Spinola with a little less than his usual suavity.

Whatever concern he had, however, was groundless, for the game ended tamely enough. Carrados ought to have won the point and divided tricks, leaving his opponent a minor quart and a solitary trio—about 15 on the hand. By a careless discard he threw away both chances and the final score stood at 205-112. Copling, who had come to regard his friend's play as rather excellent, was silent. Crediton almost shrieked his disapproval and seizing the cards demonstrated to his heart's content.

"Ninety-three and the hundred for the game—twenty-four pounds and one half-crown," said the loser, counting out notes and coin to the amount. "It has been an experience for both of us—Aurelius and myself."

"And certainly for me," added Carrados.

"Look here," interposed Crediton, "Aurelius seems off his play. If you don't mind taking my paper, Mr. Spinola, I should like another go."

"As you please," assented the old man. "Your undertaking is, of course—" The gesture suggested "quite equal to that of the cashier of the Bank of England." The venerable person had, in fact, regained his lofty pecuniary indifference. "The same point?"

"Right-o," cheerfully assented the youth.

"I will go and think over my shortcomings," said Carrados. He started to cross the room to a seat and ran into a couch. With a gasp Copling hastened to his assistance. Then he found his arm detained and heard the whisper. "Sit down with me."

Across the room the play had begun again and with a little care they could converse without the possibility of a word being over-heard.

"What is it?" asked Sir Fergus.

"The golden one will win. It is only when the cards are not exposed that you play on equal terms."

"But I won?"

"Because it is well to lose sometimes and, by choice, when the stake is low. That witless youth will have to pay for both of us."

"But how—how on earth do you suggest that it is done?"

"Look round cautiously. What eyes overlook Crediton's hand as he sits there?"

"What eyes? Good gracious! is there anything in that?"

"What is it?"

"There is a trophy of Japanese arms high up on the wall. An iron mask surmounts it. It has glass eyes. I have never seen anything like that before."

"Any others round the walls?"

"There is a stuffed tiger's head on our right and a puma's or something of that sort on the left."

"In case a suspicious player asks to have the places changed or holds his cards awkwardly. Working the automaton from other positions is probably also arranged for."

"But how can a knowledge of the opponent's cards affect the automaton? The dials—"

"The dials are all bunkum. While you were playing I took the liberty of altering them and for a whole hand the dials indicated that you must inevitably be holding eight clubs and four spades. All the time you were leading out hearts and diamonds and the automaton serenely followed suit. The only effective machinery is that indicating the display of cards on the shield and controlling the hands, and that is worked by a keyboard and electric current from the room below. The watcher behind the mask telephones the opposing hand, the discard and the take-in. The automaton's hand has already been indicated below.

"You see the enormous advantage the hidden player has? When he is the minor hand he knows everything that is to be known before he discards. When he is the elder he knows almost everything. By concentrating on one detail he can practically always balk the pique, the repique and the *kapot*, if it is necessary to play for safety. You remember what Crediton said—that he had never known Aurelius repiqued before. The leisurely manipulation of the dials gives plenty of time. An even ordinary player in that position can do the rest."

Copling scarcely knew whether to believe or not. It sounded plausible, but it reflected monstrously.

"You speak of a telephone," he said. "How can you definitely say that such a thing is being used? You have never been in the room before and we've scarcely been here an hour. It—it may be awfully serious, you know."

Carrados smiled.

"Can you hear the kitchen door being opened at this moment or detect the exact aroma of our host's *mocha?*" he demanded.

"Not in the least," admitted Copling.

"Then of course it is hopeless to expect you to pick up the whisper of a man behind a mask a score of feet away. How fearfully in the dark you seeing folk must be!"

"Can you possibly do that?" Even as he was speaking the door opened and a servant entered, bringing coffee and an assortment of viands sufficiently exotic to maintain the rather Oriental nature of entertainment.

"Stroll across and see how the game is going," suggested Carrados. "Have a look at Crediton's discard and then come back."

Sir Fergus did not quite follow the purpose, but he nodded and proceeded to comply with his usual amiable spirit.

"It stands at 137 to 75 against Crediton and they are playing the last hand. Our young friend looks like losing thirty or forty pounds."

"And his discard?"

"Oh—seven and nine of clubs and the knave of hearts."

Carrados held out a slip of paper on which he had already pencilled a few words. The baronet took it, looked and whistled softly. He had read: "Clubs, seven, nine. Hearts, knave."

"Conjuring?" he interrogated.

"Quite as simple—listening."

"I suppose I must accept it. What staggers me is that you can pick out a whisper when the room is full of other louder sounds. Now if there had been absolute stillness—"

"Merely use. There's nothing more in it than in seeing a mouse and a mountain, or a candle and the sun, at the same time. Well, what are we going to do about it?"

Copling began to look acutely unhappy.

"I suppose we must do something," he ruminated, "but I must say that I wish we needn't. I mean, I wish we hadn't dropped on this. You know, Carrados, whatever is going on, Spinola is no charlatan. He does understand mathematics."

"That makes him all the more dangerous. But I should like to produce more definite proof before we do anything. Does he ever leave us in the room?"

"I have never known it. No, he hovers round his Aurelius."

"Never mind. Ah, the game is finished."

The game was finished and it needed no inquiry to learn how it had gone. Mr. Crediton was handing the venerable Spinola a memorandum of indebtedness. His words and attitude did not convey the impression of a graceful loser.

"I wish you two men would give me the tip for beating this purgatorial image," he grumbled as they came up. "I thought that he'd struck a losing line after your experience and this is the result." He indicated the spectacle of their amiable host folding up his I.O.U. preparatory to dropping it carelessly into a letter-rack, and shrugged his shoulders with keen disgust.

"I'll tell you if you like," suggested Sir Fergus. "Hold the better cards."

"And play them better," added Carrados. "Good heavens!"

A very untoward thing had happened. They had all been standing together round the table, Spinola purring appreciatively, Crediton fuming his ill-restrained annoyance, and the other two mildly satirical at his expense. Carrados held a cup of coffee in his hand. He reached towards the table with it, seemed to imagine that he was a full foot nearer than he was, and before anyone had divined his mistake, cup, saucer and the entire contents had dropped neatly upon Mr. Spinola's startled feet, saturating his lower extremities to the skin.

"Good heavens! What on earth have I done?"

Crediton shrieked out his ill-humour in gratified amusement; Sir Fergus reddened deeply with embarrassment at his friend's mishap. Victim and culprit stood the ordeal best.

"My unfortunate defect!" murmured Carrados with feeling. "How ever can I—"

"I who have eyes ought to have looked after my guest better," replied Spinola with antique courtliness. He reduced Crediton with a glance of quiet dignity and declined Carrados's handkerchief with a reassuring touch on the blind man's arm. "No, no, my dear sir, if you will excuse me for a few minutes. It is really nothing, really nothing, I do assure you."

He withdrew from the room to change. Copling began to prepare a reassuring phrase to meet Carrados's self-reproaches when they should break forth again. But the blind man's tone had altered; he was no longer apologetic.

"Play them better," he repeated to Crediton, as if there had been no interruption, "and play under conditions that are equal. For instance, it might be worth while making sure that a Japanese mask does not conceal a pair of human eyes. If I were a loser I should be inclined to have a look."

Not until then did it occur to Sir Fergus that his friend's clumsiness had been a calculated ruse to force Spinola to withdraw for a few minutes. Later on he might be able to admire the simple ingenuity of the trick, but at that moment he almost hated Carrados for the cool effrontery with which he had duped all their feelings.

No such subtleties, however, concerned Crediton. He stared at the blind man, followed the indication of his gesture and all at once grasped the significance of the hint.

"By George, I shouldn't wonder if you aren't right!" he exclaimed. "There are one or two thing—" Without further consideration he rushed a table against the wall, swung up a chair on to it, and mounting the structure began to wrench the details of the trophy from side to side and up and down in his excited efforts to displace them.

"Hurry up," urged Copling, more nervous than excited. "He won't be long."

"Hurry up?" Crediton paused, panting from his furious efforts, and found time to look down upon his accomplices. "I don't think that it's for us to concern ourselves, by George!" he retorted. "Spinola had better hurry up and bolt for it, I should say. There's light behind here—a hole through the wall. I believe the place is a regular swindling hell."

His eyes went to the group of weapons again and the sight gave him a new idea.

"Aha, what price this?" he cried, and pulling a short sword out of its sheath he drove it in between mask and wall and levered the shell away, nails and all. "By God, if the eyes aren't a pair of opera-glasses! And there's a regular paraphernalia here—"

"So," interrupted a quiet voice behind them, "you have been too clever for an old man, Mr. Carrados?"

Spinola had returned unheard and was regarding the work of detection with the utmost benignness. Copling looked and felt ridiculously guilty; the blind man betrayed no emotion at all and both were momentarily silent. It fell to Crediton to voice retort.

"My I.O.U., if you don't mind, Mr. Spinola," he demanded, tumbling down from his perch and holding out an insistent hand.

"With great pleasure," replied Spinola, picking it out from the contents of the letter-rack. "Also," he continued, referring to the contents of his pocket-book, while his guest tore up the memorandum into very small pieces and strewed them about the carpet, "also the sum of fifty-seven pounds, thirteen shillings which I feel myself compelled to return to you in spite of your invariable grace in losing. I have already rung; you will find the front door waiting open for you, Mr. Crediton."

"'Compelled' is good," sneered Crediton. "You will probably find a train waiting for you at Charing Cross, Mr. Spinola. I advise you to catch it before the police arrive." He nodded to the other two men and departed, to spread the astounding news in the most interested quarters.

Spinola continued to beam irrepressible benevolence.

"You are equally censorious, if more polite than Mr. Crediton in expressing it, eh, my dear young friends?" he said.

"I thought that you were a genuine mathematician—I vouched for it," replied Sir Fergus with more regret than anything else. "And the extent of your achievement has been to contrive a vulgar imposture—in the guise of an ingenious inventor to swindle society by a sham automaton that doesn't even work."

"You thought that—you still think that?"

"What else is there to think? We have seen with our own eyes."

"And"—turning to his other guest—"Mr. Carrados, who does not see?"

"I am waiting to hear," replied the blind man.

"But you, Sir Fergus, you who are also—in an elementary way—a mathematician, and one with whom I have conversed freely, you regard me as a common swindler and think that this—this tawdry piece of buffoonery that is only designed to appeal to the vapid craze for novelty of your foolish friends—this is, as you say, the extent of my achievement?"

Copling gave a warning cry and sprang forward, but it was too late to avert what he saw coming. In his petulant annoyance at the comparison Spinola had laid an emphasising hand upon Aurelius and half unconsciously had given the figure a contemptuous push. It swayed, seemed to poise for a second, and then toppling irretrievably forward crashed to the floor with an impact that snapped the golden head from off its shoulders and shook the room and the very house itself.

"There, there," muttered the old man, as though he was doing no more than regretting a broken tea-cup; "let it lie, let it lie. We have finished our work together, Aurelius and I. Now let the whole world—"

It would have been too much to expect the remainder of the mysterious household, whoever its members were, to ignore the tempestuous course of events taking place within their midst. The door was opened suddenly and a young lady, with consternation charged on every feature of her attractive face, burst into the room. For the moment her eyes took in only two figures of the curious group the aged Spinola and his fallen handiwork.

"Granda!" she cried, "whatever's happened? What is it all? Oh, are you hurt?"

"It is nothing, nothing at all; a mere *contretemps* of no importance," he reassured her quickly. Then, with a recurrence of his most grandiloquent manner, he recalled her to the situation. "Mercia, our guests—Sir Fergus Copling, Mr. Carrados. Sir Fergus, Mr. Carrados—Miss Dugard."

"Then it is Mercia!" articulated the bewildered baronet. "Mercia, you here! What does it mean? What are you doing?"

"What are you doing, Sir Fergus?" retorted the girl in cold reproach. "Is this the way you generally keep your promises? Gambling!"

"Well, really," stammered the abashed gentleman, "I—I only—"

"Sir Fergus only played a game for a mere nominal stake, to demonstrate the working to his friend," interposed Spinola with a shrewd glance—a curious blend of serpentine innocence and dove-like cunning—at the estranged young people.

"And won," added Sir Fergus *sotto voce*, as if that fact condoned his offence.

"Won indeed!" flashed out Miss Dugard. "Of course you won—I let you. Do you think that we wished to take money from you now?"

"You—you let me!" muttered Sir Fergus helplessly. "Good heavens!"

"I am grateful that your consideration also extends to your friend's friend," put in Carrados pleasantly.

Miss Dugard smiled darkly at the suavely-given thrust and showed her pretty little teeth almost as though she would like to use them.

"There, there, that will do, my child," said the old man indulgently.

"Sir Fergus and Mr. Carrados are entitled to an explanation and they shall have it. The moment is opportune; the work of a lifetime is complete. You have seen, Sir Fergus, the sums that Aurelius—assisted, as we will now admit, by a little external manipulation—has gathered into our domestic exchequer. Where have they gone, these hundreds and thousands that you may estimate? In lavish living and a costly establishment? Observe this very ordinary apartment—the best the house possesses. Recall the grounds through which you entered. Sum up the simple hospitality of which you have partaken.

"In expensive personal tastes and habits? I assure you, Sir Fergus, that I am a man of the most frugal life; my granddaughter inherits the propensity. In what, then? In advancing science, in benefitting humanity, in furthering human progress. I am going to prove to you that I have perfected one of the greatest mechanical inventions of all ages, and I ask you to credit the plain statement that all my private fortune and all the winnings that you have seen upon this table—with the exception of a bare margin for the necessities of life have been spent in perfecting it."

He paused with a senile air of triumph and seemed to challenge comment.

"But surely," ventured Copling, "surely on the strength of this you would have had no difficulty in obtaining direct financial support. Well, I myself—"

Spinola smiled a peculiar smile, shaking his head sagely.

"Take care, my generous young friend, take care. You may not quite comprehend what you are saying."

"Why?"

Still swayed by his own gentle amusement, the old man crossed the room to a desk, selected a letter from a bulky pile and handed it to his guest without a word.

Copling glanced at the heading and signature, then read the contents and frowned annoyance.

"This is from my secretary," he commented lamely.

"That is what a secretary is for, is it not—to save his employer trouble?" insinuated Spinola. "He took me for a crank or a begging-letter impostor, of course." Then came the pathetic whisper. "They all took me for that."

Sir Fergus folded the letter and handed it back again.

"I am very sorry," he said simply.

"It was natural, perhaps. Still, something had to be done. My work was all arrested. I could no longer pay my two skilled mechanics. Time was pressing. I am a very old man—I am more than a hundred years old—"

The girl shot a sudden, half-frightened, pleading glance at her lover, then at Mr. Carrados. It checked the exclamation that would have come from Copling; the blind man passed the monstrous claim without betraying astonishment.

"—a very old man and my work was yet incomplete. So I contrived Aurelius. I could, of course, have perfected a model that would have done all that has been claimed for this—mere child's play to me—but what would have been the good? Such a mechanical player would have lost as often as he would have won. Hence our little subterfuge, a means amply justified by so glorious an end."

He was smiling happily—the weeks of elaborate deception were, at the worst, an innocent ruse to him—and concluded with an emphasising nod to each in turn, to Mercia, who regarded him with implicit faith and veneration, to Copling, who at that moment surely had ample justification for declaring to himself that he was dashed if he knew what to think, and to Carrados, whose sightless look agreed to everything and gave nothing in reply. Then the old man stood up and produced his keys.

"Come, my friends," he continued; "the moment has arrived. I am going to show you now what no other eye has yet been privileged to see. My mechanics worked on the parts under my instruction, but in ignorance of the end. Even Merci a—a good girl, a very clever girl—has never yet passed this door." He had led them through the house and brought them to a brick-built, windowless shed, isolated in the garden at the back. "I little thought that the first demonstration But things have fallen so, things have fallen, and one never knows. Perhaps it is for the best." An iron door had yielded to his patent key. He entered, turned on a bunch of electric lights and stood aside. "Behold!"

The room was a workshop, fitted with the highly finished devices of metal-working and littered with the scraps and debris of their use. In the middle stood a more elaborate contrivance—the finished product of brass and steel—a cube scarcely larger than a packing-case, but seemingly filled with wheels and rods, relay upon relay, and row after row, all giving the impression of exquisite precision in workmanship and astonishing intricacy of detail.

"Why, it's a calculating machine," exclaimed Sir Fergus, going forward with immense interest.

"It is an analytical engine, or, to use the more common term, a calculating machine, as you say," assented the inventor. "I need hardly remind you, of course, that one does not spend a lifetime and a fortune in contriving a machine to do single calculations, however involved, but for the more useful and practical purpose of working out involved series with absolute precision. Still, for the purpose of a trial demonstration we will begin with an ordinary proposition, if you, Sir Fergus, will kindly set one. My engine now is constructed to work to fifty places of figures and twelve orders of difference."

"If you have accomplished that," remarked Copling, accepting the pencil and the slip of paper offered him, "you have surpassed the dreams of Babbage, Mr. Spinola."

There was a sudden gasp from Mercia, but it passed unheeded in the keen excitement of the great occasion. Spinola received the paper with its row of signs and figures and turned to operate his engine. He paused to look back gleefully.

"So you never guessed, Sir Fergus?" he chuckled cunningly. "We kept the secret well, but it doesn't matter now. *I am Charles Babbage!*"

The noise of wheel and connecting-rod cut off the chance of a reply, even if anyone had been prepared to make one. But no one, in that bewildering moment, was.

"The solution," announced Spinola with a flourish, and he passed a little slip of metal stamped with a row of figures into Sir Fergus's hand. Then, with a curious indifference to their verdict, he turned away from the group and applied himself to the machine again.

"What is it? Is it not correct?" demanded Mercia in an agonised whisper. She had not looked at the solution, but at her lover's face, and her hand suddenly gripped his arm.

"It is incomprehensible," replied Sir Fergus, dropping his voice so that the old man could not overhear. "It isn't a matter of right or wrong—it is a mere *farrago* of nonsense."

"But harmless nonsense—quite harmless," interposed Carrados softly from behind them. "Come, we can safely leave him here; you will always be able to leave him safely here. Help Miss Dugard out Copling. It is better, believe me, to leave him now."

Spinola did not turn. He was bending over the machine to which he had given life, brain and fortune, touching its wheels and sliding rods with loving fingers. They passed silently from his presence and crept back to the deserted salon, where the deposed head of Aurelius leered cynically at them from the floor.

The Kingsmouth Spy Case

Not guilty, my lord!" There was a general laugh in the lounge of the Rose and Plumes, the comfortable old Cliffhurst hotel that upheld the ancient traditions unaffected by the flaunting rivalry of Grand or Metropole. The jest hidden in the retort was a small one, but it was at the expense of a pompous, pretentious bore, and the speaker was a congenial wag who had contrived in the course of a few weeks to win a facile popularity on all sides.

Across the room one of the later arrivals—"the blind gentleman," as he was sympathetically alluded to, for few had occasion to learn his name—turned slightly towards the direction of the voice and added a pleasantly appreciative smile to the common tribute. Then his attention again settled on the writing-table at which he sat, and for the next few minutes his pencil travelled smoothly, with an occasional pause for consideration, over the block of telegraphic forms that he had picked out. At the end of ten minutes he rang for a waiter and directed that his own man should be sent to him.

"Here are three telegrams to go off, Parkinson," he said in the suave, agreeable voice that scarcely ever varied, no matter what the occasion might be. "You will take them yourself at once. After that I shall not require you again tonight."

The attendant thanked him and withdrew. The blind man closed his letter-case, retired from the writing-table to the obscurity of a sequestered corner and sat unnoticed with his sightless eyes, that always seemed to be quietly smiling, looking placidly into illimitable space as he visualised the scene before him, and the laughter, the conversation and the occasional whisper went on unchecked around.

★★★★★★

Max Carrados had journeyed down to Cliffhurst a few days previously, good-naturedly, but without any enthusiasm. Indeed it had needed all Mr Carlyle's persuasive eloquence to move him.

"The Home Office, Max," urged the inquiry agent, "one of the premier departments of the State! Consider the distinction! Surely you will not refuse a commission of that nature direct from the Government?" Carrados, looking a little deeper than a Melton overcoat and a glossy silk hat, had once declared his friend to be the most incurably romantic of idealists. He now took a malicious pleasure in reducing the situation to its crudest terms.

"Why can't the local police arrest a solitary inoffensive German spy themselves?" he inquired.

"To tell the truth, Max, I believe that there are two or three fingers in that pie at the present moment," replied Mr Carlyle confidentially. "It doesn't concern the Home Office alone. And after that Guitry Bay fiasco and the unmerciful chaffing that we got in the German papers—with rather a nasty rap or two over the knuckles from the *Kölnische Zeitung*—both Whitehall and Downing Street are in a blue funk lest they should do the wrong thing, either let the man slip away with the papers or arrest him without them."

"Contingencies with which I am sure you could grapple successfully, Louis."

Mr Carlyle's bland complacency did not suggest that he, at any rate, had any doubt on that score.

"But, you know, Max, I am pledged to carry through the Vandeeming affair here in town. And—um—well, the secretary did make a point of you being the man they relied on."

"Oh! someone there must read the papers, Louis. But I wonder . . why they did not communicate with me direct."

Mr Carlyle contrived to look extremely ingenuous. Even he occasionally forgot that looks went for nothing with Carrados.

"I imagine that they thought that a friendly intermediary—or something of that sort."

"Possibly Inspector Beedel hinted to the commissioner that you would have more influence with me than a whole Government Department?" smiled Carrados. "And so you have, Louis; so you have. If it's your ambition to get the government on your books you can tell your clients that I'll take on their job!"

"By Jupiter, Max, you are a good fellow if ever there was one!" exclaimed Mr Carlyle with gentlemanly emotion. "But I owe too much to you already."

"This won't make it any more, then. I have another reason, quite different, for going."

"Of course you have," assented the visitor heartily. "You are not one to talk about patriotism, and all that, but you can't hoodwink me with your dilettantish pose, Max, and I know that deep down in your nature there is a passionate devotion to your country—"

"Thank you, Louis," interrupted Carrados. "It is very nice to learn that. But I am really going to Kingsmouth because there's a man there—a curate—who has the second best private collection in Europe of autonomous coins of Thessaly."

For a few seconds Mr Carlyle looked his unutterable feelings. When he did speak it was with crushing deliberation.

"'Mrs Carrados,' I shall say—if ever there is a Mrs Carrados, Max—'Mrs Carrados, two things are necessary for your domestic happiness. In the first place, pack up your husband's *tetradrachms* in a brown-paper parcel and send them with your compliments to the British Museum. In the second, at the earliest possible opportunity, exact from him an oath that he will never touch another Greek coin as long as you both live.'—"

"If ever there is a Mrs Carrados," was the quick retort, "I shall probably be independent of the consolation of Greek coins as, also, Louis, of the distraction of criminal investigation. In the meantime, what are you going to tell me about this case?" Mr Carlyle at once became alert. He would have become absolutely professional had not Carrados tactfully obtruded the cigar-box. The digression, and the pleasant aroma that followed it, brought him back again to the merely human.

"It began, like a good many other cases, with an anonymous letter." He took a slip of paper from his pocket-book and handed it to Carrados. "Here is a copy."

"A copy!" The blind man ran his finger lightly along the lines and read aloud what he found there:

A friend warns you that an attempt is being successfully made on behalf of another Power to obtain naval information of vital importance. You have a traitor within your gates.

Then he crumpled up the paper and dropped it half-contemptuously into the waste-paper basket. "A copy is no use to us, Louis," he remarked. "Indeed it is worse than useless; it is misleading."

"That is all they had here. The original was addressed to the Admiral-Superintendent at the Kingsmouth Dockyard. This was sent up with the report. But I am assured that the other contained no clue to the writer's identity."

"Not even a watermark, 'Jones, stationer, High Street, Kingsmouth'!" said Carrados dryly. "Really, Louis! Every piece of paper contains at least four palpable clues."

"And what are they, pray?"

"A smell, a taste, an appearance and a texture. This one, in addition, bears ink, and with it all the characteristics of an individual handwriting."

"In capitals, Max," Mr Carlyle reminded him. "Our anonymous friend is up to that."

"Yes; I wonder who first started that venerable illusion."

"Illusion?"

"Certainly an illusion. Capitals, or 'printed handwriting' as one sees them called, are just as idiomorphic as a cursive form."

"But much less available for comparison. How are you going to obtain a specimen of anyone's printed handwriting for comparison?"

Carrados reflected silently for a moment.

"I think I should ask anyone I suspected to do one for me," he replied.

Carlyle resisted the temptation to laugh outright, but mordacity lurked in his voice.

"And you imagine that the writer of this, who evidently has good reason for anonymity, will be simple enough to comply?"

"I think so; if I ask him nicely."

"Look here, Max, I will bet you a box of any cigars you care to name—"

"Yes, Louis?"

Mr Carlyle had hesitated. He was recalling one or two things from the past, and on those occasions his friend's unemotional face had looked just as devoid of guile as it did now.

"No, Max, I won't bet this time, but I should like to send across a small box of Monterey Coronas for Parkinson to pack among your things. Well, so much for the letter."

"Not quite all," interposed Carrados. "I must have the original."

The visitor made a note in his pocket diary.

"It shall be sent to you at once. I stipulated an absolutely free hand for you. Oh, I took a tolerably high tone! I can assure you, Max. You will find everything at Kingsmouth very pleasant, and there, of course, you will learn all the details. Here they don't seem to know very much. I was not informed whether the Dockyard authorities had already had their suspicions aroused or whether the letter was the first hint. At all events they acted with tolerable promptness. The letter, you will see, is undated, but it was delivered on the seventeenth—last Thursday. On Friday they put their hands on a man in the construction department—a fellow called Brown. He made no fight of it when he was cornered, but although he owned up to the charge of betraying information, there was one important link that he could not supply and one that he would not. He could not tell them who the spy collecting the information was, because there was an intermediary; and he would not betray the intermediary on any terms. And, by gad! I for one can't help respecting the beggar for that remnant of loyalty."

"A woman?" suggested Carrados.

"Even that, I believe, is not known, but very likely you have hit the mark. A woman would explain the element of chivalry that prompts Brown's attitude. He is under open arrest now—nobody outside is supposed to know, but of course he can't buy an evening paper without it being noted. They are in hope of something more definite turning up. At present they have pitched their suspicions on a German visitor staying at Cliffhurst."

"Why?"

"I don't know, Max. They must fix on someone, you know. It's expected. All the same they are deucedly nervous at this end about the outcome."

"Did they say what Brown had given away?"

"Yes, egad! Do you know anything of the Croxton-Delahey torpedo?"

"A little," admitted Carrados.

"What does it do?" asked Mr Carlyle, with the rather sublime air of casual interest which he attached to any subject outside his own knowledge.

"It's rather an ingenious contrivance. It is fired like any other uncontrolled torpedo. At the end of a straight run—anything up to ten thousand yards at 55 knots with the superheated system—the diabolical creature stops and begins deliberately to slash a zigzag course over any area you have set it for. If in its roving it comes within two hundred feet of any considerable mass of iron it promptly makes for it, cuts its way through torpedo netting if any bars its progress, explodes its three hundredweight of gun-cotton and finishes its existence by firing a 24-pound thorite shell through the breach it has made."

"'Um," mused Mr Carlyle, "I don't like the weapon, Max, but I would rather that we kept it to ourselves. Well, Mr Brown has given away the plans." Carrados disposed of the end of his cigar and crossed the room to his open desk. From its appointed place he took a book inscribed "Engagements," touched a few pages and scribbled a line of comment here and there. Then he turned to his guest again.

"All right. I'll go down to Kingsmouth by the 12.17 tomorrow morning," he said. "Now I want you to look up the following points for me and let me have the particulars before I go."

Mr Carlyle again took out his pocket diary and beamed approvingly.

★★★★★★

As a matter of fact the tenor of the replies he received influenced Carrados to make some change in his plans. Accompanied by Parkinson he left London by the appointed train on the next day, but instead of proceeding to Kingsmouth he alighted at Cliffhurst, the pretty little seaside resort some five miles east of the great dock-port. After securing rooms at the Rose and Plumes—an easy enough matter in October—he directed his attendant to take him to a sheltered seat on the winding paths below the promenade and there leave him for an hour.

"Very nicely kept, these walks and shrubberies, sir," remarked an affable voice from the other end of the bench. A leisurely pedestrian whose clothes and manner proclaimed him to be an aimless holiday-maker had sauntered along and, after a moment's hesitation, had sat down on the same form.

"Yes, inspector," replied Carrados genially. "Almost up to the standard of our own Embankment Gardens, are they not?"

Detective-Inspector Tapling, of New Scotland Yard, went rather red and then laughed quietly.

"I wasn't quite sure at first if it was you, Mr Carrados," he apologised, moving nearer and lowering his voice. "I was to report to you here, sir, and to give you any information and assistance you might require."

"How are you getting on?" inquired Carrados.

"We think that we have got hold of the right man, sir; but for reasons that you can guess the chief is very anxious to have no mistake this time."

"Muller?"

"Yes, sir. He has a furnished villa here in Cliffhurst and is very open-handed. The time he came fits in, so far as we can tell, with the beginning of the inquiries in Kingsmouth. Then, whatever his real name is, it isn't Muller."

"He is a German?"

"Oh yes; he's German right enough, sir. We've looked up telegrams to him from Lübeck—nothing important though—and he has changed German notes in Kingsmouth. He spends a lot of time over there—says the fishing is better, but that's all my eye, only the Kingsmouth boatmen get hold of the dockyard talk and know more of the movements than the men about here. Then there's a lady."

"The intermediary?"

"That's further than we can go at the moment, but there is a lady at the furnished villa. She's not exactly Mrs Muller, we believe, but she lives there, if you understand what I mean, sir."

"Perfectly," acquiesced Carrados in the same modest spirit.

"So that all the necessary conditions can be shown to exist," concluded Tapling.

"But so far you have not a single positive fact connecting Muller with Brown?"

The inspector admitted that he had not, but added hopefully that he was in immediate expectation of information that would enable him to link up the detached surmises into a conclusive chain of direct evidence.

"And if I might ask the favour of you, sir," he continued, "you would be doing us a great service if you would allow us to continue our investigation for another twenty-four hours. I think that by then we shall be able to show something solid. And if you certify what we have done, that's all to our credit, whereas if you take it out of our hands now You see what I mean, Mr Carrados, but of course it lies entirely with you."

Carrados assented with his usual good nature. His actual business was only to examine the evidence before the arrest was made and to guarantee that the Home Office should not be involved in another spy-scare fiasco. He knew Tapling to be a reliable officer, and he did not doubt that the line he was working was the correct one. Least of all did he wish to deprive the man of his due credit.

"I can very well put in a day on my own account," he accordingly replied. "And so long as Muller is here there does not appear to be any special urgency. I suppose the odds are that the papers have been got away before you began to watch?"

"There is just a chance yet, we believe, sir; and the Admiralty is very keen on recovering those torpedo plans if it's to be done. Some of these foreign spies like to keep the thing as much as possible in their own hands. There's more credit to it, and more cash, too, at headquarters if they do. Then if it comes to a matter of touch-and-go, a letter, and especially a letter from abroad, may be stopped on the way. You will say that a man may be, for that matter, but there's been another reason against posting valuable papers about here for the past week."

"Of course," assented Carrados with enlightenment.

"The Suffragettes down here are out."

"I never thought to have any of that lot helping me," said the inspector, absent-mindedly stroking his right shin; "but they may have turned the scale for us this time. There isn't a posting place from a rural pillar-box to the head office at Kingsmouth that has been really safe from them. They've even got at the registered letters in the sorting-rooms somehow. That's why I think there's a chance still." Parkinson's approaching figure announced that an hour had passed. Carrados and the inspector rose to walk away in different directions, but before they parted the blind man put a question that had confronted him several times, although he had as yet given only a glancing attention to the case.

"Now that Muller has got the plans of the torpedo, inspector, why is he remaining here?"

It was a simple and an obvious inquiry, but before he replied Inspector Tapling looked round suspiciously. Then he further reduced the distance between them and dropped his voice to a whisper.

★★★★★★

St Ethelburga's boasted the most tin-potty bell and the highest ritual of any church in Kingsmouth. Outside it resembled a brick barn, inside a marble palace, and its ministration overworked a vicar and two enthusiastic curates. It stood at the corner of Jubilee Street and Lower Dock Approach, a conjunction that should render further description of the neighbourhood superfluous.

The Rev Byam Hosier, the senior curate, whose magnetic eloquence filled St Ethelburga's from chancel steps to porch, lodged in Jubilee Street, and there Mr Carrados found him at ten o'clock on the following morning. The curate had just finished his breakfast, and the simultaneous correction of a batch of exercise books. He apologised for the disorder without justifying himself by explaining the cause, for instead of being a laggard Mr Hosier had already taken an early celebration, and afterwards allowed himself to be intercepted on his way back to attend to a domestic quarrel, a lost cat, and the arrangements for a funeral.

"I got your note last night, Mr Carrados," he said, after guiding his guest to a seat, for Parkinson had been dismissed to make himself agreeable elsewhere. "I am glad to show you my small collection, and still more so to have an opportunity of thanking you for the help you have given me from time to time."

Carrados lightly disclaimed the obligation. It was the first time the two had met, though, as the outcome of a review article, they had frequently corresponded. The clergyman went to his single cabinet, took out the top tray and put it down before his visitor on the now available table.

"Pherae," he said.

"May I touch the surfaces?" asked the blind man.

"Oh, certainly. Pray do. I am sorry " He did not quite know what to say before the spectacle of the blind expert, with his eyes fixed elsewhere, passing a critical touch over the details that he himself loved to gaze upon.

In this one thing the Rev. Byam was fastidious. His clothes were generally bordering on the shabby, and he allowed himself to wear boots that shocked or amused the feminine element in the first half-dozen pews of St Ethelburga's. He might—as he frequently did, indeed—make a breakfast of weak tea, bread and butter and marmalade without any sense of deficiency, but in the matter of Greek coins his taste was exacting and his standard exact. His one small mahogany cabinet was pierced for five hundred specimens, and it was far from full, but every coin was the exquisite production of the golden era of the world's creative art. It did not take Carrados three minutes to learn this. Occasionally he dropped a word of comment or inquiry, but for the most part tray succeeded tray in fascinated silence.

"Still Larissa," announced the clergyman, sliding out the last tray.

Under each coin was a circular ticket with written particulars of the specimen accompanying it. For some time Carrados took little interest in these commentaries, but presently Hosier noticed that his guest was submitting many of them to a close but quiet scrutiny.

"Excuse my asking, Mr Carrados," he said at length, "but are you quite blind?"

"Quite," was the unconcerned reply. "Why?"

"Because I noticed that you held some of the labels close to your eyes and I fancied that perhaps—"

"It is my way."

"Forgive my curiosity."

"I can assure you, Mr Hosier, that other people are much more touchy about my blindness than I am. Now will you do me a kindness? I should like a copy of the inscriptions on half-a-dozen of these gems."

"With pleasure." The curate discovered pen and ink and paper and waited.

"This *didrachm* of the nymph Larissa wearing earrings; this of Artemis and the stag; this, and this, and this." The trays had been left displayed upon the table and Carrados's hand selected from them with unerring precision.

Hosier took the chosen coins and noted down the legends in their bold Greek capitals. "Shall I describe the type of each as well?" he asked.

"Thank you," assented his visitor. "If you don't mind writing that also in capitals and not blotting I shall read it so much the easier."

He accepted the sheet of paper and delicately touched the lettering along each line.

"I have a friend who will be equally interested in this," he remarked, taking out his pocket-book.

The clergyman had turned to remove a tray from the table when a sheet of paper, fluttering to the ground, caught his eye. He picked it up and was returning it into the blind man's hand when he stopped in a sudden arrest of every movement.

"Good heavens, Mr Carrados!" he exclaimed in an agitated voice, "how does this come in your possession?"

"Your note?"

"You know that it is mine?"

"Yes—now," replied Carrados quietly. "It was sent to me by the Admiral-Superintendent of the Yard here. He wished to communicate with the writer."

"I am bewildered at the suddenness of this," protested the poor young man in some distress. "Let me tell you the circumstances—such at least as do not violate my promise."

He procured himself a glass of water from the sideboard, drank half of it and began to pace the room nervously as he talked.

"On Wednesday last, after taking Evensong at the church, I was leaving the vestry when a lady stepped forward and asked if she might speak to me privately. It is a request which a clergyman cannot refuse, Mr Carrados, but I endeavoured first to find out what she required, because people frequently come to one or another of us on business that really has to do with the clerk, or the organist, or something of that sort.

"She assured me that it was a personal matter and that no other official would do.

"The lights had by this time been extinguished in the church, and doubtless the apparitor had left. I gave her my address here and asked her if she would call in ten or twenty minutes. I preferred that she should present herself in the ordinary way.

"There is no need to go into extraneous details. The unhappy lady wished to unburden her conscience by making explicit confession, and she had come to me in consequence of a sermon which she had heard me preach on the Sunday before.

"It is not expedient to weigh considerations of time or circumstance in such a case. I allowed her to proceed, and she made her confession under the seal of inviolable confidence. It involved other persons besides herself. I besought her to undo as far as possible the great harm she had done by making a full statement to the authorities, but this she was too weak—too terrified—to do. This clumsy warning of mine"—he pointed to the paper now lying on the table between them—"was the utmost concession that I could wring from her."

He stopped and looked at his visitor with a troubled face that seemed to demand some sort of assent to the dilemma.

"You are an Englishman, Mr Hosier, and you know what this might mean in a conflict—you know that one of our most formidable weapons has been annexed."

"My dear sir!" rapped out the distressed curate, "don't you think that I haven't worried about that? But behind the Englishman stands something more primitive, more just—the man. I gave my assurance as a man, and the Admiralty can go hang!"

"Besides," he added, in petulant reaction, "the poor woman is dying, and then everyone can know. Of course it may be too late."

"Do you mind telling me if the lady gave you the names of her accomplices?"

"How can I tell you, Mr Carrados? It may identify her in some way. I am too confounded by your unexpected appearance in the affair to know what is important and what is not."

"It will not implicate her. I have no concern there."

"Then, yes, she did. She gave me every detail."

"I ask because a man is suspected and on the point of arrest. He may be innocent. I have no deeper motive, but if the one for whom she is working is not a German called, or passing as, Muller, you might have some satisfaction in exonerating him."

The curate reflected a moment.

"He is not, Mr Carrados," he replied decidedly.

"But please don't ask me anything more."

"Very well, I won't," said Carrados, rising. "Our numismatic conversation has taken a strange turn, Mr Hosier. There is a text for you—Money at the root of everything! By the way, I can do you one trifling service." He picked up the anonymous letter, tore it across and held it out. "You have done all you could. Burn this and then you are clear of the matter."

"Thanks, thanks. But won't it get you into trouble with the Admiralty?"

"I make my own terms," replied Carrados. "Now Mr Hosier, I have been an ill-omened bird, but I had no suspicion of this when I came. The 'long arm' has landed us this time. Will you come and dine with me one day this week, and I promise you not a single reference to this troublesome business?"

"You are very good," assented Hosier.

"I am at Cliffhurst."

"Cliffhurst?" was Hosier's quick exclamation.

"Yes, at the Rose and Plumes."

"I—I am very sorry, Mr Carrados," stammered the curate, "but, after all, I am afraid that I must cry off. This week—"

"If the distance takes up too much of your time, may I send a car?"

"No, no, it isn't that—at least, of course, one has to consider time and work. Thank you, Mr Carrados; you are very kind, but, really, if you don't mind—"

Carrados courteously accepted the refusal without further pressure. He turned the momentary embarrassment by hoping that Hosier would not fail to call on him when next in London, and the curate availed himself of the compromise to protest the pleasure that it would afford him. Parkinson was summoned and the strangely developed visit came to an end. Parkinson doubtless found his master a dull companion on the way back. Carrados had to rearrange his ideas from the preconception which he had so far tentatively based on Inspector Tapling's report, and he was faced by the necessity of discovering whose presence made the Rose and Plumes Hotel inexplicably distasteful to Mr Hosier just then. Only two flashes of conversation broke the journey, both of which may be taken as showing the trend of Max Carrados's mind, and demonstrating the sound common sense exhibited by his henchman.

"It is a mistake they often make, Parkinson, to begin looking with a fixed idea of what they are going to find."

"Yes, sir."

And, ten minutes later:

"But I don't know that it would be safe yet to ignore the obvious altogether."

"No, sir," replied Parkinson.

★★★★★★

"Not guilty, my lord!"

That was the link for which Carrados had been waiting patiently each day since his visit to Kingsmouth; or, more exactly, since the sound of a voice heard in the hotel on his return had stirred a memory that he could not materialise. Parkinson had described the man with photographic exactness and still recognition was balked.

Tapling, who found himself at a deadlock before the furnished villa, both by reason of his want of progress and at Carrados's recommendation, contributed his observation, which was guardedly negative. Everyone about knew Mr Slater—"a pleasant, open-handed gentleman, with a word and a joke for all"—but no one knew anything of him, as, indeed, who should know of a leisurely bird of passage staying for a little time at a seaside hotel?

Then across the lounge rang the mock-serious *repartee*, and enlightenment cut into the patient listener's brain like a flash of inspiration.

These were the three telegrams which immediately came into existence as a result of that ray, deciphered here from their code obscurity:

To Greatorex, Turrets, Richmond, Surrey.—Extract *Times* full report trial Henry Frankworth, convicted embezzlement early 1906, and forward express.—Carrados.

To Wrattesley, Home Office, Whitehall, S.W. —Will you please have Lincoln Authorities instructed to send me confidential report antecedents Henry Frankworth, embezzler, native Trudstone that county. Urgent.—Wynn Carrados.

To Carlyle, 72a Bampton St., W.C.—My Dear Louis,—Why not come down weekend talk things over? Meanwhile make every effort discover subsequent history Henry Frankworth convicted embezzlement Central Criminal Court early 1906. Beedel will furnish police records. Pressing.—Max.

On his way upstairs a few hours later Carrados looked in at the reception office to inquire if there were any letters.

"By the by," he remarked, after he had turned to leave, "I wonder if you happen to have a room a little —just a little—farther away from the drawing-room?"

"Certainly, sir," replied the clerk. "Does the playing annoy you? They do keep it up rather late sometimes, don't they?"

"No, it doesn't annoy me," admitted Carrados; "on the contrary, I am passionately fond of it. But it tempts me into lying awake listening when I ought to be asleep."

The young lady laughed pleasantly. It was her business to be agreeable.

"You are considerate!" she rippled. "Well, there's the further corridor; or, of course, a floor above—"

"The floor above would do nicely. Not on the front if possible. The sea is rather noisy."

"Second floor, west corridor." She glanced at her keyboard. "No. 15?"

"Is that the side overlooking the ?"

"The High Street," she prompted.

"I am such a poor sleeper," he apologised.

"No. 21 on the other side, overlooking the gardens?" she suggested.

"I am sure that will do admirably," he said, with the gratitude that is always so touching from the blind. "Thank you for taking so much trouble to pick it for me. Goodnight."

"I will have your things transferred tomorrow," she nodded after him.

An hour later Mr Slater, generally the last man to leave the lounge, strolled across to the office for his key.

"No. 22, sir, isn't it?" she hazarded, unhooking it without waiting for the number.

"Good little girl," he assented approving. "What a brain beneath that fascinating aureola. *Eh bien, au revoir, petite!* You ought to be about snuffing the candle yourself, my dear."

The young lady laughed just as pleasantly. It was her business to be equally agreeable to all.

******

Mr Carrados was sitting in an alcove of the lounge on the following morning when Parkinson brought him a letter. It proved to be the extract from *The Times*, written on the special typewriter. The day was bright and inviting and the room was deserted. On his master's instruction Parkinson sat down and waited while the blind man rapidly deciphered the half-dozen sheets of typewriting.

"You have been with me to the Old Bailey several times," remarked Carrados, as he slowly replaced the document. "Do you remember an occasion in February 1906?"

Parkinson looked unnecessarily wise, but was unable to acquiesce. Carrados gave him another guide.

"A man named Frankworth was sentenced to eighteen months' imprisonment for an ingenious system of theft. He had also fraudulently disposed of information to trade rivals of his employer."

"I apprehend the circumstances now, sir."

"Can you recall the appearance of the prisoner?" Parkinson thought that he could, but he did not rise to the suggestion and Carrados was obliged to follow the direct line.

"Have you seen anyone lately—here in the hotel—who might be Frankworth?"

"I can't say that I have, sir."

"Take Mr Slater now. Shave off his beard and moustache."

Parkinson began to look respectfully uncomfortable.

"Do you mean, sir—?"

"By an effort of the imagination, Parkinson. Close your eyes and picture Mr Slater as a cleanshaven man, some years younger, standing in the dock—"

"Yes, sir. There is a distinct resemblance."

With this Max Carrados had to be satisfied for the time. Long memory was not Parkinson's strong point, but he had his own pre-eminent gift, and of this his master was to have an immediate example that outweighed every possible deficiency.

"Speaking of Mr Slater, sir, I noticed a curious thing that I intended to mention, as you told me to be particularly observant."

Carrados nodded encouragingly.

"I was talking to Herbert early this morning as he cleaned the boots. He is a very bigoted Free Trader, sir, and is thinking of becoming a Mormon, and I was speaking to him about it. Presently he came to No. 22's—Mr Slater's. They were muddy, for Mr Slater went out for a walk last night—I saw him as he returned. But the boots that Mr Slater put out to be cleaned last night were not the boots that he went out in and got wet, although they were exactly the same make."

"That is certainly curious," admitted Carrados slowly. "There was only one pair put out?"

"That is all, sir; and they were not the boots that Mr Slater has worn every day since I began to notice him particularly. He always does wear the same pair, morning, noon and night."

"Wait," said Carrados briskly. An idea bordering on the fantastic flashed between a sentence in the report which he had just been reading and Parkinson's discovery. He took out the sheets, ran his finger along the lines and again read—"stated that the prisoner was the son of a respectable bootmaker, and had followed the occupation himself." "I know how accurate you are, Parkinson, but this may be of superlative importance. You see that?"

"I had not contemplated it in that light, sir."

"But what did the incident suggest to you?"

"I inferred, sir, that Mr Slater must have had some reason for going out again after the hotel was closed."

"Yes, that might explain half; but what if he did not?" persisted Carrados.

Parkinson wisely dismissed the intellectual problem as outside his sphere.

"Then I am unable to suggest why the gentleman cleaned his muddy boots himself and muddied his clean boots, sir."

"Yes, that is what it comes to. He is wearing the same pair again this morning?"

"Yes, sir. The boots that were dirty at ten o'clock last night."

"Pay particular attention to Mr Slater's boots in future. I have transferred to No. 21, so you will have every opportunity. Talk to Herbert about Tariff Reform tomorrow morning. In the meanwhile—Are they any particular make?"

"'Moorland hand-made waterproof,' a heavy shooting boot, sir. Size 7. Rossiter, of Kingsmouth, is the maker."

"In the meanwhile go to Kingsmouth and buy an identical pair. Before you go cut the sole off one of your oldest boots and bring me a piece about three inches square. Buy yourself another pair. Here is a note. Do you know which chamber-maid has charge of No. 21?"

"I could ascertain, sir."

"It would be as well. You might buy her a bangle out of the change—if you have no personal objection to the young lady's society. And, Parkinson—"

"Yes, sir?"

"I know you to be discreet and reliable. The work we are engaged on here is exceptionally important and equally honourable. A mistake might ruin it. That is all."

"Thank you, sir." Parkinson marched away with his head a little higher for the guarded compliment. It was the essence of the man's extraordinary value to his master that while on some subjects he thought deeply, on others he did not think at all; and he contrived automatically to separate everything into its proper compartment.

"Here is what you require, sir," he said, returning with the square of leather.

"Come across to the fireplace," said Carrados. "There is still no one else in the lounge?"

"No, sir."

"Who would be the last servant to see to this room at night—to leave the fire safe and the windows fastened?"

"The hall porter, sir."

"Where is he now?"

"In the outer hall."

Carrados bent towards the fire. "It's a million-to-one chance," he thought, "but it's worth trying." He dropped the leather on to the red coals, waited until it began to smoke fiercely, and then, lifting it out with the tongs, he allowed the pungent aromatic odour to diffuse into the air for a few seconds. A minute later the charred fragment had lost its identity among the embers.

"Go now, and on your way tell the hall porter that I want to speak to him."

The hall porter came, a magnificent being, but full of affable condescension.

"You sent for me, sir?"

Carrados was sitting at a table near the fire.

"Yes. I am a little nervous. Do you smell anything burning?"

The porter sniffed the air—superfluously but loudly, so that the blind gentleman should hear that he was not failing in his duty. Then he looked comprehensively around.

"There certainly is a sort of hottish smell somewhere, sir," he admitted.

"It isn't any woodwork about the fireplace scorching? We blind are so helpless."

"That's all right, sir." He laid a broad hand on the mantelpiece and then rapped it reassuringly. "Solid marble that, sir. You needn't be afraid; I'll give a look across now and then."

"Thank you, if you will," said Carrados, with relief in his voice. "And, by the way, will you ring for Maurice as you go?"

A distant bell churred. Across the room, like a strangely balancing bird, skimmed a waiter.

"Sair?"

"Oh, is that you, Maurice? I want By the way, what's that burning?"

"Burning, sair?"

"Yes; don't you smell anything?"

"There is an odour of smell," admitted Maurice sagely, "but it is nothing to see."

"You don't know the smell?"

The waiter shook his head and looked vague. Carrados divined perplexity.

"Oh, I dare say it's nothing," he declared carelessly. "Will you get me a sherry and khoosh?"

The million-to-one chance had failed.

"Sherry and bittaire, sair." Maurice deposited the glass with great precision, regarded it sadly and then moved it three inches to the right.

"I 'ave recollect this odour, sair," he remarked, "although I cannot give actuality. I 'ave met him here before, but—less—less forcefully."

"When?"

"Oh, one week since, perhaps."

"Something in the coals?" suggested Carrados.

"I imagine yes," pondered Maurice conscientiously.

"I was 'brightening up,' you say, for the night, and the fire was low down. I squash it with the poker still more for safety."

"Oh, then the lounge would be empty?"

"Yes—of people. Only Mr Slataire already departing."

Carrados indicated that he did not want the change and dismissed the subject.

"So long as nothing's on fire," he said with indifference.

"Thank you, sair."

The million-to-one chance had come off after all.

★★★★★★

Two days later, walking beyond the usual limit of the conventional promenade, Carrados reached a rough wooden hut such as contractors erect during the progress of their work. Having accompanied his master to the door, Parkinson returned towards the promenade and sat down to admire the seascape from the nearest bench.

Inside the hut three men had been waiting. One of the trio, a tall, military-looking man with the air of a personage, had been sitting on a whitewash-splashed trestle reading *The Times*. Of the others, one was Inspector Tapling, and the third a dwarfish, wizened creature with the air of a converted ostler. He had passed the time by watching the Cliffhurst side through a knot-hole in a plank. With the entrance of Carrados the tall man folded his newspaper and a period of expectancy seemed to have come to an end.

"Good-morning, colonel, inspector and you there, Bob."

"You found your way, Mr Carrados?" remarked the colonel.

"Yes; it is not really I who am late. I had a letter this morning from Wrattesley holding me up for a wire at 10.30. It did not arrive till 10.45."

"Ah, it did come! Then we may regard everything as settled?"

"No, colonel. On the contrary, we must accept everything as upset."

"What, sir?"

Carrados took out the slim pocket-book, extracted a telegram and held it out.

"What is this?" demanded the colonel, peering through his glasses in the indifferent light. "'Laburnum edifice plaster dark dark late herald same dome aurora dark vitiate camp encase.' I don't know the code."

"Oh, it's Westneath's arrangement," explained Carrados. "'The individual with whom we are concerned must not be arrested on charge, but it is of the gravest importance that the papers in question be recovered. There must be no public proceedings even if conviction assured.'"

There was a moment of stupefaction.

"This—this is a bombshell!" exclaimed the colonel. "What does it mean?"

"Politics," replied Carrados tersely.

"Ah!" soliloquised Tapling, walking to the door and looking sympathetically out at the gloomy prospect of sea and sky.

"But I've had no notification," protested the colonel. "Surely, Mr Carrados—"

"The wire is probably at the station."

"True; you said 10.45. Well, what do you propose doing now?"

"Scrapping all our arrangements and recovering the papers without arresting Slater."

"In what way?"

"At the moment I have not the faintest idea."

The inspector left the door and came back moodily to his old position.

"We have reason to think that he is becoming suspicious, Mr Carrados," he remarked. "He may decide to go any hour."

"Then the sooner we act the better."

The stunted pygmy in the background had been listening to the conversation with rapt attention, fastening his eyes unwinkingly on each face in turn. He now glided forward.

"Listen to me, gents," he said, throwing round a cunning leer; "how does this sound? This afternoon ..."

★★★★★★

That afternoon Mr Slater had been for what he termed "a blow of the briny," as his custom was on a fine day. He was returning in the dusk and had crossed the spacious promenade when, at a corner, he almost ran into the broad figure of a policeman who stood talking to a woman on the path.

"That's the man!" exclaimed the woman with almost vicious certainty.

Mr Slater fell back a step in momentary alarm; then, recovering his self-control, he went forward with admirable composure.

"Beg pardon, sir," explained the constable, "but this young lady has just lost her purse. She says she was sitting next to you on a seat—"

"And the minute after he had gone—the very minute—my bag was open like you see it now and my purse vanished," interposed the lady volubly.

"On the seat by the lifeboat where I passed you, sir," amplified the constable.

"This is ridiculous," said Mr Slater with a breath of relief. "I am a gentleman and I have no need to steal purses. My name is Slater, and

I am staying at the Rose and Plumes."

"Yes, sir," assented the policeman respectfully. "I know you by sight, sir, and have seen you go there. You hear what the gentleman says, miss?"

"Gentleman or no gentleman, I know my purse has gone," snapped the girl. "If he hasn't got it why did it vanish—where is it now? That's all I ask—where is it now?"

"You've seen nothing of it, I take it, sir?"

"No, of course I haven't," retorted the gentleman contemptuously. "I was sitting on a seat. The woman may have sat next to me—someone reading certainly did. Then I got up, walked once or twice up and down and came across. That's all."

"What was in the purse, miss?" inquired the constable.

"A postal order for a sovereign—and, thank the Lord, I've got the tag of it—a half-crown, two shillings and a few coppers, a *Kruger* sixpence with a hole through, a gold gipsy ring with pearls, the return half of my ticket, some hairpins and a few recipes, a book of powder papers, a pocket mirror—"

"That ought to be enough to identify it by," said the constable, catching Mr Slater's eye in humorous sympathy. "Well, miss, you'd better come to the station and report the loss. Perhaps you'll look in as well, sir?"

"Does that mean," demanded Mr Slater with a dark gleam, "that I am to be charged with theft?"

"Bless you, no, sir," was the easy reassurance. "We couldn't take a charge in the circumstances—not with a gentleman of respectable position and known address. But it might save you some inquiry and bother later, and if it was myself I should like to get it done with while it was red-hot, so to speak."

"I will go now," decided Mr Slater. "Do I walk with—?"

"Just as you like, sir. You can go before or follow on. It's only just down Bank Street."

The two went on and the gentleman followed at a few yards' interval. Three minutes and a blue lamp indicated their destination. No other pedestrian was in sight; the door stood hospitably open and Mr Slater walked in.

The station inspector was seated at a desk when they entered and a couple of other officials stood about the room. The policeman explained the circumstances of the loss, the Inspector noting the details in the record-book.

"This gentleman voluntarily accompanied us as he had been brought into the case," concluded the policeman.

"Here is my card, superintendent," said Mr Slater with some importance. He had determined to be agreeable, but dignified, and to enlist the inspector on his side. "I am staying at the Rose and Plumes. It's deuced unpleasant, you know, for a gentleman in my position to have to answer to a charge like this. That's why I came at once to clear the matter up."

"Quite so, sir," replied the inspector; "but there is no charge at present." He turned to the girl. "You understand that if you sign the charge-sheet and it turns out that you are mistaken it may be a serious matter?"

"I only want my purse and money back," replied the young woman mulishly.

"We will try to find it for you; but there is nothing beyond your suspicion that this gentleman has ever seen it. Probably, sir, you don't possess a sovereign postal order, or a *Kruger* coin, or any of the other articles, even of your own?"

"I don't," replied Mr Slater. "Except, of course, some silver and copper. If it will satisfy you I will turn out my pockets."

The inspector looked at the complainant.

"You hear that, miss?"

"Oh, very well," she retorted. "If he really hasn't got it I shall be the one to look silly, shan't I?"

On this encouragement Mr Slater made a display of his various possessions, turning out each pocket as he emptied it. The contents were laid before the inspector, who satisfied himself by a glance of their innocent nature.

"I should warn you that I am going to bring out a loaded revolver," said Mr Slater when he came to his hip-pocket. "I travel a good deal abroad and often in wild parts, where it is necessary to carry a pistol for protection."

The inspector nodded and examined the weapon with a knowing touch. The last pocket was displayed.

"That's not what I mean," objected the girl with a dogged air, as everyone began to regard her in varying degrees of inquiry. "You don't suppose that anyone would keep the things in their pocket, do you? I thought you meant properly."

The inspector addressed himself to Mr Slater again in a matter-of-fact, business manner.

"Perhaps you would like one of my men to put his hand over you to settle the matter, sir?" he asked. For just a couple of seconds there was the pause of hesitation.

"If nothing is found you withdraw all imputation against this gentleman?" demanded the inspector of the girl.

"Suppose I must," she admitted with an admirable pose of sulky acquiescence. In less exciting moments the young lady was a valued member of the Kingsmouth Amateur Dramatic Society.

"Oh, all right," assented Mr Slater. "Only get it over."

"You quite understand that the search is entirely voluntary on your part, sir. Hilldick!" One of the other policemen came forward.

"You can stand where you are, sir," he directed. With the practised skill of, say, a Custom House officer from Kingsmouth, he used his fingers dexterously about the gentleman's clothing. "Now, sir, will you sit down and remove your boots for a moment?"

"My boots!" The man's eyes narrowed and his mouth took another line. He glanced at the inspector.

"Is it really necessary ?"

"That's it!" came from the girl in a fiercely exultant whisper. "He's slipped them in his boots!"

"Idiot!" commented Mr Slater. He sat down and slowly drew slack the laces.

"Thank you," said Hilldick. He picked up both boots and with them turned to the table underneath the light. The next moment there was a sound like the main-spring of a clock going wrong and the sole and the upper of one boot came violently apart.

"You scoundrel!" screamed Slater, leaping from the chair.

But the grouping of the room had undergone a quiet change. Two men closed in on his right and left, and Mr Slater sat down again. The inspector opened the desk, dropped in the revolver and turned the key. Then all eyes went again to Hilldick and saw—nothing.

"The other boot," came in a quiet voice from the doorway to the inner room. "But just let me have it for a second."

It was put into his hands, and Carrados examined it in unmoved composure, while unpresentable words flowed in a blistering stream from Slater's lips.

"Yes, it is very good workmanship, Mr Frankworth," remarked the blind man. "You haven't forgotten your early training. All right, Hilldick."

The tool cut and rasped again and the stitches flew. But this time from the opening, snugly lying in a space cut out among the leathers, a flat packet slid down to the ground.

Someone tore open the oiled silk covering and spread out the contents. Six sheets of fine tracing paper, each covered with signs and drawings, were disclosed. The finality of the discovery acted on the culprit like a douche of water. He ceased to revile, and a white and deadly calm came over him.

"I don't know who is responsible for this atrocious outrage," he said between his clenched teeth, "but everyone concerned shall pay dearly for it. I am a naturalised Frenchman, and my adopted country will demand immediate satisfaction."

"Your adopted country is welcome to you, and it's going to have you back again," said the inspector grimly. "Here is a pair of boots exactly like your own—we only retain the papers, which do not belong to you. You are allowed twenty-four hours to be clear of the country. If you have not sailed by this time tomorrow you will be arrested as Henry Frankworth for failing to report yourself when on licence and sent to serve the unexpired portion of your sentence. If you return at any time the same course will be followed. Inspector Tapling, here is the warrant. You will keep Frankworth under observation and act as the circumstances demand."

Henry Frankworth glared round the room vindictively, drew himself up and clenched his fists. Then his figure drooped, and he turned and walked dully out into the darkening night.

★★★★★★

"So you let the German spy slip through your fingers after all," protested Mr Carlyle warmly. "I know that it was on instructions, and not your doing, Max; but why, why on earth, why?"

Carrados smiled and pointed to the heading of a column in an evening paper that he picked up from his side.

"There is your answer, Louis," he replied.

"'Position of the *Entente*. What Does France Mean?'" read the gentleman. "What has that got to do with it?"

"Your German spy was a French spy, Louis, and just at this moment a certain section of the public, led by a certain gang of politicians and aided by a certain interest in the Press, is doing its best to imperil the *Entente*. The government has no desire to have the *Entente* imperilled. Hence your wail. If the dear old emotional, pig-headed, Rule-Britannia! public had got it that French spies were stalking through the land at this crisis, then, indeed, the fat would have been in the fire!"

"But, upon my soul, Max Well, well; I hope that I am the last man to be led by newspaper clap-trap, but I think that it's a deuced queer proceeding all the same. Why should our ally want our secret plans?"

"Why not, if he can get them?" demanded Max Carrados philosophically. "One never knows what may happen next We ought to have plans and knowledge of all the French strategic positions as well as of the German. I hope that we have, but I doubt it. It would be a guarantee of peace and good relations."

"There are times, Max," declared Mr Carlyle severely, "when I suspect you of being—er—paradoxical."

"Can you imagine, Louis, an Archbishop of Canterbury, or a Poet Laureate, or a Chancellor of the Exchequer being friendly—perhaps even dining—with the editor of *The Times*?"

"Certainly; why not?"

"Yet in the editor's office, drawn up by his orders, there is probably a three-column obituary notice of each of those impersonalities. Does it mean that the editor wishes them to die—much less has any intention of poisoning their wine? Ridiculous! He merely, as a prudent man, prepares for an eventuality, so as not to be caught unready by a misfortune which he sincerely hopes will never take place—in his time, that is to say."

"Well, well," said Mr Carlyle benignantly—they were lunching together at Vitet's, on Carrados's return —"I am glad that we got the papers. One thing I cannot understand. Why didn't the fellow get clear as soon as he had the plans?"

"Ah," admitted the blind man, "why not, indeed? Even Inspector Tapling bated his breath when he suggested the reason to me."

"And what was that?" inquired Carlyle with intense interest.

Mr Carrados looked extremely mysterious and half-reluctant for a moment. Then he spoke.

"Do you know, Louis, of any great secret military camp where a surprise fleet of dirigibles and flying machines of a new and terrible pattern is being formed by a far-seeing government as a reserve against the day of Armageddon?"

"No," admitted Mr Carlyle, with staring eyes, "I don't."

"Nor do I," contributed Carrados.

The Eastern Mystery

It could scarcely be called Harris's fault, whatever the driver next behind might say in the momentary bitterness of his heart. In the two-fifths of a second of grace at his disposal Mr Carrados's chauffeur had done all that was possible and the dent that his radiator gave the stair-guard of the London General in front was insignificant. Then a Railway Express Delivery skated on its dead weight into his luggage platform and a Pickford, turning adroitly out of the *mêlée*, slewed a stationary Gearless round by its hand-rail stanchion to spread terror among the other line of traffic.

The most unconcerned person, to all appearance, was the driver of the London General, the vehicle whose sudden stoppage had initiated the riot of confusion. He had seen a man, engrossed to the absolute exclusion of his surroundings by something that took his eye on the opposite footpath, dash into the road and then, brought up suddenly by a realisation of his position, attempt to retrace his steps. He had pulled up so expertly that the man escaped, so smoothly that not a passenger was jarred, and now he sat with a dazed and vacant expression on his face, leaning forward on his steering wheel, while caustic inquiry and retort winged unheeded up and down the line behind him.

It was not until the indispensable ceremony of everyone taking everyone else's name and number had been observed under the authority of the tutelary constable that the single occupant of the private car stirred to show any interest in the proceedings.

"Parkinson," he called quietly, summoning his attendant to the window. "Ask Mr Tulloch if he will come round here when he has finished with the policeman."

"Mr Tulloch, sir?"

"Yes; you remember Dr Tulloch of Netherhempsfield? He is on in front there."

A moment later Jim Tulloch, as genial as of old, but his exuberance temporarily damped by the cross-bickering in which he had just been involved, thrust his head and arm through the sash.

"Lord, lord, it really is you then, Wynn, old man?" he cried. "When your Parkinson came up I couldn't believe it for a minute, simply couldn't believe it. The world grows smaller, I declare."

"At all events this car does," responded Carrados, wringing the hearty, outstretched hand. "They've got us two inches less than the makers ever intended. Is it really your doing, Jim?"

"Did ever you hear such a thing?" protested Tulloch. "And yet that wall-eyed atrocity yonder has kidded the copper that if he hadn't stopped dead—well, I should."

"Was it a near thing?" asked Carrados confidentially.

"Well, strictly between ourselves, I don't mind admitting that it might have been something of a shave," confessed Tulloch, with a cheerful grin. "But, lord bless you, Wynn, the streets of London are paved with 'em nowadays, paved with them. You don't merely take your life in your hands if you want to get about; you carry it on each foot."

"Look here," said Carrados. "You never let me know that you were up in town, Tulloch. What are you doing today?"

"I beg your pardon, sir," interrupted Parkinson's respectful voice, "but the policeman wishes to speak with you, sir."

"With me?" queried Tulloch restlessly. "Oh, good lord! have we to go into all that again?"

"It's only the bus-driver, sir," apologised the constable with the tactful deference that the circumstances seemed to demand. "As you are a doctor—I think there's something the matter with him."

"I'm sure there is," assented Tulloch. "All right, I'm coming. Are you in a hurry, Wynn?"

"I'll wait," was the reply.

The doctor found his patient propped up on a doorstep. Having, as he expressed it afterwards, "run the rule over him," he prescribed a glass of water and an hour's rest. The man was shaken, that was all.

"Nerves, Wynn," he announced when he returned to his friend. "I don't quite understand his emotion, but the shock of not having run over me seems to have upset the poor fellow."

"I was asking you whether you were doing anything today," said Carrados. "Can you come back with me to Richmond?"

"I'm not doing anything as far as that goes," admitted Tulloch. "In fact," he added ruefully, "that's the plague of it. I'm waiting to hear from a man who's waiting to hear from another man, and he's depending on something that may or mayn't, you understand."

"Then you can come along now anyway. Get in."

"If it's dinner you mean, I can't come straight away, you know," protested Tulloch. "Look at me togs"—he stood back to display a serviceable Norfolk suit—"all right for the six-thirty sharp of a Bloomsbury boarding-house, but—eh, what?"

"Don't be an ass, Jim," said the blind man amiably. "I can't see your silly togs."

"No ladies or any of your tony friends?"

"Not a soul."

"The fact is," confided Tulloch, taking his place in the car, "I've been out of things for a bit, Wynn, and I'm finding civilisation a shade cast-iron now. I've been down in the wilds since you were with me."

"I wondered where you were. I wrote to you about six months ago and the letter came back."

"Did it actually? Now that must have been almighty careless of someone, Wynn. I'm sorry; I'm a bit of a rolling stone, I suppose. When Darrish came back to Netherhempsfield my job was done there. I felt uncommonly restless. I hadn't much chance of buying a practice or dropping into a partnership worth having and I jibbed at setting up in some God-forsaken backwater and slipping into middle age 'building up a connection.' Lord, lord, Carrados, the tragic monotony of your elderly professional nonentity! I've known men who've whispered to me between the pulls at confidential pipes that they've come to hate the streets and the houses and the same old everlasting silly faces that they met day after day until they began to think very queer thoughts of how they might get away from it all."

"Yes," said Carrados.

"Anyway, 'Not yet,' I promised myself, and when I got the chance of a temporary thing on a Red Cable liner I took it like a shot. That was something. If there was a mighty sameness about it after a bit, it wasn't the sameness I'd been accustomed to. Then, as luck of one sort or another would have it, I got laid out with a broken ankle on a Bombay quay."

Carrados voiced commiseration.

"But you made a very good mend of it," he said. "It's the left, of course. I don't suppose anyone ever notices it."

"I took care of that," replied Tulloch. "But it was a slow business and threw all my plans out. I was on a very loose end when one day, outside the Secretariat, as they call it, I ran up against a man called Fraser whom I'd known building a viaduct or something of that sort in the Black Country.

"'What on earth are you, doing here?' we naturally both said at once, and he was the first to reply.

"'I'm just off to repair an irrigation "bund" a thousand miles more or less away, and I'm looking for a doctor who can speak six words of Hindustani, and doesn't mind things as they are, to physic the camp. What are you doing?'

"'Good lord! old man,' I said, 'I was looking for you!'"

It only required an occasional word to keep Tulloch going, and Carrados supplied it. He heard much that did not interest him—of the journey inland, of the face of the country, the surprising weather, the great work of irrigation and the other impressive wonders of man and nature. These things could be got from books, but among the weightier cargo Tulloch now and again touched off some inimitable phase of life or told an uninventable anecdote of native character that lived. Yet the buoyant doctor had something on his mind, for several times he stopped abruptly on the edge of a reminiscence, as though he was doubtful, if not of the matter, at least of the manner in which he should begin. These indications were not lost on his friend, but Carrados made no attempt to press him, being very well assured that sooner or later the ingenuous Jim would find himself beyond retreat. The occasion came with the cigarettes after dinner. There had been a reference to the language.

"I often wished that I was a better stick at it," said Tulloch. "I'd picked up a bit in Bombay and of course I threw myself into it when Fraser got me the post. I managed pretty well with the *coolies* in the camp, but when I tried to have a word with the *ryots* living round —little twopenny ha'penny farmers, you know—I could make no show of it. A lot of queer fish you come across out there, in one way or another, you take my word. You never know whether a man's a professional saint of extreme holiness or a hereditary body-snatcher whose shadow would make a begging leper consider himself unclean until he had walked seventy miles to drink a cupful of filthy water out of a stinking pond that a pock-marked ascetic had been sitting in for three years in order to contemplate quietly."

"Possibly he really was unclean—in consequence or otherwise," suggested Carrados.

"Help!" exclaimed Tulloch tragically. "There are things that have to be seen. But then so was the sanctified image, so that there's nothing for an outsider to go by. And then all the different little lots with their own particular little heavens and their own one exclusive way of getting there, and their social frills and furbelows—Jats and Jains and Thugs and Mairs and Gonds and Bhills and Toms, Dicks and Harrys—suburban society is nothing to it, Wynn, nothing at all. There was a strange old joker I've had in mind to tell you about, though it was no joke for him in the end. God alone knows where he came from, but he was in the camp one evening juggling for stray coppers in a bowl.

"Pretty good juggling too it seemed to be, of the usual Indian kind—growing a plant out of a pumpkin seed, turning a stick into a live snake, and the old sword and basket trick that every Eastern conjurer keeps up his sleeve; but all done out in the open, with people squatting round and a simplicity of appliance that would have taken all the curl out of one of your music-hall magicians. With him he had a boy, his son, a misshapen, monkey-like anatomy of about ten, but there was no doubt that the man was desperately fond of his unattractive offspring.

"That night this ungainly urchin, taking a cooler in one of the big irrigation canals, got laid hold of by an alligator and raised the most unearthly screech anything human—if he really was human—ever got out. I seemed to have had something prominent to do with the damp job of getting as much of him away from the creature as we could, and old Calico—that's what we anglicised the juggler's name into—had some sort of idea of being grateful in consequence. Although I don't doubt that he'd have put much more faith in a local wizard if one had been available, he let us take the boy into the hospital tent and do what we could for him. It wasn't much, and I told my assistant to break it to poor old Calico that he must be prepared for the worst. A handy man, that assistant, Wynn. He was a half-bred 'Portugoose,' as they say in Bombay, with the name of Vasque d'Almeydo, and I understood that he'd had some training.

"When we got out there he said that it was all the same to him, but he admitted quite blandly that he was really a cook and nothing more. What about his excellent testimonials? I asked him, and he replied with cheerful impenitence that he had hired them in the open market for one *rupee* eight, adding feelingly that he would willingly have given twice as much to qualify for my honourable service. In the end he did pretty much as he liked, and as he could speak five languages and scramble through seven dialects I was glad to have him about on any terms. I don't quite know how he broke it, but when I saw him later he said that Calico was a 'great dam fool.' He was a conjurer and knew how tricks were done and yet he had set out at once for some place thirty miles away-to procure a charm of some sort, the Portuguese would swear from a hint he had got.

"Vasque—of course by this time he'd become Valasquez to us—laughed pleasantly as he commented on native credulity. He was a Roman Catholic himself, so that he could afford it. The next day the boy died and an hour later poor Calico came reeling in. He'd got a nasty cut over the eye and a map of the route drawn over him in thorns and blisters and sand-burns, but he'd got something wrapped away in a bit of rag carried in the left armpit, and I felt for the poor old heathen. When he understood, he borrowed a spade and, taking up the child just as he was, he went off into the pagan solitude to bury him. I'd got used to these simple ways by that time.

"I thought that I'd seen the end of the incident, but late that night I heard the sentry outside challenge someone—we'd had so many tools and things looted by 'friendlies' that they'd lent us half a company of Sikhs from Kharikhas—and a moment later Calico was *salaaming* at the tent door. As it happened, Valasquez was away at a thing they called a village trafficking for some ducks, and I had to grapple with the conversation as best I could—no joke, I may tell you, for the juggler's grasp on conventional Urdu was about as slender as my own. And the first thing he did was to put his paws on to my astonished feet, then up to his forehead, and to prostrate himself to the ground.

"'*Sahib*,' he protested earnestly, 'I am thy slave and docile elephant for that which thou hast done for the man-child of my house.'

"Now you know, Carrados, I simply can't stand that sort of thing. It makes me feel such a colossal ass. So I tried, ungraciously enough I dare swear, to cut him short. But it couldn't be done. Poor old Calico had come to discharge what weighed on him as a formidable obligation and my 'Don't mention it, old chap,' style was quite out of the picture. Finally, from some obscure fold of his outfit, he produced a little screw of cloth and began to unwrap it.

"'Take it, O *sahib*, and treasure it as you would a cup of water in the desert, for it has great virtue of the hidden kind. Condescend to accept it, for it is all I have worthy of so great a burden.'

"'I couldn't think of it, Khaligar,' I said, trying to give his name a romantic twist, for the other sounded like guying him. 'I've done nothing, you know, and in any case this is much more likely to work with you than with me—an unbeliever. What is it, anyway?'

"'It is the sacred tooth of the ape-god Hanuman and its protects from harm,' he replied, reverently displaying what looked to me like an old rusty nail. 'Had I but been able to touch so much as the hem of the garment of my manlet with it before the hour of his outgoing he would assuredly have recovered.'

"'Then keep it for your own protection,' I urged. 'I expect that you run more risks that I do.'

"'When the flame has been extinguished from a candle the smoke lingers but a moment before it also fades away,' he replied. 'Thy mean servant has no wish to live now that the light of his eyes has gone out, nor does he seek to avert by magic that which is written on his forehead.'

"'Then it is witchcraft?' I said, pointing to the amulet.

"'I know not, my lord,' he answered; 'but if it be witchcraft it is of the honourable sort and not the goety of Sahitan. For this cause it is only of avail to one who acquires it without treachery or guile. Take it, *sahib*, but do not suffer it to become known even to those of your own table.'

"'Why not?' I asked.

"'Who should boast of pearls in a camp of armed bandits?' he replied evasively. 'A word spoken in a locked closet becomes a beacon on the hill-top for men to see. Yet have no fear; harm cannot come to you, for your hand is free from complicity.'

"I hadn't wanted the thing before, but that settled me. I very much doubted how the conjurer had got possession of it and I had no wish to be mixed up in an affair of any sort. I told him definitely that while I appreciated his motives I shouldn't deprive him of so great a treasure. He seemed really concerned, and Fraser told me afterwards that for one of that tribe to be under what he regarded as an unrequited obligation was a dishonour. I should probably have had some trouble to get him off, only just then we heard Valasquez returning. Calico hastily wrapped up the relic, stowed it away among his wardrobe and, with his most ceremonious *salaam*, disappeared.

"'Do you know anything about the tooth of the ape-god Hanuman, Valasquez?' I asked him some time later. The 'Portugoose' seemed to know a little about everything and in consequence of my dependence on him he strayed into a rather more free and easy manner than might have passed under other conditions. But I'm not ceremonious, you know, Wynn." And Carrados laughed and agreed.

"'The sacred tooth of Sira Hanuman, sir?' said Valasquez. 'Oh, that's all great tom dam foolery. There are a hundred million of them. The most notable one was worshipped at the Mountain of Adam in Ceylon until it was captured by my ancestor, the illustrious Admiral d'Almeydo, who sent it with much pomp and circumstance to Goa. Then the Princes of Malabar offered a ransom of *rupees*, forty *lakhs*, for it, which the Bishop of Goa refused, like a dam great fool!'

"'What became of it?' I asked, but Valasquez didn't know. He was somewhat of a liar, in fact, and I dare say that he'd made it all up to show off his knowledge."

"No," objected Carrados; "I think that Baldseus, the Dutch historian, has a similar tale. What happened to Calico?"

"That was the worst of it. Some of our men found his body lying among the tamarisk scrub two days later. There was no doubt that he'd been murdered, and not content with that, the ghouls had mutilated him shamefully afterwards. Even his cheeks were slashed open. So, you see, the tooth of Hanuman had not protected him."

"No," assented Carrados, "it had certainly not protected him. Was anything done—anyone arrested?"

"I don't think so. You know what the natives are in a case like that: no one knows anything, even if they have been looking on at the time. I suppose a report would be sent up, but I never heard anything more. I always had a suspicion that Calico, with his blend of simple faith and gipsy blood, had violated a temple, or looted a shrine, to save his son's life, and that the guardians of the relic tracked him and revenged the outrage. Anyway, I was glad that I hadn't accepted it after that, for I had enough excitement without."

"What was that, Jim?"

"Oh, I don't know, but I always seemed to be running up against something about that time. Twice my tent was turned inside out in my absence, once my clothes were spirited away while I was bathing, and the night before we broke up the camp I was within an ace of being murdered."

"You bear a charmed life," said Carrados suggestively, but Tulloch did not rise to the suggestion.

"It was a bit of luck. Those *dacoits* are as quiet as death, but for some reason I woke suddenly with the idea that devilment was brewing. I slipped on the first few things that came to hand and went to reconnoitre. As I passed through the canvas I came face to face with a native, and two others were only a few yards behind. Without any ceremony the near man let drive at my throat with one of those beastly wavy daggers they go in for. I suppose I managed to dodge in the fraction of a second, for he missed me. I gave a yell for assistance, landed the leader one in the eye and backed into my tent for a weapon. By the time I was out again our fellows were running up, but the precious trio had disappeared."

"That was the last you saw of them?" asked Carrados tentatively.

"No, queerly enough. The day I sailed I encountered the one whose eye I had touched up. It was down by the water—the Apollo Bander—at Bombay, and I was so taken aback, never thinking but that the fellow was hundreds of miles away, that I did nothing but stare. But I promised myself that in the unlikely event of ever seeing him again I would follow him up pretty sharply."

"Not under the wheels of a London General again, I hope!"

Tulloch's brown fist came down upon the table with a crash.

"The devil, Carrados!" he exclaimed. "How did you know?"

"Parkinson was just describing to me a rather exotic figure. Then the rest followed."

"Well, you were right. There was the man in Holborn, and of all the fantastic things in the world for a bloodthirsty thug from the back wilds of Hindustan, I believe that he was selling picture post cards!"

"Possibly a very natural thing to be doing in the circumstances."

"What circumstances, Wynn?"

"Those you are telling me of. Go on."

"That's about all there is. When I saw the man I was so excited, I suppose, that I started to dash across without another thought. You know the result. Of course he had vanished by the time I could look round."

"You are quite sure he is the same?"

"There's always the possibility of a mistake, I admit," considered Tulloch, "but, speaking in ordinary terms, I should say that it's a moral certainty. On the first occasion it was bright moonlight and the sensational attack left a very vivid photograph on my mind. In Bombay I had no suspicion of doubt about the man, and he was still carrying traces of my fist. Here, it is true, I had less chance of observing him, but recognition was equally instantaneous and complete. Then consider that each time he has slipped away at once. No, I am not mistaken. What is he after, Carrados?"

413

"I am very much afraid that he is after you, my friend," replied Carrados, with some concern lurking behind the half-amused level of his voice.

"After me!" exclaimed Tulloch with righteous indignation. "Why, confound his nerve, Wynn, it ought to be the other way about. What's he after me for?"

"India is a conservative land. The gods do not change. A relic that was apprised at seven hundred thousand *ducats* in the days of Queen Elizabeth is worth following up today—apart, of course, from the merit thereby acquired by a devotee."

"You mean that Calico's charm was the real original thing that Valasquez spoke of?"

"It is quite possible; or it may be claimed for it even if it is not. Goa has passed through many vicissitudes; its churches and palaces are now in ruins. What is more credible—"

"But in any case I haven't got the thing. Surely the old ass needn't murder me to find out that." The face he appealed to betrayed nothing of the thoughts behind it. But Carrados's mind was busy with every detail of the story he had heard, and the more he looked into it the less he felt at ease for his impetuous friend's safety.

"On the contrary," he replied, "from the pious believer's point of view, the simplest and most effective way of ascertaining it was to try to murder you, and your providential escape has only convinced them that you are now the holder of the charm."

"The deuce!" said Tulloch ruefully. "Then I have dropped into an *imbroglio* after all. What's to be done?"

"I wonder," mused the blind man speculatively, "I wonder what really became of the thing."

"You mean after Calico's death?"

"No, before that. I don't imagine that your entertaining friend had it at the end. He had nothing to look forward to, you remember; he did not wish to live. His assassins were those who were concerned in the recovery of the relic, for why else was he mutilated but in order to discover whether he had concealed it with more than superficial craft—perhaps even swallowed it? They found nothing or you would not have engaged their attention. As it was, they were baffled and had to investigate further. Then they doubtless learned that you had put this man under an undying obligation, possibly they even knew that he had visited you the last thing before he left the camp. The rest has been the natural sequence."

"It seems likely enough in an incredible sort of way," admitted the doctor. "But I don't see why this old sport should be occupying himself as he is in the streets of London."

"That remains to be looked into. It may be some propitiatory form of self-abasement that is so potent in the Oriental system. But it may equally well be something quite different. If this man is of high priestly authority there are hundreds of his co-religionists here at hand whose lives he could command in such a service. He may be in communication with some, or be contriving to make himself readily accessible. Are there any Indians at your boarding-house?"

"I have certainly seen a couple recently."

"Recently! Then they came after you did?"

"I don't know about that. I haven't had much to do with the place."

"I don't like it, Jim," said Carrados, with more gravity than he was accustomed to put into the consideration of his own risks. "I don't like the hang of it at all."

"Well, for that matter, I'm not exactly pining for trouble," replied his friend. "But I can take care of myself anyway."

"But you can't," retorted Carrados. "That's just the danger. If you were blind it would be all right, but your credulous, self-opinionated eyes will land you in some mess. . . . Tomorrow, at all events, Carlyle shall put a watch on this enterprising Hindu and we shall at least find out what his movements are." Tulloch would have declined the attention, but Carrados was insistent.

"You must let me have my way in such an emergency, Tulloch," he declared. "Of course you would say that it's out of your power to prevent me; but among friends like you and I one acquiesces to a certain code. I say this because I may even find it necessary to put a man on you as well. This business attracts me resistlessly. There's something more in it than we have got at yet, something that lies beyond the senses and strives to communicate itself through the unknown dimension that we have all stood just upon the threshold of, only to find that we have lost the key. It's more elusive than Macbeth's dagger: '*I have thee not and yet I see thee still*'—always just out of reach. What is it, Jim; can't you help us? Don't you feel something portentous in the air, or is it only my blind eyes that can see beyond?"

"Not a bit of it," laughed Tulloch cheerfully. "I only feel that a blighted old heathen is leading himself a rotten dance through his pig-headed obstinacy. Well, Wynn, why can't he be rounded up and have it explained that he's on the wrong tack? I don't mind crying quits. I did get in a sweet one on the eye, and he's had a long journey for nothing. Eh, what?"

"He would not believe." Carrados was pacing the room in one of his rare periods of mental tension. Instinct, judgment, experience and a subtler prescience that enveloped reason seemed at variance in his mind. Then he swung round and faced his visitor.

"Look here, Tulloch, stay with me for the present," he urged. "You can go there for your things tomorrow and I can fix you up in the meantime. It's safer; I feel it will be safer."

"Safer! Good lord! what could you have safer than a stodgy second-rate boarding-house in Hapsburg Square? The place drones respectability. Miss Vole, the landlady, is related to an arch-deacon and nearly all the people there are on half-pay. The two Indians are tame *baboos*. Besides, if I get this thing I told you of, I shall be off to South America in a few days, and that ought to shake off this old man of the tooth."

"Of course it won't; nothing will shake him off if he's made the vow. Well, have your own way. One can't expect a doctor of robust habit to take any reasonable precautions, I know. How is your room situated?"

"Pretty high up. Next to the attics, I imagine. It must be, because there is a little trapdoor in the ceiling leading there."

"A trapdoor leading to the attics! Well, at all events there can't be an *oubliette*, I suppose? Nor a four-post bed with a canopy that slides up and down, Jim; nor a revolving wardrobe before a secret passage in the oak panels?"

"Get on with you," retorted Tulloch. "It's just the ordinary contrivance that you find somewhere in every roof when the attics aren't made into rooms. There's nothing in it."

"Possibly; but there may be some time. Anyway, drive a tack in and hang up a tin can or something that must clatter down if the door is raised an inch. You have a weapon, I suppose?"

"Now you're talking, Wynn. I do put some faith in that. I have a grand little revolver in my bag and I can sleep like a feather when I want."

"Little? What size does it take?"

"Oh, well, it's a .320, if it comes to that. I prefer a moderate bore myself."

Carrados opened a drawer of his desk and picked up half-a-dozen brass cartridges.

"When you get back, throw out the old ones and reload with these to oblige me," he said. "Don't forget."

"Right," assented Tulloch, examining them with interest; "but they look just like mine. What are they?—something new?"

"Not at all; but we know that they are charged and you can rely on them going off if they are fired."

"What a chap you are," declared Tulloch with something of the admiring pity that summed up the general attitude towards Max Carrados. "Well, for that matter, I must be going off myself, old man. I'm hoping for a letter about that little job and if it comes I want to answer it tonight. You've given me a fine time and we've had a great talk."

"I'm glad we met. And if you go away suddenly don't leave it to chance the next time you are back." He did not seek to detain his guest, for he knew that Tulloch was building somewhat on the South American appointment. "Shall Harris run you home?"

"Not a bit of it. I'll enjoy a walk to the station, and these Tubes of yours'll land me within me loose-box by eleven. It's a fine place, this London, after all." They had reached the front door, opened it and were standing for a moment looking towards the yellow cloud that arched the west end of the city like the mirage of a dawn.

"Well, goodbye, old man," said Tulloch heartily, and they shook hands. At the touch an extraordinary impulse swept over Carrados to drag his friend back into the house, to implore him to remain the night at all events, or to do something to upset the arranged order of things for the next few hours. With the cessation of physical contact the vehemence of the possession dwindled away, but the experience, short as it was, left him white and shaken. He could not trust himself to speak; he waved his hand and, turning quickly, went back to the room where they had sat together to analyse the situation and to determine how to act. Presently he rang for his man.

"Some notes were taken after that little touch in Holborn this afternoon, Parkinson," he said. "Have you the address of the leading motor-bus driver among them?"

"The London General, sir?"

"Yes; the man who was the first to stop." Parkinson produced his memorandum book and referred to the latest of its entries.

"He gave his private residence as 14 Cogg's Lane, Brentford, sir."

"Brentford! That is fortunate. I am going to see him tonight if possible. You will come with me, Parkinson. Tell Harris to get out the car that is the most convenient. What is the time?"

"Ten-seventeen, sir."

"We will start in fifteen minutes. In the meanwhile just reach me down that large book labelled *Xavier* from the top shelf there."

"Yes, sir. Very well, sir. I will convey your instructions to Harris, sir."

It was perhaps rather late for a casual evening call, but not, apparently, too late for Cogg's Lane, Brentford. Mr Fitzwilliam—Parkinson had infused a faint note of protest into his voice when he mentioned the bus-driver's name—Mr Fitzwilliam was out, but Mrs Fitzwilliam received the visitor with conspicuous felicity and explained the circumstances. Fitzwilliam was of a genial, even playful, disposition, but he had come home brooding and depressed. Mrs Fitzwilliam had not taken any notice of it—she put it down to his feet-but by cajolery and innuendo she had persuaded him to go to the picture palace to be cheered up, and as it was now on the turn of eleven he might be expected back at any moment.

In the meantime the lady had a favourite niece who was suffering—as the doctor himself confessed—from a very severe and unusual form of adenoids. Carrados disclosed the fact that the subject of adenoids was one that interested him deeply. He knew, indeed, of a case that was thought by the patient's parents to be something out of the way, but even it, he admitted, was commonplace by the side of the favourite niece. The minutes winged.

"That's Fred," said Mrs Fitzwilliam as the iron gate beyond the little plot of beaten earth that had once been a garden gave its individual note. "Seems strange that they should be so ignorant at a hospital, doesn't it?"

"Hallo, what now?" demanded Mr Fitzwilliam, entering.

Mrs Fitzwilliam made a sufficient introduction and waited for the interest to develop. So far the point of Carrados's visit had not appeared.

"I believe that you know something about motors?" inquired the blind man.

"Well, what if I do?" retorted the bus-driver. His attitude was protective rather than intentionally offensive.

"If you do, I should be glad if you would look at the engine of my car. It got shaken, I fancy, in a slight accident that we had in Holborn this afternoon."

"Oh!" The driver looked hard at Mr Carrados, but failed to get behind an expression of mild urbanity. "Why didn't you say so at first?" he grumbled. "All right; I'll trot round with you. Shan't be long, missis." He led the way out and closed the door behind them, not ceasing to regard his visitor with a distrustful curiosity. At the gate he stopped, having by that time brought his mind round to the requirements of the situation, and faced Carrados.

"Look here," he said, "what's up? You don't want me to look at no bloomin' engine, you know. I don't half like the whole bally business, let me tell you. What's the game?"

"It's a very simple game for you if you play it straightforwardly," answered Carrados. "I want to know just how much you had to do with saving that man's life in Holborn today."

Fitzwilliam instinctively fell back a step and his gaze on Carrados quickened in its tensity.

"What d'yer mean?" he demanded with a quality of apprehension in his voice.

"That is complicating the game," replied Carrados mildly. "You know exactly what I mean."

"And what if I do?" demanded the driver. "What have you got to do with it, may I ask?"

"That is very reasonable. I happened to be in the car following you. We were scraped, but I am not making any claim for paint whatever happened. I am satisfied that you did very well indeed in the circumstances, and if a letter to your people—I know one of the directors—saying as much would be of any use to you—"

"Now we're getting on, sir," was the mollified admission. "You mustn't mind a bit of freshness, so to speak. You took me by surprise, that's what it was, and I've been wound up ever since that happened." He hesitated, and then flung out the question almost with a passionate directness: "What was it, sir; in God's name, what was it?"

"What was it?" repeated the blind man's level voice persuasively.

"It wasn't me. I couldn't have done nothing. I didn't see the man, not in time to have an earthly. Then we stopped. Good Gawd, I've never felt a stop like that before. It was as though a rubber band had tightened and pulled us up against ten yards squoze into one, so that you didn't hardly know it. I hadn't nothing to do with it. Not a brake was on, and the throttle open and the engine running. There we were. And me half silly."

"You did very well," said Carrados soothingly.

"I did nothing. If it had been left to me there'd have been a inquest.

You seem to have noticed something, sir. How do you work it out?" Carrados parried the question with a disingenuous allusion to the laws of chance. He had not yet worked it out, but he was not disposed to lay his astonishing conclusions, so far as they went, before the bus-driver's crude discrimination. He had learned what he wanted. With a liberal acknowledgment of the service and a reiteration of his promise to write, he bade Mr Fitzwilliam goodnight and returned to his waiting car.

"Back home, Harris," he directed. He had gone out with some intention of including Hapsburg Square in his peregrination. He was now assured that his anxiety was groundless.

But the next morning all his confidence was shattered in a moment. It was his custom before and during breakfast to read by touch the headings of the various items in the newspapers and to mark for Greatorex's later reading such paragraphs as claimed his interest. Generally he could, with some inconvenience, distinguish even the ordinary type by the same faculty, but sometimes the inequality of pressure made .this a laborious process. There was no difficulty about the larger types, however, and with a terrible misgiving finger-tip and brain had at once grasped the significance of a prominent heading:

Fatal Gas Explosion
Hapsburg Square Boarding-House in Flames

"Are you there, Parkinson?" he asked. Parkinson could scarcely believe his well-ordered ears. Not since the early days of his affliction had Carrados found it necessary to ask such a question.

"Yes, sir, I'm here," he almost stammered in reply.

"I hope you are not unwell, sir?"

"I'm all right, thanks," responded his master dryly —unable even then not to discover some amusement in having for once scared Parkinson out of his irreproachable decorum. "I was mentally elsewhere. I want you to read me this paragraph."

"The one about Dr Tulloch, sir?" The name had caught the man's eye at once. "Dear, dear me, sir."

"Yes; go on," said Carrados, with his nearest approach to impatience.

Parkinson read:

During the early hours of this morning 52 Hapsburg Square was the scene of a gas explosion which was unhappily attended by loss of life. Shortly after midnight the neighbourhood was alarmed by the noise of a considerable explosion which appeared to blow out the window and front wall of one of the upper bedrooms, but as the part in question was almost immediately involved in flames it is uncertain what really happened. The residents of the house, which is a boarding establishment carried on by Miss Vole (a relative, we are informed, of Archdeacon Vole of Worpsley), were quickly made aware of their danger and escaped. The engines arrived within a few minutes of the alarm and soon averted any danger of the fire spreading. When it was possible to penetrate into the upper part of the house it was discovered that the occupant of the bedroom where the explosion took place, a Dr Tulloch who had only recently returned to this country from India, had perished. Owing to the charred state of the body it is impossible to judge how he died, but in all probability he was mercifully killed or at least rendered unconscious by the force of the explosion.

"That is all, sir."

"I ought to have kept him," muttered Carrados reproachfully. "I ought to have insisted. The thing has been full of mistakes." He could discover very little further interest in his breakfast and turned to the other papers for possible enlargement of the details.

"We shall have to go down," he remarked casually. "Say in half-an-hour. Tell Harris."

"Very well, sir."

Greatorex, just arrived for the day, and diffusing an atmosphere of easy competence and inoffensively general familiarity, put his head in at the door.

"Morning, sir," he nodded. "Tulloch's here and wants to see you. Came in with me. Hullo, Parkinson, seen a ghost?"

"He hasn't yet," volunteered his master. "But we both expect to. Yes, send him in here. Only one mistake the more, you see," he added to his servant, "And one the less," he added to himself.

"I might just as well have stayed, you know," was Tulloch's greeting. He included the still qualmish Parkinson in his genial domination of the room, and going across to his friend he dropped a weighty hand upon his shoulder.

"'There are more things in heaven and earth than in your philosophy, Horatio,'" he barbarously misquoted with significance. "There, you see, Wynn, I can apply Shakespeare to the situation as well as you."

"Quite so," assented Carrados. "In the meanwhile will you have some breakfast?"

"It's what I came in the hopes of," admitted the doctor. "That and being burned out of hearth and home. I thought that I might as well quarter myself on you for a couple of days. You've seen the papers?" His friend indicated the still open sheet.

"Ah, that one. *The Morning Reporter* gave me a better obituary. I often had a sort of morbid fancy to know what they'd say about me afterwards. It seemed unattainable, but, like most things, it's a sad disappointment when it comes. Six lines is the longest, Wynn, and they've got me degree wrong."

"Whose was the body?" asked Carrados.

Gravity descended upon Tulloch at the question. He looked round to make sure that Parkinson had left the room.

"No one will ever know, I'm hoping," he replied. "He was charred beyond recognition. But you know, Wynn, and I know and we can hold our tongues."

"The Indian avenger, of course?"

"Yes. I went round there early this morning expecting nothing and found the. place a wreck. One can only guess now what happened, but the gas-bracket is just beneath that trap-door I told you of and there's a light kept burning in the passage outside. One of the half-pay men brought me a nasty wavy dagger that had been picked up in the road. 'One of your Indian curiosities, I suppose, Dr Tulloch?' he remarked. I let it pass at that, for I was becoming cautious among so much devilment. 'I'm afraid that there's nothing else of yours left,' he went on, 'and there wouldn't have been this if it hadn't been blown through the window.' He was quite right. I haven't a thing left in the world but this now celebrated Norfolk suit that I stand up in, and, as matters are, I'm jolly well glad you didn't give me time to change yesterday."

"Ah," assented Carrados thoughtfully. "Still the Norfolk suit, of course. Tell me, Jim—you had it in India?"

"To be sure I had. It was new then. You know, one doesn't always go about there in white drill and a cork helmet, as your artists here seem to imagine. It's cold sometimes, I can tell you. This coat is warm; I got very fond of it. You can't understand one getting fond of a mere suit, you with your fifty changes of fine raiment."

"Of course I can. I have a favourite jacket that I would not part from for rubies, and it's considerably more of an antique than yours.

That's still a serviceable suit, Jim. Come and let me have a look at it."

"What d'ye mean?" said Tulloch, complying half reluctantly. "You're making fun of me little suit and it's the only thing in the world that stands between me and the entire."

"Come here," repeated Carrados. "I am not in the least guying. I'm far too serious. I am more serious, I think, than I have ever been in my life before." He placed the wondering doctor before him and proceeded to run a light hand about the details of his garments, turning him round until the process was complete.

"You wore these clothes when the native you call Calico came to you that night?"

"It's more than likely. The nights were cold." Carrados seemed strangely moved. He got up, walked to the window, as his custom was, for enlightenment, and then, after wandering about the room, touching here and there an object indecisively, he unlocked a cabinet and slid out a tray of silver coins.

"You've never seen these, have you?" he asked with scanty interest.

"No, what are they?" responded Tulloch, looking on.

"Pagan art at its highest. The worship of the strong and beautiful."

"Worth a bit?" suggested Tulloch knowingly.

"Not what they cost." Carrados shot back the tray and paced the room again. "You haven't told me yet how you were preserved."

"How ?"

"Last night. You know that you escaped death again."

"I suppose I did. Yes. . . . And do you know why I have been hesitating to tell you?"

"Why?"

"Because you won't believe me."

Carrados permitted himself to smile a shade.

"Try," he said laconically.

"Well, of course, I quite intended to. ... The sober truth is, Wynn, that I forgot the address and could not get there. It was the silliest and the simplest thing in the world. I walked to the station here, booked for Russell Square and took a train. When I got out there I started off and then suddenly pulled up. Where was I going? My mind, I found, on that one point had developed a perfect blank. All the facts had vanished. Drum my encephalon how I might, I could not recall Miss Vole, 52, or Hapsburg Square. Mark you, it wasn't loss of memory in the ordinary sense. I remembered everything else; I knew who I was

423

and what I wanted well enough. Of course the first thing I did was to turn out my pockets. I had letters, certainly, but none to that address and nothing else to help me. 'Very well,' I said, 'it's a silly game, but I'll walk round till I find it.' Had again! I walked for half-an-hour, but I saw nothing the faintest degree familiar. Then I saw 'London Directory Taken Here' in a pub. window. 'Good,' I thought. 'When I see the name it will all come back again.' I went in, had something and looked through the 'Streets' section from beginning to end." He shook his head shrewdly. "It didn't work."

"Did it occur to you to ring me up? You'd given me the address."

"It did; and then I thought, 'No, it's midnight now' —it was by then—'and he may have turned in early and be asleep.' Well, things had got to such a pass that it seemed the simplest move to walk into the first moderate hotel I came to, pay for my bed and tell them to wake me at six, and that's what I did. Now what do you make of that?"

"That depends," replied Carrados slowly. "The scientist would perhaps hint at a telepathic premonition operating subconsciously through receptive nerve centres. The sceptic would call it a lucky coincidence. The Catholic—the devout Catholic—would claim another miracle."

"Oh, come now!" protested Tulloch.

"Yes, come now," struck in Carrados, rising with decision and moving towards the door. "Come to my room and then you shall judge for yourself. It's too much for any one man to contemplate alone. Come on." He walked quickly across the hall to his study, dismissing Greatorex elsewhere with a word, and motioned the mystified doctor to a chair. Then he locked the door and sat down himself.

"I want you to carry your mind back to that night in your tent when the native Khaligar, towards whom you had done an imperishable service, presented himself before you. By the inexorable ruling of his class he was your bondsman in service until he had repaid you in kind. This, Jim, you failed to understand as it stood vitally to him, for the whole world, two pantheons and perhaps ten thousand years formed a great gulf between your mind and his. You would not be repaid, and yet he wished to die."

The doctor nodded. "I dare say it comes to that," he said.

"He could not die with this debt undischarged. And so, in the obscurity of your tent, beneath your unsuspecting eyes, this conjurer did, as he was satisfied, requite you. You thought you saw him wrap the

424

relic in its covering. You did not. You thought he put it back among his dress. He did not. Instead, he slipped it dexterously between the lining and the cloth of your own coat at the thick part of a band. You had seen him do much cleverer things even in the open sunlight."

"You don't say," exclaimed Tulloch, springing to his feet, "that even now—"

"Wait!" cried the blind man warningly. "Don't seek it yet. You have to face a more stupendous problem first."

"What is that?"

"Three times at least your life has been—as we may say—miraculously preserved. It was not your doing, your expertness, my friend. What is this sacred relic that once was in its jewelled shrine on the high altar of the great cathedral at Goa, that opulent arch-bishopric of the East to which Catholic Portugal in the sixteenth century sent all that was most effective of treasure, brain and muscle to conquer the body and soul of India?"

"You suggested that it might be the original relic to which Valasquez had referred."

"Not now; only that the natives may have thought so. What would be more natural than that an ignorant despoiler should assume the thing which he found the most closely guarded and the most richly casketed to be the object for which he himself would have the deepest veneration?"

"Then I don't follow you," said Tulloch.

"Because I have the advantage of having turned to the local and historical records bearing on the circumstances since you first started me," Carrados replied. "For instance, in the year 1582 Akbar, who was a philosopher and a humorist as well as a model ruler, sent an invitation to the 'wise men among the Franks' at Goa to journey to Agra, there to meet in public controversy before him a picked band of Mohammedan *mullas* and prove the superiority of their faith. The challenge was accepted. Abu-l-Fazl records the curious business and adds a very significant detail. These Catholic priests, to cut the matter short in the spirit of the age, offered to walk through a fiery furnace in the defence of their belief. It came to nothing, because the other side backed out, but the challenge is suggestive because, however fond the priesthood of those times was of putting other people to the ordeal of fire and water, its members were singularly modest about submitting to such tests themselves. What mystery was there here, Tulloch? What had those priests of Goa that made them so self-confident?"

"This relic, you suggest?"

"Yes, I do. But, now, what is that relic? A monkey's or an ape-god's tooth, an iron-stained belemnite, the fragment of a pagan idol—you and I can smile at that. We are Christians. No matter how unorthodox, no matter how non-committal our attitude may have grown, there is upon us the unconscious and hereditary influence of century after century of blind and implicit faith. To you and to me, no less than to every member of the more credent Church of Rome, to everyone who has listened to the story as a little child, it is only conceivable that if miraculous virtues reside in anything inanimate it must pre-eminently be in the close accessories of that great world's tragedy, when, as even secular and unfriendly historians have been driven to admit, something out of the order of nature did shake the heavens."

"But this," articulated Tulloch with dry throat, leaning instinctively forward from the pressure of his coat, "this—what is it, then?"

"You described it as looking like a nail," responded Carrados. "It is a nail. Rusty, you said, and it could not well be otherwise than red with rust. And old. Nearly nineteen hundred years old; quite, perhaps."

Tulloch came unsteadily to his feet and slowly slipping off his coat he put it gently away on a table apart from where they sat.

"Is it possible?" he asked in an awe-struck whisper. "Wynn, is it—is it really possible?"

"It is not only possible," he heard the blind man's more composed voice replying, "but in one aspect it is even very natural. Physically, we are dealing with an historical fact. Somewhere on the face of the earth these things must be enduring; scattered, buried, lost perhaps, but still existent. And among the thousands of relics that the different churches have made claim to it would be remarkable indeed if some at least were not authentic. That is the material aspect."

"Yes," assented Tulloch anxiously, "yes; that is simple, natural. But the other side, Carrados—the things that we know have happened—what of that?"

"That," replied Carrados, "is for each man to judge according to his light."

"But you?" persisted Tulloch. "Are you convinced?"

"I am offered a solution that explains everything when no other theory will," replied the blind man evasively. Then on the top of Tulloch's unsatisfied "Ah!" he added: "But there is something else that confronts you. What are you going to do?" and his face was towards the table across the room.

"Have you thought of that?"

"It has occurred to me. I wondered how you would act."

It was some time before either spoke again. Then Tulloch broke the silence.

"You can lend me some things?" he asked.

"Of course."

"Then I will decide," he announced with resolution.

"Whatever we may think, whatever might be urged, I cannot touch this thing; I dare not even look on it. It has become too solemn, too awful, in my mind, to be seen by any man again. To display it, to submit it to the test of what would be called 'scientific proof,' to have it photographed and 'written up'—impossible, incredible! On the other hand, to keep it safely to myself—no, I cannot do that either. You feel that with me?"

The blind man nodded.

"There is another seemly, reverent way. The opportunity offers. I found a letter at the house this morning. I meant to tell you of it. I have got the appointment that I told you of and in three days I start for South America. I will take the coat just as it is, weight it beyond the possibility of recovery and sink it out of the world in the deepest part of the Atlantic; beyond controversy, and safe from falling to any ignoble use. You can supply me with a box and lead. You approve of that?"

"I will help you," said Carrados, rising.

The Secret of Headlam Height

Parkinson, the unquenchable stickler for decorum, paused after receiving the general instructions for the day just long enough to create a sense of hesitation. Mr Carrados, merely concerned with an after-breakfast cigarette, divined the position with his usual unerring instinct.

'Yes, Parkinson,' he remarked encouragingly; 'is there anything going on?'

A clumsily-folded newspaper enabled the punctilious attendant to salve his conscience as he returned slowly to the table. He shook out the printed sheets into a more orderly arrangement by way of covering the irregularity.

'I understand, sir,' he replied in the perfectly controlled respectful voice that accorded with his deliberate actions 'I understand that this morning's foreign intelligence is of a disquieting nature.'

The blind man's hand went unfalteringly to an open copy of *The Times* lying by him and there a single deft finger touched off the headlines with easy certainty.

'"On the Brink of War." "Threatened German Mobilisation",' he read aloud. '"The Duty of Great Britain." Yes, I don't think that "disquieting" over-states the position.'

'No, sir. So I gathered from what I had already heard. That is why I thought it better to speak to you about a trifling incident that has come under my notice, sir.'

'Quite right,' assented Mr Carrados. 'Well?'

'It was at the museum here, sir—a very instructive establishment in Market Square. I had gone there in order to settle a small matter in dispute between Herbert and myself affecting the distinction between shrimps and prawns. I had always been under the impression that prawns were unusually well-grown shrimps, but I find that I was mistaken. I was directed to the cases of preserved fish by a gentleman with a cut across his cheek. Subsequently I learned from the hall-keeper, to whom I spoke about the weather, that the gentleman was the assistant curator and was called Vangoor, being a native of Holland.'

'Vangoor,' mused Mr Carrados. 'I have never heard the name before.'

'No, sir. When I saw the gentleman last we were at Kiel, and he was then a Lieutenant von Groot. I thought perhaps I had better mention it, sir.'

Carrados's half-smiling expression did not change in its placid tone and he continued to smoke with leisurely enjoyment. His mind turned back to the details of the Kiel visit of a few years previously as one might turn to a well-kept diary.

'The man you mean called on me once with a complimentary message from the Admiralty department there. I was not in the hotel at the time and he left his card with a few words of explanation in perfect English. We never met and I cannot suppose that he has ever seen me.'

'No, sir,' acquiesced Parkinson. 'You sent me the next day to the Dockyard with a reply. That is the only time I have ever seen the gentleman before today.'

'Have you any reason to think that he may have remembered you again?'

'I formed a contrary opinion, sir. On the other occasion, although it was necessary for us to hold some slight conversation together, Lieutenant von Groot did not seem to be aware of my presence, if I may so define it, sir. I received the impression that the gentleman imagined he was talking to someone taller than I am, sir; and I doubt if he really saw me at all.'

'You are sure of him, though?'

'I was then making a study of detailed observation under your instruction, sir, and I have no misgiving on the point.'

'Very well. It was quite right of you to tell me of this; it may be really important. We are only five miles from a vital naval port, we must remember. Don't say anything to anyone else and I will consider it meanwhile.'

'Thank you, sir,' replied Parkinson, modestly elated.

In the past, whenever the subject of the English Secret Service came up it was patriotically assumed on all hands that nothing much was to be expected from that quarter, and we were bidden to lift our admiring eyes to German and other continental models. As a matter of history, when the test came the despised organisation proved itself signally efficient. In a small way there was evidence of this that same July day, for within a couple of hours of sending a curiously-worded telegram to an official whose name never appeared in any official list Mr Carrados received an equally mysterious reply from which, after a process of disintegration, he extracted the following information:

Ref. Fff. C/M.107.
Groot, Karl von. Born Friedeberg (Prussia) about 1880. Mother English. Educated Heidelberg and (?) Kiel. Entered navy. Torpe-do-lieutenant (staff) 1907. Resigned in doubtful circumstances 1910. Drawn into espionage system under Bluthmel in con-nexion with resignation. Expelled Holland 1912. Visited Russia 1913. Recognised in Cork, June, 1913. Speaks German, French, Dutch, Russian, English (excellent). Blonde, tall, grey eyes, di-agonal sword-cut left cheek. Description ends. Please report anything known further.

Carrados read the decoded message twice, and then thoughtfully crushing the thin paper into a loose ball he dropped it upon an ash-tray and applied a match.

'A telegram form, Parkinson.'

With his uncanny prescience the blind man selected a pencil from the rack before him, adjusted the paper to a more convenient angle and, not deviating the fraction of an inch beyond the indicated space, wrote his brief reply:

Ref. Fff. C/M.107.
Information received. Regret have nothing further to report. M.C.

'We will investigate Mr Vangoor for ourselves a little first,' he re-marked, passing across the slip. 'London will have its hands pretty full for the next few days and we are on the spot.'

'Very well, sir,' replied Parkinson with the same trustful equanimity with which he would have received an order to close a window. 'Shall I dispatch this now, sir?'

'Yes—from the head office: head offices are generally too busy to be inquisitive. Read it over first in case of an inquiry. . . . Yes, quite right. Something of a feather if we can circumvent a German spy off our own bats, eh, Parkinson?'

'Yes, sir.'

'At all events we will open the innings without delay.'

'I quite appreciate the necessity of expedition, sir,' replied Parkinson, with his devastating air of profound wisdom.

It is doubtful if anyone had yet plumbed the exact limits of the worthy fellow's real capacity. There were moments when he looked more sagacious than any mortal man has any hope of ever being, and there were times when his comment on affairs seemed to reveal a greater depth of mental vacuity than was humanly credible. Carrados found him wholly satisfactory, and Parkinson on his side had ignored a score of hints of betterment.

'Pack a couple of bags with necessaries,' was the instruction he received on his return from the post office. 'Von Groot may likely enough remember my name, and I can't very well change it while staying at a public hotel. We will keep on our rooms here and go into apartments at the other end of the town for a time. There my name will be Munroe and yours can be—say Paxton. I will tell the office here all that is necessary.'

'Very good, sir,' assented Parkinson. 'I did not think the woodcock toast sent up for your breakfast entirely satisfactory, sir.'

In years to come generations now unborn will doubtless speculate how people lived in those early days of August, 1914. The simple truth, of course, is that to the vast majority external life went on almost precisely as before. It is as exacting for the moving machine to stop as for the quiescent one to start, and *'Business as usual'* was one of the earliest *clichés* coined. The details of the situation that most impressed the citizen of 1914 are not the details to which the inquirer of 2014 will give a second thought. Individually, it was doubtless very intriguing to have to obtain change for a five-pound note by purchasing postal orders to that amount and immediately cashing them singly again. . . .

Mr Carrados found the Castlemouth Museum open as usual when his leisurely footsteps turned that way on the following morning, and, as usual, the day being fine, deserted. Before they had—Parkinson describing as they went—made the circuit of the first room they were approached by a sociable official—the curator it soon appeared—drawn from his den by the welcome sight of two authentic visitors.

'There are a certain number of specimens that we have to store away for want of space,' he remarked hopefully. 'If there is any particular subject that you are interested in I should be very pleased—'

This suited Mr Carrados's purpose well enough, but before committing himself he not unnaturally preferred to know what the curator's particular subject was. An enthusiast is always vulnerable through his enthusiasm and no man becomes curator of an obscure museum in order to amass a fortune.

'I understand,' he replied tentatively, 'that you are rather strong here in—' An impatient gesture with the expressive fingers conveyed the speaker's loss. 'Dear me—'

'Palaeontology?' suggested the curator. 'My predecessor was a great collector and our series of local fossils is unsurpassed. If you—'

'Ah,' replied Mr Carrados; 'very instructive no doubt.' His alert ear recognised the absence of the enthusiast's note. 'But somehow there always seems to me about fossils a—'

'Yes, yes,' supplied the curator readily; 'I know. No human touch. I feel just the same myself about them. Now flints! There's romance, if you like.'

'That is the real thing, isn't it?' exclaimed Mr Carrados with unqualified conviction. 'There's more interest to my mind in a Neolithic scraper than in a whole showcase full of ammonites and belemnites.'

The curator's eyes sparkled; it was not often that he came across another.

'Brings you face to face with the primeval, doesn't it?' he said. 'I once picked up a spearhead, beautifully finished except the very last chippings of the point. Not broken off, you understand—just incomplete. Why? Well, one might risk a dozen likely guesses. But there it was, just as it had dropped from the fingers of my prehistoric forefather ten thousand years before—no other hand had touched it between his and mine.'

'I should very much like to see what you have here,' remarked the affable visitor. 'Or, rather, in my case, for I am practically blind, I should ask to be allowed to handle.' There were occasions when Mr Carrados found it prudent to qualify his affliction, for more than once astonished strangers had finally concluded that he must be wholly shamming. In his character as an American tourist of leisure—a Mr Daniel Munroe of Connecticut, as he duly introduced himself—the last thing he desired was that ex-Lieutenant von Groot or any of that gentleman's associates should suspect him of playing a part.

For the next half-hour Mr Lidmarsh—his name marked the progress of their acquaintanceship—threw open cabinets and showcases in his hospitable desire to entertain the passing stranger. Carrados knew quite enough of flint implements—as indeed he seemed to know enough of any subject beneath the sun—to be able to talk on level terms with an expert, and he was quite equal to meeting a reference to Evans or to Nadaillac with another.

'I'm afraid that's all,' said the official at length, '—all that's worth showing you, at any rate. We are so handicapped for means, you see—the old story with this sort of institution. Practically everything we have has been given us at one time or another—it has to be, for there is simply no fund to apply to purchasing.'

'Surprising,' declared Carrados. 'One would have thought—'

'We arrange lectures in the winter and try to arouse interest in that way, but the response is small—distressingly small. A great pity. Theatres, cinemas, dancing halls, all crowded—anything for excitement. If we get nine adults we call it a good meeting—free, of course, and Mrs Lidmarsh has tried providing coffee. Now in Holland, my assistant tells me—'

It was the first mention of the absent Karl, for Carrados was too patient and wily a tracker to risk the obliquest reference to his man until he knew the ground he stood on. He listened to a commonplace on the unsophisticated pleasures of the Dutch.

'But surely you have more help for a place like this than a single assistant, Mr Lidmarsh? Why, in the States—'

'It has to be done; it's as much as our endowment and the ha'penny rate will run to,' replied the curator, accepting his visitor's surprise in the sense—as, indeed, it was intended—of a delicate compliment to his own industry. 'Vangoor, myself, and Byles, the caretaker, carry everything upon our shoulders. I count myself very fortunate in having a helper who makes light of work as Mr Vangoor does. Englishmen, unfortunately, seem mostly concerned in seeing that they don't put in half an hour more than they're paid for, Mr Munroe. At least that's my experience. Then he just happens to be keen on the subjects that I'm most interested in.'

'That's always nice,' admitted Mr Carrados, unblushingly.

'Well, it all helps to give an added interest, doesn't it? Not that any department of the work here is neglected or cold-shouldered, I hope—no, I am sure it isn't. For instance, neither of us really cares for natural history, but we recognise that others will think differently, so natural history in all its branches receives due attention. As a seaside town, of course, we give prominence to marine zoology, and our local fishermen and sailors are encouraged to bring in any curious or unusual specimen that they may light upon.'

'Do they much?' inquired the visitor.

'I am afraid not. Lack of public spirit and the suspicion that something is being got out of them for nothing, I suppose. Why, I have even found Vangoor rewarding them out of his own slender pocket to encourage them to come.'

'Fine,' was Mr Carrados's simple comment.

'Yes—when you consider that the poor fellow is none too well paid at the best and that he sends a little every week to his old people away in Holland—all that he can save, in fact—and he lives in a tiny, out-of-the-way old cottage quite by himself so as to do it as cheaply as possible.'

'Vangoor,' considered the blind man thoughtfully; 'Vangoor—there was a fellow of that name I used to meet at times up to six months ago. Now I wonder—'

'In America, you mean?'

'Yes. We have a good sprinkling of Dutch of the old stock, you know. Now what was my man's front name—'

'Then it couldn't have been this one, for he has been here just a year now. I wish he was about so that I could introduce him to you, but he won't be back yet.'

'Well, as to that, I've been thinking,' remarked Mr Carrados. 'I've had a real interesting time here, and in return I'd like to show you a few good things in the flint line that I've picked up on my tour. Could you come around to dinner tomorrow—Sunday?'

'That's very kind indeed.' Mr Lidmarsh was a little surprised at the attention, but not unflattered. 'Sure it won't be—'

'Not a shred,' declared the new acquaintance. 'Bring Vangoor along as well, of course.'

'I'll certainly give him your invitation,' promised the curator; 'but what his arrangements are, naturally I cannot say.'

'Seven o'clock tomorrow then,' confirmed Mr Carrados, referring to the fingers of his own rather noticeable watch as he spoke. '"Abbotsford," in your Prospect Avenue here, is the place. So long.'

At the slightest of gestures Parkinson broke off his profound meditation among Egyptian mummy-cloth and took his master in charge. Together they passed down the flight of stairs and reached the entrance hall again.

'Let them know at the house that I expect two guests to dinner tomorrow,' said Mr Carrados as they crossed the hall. 'Mr Lidmarsh will be coming, and very likely Mr Vangoor as well.'

'I don't think you'll find the last-named gentleman will favour you, Mr Carrados,' said a discreetly lowered and slightly husky voice quite close to them. 'Not much I don't.'

Parkinson started at the untimely recognition, but Carrados merely stopped.

'Ah, William,' he said, without turning, 'and pray why not?'

Mr William Byles, caretaker, doorkeeper, and general *factotum* of the Castlemouth Museum, disclosed himself from behind an antique coffer smiling broadly.

'So you knew me, sir, after all?' he remarked, with easy familiarity. 'I thought to surprise you, but it's the other way about, it seems.'

'Your voice has much the same rich quality as when you looked after my cellar, a dozen years ago, William,' replied Mr Carrados. 'Making due allowance for a slight—erosion. One expects that with the strong sea air.'

'I wondered what you was up to, sir, when I hear you pitch it to the governor you were Mr Munroe from America. Made me laugh. Now that you're inviting Mr Dutch Vangoor to dinner I can give a straightish guess. You needn't trouble, sir. I'm keeping an observant eye on that identical piece of goods myself.'

'Come to the door and point out the way somewhere,' directed Mr Carrados, moving on from the dangerous vicinity of the stairs. 'What do you know about Vangoor?'

'Not as much yet as I'd like to,' admitted Mr Byles, 'but I can put two and two together, Mr Carrados, as well as most.'

'Yes,' mused the blind man reminiscently, 'I always had an idea that you were good at that, William. So you don't exactly love him?'

''Ate isn't the word for it,' replied the caretaker frankly. 'Too much of the bleeding Crown Prince about Jan Van for my vocabulary. Ready to lick his superior's boots three times a day if requisite, but he's done the double dirty on me more than once. And I don't forget it neither.'

'But why do you think he won't come tomorrow?'

'Well, if it's going to be war in a day or two, as most people say, depend on it, sir, Jan Van knows already and it stands to reason that he's busy now. And so shall I be busy, and when he least expects it too.'

'Then I can safely leave him in your hands, William,' said Mr Carrados pleasantly. 'By the way, how do you like it here?' and he indicated the somnolent institution they were leaving.

'Like?' repeated Mr Byles, swallowing with difficulty. 'Like it! Me that's been butler in superior West End families the best part of my life to finish up as "general" in what's nothing more or less than a sort of mouldy peep-show? Oh, Mr Carrados!'

The blind man laughed and a substantial coin found its billet in the caretaker's never-reluctant palm.

'Not "Mr Carrados" here, William, remember. Please preserve my alias or you'll be doing Mr Vangoor a kindness. And whatever you are at, don't let him guess you're on his track.'

Mr Byles's only reply was to place a knowing forefinger against an undeniably tell-tale nose and to close one eye significantly—a form of communication that was presumably lost on the one for whom it was intended though it shocked Parkinson not a little. But the tone and spirit of the whole incident had been a source of pain to that excellent servitor all through.

Another member of Mr Carrados's household—though in point of miles a distant one—was also adversely affected by his employer's visit to the Castlemouth Museum. Less than an hour after Mr Byles's parting gesture a telegram addressed 'Secretary' was delivered at 'The Turrets' and threw Annesley Greatorex, who was contemplating a bright week-end, into a mild revolt.

'My hat, Auntie! just listen to this,' exclaimed Mr Greatorex, addressing the lady whose benevolent rule as Mr Carrados's housekeeper had led to the mercurial youth conferring this degree of honorary relationship upon her. 'Here you have M.C.'s latest:

Borrow few dozen flint implements any period but interesting and dispatch fully insured post or rail to reach me first tomorrow. Try Vicars, Bousset, Leicester (Oxford Street), Graham, etc. Wire advice; then stand by.

Stand by! That means ta-ta to mirth and melody by moonlit streams, until our lord returns, forsooth.'

'And not a bad thing either, Mr Greatorex,' declared the lady, without pausing in her work. 'If there's going to be a war any minute and that German family in Canterbury Road who've got an airship hidden away in their coachhouse fly out and start dropping bombs about, you're much better here safe in bed than gallivanting up and down the open river.'

'Then what about Mr Carrados right on the coast and near a naval harbour?'

'I'm no' troubling about Mr Carrados,' replied the housekeeper decisively. 'If the Germans come they'll come by night. So long as it's in the dark Mr Carrados won't be the first one to need the ambulance, ma lad.'

Carrados duly received his few dozen flints and smiled as he handled them and removed the labels. Promptly on the stroke of seven the curator arrived, but he came alone; whatever the true cause might be, William Byles was right.

'I'm sorry about Vangoor,' apologised Mr Lidmarsh as they greeted. 'He quite intended to come and then at the last found that he had an appointment. I'm sorry, because I should like you to have met him, and he isn't having the pleasantest of times just now.'

'Oh! How is that?'

'Foolish prejudice, of course. People are excited and regard every neutral as an enemy *in esse* or *in posse*. And the irony of it is that Vangoor hears positively that Holland will be in on our side within a month.'

They fell to talking of the war-cloud, as everybody did that day. It was known from the special issues that Germany had formally declared war on Russia, and had launched an ultimatum against France; that here and there fighting had actually begun. The extent of our own implication was not yet disclosed, but few doubted that the die was irrevocably cast.

'Will it make any difference to you up at the museum?' inquired the host. Enlisting had suddenly become a current topic.

'I don't see how it can,' replied Mr Lidmarsh, with regret expressed very largely in his tone. 'At my age—I've turned thirty-nine, though you mightn't think it—I'm afraid there would be no earthly chance of being accepted even if the war lasted a year.'

'A year,' repeated the blind man thoughtfully.

'Well, of course, that's an absurdly outside limit. Mrs Lidmarsh comes of a military family, and she has it privately from an aunt, whose daughter is engaged to the nephew of a staff officer, that the Russian commander-in-chief has sent a map of Germany to Lord Kitchener with the words "Christmas Day" written across Berlin. Naturally everyone at the War Office can guess what that means!'

Carrados nodded politically. Every second person whom he had met that day had a string leading direct to Whitehall.

'Vangoor would go like a shot if they'd raise a Foreign Legion. But of course—Then there's only old Byles—So I'm afraid that we shall have to carry on as usual. And, after all, I don't know that it isn't the most patriotic thing to do. People will want distraction more than ever—not hectic gaiety: no one would dream of that, but simple, rational amusement. Soldiers on leave will need entertainment and somewhere to pass their time. A museum—'

Mr Carrados got out his flints and the curator brightened up, but something was plainly on his mind. He hemmed and hawed his intention to confide half a dozen times before the plunge was taken.

'There's one thing I should like to tell you about, Mr Munroe, although in a sense I'm—well, I won't say bound to secrecy, but confidentially placed.'

'Of course anything that you might say—' encouraged his auditor, discreetly occupied with the cigars.

'Yes, yes; I'm sure of that. And you have been so extremely kind and—er—reciprocal and would, I know, be deeply interested in the find that—well, I feel that if you went away without my saying anything and you afterwards—perhaps when you are back in America— read of what we had been doing, you would think that in the circumstances I had not been quite—eh? Certainly, I know that I should in your place.'

'A find,' commented Mr Carrados, with no very great hope in that direction—'a find is always exciting, isn't it?'

'Well, perhaps I spoke prematurely in the fullest sense—though something we undoubtedly shall find—Did you ever hear of the golden coffin of Epiovanus?'

'I'm afraid,' admitted the other, 'that I never even heard of Epiovanus himself. Stay though—doesn't Roger of Wimborne mention something of the sort in his *Chronicle*?'

'The tradition of an early British chief or king being buried in a gold coffin seems to have been curiously persistent, and that would go to give it a certain degree of credibility. Personally, I take it *cum grano*, I am quite prepared for a gold-mounted coffin or a coffin containing certain priceless gold adornments or treasure of gold coin. I question if the richest tribe could at that time disclose sufficient gold to fashion a solid case of the size required.'

'There was fairly extensive gold coinage at that period, and then the metal practically disappears from the mints for the next thousand years,' suggested Carrados.

'It having gone into the manufacture of royal coffins? I should like to think so, for we believe that we are in fact on the track of something of the kind.'

'You are?' exclaimed the sympathetic listener. 'That would be great—real unique, I suppose. But I don't quite take it home, you know.' Actually he was only bridging conversation out of politeness to a guest. All the treasure of the Indies was of less interest than Vangoor's moves just then.

'Perhaps it sounds too good to be true, but Vangoor is thoroughly convinced, and he is exceptionally well up on the subject and has a veritable craze for digging.'

'Go on,' said Carrados mechanically. For one concentrated moment he even forget his American citizenship in the blinding inspiration that cleft without warning, shapeless but at the same time essentially complete, into his mind. 'I'm tremendously intrigued.'

'Nothing is known of Epiovanus beyond the existence of a unique copper coin reading *EPIOV. REX.* But among the country-people back in the valleys here—the peasants and labourers in whose names you can trace a Saxon ancestry—you will often get a shamefaced admission that they have "heard tell" from their grandfathers of a golden coffin containing the bones of a great chief. But where? That was the difficulty, Mr Munroe. But, to cut short a long story—nearly two thousand years long, in fact—I may say that we have at last linked up the golden coffin legend with Epiovanus, Epiovanus with this part of the land, and now, finally, Vangoor has established that the solitary mound on Headlam Height is undoubtedly an early British sepulchural barrow of very unusual size and importance.'

'Headlam Height?'

'It is a small, rugged promontory a mile or two along the coast here. The barrow is almost on the edge of the land, for the cliff has been falling away for ages—indeed, in another fifty years or less the tumulus would have gone over and whatever it contains been dumped into the sea.'

'And you have opened it?'

'We have made a start. There was considerable difficulty in fixing up a reasonable arrangement at first. You would think it a simple and harmless enough undertaking, but there was the lord of the manor to be approached, the landlord to be got round, and the farmer—well, he had to be bought over, and I am sorry to say that Vangoor in his scientific zeal has in the end promised him the greater part of his own share.'

'Of the golden coffin?' remarked Mr Carrados. 'A very weighty argument.'

'Well, of course, we should hope to retain the best things for the museum, but there would have to be some pecuniary adjustment. If it turns out at all as we anticipate, the find would create a stir beyond anything of the kind before—at least, it would have done if it hadn't been for this wretched war.'

'It opens dazzling possibilities,' admitted the blind man. 'Have you found anything yet?'

'Nothing important but plenty of encouraging trifles—burnt bones and other remains of a funeral feast, fragments of pottery, and so on. We have only been at work a fortnight, and partly from motives of economy, but more because of the extreme care that must be taken, Vangoor has done nearly all the work himself.'

'Driving a tunnel from the shore side?' suggested Mr Carrados.

'Why, yes,' admitted the curator, looking rather surprised, 'but surely you haven't heard it spoken of?'

'Not at all,' Carrados hastened to assure him. 'Merely an interested guess.'

'I hoped it wasn't getting about generally or we shall have all sorts of prying busybodies up there. As it is, we have railed off the part and placarded it "Dangerous"—which it really is. But it struck me as curious you saying that, because at first we thought of making a sectional cutting right down. Then it was only after trials that Vangoor found the seaward side the safest to tunnel in.'

When Carrados decided that there was nothing more of value to be learned—a few aimless remarks elicited this—the conversation imperceptibly slid off to other and less personal themes. The wary investigator had no wish to stir the suggestion that he was curious about Vangoor, and, indeed, the impression that Mr Lidmarsh took away with him was that his host's real hobby in life was the promulgation of phonetic reform.

But what had before been merely a general precautionary suspicion on the blind man's part had now fined down to a very definite conviction, and from whichever side he approached the problem the road led to Headlam Height His first impulse was to investigate that secluded spot at once, but a moment's reflection suggested that the chance of encountering Vangoor there was too substantial to be risked at that stage of the quest. Mr Byles's rather burlesque intervention now began to wear another and a more important face. Was it possible that the disgruntled caretaker knew anything definite of what was going on at Headlam Height?

'This is your affair, Parkinson, and you ought to know all that I do,' said Mr Carrados five minutes later, as he retold Lidmarsh's disclosure. 'On the one hand we have a harmless Dutch scientist, wholly taken up with investigating a lonely burial mound; on the other a dangerous German spy, constructing to some hostile end a retreat that directly overlooks the Channel while it is itself cunningly hidden from every point of land. What do you think about it?'

'I apprehend that we ought to be prepared for the latter eventuality, sir,' replied Parkinson sagely.

'I quite agree with you,' assented his master, with all the air of receiving a valuable suggestion. 'We will stroll round by the Market Square, as any casual visitors might before turning in. If we encounter Mr Byles it may lead to something further. If not, another time will do.'

They made their leisurely perambulation, but nothing came of it. Not only did they fail to encounter Mr Byles but the small curtained upper windows that inevitably suggested his modest suite of rooms displayed no light. The two outstanding hypotheses had to be dismissed, for William had never been an early sleeper in the past, while the public-houses had now been closed some time. Plainly there was nothing left but to retrace their steps.

'Tomorrow morning we will come again,' arranged Mr Carrados. 'Fortunately the museum will be open as usual, so that William cannot very well elude us. Afterwards . . . I expect it will be Headlam Height.'

'Tomorrow' was the last day of peace—Monday, the 3rd of August, and thereby a bank holiday. 'Five Nations at War', 'Invasion of France', and 'British Naval Reserves Mobilized', ran the burden of the morning papers. It was no longer a question of peace trembling in the balance: it was merely the detail of when it would kick the beam.

But 'Business as usual' was now held to be the thing; and Castlemouth's business being largely that of providing amusement for its visitors, there was very little indication of stress or crisis on its joyous sands or along its glittering front that day. At the railway station perhaps the outward trains were crowded and the inward ones were light, while in every chatting group a single word prevailed, but so far Castlemouth was resolved to take war peacefully.

'I believe, sir,' reported Parkinson, as they crossed the Market Square—'I believe that the place is closed.'

'The museum, you mean?'

'Yes, sir. The outer doors are certainly shut.'

'Curious. I made a point of asking about today. Mr Lidmarsh was explicit.'

'There is Mr Lidmarsh, sir. He has just come up. He is fastening a paper to the door.'

Carrados's heart gave a thud, but his pace did not alter, and the curator, looking up, judged the meeting accidental.

'Oh, Mr Munroe,' he exclaimed, 'this is a shocking business. Have you heard?'

'Not a solitary word,' replied the blind man. 'What is it?'

'Poor Byles. He was found dead on the shore this morning.'

'Where?' dropped from Mr Carrados's lips. A good deal might depend on that.

'Just below Headlam Height, I understand. "*De mortuis*", and all that, you know, but the man certainly had himself largely to blame, I fear. He wasn't supposed to know anything about our work up there, but he had evidently got wind of something. He was a curious, secretive old fellow, and, as I read it, he went up there in the dark last night, and, prying about, he either slid on the slippery grass or did not see the edge. And late at night Byles was sometimes just a little—you understand? However, we have closed the museum today as a mark of respect. But of course if you want to go in—'

'Thank you,' replied Mr Carrados, 'but I guess not. I was thinking. . . . Where have they put him?'

'In the mortuary close by. He's fearfully knocked about. He had a couple of rooms up there'—indicating the windows Parkinson had observed the night before—'but he has no wife or people; and in any case the mortuary is the proper place. There'll have to be an inquest, of course; I've sent Vangoor to make inquiries now.'

'I was thinking'—he had undoubtedly been thinking, but he had not yet had time to review every possibility—'this Byles did me a service as we left the museum on Saturday—saved me perhaps from what might have been a nasty fall—and a few friendly words passed afterwards. And now. . . . Dear me; how sad! . . . Well, I'm not up in the customs of your sarcophagi, but if a trifling bouquet—Why, I've a notion that I'd like to.'

This impressed Mr Lidmarsh with the sentimentality of masculine America—an attribute he had frequently heard it credited with.

'Why, of course,' he replied, 'there could be no difficulty about that if you wish it. But did you mean—right now?' The last two words were in the nature of a spontaneous tribute to the visitor's nationality.

'Sure. You see, I might have moved on tomorrow or the day after. There seems to be a flower store open that we passed just back—'

Even as he purchased the sheaf of lilies to lay on William Byles's shroud, Carrados was not altogether free from an illusion of sharing a rather exquisite joke with that mordant individual. How would William have regarded the touching act on the part of his old employer? By whatever means it reached his insight the blind man's mind immediately envisioned the flashlight of a tight-closed humid eye and a nose and finger placed in close conjunction. But, in truth, Carrados had felt the necessity of investigating further, and no other excuse occurred to him at once. He could hardly affect that he wished to see the doorkeeper once more. . . . The sudden intuition that Parkinson was tentatively regarding a wreath of white moss-roses hastened their departure.

'One curious feature is the time this must have happened,' remarked Mr Lidmarsh as they walked on. 'He was found by the merest chance early this morning—almost as soon as it was light, in fact—and his clothing was not wet. That shows that he could not have fallen down before midnight at any rate. Now, whatever possessed the man to be there at that hour when nothing could be seen? He had the whole of Sunday on his hands if he wished to look about.'

'Singular, isn't it?' assented Carrados. 'No one saw him up there, I take it?'

'Oh, no—at least we have heard of no one. Who would be likely to be there? Even Vangoor doesn't dig on Sunday—he wouldn't think it right.'

The mortuary proved to be quite near—a corner of the market hall in fact. Mr Lidmarsh procured the key from the police station, with no more formality than a neighbourly greeting on either side, and Carrados was free to perform his thoughtful office.

The body lay, outlined beneath a single covering, on one of the two stone benches that the place contained. On the other were arranged the dead man's clothes, with the few trumpery belongings that his pockets had yielded set out beside them.

'They told me that his watch, purse, and keys were taken for safety to the station,' remarked their guide, as Carrados's understanding hands moved lightly to and fro. 'The rest is of no consequence.'

'String, pipe, tobacco-box, matches, small folding measure, odd

443

cuff-link, silver mariner's compass, handkerchief,' checked off the leisurely fingers. 'How stereotyped we he-things are: my own pockets would show almost the same collection—in a liberal sense, of course.'

'It is rather odd about the book,' volunteered the curator, pointing to a worn volume of pocket size. It was lying a little apart, and apparently the gesture was for Carrados's eyes to follow—and strangely enough they did seem to follow, for he picked up the book unfalteringly. 'It was still tightly held in Byles's hand when he was found. Now, why should the man be holding a book in his hand—one that would obviously go into his pocket—on a dark night? If there was any mystery about the case I suppose this ought to be one of the clues that those wonderful detectives we read about, but never meet in real life, would unravel the secret by.'

Mr Carrados laughed appreciatively as he turned the pages of the book.

'*Stories from the Studios of Paris,*' he read aloud. 'At all events this throws some light on the literary calibre of our departed friend. . . . . The only thing that would seem to be missing from the average pocket is a pen-knife.'

'Pen-knife?' repeated Mr Lidmarsh looking about. 'To be sure he had a knife generally; I've seen it often enough. Well, I don't suppose it matters—a shilling at the outside.'

Everything had been seen—everything except the chief 'exhibit' lying beneath the merciful coverlet. The curator understood that his new friend relied chiefly on a highly-trained sense of touch—he had marvelled more than once during this short intercourse at what it told—but he was hardly prepared to see Mr Carrados raise the sheet and begin to pass his hand over the—his own eyes perforce went elsewhere—over the dreadful thing which the day before had been William Byles's face.

'I think,' said the blind man, turning away suddenly, 'that this is rather too much—' His left hand came into contact with his attendant's sleeve and Parkinson felt himself detained by a robust grasp. 'Is there anywhere, Mr Lidmarsh, where . . . a glass of water?'

'Yes, yes.' Almost with a feeling of self-reproach that he had allowed the mishap Mr Lidmarsh was off to the nearest house. He ought to have warned. . . .

'The book, Parkinson,' said Carrados in his usual easy tone, and before Parkinson (who would carry his own blend of simplicity and shrewdness to the grave) quite knew what was happening, *Stories from the Studios of Paris* had disappeared into his master's coat pocket.

'I don't think that there is anything more to detain us here,' remarked the strategist dispassionately. 'We may as well await our friend outside.' He closed the door, locked it, and took out the key in readiness. When Mr Lidmarsh returned with the water he found Carrados seated on a market truck.

'I am glad you came away from the ghastly place,' he declared. 'I ought to have thought of that.' Still accusing himself of some remission, he insisted on accompanying the two halfway through the town and hoped that they might meet again.

As they stood there, exchanging these amiable formalities, an acquaintance of the curator's passed along on the other side of the road and could not forbear to give the news.

'The Germans have invaded Belgium,' he called across. 'They've just got it at the post office. I bet that means we're in the soup!'

★★★★★★

'What happened, Parkinson, is as clear as day,' explained Mr Carrados. 'The important thing now is to decide what to do ourselves.'

They were seated in the private sitting-room at 'Abbotsford,' a table between them and on the table, with Mr Carrados's eerie fingers never long away from it, the copy of *Stories from the Studios of Paris*.

'We know from Byles's own lips that he only had a general suspicion of Vangoor's business here. Doubtless last night he watched the secluded cottage, and when Jan crept out about midnight he followed him to Headlam Height. Or, of course, he may have gone there earlier and waited. Evidently he did not know what he was going to see or he would have gone better prepared. As it was he had no pencil and he had no proper paper. . . . We are overdue at Headlam Height, Parkinson.'

'Yes, sir,' acquiesced the model confederate.

'Obviously there is some ground from which Vangoor's signals can be seen, carefully as he has planned his burrow. Byles saw something, and recognising the importance of what he saw he tried to take it down. These cuts and pricks made with a pocket-knife (which we shall doubtless find up there) on the covers of this book represent quite intelligently a rendering of morse. What that meant he did not know; what this means we do not know, but Byles has done his bit and passed on the responsibility to us.'

'I think I appreciate the obligation, sir. Mr Vangoor should not be allowed to remain at large.'

445

'That is the difficulty. We can have a spy snapped up and possibly hanged for murder, or, what would be simpler, he might slip on Headlam Height—in the same way that William Byles did. But we must not lose sight of the fact that the man has been signalling out to sea. That definitely suggests a submarine—a submarine lying off Pentland Harbour, full of battleships. What has he signalled, and, if we give him rope, *what will he signal next?*' The blind man came to his feet and strode to the window, where before him lay the broad waters of the Channel still carrying their wealth of shipping—the panorama he would never see again. Seldom before had Parkinson known his master so visibly concerned as he stood there in the hot sunlight, moodily beating his palm with the thin edge of the book. 'Here in my hand are the very words he flashed—the key to every other message he may send—and we cannot read a letter of it. The system is capable of a thousand changes and ten thousand shifts of code. And the time is slipping by. It's maddening, maddening....Suggest something, Parkinson, there's a good fellow.'

Parkinson might be conscious of a complete mental destitution at that moment, but he had never yet failed to comply with an order reasonably given.

'I recollect, sir, reading about a Bristol baker who murdered his wife because she had been communicating with a young gentleman by means of secret marks on the rolls delivered at the house. He discovered—'

'Enough!' exclaimed Mr Carrados, making for the writing-table with his indecision vanished. 'That's it. You were inspired, Parkinson. Clifton Baker, of course!'

'Thank you, sir,' replied Parkinson, much gratified.

In those days the name of Clifton Baker appeared on the frosted glass of the outer door belonging to a small top-floor office in Chancery Lane. There was nothing more to indicate who Clifton Baker was or the nature of the business carried on there. Few callers appeared at the dingy office, but those who did almost invariably left instructions to proceed, and as each order meant a substantial cheque eventually, Clifton might be assumed to be not so unsuccessful after all.

In almost every case the new client experienced a mild shock on opening his business. Generally he had been sent there by a firm of responsible solicitors, and the matter on which he required assistance was confidential, extremely technical, and beyond the capacity of any other specialist. He expected to see—well, at all events he did not expect a slight, sallow-complexioned, glad-eyed, deep-browed young woman who dressed rather skittishly and struck him as being more than a shade rattle-pated. He might have left the commission somewhat dubiously, but he did leave it, and it was duly carried out: done to time, done as required, and done perfectly.

At the age of fifteen Clifton Baker had made up her mind—a considerable achievement of itself in that era. At twenty-five she spoke all the most useful living languages and wrote the four most important dead ones. Eight letters (which she never by any chance used) after her hermaphroditic name were some evidence of a scientific grounding, while the recital of her attainments in the higher planes of mathematics made elderly professors who were opposed to the movement ooze profusely in the region of the collar. Then chance, in the shape of a baffling testamentary puzzle, threw destiny across her path, and on the assumption that there was room for one professional lady cryptologer in the world Clifton took an office and passed the word round among her friends.

Up to that time the girl had never really done her hair, and she regarded boots merely as things to protect the feet. Suddenly it dawned on her that she was considered plain and that she diffused an atmosphere of intellectual frost. A morbid terror of being thought learned seemed from that moment to possess Clifton, and to make up for her neglected youth she began to outflap the veriest flapper in a stern resolve not to be taken seriously. Had she been less brilliantly efficient it might have ruined her business; had she been less impossibly absurd it would have spoiled her pleasure, but the two things simply antidoted one another. Everybody smiled indulgently and said how typical a product of the age Miss Baker was, and how hopeless it would be, except in this London of nineteen-dash, to look for such another.

Thus it came about that Mr Greatorex, dutifully 'standing by' on Monday afternoon, was startled to receive a duplicated telegram as follows:

Find Clifton Baker and get her here on any terms by breakfast-time tomorrow. Report progress. Carrados.

'Whew!' ejaculated Annesley, who was not altogether ignorant of the lady's personality, 'that puts the top-knot on the pan-lid with a vengeance! Bank holiday, too, *ecog!*' He went through the various rooms of the almost empty house vainly bleating for suggestions. 'Where on earth am I to find Clifton Baker, on this of all days, Auntie?'

The housekeeper looked up over the top of her reading glasses a trifle dourly. She had a niece at school somewhere near Dinant. . . .

'What should you want Miss Baker for?' she asked.

'I don't want her; I fear and shun her. But Mr Carrados does. He's just wired.'

'Oh, that will be all right then. Well, my laddie, I can't tell you where Miss Baker is, but I can tell you this; if she's not verra hard at work somewhere she's somewhere verra hard at play.'

It was at breakfast-time that Greatorex delivered her. Mr Carrados was standing in the loggia of the Hotel Beverley when a not unfamiliar sound claimed his attention. It announced to him the arrival of his own touring car, and the next moment a squeal of maidenly delight indicated that Miss Baker had espied him.

'You monster!' she exclaimed vivaciously, while a dozen yards away. 'To inveigle me into travelling all night with that delightfully wicked-looking young secretary of yours! I declare I don't know what people will say when I get back.'

'I thought it better to bring her down by car, sir,' explained Annesley in an aside of moody resignation. 'I only dug her out at something past eleven last night, and all the trains are at sixes and sevens just now.'

'Quite right,' assented Carrados. 'I suppose you can be ready for breakfast in about ten minutes, Miss Baker?'

Clifton drooped one eyelid thoughtfully as she considered this—a device she had lately taken up.

'Do I really require breakfast?' she confided to the hotel front generally. 'Mr Greatorex was most attentive all the way. He insisted on stopping at a charmingly romantic cabman's shelter somewhere, at five o'clock this morning, and we had a surfeit of hot cocoa and currant buns. I simply can't imagine why he should take such enormous care of small me.'

'I think I'll go up and wash, sir,' announced Mr Greatorex abruptly, 'if you don't require me just now.'

'Not until after breakfast,' said Carrados. 'In the meanwhile Miss Baker and I will talk business.'

Breakfast at a little table in the Fountain Court provided an opportunity (the discovery of filleted sole à la Normande restored Clifton's appetite), for the hotel was no longer full. . . .

'Yes, I see,' nodded the girl at intervals, forgetting to be coy, and Carrados deployed the facts. When he had finished she held out her hand for the transcript of the message that he had already made.

'H'm. It looks rather hopeless, doesn't it, Mr Carrados?' she remarked professionally. 'When do you want it by?'

'Three o'clock if possible,' he replied brazenly. 'Six o'clock in any case.'

Clifton gave a little shriek of young-ladylike dismay.

'Mercy! Today?' she exclaimed. 'Why, you dear creature, do you know—'

'I know what you can do when you like,' he got in.

'And I know that perhaps it can't be done at all, sir.'

'And I know that Edgar Allan Poe said—'

'He said nothing about doing it in six hours.' Miss Baker had had that celebrated *dictum* quoted to her quite often enough to be able to dispense with it. 'Are you sure that you have even got this Morse the right way up?'

'Yes, I can guarantee you that. But the message certainly begins incomplete and it probably ends so.'

'In German, we assume? Oh, yes; I think it must be. Well—'

'I knew you would. My sitting-room here is at your disposal. You'll find most things you may require already there. Anything else—'

'By the way, was there no later message sent? What was the man doing last night?'

'No. I have him watched now, of course. Last night after leaving the museum he was at Pentland until quite late, and returning he went home and stayed there.'

'Then I should like a full list of the warships in Pentland Harbour, recent sailings, and those expected, please. The "Navy List" I suppose you have here?'

'Good girl!' smiled Carrados approvingly. 'You shall have it if it's humanly possible. If I am caught in the act and my motives doubted I shall certainly be shot at dawn—and you will be transported. . . . Will they insist on blindfolding me, I wonder? Probably. . . . Regulations, you know, Miss Baker. Nothing else?'

'No, thank you.' Clifton still wriggled about the open door of the private room. 'Well—please keep Mr Greatorex away while I am busy, won't you? He will be sure to want to bring me ices and things like that; he's so absurd, poor boy!'

So much for that particular Clifton Baker. About three o'clock Carrados tapped lightly on his own door and a very faint voice bade him enter. Clifton was lying prostrate on the couch, a napkin round her head, and the reek of eau-de-Cologne filling the room. A single written sheet of paper was on the table near her—but there were more than a hundred others, torn across, littering the floor. Without a word she picked up the single sheet and, rattling it slightly to call his attention, held it towards him.

'You have?' he exclaimed, scarcely daring to believe it. 'You are really a wonderful woman, Clifton. This is splendid.' Neatly set out on the paper were three separate details—the alphabet in Morse code as she had finally resolved it; the message William Byles had intercepted (including three textual errors to be discounted), as it was sent in German; and the same rendered into English.

'"— — — instruction. Your presence not yet suspected. *Virulent, Delhi,* and *Telemachus* left today for unknown. *Westmorland* for repairs expected tonight. Supply arrangements stand, VJ.372 will be trawling — — —"' he read aloud. 'Yes; we have it now. Mr Vangoor's bulletin tonight should be more interesting still.'

'I think you really are a wonderful man, Mr Carrados,' retorted Clifton, watching his shifting fingers as he touched her firm, bold handwriting word after word without a pause. 'I suppose you always get your way? I wonder what you are going to do with me now?'

'I am going to prescribe a cup of tea at once, an early dinner, and twelve hours' good solid sleep after all this excitement. Tomorrow I shall pack you off back to town by the car again, with Mr Greatorex to beguile the way.'

'Oh, please, please, please, Mr Max!' wailed Clifton in appealing tones. 'Can't you leave Mr Greatorex here and come instead? I should feel ever so much safer with you in these dreadful times!' But Mr Max laughed indulgently and shook his head. He had heard Miss Baker at work before.

'Not yet, I'm afraid,' he said. 'I am here for another fish, only Vangoor came along. And while I remember'—he took a slip of tinted paper from his wallet and held it out—'I hope that will be all right.'

'Oh, Mr Carrados,' she tittered. 'Ought I to, really? It doesn't seem at all like business with *you*! I hope no one will think—'

'I should like you to—it's certainly well earned,' he said. 'But, of course,' he added maliciously, 'if you prefer the satisfaction of serving your country for nothing you can always burn the cheque.'

'Burn it!' shrieked Clifton, scrambling the paper into her handbag. 'And my visit to the Cosmo-Croxtons in Scotland only ten days off! Why, you delightfully opportune being, this means four new frocks to me!'

'Well, make the most of them,' he advised, a trifle grimly. 'There won't be any country-house parties next year.'

'Why ever not?'

'When you wake up tomorrow you will find that we are at war. Before long most of your fair friends will be wearing white caps and aprons—or black dresses.'

★★★★★★

Carrados had quite intended to climb up to Headlam Height on Monday afternoon, he had fully determined to do so on Tuesday morning, but each time the more important post lay elsewhere. When, therefore, taking Parkinson with him, he turned his inquiring footsteps in that direction after leaving Miss Baker, it was his first reconnaissance.

'Admirably chosen, Parkinson,' he remarked as they made the circuit of the acre or so of grass and heather that comprised the Height. 'No path or roadway near; cut off from Castlemouth's view by cliffs, and not a house or habitation in sight anywhere. . . . And this thing may really be an early British grave for all that we can say.'

'Yes, sir,' agreed Parkinson. 'I have always understood that the early natives of these parts were peculiar in their habits. But if I may mention it, sir, the ground here is very broken and there is little beyond a crevice, almost a yard wide, between us and the edge.'

'Quite right,' assented the other, turning back; 'we must be careful. The British Empire doesn't exactly hang on us today, but a British ironclad may. I suppose that crevice was the unfortunate William's retreat—there seems no other cover that would serve up here. We have a better arrangement for tonight. Now for the excavation.'

A couple of rough balks of timber across the entrance were the only barrier. The tumulus itself rose to nearly thirty feet, and the cutting was sufficiently roomy for a tall man to stand in.

'Are we to imagine that our enthusiastic friend contemplated driving an unpropped tunnel clean through?' reflected Mr Carrados, touching the loose earth sides. 'What does the view seaward give us, Parkinson?'

'There is a flat-topped rock visible a little way out at sea, and, farther away, the extremity of Pentland Rump—as I understand it is designated, sir.' Privately, Parkinson thought the name lacking in delicacy, and he wished to make it clear that the expression was none of his.

'Aye. And the extremity of Pentland Rump and the flat-topped rock line this point of course. Ah, what have we here?'

Evidently the excavator's tools, piled at the far end of the tunnel and covered with tarpaulin: a spade, a pick, a riddle, a wheelbarrow, rope, and the usual odds and ends—that was all; no, there remained a wooden tripod, such as may serve a score of uses, lying with the rest—a tripod with rough, substantial wooden legs but a nicely-finished metal top. Smooth metal is rather pleasant to the touch, and the blind man's hand lingered on its construction thoughtfully.

'We must put all these back just as they were,' he observed, busying himself. 'Parkinson!'

There was no answer for a moment; then Parkinson appeared at the entrance to the tunnel.

'I was looking out beyond the mound, sir. I felt apprehensive. . . . There is someone coming.'

Carrados replaced the last tool and rearranged the covering.

'Von Groot?' he asked quietly.

'Yes, sir.'

The two timbers fell into their proper places; everything was as they had found it. They stood, hidden from the land side by the mass of earth rising above them.

'How far off is he?' said Carrados.

'Nearly half a mile, sir. I saw him with the glasses on the skyline of the hill we had to cross. That means ten minutes yet.'

'He may have seen you also.'

'I was careful to keep in the shadow of the mound. I don't think you need entertain that, sir.'

'It doesn't matter.' For once the blind man's voice had lost its wonted suaveness. 'I've made a hash of it this time, Parkinson. I took it for granted that he'd not venture on anything before it was night again. We were prepared to deal with that, but he's going to steal a march on us. He isn't waiting for the dark—he's going to heliograph. We can stop him, of course,' he went on, sensing the unspoken question; 'we shall have to stop him. But we lose the message and whatever hangs upon it. No matter how plausibly we put him off it now, after finding us up here he won't risk it again—not on the top of William Byles's affair.'

'Excuse me, sir,' volunteered Parkinson, 'but I see no reason why we should not attempt to obtain the message still.'

'We—how?' demanded Carrados sharply.

'I understand, sir, that the system is merely a succession of long and short flashes of a mirror, and that one may commit it to paper without any understanding of the meaning.'

'Quite so—as William doubtless did. But where are you going to see it from?'

Parkinson's backward nod indicated the crevice on the very edge of the sheer precipice. 'I think it might succeed, sir.'

'No, no,' exclaimed Carrados, with a sharp pang of misgiving in his voice; 'it would be madness in broad daylight. Besides, here am I—'

'There are suitable clumps of gorse a little way back, sir. I anticipate that you would be quite safe there, or I would not suggest it, sir. And lying in the crevice I could watch through the grass and heather.'

'I can't allow it,' insisted Carrados, moved by the horror of what he saw impending. 'The man discovered Byles there ever in the dark, and we know how that encounter ended. No, Parkinson, I won't have you sacrificed in the forlorn hope of patching up my bungle.'

'I beg your pardon, sir,' said Parkinson, without a hair's deviation from his invariable tone of dignified respect, 'but I was not thinking of you—or of myself. I understand that we are on the point of war, sir, and that if we lose this message it may involve a misfortune to our arms. And I must remind you, sir, that yesterday you described this affair as mine.'

'By heaven, you have me there!' exclaimed his master, in an access of fine emotion. 'Go if you must—and God go with you!'

'The gorse, sir.' Parkinson took his arm and began to hurry him across the slope that led from the Height to the rolling land behind. 'I must be satisfied that you are safe there first.'

'Not so fast.' Carrados checked his pace to the deliberate walk at which he tried the unfamiliar. 'I may need to know this ground again.' His hand went to a pocket and came out with something in it. 'You are the one to have this now.'

'I would rather not, sir', if I may say so,' declared Parkinson with naive reluctance. 'I have never discharged a firearm in my life and the consequences might be unpropitious.' So Carrados retained the weapon, and a moment later he was lying in a natural bower of undergrowth, listening to the swish and crackle of Parkinson's diminishing footsteps.

It was perhaps three minutes before any sound other than the cheeping of a linnet or the rasping of a dead leaf on its bough reached the straining ears. Then, away on the left, Carrados heard the approaching beat of a heavy foot. There was little chance of reading any of the subtler indications on that luxuriant carpet, but the blind listener interpreted haste and the strain of an alert caution. The intruder passed within ten yards of the unsuspected lair—within easy pistolshot, and the steady hand went again to the pocket, but this time it came out empty.

From the direction of the mound no sound came through; the day was drowsy, with occasional puffs of warm air and the smell of honey, and time began to hang like lead.

'He must get on, from every point of view,' argued Carrados to pass the seconds. 'Five minutes to fix the rig, ten more to send his message, five to pack up. Heavens! it seems an hour already.' He touched the fingers of his watch and found that barely twelve minutes had gone. 'But that's only if the submarine is here. He may have to wait....At any rate, he hasn't spotted Parkinson at the outset or I should have heard something.'

And then, as if his action had been a continuation of the unspoken words, Carrados was on his feet and racing across the glacis. He had heard 'something,' and that sound the echo of his worst forebodings, for the sharp crack of a pistol had whipped the flagging afternoon— and that could mean one thing only. It was with this return in view that the blind man had marked his way, and he covered the ground with confidence, making directly for the barrow. When the difference of the air against his face told him that he was by it he dropped into a walk and moved with caution. Beyond it he was in full view, and the sheer drop hardly twenty yards away. Everything was now poised on the edge of chance.

'Damn!' came the low murmur to his ear. '*Ein anderer!*'

It was not the time to ask for explanations. Carrados—conscious even then of the irony of the phrase—had to take the risk. As he once stopped to explain to Monsieur Dompierre, upon an occasion less hurried but quite as tense, he aimed by sound and practised round a watch.

He fired now into the centre of the 'Damn!' and on the overhanging lip of the cliff there was a little scurry of movement among the loose stones and earth. He did not fire again. He waited, listening. . . .

'Parkinson!' he called, without moving from the spot. 'Parkinson, are you—'

There was no response. The disturbed seagulls wheeled overhead, raising a plaintive clamour at the violation of their homes; a string of swift shorebirds cleft a zigzag course right out to sea; at his feet the untroubled bees continued in their humble toil.

'Gone!' whispered the blind man to himself. 'Gone, and I'm left alone. The best fellow—Good heavens!'

From the bowels of the earth, apparently, a wild echoing sound had come with startling suddenness—a sound so truculent and formless that it baffled perception. The next moment it revealed itself: a human being had sneezed with appalling vigour.

'Parkinson!' exclaimed Carrados, dropping on hands and knees and crawling to the crevice. 'Where the devil are you?'

'I'm down here, sir,' replied the welcome voice from somewhere below. 'I was unable to reply when you called before as I was on the point of sneezing. The dust, sir—'

'Wait; don't try to get out,' directed his master. 'I'll get that rope.'

It was the rope that Mr Vangoor had thoughtfully provided to give an air of conviction to his labours. By its aid Parkinson was soon hauled to safety. Once there he looked apprehensively around.

'Has anything happened to Mr Vangoor, sir?'

'Yes,' replied Carrados. 'He was too talkative. If you do not see anything of him about we must conclude that he has gone down the same way William Byles went . . . . What happened to *you?*'

'Unfortunately, when he had finished his message the gentleman seemed to be looking my way. I endeavoured to obliterate myself more thoroughly and evidently attracted his attention. I infer that he was rather nervous, sir, for he shot at me without saying a word.'

'If only he'd had the sense to do that in my case we might both be in Kingdom Come now.'

'Yes, sir? I may say that I didn't like it, sir, and as he fired I made a considerable effort to get down still lower. I imagine that something must have given, for the next moment I found myself wedged in some twenty feet down. I believe that the gentleman was much concerned what to do next as he could not discover me. . . . What is that?'

'Back!' cried Carrados. 'The cliff is going!'

The cliff, as Mr Lidmarsh had remarked, had been going for centuries—going by inches, by feet, or by yards. Possibly William Byles's activity had started a movement that Parkinson's struggles had consummated; perhaps, even, the pistol-shots had vibrated a responsive tremor. Now the cliff face—all the ground beyond the fissure—began to fall rigidly away from Headlam Height, as a ladder falls; then, as its base gave way, to change and to collapse, in hundreds of tons of shattered rock, upon the beach. In Castlemouth it was thought that the war had begun.

'Excellent,' remarked Carrados, when voices could be heard again. 'That should save much inconvenient inquiry about Mr Vangoor's unfortunate end. I suppose, Parkinson, that any notes you made are down there also?'

'No, sir. I managed to get the notebook back into my pocket. I trust that my efforts will have been adequate.'

'That is easily proved. If you really have got the message, Parkinson, you will deserve a knighthood.'

'Thank you, sir, but I hope you won't mention it to anyone. It would be very uncongenial to me to become notorious in any way.'

Carrados laughed as he took the notebook. Then he sat down at the base of the mound, and with Miss Baker's key before him he began to test the notation.

'Yes,' he reported presently, 'you seem to have hit it off all right, "*Kriegserklärung*" this begins.'

'I beg your pardon, sir?'

'It's in German of course—"War declaration". I'll give you the whole thing in a few minutes.'

'You left your hat in the gorse, sir,' said Parkinson thoughtfully. 'I will get it while you are engaged.'

'Thank you—do,' murmured Mr Carrados, again deep in the code. 'Now what—oh, "*hafen*", of course.'

When Parkinson returned—he had taken the opportunity to wisp himself down—Carrados was already on his feet and impatient to get away.

'We don't want to be here when the town comes out to find what the row was about,' he explained. 'We are not going to appear in this, Parkinson. We will make a wide detour—in fact, we may as well make Pentland direct while we are about it.'

'Very well, sir.'

'The message—you only got two letters wrong, which was better than William and less important, of course, as we have the code now. Well, here it is:

Declaration of war midnight. *Inexorable* leaves western harbour one a.m. by Viking Channel and from Gnome Lightship will proceed S.S.W. Rendezvous as arranged.

'The *Inexorable* it was to have been, Parkinson.'

'Yes, sir. What had we better do now, sir?'

'Nothing, practically. We have done. At Pentland I shall hand this over to the naval authorities with so much explanation as they may desire. It will then rest with them to do the doing. I venture to predict that *Inexorable* will not leave the western harbour at one a.m. by the Viking Channel. At the same time I think that a rendezvous will be kept. But so far as we are concerned it is *Finis*. You, Parkinson, have already done your bit.'

'Thank you, sir,' replied Parkinson, entirely satisfied.

The Mystery of the Vanished Petition Crown

Max Carrados always seemed inclined to laugh quietly if anyone happened to mention the curious disappearance of the Willington Petition Crown. Why he should have been amused rarely came out at such times, perhaps because it is not expedient for one private collector openly to accuse another private collector of barefaced theft (whatever misgivings the majority may secretly admit of one another's morals), but the extent of his knowledge in the affair will emerge from the following pages.

As a specialist in Greek *tetradrachms* Carrados would naturally only have a condescending interest in any of the non-classical branches of numismatics, but it was an interest that drew him to every word of coin news that appeared. As his delicate fingertips skimmed the morning paper headings at breakfast one day they 'read' for him a line that promised some entertainment, and the item was duly blue-pencilled for consideration later. It was no effort for the blind man to pick out all the essentials of the newspaper's contents in this way; he could even, though not with the same facility, read the ordinary smaller type, but where there was no special reason for this it was his custom to mark off such paragraphs for his secretary's subsequent attention. This was in the nature of their ordinary daily routine, and an hour later Greatorex noticed and read aloud the following extract from the *Daily Record*:

RARE COIN DISAPPEARS
AUCTION ROOM SENSATION

Collectors and dealers who forgathered at Messrs Lang & Leng's well-known sale-rooms yesterday in the hope of bidding for an exceptionally fine specimen of the celebrated Petition Crown of Charles II were doomed to disappointment. When the lot in question was reached and the coin was displayed at the tables it was discovered that something was wrong. The Petition Crown, which had previously been on view for several days and up to the hour of the sale, had disappeared and a comparatively valueless coin of a somewhat similar type occupied its numbered receptacle.

Immediate search among the other lots, both sold and unsold, failed to reveal any trace of the missing rarity and the whole affair is so far shrouded in mystery.

Piquancy is added to the incident by the fact that the last person to see and handle the coin was a well-known lady journalist, who, however, disclaims any numismatic cravings. After inspecting the coin merely as a rare and valuable curiosity the lady in question returned the tray containing it to the attendant in charge, who at once replaced it in the cabinet. As already stated, when it was next required the crown had vanished.

The Petition Crown holds the auction record among English coins, an example having realized £500 some years ago. It is generally stated that only fifteen specimens of this excessively rare coin were ever struck, and all but two or three are now in public collections and therefore out of the reach of enthusiasts. The crown owes its name to the interesting circumstances of its origin. The English engraver, Thomas Simon, having been supplanted in Charles II's favour by his Dutch rival, Roettier, the former put all his skill and genius into the creating of a supercoin, which took the form of a crown piece, with the following quaint inscription neatly engraved around the edge:

Thomas Simon most humbly prays your Majesty to compare this his tryall piece with the Dutch, and if more truly drawn and embossd, more gracefully ordered, and more accurately engraven, to relieve him.

Sad to relate, although Simon's work is admittedly superior to that of "the Dutch", his petition was in vain. Still worse, the royal patron of the arts allowed his "most humble's" salary and working expenses for several years to remain unpaid, so that after the engraver's death his widow had also to "petition"—for £2,164 long overdue."

'That's rather like another plant where a string of pearls was changed some years ago,' volunteered Greatorex, laying aside the paper in favour of his own reminiscences. He was a cheerful, mercurial youth who conceived that the more important part of his duty was to regale Mr Carrados with his personal views on life and affairs, nor, strange to say, did his employer very often undeceive him. 'Do you remember the one I mean, sir?'

'Yes; they mulled that by not copying the sale label closely enough, and the attendant noticed it when the necklace was laid down again. There was a woman in that business also. But the two cases have nothing in common really.'

'How do you mean? Both were at auction sales; both—'

'True,' interrupted Carrados, 'but those things are only superficial. The essential motives fall into two quite different classes. Good pearls are always readily saleable, and it is simply a matter of rearranging them and making them up in a different form. But what is a man going to do with a Petition Crown? Wear it on his watch-chain? As a marketable piece of loot he might as well carry off a Turner from the National Gallery, or, indeed, one of the lions from Trafalgar Square. Its trade value is about one and ninepence for the melting-pot.'

'Oh, come, sir,' protested Greatorex. 'This account speaks of a few other specimens knocking about. Surely in a year or two's time this one couldn't be positively identified as stolen?'

Max Carrados turned to pull open a drawer of his desk and took out the top pamphlet of a number it contained.

'Here is Lang's catalogue of this sale,' he said, passing it across. 'I haven't gone into it, but very likely that crown will be illustrated among the plates at the end. Just see.'

'Quite right, sir. It is Lot 64, and it is reproduced in one of those photographic process types here on Plate 2.'

'Take a glass and look into it. It is described as exceptionally fine, but you will almost certainly find a number of small cuts and dents here and there on the surface.'

'Yes; I see what you mean. They don't show ordinarily.'

'All the same they label the specimen as definitely as if it was a numbered banknote. The simplest way out of that would be to carry it loose in your pocket for a few years. That would reduce its cabinet value to one-half, but it would effectually wipe out its identity. The trouble would be that whenever you started to dispose of it you would be pointedly asked for the pedigree. What collection had it come from last? All these little details are on record and easily available. No, it's amateur work, whoever it may be, Greatorex.'

'I was rather hoping that perhaps someone would bring it round here to offer sooner or later,' remarked the adventurous Greatorex, still examining the plate. 'I'll bet I could spot it by that scratch over His Majesty's eye.'

'Then you will certainly be disappointed,' was the unpromising reply. 'If the coin really has been stolen—and that's a palpable "if" so far—ten to one its immediate destination is the private drawer of some collector who will be content to handle and gloat over it in secret for the remaining days of his life.'

'And then I suppose it all comes out when he goes off?'

'It may. But I have heard a curious story of an old fellow who had a few pieces in his collection that he never showed. When he thought that he only had a short time left he took a coal hammer and in five minutes the rarities were effectually put beyond any fear of identification.'

'My Sunday hat!' exclaimed Mr Greatorex, compelled to a generous admiration. 'Some collectors are hot stuff!'

With that decorous epitaph the subject was laid to rest, with no indication that it would ever be raised again. But—just as one may meet three piebald horses in the course of one short walk—the Petition Crown was fated to persist, and before lunch-time a telephone call from Mr Carlyle had resurrected it. The period of interment had been just short of three hours.

'Busy, Max?' chirruped the familiar voice of his friend the inquiry agent—incurably brisk and debonair even after its ten miles' journey along the wire. 'Not to me? Dear old chap! Well, I dare say you've read all about the disappearance of Lord Willington's—er—Petition Crown in the paper this morning? I thought you might be interested as it's something in your line.'

'Greatorex is, at all events,' replied Mr Carrados. 'He was half expecting that someone might bring it here in the course of the day. Do you—strictly between ourselves, of course—do you happen to have it for disposal, Louis?'

'Do I happen to have it for disposal?' repeated Mr Carlyle in a slightly mystified tone. 'I thought you would have read that the coin has been stolen. However, Max, in my office at this moment there is a young lady who is very much concerned at being implicated in the affair. Frankly, as the auctioneers are naturally doing all that can be done to solve the riddle, I did not see how I could be of any real service to her, and I told her so. But she seemed so disappointed that as a—er—well—'

'As a sort of forlorn hope?' suggested the listener maliciously.

'Not at all; most certainly not!' protested Mr Carlyle indignantly. 'I explained that as you were both a keen coin collector yourself and an enthusiast in certain branches of criminal research, if—if, mind you, Max—you cared to hear what she had to say, you would be in an exceptional position to give her a word of advice. And that is really the long and the short of the whole matter, my mordacious friend.'

'Very likely, my ingenious sleuth, but I imagine that there is a small piece missing somewhere. You were not wont to turn young and beautiful suppliants from your office door. What is the real reason of this professional reluctance on your part?'

'Max,' came along Mr Carlyle's cautiously-restrained voice—the listener could divine how near the moving lips were to the mouthpiece—'I will speak to you as one gentleman to another when there is no danger of being overheard. Miss Frensham is young, but she is not beautiful, and to put it in that way is to pay her a noticeable compliment. She is also, I gather, regrettably hard up. Now, as I never conceal from my clients, my business is conducted on a purely financial basis, whereas you amuse yourself for—the other thing. Doubtless I could earn a few honest but ill-spared guineas at this young lady's expense, but I cannot satisfy myself that she would be any the wiser for the outlay. And so—'

'All right, you old humbug,' said Carrados amiably; 'send her along. So far as the portents go I am with you in not seeing that there is much to be done for her, but if she finds any satisfaction in talking about it you can tell her that I shall be here for the next few hours.'

Miss Frensham evidently did foresee some satisfaction in talking about it, for she came at once. In view of her circumstances, Carrados could not but deem her rather extravagant, for nothing but a taxi from door to door could explain the promptness of her arrival. Mr Carlyle had not maligned her looks: plain she undoubtedly was, not in any sense describably ugly but with a sort of pug-dog grotesquery. Her dress made no attempt to counteract physical deficiencies, but when she spoke Carrados's unemotional face instantly lit up with pleasure, for, unexpected in such a setting, her voice had the rare quality of gracious music.

'How good of you to let me come in this way, Mr Carrados!' she exclaimed as they shook hands. 'I don't know which I have to thank the more—you or Mr Carlyle.'

'I think I shall claim the major share,' said the blind man lightly. 'Not for any particular merit, but because I am so very pleased to hear you.'

'To hear—Oh, yes; of course he told me or I really should not have guessed. You know what it's all about?'

'I infer that you are the lady of the paragraph,' and the lifted hand indicated the open sheet of the *Record* lying nearby.

'Yes, in a sense I am.' Miss Frensham seemed troubled for a moment. 'But I am not really a "well-known lady journalist", Mr Carrados. I am only a very obscure one—hardly a real journalist at all. That was just swank, and also because I felt sure that under that description no one who knew would ever think of *me*.'

'Oh,' said Mr Carrados with an amused and deepening interest, 'so in addition to being the heroine of the adventure you wrote it up?'

'Yes, ultimately I did. At first I was too upset to think about that. But I had gone to the place yesterday to see if there wasn't a "news-story" in this Petition Crown—nothing but "news-stories" are worthwhile, you know—and it seemed rather a pity to miss it when it turned out to be a very much better "news-story" than I had ever expected. And then I knew that if I got my "copy" taken I could keep my own name out. I had particular reasons for wishing that.'

Carrados nodded without showing any curiosity about the reasons. 'What is it exactly that you want to do now?' he asked.

'Well, I feel that I am really under suspicion of having taken the coin—I don't see how they can think anything else in the circumstances—and the only way of clearing myself is to find out who did take it. Knowing that I didn't, I naturally think that it must be the attendant there, because he seems to have been the only other person who could have done.'

'Reverse the argument, and the attendant, knowing that he didn't, naturally thinks that it must be you, because you seem to be the only other person who could have done. And so both sides get into difficulties along that obvious line. Suppose we ignore the two palpable suspects—yourself and the attendant. Now who else might it have been?'

'That is the difficulty, Mr Carrados; it could have been no one else. I returned the coin to the attendant; he put it back in the case and remained on duty there until he displayed it on the tray to show round. Then it was discovered to have been taken.'

'I suppose,' said Carrados tentatively, 'you really were the last to inspect the coin? Sitting there you would probably have noticed if anyone else had asked for it?'

'I only know what they said, but no one seemed to have any doubt about it. I went out to—to get some lunch and when I got back the sale was going on.'

'Ah,' said the blind man thoughtfully. 'Of course you would have to. Suppose you tell me the—the "news-story" all through.'

'I hoped that you would let me,' replied the girl. 'But I was afraid of taking up too much of your time. Well, I have been living by journalism for some time now. Rather suddenly I had to support myself by some kind of work, and there was nothing else that I seemed able to do. I have always been fond of writing, and I had quite a lot of stories and articles and poems that I had been told by friends were quite good enough to print. I brought them to London with me, but somehow they didn't seem so much thought of here. I got to know one or two other girls who wrote, and they told me that my sort of stuff would be all right when I got into the peerage or became a leading lady, but if I wanted to live meanwhile it was absolutely necessary to cultivate a "news-nose". I soon saw what they meant: it wasn't absolutely necessary that it should be news you wrote, but it had to give the impression that it was.'

'Miss Frensham, I have been a practical journalist myself,' remarked Carrados. 'You had grasped the sacred torch.'

'At all events, I could just keep the domestic pot boiling after that. It was rather a near thing sometimes, but there was someone—he is a sub-editor on the *Daily Record* actually—who helped me more than I can ever say. He told me of this sale. "There's a coin to be sold that's expected to break the record," he said; and he explained to me which it was. "There ought to be a 'news-story' in it if it does—say two hundred words in the ordinary way, four hundred if you can make it kick. I'll try and put it through." I thought that I had made it kick, so I went to four hundred.'

'Yes,' agreed her auditor, 'I certainly think you can claim that amount of movement.'

'I didn't know anything about a coin auction, of course, but I looked up Simon in the biographical dictionary at the B.M. reading-room and then went on to the place. That was yesterday—the morning of the sale. There were two or three others—men—looking at the coins—nothing to what I had expected—and one attendant who gave out the drawers in which they were arranged as they were asked for.

'I expected some sort of formality before they let me see the crown—so valuable—but there was really nothing at all. I just said, "Can I see No. 64, please?" and he simply pulled one of the shallow drawers out of its case and put it down before me on the table. There were about a dozen other lots in the drawer, each in its separate little box. Then he turned his back on me to attend to something else. I believe that I could have picked up the coin and walked out of the place with it.'

'We are a trustful people both in war and peace,' conceded Mr Carrados. 'But I think you would have found that you couldn't quite do that.'

'Well, I didn't try—though it certainly did occur to me that there might be a stunt of some sort in it: you look out for them when one means a week's good keep. I made a few notes that I thought I could work in and then found that it was just one o'clock—the sale was to begin at a quarter past. As the attendant took the coins away I asked him how fast they sold them.

'"If you only want to see that lot sold, miss, a quarter to two will be in plenty of time. If you reckon a hundred lots to the hour you'll be well on the safe side."

'I thanked him and went out. That was really all I had to do with the coin. I never saw it again. When I got back to the sale room the auction was going on. Even then there were only about twelve or fifteen people there. They sat at the tables—I suppose you know how they are arranged, as a sort of hollow oblong, with the auctioneer at one end and the attendant showing the coins up and down in the middle?—and a few sitting here and there about the room. I didn't sit down; I stood between the table and the door waiting for the price of Lot 64, which was the only thing I wanted.

'When he got to it there was a slight stir of interest, though a more lethargic set of enthusiasts I never saw. I always imagined that collectors were a most excitable race who lost their heads at bidding and went on and on madly. These might have been buying arrowroot for all the emotion they showed.'

'Half of them would be dealers who had long ago got over all human enthusiasms; the remainder would be collectors, too afraid lest the others should think that they were keen on something. And then?'

'The attendant was carrying the coin round on a little tray when one man picked it up and looked at it. "Hullo!" he said and passed it to the next. "This is the wrong lot," said that one, and then the auction-eer leaned over and called to the attendant, "Come, come, my lad—No. 64," and the attendant said, "This is No. 64," in an aggrieved way and showed him the numbered box. Then the attendant and those near that end began to look among the unsold lots, and after that they all turned out the sold lots—they had mostly been put into little envelopes—and when they came to the end of these everyone looked at everyone else and said nothing. Then I think they began it all over again—the hunting, I mean—when the auctioneer hit on his desk.

'"This is an important lot. Very sorry, but we can't go on with the selling until we know more where we are. I suppose someone did see the Petition Crown this morning?"

'Two or three men said that they had, and the attendant, looking round, recognised me.

'"That lady was the last to see the lot before the sale, sir," I heard him say. "Better ask her."

'"Did you—" began the auctioneer, and then, I suppose, recognis-ing that I mightn't like to carry on a shouting conversation across the room, he added, "Do you mind coming round here?"

'I went round the tables to where he was sitting, and he contin-ued:

'"Did you see this lot before the sale? Our man thinks that you were the last to have it out."

'"Yes," I admitted. "I saw it, and it was there when I returned the drawer. Of course I don't know that I was the last, but it was about one o'clock."

'"No one had it out later, Muir?"

'"No, sir. I've been on this spot ever since, and that tray hasn't been asked for."

'The auctioneer seemed to consider, and everyone else looked first at one and then the other of us. I began to feel very uncomfortable.

'"I suppose it really was the Petition Crown you saw at one o'clock?" he asked after a bit.

'"I suppose it must have been," I replied. "I copied the 'Petition' from the edge into this notebook."

'"Well, that fixes it all right. You see how awkward it is for us, Miss—Miss—"

'I gave him my name.

'"Miss Frensham. We have to do the best we can in the circum-stances. I can't say at the moment on whom the loss will fall—if the coin really proves to have disappeared—but the figure is considerable. Now everyone else in the room is known to us by sight; we have the names and addresses of them all"

'"You have my name," I said, "and I am living at the Allied Arts Hostel in Lower Gower Street."

'"Thank you," he replied, writing it down. "But of course that means very little to us. Is there anyone convenient who knows you personally to whom we can refer? You must understand that this does not imply any sort of suspicion of your *bona fides*: it is only putting you on equal terms with the rest of the company."

'I thought for a moment. I saw a great many unpleasant possibilities. Most of all I knew that I wanted to keep this from my people.

'"The editor of the *Daily Record* knows me slightly," I replied; "but I don't see that he can say anything beyond that. And as to suspicion, I am afraid that you already have some. If you have any ladies on your staff I am quite willing to turn out everything I have before them"—I thought that perhaps this would settle the matter off-hand, and I couldn't help adding rather viciously: "and after that I dare say the rest of the company will do the same before you."

'"Yes," he considered, "but you've been out for half an hour, so that would really prove nothing. At lunch, I suppose?"

'I began to see that things were fitting in rather unpleasantly for me.

'"Yes," I said.

'"Perhaps I had better note where you went. We don't know where this may land us, and in the end it may be to your interest to have a waitress or someone who can identify you over that time."

'"I'm afraid I can't do that," I had to say. "There was no one who noticed me."

'"Surely—Well, anyhow, the place?"

'I shook my head. He looked at me for a moment and then wrote something down. . . . You think that was very suspicious, Mr Carrados?'

'Your advocate never thinks that anything you do is suspicious,' replied the suave listener. 'Probably they would.'

'They seemed to. Well, Mr Carrados, I don't mind telling you, but somehow I couldn't say it before that—I felt—unfriendly battery eyes . . . . My lunch consisted of three very unladylike thick slices of bread-and-butter, and I ate them as I walked slowly up and down the stairs at a tube station. So, you see, there could be no corroboration.'

'Perhaps we shall do better—not even require it,' he replied quietly. 'What happened next?'

'I don't think that there was much more. They gave up looking for the coin. The auctioneer said that he had telephoned to someone—his solicitor or Scotland Yard, I imagined, but I didn't hear which—to know what ought to be done, and he hoped that everyone would remain until they knew. The sale began again. I went across and sat down on a chair away from the table. I had no interest in the sale—in fact I hated it—and after a time I took out my pad and tried to write the paragraph. Very soon the sale came to an end and the men began to go—I suppose they had been told to. I waited, for I wasn't going to seem in a hurry, until I was the only person left. After a bit the man who had been selling came in and seemed rather surprised to see me still there. He said he hoped I didn't think that I was being detained, and I said, "Oh, no, I was just finishing something." He said that that was all right, only they were going to lock up the room then and have it thoroughly looked over today—it was just possible that something might turn up, though he was rather afraid that it would remain a mystery to the end. He was quite nice about it, and told me several curious things that had happened in connexion with sales in the past. Then I left and he locked the door after us and, I believe, took the key.'

Carrados laughed appreciatively.

'Yes, it was rather like the proverb about the stolen horse, wasn't it?' said the girl. 'But I suppose they felt that even the unlikeliest chance must be taken. Anyway, they have certainly sent inquiries both to my Hostel and to the Record office. That's chiefly why I want to have my poor character restored. Everyone says, "Of course, Miss Frensham, nobody would think for a moment—" But what else are they to think privately? The thing has gone and I am branded as the last to handle it.'

'Yes, yes,' said Carrados, beginning to walk about the room and to touch one familiar object after another in his curiously unhesitating way. 'That unfortunate "last" has obsessed you and all the others until it has shut out every real consideration. Your account of the whole business—quite clear so far as it goes—is entirely based on the fact that you were the last, and the attendant knew you were the last, and the auctioneer was told you were the last, and all the others grasped it, and you all proceeded to revolve round that centre. There stands the man we want, as plain as a pikestaff for us, only you and your lastness get between so persistently that we cannot see him.'

'I'm very sorry,' faltered Miss Frensham, rather taken aback.

'That's all right, my dear young lady,' said an entirely benevolent Carrados. 'We are getting on very nicely on the whole, and soon you will begin to tell me the things I really want to know.'

'Indeed I will tell you anything,' she protested.

'Of course you will—as soon as I have the gumption to ask. In the meantime what do you really think of the celebrated Petition Crown now that you've seen it?'

This light conversational opening struck Miss Frensham as rather an unpropitious way of grappling with the problem of the theft, but she had just professed her general willingness.

'Well,' she replied with conscientious effort, 'it chiefly struck me as rather absurd that people should be willing to pay so much for this one when other coins, apparently almost like it, could be had for a few shillings.'

'Yes; very true.' The blind man appeared to consider this naive expression deeply. 'As a collector myself of course that goes home. You are not a collector, in any sense, Miss Frensham?'

'No, indeed.'

'I was wondering,' speculated Carrados in the same idle vein, 'how you happened to know that.'

'Oh, very simply. There were about a dozen other lots in the drawer the man put before me. One of them consisted of quite a number of crown pieces, and they struck me as being so like the Petition Crown at a glance that out of curiosity I compared them. When it came to the sale they made only a few pounds for the lot.'

'You compared them—side by side?'

'Yes. I—I—' As she spoke Miss Frensham suddenly went very white, half rose from her chair, and sat down again. The charming voice trailed off into a gasp.

'You remember something now? You—possibly—changed them somehow?'

'*I did!* I see it all. I remember exactly how it went. What a dreadful thing!'

'Tell me what happened.'

'I was waiting for the attendant to turn so that I could tell him I had finished. It was then that I took up these two coins—the Petition Crown and one from another box—to compare. There was a man near me who had seemed to be watching—at least I thought so—and just then I looked up and caught his eyes on me. I suppose it made me nervous; anyway I dropped one of the crowns back into the drawer. It made a great clatter as it fell among the others and I felt that it would be almost a crime there to knock a coin like that. I just slipped the other into its place and pushed the drawer away as the attendant turned. And now I see as clearly as can be that I returned them wrong.'

'That is our real starting-point.' said Carrados happily. 'Now we can proceed.'

'But it must have been found out. All the sold lots were looked over again.'

'Oh, yes; it must have been found out. But exactly when? The man who was observing you—did you hear his name?'

'No.'

'Where did he sit during the sale?'

'He sat—yes, that's rather curious. You remember that after talking to the auctioneer I went and sat down away from the table? Well, when the selling was going on again this man kept hovering round. Presently he bent down to me and said, "Excuse me, but you have taken my seat." "What on earth do you mean?" I retorted, for it was just at the time that I was feeling exasperated. "There was nothing on the chair, and there are a dozen others there," and I pointed to the whole empty row. Then he said, "Oh, I beg your pardon," and went and sat down on another.'

'Isn't it splendid!' exclaimed Carrados in one of his rare bursts of enthusiasm. 'No sooner have we got rid of you and the attendant as the only possible culprits than we find the real man absolutely fighting to make himself known—doing everything he can to attract our attention—struggling like a chicken emerging from its shell. Soon you will tell me that you found his hand on the back of your chair.'

'Oh!' cried Miss Frensham in sharp surprise. 'How can you possibly know that?'

'I did not; but it was worth while suggesting to you.'

'It's absolutely true. I certainly shouldn't have thought it worth while mentioning, but just at the end of the sale, when everyone got up, he passed behind me, and stopping, he put his hand—rather gratuitously it seemed—on my chair and asked me if I had heard what the last lot made. I said that I wasn't taking the least notice, and he went away. What does it mean?'

'At the moment it means that we must telephone to Lang's to

keep the stable door locked—don't put your trust in proverbs, Miss Frensham. And there are a few questions I want them to have settled before I call there.'

'I dare say I'm an idiot,' said the lady frankly, 'but I'm beginning to get rather excited. Isn't there anything that I can do to help?'

'Why, yes,' he smiled with friendly understanding. 'Make out the list for me. We need the catalogue—it's over there. Now which was the lot of crowns you compared with?'

'This one—No. 56,' she replied, after studying the pages. '"Charles II, Crowns, various dates, in fine condition generally, 7."'

'That's sufficient. You have your pad? Now write:

CONFIDENTIAL. PLEASE ASCERTAIN

(1) Who bought Lot 56?
(2) What man, if any, left the sale-room about one o'clock and returned before Lot 56 was sold?
(3) What man, if any, returned after the sale for something he had left in the room?

'Of course,' he seemed to apologise, 'that gives away the whole show to you.'

'Ye—es,' replied Miss Frensham dutifully.

Mr Carrados insisted on his visitor remaining to lunch. He even arranged that no one else should be present on the occasion, and the guest, justly annoyed at this characteristic masculine act of delicacy, repaid him by discovering the appetite of the proverbial fairy. The ghosts of three slabs of bread-and-butter stood between her and that generous table; and, reflecting on that, the whimsical maiden sought her own means to dispel the spectre.

'It is really my fault that the coin has gone,' she found occasion to remark. 'Almost as much as though I had taken it. If it never turns up again I can't be satisfied until I have made it good.'

Carrados was naturally horrified. Was she mad? Had she forgotten its record?

'My dear young lady, don't be romantic. The coin is insured, or ought to be. Why, it would cripple you for years—for ever.'

'Oh, no,' she retorted airily. 'We all expect to make our fortunes. And I really have some money that I don't use.'

'Yes?' he smiled, and in the character of her intimate adviser the words slipped out: 'How much?'

'Well,' she considered with deliberate effect, 'I think it varies....

But'—with devastating clearness—'it is somewhere about three thousand pounds a year.'

'I beg your pardon?' stammered Carrados. 'No, no; don't say it again. I heard perfectly. I see. I understand. You ran away from it?'

'I ran away—if you call it running away—from several things. If you could see me, Mr Carrados, you would understand that I am endowed with an almost supernatural plainness. It is too obvious even for the glass to conceal from me. At school, where politeness is not one of the compulsory subjects, I was "Pup", "Puggy", "Ki-ki", "Balcombe Beauty", "Snarleywow", and other shafts of endearment. I was not petted. Even my mother found it a little trying. . . . And yet as I grew up I learned that I could be astonishingly popular with most men. The things I said were witty, the things I did were clever, my taste was exquisite, and they were all prepared to marry me . . . . But when I happened to wander into the society of strange men who had missed hearing of my pecuniary worth, my word! No one noticed that I hadn't a seat, no one thought of asking me to dance, to sing, to skate. They didn't see me.

'And if I opened my mouth they very rarely even heard me. And then if a really pretty girl happened to come into the circle! What an instant preening up of the fishy-eyed old men and a strutting round of the bored-to-death young ones! They didn't even take the trouble to hide anything from me: I might have been a man too. I could watch them licking their lips and arranging their attractions. Oh—h! do you wonder that I went sick among it all? There was a man my father wanted me to marry; well, at all events a decent sort of male, it seemed. I was beginning to think that I might as well when that came out. No, it doesn't really matter what. My father thought it needn't make any difference! Mother assured me that it was nicer not to notice these things!

'When I said that it made all the difference and that I had already noticed a great many things and that I was going away out into the world to see if it was the same everywhere and meant to begin by earning my own living of course I raised a tremendous storm. Then— if I must go—they wanted to arrange things for me, so that everything should be quite nice. But they'd been arranging for me all my life and that was just what I wanted to disarrange. In the end I got my way— you see, I was in rather a strong position—subject to certain conditions. Father stipulated that I didn't get into any "damned mess", or back I should have to go. Mother hoped that her girlie would remain unspotted from the world. So here I am. And that's the whole story, Mr Carrados, and the reason why I'm so anxious to keep out of what I am sure my father would call a—ahem—mess.'

'Poor Louis!' thought his friend. Then aloud, 'And is human nature entirely transformed by the five-mile radius, Miss Frensham?'

'No,' she admitted seriously. 'But at least I know exactly where I am. There is no competition to carry my parcel or to run my errands—I hope I haven't given the impression that I want it?—but if anything I do does happen to get praised I can believe it honest; if I make a friend I can really feel that it is for myself. . . . I am no longer, as I heard of one "admirer" dubbing me, "The Girl with the Golden Mug".'

Both laughed. Then he grew almost pensive.

'After laughing at that let me say something,' he ventured at length. 'When you needn't fear having to meet a man's eyes ever he may be privileged to an unusual frankness . . . . Think as little of looks as you do of lucre, Miss Frensham. I can know nothing of the features you so dispraise: to me you would always be the girl with the golden voice. I am sure that someone else will see you—as you think you are—as little as I do, and to him you will always be the girl with the golden heart.'

'You kind man!' she responded. 'Well. . . . perhaps there is!'

******

When Carrados got down to Lang & Leng's a few hours later he found that the seller on the previous day had been Mr Travis, a gentleman to whom he was by no means a stranger.

'Very glad to have your suggestions, of course, Carrados,' remarked Mr Travis graciously. 'Are you looking into it on Lord Willington's behalf? Miss Frensham's! You don't say so!'

'I have a weakness for being on the winning side,' remarked the blind man.

'Well, as to that, I don't know that it's exactly a case of a winning side or a losing side. Unless you call us the losing side, egad! This is the room. You want to look—to go round it?'

'I should like to. One never knows.'

'Oh, we've been thoroughly over it this morning. Heaven knows what we could expect, but it seemed the natural thing to do. Yes, it's still being kept locked, since you asked.'

'Anyone wanting to go in for anything?'

'No—only Mr Marrabel, who called for his gloves after the sale; they'd been taken to the office though.'

'Marrabel!' thought the patient worker in the dark. 'Yes, of course—Marrabel the *dilettante.*'

'And, by the way, that reminds me,' continued Mr Travis. 'Oh yes, sit anywhere you like. That list you sent through. You're not going to suspect Marrabel of any connexion? Because, strangely enough, his name is the answer to each of your inquiries.'

'I should scarcely describe it as a case for suspicion,' replied Carrados. 'Still, one thinks of everyone.'

'We can eliminate Mr Marrabel at all events, I think. He did not look at any of the lots yesterday. He only bought No. 56, and both Muir and I noticed that he did not touch the coins when he got them–just put them on an empty chair by his side until the hue and cry was raised, and then he passed the box over to the table for someone to verify—all there and the correct number.'

'Very convincing,' assented Carrados.

'I mean it rather shows that there isn't much to be gained by looking for so-called "clues" at this end, don't you think? Marrabel as a case in point. Of course we shall be delighted to put any information or facilities that we may have at your disposal, Carrados, both out of consideration for yourself and as due to your client. But what *we* chiefly want is to get the coin back. And the people we have put on to it seem to be extending themselves in that direction. By tomorrow every curio-dealer, pawnbroker, and leading collector will be on the look out, America will be notified, for they think that the coin may be quite likely offered there. A reward is being offered to make it worth anybody's while. In the next number of the *Bric-à-brac Collector* there will be an ingenuous advertisement from a wealthy colonial anxious to buy rare milled silver coins; don't be deceived by it.'

'I won't,' promised Mr Carrados. 'But all this must come rather expensive.'

'Doubtless it is. But the fact is, since the thing has gone, Willington's people are persuading themselves that it might have made a fantastic price. That is why we are only anxious to get it back again.'

'Oh!' Polite unconcern was Carrados's note. He seldom denied himself these rare moments when, perhaps, a week's patient labour ran down to a needle-point. 'Of course I'm more interested in my client. But as the coin is all you want—why, here it is!'

'What—what's—that?' articulated Mr Travis.

'The Petition Crown,' replied the arch-humbug, continuing to hold out his hand. 'Delighted to be the means of restoring it to you,

Travis.'

'It is the Petition Crown,' murmured Travis. 'Good God! You brought it?'

'On the contrary, I found it here.'

'Found it? Where?'

'Beneath the seat of this chair.'

'You knew that it was there? Do you mean that Miss Frensham told you?'

'I knew that it should be here, and Miss Frensham certainly told me.'

'She hid it there?'

'Not at all. She did not know that it was here. She told me where it was, but she did not know that she was telling me.'

'Then I'm hanged if I understand,' complained Mr Travis. 'Can't you be human once in a way, Carrados? Damn it all, man, we went to school together!'

'Sit down,' said Carrados, 'and I'll be as human as you like.... Did you ever commit a crime, Travis?'

'Not really,' confessed the auctioneer with admirable sang-froid. 'I robbed an orchard when I was ten, but that—'

'Robbing orchards at ten scarcely counts, does it? Well, I have the advantage because there is no form of villainy that I haven't gone through in all its phases. Theoretically, of course, but so far as working out the details is concerned and preparing for emergencies, efficiently and with craftsmanlike pride. Whenever I fail to get to sleep at night—rather frequently, I'm sorry to say—I commit a murder, forgery, a robbery or what not, with all its ramifications. It's much more soothing than counting sheep and it never fails to get me off. The point is, that the criminal mind is rarely original, and I find that in nine cases out of ten that sort of crime is committed exactly as I have already done it. Being a collector myself, of course, I've robbed coin auctions frequently. I know precisely how it should be done and what is to be avoided. Marrabel did the correct things, but he overlooked the contingency of someone else also thinking of them.'

'But Marrabel, my dear fellow! He must be almost in Debrett. Think!'

'Oh, yes. But he makes a speciality of getting choice things for nothing, provided there is no risk.'

'And is there no risk here?'

'None at all; practically none if he's content to take his loss. But is he? We shall see. However, this is what has happened so far:

'Miss Frenshaw started the business by mixing Lots 56 and 64 without knowing it at the time. She had come to get a newspaper par out of the sale if she could, and was taking an intelligent interest in the subject when she happened to catch Marrabel overlooking her. Well, being nervy and rather touchy she dropped the Petition Crown on to the other crowns in Lot 56 and put the one from that lot into box No. 64.

'Marrabel evidently grasped that. It might prove a golden opportunity. Doubtless he took five minutes to consider the position. Then he hied him off to his Mayfair flat and returned with an appropriate coin in his pocket, well in time to purchase Lot 56. What did it cost him?'

'Three-fifteen,' said Mr Travis.

'You know well enough, Travis, that although a single-coin lot is generally taken up by someone as it goes round the table, half a dozen coins, like Lot 56, are seldom touched. At the most they are glanced at. When Muir turned them out on to his tray, what had been at the top naturally got hidden. When he returned them to the box, to hand over to the buyer, the Petition Crown perhaps came to the top again. Marrabel, seated in an unusually retiring position, doubtless received his booty with an appropriate gesture of unconcern and laid it carelessly on the next chair. Good. No risk so far.

'He had at least four minutes in which to act. You and Muir thought he paid no attention to the purchase because he didn't hold the box and examine the contents. Quite natural; but of course you weren't actually watching him and he was out to mask his movements. All in good time the exchange was made. But now the element of risk came in: he had the thing in his possession.

'Your amateur is always self-conscious. Marrabel could have walked off then, but that would certainly have put him in an equivocal position. Yet supposing it came to being searched? And Miss Frensham, you may remember, did throw out the suggestion. Whether he had reconnoitred in advance we need not speculate; but here beneath his chair, without moving, Marrabel found an ideal crevice for his loot: tight, hidden, accessible.

'He could now move away from the dangerous spot, and he did when the chase began, putting his purchase on the table with a fine indifference for someone else to verify. He stayed away from this chair so long that a curious thing occurred. Miss Frensham took it.

'In one way Marrabel was now on velvet. The leading suspect had drawn a red herring across his tracks, for if by any chance the crown should come to light here Miss Frensham was hopelessly involved. Then presently the situation eased; the sale was coming to an end and there was no suggestion now of search or of anyone being detained. His only desire was to recover the coin and get away. But the lady seemed set here, and Marrabel, ignorant of her intentions, made his first bad move. He claimed the chair, fully expecting to be given it at once.

'As it happened Miss Frensham didn't budge. She is far from being an ordinary meek young person, and the immediate events hadn't gone to soothe her. She was sitting there quietly writing, and, taken on the surface, it was sheerly an impertinence on the man's part. She had had occasion to notice Marrabel already. In strictly feminine terms she told him to go to the devil, and Marrabel, now beginning to feel jerky, veered off.

'The sale comes to an end. Everyone begins to go. Is Marrabel to hang about aimlessly until this chair is vacant and then deliberately come and sit here for no obvious reason? The man's tightened nerves won't hear of it. Act naturally and there is no risk at all. Return later—tomorrow, next week, it doesn't matter, the coin is snugly waiting. And then, good heavens! the thing flashes on him. The chairs are all alike! Next week, tomorrow, even after the sale they may be rearranged, moved, taken to another room, and he will have to go sitting on one after another, an object for all to marvel at. What's to be done? Why, plainly to mark the chair before it is too late, and here, Travis, under my fingers, is the cross that our man broke his pencil on.'

'Very ingenious,' admitted Mr Travis, 'and in the face of this evidence'—delicately balancing the recovered crown upon a finger-tip—'it would be mean to argue. But, you know, Carrados, Miss Frensham *did* sit here last.'

'Inflexible man!' replied Carrados. 'Well, when is your next sale?'

'Friday—enamels. On view for one day only.'

'So much the better. You can have it in here? Keep it closed till then and I will be here early. And just make sure that Marrabel is sent his catalogue, won't you?'

★★★★★★

There was nothing at all unusual to be noticed about the sale-rooms on Thursday morning, and Mr Marrabel strolled round in perfect composure. With praiseworthy restraint he had not hastened there, and the group of conspirators in the private office had to amuse themselves as best they could for at least two hours.

Marrabel was interested in enamels, as he was in all precious things, and he wandered from point to point consulting his catalogue, examining a piece and marking a price as he had done a score of times before—as everyone else was doing then. Finally he sat down to review his list: nothing could be more natural. Satisfied, he rose to go.

Outside the room an attendant came across to speak to him: the signal had been passed.

'Do you mind stepping into Mr Travis's office, sir? I think he wants to see you about something.'

The message was polite and not wholly unusual, but Marrabel's throat went dry.

'Not now,' he said, quickening his step. 'I have an important—. Back in half an hour, tell him.'

It was too late for that easy manoeuvre to carry. Across the hall there was another form between him and the outer door. Nor did the first one obligingly retire.

'Beg pardon, sir, but I understand it's rather particular, sir.'

Then Marrabel must have known that something had miscarried.

'Oh, curse it, all right,' he snapped and, watched at every step, he went.

'It's about the Petition Crown that disappeared at the last coin sale.' The urbane Travis never had a less relished job. 'We have received certain information and we may have to take proceedings. Do you wish to make any statement?'

Marrabel had dimly foreseen this possibility and he had given some thought to a satisfactory explanation, but in the end he had left it to be decided by the circumstances of the moment, because there was no perfectly satisfactory explanation to be thought of.

'Well,' he said, affecting a light laugh, 'that's an unnecessarily brutal way of putting it, because, as a matter of fact, I was bringing the crown to return to you, and I have it in my pocket at the moment. It was only this morning I discovered it when I came to look into that lot I bought. How it got there and how it came to be missed by the dolts who looked I can't say. Personally I didn't examine one of the coins until today.'

'I see,' remarked Mr Travis. 'But I understand that you were leaving the place just now?'

'You understand quite right. I intended handing you the crown, but when I got here and realised how cursed unpleasant it might be I funked it. I decided to send the damned thing back by post without a word.'

'At all events you have it for us now?'

'Yes, here it is,' and Marrabel took a coin from his pocket with alacrity, and laying it on the desk turned hopefully to go.

'Thanks, but—one moment—what is this?'

The unhappy man looked at the coin he had just produced and turned paler than before.

'I must have picked up the wrong one,' he muttered, beginning to recognise the hopeless morass he was floundering into.

'Look again,' said a quiet voice as Mr Carrados appeared on the scene. 'Look closer at the coin you brought from your room this morning!'

'You blind devil!' Lightly scratched on the surface of the silver he found the signature 'Max Carrados' and the date of that very day. 'This is your doing all through!'

'If it is it is only to show up a scoundrel. You didn't stick at getting two innocent people suspected by your scheme. Let them see you now.'

As if worked by machinery an inner door fell open and Miss Frensham and Muir walked in and stood silently regarding him.

'At the sale,' continued Carrados pitilessly, 'you were both publicly put in a position of some suspicion by the disappearance of a coin. It is right that you should now know that it was deliberately stolen by Mr Marrabel here. He is the thief and your perfect innocence is established.'

'Well, curse it all, it wasn't entirely my fault,' snarled Marrabel. 'I only accepted what was given me.'

'That will be for a judge and jury to assess. You'll give him in charge now, Travis?'

At this prospect Marrabel's last vestige of pretence broke down. All the poltroonery in the man came to the surface with a rush.

'For God's sake don't do that, Travis,' he cried, clutching him by the sleeve. 'I'll do anything you wish—confess anything you like—only don't have me sent to prison. I'll put all sorts of things your way, and I know crowds of people. Heavens! man, consider what it would mean to me—one of your own class.'

'What shall we do, Carrados? We never like to prosecute.'

'I know you don't,' replied the blind man. 'I've already drawn up his confession. Read this and then sign it, Mr Marrabel, and we will all be witnesses of the spontaneous act of reparation on your part.'

'What are you going to do with it?' asked the unfortunate wretch.

'Keep it as a guarantee of future good behaviour, and to vindicate these others if the necessity occurs. And you needn't think of having me knifed to get it back again, because I shan't carry it in my pocketbook.'

Marrabel slowly signed and then stabbed the polished desk with the pen he held in a gust of passion that left his fingers pierced and bleeding.

'I'd go willingly to hell if I could first see you skinned alive, Carrados,' he said as he turned to leave.

'I am sure you would,' retorted Max Carrados pleasantly. 'But I don't think that anything to do with me need affect your destination. Now go.'

This did not happen last year nor yet the year before. Miss Frensham married her sub-editor, and their children—now old enough to go to school—frequently take prizes at quite important beauty competitions. Mr Marrabel almost immediately left these inhospitable shores, and after a seemly interval appeared in flourishing conditions in New York. Not that American connoisseurs know less than English ones do, but they know less of Mr Marrabel.

The Holloway Flat Tragedy

A good many years ago, when chance brought Max Carrados and Louis Carlyle together again and they renewed the friendship of their youth, the blind man's first inquiry had been a jesting, 'Do you unearth many murders, Louis?' and the private detective's reply a wholly serious, 'No; our business lies mostly on the conventional lines among defalcation and divorce.' Since that day Carlyle's business had increased beyond the fondest dreams of its creator, but 'defalcation and divorce' still constituted the bulwarks of his prosperity. Yet from time to time a more sensational happening or a more romantic course raised a case above the commonplace, but none, it is safe to say, ever rivalled in public interest the remarkable crime which was destined to become labelled in the current Press as 'The Holloway Flat Tragedy.'

It was Mr Carlyle's rule to see all callers who sought his aid, for the very nature of their business precluded clients from willingly unbosoming themselves to members of his office staff. Afterwards, they might accept the discreet attention of tactful subordinates, but for the first impression Carlyle well knew the value of his sympathetic handshake, his crisply reassuring voice, his—if need be—humanly condoning eye, and his impeccably prosperous person and surroundings. Men and women, guilty and innocent alike, pouring out their stories felt that at last they were really 'understood', and, to give Louis Carlyle his due, the deduction was generally fully justified.

To the quiet Bampton Street establishment one September afternoon there came a new client who gave the name of Poleash and wished to see Mr Carlyle in person. There was, as usual, no difficulty about that, and, looking up from his desk, Louis registered the impression of an inconspicuous man, somewhere in the thirties. He used spectacles, wore a moustache, and his clothes were a lounge suit of dark material, cut on the simple lines affected by the prudent man who reflects that he may be wearing that selfsame garment two or three seasons hence. There was a slight air of untidiness—or rather, perhaps, an absence of spruceness in any detail—about his general appearance, and the experienced observer put him down as a middle-class worker in any of the clerical, lower professional, or non-manual walks of life.

'Now, Mr Poleash, sit down and tell me what I can do for you,' said Carlyle when they had shaken hands—a rite to which the astute gentleman attached no slight importance and invariably offered. 'Some trouble or little difficulty, I suppose, umph? But first let me get you name right and have your address for reference. You can rely on this, Mr Poleash'—the inclination of Mr Carlyle's head and the arrest of his lifted pen were undeniably impressive—'every word you utter is strictly confidential.'

'Oh, that'll be all right, I'm sure,' said the visitor carelessly. 'It is rather out-of-the-way all the same, and at first—'

'The name?' insinuated Mr Carlyle persuasively.

'Albert Henry Poleash: P-o-l-e-a-s-h—twelve Meridon House, Sturgrove Road, Holloway.'

'Thank you. Now, if you will.'

'Of course I could tell you in a dozen words, but I expect you'd need to know the circumstances, so perhaps I may as well begin where I think you'll understand it best from.'

'By all means,' assented Mr Carlyle heartily; 'by all means. In your own words and exactly as it occurs to you. I'm entirely at your service, so don't feel hurried. Do you care—' The production of a plain gold case completed the inquiry.

'To begin with,' said Mr Poleash, after contributing a match to their common purpose, 'I may say that I'm a married man, living with my wife at that address—a smallish flat which suits us very well as we have no children. Neither of us has any near relations either, and we keep ourselves pretty much to ourselves. Our only servant is a daily woman, who seems able to do everything that we require.'

'One moment, if you please,' interposed Mr Carlyle briskly. 'I don't want you to do anything but tell your story in your own way, Mr Poleash, but if you would indicate by a single word the nature of the event that concerns us it would enable me to judge which points are likely to be most vital to our purpose. Theft—divorce—blackmail—'

'No—murder,' replied Mr Poleash with literal directness.

'Murder!' exclaimed the startled professional. 'Do you mean that a murder has been committed?'

'No, not yet. I am coming to that. For ordinary purposes I generally describe myself as a rent-collector, but that is because official Jacks-in-office seem to have a morbid suspicion of anyone who is obviously not a millionaire calling himself independent. As a matter of fact, I have quite enough private income to serve my purpose. Most of it comes from small house property scattered about London. I see to the management of this myself and personally collect the rents. It takes a few days a week, gives me an interest, keeps me in exercise, and pays as well as anything else I could be doing in the tune.'

'Quite so,' encouraged the listener.

'That's always there,' went on Mr Poleash, continuing his leisurely narrative with no indication of needing any encouragement, 'but now and then I take up other work if it suits me—certain kinds of special canvassing; sometimes research. I don't want to slave making more money than we have the need of, and I don't want ever to find that we haven't enough money for anything we may require.'

'Ideal,' contributed Mr Carlyle. 'You are a true philosopher.'

'My wife also has no need to be dependent on anyone either,' continued Mr Poleash, without paying the least attention to the suave compliment. 'As a costume designer and fashion artist she is fully qualified to earn her living, and in fact up to a couple of years ago she did work of that kind regularly. Then she had a long illness that made a great change in her. This brings me to one of the considerations that affect whatever I may wish to do: the illness left her a nervous wreck—jumpy, excitable, not altogether reasonable.'

'*Neurasthenia*,' was Mr Carlyle's seasonable comment. 'The symptom of the age.'

'Very likely. It doesn't affect me—at least it doesn't affect me directly. Living in the same house with Mrs Poleash, it's bound to affect me, because I have to consider how every blessed thing I do will affect her. And just lately something very lively indeed has come along.

'There is a girl in a shop that I got friendly with—no, I don't want you to put her name down yet. It began a year or eighteen months. . . . But I don't suppose that matters. The only thing I really think that I'm to blame about is that I never told her I was married. At first there was no reason why I should; afterwards—well, there was a certain amount of reason why I shouldn't. Anyhow, I suppose that it was bound to come out sooner or later, and it did, a few weeks ago. She said, quite nicely, that she thought we ought to get married as things were, and then, of course, I had to explain that we couldn't.

'I really hadn't the ghost of an idea that she'd take it so terribly to heart as she did. There's nothing of the Don Juan about me, as you can see at a glance. The thing had simply come about—one step leading to another. But she faulted clean away, and when she came to again she was like a solid block of ice to everything I said. And then to cap matters who should appear at that moment but a fellow she'd been half engaged to before I came along. She'd frequently spoken about this man—his jealousy and temper and so on—and begged me never to let him pick a quarrel with me. "Peter" was the only name I ever heard him called by, but he was a foreign-looking fellow—an Italian, I think.'

'"Pietro", perhaps?' suggested Mr Carlyle.

'No; "Peter" she called him. "Please take me back home, Peter," was all she said, and off they went together without a word from either to me. Whenever I've seen her since it's been the same. "Will I please leave her as there is nothing to be said?" and I've been trying to think of all manner of arrangements to put things right.'

'The only arrangement that would seem likely to do that is the one that's out of your power to make,' said Mr Carlyle.

'I suppose so. However, this Peter evidently had a different idea. This is what happened two nights ago. I woke up in the dark—it was about three o'clock I found afterwards—with one of those feelings you get that you've forgotten to do something. It was a letter that I should have posted: it was important that it got delivered some time the next day—the same day by then—and there it was in my breast pocket. I knew if I left it that I should never be up in time for the first morning dispatch, so I determined to slip out then and make sure of it.

'It would only be a matter of twenty minutes or so. There is a pillar-box nearer, but that isn't cleared early. I pulled on a few things and prepared to tiptoe out when a fresh thought struck me.

'Mrs Poleash is a very uncertain sleeper nowadays, and if she is disturbed it's ten to one if she gets off again, and for that reason we use different rooms. I knew better than wake her up to tell her I was going out, but at the same time there was just the possibility that she might wake and, hearing some noise, look in at my door to see if I was all right. If she found me gone she would nearly have a fit. On the spur of the moment I pushed the bolster down the bed and rucked up my dressing gown—it was lying about—above it. In the poor light it served very well for a sleeping man, and I knew that she would not disturb me.

'In less time than I'd given myself I had done my business and was back again at the building. I was entering—my hand was on the knob of the outer door in fact—when the door was pulled sharply open from the other side and another man and I came face to face on the step. We both fell back a bit, I think, but the next moment he had pushed past me and was hurrying down the street. There was just enough light from the lamp across the way for me to be certain of him; it was Peter, and I'm pretty sure that he was equally sharp in recognising me.

'Of course I went up the stairs in double quick time after that. The door of the flat was as I had left it—simply on the handle as I had put up the latch catch, never dreaming of anyone coming along in that time—and all was quiet and undisturbed inside. But one thing was different in my room, although it took me a few minutes to discover it. There was a clean cut through my dressing gown, through the sheet, through the bolster. Someone, Mr Carlyle, had driven a knife well home before he discovered his mistake.'

'But that was plain evidence of an attempt to murder,' declared Mr Carlyle feelingly—he disliked crimes of violence from every point of view. 'Your business is obviously to inform the police.'

'No,' replied the visitor slowly, 'no. Of course I thought of that, but I soon had to let it slide. What would it mean? Visits, inquiries, cross-examinations, explanations. Everything must come out. After a sufficient exhibition of nerve-storm Mrs Poleash would set about getting a divorce and I should have to go through that. Then I suppose I should have to marry the other one, and, when all's said and done, that's the last thing I really want. In any case, my home would be broken up and my whole life spoiled. No, if it comes to that I might just as well be dead.'

'Then what do you propose doing, may I ask? Calmly wait to be assassinated?'

'That's exactly what I came to see you about. You know my position, my difficulty. I understand that you are a man of wide experience. Putting aside the police and certain publicity, what should you advise?'

'Well, well,' admitted the expert, 'it's rather a formidable handicap, but we will do the best for you that is to be done. Can you indicate exactly what you want?'

'I can easily indicate exactly what I don't want. I don't want to be murdered or molested and I don't want Mrs Poleash to get wind of what's been going on.'

'Why not go away for a time? Meanwhile we could find out who your man is and keep him under observation.'

'I might do that—unless Kitty took it into her head that she didn't want to go, and then, of course, I couldn't leave her alone in the flat just now. After Tuesday night's business—this is what concerns me most—should you think it likely that the fellow would come again or not?'

Mr Carlyle pondered wisely. The longer he took over an opinion, he had discovered—providing he kept up the right expression—the greater weight attached to his pronouncement.

'No,' he replied with due authority. 'I should say not—not in anything like the same way. Of course he will naturally assume that you will now take due precautions—probably imagine that the police are after him. What sort of fastenings have you to your doors and windows?'

'Nothing out of the way. They are old flats and not in very good repair. The outer door is never kept locked, night or day. The front door of our flat has a handle, a latch lock, and a mortice lock. During the day it is simply kept on the latch; at night we fasten the other lock, but do not secure the latch, so that the woman can let herself in when she comes—she has one set of keys, I another, and Mrs Poleash the third.'

'But when you were out on Tuesday night there was no lock fastened, I understand?'

'That is so. Simply the handle to turn. I purposely fastened the latch lock out of action as I found at the door that I hadn't the keys with me and I didn't want to go back to the room again.'

'And the inner doors?'

'They have locks, but few now work—either the key is lost or the lock broken. We never trouble about them—except Kitty's room. She has scrupulously locked that at night, since she has had burglars among other nerve fancies.'

Mr Carlyle shook his head.

'You ought at the very least to have the locks put right at once. Practically all windows are fitted with catches that a child can push back with a table-knife.'

'That's all very well, but, you see, if I get a locksmith in I shall have to make up some cock-and-bull story about house-breaking to Mrs Poleash, and that will set her off. And, anyway, we are on the third storey up.'

'If you are going to consider your wife's nerves at every turn, my dear sir,' remarked Mr Carlyle with some contempt, from the security of his single state, 'you will begin to find yourself in rather a tight fix, I am afraid. How are you going to account for the cut linen, for instance?'

'Oh, I've arranged all that,' replied Mr Poleash, nodding sagaciously. 'My dressing gown she will never notice. The sheet and bolster case—it was a hot night so there was only a single sheet fortunately—I have hidden away in a drawer for the present and put others in their place. I shall buy another of each and burn or lose these soon—Kitty doesn't keep a very close check on things. The bolster itself I can sew up well enough before it's noticed.'

'You may be able to keep it up,' was Mr Carlyle's dubious admission. 'At all events,' he continued, 'as I understand it, you want me to advise you on the lines of taking no direct action against the man you call Peter and at the same time adopting no precautions that would strike Mrs Poleash as being unusual?'

'Nothing that would suggest burglars or murder to her just now,' assented Poleash. 'Yes; that's about what it comes to. You may be able to give me a useful tip or two. If not—well, I know it's a tough proposition and I don't grudge the outlay.'

'At least let us see,' replied the professional man, never failing on the side of lack of self-confidence. 'Now as regards—'

It redounds to Louis Carlyle's credit as an inquiry agent that in an exacting world no serious voice ever accused him of taking unearned money; for so long as there was anything to be learned he plied his novel client with questions, explored surmises and bestowed advice. Even when they had come to the end of useful conversation and the prolific notebook had been closed Carlyle lingered on the topic.

'It's an abnormal situation, Mr Poleash, and full of professional interest. I shall keep it in mind, you may be sure, and if anything further occurs to me, why, I will let you know.'

'Please don't write on any account,' begged Mr Poleash with sudden earnestness. 'In fact, I'd ask you to put a line to that effect across my address. You see, I'm liable to be out at any post time, and if my wife should happen to get curious about a strange letter, why, that, in the language of the kerb, would blow the gaff.'

'I see,' assented Mr Carlyle. 'Very well; it shall be just as you like.'

'And if I can settle with you now,' continued Poleash; 'for of course I don't want to have an account sent. Then some day—say next week—I might look in to report and to hear if you have anything further to suggest.'

'You might, in the meanwhile, consider the most practical course—that of having your man kept under observation.'

'I will,' promised the other. 'But so far I'm all in favour of letting sleeping dogs lie.'

Not unnaturally Mr Carlyle had heard that line before and had countered it.

'True, but it is as well to know when they wake up again,' he replied. With just the necessary touch of dignity and graciousness he named and received the single guinea at which he assessed the interview and began to conduct Mr Poleash towards the door—not the one by which he had entered from the waiting-room but another leading directly down into the street. 'Have you lost something?'

'Only my hat and things—I left them in your ante-room.' He held up his gloved left hand as though it required a word of explanation. 'I keep this on because I am short of a finger, and I've noticed that some people don't like to see it.'

'We'll go out that way instead then—it's all the same,' remarked Carlyle, as he crossed to the other door.

Two later callers were sitting in the waiting-room, and at the sight of them Mr Carlyle's somewhat cherubic face at once assumed an expression of the heartiest welcome. But beyond an unusually mellifluent 'Good afternoon!' he said nothing until his departing client was out of hearing. Names were not paraded in those precincts. With a muttered apology Mr Poleash recovered his belongings from among the illustrated papers and hurried away.

'And why in the world have you been waiting here, Max, instead of sending in to me?' demanded the hospitable Carlyle with a show of indignation.

'Business,' replied Mr Carrados tersely. 'Tour business, understand. Your chief minion was eager to blow a message through to you but "No," I said, "we'll take our proper turn". Why should I interrupt the Bogus Company Promoter's confession or cut short the Guilty Husband's plea?'

'Joking apart, that fellow who just went brought a very remarkable story,' said Mr Carlyle. 'I should be glad to know what you would have had to say to him when we have time to go into it.' (Do not be too ready to condemn the gentleman as an arrant humbug and this a gross breach of confidence: Max Carrados had been appointed Honorary Consultant to the firm, so that what would have otherwise been grave indiscretions were strictly business discussions.)

'In the meantime the suggestion is that you haven't taken a half-day off lately and that Monday morning is a convenient time.'

'Generous man! What is happening on Monday morning then?'

'Something rather surprising in wireless at the Imperial Salon—ten to twelve-thirty. I know it's the sort of thing you'll be interested in, and I have two tickets and want someone fairly intelligent to go with.'

'An ideal chain of circumstances,' rippled Mr Carlyle. 'I shall endeavour to earn the price of my seat.'

'I am sure you will succeed,' retorted Carrados. 'By the way, it's free.'

To a strain of this intellectual horseplay the arrangements for their meeting were made, and that having been the only reason for the call, Mr Carrados departed under Parkinson's watchful escort. In due course the wireless demonstration took place, but (although an invention then for the first time shown bore no small part in one of the blind man's subsequent cases) it is unnecessary to accompany them inside the hall, for with the enigma centring in Mr Poleash that event had no connexion. It is only touched upon as bringing Carrados and his friend together at that hour, for as they walked along Pall Mall after lunching Mr Carlyle suddenly gave a whistle of misgiving and surprise and stopped a hurrying newsboy.

'Holloway Flat Tragedy,' he read from the bill as he investigated sundry pockets for the exact coin. 'By gad, if that should happen to be—'

'Poleash! My God, it is!' he exclaimed as soon as his eye had found the paragraph concerned—a mere inch in the 'Stop Press' news. 'Poor beggar! Tshk! Tshk!'—his clicking tongue expressed disapproval and regret. 'He ought to have known better after what had happened. It was madness. I wonder what he actually did—'

'Your remarkable caller of last Thursday, Louis?'

'Yes; but how do you come to know?'

'A trifling indiscretion on his part. With a carelessness that must be rare among your clients I should say, Mr Poleash dropped one of his cards under the table in your writing-room, where the conscientious

Parkinson discovered it.'

'Well, the unfortunate chap doesn't need cards now. Listen, Max.

North London Tragedy

Early this morning a charwoman going to a flat in Meridon House, Holloway, made a gruesome discovery. Becoming suspicious at the untouched milk and newspapers, she looked into a bedroom and there found the occupier, a Mr Poleash, dead in bed. He had received shocking injuries, and everything points to deliberate murder. Mrs Poleash is understood to be away on a holiday in Devonshire.

'Of course Scotland Yard takes it up now, but I must put my information at their service. They're devilish lucky, too. I can practically hand over the miscreant to them and they will scoop the credit.'

'I was to hear about that,' Carrados reminded him. 'Suppose we walk across to Scotland Yard, and you can tell me on the way.'

At the corner of Derby Street they encountered two men who had just turned out of the Yard. The elder had the appearance of being a shrewd farmer, showing his likely son the sights of London and keeping a wide-awake eye for its notorious pitfalls. To pursue appearances a step farther they might even have been calling to recover the impressive umbrella that the senior carried.

'Beedel,' dropped Mr Carlyle beneath his breath, but his friend was already smiling recognition.

'The very man,' said Carrados genially. 'I'll wager you can tell us something about the Poleash arrangements, inspector.'

The two plain-clothes men exchanged amused glances.

'I can tell you this much, Mr Carrados,' replied Inspector Beedel, in unusually good spirits, 'my nephew George here is going to do the work and I'm going to look after the bouquets at the finish. We're on our way there now.'

'Couldn't be better,' said the blind man. 'Perhaps you wouldn't mind us going up there with you?'

'Very pleased,' replied Beedel. 'We were making for the station.'

'You may as well help to fill our taxi,' suggested Carrados. 'Mr Carlyle may have something to tell you on the way.'

On the whole Mr Carlyle would have preferred to make his disclosure to headquarters, but the convenience of the arrangement was not to be denied, and with a keen appreciation of the astonishing piece of luck Beedel and George heard the story of the inquiry agent's client.

'It looks like being simply a matter of finding this girl, if the conditions up there bear out his tale,' remarked George, between satisfaction at so veritable a clue and a doubt whether he would not have preferred a more complicated case. 'Did you happen to get her name and address, sir?'

'No,' admitted Mr Carlyle with a slight aloofness, 'it did not arise. Poleash was naturally reluctant to bring in the lady more than he need and I did not press him.'

'Makes no odds,' conceded George generously. 'Shop-girl—kept company with a foreigner—known as Peter. Even without anything else there ought to be no difficulty in finding her.'

Sturgrove Road was not deserted, and there was a rapid concentration about the door of Meridon House 'to see the 'tecs arrive.' On the whole, public opinion was disappointed in their appearance, but the action of George in looking up at the frontage of the building and then glancing sharply right and left along the road was favourably commented on. The policeman stationed at the outer door admitted them at once.

A sergeant and a constable of the local division were in possession of No. 12, and the scared daily woman, temporarily sustained by their impression of absolute immobility, was waiting in the kitchen to indicate whatever was required. Greetings on a slightly technical plane passed between the four members of the force.

'Mrs Poleash has been sent for, I suppose?' asked Mr Carlyle.

'We telephoned from our office to Torquay some hours ago,' replied the sergeant. 'They'll send an officer to the place she's staying at and break it to her as well as possible. That's the course we usually follow.' He took out a weighty presentation watch and considered it. 'Torquay. I don't suppose she could be here yet.'

'Not even if she was in first go,' amplified his subordinate.

'Well,' suggested George. 'Suppose we look round?' The bedroom was the first spot visited. There was nothing unusual to be seen, apart from the outline of the bed, its secret now hidden beneath a decorous covering—nothing beyond the rather untidy details of the occupant's daily round. All these would in due course receive a careful scrutiny, but at the moment one point drew every eye.

'Hold one another's hands,' advised the sergeant, as he prepared to turn down the sheet. The hovering charwoman gave a scream and fled.

'That's a wild beast been at work,' said Inspector Beedel, coolly drawing nearer to appreciate the details.

'My word, yes!' agreed George, following a little reluctantly.

'Shocking! Shocking!' Mr Carlyle made no pretence about turning away.

'Killed at the first blow,' continued the sergeant, indicating, 'though it's not the only one. Then his face slashed about like a fancy loaf till his own mother wouldn't know him. Something dreadful, isn't it? Finger gone? Oh, that's an old affair. What're you to make of it all?'

'Revenge—revenge and rage and sheer blood-thirstiness,' summed up Mr Carlyle. 'Was anything taken?'

'Nothing disturbed so far as we can see, and the old party there'—a comprehensive nod in the direction of the absent charlady—'says that all the things she knows of seem to be right.'

'What time do they put it at?' asked Beedel.

'Dr Meadows has been here. Midnight Saturday to early Sunday morning, he said. That agrees with the people at the flat opposite hearing the door locked at about ten on Saturday night and the Sunday morning milk and paper not being touched.'

'Milkcan on the doorstep all day, I suppose?' suggested someone.

'Yes; people opposite noticed it, but thought nothing of it. They knew Mrs Poleash was going away on Saturday and thought that he might have gone with her. Mrs Jones, she doesn't come on Sundays, so nothing was found but till this morning.'

'May as well hear what she has to say now,' said Beedel. 'No need to keep her about that I know of.'

'Just one minute, please, if you don't mind,' put in Mr Carlyle, not so much asking anyone's permission as directing the affair. The sight of a wardrobe had reminded him of the dead man's story, and he was now handling the clothes that hung there with keen anticipation. 'There is something that I really came especially to see. This is his dressing gown, and, yes, by Jupiter, it's here!'

He pointed to a clean cut through the material as they gathered round him.

'What's that?' inquired the sergeant, looking from one face to another.

'Previous attempt,' replied Beedel shortly.

'There ought to be a sheet and a bolster case somewhere about,' continued the eager gentleman, now thoroughly intrigued, and under the impulse of his zeal drawers and cupboards were opened and their contents gingerly displaced.

'Something of the sort here among the shirts,' announced George.

'Have them out then. Not likely to be any others put away there.' The hidden things were unfolded and displayed and here also the tragic evidence lay clear before them.

'By gad, you know, I half thought he might have dreamt it until this came,' confided Mr Carlyle to the room at large. 'Tshk! Tshk! How on earth the fellow could have gone——' He remembered the quiet figure lying within earshot and finished with a tolerant shrug.

'Let's get on,' said Beedel. These details could very well have waited had been his thought all along.

'I'll fold the things,' volunteered Mr Carrados. All the others had satisfied their curiosity by glance or scrutiny and he was free to take his time. He took up the loose bundle in his arms and with the strange impulse towards light that so often moved him he turned away from them and sought the window.

'Now, missis, come along and tell us all about it,' called out the young constable.

'No,' interposed the inspector kindly, 'the poor creature's upset enough already without bringing her in here again. Stay where you are, Mrs Jones, we're coming there,' he announced from the door, and they filed along the skimpy passage into the dingy kitchen. 'Now can you just tell us quietly what you know about this bad business?'

Mrs Jones's testimony, given on the frequently expressed understanding that she was quite prepared to be struck dead at any point of it if she deviated from the strictest line of truth, did not disclose any new feature, while its frequent references to the lives and opinions of friends not concerned in the progress of the drama threatened now and then to stifle the narrative with a surfeit of pronouns. But she was listened to with patience and complimented on her nerve. Mrs Jones sadly shook her antique black bonnet and disclaimed the quality.

'I could do nothing but stand and scream,' she confessed wistfully, referring to the first dreadful moment at the bedroom door, 'I stood and screamed three times before I could get myself away. The poor gentleman! What harm was he, for to be done in like that!'

There was a string of questions from one or another of the company before she was finally dismissed—generally from Beedel or George with Mr Carlyle's courteously assertive voice intervening once or twice: the Poleashes had few visitors that she had ever seen—she was only there from eight to six—and she had never known of anyone staying with them; no one had knocked at the door for anything on Saturday; she had not noticed anyone whom she could call to mind as 'a foreigner' loitering about or at the door recently (a foreign family lived at No. 5, but they were well spoken of); neither Mr nor Mrs Poleash had talked to her of anything uncommon of late—the gentleman was mostly out and 'she' wasn't one of the friendly sort; the couple seemed to get on together 'as well as most', and she had never heard a 'real' quarrel.

Mrs Poleash had gone off for a week (she understood) about noon on Saturday, and Mr Poleash had accompanied her to Paddington (as he had mentioned on his return for tea); she had last seen him at about five o'clock on Saturday, when she left, a little earlier than usual; she knew nothing of the ashes in the kitchen grate, not having had a fire there for weeks past; the picture post card (passed round) from Mrs Poleash, announcing her arrival at Torquay, she had found on the hall floor together with the Sunday paper; she was to go on just the same while Mrs Poleash was away, coming daily to 'do up', and so on; it was a regular arrangement 'week in and week out'.

'That seems to be about all,' summed up Inspector Beedel, looking round. 'We have your address, Mrs Jones, and you're sure to hear from us about something pretty soon.'

'Before you go,' said a matter-of-fact voice from the door, 'do you happen to remember what you were doing last Thursday afternoon?' It was the first question that Mr Carrados had put, and they had scarcely noticed whether he had re-joined them yet or not.

'Last Thursday afternoon?' repeated Mrs Jones helplessly. 'Oh, Lor', sir, my head's in that whirl—'

'Yes, but it isn't so difficult if you think—early closing day, you know.'

This stimulus proved effective and the charwoman remembered. She had something special to remember by. On Thursday morning Mrs Poleash has passed on to her a single ticket for that afternoon's performance at the Parkhurst Theatre, and told her that she could go after she had washed up the dinner things.

'So that you were not here at all on Thursday afternoon? Just one more thing, Mrs Jones. Sooner or later a photograph of your master will be wanted. Is there one anywhere about?'

'The only one I know of stands on the sideboard in the little room. There may be others put away, but not being what you might call curious sir—'

'I'm sure you're not,' agreed Carrados. 'Now, as you go you shall point it out to us so that there can be no mistake.'

'You couldn't make no mistake because there's only that and one of her stands there,' explained Mrs Jones, but she proceeded to comply. 'There it—'

'Yes?' said the blind man, close upon her.

'I'm sorry, sir, indeed. I must have made a mistake—'

'I don't think you made any mistake,' he urged. 'I don't think you really think so either.'

'I'm that mithered I don't rightly know what to think,' she declared. 'That isn't him.'

'Is it the frame? No, don't touch it—that might be unlucky, you know—but you can remember that.'

'It's the frame, right enough. I ought to know, the times I've dusted it.'

'Then the photograph has been changed: there's nothing unlikely in that. When was the last time that you noticed the other one there?'

Quite recently, it would seem, but taking refuge behind her whirling head Mrs Jones held out against precision. It might have been Friday or it might have been Saturday. Carrados forbore to press her more exactly, and she departed, sustained by the advice of Authority that she should have nothing to say to nobody, under the excuse, if need be, that she had answered enough questions already for one day.

'While we are here,' said the sergeant—they were still in the 'little room', the only one that looked out on the front 'you might as well see where he got in.' He went to the window and indicated certain marks on the wood- and stone-work. 'We found the lower sash still a few inches up when we came.'

'Went the same way as he came, I suppose?' suggested George.

'Must have done. All the keys are accounted for, and Mrs Jones found the front door locked as usual. And why not; why shouldn't he? There's the balcony, and you hardly have to lean out to see the stairway window not a yard away. Why, it's as easy as ring-a-roses. Might have been made for it.'

'Tshk! Tshk!' fumed Mr Carlyle unhappily. 'After what I said. And not one of the locks has been seen to.'

'Locks?' echoed the young policeman, appearing that moment at the door. 'Why, here is a chap with tools, says he's come to repair and fit the locks!'

'Well, if this isn't the fair *nefus ultra!*' articulated the sergeant. 'However, show him in, lad.'

The locksmith, looking scarcely less alarmed than if he had fallen into a den of thieves, had a very short and simple tale to tell. His shop was in the Seven Sisters Road, and on Friday afternoon a gentleman had called there and arranged with him to come on Monday and repair some locks. He had given the name of Poleash and that address. The man knew nothing of what had taken place and had come as fixed.

'It's a pity you didn't happen to make it Saturday, Mr Hipwaite,' said Inspector Beedel, as he took a note of this new evidence. 'It might—I don't say it would, but it might—have prevented murder being done.'

'But that's the very thing I was not to do,' declared Hipwaite, with some warmth. '"Don't come on Saturday because the wife is very nervous, and if she thinks burglars are about she'll have a fit," he said—those very words. "She'll be away on Monday, and then by the time she comes back she mayn't notice." Was I likely to come on Saturday?'

Plainly he was not. 'That's all right,' it was conceded, 'but there's nothing in your line doing today.' So Mr Hipwaite departed, more than half persuaded that he had been hardly used and not in the least mollified by being concerned in so notable a tragedy.

'Before I go,' resumed the sergeant, leading the way back to the kitchen, 'there's one other thing I must hand over. You heard what Mrs Jones said about the fire—that there hadn't been one for weeks as they always used the stove?'

'That's what I asked her,' George reminded him. 'Someone has had a fire here.'

'Correct,' continued the officer imperturbably. 'It's also what I asked her a couple of hours before you came. Someone's had a fire here. Who and what for? Well, I've had the cinders out to see and now I'll make over to you what there was.'

'Glove fasteners,' commented the inspector, 'All the metal there was about them. Millions of the pattern, I suppose.'

'Burned his gloves after the job—they must have been in a fair mess,' said George. '"*Audubon Frères*" they're stamped—foreign make.'

'That reminds me—there's one thing more.' It was produced from the sergeant's pocket-book, a folded fragment of paper, charred along its edge. 'It's from the hearth; evidently a bit that fell out when the fire was made. Foreign newspaper, you will see; Italian it looks to me.'

Mr Carlyle, Inspector Beedel, and George exchanged appreciative glances. Upon this atmosphere of quiet satisfaction there fell something almost like a chuckle.

'Did anyone happen to notice if he had written "*Si parla Italiano*" in red on the wall over the bed?' inquired the guileless voice.

The young constable, chancing to be the nearest person to the door, rose to this mendacious suggestion by offering to go and see. The others stared at the blind man in various stages of uncertainty.

'No, no,' called out Mr Carlyle feelingly. 'There is no need to look, thank you. When you know Mr Carrados as well as I do you will understand that although there is always something in what he says it is not always the something you think it is. Now, Max, pray enlighten the company. Why should the murderer write "Italian spoken" over the bed?'

'Obviously to make sure that you shouldn't miss it,' replied Mr Carrados.

'Well,' remarked the sergeant, demonstrating one or two simple exercises in physical drill as a suitable preparation, 'I may as well be going. I don't understand Italian myself. Nor Dutch either,' he added cryptically.

Mr Carlyle also had nothing more to stay for. 'If you have done here, Max—' he began, and turned only to find that Carrados was no longer there.

'Your friend has just gone to the front room, sir,' said the constable, catching the words as he passed. 'Funny to see a blind man getting about so—' But a sudden crash of glass from the direction referred to cut short the impending compliment.

It was, as Carrados explained, entirely his own preposterous fault. Nothing but curiosity about the size of the room had impelled him to touch the walls, and the picture, having a weak cord or an insecure nail . . . had it not brought something else down in its fall?

'Only the two frames from the sideboard, so far as I can see,' replied Carlyle. 'All the glass is shattered. But I don't suppose that Mrs Poleash will be in a condition to worry about trifles. Jolly good thing you aren't hurt, that's all.'

'Of course I should like to replace the damage,' said the delinquent.

Inspector Beedel said nothing, but as he looked on he recalled one or two other mischances in the past, and being of an introspective nature he continued to massage his chin thoughtfully.

Three days later the inquest on the body of Albert Henry Poleash was opened. It was of the merest formal description, proof of identity and a bare statement of the cause of death being the only evidence put forward. An adjournment for a week was then declared.

At the resumed inquiry the story of Poleash's death was taken forward, and the newspaper reader for the first time was encouraged to see in it the promise of a first-class popular sensation. Louis Carlyle related the episode of his unexpected client. Corroboration of that wildly romantic story was forthcoming from many sides. Mr Hipwaite carried the drama two days later by describing the dead man's visit to his shop, the order to repair the locks, and his own futile journey to the flat. Mrs Jones, skilfully piloted among dates and details, was in evidence as the discoverer of the body. Two doctors—a private practitioner called hurriedly in at the first alarm and the divisional surgeon—agreed on all essential points, and the police efficiently bridged the narration at one stage and another and contrived to present a faithful survey of the tragedy.

But the most arresting figure of the day, though her evidence was of very slight account and mainly negative, was the unhappy widow. As she moved into the witness-box, a wan, graceful creature in her unaccustomed, but, it may be said, not unattractive *crêpe*, a rustle of compassion stirred the court and Mr Carlyle, who had come prejudiced against her, as an automatic reflex of his client's fate, chirruped sympathy.

Mrs Poleash gave her testimony in a low voice, not particularly attractive in its tone, and she looked straight before her with eyes neither downcast nor wandering. Her name, she said, was Katherine Poleash, her age twenty-nine. She knew nothing of the tragedy, having been in Torquay at the time. She had gone there on the Saturday afternoon, her husband seeing her off from Paddington. Their relationship was perfectly friendly, but not demonstrative. Her husband was a considerate but rather reserved man with no especial interests. Up to two years ago she had been accustomed to earn her own living, but a nervous breakdown had interfered with her capacity for work. It was on account of that illness that she had generally occupied a separate bedroom; it had left her nervous in many ways, but she was surprised to hear that she should have been described as exacting or ill-tempered.

"'Not wholly reasonable and excitable" were the precise terms used, I think,' put in Mr Carlyle gallantly.

'It's much the same,' she replied apathetically.

Continuing, she had no knowledge at all of any intrigue between her husband and a shop-girl, such as had been referred to, nor had she ever heard of the man Peter, either by name or as an Italian. She could not suggest in what quarter of London the shop in question was likely to be as the deceased was accustomed to go about a good deal. The police already had a list of the various properties he owned. At the conclusion of her evidence Mrs Poleash seemed to be on the point of fainting and had to be assisted out.

There was nothing to be gained by a further adjournment. The cause of death—the real issue before that court—was reasonably clear. The jury brought in a verdict of 'Wilful Murder against Some Person or Persons Unknown.' Before the reporters left the police asked that the Press should circulate a request for anyone having knowledge of a shop-assistant who had been friendly with a foreigner known as Peter or Pietro, or with a man answering to Mr Poleash's description, to communicate with them either at New Scotland Yard or to any local station. The Press promised to comply and offered to publish photographs of Mr Poleash as a means towards that end, only to learn that no photograph possessing identification value could be found. So began the memorable paper-chase for an extremely nebulous shop-assistant and a foreigner whose description began and ended with the *sobriquet* 'Peter the Italian'.

★★★★★★

'I was wondering if you or Inspector Beedel would come round one day to see me,' said Mr Carrados as George was shown into the study at The Turrets. Two full weeks had elapsed since the conclusion of the inquest and the newspaper value of the Holloway Flat Tragedy had sunk from a column opposite the leader page to a six-line fill-up beneath 'Home and General'. 'Your uncle used often to drop in to entertain me with the progress of his cases.'

'That wasn't his way of looking at it, Mr Carrados. He used to say that when it came to seeing through a brick wall you were—well, hell!'

'Curious,' remarked Mr Carrados. 'I don't remember ever hearing Inspector Beedel make use of that precise expression.'

George went a trifle red and laughed to demonstrate his self-possession.

'Well, perhaps I dropped a word of my own in by accident.' he said.

'But that was what he meant—in a complimentary sense, of course. As a matter of fact, it was on his advice that I ventured to trouble you now.'

'Not "trouble",' protested the blind man, ever responsive to the least touch of diffidence. 'That's another word the inspector wouldn't use about me, I'm sure.'

'You're very kind,' said George, accepting a cigarette, 'and as I had to come this way to see another—oh, my Lord, another!—shop-girl, why, I thought—'

'Ah; how is the case going?'

'It's no go, Mr Carrados. We've seen thousands of shop-girls and hundreds of Italian Peters. I'm beginning to think,' said the visitor, watching Mr Carrados's face as he propounded the astonishing heresy, 'that there is no such person.'

'Yes?' replied Carrados unmoved. 'It is always as well to look beyond the obvious, isn't it? What does the inspector say?'

'He says, "I should like to know what Mr Carrados really meant by 'Italian spoken', and what he really did when he smashed that picture".'

Carrados laughed his appreciation as he seemed actually to watch the blue smoke curling upwards.

'How easy it is to give a straightforward answer when a plain question is asked,' he replied. 'By "*Si parla Italiano*" I ventured to insinuate my own private opinion that there was no Italian Peter; when I broke the picture I tried to obtain some definite evidence of someone there was.'

George waited in the hope of this theme developing, but his host seemed to consider that he had said all that was necessary, and it is difficult to lead on a man into disclosures when you cannot fix him with your eye.

'Poleash may have been mistaken himself,' he continued tentatively; 'or he may have purposely misled Mr Carlyle on details, with the idea of getting his advice but not entirely trusting him to the full extent.'

'He may,' admitted the placid smoker.

'One thing I can't understand is however the man set about keeping company with a girl without spending more on her than he seems to have done. We found a small pocket diary that he entered his current expenses in, and there isn't a single item for chocolates, flowers, theatres, or anything of that sort.'

'A diary?'

'Oh, he didn't keep a diary; only entered cash, and rents received, and so on. Here it is, if you care to—examine it.'

'Thank you, I should. I wonder what our friend Carlyle charged for the consultation?'

'I don't remember seeing that,' admitted George, referring to the pages. 'Thursday, the 3rd, wasn't it? No, curiously enough, that doesn't appear.... I wonder if he never put down any of these what you might call questionable items for fear of Mrs Poleash seeing?'

'Not unnaturally,' agreed Carrados. 'You found nothing else of interest then—no addresses or new names?'

'Nothing at all. Oh, that page you've got is only his memorandum of sizes and numbers and so on.'

'Yes; quite a useful habit, isn't it?' The long, vibrant fingers touched offline after line without a pause or stumble. 'When he made this handy list Albert Henry Poleash little thought—Boots, size 9; hat, size 71/8; collars, size 16; gloves, size 8¾; watch, No. 31903; weight, 11st. 8lbs. There we have the man: *Ex pede Herculem*, as the motto has it— only in this case of course the hat and gloves are more useful.'

'Very true, sir,' said George, whose instinct was to keep a knowing front on all occasions.

When Parkinson was summoned to the room some time later he found his master there alone. Every light was blazing on, and, sitting at his desk, Mr Carrados confronted a single sheet of paper. With his trained acuteness for the minutiae of every new condition, Parkinson immediately took mental photographs of the sheet of paper with its slim written column, of the position and appearance of the chair George had used, of the number and placing of cigarette ends and matches, of all the details connected with the tray and contents, and of a few other matters. It was his routine.

'Close the door and come in,' said Carrados. 'I want you to carry your mind back about four weeks to the last occasion when we called at Mr Carlyle's office together. As we sat in the waiting-room I asked you if the things left there belonged to anyone we knew.'

'I remember the circumstances perfectly, sir.'

'I want the articles described. The gloves?'

'There was only one glove—that for the right hand. It was a dark grey suede, moderately used, and not of the best cut. The fastening was a press button stamped "Audubon Frères". The only marking inside the glove was the size, 7½.'

Carrados made a note on the sheet before him. The hat?' he said.

'What size was that?'

'The size of hat, printed on an octagonal white ticket, was 6¾, sir.'

'Excellent, so far. When the caller passed through you saw him for a moment. Apart from clothes, which do not matter just now, was there any physical peculiarity that would identify him?'

'He had a small dark mole beneath the left eye. The lobe of his right ear was appreciably less than the other. The nail of the middle finger of the right hand was corrugated from an injury at some time.'

Carrados made a final note on the paper before him.

'Very good indeed, Parkinson,' he remarked. 'That is all I wanted.'

★★★★★★

A month passed and nothing happened. Occasionally a newspaper, pressed for a subject, commented on the disquieting frequency with which undetected murder could be done, and among other instances mentioned the Holloway Flat Tragedy and deplored the ease with which Peter the Italian had remained at large. The name by that time struck the reader as distantly familiar.

Then one evening early in November Beedel rang Mr Carrados up. The blind man happened to take the call himself, and at the first words he knew that the dull, patient shadowing of weeks was about to fructify.

'Yes, Inspector Beedel himself, sir,' said the voice at the other end. 'I'm speaking from Beak Street. The two you know of have just gone to the Restaurant X in Warsaw Street. The lady has booked two seats at the Alhambra for tonight, so we expect them to be there for the best part of an hour.'

'I'll come at once,' replied Carrados. 'What about Carlyle?'

'He's been notified. Back entrance in Boulton Court,' said the inspector. 'I'm off there now myself.'

It was the first time that the two the blind man 'knew of' had met since the watch was set, and their correspondence had been singularly innocuous. Yet not a breath of suspicion had been raised, and the same elaborate care that had prompted Mr Carrados to bring down a picture to cover the abstraction of a small square of glass had been maintained throughout.

'Nice private little room upstairs, saire,' insinuated the proprietor as 'the two' looked round. He guessed that they shunned publicity, and he was right, although not entirely so. With a curt nod the man led the way up the narrow stairway to the equivocal little den on the first floor. The general room below had not been crowded, but this one was wholly empty.

'Quite like old times,' said the woman with an unmusical laugh as she threw off her cloak—there was little indication of the sorrowing widow now, 'I thought we had better fight shy of the "Toledo" for the future.'

"M yes,' replied her companion slowly, looking dubiously about him—he no longer wore glasses or moustache, nor was his left hand, the glove now removed, deficient of a finger. 'The only thing is whether it isn't too soon for us to be about together at all.'

'Pha!' she snapped expressively. 'They've gone to sleep again. There isn't a thing—no not a single detail—gone wrong. The most that could happen would be a raid here to look for Peter the Italian!'

'For God's sake don't keep on that,' he urged in a low voice. 'Your husband was a brute to you by what you say, and I'm not sorry now it's done, but I want to forget it all. You had your way: I've done everything you planned. Now you are free and decently well off and as soon as it's safe we can really marry—if you still will.'

'If I still will,' she repeated, looking at him meaningly. 'Do you know, Dick, I think it may become desirable sooner even than I thought.'

'Sssh!' he warned; 'here comes someone. You order, Kitty—you always have done! Anything will suit me.' He turned to arrange his overcoat across an empty chair and reassured his hand among the contents of the nearest pocket.

Downstairs, in his nondescript living-room, the proprietor of the Restaurant X was being very quickly and efficiently made to understand just so much of the situation as turned on his immediate and complete acceptance of it. In the presence of authority so vigorously expressed the stout gentleman bowed profusely, lowered his voice, and from time to time placed a knowing finger on his lips in agreement.

'Hallo,' said the man called 'Dick' as a different attendant brought a dish. 'Where has our other waiter got to?'

'Party of regular customers as always has him just come in.' explained the new one. 'Ope you don't mind, sir.'

'Not a brass button.'

'It's all right, inspector,' reported the 'waiter'. 'He has the three marks you said—mole, ear, nail.'

'Certain of the woman?'

'Mrs Poleash, sure as snow.'

'Any reference to it?'

'Don't think so while I'm about. Drama just now. Has his little gun handy.'

'Take this in now. Leave the door open and see if you can make him talk up. . . . If you two gentlemen will step just across there I think you'll be able to hear.'

Carrados smiled as he proceeded to comply.

'I have already heard,' he said. 'It is the voice of the man who called on Mr Carlyle on September the third.'

'I think it is the voice,' admitted Mr Carlyle when he had tiptoed back again. 'I really think so, but after two months I should not be prepared to swear.'

'He is the man,' repeated Carrados deliberately.

Inspector Beedel, clinking something quietly in his pocket, nodded to his waiter.

'Morgan follows you in with the coffee,' he said. 'Put it down on the table, Morgan, and stand beside the woman. Call me as soon as you have him.'

It was the sweet that the first waiter was to take, and with it there was a sauce. It was not exactly overturned, but there was an awkward movement and a few drops were splashed. With a clumsy apology the waiter, napkin in hand, leaned across the customer to remove a spot that marked his coat-sleeve.

'Here!' exclaimed the startled man. 'What the devil are you up to?'

It was too late. Speech was the only thing left to him then. His wrists were already held in a trained, relentless grasp; he was pressed helplessly back into his chair at the first movement of resistance. Kitty Poleash rose from her seat with a dreadful coldness round her heart, felt a hand upon her shoulder, cast one fearful glance round, and sank down upon her chair again. Before another word was spoken Inspector Beedel had appeared, and the grip of bone and muscle on the straining wrists was changed to one of steel. Less than thirty seconds bridged the whole astonishing transformation.

'Richard Crispinge, you are charged with the murder of this woman's husband. Katherine Poleash, you are held as an accessory,' The usual caution followed. 'Get a taxi to the back entrance, Morgan.'

Half a dozen emotions met on Crispinge's face as he shot a glance at his companion and then faced the accuser again.

'You're crazy,' he panted, still labouring from the effort. 'I've never even seen the man.'

'I shouldn't say anything now, if I were you,' advised Beedel, on a quite human note. 'You may find out later that we know more than you might think.'

What followed could not have been charged against human foresight, for at a later stage it was shown that a certain cable failed and in a trice one side of Warsaw Street was involved in darkness. What happened in that darkness—where they had severally stood before and after—who moved or spoke—whose hand was raised—were all matters of dispute, but suddenly the black was stabbed by a streak of red, a little crack—scarcely more than the sharp bursting of a paper bag—nearly caught up to it, and almost slowly to the awaiting ears came the sound of strain and the long crash of falling glass and china.

'A lamp from down there!' snapped Beedel's sorely-tried voice, as the ray of an electric torch whirled like a pygmy searchlight and then centred on a tumbled thing lying beyond the table. 'Look alive!'

'They say there is gas somewhere,' announced Mr Carlyle, striking a match as he ran in. 'Ah, here it is.'

No need to ask then what had happened, though how it had happened could never be set quite finally at rest; for if Kitty Poleash was standing now, whereas before she had sat, the weapon lay beyond her reach close to the shackled hands. A curious apathy seemed to fall upon the room as though the tang of the drifting wisp of smoke dulled their alertness, and when the woman moved slowly towards her lover Beedel merely picked the pistol up and waited. With a terrible calmness she knelt by the huddled form and raised the inert head.

'Goodbye, my dear,' she said quietly, kissing the dead lips for the last time; 'it's over.' And with a strange tragic fitness she added, in the words of another fatal schemer, 'We fail!'

She seemed to be the only one who had any business there; Beedel was abstracted; Carlyle and Carrados felt like spectators walking on a stage when the play is over. In the street below the summoned taxi throbbed unheeded; they were waiting for another equipage now. When that had moved off with its burden Kitty Poleash would follow her captors submissively, like a dog without a home.

'It isn't a feather in our caps to have a man slip away like that,' remarked the inspector moodily as the two joined him for a word before they left; 'but, of course, as far as they are both concerned, it's the very best that could have happened.'

'In what way do you mean the best?' demanded Mr Carlyle with a professional keenness for the explicit.

'Why, look at what will happen now. He's saved all the trouble and thought of being hanged, which it was bound to be in, the end, and has got it over without a moment's worry. She will get the full benefit of it as well, because her counsel will now be able to pile it all up against the fellow and claim that he exercised an irresistible influence over her. Personally, I should say that it's twelve of one and thirteen of the other, and I don't know that she isn't the thirteen, but she is about as likely to be hanged as I am to be made superintendent tomorrow.'

★★★★★★

'Max,' said Mr Carlyle, as they sat smoking together the same night, 'when you think of the elaboration of that plot it was appalling.'

'Curious,' replied Carrados thoughtfully. 'To me it seems absolutely simple and inevitable. Perhaps that is because I should have done it—fundamentally, that is–just the same way myself.'

'And got caught the same way?'

'There were mistakes made. If you decide to kill a man you must do it either secretly or openly. If you do it secretly and it comes to light you are done for. If you do it openly there is the chance of putting another appearance on the crime.

'These two—Crispinge and Mrs Poleash—knew that in the ordinary way the killing of the husband would immediately attract suspicion to the wife. Under that fierce scrutiny it could not long be hidden that the woman had a lover, and the disclosure would be fatal. Indeed, if Poleash had lived, that fact must shortly have come to light, and it was the sordid determination to secure his income for themselves before he discovered the intrigue and divorced his wife that sealed his fate and forced an early issue.

'If you intend to commit a murder, Louis, and know that suspicion will automatically fall on you, what is the first thing that you would wish to effect? Obviously that it should fall on someone else more strongly. But as the arrest of that someone else would upset the plan, you would naturally make his identity such that he would have the best chance of remaining at large. The most difficult person to find is one who does not exist.

'There you have the whole strategy of the sorry business. Everything hinged on that, and when you once possess that clue you not only see why everything happened as it did but you can confidently forecast exactly what will happen. To go on believing that you had talked with the real Poleash it was necessary that you should never actually see the man as he was. Hence the disfigurement. What assailant would act in that way? Only one maddened by a jealous fury. The

506

Southern people are popularly the most jealous and revengeful, so we must have a native of Italy or Spain, and the Italian is the more credible of the two. Similarly, Mr Hipwaite is brought in to add another touch of corroboration to your tale. But why Mr Hipwaite from a mile away? There is a locksmith quite near at hand; I made it my business to call on him, and I learned that, as I expected, he knew Poleash by sight. Plainly he would never have served the purpose.'

'Perhaps I ought to have been more sceptical of the fellow's tale,' conceded Mr Carlyle; 'but, you know, Max, I have a dozen fresh people call on me every month with queer stories, and it's not once in a million times that this would happen. I, at any rate, saw nothing to rouse suspicion. You say he made mistakes?'

'Crispinge, among divers other things he's failed in, has been an actor, and with Mrs Poleash's coaching on facts there is no doubt that he carried the part all right. Being wise after the event, we may say that he overstressed the need of secrecy. The idea of the previous attack, designed, of course, to throw irrefutable evidence into the scales, was too pronounced. Something slighter would have served better. Personally, I think it was excess of caution to send Mrs Jones out on the Thursday afternoon. She could have been relied upon to be too "mithered" for her recollections to carry any weight. It was necessary to destroy the only reliable photograph of Poleash, but the risk ought to have been taken of burning it before she went off to establish her unassailable alibi, and not leaving it for her accomplice to do. In the event, by handling the frame after he had burned his gloves, Crispinge furnished us with the solitary fingerprint that linked up his identity.'

'He had been convicted then?'

'Blackmail, six years ago, and other things before. A mixture of weakness and violence, he has always gravitated towards women for support. But the great mistake—the vital oversight—the alarm signal to my perceptions—'

'Yes?'

'Well, I should really hardly like to mention it to anyone but you. The sheet and the bolster-case that so convincingly turned up to clinch your client's tale once and for all demolished it. They had never been on Poleash's bed, believe me, Louis. What a natural thing for the woman to take them from her own, and yet how fatal! I sensed that damning fact as soon as I had them in my hands, and in a trice the whole fabric of deception, so ingeniously contrived, came down in ruins. Nothing—nothing—could ever retrieve that simple, deadly blunder.'

The Curious Circumstances of the Two Left Shoes

At the time when the Enderleighs lost their silver the Monkey Burglar was at the height of his fame. The Monkey Burglar, should you by this date have forgotten, was the one who invariably gained access by leaping from a tree on to an upper-storey windowsill. So strong was habit that there were said to be cases of the Monkey Burglar going through this performance at houses where the front door stood open, or where a builder's ladder, left in position overnight, was reared against the very point he gained by the more sensational flight. During the thick of the burglary season that year each number of *Punch* regularly contained one or more jokes about the Monkey; no pantomime was complete without a few references to him; and the burgled invariably tried to claim distinction as authentic victims. In this, the Press, to do it justice, worthily seconded their endeavours.

The Enderleighs lived near Silver Park at that time, in one of the old-fashioned cottages that have long, delightful gardens running down to the river edge. They were a young couple, setting themselves a very moderate standard until the day when Enderleigh's wonderful qualities should be suitably recognised by a partnership. In the meanwhile he was something exceptionally responsible but not so exceptionally rewarded in connexion with a firm of estate agents and surveyors. Max Carrados had heard of him favourably from one or two friends and was not unwilling to put business in the young man's way. An opportunity came when the blind criminologist had, as trustee, to deal with an estate down in Warwickshire. He ascertained that Enderleigh was not debarred from doing work on his own account, and gave him a commission to inspect the property and make a general report. Business being slack, there was no difficulty in arranging a few days' leave of absence from the office, and the proposal was gratefully accepted.

On his return—he had conscientiously managed to cover the ground within two days—Enderleigh looked in at The Turrets before proceeding home and found Mr Carrados at leisure.

'I thought that I would leave the report with you now,' he explained, 'in case you cared to glance over it and ask me about any details while it's all fresh in my mind. I wrote up my notes in the train on the way back.'

'Good man,' smiled Carrados, accepting the docket. 'I should have liked you to stay while we discussed the matter, but I am afraid that someone else has a prior lien on your time.'

'In what way?'

'A few hours ago Mrs Enderleigh rang me up on the phone, and there is what I might describe as a standing order for you to communicate with her from here at the earliest moment.'

'Good heavens!' exclaimed Enderleigh in some trepidation. 'What's up, I wonder? Nothing wrong that you know of?'

'Nothing at all,' replied Carrados with reassuring unconcern. 'Your wife was in exceptional spirits, I gathered, but somewhat cryptical. However, there is the means of setting your mind at rest,' and he indicated the instrument. 'I'll leave you to it.'

'Please don't go.' Enderleigh seemed to be toying with the moment as if rather unwilling to set his mind at rest. 'I was startled for a second, but if my wife herself spoke to you there can't be anything much the matter. The fact is,' he confided with a certain shy complacency, 'she has been getting rather fanciful of late—not an unusual phase of the situation, I understand.'

Mr Carrados murmured his discreet congratulations, and his visitor summed up enough indifference to make the call.

'Holy Moses!' the blind man heard him mutter, and there followed a rapid fusillade of 'How?' and 'When?' and 'What?' and 'You don't mean it!' all indicating consternation and surprise, as long as the colloquy lasted.

'Here's a pretty go,' announced Mr Enderleigh, hanging up the receiver. 'We've been burgled!'

'The deuce!' exclaimed Carrados sympathetically. 'I hope your wife isn't much upset?'

'No, I don't think so. In fact, she seems rather set up, because some of our neighbours were robbed in a very commonplace way lately, and she's determined that this must have been the authentic Monkey.'

'Much taken?'

'Apparently the silver chest and nothing else. Myra rather fancied that I would call here on my way from something I had said—that's why she rang you up—and she wants me to go straight on. I hope you don't mind?'

'Of course not. I had hoped that you would keep me company for an hour or two, but that's out of the question now.... I'll tell you what, though: I will make a bargain with you. Stay another fifteen minutes, in which we can have a snack of some kind in place of dinner. In the meanwhile I will have a car got out that will land you at your place quicker than any other way you could go; and in return you shall invite me to inspect the depredation.'

'That's certainly a bargain from my side of the transaction,' replied Enderleigh. 'If it isn't putting you out, I'll accept like a shot.'

'Not a bit,' declared his host with more than polite formality. He moved across to the house telephone and quickly distributed the necessary orders. 'I love anything that comes suddenly along. It may be the beginning of—what adventure?'

'Well, as to that, of course there are two sides,' said the domesticated Enderleigh. 'This is quite sudden enough for men, but I certainly don't love it.'

Carrados was as good as his literal word, and fifteen minutes after he had spoken the lean form of his speedy Redshank car glided down the drive into the high road and then stretched out for Silver Park.

'Now that it's come to this, I may as well tell you about our silver,' explained Mr Enderleigh to his companion, on a confidential impulse. 'We happen to have rather a lot—more than people in our modest way generally sport, I mean. Myra's father was a fruit-grower and won a lot of cups and plates in his time. I used to be something of a runner and I amassed a few more, and when we got married our friends showered cruets and cake baskets down on us galore. The consequence is that there was a solid half-hundredweight of the metal reposing in a specially made case in the dining-room at Homecroft. Of course it ought to have been kept at the bank, and at first it was, but Myra liked to see an assortment out on the sideboard, so that it got to be a nuisance sending it backwards and forwards.

'Then I said that if we had it in the house it ought to be kept up in the bedroom for safety, and Myra found that she couldn't even lift the chest and decided that it would be too inconvenient to have it

510

there. What with one thing and another, the confounded silver got to become a bit of a sore point between us—it brought on the first unpleasantness we had. Then, as bad luck would have it, just when I was leaving the other morning to go on this job we must needs get arguing about it again. I suggested that as there would be only two women alone in the house—herself and the servant—it would be safer if I carried the box up and hid it under the bed. Myra—God know why—retorted that if the silver was the danger-point it wasn't very kind to want to put it just under where she would be. One silly word led to another until I finally went off saying that I wished the damned stuff was at the bottom of the river.'

'You seem to have got the next thing to what you asked for then,' remarked Carrados. 'The silver apparently won't trouble you again.' But Enderleigh demurred at this cheerful summary and shook his head.

'Oh, yes,' he replied, 'but when you wish a thing like that you don't really mean that you want it to happen.'

'You are insured, I suppose?'

'Only partly, I'm afraid, because the value of the silver now exceeds the percentage allowed. And of course a lot of the things have associations, although there is nothing of antique value. I'm really wondering how Myra will take it when the excitement wears off.'

But so far the excitement was on, and she welcomed them radiantly, albeit a shade mystified that Mr Carrados should have chosen that moment to pay his call. It does not say much for the criminal expert's sense of publicity that neither his host nor hostess had the faintest idea of his uncanny reputation. To them he was simply the rich blind man who seemed as though he might be useful to Guy.

'But isn't it a shame, Mr Carrados?' she cooed, when the first round of wonder and exclamation had been gone through. 'Sergeant Lapworth declares that it can't possibly be the Monkey Burglar. And I was so relying on that to squelch the Higgses with.'

Carrados divined an exchange of private glances, expostulatory from the husband, playfully defiant on her part.

'I have met Sergeant Lapworth once or twice and he seemed to know his work,' said the visitor. 'Did he say why it couldn't be?'

'Well, the only way they could have got in was by the side door. No fastenings have been forced or windows opened. And the Monkey wouldn't ever dream of using a side door.'

'But how on earth could they do that?' demanded Enderleigh. 'I mean without using force. Chloe fastens the door at night, doesn't she?'

'I'll show you if you don't mind accompanying me to the nether regions,' said the light-hearted girl. 'Chloe only locks the door it seems—the bolts are too stiff to work—and Sergeant Lapworth says that these people—he's almost sure he knows the gang—have all manner of ingenious tools. There's a sort of pincers that you catch hold of a key with from the other side and turn it quite easily. You can see that the lock has been oiled to make it go.'

'You found the door unlocked this morning?'

'No—I don't know. I never thought of that. But I suppose they could just as easily lock it again to cover their tracks, and as it happened it was not until this afternoon that I missed the silver chest. Then there are footprints on the bed from the gate to the side door. He found those as well. It's most wildly exciting discovering clues; I've been looking for some all the afternoon, but so far without success.'

'Come on then,' suggested Enderleigh. 'You have a lamp or candle, I suppose?'

'Yes. Do you care to see our private morgue, Mr Carrados—oh, I am sorry: I forgot!'

'That's very nice of you—to forget,' smiled the blind man. 'It shows that I'm not so helpless after all. Certainly I should like to come; I'm as keen on clues as you are.'

The side door was the chief point of interest. It opened on to the garden from the scullery. The scullery—a dank and forbidding chamber that almost justified its epithet—in turn led into the kitchen, and the kitchen into the hall. But there were other ways of getting about, for it was an old house with many passages and on various levels. Most of the rooms appeared to have at least two doors. 'I think that the man who built it must have been fond of French farces,' remarked Mr Enderleigh, pointing out this feature.

But even at the side door there was very little to see, the Enderleigh burglary being chiefly remarkable for its negative features. There was the oiled lock, and the key bore certain recent scratches, and that was all.

'If the bolts had been shot this would never have happened,' said the master of the house. 'Perhaps in future—'

'But the bolts can't be stirred, dear,' protested Myra. 'I've tried myself until my poor thumbs are nearly dislocated. And everyone says that if burglars want to get in they will, even if they have to come down the chimney.'

'I think the bolts might move if they were simply oiled,' suggested Carrados. 'The level is all right, you see.'

'Chloe,' called out Mr Enderleigh—the kitchen door stood open—'is there any oil about?'

A young girl in cap and apron—a girl of quite unusual prettiness—appeared at the door.

'Oil, sir?' she repeated faintly, and she continued to look from one to another of them as though something was amiss.

'Yes, oil—ordinary oil—the sort you oil with, you know. There must be some about somewhere.'

'Oh, yes—for the sewing machine,' she replied, and disappeared to return with it in a moment.

'Now a feather.'

The girl's eyes shot to a bucket holding kitchen refuse that stood beneath the sink; then rose to the level again as she continued to stand there.

'Feathers: in the middle dresser drawer, Chloe,' prompted her mistress tartly. 'Bless me,' she confided to the others, 'the girl's going dotty, I believe. Over-excitement isn't good for our poor sex.'

'Now we want a chair or something for the top bolt,' said Enderleigh.

'I think I can do it without, if you will allow me,' put in Carrados. 'I fancy that I am just a few inches to the good in that respect.'

'But really, Mr Carrados,' protested the lady, 'won't you get it on your clothes—or something?'

That is only a matter of carelessness, not vision,' replied Carrados. He gave the feather a dexterous turn in the neck of the bottle to remove the excess of oil before he withdrew it. 'Children have the keenest sight, Mrs Enderleigh, and yet look how they drop the jam about!'

'It's quite marvellous,' she murmured, watching him apply the oil and then work the action until the bolt slid easily.

'Not so much as you might think,' he assured her. 'Frequently you are indebted to other senses when you think you are using your eyes, and they get all the credit. Several men have told me that they always close their eyes when they are doing certain delicate adjustments.'

'I once knew a lady who always shut her eyes before she fired a gun off,' contributed Enderleigh. 'Yet she was fond of shooting, and often hit things.'

'Dogs or keepers?' inquired Myra politely.

Certainly the burglary did not seem to have damped anyone's spirits. Presently they went out to look at the incriminating footprints—'viewing the body' Myra called it—by candlelight until they were tired of striking matches and the friendly darkness put Carrados at liberty to go down on hands and knees and touch the well-marked impressions with his eerily perceptive fingers in his own peculiar way.

'What's this—snowing?' Enderleigh had exclaimed as he opened the door to lead the way into the garden. A sprinkling of white showed on the bare earth before them.

'Goose!' retorted Myra fondly, 'it's lime, of course. Old Benjamin—he's a sort of local unhandyman, Mr Carrados, whom Guy employs one day a week to sit in the garden and smoke shag—put it on only yesterday. He said the soil was too "thodden" for bulbs: it's always too something for Ben.'

'It came in useful, all the same,' said her husband. 'You see, the lime being crushed down in the footprints shows that they were made after it was put there. That's important.'

'Lapworth the Sleuth had already diagnosed that, O Fountain of Wisdom,' mocked his wife. She leaned forward and struck him lightly on the arm. 'You're it! Race you to the river, Guy!'

'Ssh!' warned Enderleigh with a nod towards their guest.

'Go, children—run,' urged Carrados benignly. 'I will follow at a pace more suited to my years.'

'Hold up!' cried Myra, limping into a walk before they were fairly off. 'I forgot; my feet are as soft as mush today. Besides, I oughtn't to now.'

'No, of course you oughtn't to,' said Guy severely. 'And we oughtn't to leave Mr Carrados like that. God knows what sort of a lunatic asylum he'll think he's dropped on.'

'Never mind: I got you away. Just one, Guy. And don't worry about him. He said his ears, but he meant his eyes, of course: his ears are sharp enough. That old man wouldn't take any harm if you put him down in the middle of a sawmill.'

'Old!' exclaimed Mr Enderleigh indignantly. 'Great Scott! What next?'

They walked back to meet the advancing Carrados, and then they all strolled soberly down to the extremity of the garden and stood contemplating the slow, muddy river before they turned back again.

'You take Mr Carrados into the dining-room, Guy,' said Myra, hastening on ahead as they neared the house. 'I'm going up to change my shoes—these are soaked.'

'Yes, my lady, you are pretty high up already, I'm afraid,' apostrophized her husband as they followed. 'That's the way of it, Mr Carrados. I shall think myself lucky if she isn't down below zero before the night is out.'

'I've taken hot water up to the spare room, sir,' said Chloe, as they passed her in the hall.

They washed their hands leisurely and went down to the dining room. The maid had lit the lamp and was replenishing the fire. Still Mrs Enderleigh did not appear. A few minutes passed rather flatly. Enderleigh made a half-hearted show of asking his guest if he was fond of this and that, but Carrados divined his vague uneasiness and soon they both frankly waited.

'Guy,' said a queer little voice just outside the door—it had been left somewhat ajar—'do you mind coming here a minute.'

Enderleigh threw a quick, inquiring look across, and the blind man—informed by what sense, who shall say?—nodded mute assent. Then the door closed and Carrados slowly turned his face to the four points of the room.

It was perhaps five minutes later that Enderleigh returned. He came thoughtfully across the room and stood close to his guest's chair.

'It's just as I was afraid,' he said, pitching his voice cautiously. 'Myra is now at a very minus stage indeed. And a curious thing—curious and trivial, and yet, I must admit, extraordinary—has happened to upset her. It's mixed up with one or two other matters, and I suppose that this burglary also—although that has nothing to do with it—has helped to put the emotional screw on. If you care to hear I will tell you with pleasure, especially as you have seen how bright she was a few minutes ago, but I don't want to bore you.'

'Go on,' said Carrados. 'Curious and trivial things that are extraordinary have never bored me yet.'

'Well, you shall judge. I indicated, over at your place, that we are expecting our little household to be increased in the course of a few months. Not unnaturally, Myra has to pass through a variety of new emotions on the subject, and she also has an unfortunate misgiving. It happened that her father was born club-footed and his father was disfigured in the same way. Of course, we tell her that it's all nonsense, but there is undeniably an element of heredity in that sort of thing, and she knows it well enough. Just now she is doubly prone to take notice of any kind of suggestion or premonition that may come along, especially on that one unlucky possibility. You heard her say that she was going up to change her shoes?

'Well, this is what has happened: she went upstairs, kicked off her wet shoes, and proceeded to pull on another pair. They are shoes that she has worn quite comfortably at intervals for the past few weeks, but now one—the right foot—would not go on. Thinking nothing of it, she picked up a shoe-lift and tried again. Still it refused to accommodate, and then she went to the light and looked more closely. . . . It wasn't likely to fit, Carrados, for the extraordinary thing is that those shoes, which she has worn quite easily and naturally a dozen times in the last few weeks, are both for the left foot!'

There was a rattle of cups and glasses as the attractive maid nearly dropped the tray she was bringing in. Enderleigh looked sharply round, but the girl kept her face averted and quickly went out again.

'There's another who's certainly got the jumps,' said her master. 'But about those shoes. Of course it's ridiculous, but you see the inference? In each forerunning case it was the right foot that was wrong, and so poor Myra is miraculously endowed with two left shoes at this moment as a sort of admonition than an ordinary right will not be needed. . . . But you don't see anything in it, I expect?'

'On the contrary,' replied Carrados slowly, 'I see so much in it—so many thousand possibilities, all wrong but one—that I should like to go up into a very large, perfectly bare attic, lit by several twenty thousand candle-power arc-lamps, and there meditate.'

'And the nearest thing I can offer you,' said Enderleigh, 'is the coal cellar. It's roomy as such places go and certainly practically empty now. For the rest—' He found the pleasantry difficult to sustain.

'So,' continued the blind man seriously, 'we must still proceed on directly material lines. I should very much like to handle the pair of shoes that has caused the trouble. Do you think Mrs Enderleigh would allow me?'

'Why not?' assented the lady's husband. 'I'll go and get them.'

He went, and returned almost immediately—but empty-handed.

'She's coming down now. Much better,' he whispered in the voice of a conspirator. 'Bringing them.' And almost at his heels a sobered Myra reappeared.

'I'm a hopeless little rabbit, Mr Carrados,' she apologised. 'Please don't say anything nice about it, because I am.'

'Rabbit!' ejaculated her natural protector loyally; 'rabbit! Why, Mr

Carrados, that—that sylph has the heart of a—a—well, I'm not strong on the faunas, but of whatever is the antithesis of rabbit.'

'That would be a ferret, wouldn't it?' asked Myra in her funny way. 'What a sad flatterer you are, Guy!'

'Go on,' said Guy happily. 'So long as you can laugh—'

She waved a reassuring hand to him across the room as she addressed their guest again.

'Of course, I know that he has told you all about it, Mr Carrados,' she said. 'Because when I taxed him he began by saying, "I only just—" Here is the mystery.'

It was a pair of pretty bronze shoes, neat yet not fragile, that she put into the blind man's hands. He held them one by one, and as his long, delicately-formed fingers brushed across their surface the two watchers received a curious impression of seeing something read.

'I shouldn't mind-I shouldn't mind the shoes a particle,' declared Myra—she felt compelled to speak to break the almost hypnotic quest of those understanding hands 'though, of course, they're no earthly use. But for weeks I've been wearing them all right, and now I know perfectly well that I couldn't. There's something wrong with me somewhere, don't you see?'

'But, dearest,' pleaded Guy soothingly, 'there's some perfectly simple explanation if only we could see it. Why, only just now you said that your feet were tender. That's probably it. You've got them sore, and so you can't put on the shoe. If they were all right you'd jump into them and not notice that anything was the matter, just as you have been doing up to now.'

'Don't talk tommy, Guy!' she exclaimed half wrathfully. 'As if I could possibly put on two left shoes without knowing it, even if I could get them on. And yet,' she wailed, 'I have been putting them on—that's the horrible thing about it.'

Carrados had apparently finished his scrutiny, for he was listening to this exchange in his usual benign complacency, and as he listened he absently rubbed his nose gently with the polished toe of a shoe.

'Set your mind at rest, Mrs Enderleigh,' he remarked quietly, as he offered her the other one. 'There is nothing wrong. You have never worn that shoe.'

'I have never worn it?'

'Neither you nor anybody else. The shoe has not been worn.'

'But look at the wear,' she persisted, displaying the scarified sole. 'Look at this worn lace.'

'The lace, yes,' he admitted, with unshaken confidence. 'But not the shoe.'

'But how can you possibly know that?'

'In exactly the same way that I could oil the bolt—by using other powers than that of sight.'

'Do you mean—' began Enderleigh, but Carrados interrupted him with uplifted hand.

'If I may suggest, please don't say anything more about the shoes just yet. At this moment Sergeant Lapworth has come to the door and your servant is admitting him. Let us hear what he has to say.'

Myra and Guy exchanged looks of bewilderment—almost of alarm—and then the girl's face cleared.

'Yes,' she exclaimed, 'I had forgotten to tell you. He did say that he would look in again after you got back, Guy.'

'If you please, m'm,' said Chloe at the door, 'there's the detective here again, and he would like to see the master if it's convenient.'

'Quite right,' replied Myra. 'Show him in here.'

Sergeant Lapworth was a plain-clothes man of the local staff. If he had a fault it was that of giving the impression of knowing more than he would tell, a suggestion that resulted in people sometimes finding him less omniscient in the end than they had expected. The Enderleighs were rather surprised at the sudden respect that came over him when he recognised their blind visitor.

'One or two small matters I thought I'd like to see you about, sir,' he said, addressing Mr Enderleigh. 'Those footprints by the side gate. I understand that no one came along that way between the time your gardener put the lime there yesterday and my seeing them this afternoon?'

'That is quite right,' agreed Myra. 'We allow the milkman to come in at the front gate and go to the side door, to save him carrying his can right round the other way. No one else came; I asked Chloe particularly.'

'You see the point, sir?' continued the sergeant, directing his voice at Mr Carrados this time. 'Whoever left those footprints is the man we want to put our hands on. We should like him to account for his movements last night at all events. Old Ben certainly never made those prints, sir. Now, I wonder,' the sergeant's voice became softly speculative as he leisurely felt in one or two pockets and finally produced a neat paper template of a boot, 'I wonder if this suggests anything to either of you?'

Myra shook her head and passed the paper on to Enderleigh.

'It's a man's boot, I suppose,' she said. 'It is broader than a woman's and the heel is twice as large. It's much smaller than any of yours, Guy.'

'Lord, yes,' he agreed. 'I'm miles beyond that.'

'Perhaps,' continued Sergeant Lapworth, becoming almost dreamy in his quiet detachment, 'perhaps this might help you more if you should ever have seen the original.' It was a small fancy button that he mysteriously produced this time from the Aladdin's cave among his garments. Myra's spirits went up.

'What a splendid clue, Mr Lapworth!' she exclaimed. 'Where did you find it?'

'I don't want anything said about it just yet,' he stipulated. 'As a matter of fact I picked it up in your scullery this afternoon.'

'It is a boot button, I suppose?' questioned Enderleigh. 'It strikes me as rather dressy.'

'It is the top of a pearl boot button undoubtedly, I should say,' pronounced the sergeant. 'One of those metal-shanked things that they wire into the boot nowadays. First question is, Does it belong to anyone of the house? I dare say you have plenty of pairs of fancy boots and shoes in use or put by, but it isn't a button that you would readily forget.'

Myra breathlessly agreed that if she had had boot buttons like that she would never have forgotten it, and added that if Guy had appeared with them she could never have forgiven it—a *sotto-voce* effort that elicited nothing more than an anxious look from her husband.

'And how about the young person in the kitchen?' suggested Lapworth.

'I know Chloe's boots, and it certainly doesn't come from there,' replied Chloe's mistress. 'However, you had better ask her, to make sure. Shall I ring now?'

'Don't trouble,' he replied, with a quite spontaneous glance towards the decanters on the table, as he returned the precious relic to its hiding-place. 'I can have a word with her as I go out. Now as regards the silver. Your good lady said that you would be able to make me out a list, sir.'

'Of course,' assented Enderleigh; 'that's got to be done, hasn't it? And then there'll be the insurance people. And then a young man introducing himself as "The Press". I'll tell you what, sergeant, this being burgled isn't such a soft thing after all.'

'I don't know, sir. It strikes me that you have come off uncommonly easy, seeing as how things were. No mess, no breakages, no odds and ends from every room that you can't remember until it's too late to claim. Just one big lot taken clean.'

'It would be about as much as he could take, anyway,' said the owner. 'I shouldn't like to heft that case far.' He casually indicated the group of liquors. 'What shall it be, sergeant?'

'I'll leave that to you, sir,' said the sergeant modestly. 'Yes, it would be a tidy load. I don't know that I ever remember the case being taken before. Reckon they had a car somewhere near.'

'Anyway, nothing was overlooked,' said Myra. 'There were some tankards out on the sideboard here, and three dozen spoons of various sizes in the drawer, and they went too. I put them—'

'You put them what?' prompted her husband, for Myra had stopped as though she had said her say.

'I haven't the faintest notion, dear,' she replied frankly. 'To tell the truth I think I was half asleep. Put what what?'

'Well, I think I'll be getting on along, sir,' said Lapworth, reading in this a pretty obvious hint. 'As soon as we hear from you—'

'Nonsense,' interposed Enderleigh, rather put out at the turn; 'have another first,' and he refilled the not altogether inflexible sergeant's glass.

There was a hesitating knock at the door and Chloe entered with a card.

'Please, m'm,' said the girl—Mrs Enderleigh happened to be seated nearest to her—'there's a gentleman would like to see the master for a minute.'

'"Wich"—"Mr William Wich",' read Myra. 'Isn't there a Lady Wich a few houses away?'

'Trefusis—Lady Wich, madam,' volunteered Lapworth. 'There is a Mr William, the son.'

'I'd better go out and see what it is,' said Enderleigh. 'Probably only a minute—excuse me, won't you?'

For so short a gap it did not seem worth while discovering a topic of conversation, and so no one broke the minute's silence. If they had spoken their thoughts the exchange would have been something after this fashion:

'I wonder if Lady Wich ever intends to call—city knight's widow, I suppose. Now will Mr Carrados go when the fat sergeant leaves, or does he expect that we have proper supper?'

'Bit of a card this Mr Willie Wich from what I hear. Old party keeps him in pretty tight by all accounts. Larky; girls. Damn fine stuff this Scotch here. Wonder if it'd be all right, if he does give the nod again, for me to—'

'She must stand five feet five—possibly six. At that, with the tread she has, she will take a 4½ to 5. Yes, under any vigorous exercise she might reasonably split a pliant 3½. There were certainly two definable personal exudations about the other shoe, and associable with them *syringa*—that's the girl—and *cheiranthus*—this one.'

The door opened and Enderleigh entered, then standing aside he waited for someone else.

'Rather curious,' he announced. 'Mr Wich has come to give us some information about our friend last night; so as we are all here— My wife; Mr Wich; Mr Carrados; Sergeant Lapworth.'

'It's really from my mother, you know,' said the dapper youth who followed the host in. 'She's a frightful invalid—heart and all that—so she sent me to tell you. We only just heard of what had happened: beastly shame—'

'We didn't know that you'd be interested,' ventured Myra graciously.

'Eh? Oh, I mean rotten luck being burgled like that. Well, it seems that last night the mater was having a bad turn and she had to get up and sit at the open window to have air. That's how it takes her. It seems that from her bedroom window one can see most of your garden— we live a couple of houses along: Trefusis, you know—and as she sat there she distinctly saw someone go down your garden towards the river and disappear among the trees. She says she wasn't taking much notice of it at the time, because there was no reason why there should be anything wrong in that, and it being dark she didn't see a lot, and she was feeling pretty washed out as well. But she did notice that it seemed to be a man carrying something large and heavy, and when she heard of this she thought you'd better know.'

'It's most awfully good of Lady Wich to send,' gushed Myra; 'and of you to come. We are just celebrating the event with frugal hospitality. Will you drink the toast "Our Absent Friend" in whisky, port, or coffee, Mr Wich?'

'Eh? Oh, I don't mind. The first for choice, thank you.'

'The river,' mused Lapworth. 'That's certainly an idea now: we couldn't find any likely motor wheel-tracks down the side road here. A boat waiting, you see. What time about would this be, sir?'

'Oh, about half-past twelve, she said.'

'Ah!' The sergeant continued to regard Mr Wich with an air of distant speculation while at the same time his hand went mechanically to his mysterious pocket. 'I suppose you didn't by any chance happen to be in the neighbourhood yourself at about that hour, sir?'

The perfect respect of the tone could not wholly disguise a certain significance in the question, and Willie Wich looked up to meet the sergeant's eyes on level terms. Enderleigh also found something arresting in the sudden tension that seemed to have involved two of his guests, while Carrados continued to gaze into unseen space with the faint half smile of placid contemplation. Myra alone appeared to have no interest in the passage, and her face was turned away, but her lips were tight pressed to hold back a cry of generous warning and her heart was thudding like an engine beat, for in a flash her eyes had followed Lapworth's and in a flash had seen on her spruce guest's extended foot a boot with identical pearl buttons, of which the upper one was missing.

The gap between the question and the answer was almost as long as it takes to tell of it, for with their eyes meeting Wich paused to consider his reply as though a thought urged caution.

'What do you quite mean by that?' he asked guardedly. 'You know, of course, that I live in the neighbourhood. Do you mean, was I at home?'

'Not exactly, sir,' replied the sergeant. 'You might have been passing this very house on your way home and thought you saw or heard something suspicious here and come nearer to investigate. Or you might have had a dog stray into this garden and come in to call it back, or a dozen things. What I should like to know is, did you come into this house or garden last night for any purpose?'

'I did not,' said Wich, his face relaxing into something like an amused grin. 'What is more, sergeant, I have never before been in this house or garden in the course of my long and industrious life.'

'That's quite definite, sir,' Lapworth admitted. 'In the circumstances would you mind stating where you were between the hours of eleven last night and two o'clock this morning?'

To those who knew him pretty well young Mr Wich was something of a puzzle, and they complained that you never knew how he would take it and whether the fellow was quite the fool he sometimes seemed.

'"In the circumstances", sergeant, seems to imply the existence of certain conditions of which I have no knowledge,' he now replied. 'Should I ever find myself in the dock of the Old Bailey, charged with the murder of a constable, or before the Surrey Petty Sessions accused of appropriating Mr Enderleigh's ancestral plate, either of those eventualities would constitute an aggregation of circumstances that would enforce my acquiescence. At present I fail to see any reason why I should render an account of my trivial life and movements.'

Sergeant Lapworth took out an irreproachably white pocket handkerchief and wiped his face profusely.

'Very good, sir,' he remarked with dark significance. 'Should you have any objection to my comparing this form'—here the sergeant dramatically produced his first exhibit—'with the boots you are now wearing?'

'Not the least,' replied the buoyant young man, raising his right foot to facilitate the operation; 'though I must protest against the attention thus gratuitously directed to my very unprepossessing footwear. Anything to assist the legitimate ends of justice. But not,' he added severely, 'of mere vulgar curiosity.'

Without deigning to reply, Sergeant Lapworth went down on one knee and from that position fitted the paper impression against the proffered boot. It was at once plain to everyone that the two outlines coincided perfectly. But an even more significant piece of evidence was to emerge, for as the sergeant performed this office he slyly inserted a nail in the angle of the instep and an appreciable sprinkling of white-peppered soil fell down into his hand.

'I must call your attention, sir, to the fact that this earth from your boot appears to correspond with the soil of the garden here.'

'I say!' exclaimed Mr Wich aghast, 'I am sorry, Mrs Enderleigh—bringing stuff like that into your pretty room!' Then with a bright look of toleration, 'But I expect you know what servants are!'

'Lastly,' said Sergeant Lapworth with admirable composure in spite of a rather flushed complexion, 'I shall be glad if you will look at this button which corresponds exactly with those on your boot, where one is missing.'

'Thank you,' replied young Mr Wich, passing it back again; it's very good of you to have kept it for me, but it's really no use. It isn't a button you sew on, but one of those metal-shanked affairs and the shank is broken.'

'Then I understand, sir, that you decline to assist us with any information?'

'Oh, no, you don't, sergeant—not if you understand the common or vernacular tongue, that is,' retorted his antagonist. 'So far, what I have declined is to give an account of my movements on the strength of an old button hypothetically lost at some time from my boot and a little piece of paper traced to measure. It may be the law that I have to if anyone shows me those: I must look that up. But you may remember that the only reason for my being here was to bring you information.'

'Oh, yes,' exclaimed Myra, completely won over by the suspect's ready nonchalance, 'we are all sure that Mr Wich is quite all right, Sergeant Lapworth. Aren't we, Guy?'

'Mrs Enderleigh,' put in Wich, gazing at her with melancholy admiration, 'before I go I must unburden my mind, and I'm afraid you may think very poorly of me in consequence. I did not purloin your silver and I have not the faintest idea who did. Goodbye.'

'Must you really go?' she asked. 'Please be sure and thank Lady Wich from me, won't you? And any Thursday.'

'If you would be so kind as to help a blind man to his car, Mr Wich,' interposed Carrados, and Enderleigh found his own proffered services quietly brushed aside.

'You don't say you are!' exclaimed Wich. 'I never tumbled to it. And that's your little jigger waiting then? I'm looking forward to something on four wheels myself, but so far I have to be content with two.'

'It's hardly worth while offering you a lift,' said Carrados, when they were in the road, 'but if you don't mind I should like to walk with you as far as your gate.'

'Right-o,' said Mr Wich, wondering who this queer customer who had made up to him might be. 'Lovely night, isn't it? What about your car?'

'It will follow presently; my driver understands. I have been trying to think where we have met before. Are you by any chance the Wich who made forty-nine for The Rest against Lord's Schools five years ago?'

'Oh, I say!' exclaimed his companion, becoming quite boyishly shy at the reference to this exploit. 'You don't mean to say that you remember that? Were you at Lord's?'

'Yes. I am fond of the minor fixtures; I can hear more play in them than often comes out in first-class matches. We did not speak, but you passed, and I thought I recognised your step again. A Winchester fellow was commenting on the game for me. You were given run out.'

'You must simply be a walking Wisden, sir.' said Wich, brimming with admiration. And then with a curious intonation in his voice he added, 'But why "given"?'

'I remember some reference to it. . . . Were you out?'

'As a matter of fact I was not,' he admitted.

'I don't think you made any fuss about it—quarrelled with the umpire or groused about the pavilion?'

'Well, should I be likely? . . . It was cricket.'

'Yes. . . . And now about this business?'

They had reached the gate of Trefusis, but the young man made no movement towards it, and presently they fell to walking slowly on again.

'That isn't so easy. Not by a long, long way. I was taken by surprise, I must admit; I hadn't a notion that there'd be any trace. Of course it would have been simple enough to tell the sergeant how it came about, if that was all.'

'You mean the lady in the case; or shall we say the girl in the shoes?'

'Partly; and then there is my mother. She would certainly have a heart-attack if she found that William had been taking her neighbour's handmaiden out to midnight carnivals and other forms of penance.'

'Is that quite—cricket?'

'Not absolutely M.C.C., perhaps, but it isn't to be inferred that I had the inklingest of who she was at first. And Chloe really is an awfully pretty girl, you know. What has she let out?'

'Nothing at all, so far as I am aware.'

'Then how on earth do you come to know of her—and the shoes?'

'Very much, I suppose, in the same way that Sergeant Lapworth has come to know of you and the boot—because the traces are so obvious.'

'I must say I think Chloe was a bit of a mutt to walk on the bed and then leave a button somewhere about. She might have learned better than that from the pictures surely.'

'Chloe naturally had not foreseen that the escapade would coincide with a burglary. But I would not be too ready to blame her, my young friend,' advised Carrados dryly. 'The most disastrous blunder of all was made by someone else.'

'That's a straight one,' said Mr Wich. 'What did I do?'

'Suppose you tell me about it?' suggested Mr Carrados. 'Under the seal of confidence.'

'I don't mind. I was going to see a lawyer first thing tomorrow to find out what I'd better do to circumvent the forces of law and order. Perhaps you could advise me?'

'Perhaps I could,' admitted Carrados. 'At all events I will.'

'There really isn't very much to tell,' said young Mr Wich pensively. 'I happened to be on the river alone a few months ago when I noticed a dazzling creature watching my feeble efforts from the bank. To have a nearer look I landed and asked her if she was not, excuse me, Miss Prendergast? She said no, but, how curious, she had been almost sure that I was a certain Mr Johnson. This constituting a deputy introduction on established lines I prevailed upon the bright vision to go for a short cruise and even to accept some slight refreshment of a light and portable nature.

'Under the auspices of the gods the idyll proceeded with exemplary propriety to run its normal course. So far as I was concerned the chief attraction was the extreme likelihood of detection and the certainty that everyone concerned would impute the very worst motives to my conduct when they did find out.

'On our usual "evening" last week I was indulging the delightful being's passion for a harmless beverage known as Tango Teaser when she espied a handbill announcing a cheap fancy dance at one of the public halls a few miles away and artlessly exclaimed:

'"I should love to go to one of those".

'Of course there was only one humanly possible reply to a heart-cry like that, and I gallantly made it.

'"And I should love to take you. Why not?"

'To this she said that it was absolutely impossible and we fell to making the arrangements. She was to creep out quietly by a side door after the others had gone to bed, lock the door after her and bring the key, and meet me at our usual trysting place—a spot a few hundred yards from our respective abodes. I would be there with my iron steed, and on the pillion thereof would whirl her into fairyland.

'Everything went off as per schedule. The only contretemps was that Chloe—have I mentioned that the heroine was Chloe, by the way?—ripped one of her shoes across and thus passed automatically into the retired list. I confess that I was surprised at the consternation the mishap occasioned the sweet chit, and then she told me. Ashamed at the deficiency of her own pedal outfit she had surreptitiously "borrowed" a pair belonging to her mistress. Detection would now inevitably follow, disgrace, possibly dismissal. Sighs, tears—heavens!—reproaches. Again I did the insane chivalrous thing and swore to replace the shoe within twelve hours or perish.'

'The rest is obvious. Chloe knew where they had been bought—a shop in Oxford Street—and I was to his me off at dawn and duplicate them. As there would be the business of giving the shoes the necessary "wear" it would be simpler to keep only one, and this I was to put into a clump of ivy on the garden side wall. But when it came to parting a difficulty arose: it was essential for me to have the split shoe as a pattern; I could not allow the fair penitent to walk stocking-footed along the stony road; and it wasn't wise to risk being seen together any nearer our houses. The simple way out was for me to lend her one of mine, and this I recovered from the ivy bush when I put the other one in. And there, Mr Carrados, you have the whole egg in a nutshell.'

'Everything went off all right then?' inquired Carrados maliciously.

'Like a clock. I obtained the exact thing in the exact size, scrubbed it down to the exact appearance of the other and put in the old lace. The superfluous shoe was flung over into an orchard somewhere Isleworth way. There was nothing much in all that. But now you see why it was impossible to satisfy Sergeant Lapworth's inopportune curiosity.'

'You may perhaps find it difficult to satisfy one or two other people as well. Did Chloe say anything when she let you in just now?'

'Why, yes; it struck me as ungracious at the time. The angel looked at me very weirdly and just said "Idiot!" I thought she must be overwrought.'

'I think it very likely. I told you that there had been other blunders besides Chloe's. What she wished to indicate by a single appropriate word, my budding Lothario, was that you had thrown away the wrong shoe, with the consequence that Mrs Enderleigh is now on the verge of hysterics at an apparent miracle.'

'No!' exclaimed Wich incredulously, 'I could not. And yet, surely, Oh, good Lord, I did! I kept them to make a pair—the new one and the other, instead of. . . . Well, I am a prize fathead! What will happen now?'

'What? Why the extreme probability that you have had your trouble for nothing and that Chloe will be sacked after all.'

'Oh, I don't think that—not after seeing Mrs Enderleigh. You and

Chloe both misjudge her strangely. She seems the jolliest sort of girl to me. I bet she'll understand.'

'I'll bet she will,' assented Carrados grimly. 'And when she understands that her pretty servant has been wearing her things, sneaking out at nights (to say nothing about giving burglars the chance of sneaking in) to foot it at dance-halls with the young spark from next-door-but-one, you may not find her quite so sympathetic as she was half an hour ago. If she doesn't take the opportunity of calling upon Lady Wich about it I'm badly out.'

'It's a mug's business,' said Mr Wich with a qualmish note in his voice. 'What had I better do?'

'What you had better do is to leave it in my hands and agree to my condition.'

'What condition?'

'That you never go gallivanting with Chloe again. You both "don't mean anything", but suppose you did happen to get the girl discharged with a very dubious character? Should you see any alternative to behaving either as a fool or a knave to put it right?'

'Whew!' exclaimed Mr Wich, easing the collar against his neck, 'that's heart-to-heart stuff. Well, if you can bring it off I'm good for my part. Chloe certainly is a dazzling thing, but, strictly between ourselves, her mind is little more than an assortment of obsolete film captions.'

★★★★★★

When Mr Enderleigh returned from business the next day Myra greeted him with a subdued note. It was plain that the excitement had quite worn off.

'If Mr Carrados is really going to be useful to you, Guy, of course I shall do my best to amuse him. But I wonder all the same if he is going to make a practice of dropping in every evening.'

'How so?' demanded Guy.

'He rang me up this afternoon and hoped that we should both be in later as he would like to call. I had to say we should be charmed.'

'Just as well you did, my lady,' remarked Guy. 'Do you know that quite important people have a most extraordinary opinion of the man, and I am told that Scotland Yard will do anything to oblige him. That's what I've come across today.'

'My gracious!' said Myra, deeply impressed; 'it's just as well I fawned. Talking about police, I met Sergeant Lapworth in the road this morning and he seemed very odd. He said they had received instructions to go slow in taking any steps.'

'That ought to suit them down to the ground,' suggested Guy pessimistically. 'We don't look like seeing any of our plate again, old girl.'

'I don't know, Guy. It struck me that Sergeant Lapworth knew more than he would tell. He said that they expected developments.'

'It used to be "were investigating a clue",' said the unimpressed gentleman.

Mrs Enderleigh had named nine o'clock as a convenient hour and with the busy man's punctuality nine o'clock found Mr Carrados walking up the Homecraft garden path. Looking out, the lady of the house felt a pleasant access of importance, arising from the notable proportions of the car waiting at her gate.

'How nice of you to come again!' she exclaimed playfully. 'After the alarms and excursions of yesterday I hardly dared to hope it.'

'Oh, yes,' he replied prosaically, 'your husband and I have some small business details to discuss.'

'Of course,' she assented quickly. 'I am going to leave you at it.'

'But first,' he continued, 'I have a bargain to offer you.'

'Offer me? How exciting! Whatever can it be?'

'You really want to get your silver back again?'

'Why, naturally. Guy tells me that we shall only receive about half the value the way our policy goes—isn't it, Guy?'

'I'm afraid it is,' admitted her husband.

'And that's only money. To both of us many of the things are priceless.'

'While you have no particular affection for that odd pair of shoes?'

'Shoes? Oh, *those*! How ridiculous, Mr Carrados! You are not coming like an up-to-date genie to offer silver plates for old shoes, are you?'

'You have guessed. But there's always a catch about these attractive bargains, you remember. If you agree to let the shoes go, everything connected with them goes also. You have no curiosity, make no inquiries, entertain no suspicions: it is to be as though they and all that appertains to them had never been.'

'I wonder if I understand?' mused Myra with a sharp little look in his direction.

'I think you do,' replied Carrados. 'You are—forgive the homely phrase—no fool, Mrs Enderleigh. If you do not quite understand yet it's only because you have not had time to think about it. You soon would.'

'All right; I'll take it,' said Myra, with a very sporting air.

'But do you mean that you actually know now where the silver is?' demanded Enderleigh.

'I know where the silver is,' Carrados admitted.

'Where?' exclaimed two simultaneous voices.

'When you went off a few days ago, you expressed a wish as to where it might be, Mr Enderleigh, didn't you?'

'What was that?' asked Myra, from whose mind the malediction had apparently faded. Her husband, on the contrary, remembered very well and he coloured at the recollection.

'I am sorry to be reminded of that,' he said moodily. 'Something happened to put me out, Myra, and in a moment of irritation, without meaning it, I said I wished the stuff at the bottom of the river. That's all.'

'Yes; that's the way with you impulsive people, as we *genii* are always finding. You want a thing and then discover that you don't. Well, my friend, you have got your wish, willy-nilly. The stuff is at the bottom of the river.'

'What a lark!' exclaimed the lady.

'The burglars dropped it or hid it there?' said her husband, keenly intrigued. 'How on earth did you find that out?'

'The burglars had nothing to do with it, because there was no burglar—no burglary,' was the reply.

'Oh, but I say! Besides, it's gone. No, Mr Carrados! And then the side door key, you know.'

'Hush!' said Carrados mysteriously. 'That doesn't count. The side door key went, according to our bargain, with the shoes.'

'Very well,' acquiesced Myra, with something very like a giggle, 'but if there was no burglar how did the silver get into the river?'

'How?' Carrados raised an accusing finger and slowly brought it dead level on his hostess. 'How? Behold the culprit! You, my dear lady, threw it there!'

Moved by a common impulse Guy and Myra came slowly to their feet. Looking at Max Carrados's quietly smiling face it seemed impossible to believe that he—to doubt that he—to know what to think.

'I—threw—it—there?' articulated Myra queerly.

'You deliberately cast the "damned stuff" in. Rising in the dead of night, without staying to put on slippers or to cover those inadequate garments that are no longer the prerogative of my sex, you crept down, carefully replaced the silver lying about, took up the burden, let yourself out by the French window in the drawing-room, crossed the lawn, reached the silent river, and with a sigh of relief at accomplishing so meritorious a task, tipped the whole bag of tricks into the water. All in a profound sleep, of course. By the way, I hope your feet are better today?'

Myra sat down again with a strange look in her eyes.

'But I could not—I could not even move the box,' she whispered.

'Not when you are awake,' he replied, becoming grave again. 'And do you know why that is? It is because you know that you cannot, and so, your slavish body assenting, you really cannot. But in your sleep you do not know it; your unbound mind admits no limits, and so—'

'Do you know,' interposed Enderleigh sagely, 'I've heard something like that several tunes lately. I suppose there may be something in it after all.'

'Anyway,' said Mr Carrados, 'there is one thing you can congratulate yourself on. A wife who carries out her husband's slightest wish even in her sleep is a woman in a thousand.'

The Ingenious Mind of Mr Rigby Lacksome

The mysterious affair of the anatomical subject, that ended in a Great Western corridor express, really began in a New York Mansion when Mr Hiram S. Nogg, wearing noiseless slippers, inconsiderately wandered into the remotest of his five palatial drawing-rooms, to the embarrassment of his niece Sabina and the even more pronounced dismay of Rigby Lacksome. In the terms of Mr Lacksome's unspoken comment, the premature discovery of the idyll 'knocked a piece of varnish off the mudguard,' and he rapidly speculated that unless something drastic and convincing could be brought into the situation not only his excellent chance of winning Miss Craddock's hand, together with a reasonable settlement, but even his tenure of usefulness as Mr Nogg's third secretary stood in jeopardy. But having been modelling himself on the strong silent pattern for some time past, nothing really useful occurred to him.

'Well, Pop,' remarked the maiden, after she had nicked her hair into position (long residence in the Nogg household had led to the adoption of this unpleasant form of endearment at her lips), 'what you gotta say about it?'

'Rainproof' Nogg fingered his scanty goatee dubiously and looked from one to the other of the young people in mild reproach. He had been warned by his private specialist that strong emotion consumed tissue, so he never ran to it now that he was seventy-five. He just acted in the same way, but without the excuse of deep feeling.

'Don't know that I've anything much to say, Sabbie,' he replied guardedly. 'Leastways, not in words. Rigby was going to Europe for the sales next week. Reckon he'd better go over just the same—and maybe stay there.'

'I guess not,' speculated Miss Craddock in an equally level voice, 'England's all right for a trip, but I don't congeal to the idea of a permanency. I must have room to reverse in.'

'I wasn't exactly thinking of you, Sabbie,' said the old man.

'No,' agreed Sabina. 'But from a child onwards I've always been encouraged to think for myself. And from what Rigby's just said I understand that if he went he'd wish to take me with him.'

'I hope, sir, you won't consider that there's anything clahndestine in my cawnduct beneath your roof.' Bracing himself against the Sicilian marble mantelpiece Rigby began to recover something of the attitude of the Noble Lover, a pose necessarily checked as yet by the uncertainty of the old man's real feelings. 'For some time past I have regarded Miss Craddock with sentiments of respectful admiration, but until this morning, when speaking of my forthcoming trip to Yurrup, I have never—'

'That so?' interrupted Mr Nogg enigmatically. 'Well we'll leave it there. Now, did that Shrubworth sale catalogue come in from Sotheby's by this morning's mail?'

'Yes, sir,' replied Rigby rather blankly. That was old Nogg all over—until it suited his own convenience the young man wouldn't have the least indication whether it was going to be the foot of ignominious expulsion or the hand of golden blessing.

'I want to go through it with you then,' said Hiram briskly. 'Bring it to my room when Johnson leaves.' He slid noiselessly away again, and after a very subdued exchange of protestations with his *inamorata* Rigby followed him. As he went to find the catalogue of the celebrated Shrubworth collection of Shakespeariana he was thinking harder and more rapidly than he had perhaps ever done before.

★★★★★★

Max Carrados, you may remember, had some connexion with the United States. He had inherited his not inconsiderable fortune from an American cousin, who had in his time been a successful speculator—a speculator not exactly in crops, which are notoriously kittle-cattle, but in official crop reports. With a select few of his friends out there the blind man endeavoured to hold for a little longer a solitary outpost of the lost cause of polite correspondence. It is to be inferred that his contributions were acceptable; in return he certainly learned much that even the sleuths of American journalism failed to get on to, and once or twice his information was curiously effective.

'I doubt if you will ever have met "Rainproof" Nogg,' wrote one about this time—a shrewd old lady whose Dutch-sounding name caused pushful young hostesses to prick up their ears even when it reached them at third hand. 'Not a great many years ago he was living precariously on the crumbs that fall from rich men's waste-paper baskets, but during the last decade or two he has shot forward amazingly. I don't quite know what he does, but if I had a son—no, I should prefer it to be my grandson—I think I would put him to it. We have wheat "kings" and cotton "kings" and coal "kings"; railroad "kings", stationary engine "kings", and Mr Ford; "kings" in the realms of hardware, software, sectional bookcases, crime, and canned tomatoes. But all these sovereigns have some connexion with the domains they represent. I have never heard that Rainproof Nogg had any connexion with anything. I believe that people just bring schemes to him and if he approves of them they give him a share of the scheme for approving. It seems an easy way.

'At any rate, Mr Nogg is vastly wealthy, but he is growing old. This disease, I am told, has brought a morbid affection in its train: a dread that when he is dead he will be forgotten. It has become a terrible thing that in spite of his power and influence now, when he is gone his memory will soon be utterly effaced. I suppose he has been thinking. True, he has three thin-lipped, razor-jawed, stern-faced Wall Street sons, who will doubtless go on gathering more and more moss around the name of Nogg until the Constitution is amended to suppress them. ("So long as I can keep the money-making in the family, I can afford to pay other people to do the spending," is a golden Noggett.) But that only raises the problem one power higher: Rainproof, poor romanticist, wants to be remembered in the way that George Washington, Col. W. F. Cody, Pocahontas, and Mary Garden will always be.

'You have heard of his National Temple out in Virginia? That we possessed no Westminster Abbey must have touched his native pride somewhere, and he has set out to remove the slur by building and endowing a lordly private Valhalla on one of his seventeen estates for the last sleep of the great. Eminent Americans are to be invited to direct by will their interment there; and in the case of Americans not so eminent as to be invited, but who have nevertheless expressed a wish to join the others, a committee will decide. It seems a touchy business all along. . . . One cannot but think that Rainproof will have established a lien on the verdict of that committee when his own case comes up. A long shot, it may be, at immortality, but longer ones have hit; or Guido

Fawkes, William Tell, and Samuel Pepys were forgotten now.

'In another direction Mr Nogg has found what I imagine has been signally lacking in his life hereto—amusement. And this brings me at last back to my original sheep—a fleece in which you may discover the predatory Rainproof's lupine form. You collect something I know, but what it is between cigarette pictures and stuffed mammoths I can plead the most benighted ignorance. But I know that you will have the best of them whatever they are—and so, hark ye, my friend, a word in your judicious ear. If-if they should be Shakespeariana by any chance, lock them up until you hear that a young man called Rigby Lacksome has returned to the land of his fathers.

'For by this time Rainproof is quite slightly Shakespeare mad. A while ago he was advised by a prominent nerve and stomach consultant (the two things go together here it seems) to "cultivate more interest outside business". Rainproof made the one recorded joke of his existence then, but let that pass. Whether the poor old gentleman heard the Bard's curious name for the first time about that period, or whether it was because his great financial rival "Slogger" Macmahomet was commissioning Frissman to corner First Folios matters not. At all events, Rainproof went down into the Shakespeariana pit and became a bull power.

'His first acquisition was a wistful young expert who had been in the ancient book business but who was quite content to get out of it—Mr Lacksome, to wit. He was to be Rainproof's librarian and Shakespeare secretary. This, I glean, is how they got to work.

'"See here," said Mr Nogg, "I hear that fellow on the other side the street has just given fifteen hundred dollars for a book called Hamlet, printed way back in the Dark Ages. Now I shall expect you to go one better."

'R.L. considered.

'"I know of a copy that might be got," he replied. "But you would have to go at least two hundred dollars more because it is half an inch taller than Macmahomet's example."

'"Inch!" snapped Rainproof, "I don't do things by inches now, young man. Find me one that's about half a yard taller and I won't jib at two thousand dollars more".

'He has been put wiser since then. You will have heard of the anonymous purchase last fall of the Croxton Park First Folio for four thousand guineas (he buys anonymously on Wall Street principles). Yes, like Macheath's Polly, Mr Nogg by now is "most confoundedly bit."

'Will I bring this disquisition to a seemly close? I will, sir, and then only will you plumb its dark significance. R.L. is on his mettle, and the attitude of Rainproof is that of an expectant child with its mouth open and its eyes closed. For the engaging young librarian has fallen beneath the charm of Rainproof's not wholly guileless niece, and in return has found favour in her eyes. But what, everyone will naturally ask, what about the expression of old man Nogg's eyes, for on that the exact complexion of love's young dream must turn? Well, our quite astute Romeo has thrown out a very effective fly and the poor fish has risen. It is to be something so rarely and preciously Shakespearian that our hero begs the continuance of his employer's confidence until his return. Is this mere bluff for time? Or what—a manuscript, a signature, another portrait, a counter-cryptogram? However, young Lochinvar has gone out of the West—*verbum sap.*

'For you collectors are—well, how shall I put it? Rainproof will do it for me.

'"Reckon even in England they take some stock of W. Shakespeare as an asset. So if you get a safe chance at anything unique, Rigby, don't think that I shall worry you any about just how it happened—so long as I don't come in it," he remarked.

'"I just bet you won't sir," replied R.L. frankly.

'So now you know.'

******

Mr Carrados dropped the copy of the *Pall Mall Gazette* that he had been reading and turned to light a cigarette.

'Greatorex,' he remarked across the room; 'this is the Suffragettes' latest: they have tried to blow up Stratford-on-Avon Church.'

'My Sunday hat!' exclaimed the secretary, deeply impressed. 'So that was it!'

'Was what?'

With no particular appearance of regret Annesley Greatorex detached himself from the occupation of typing letters and came across to his employer's chair.

'In a sort of way I suppose I am an accessory before the fact,' he remarked with some complacency. 'At least, I knew that they were up to some special brand of devilment from Moya's hints and general air of mystery and triumph. Began about last Friday.'

'Moya?' repeated Mr Carrados. 'Do you mean to say that your shy little sister has become a "militant"?'

Mr Greatorex essayed a hollow laugh with considerable success.

'"Shy", you said, sir! And I think you saw Moya less than six months ago? Well, the shrinking violet has been "had" twice since then for brawling, and if her mother hadn't contrived influenza in the very nick of time I understand that the timid fawn had arranged to chain herself to the minute hand of Big Ben.'

'To prove that women are moving with the time, I suppose? Fine spirit, Greatorex.'

'Moral hashish, I tell her, sir,' amended Annesley with severity. 'It's a pretty grey outlook for England if these are a sample of the mothers of the coming generation.'

Max Carrados turned away from his ingenuous young assistant in order to strike a match for which he had no use.

'What did you hear about this business?' he asked, indicating the open paper.

'Well, you know what these young women are. I won't say they can't keep a secret, but at the same time they like to let it out on a string and then pull it back again. Now that Moya is on the active list of the precious "cause" she and half a dozen other hectics are in and out of our place like rabbits all day long. And ever since Friday there's been a sort of "We could and if we would" *innuendo* in the air.'

'Hallo!' exclaimed Mr Carrados with interest. 'Shakespeare again. How the Bard persists.'

'Force of example, sir. Moya and her new friend Mamie have been shrieking appropriate quotations at one another, upstairs and down, for days past. Of course, I didn't see the exact point of the various shafts of wit until now, but this is evidently what was brewing.'

'Oh,' thought Mr Carrados speculatively, 'Mamie!' 'Trust an American,' he said aloud, 'to know more Shakespeare than nine out of ten of us. I suppose your sister's friend is from the States?'

'She just is sir,' replied Mr Greatorex, pitching his voice into what he considered an appropriate twang. 'And devoted to the emancipation of her downtrawd'n Bri'sh sisters. Says they are real ladies but want gingering some. Seems to be doing it too. I'll bet this last affair was her idea.'

'Do you know what she is doing here?'

She says she is the European representative of the *Bluff Folly Weekly Rapier*. My holy aunt!'

All rather slack and jejune doubtless. But Annesley Greatorex was no fool despite his occasional lapses of exuberance. He knew precisely to the dot of an 'i' and the crossing of a 't' where he stood with Mr Carrados, and when the blind man merely indicated the newspaper paragraph that had started the digression it was read aloud to him with excellent clearness and diction by an entirely staid and businesslike assistant.

ATTEMPT TO BLOW UP

STRATFORD-ON-AVON CHURCH

SUFFRAGETTES' LATEST OUTRAGE

Shortly after midnight a determined attempt was made to wreck a portion of Holy Trinity Church, Stratford-on-Avon, by means of an explosive bomb. Many residents in various parts of the town were awakened about that hour by a loud report, and on investigation being made it was discovered that a sensational attack had been carried out with the parish church as its objective. Both the fire brigade and the police were quickly on the spot, but the services of neither were immediately required, for no conflagration resulted from the explosion and the dastardly perpetrators of the outrage were clear of the scene before the earliest investigators arrived. Copies of suffragette leaflets strewn about clearly indicate the purpose of this discreditable affair.

Detailed examination made when it was light reveals the extent of the damage is less than might have been expected. The spot chosen for the attack is on the north side of the chancel, and here several courses of masonry are shattered, much glass— fortunately all modern—broken, and the tracery of one window destroyed. The exact point of the explosion was against the walled-up doorway of what is known as the old "charnel house", and here the force of the bomb is shown by the dummy door on the interior being blown out. Those familiar with the sacred edifice will recognise from this description that the explosion took place within a few feet of Shakespeare's monument. It may be assumed, indeed, that this was the real objective, and that nothing but a slight miscalculation due to the darkness of the night, and, possibly, the nature of the explosive used, saved it from destruction. Fortunately we are spared this crowning act of vandalism; the monument is absolutely untouched and the actual damage can be made good without any loss of historic association."

538

That is all, sir—no, here is something more about it in the "fudge".

Greatorex rearranged the paper to display the 'Stop Press' space and read on.

Stratford-on-Avon Explosion—Later

A representative of Mr Hiram S. Nogg, the American millionaire and Shakespearian enthusiast, who happens to be staying in the town, communicated with his principal as soon as the news of the outrage reached him. As a result of this timely intervention Mr Nogg has generously undertaken to defray the entire cost of repairs. The work will be put in hand immediately, the church meanwhile being closed to the public.

'I think that really is all, sir.'

'Thank you, said Mr Carrados; 'that will do. Now bring me Valp's *First Empire*, will you. I want a reference.'

Greatorex stared at his employer almost with concern.

'I'm sorry, but don't you remember? You advised me to read it and—'

'True. I told you to take it home with you. It's still there?'

'Yes, sir. . . . But I could cut out and be back under the hour—time to do these letters for the post.'

'No; I want you for something else. . . . And Parkinson is out. I wonder—'

'I could phone to some people who live next door. They'd take a message in, and if Moya is about she'd bring it like a shot.'

'Do you think so? That would be very convenient, but it seems rather too bad—'

'Not a bit, sir,' declared Annesley with easy generosity. 'She thinks no end of you; in fact, only the other day she said that if she was put on to set this house on fire she wouldn't—'

'Really?' said Max Carrados, much gratified apparently.

'Yes; she said she'd certainly persuade someone else to do the job. But, of course, at this hour it's just a toss up—'

As it happened, however, Mr Carrados might be said to have won the toss, for Miss Greatorex was discovered to be at home, and as she arrived at The Turrets within forty minutes she may be judged to have come 'like a shot'. She was a small, elfin creature (the good looks of the family had begun and ended with Annesley), who in intimate political circles was generally referred to as 'The Vole'.

'Come and have some tea, Miss Greatorex, and tell me all the Secret History of the day,' suggested Mr Carrados, and grinning amiably the Vole complied—to the extent of taking tea, at all events.

'I know that you don't quite approve of us yet, Mr Carrados,' she remarked, 'but that's only because you've never really thought it out. None but the very young and the very stupid are actually hostile.'

'They're all as pert as poll parrots, sir,' apologised Annesley. 'That's a fair sample.'

Moya showed her splendid little teeth at him across the table, but refrained from any of the half-dozen appropriate retorts provided by the textbook for the occasion. After all, there would be no particular sense in exposing Annesley's intellectual shallowness to his employer; and she was quite reasonably fond of her brother—although he would come on the forthcoming Register, with lodger qualification.

'I suppose this is some of your fatuous work?' he remarked presently, pointing to the open evening paper. 'I hope you are proud of it.'

'Officially, I know nothing of it, Buttons,' she replied graciously. 'But it seems to have made some stir. Good heavens! Can that possibly be what the idiots intended?'

'Well, for mercy's sake don't call me by that ridiculous name, now we're grown up,' he besought. 'At least, I am.'

'You certainly came within an ace of making a much greater stir,' interposed the host, as peacemaker. 'I wonder how your friends came to miss the monument.'

'Perhaps they didn't want to hit it,' suggested the girl cryptically.

'Don't you believe it, sir,' put in Annesley with vigour. 'They'd blow up old Shakespeare himself, if they could, to keep in the limelight.'

'Mr Carrados, do you think that the man who created Portia would object in the least to having that smug, fat-headed image of a retired pork-butcher blown into atoms, if it would help to get her the vote?'

'I think,' replied Mr Carrados with a laugh, 'that he would recommend you to make better bombs—if you want to prove that you can do anything.'

'Hear, hear,' applauded Annesley, somewhat at a venture.

Moya Greatorex shot a curious little glance at the smiling Carrados and a quizzical expression twisted her small face.

'I don't mind telling you something, Mr Carrados,' she remarked, looking down upon her plate demurely. 'It was a man who contrived this particular demonstration.'

'Oh, we Englishmen can't,' he hastened to declare. 'Too law-abiding, I suppose. You ought to get an Irishman—or an American—to do that sort of job.'

'How sharp you are,' she laughed. 'Well, as it happens, he *is* an American!'

In the pause—of indignation on one gentleman's part but of signal complacency on the other's—that followed this little note of triumph, Miss Greatorex rose to go.

'Goodbye,' she said, giving Carrados her hand. 'I'm very glad to have been of this slight service to you.'

'Thank you,' he replied. 'It was most good of you to bring the book.'

'Oh, the book.' She dismissed that casually. 'Yes. But of course I was referring to the information that you wanted. Frankly, Mr Carrados, I'm not at all satisfied with the ins-and-outs of that affair myself.'

She nodded luminously and under the escort of a rather mystified brother took her departure.

'Greatorex,' remarked the blind man, when his secretary returned, 'I am not subscribing to a general principle at all, but it would be absurd to deny that your sister ought to have a vote.'

It was in this haphazard way that Mr Carrados was fated to be drawn into the curious Shakespeare case—a gossipy letter from an American friend coupled with the Stratford-on-Avon outrage, and the contiguous circumstance that his secretary's sister happened to be in the council of the 'militants'. Personally, it was no affair of his: whatever Rigby Lacksome had in mind, a cabinet of Greek *tetradrachms* did not attract him; and it would be idle to pretend that the amateur criminologist was stirred by public spirit to interest himself in a felony that he saw impending. He would be just as likely to assist in it if his sympathy went that way. No, as he himself would be the first to admit, it was nothing but the element of mystery that attracted here; until that had been set at rest something unsatisfied would continue to disturb the even balance of his mind.

'That is well enough, my friend,' he said to himself that night, 'but you have precious little to go on. Coincidence is simply the meeting of two straight lines, and they, we all know, can never enclose a space. Before going any farther on a wild goose chase I should advise you to verify the admitted American influence in the affair as connectible with Rigby Lacksome, the get-Shakespeariana-anyhow figure in the drama. Until that point is settled both wings of your deductions are purely in the air.'

'All right,' replied the other moiety. 'I will. That strange young creature certainly will know, and if I ask her nicely (as I might have had the sense to do before) I think she may have enough originality to tell me.'

'Do you?' scoffed the negative participant. 'Well, I very much doubt it.'

Without wasting any more time in arguing, Mr Carrados sat down and wrote his diplomatic little note. He had to wait several posts for any answer—he heard incidentally from Greatorex that his sister was 'out for scalps' somewhere—but one at length arrived. This was the form it took:

Dear Mr Carrados,
In reply to yours, the reference you require would seem to be in Brutus's third speech, *Julius Caesar*, Act i, scene 2.
Yours truly,
Moya Greatorex

'Reference I require?' pondered the recipient dubiously, walking to a bookcase. 'Now, did I—' By this time his hand had gone unerringly to the book he sought, and he was turning the pages among the Tragedies. 'Well, anyhow, here is the reference I require, whatever it is:

Brutus: I am not gamesome; I do lack some part
Of that quick spirit that is in Antony.

A sudden light broke upon him and he repeated the first line with expression.

'"Lack some part." Lacksome, of course. That girl is a born conspirator, I'll take oath. In fifteenth-century Italy she'd have been up to the neck with some ring-and-dagger party. . . . In these prosaic days she has to be a militant suffragette. . . . Well, that settles it.'

But what did it settle, after all? Assuming the accuracy of his information, the curious fact was established that Mr Rigby Lacksome, ostensibly in England to attend the book sales, had prompted a convenient organisation to carry out a raid on a certain historic building, while he himself immediately appeared on the scene with an arrangement to make good the damage. It could scarcely be an elaborate plan to get Rainproof's name associated with Stratford; that result could have been obtained in a hundred showier and less expensive ways. There was also a detail that might begin to assume significance: one gathered that on the whole the demonstration had somehow missed its full point. The local reports suggested so much, and Moya's suspicions might very well have been awakened by that very fact. Carrados was inclined to agree with his outspoken secretary that the 'militants', then at the apex of their frenzy, would be much more likely to blow up the poet's tomb itself, rather than to spare his effigy. Was there, indeed, some double purpose here at work?

In a reflective mood Robinson Crusoe made a tabulated statement of the prospects of his case. In much the same vein Max Carrados now drew a sheet of foolscap before him and stated the position:

'What does Rigby Lacksome need?

'He must procure an incomparable Shakespeare item before he returns—fair means or foul allowed.

'What has he achieved already?

'He had gained the most privileged access to Stratford-on-Avon church under unique conditions. The church and grounds will be closed against further "militant" attacks. The portions under repair may be screened off if he requires it, and there is no reason to suppose that he cannot introduce workmen of his own selecting.

'What special points will be under his direct control?

'Shakespeare's monument and Shakespeare's grave are both at this spot.'

Carrados creased and recreased the sheet of paper a dozen times with absent-minded precision as he began to pace the room, making his way among the scattered furniture with startling certainty; pausing now and then to touch a special piece of ivory or bronze, just as another's eyes might linger for a moment on a possession in half-unconscious satisfaction.

The monument; the grave.....The grave; the monument.

Among the many very baffling inconsistencies of Shakespeare's life the outstanding mystery is surely this: that of all his prolific work ('in bulk almost equal to the English Bible; in importance second only to that book'), not a line of manuscript is known to exist today. Nothing approaching this complete effacement can be paralleled in literary history, and to equip legend, when the poet who scrupulously particularized his worn wearing attire and his second-best bed came to the making of a will, not the obliquest reference to the contingencies of thirty-seven dramas finds a place therein. If William Shakespeare had been the greatest exponent of the modern method he could scarcely have planned a more effective 'stunt'. The Baconian heresy is one of its first-born—certainly the lustiest of its offsprings—but the curious inquirer among the byways of literary credulity will start many another hare.

The monument; the grave. . . .

What, for instance, was that American theory (most of the Shakespeare heterodoxies spring from that vigorous soil) that in the poet's tomb, secure beneath the everlasting curse—though too much strain should not be put on that protection in these material days—the missing manuscripts may still be found, *in extenso* and intact? Well, as to that, both before Shakespeare's time and after, poets have buried their lyrics in their own graves or someone else's—and one at least of the greatest of the latter has repented and dug them up again.

'I don't feel drawn to that particular line,' mused the blind man, wheeling short on his beat to seek his bookshelves again. 'No one believed it here, and I doubt if anyone now does in the States. No, Judith made greased cake-papers of the sheets of *Romeo and Juliet* that she found about, and practical-minded W.S. nodded approval. But, ye gods! imagine a complete and original MS. of, say, *Hamlet* today! Would gold, literally in millions, buy it?' He drew from its shelf a volume of that useful series *The American Catalogue* and soon found the entry he required.

"Where are Wm. Shakespeare's Manuscripts?" By Hasdrubal Pott. Philadelphia. 1866. It might be worth while to look it up. Lacksome will certainly know of it, and one must be on equal terms with him.

He copied the details with his invariable precision and added a line for Greatorex's guidance:

'Shadrock, of Museum Street, will be the likeliest to have this.

'It's wrong, wrong, wrong,' he repeated softly as he put back the book. 'I should feel it down to my finger-ends if I was going right; but what else can there be? The monument . . . . no earthly use or chance there. After all, Lucy Heemskerk did specify manuscript, and she may have had an inkling. Perhaps I'd better make sure of what she really says.'

It was easy in that room of perfect system to refer to anything, and in another minute Carrados was reading again the faintly ironic commentary on Rainproof Nogg's lamentable ambitions. At the time that he had received the letter he had attached only the interest of amusement to a warning that was plainly half or wholly jest, but now, as he touched line after line, his long delicate fingers seemed to linger for an inspiration.

And then in a flash it came.

'. . . You have heard of his National Temple out in Virginia . . . a lordly private Valhalla . . . for the last sleep of the great . . . . For by this time Rainproof is quite slightly Shakespeare made....'

The paper fell unheeded from the blind man's hand; he was caught up in the magnificence of the brazen enterprise.

'My gosh!' he exclaimed at last; 'but that would lick creation, wouldn't it, Uncle Sam?'

★★★★★★

It is one thing to 'know' that you are right; it is rather another to go to the length of putting your entirely unsupported conviction into practice. Before he had bargained for quite so astonishing a revelation, Mr Carrados had pledged himself in his note to Moya Greatorex that there should be no prosecution. He nearly always kept that sort of undertaking, and in the present case he had no intention of departing from it, but it might mean that he would be able to avail himself very little of any official help.

But in the first place it would be desirable to strengthen the case somewhat, not so much on his account as against the contingency that he might have to lay his suspicions before other and less romantic-minded people before he had done with it. If he had entered upon the adventure casually he was now in it up to the neck, and with no intention of being left behind.

There were two ends at which he could begin—in London or in Stratford. The latter was the more conclusive ground, but at the same time the more delicate. No harm would be likely to come of any sort of indiscreet move made here in London, but on the scene of the exploit a single false step might easily be fatal. For, be it noted, with his keen appetite for crime, Max Carrados was not so much concerned to scotch a plot before it came to fruition as to demonstrate—if only to himself—that his deductions had been correct. In the meanwhile he took certain simple precautions against being forestalled by Lacksome's sudden departure, and then, satisfied that he had made the position safe, he turned with leisurely deliberation to the more delicate lines of investigation.

For this theoretical side of the business there was one formula alone. To the extent that Carrados was able to merge himself within the skin of Rigby Lacksome would success or failure attend him. Rigby Lacksome, arrived in London, his plan well in train, certain things assured, certain difficulties ahead, a keen appreciation that the stake was a high one, and that at the last moment, when it might be touch and go, no untoward irregularity must arise to rob him of the prize with the goal in sight. Come now, what would Rigby do?

From this starting-point Carrados launched four entirely different lines of inquiry. Not one of them came to anything and the time was slipping by. It looked very like having to go on to Stratford and take up the case by the thick end. Before admitting this measure of defeat the blind man sent the arrow of venture on one more flight.

'I want you to hunt round and see if it's possible to pick up a fairly complete human skeleton,' he said to Greatorex the next morning. 'I shan't need you again today, so you can go off and let me know to-morrow how you got on.'

'Right-o,' assented Mr Greatorex cheerfully—he had 'hunted round' after rather out-of-the-way things for his employer too often to be startled. 'What about the price?'

'There won't be any price. I don't propose to go to the length of buying one—but you needn't let that out. Just talk to anyone who seems to have anything to say. Even if you come across one for sale you can go on trying, all the same. I want to cut across a similar inquiry—successful or unsuccessful—in the past few weeks. It is not impossible that Lacksome may have bought one. If you strike that, get all you can about it. Anyone who's been asked for another skeleton so recently is sure to want to mention it.'

Annesley smiled his usual happy smile of charmed agreement and got as far as the door.

'Oh, where had I better try, sir?' he asked, pausing there.

'That's just what I'm not going to tell you,' replied Mr Carrados with decision. 'Your chief asset in this business is that you know nothing about it and you are quite likely to go where any other stranger in the same position might get. Now see what you can make of it.'

The wanderings of Annesley Greatorex throughout that livelong day (he was a generous worker on occasions) might be treated from a variety of dramatic standpoints, being tragic, comic, farcical, melo-dramatic, or extravaganzic alternately—or even several at once—nor could the claims of pantomime and mystery justly be omitted. Annesley's own considered verdict was that any account, from its lack of cohesive plot, its tenuous thread of connecting interest, and its wealth of varied and irrelevant detail, could only be done justice to as a musical comedy. It began in the back parlour of Miss Poppington's surprising establishment in Putney High Street and ended in the Lost Property Office at London Bridge.

Between those limits Annesley visited two general hospitals, a phrenologist off Fleet Street, an eminent naturalist in Piccadilly, a metal dealer down the Elephant and Castle way, Madame Tussaud's, a theatrical costumier in Convent Garden, a wholesale toy merchant near Aldgate Pump, a Harley Street specialist, a firm of auctioneers, a museum in Lincoln's Inn Fields, a housebreaker (the legal variety), a retired conjurer and about eight other people less easy to define. In most cases he had sought these at someone else's suggestion, and the abiding impression he retained of that wonderful day was of the extraordinary good-nature of nearly everybody. Annesley certainly had a pleasant way with him.

And in the end he had the most astonishing success. It came as the result of one of these kind suggestions—the housebreaker's, in point of fact.

'Look here, mate,' said the giant in charge. 'What about the big west-end stores? Tried any yet?'

'No,' admitted Annesley, who had come on there from an educational appliance maker. 'Do you think it would be any good?'

'Why not give it a run? I should. There's Blackley & Whiteing now, up Kensington way. My missus isn't an easy one to please and *she* says they have nearly everything there that she can even think of. Can't do no harm, anyway.'

Annesley thanked the dusty giant gracefully and withdrew. Blackley & Whiteing, whose proud boast it was that anything from a troupe of performing earwigs to a desert island would not find them wanting, ought certainly to be on his list. None the less he felt some of the diffidence of youth at stating his business when ah unconsidered entrance brought him face to face with a tall, blonde lady in the glove department. These big, busy shops, thought Annesley, expect one to be precise, and yet. . . . The tall, blonde guide would probably, he feared, emit a piercing shriek. He asked to see the manager.

It would be meticulous to cavil about a definite article. Annesley, at all events, saw an important-looking gentleman with a managerial air. He listened gravely and patiently to his visitor's recital and then struck a desk-bell.

'Mr Chadbeate!'

That is the worst of these big, busy shops. Annesley had imagined that he was getting on. He now had to repeat word for word to Mr Chadbeate all that he had just said to the manager. Mr Chadbeate listened gravely and patiently and then with a dignified 'Kindly step this way, sir,' led the inquirer to a third compartment.

'Mr Noate!'

'Heavens,' murmured Annesley, as the prospect of an unending recital faced him. 'I ought to have got it printed.'

Mr Noate, however, really was the man. He understood. He even sympathized. It was like that. You never could tell. Curious, too. Within the past few weeks they had had a similar inquiry. Yes, in that case they had been able to supply the order. . . .

'Really? Then there is a sort of demand?'

Scarcely that—not so far as Blackley & Whiteing were concerned, at any rate. Of course they had a reputation, and jokers now and then —But it must have been years ago that the last. . . . .

'Scientific requirement of course?' suggested Annesley.

'Oh, yes. An American. Singular idea. Theory that the English and American races, starting from a common stock, are diverging structurally. Wants to be able to demonstrate it by an English skeleton.'

'I recently struck a man,' volunteered Annesley, 'who was on that tack. Fellow called Lacksome; sort of confidential secretary to old Nogg, the U.S.A. millionaire.'

'That *is* the chap,' cried Mr Noate joyfully. 'So you know him? Well, it just happened that we were able to meet his requirement.'

'Quite casually,' admitted the caller. 'He didn't mention this to me. Awkward piece of luggage, won't it be?'

'Of course we had a proper box made; and nicely packed. . . . What he seemed most concerned about was the idea of trouble with the steamship company or at the customs somewhere. Didn't know anything about that sort of thing, and appeared to have an idea that someone might think it fishy and hold him up.'

'Yes; that might have occurred to me.'

'Quite an ordinary matter, of course. We obtained and filled up a special customs declaration form so that there will be no trouble on that score, and as he still seemed anxious we wrote to the Cunard Company and got their express acceptance of the freight on our voucher. Now as regards—'

'Thank you,' interposed Annesley with a grateful air. 'I think that should be something for my people to go on. It's a little doubtful, as I said, but if anything—'

'We should do our best, rely on it,' acquiesced Mr Noate, with suave dignity.

★★★★★★

Carrados retrieved a creased sheet of foolscap from his waste-paper basket, thoughtfully straightened it out, and added a few more lines of writing to round off the new position.

'What precaution has he taken against inconvenient curiosity?'

'He has provided himself with a perfectly *bona fide* receipt for what he may be suspected of unlawfully possessing, and he has insured against an unusual property leading to awkward inquiry. He has created a sort of proprietorial alibi, which, like all fictitious alibis, may prove disastrous when it begins to crumble.

This time he burned the sheet. The *précis* was complete.

The last up-train from Stratford-on-Avon with any tolerable connexion for Paddington (the 6.32 in those days) had just pulled out of Leamington. There was no lack of accommodation and the single occupant of a smoking compartment well towards the rear was congratulating himself that he would be undisturbed for the remainder of the journey when two men passed slowly along the corridor, dropping an occasional word of comment.

'This will do quite nicely,' said Mr Carrados, stopping at the compartment indicated and Parkinson slid the door open for him. 'Come back as we reach Westbourne Park.'

'Very well, sir,' replied Parkinson, as he closed the door and moved on again.

The blind man settled down in his corner seat and lifted his face towards the other passenger.

'Ah, Mr Lacksome, I believe,' he remarked sociably. 'Delightful old place, Stratford, isn't it?'

Rigby Lacksome lowered the late evening paper that he had provided himself with at Leamington station and favoured the intruder with a long, cool stare.

'That's my name, sir,' he replied with deliberation. 'But you have the advantage of me.'

'Scarcely,' smiled Mr Carrados. He appeared to be in excellent spirits, as though the interview promised some entertainment.

'I mean,' explained the other man distantly, 'that I have no recollection of ever having seen you before.'

'That gives me no advantage, for I do not even see you now.'

'What do you mean?'

'Simply that I am blind.' Mr Carrados beamed benignly on his startled fellow-traveller. 'There is no question of who holds the ace, you see, if it should come to violence.'

'Just a modicum of breathing time, sir,' pleaded Mr Lacksome. 'You cut the ice considerably quicker than I can stack it . . .. Why violence?'

'One never knows. . . . I was talking to a man about a murder recently–just as casually as I am talking now to you. He became very violent.'

Lacksome's vaguely calculating glance went round the narrow place they were enclosed in and came back to the self-possessed figure in the other corner without losing a shred of its own slightly arrogant assurance.

'There's some mistake, I guess,' he remarked. 'Are you one of the Scotland Yard outfit?'

Mr Carrados laughed appreciatively. 'No, no,' he said; 'you mustn't poke fun at our national institutions, Mr Lacksome. I am really no one. I ought to have introduced myself before. My name is Carrados— Max Carrados. I am just interested in things.'

'I see,' commented the other reflectively. Then he added, 'Any particular sort of things, might I inquire, sir?'

'Crime in general, if it promises originality. At the moment I am curious to clear up one or two points in what I might call the Mystery of the Anatomical Specimen.'

Rigby Lacksome stretched his limbs and yawned slightly to demonstrate indifference.

'It sounds like a three-reel thrill all right, Mr Cahrados,' he said. 'What does it hinge on?'

'I'm afraid,' apologised Mr Carrados, 'that it hinges on one of your own articles of luggage. . . . No, the communication cord, if that is what you are looking for, is on your side.'

'I guessed you were trying to put it across me about being blind,' said Mr Lacksome cutely. 'I don't want the cord, but I want to know right here before we go any further how you come into this.'

'It's a detail of our old-fashioned judicial system,' explained Mr Carrados. 'According to these antiquated laws it is the duty of the merest outsider—myself, for instance—to arrest and give into custody anyone whom he reasonably suspects of having committed a felony.'

'Is that so?' drawled Mr Lacksome, moving a careless hand. 'How does he get on with it if he finds himself looking down the barrel of a gun?'

'What, violence already!' chid Mr Carrados amiably. 'And after I had warned you, too! But the answer to that, Mr Lacksome, is that a blind man—and you may take my word for it—never knows, of course that he *is* looking down the barrel of a gun.'

Rigby Lacksome's hand went back again to its former position.

'Excuse me relapsing into the vernacular, Mr Cahrados,' he remarked, not without a streak of admiration, 'but you certainly are the gelidest brand of guy I've ever struck.'

'Of course,' assented his companion; 'why not? I am sure it would shock you immeasurably if you met an Englishman who began to show traces of emotion under any circumstances whatever. You, for your part, are the most accomplished body-snatcher I have so far had to do with. Something like an hour must elapse before we reach Paddington. Why should we not entertain one another like two travellers in a mid-Victorian Christmas Annual?'

'Preparatory to being handed over to a posse of the station police at the terminus?'

The blind man raised a deprecatory gesture.

'Surely you must have misunderstood me, Mr Lacksome. I said that such was the *duty* of every citizen. . . . Alas; how few of us do our duty nowadays!'

'Just put it into English for me, sir,' said Mr Lacksome wearily. 'I'm late on the gear-clutch, I admit.'

'It is quite simple. You will find that at Westbourne Park we shall slow down almost to nothing. There will be a couple of plainclothes men waiting on the platform. If I show a white handkerchief at the window they will just step on to the footboard and take instructions. If I show a coloured one—a certain coloured one—they will know that the case has dropped through and they are not wanted.'

'Great,' admitted Mr Lacksome with suspicious fervour. 'I had no idea that we were doing this for the movies, sir. . . . And now let me tell you, Mr Cahrados, that you've given yourself the devil of a lot of trouble over nothing. The particular equipment that you seem to have had your nose into when no one was looking is a scientific exhibit that I've bought here for anthropological use in America. . . . Like to see Blackley & Whiteing's receipt for it?'

551

'Not just now, thank you,' replied Mr Carrados. 'Mr Noate showed me the counterfoil. And we needn't waste time over the arrangement made at the Claverhill Street branch of the S.W.L.; or your understanding with Rainproof Nogg; nor the engagement of Sam Barbel to be foreman of repairs.'

'Hell!' was wrung from Rigby, 'that makes a bobtail flush, I must allow, sir. I can only put up one card against a hand like that, but I guess he is the joker.'

'Well?'

'You think I've lifted the mortal remains of old man Shakespeare to join the rest of Great Britain that we've accumulated over there, don't you, sir?'

'I think you set out with that idea.'

'Say "Yes", Mr Cahrados, won't you?' pleaded Lacksome. 'I should love you to guess wrong just once.'

'Was it the curse you weakened on?'

Mr Lacksome smiled his pagan superiority to such a failing.

'It was not, sir. I wouldn't deviate one jot, tittle, or iota for a sackful of best assorted medieval curses. Besides, do you think that the man who heart-throbbed to the tune of Romeo and Juliet, of Rosalind and Orlatido, and of Florizel and Perdita would care a banana-skin what became of his loose parts after three centuries if it would help me to win Sabina Craddock? No, sir; there wasn't a milligram of gall in old man Shakespeare's constitution.'

'It seems to me,' remarked Mr Carrados, remembering something very similar not long before, 'that whatever anyone wants to do about Shakespeare, it is easy to find authority in his works for doing it.'

'That is so,' agreed Rigby simply. 'W. Shakespeare was not for an age, but for all time; not of one country but common to the world, and he said everything that there is to be said on every subject. That's where old man Nogg left the track. He has worked it out that Shakespeare was an American citizen, and he's tickled to death at the idea of getting him for his National Temple.'

'I think someone else has already proved that he was a German,' said Mr Carrados. 'So why not a German-American?'

'Both wrong, sir,' replied Mr Lacksome. 'Shakespeare was really a Literary Syndicate. Rainproof is demonstrably *non compos mentis* on that subject, and his infirmity is spreading. My own concern is to get my matrimonial—and I may add financial—arrangements put through before he is actually certified. You see how I am fixed?'

Carrados nodded sympathetically. 'But you haven't yet told me how you came to fail,' he said.

'Fail . . .' considered Rigby dubiously. 'Well, as to that. . . You are quite satisfied about it, Mr Cahrados?'

'Life is full of surprises,' admitted Carrados, 'but I must stand by my opinion. The stone had not been raised—the joint wouldn't even take water—and you certainly had not tunnelled.'

'You are right sir. The paralysing truth is that the stone can't be raised.'

'Can't? Why not?'

'That will have to wait for another generation to find out, I guess. All I know is that we had a patent suction jack—for of course we daren't use leverage—capable of raising five tons dead weight drawing on a stone weighing something less than five hundredweight and it couldn't budge it a hair. No, sir; do what we might it had us beaten to cold cinders. And if you want my *obiter dictum* I should say the biggest thing in W.S. enigmas is waiting patiently there for some bright boy to come along and scoop it.'

'Quite likely,' agreed Max Carrados. 'You aren't the first to have a try by any means. And you are not going away absolutely empty-handed, I imagine?'

Mr Lacksome's face relaxed appreciably from its smart, purposeful expression into something suspiciously like a genial grin.

'Well, come now, Mr Cahrados,' he replied. 'What should you say! You know that right beneath my feet there, by what they call the old charnel house, there were enough ancient bones of every sort and kind to stock the field of Waterloo. Sculls, arms, legs, middles, toes, fingers, ribs and what not. And there on the other side Hiram S. Nogg is lapping up my cables and biting his nails to keep calm about it. Why should we disappoint the poor old mono-maniac in the midst of plenty? Why, I've even rooted out a few odds and ends of antique coffins and a brass plate with something that you couldn't say wasn't a spear cut on it. Oh, Rainproof will be satisfied, never fear, and Sabina will be satisfied, and I don't see why Rigby Lacksome shouldn't be satisfied too. And in about another century there'll be the dandiest Shakespeare mystery spring up at Nogg's National Temple that ever was!'

The suburban lights had been growing thicker for the last few miles and the slackening train now began to dodge its way across the maze of points and switches. Parkinson's restful face appeared at the window and the corridor door was pushed open.

'We are approaching Westbourne Park, sir.'

Lacksome started at the name, and despite the amiable relations that had occupied the journey his face was not without a shade of anxiety as he spoke.

'I hope you are satisfied as well, sir. After all—no one's a red cent worse off.'

'Rather a fine point though, isn't it?' conceded Mr Carrados. 'However—you're on the platform side—perhaps you'll show this from the window.'

Rigby snatched the dark silk handkerchief from the blind man's hand and turned to wave it vigorously at the open window.

'But there's not a soul along the platform!' he exclaimed blankly, looking back. 'Say, Mr Cahrados, have you been patting one over on me?'

'Dear me,' confessed Mr Carrados, quite crestfallen. 'Can I have dreamt that part of it, after all?'

The Crime at the House in Culver Street

The garden gate of Thornden Lodge stood open as the Bellmarks walked past, and from the path beyond there came the sharp aggressive click of decisive shears at work. Elsie Bellmark grew irresolute, then stopped.

'Do you mind if I just pop in for a wee moment, Roy?' she asked. 'I expect that it's Miss Barrowford gardening, and it will save me writing. G.F.S. business, you know.'

'All right,' her husband replied. 'Only don't forget me and stay to supper.'

'The idea! As if I ever—I'll catch you up—or won't you come in too? You know her.'

'No,' he decided. 'If I do we shall be talking there for an hour. I won't go right on either. I'll just hang about in the middle distance to keep you up to the mark.'

With a nod and a smile she left him, and almost immediately the sound of the shears ceased and through the privet hedge came the rather ecstatic interchange of greetings. A grin of affectionate amusement came into Bellmark's face as he slowly lit a cigarette.

'It's long odds on my finishing this undisturbed,' ran his speculation; but he was wrong, for before the first ash had fallen an insinuating 'Roy!' from beyond the privet hedge summoned him inside.

'All bets off,' he murmured, as he cheerfully complied. 'That isn't according to the rules, my dear.'

'Oh Roy,' exclaimed Elsie, signalling. 'Sorry, couldn't help it,' with her eyes, 'Miss Barrowford wondered whether you had seen her brother. He didn't come by your train, did he?'

'You do know Vernon by sight, don't you, Mr Bellmark?' put in the

555

lady of the garden. 'It's unusual for him to be so late on Saturday.'

'I think I know him,' admitted Roy. 'First class, non-smoking; *Morning Post*: never in a hurry; nine-thirty-seven, isn't he?'

'Spats; black tie: neat umbrella,' smiled Miss Barrowford. 'Has been in the Civil Service. Yes?'

'At all events he didn't come, or he would have been here long ago—this young lady has been shopping as we came along, and leisurely at that. And when I come to think of it, there was only one other man got off the train at Stanthorpe—an oldish fellow, who didn't quite seem as though he knew what he was doing here. Women and children in plenty, but no other man.'

'Well, I don't think that anyone would describe Vernon as exactly old,' hazarded his sister. 'We are neither of us children certainly, but—'

'No, indeed,' exclaimed Elsie with great fervour. 'I mean,' she added hastily, as she realized that her well-meant disclaimer had got belated, 'I mean about your brother, of course. Why I feel ages older than he looks, I'm sure.'

'All the same, my dear,' confided Miss Barrowford dropping her voice, 'I think he feels the stress of business life of late. I often wonder if he was quite well advised in giving up the Civil Service for commerce. Somerset House is so assured; the feeling of permanency must be very tranquillizing.'

'I suppose he has to work hard now?' suggested Elsie politely. She had very little interest in the absent Vernon and still less in his occupation, but Miss Barrowford was 'a dear', and the surest way to her good opinion was to turn a sympathetic ear to amiable garrulities on her two subjects—her wonderful garden and her exceptional brother.

'Yes,' agreed the sister with a slightly dubious look; 'I suppose he has. But it is more the weight of responsibility that I was thinking of. Vernon, you see, was never brought up to the business—to any business, in fact—and when an uncle left it entirely to him on condition that he carried it on, it was like beginning life over again. His real tastes are literary and artistic, and he had to overcome something like a positive aversion to trade—though it is strictly wholesale trade of course.'

'I don't think that I even know what he does,' admitted Elsie. 'But perhaps I oughtn't to be inquisitive—'

'Oh, yes, my dear; there's no secret at all about it.' Miss Barrowford's shrewd, good-natured eyes opened wide at the implication. 'It's a wholesale fancy leather business—Widdowson & Stubb in Culver Street, though Uncle Con was the last Stubb and there hasn't been a Widdowson in it for half a century. They do with all the finer sorts of leather. Vernon didn't know the least thing about either leather or business when he took it up, but he had a very capable manager and reliable staff, or I don't know what might have happened.'

'It sounds nice—fine leather: bindings have such a lovely smell. Do you ever go and revel among it, Miss Barrowford? I should.'

'I have been once or twice, but I am not fond of going,' confessed the lady. 'The place was formerly a large, rambling old house—it was a good residential district once—and many years ago a very dreadful murder was committed there. Of course'—with an appropriate smile—'it is now haunted. But, seriously, I do not care about the place; it is a little errie after dusk.'

'How gruesome! And your brother really likes it now?'

Miss Barrowford indicated the complexity of her opinion by a shrug and a ladylike little move before she committed herself on this. She even snipped off a superfluous leaf enigmatically as she glanced slyly at her other visitor.

'Men are strange beings, my dear,' she replied. 'Do we ever know what they really like—or, for that matter, do they know themselves? But who have we here?'

The gate, which had been pushed to on Mr Bellmark's entrance, was very slowly opened by an unfamiliar hand and along the immaculate path there advanced a peculiar figure—curious not by reason of anything outlandish in dress or feature but by his odd detachment from the scene and his pathetic air of being in some way lost. A trite synonym for witlessness is 'not all there', and no phrase could better describe the impression that the stranger made: some essential thing was missing.

'Now, who in the world—' speculated Miss Barrowford with a queer afarness in her voice, and then suddenly she gave a startled little cry and ran a few steps forward, only to stop again in a nameless fear.

'Vernon. *Vernon!*' was wrung from her, though scarcely heard. 'What is it? Oh, my dear, what ever can have happened?'

'Good God!' whispered Bellmark to his wife. 'This is the man I spoke of-the one who came by the train. It isn't the fellow I took to be her brother, and yet it somehow is. Do you catch on to it?'

'I don't know what you are saying,' replied Elsie, hypnotized by the two before her. 'But there is something dreadful.'

'Oughtn't we to go away?' he asked.

'I'm too bewildered to know. I shouldn't like her to think—And yet she may want us.'

Very slowly Vernon Barrowford walked up the familiar path to the door of his house, looking to the right and the left occasionally as he seemed to verify some half-forgotten landmark. He passed his sister, he passed the others, without a sign of recognition, but when Miss Barrowford caught him up and took his hand with a passionate cry to be spoken to he did not shake her off. Only he never spoke. Docilely he allowed himself to be led up the steps to the closed front door. Standing there, with the same monotonous precision that had marked his passage through the garden, he took out his bunch of keys, selected the right one with slow deliberation, and unlocked the door.

'I must go in to her,' said Elsie, as the two passed out of sight. 'Whatever it is, we've seen it now, so it can't much matter. You will wait, won't you?'

'Of course I'll wait,' he replied half gruffly. 'Tell her we'll do any-thing—'

In three minutes she was back again. Bellmark had discovered a garden seat and was meditating. He looked at her with inquiry in his eyes.

'He's sitting there in the morning-room, and he does nothing. He won't speak. And, Roy—don't laugh—she whispered to me would I ask you how you can tell if people are drunk or not. She thinks it may be that, but I'm sure it isn't.'

'You ask them,' replied Roy gravely. 'In either case they deny it, but if they are drunk they begin to argue about it and want to prove that they're not, and the more you agree and say, "It's all right, old man; don't shout and nobody will notice anything," the warmer they become, until you can hear a very intoxicated man a mile away pro-testing how sober he is.'

'Well, that's no good because he certainly wouldn't speak. She'd be only too relieved if he would, whatever he might say.'

'He looked sober enough just now—too sober, in fact. If you want my opinion, it's a doctor's job.'

'I think so too, Roy. I'm sure she'd be glad to be encouraged to send, so I'll go in again and tell her what you say.'

'Wait a minute,' he advised, looking over her shoulder. 'I think—yes, here she comes.'

'What does he say?' asked Miss Barrowford, as Elsie went to meet her.

'He thinks you ought to have a doctor at once. I think so too, dear. We are afraid that you brother is really ill in some way.'

'I am sure that you are right. Yes, I will send for Dr Page at once. It is all very sudden, and for the moment I wished to keep it from the servants if it had been—anything disgraceful. I ought to have known Vernon better, but it is so inexplicable.'

'We'll go straight there and tell Dr Page to come. I'm sure Roy will get him as soon as anyone could.'

'Would you? That's very kind of you,' said Miss Barrowford quite gratefully.

'Oh, how can you talk like that!' exclaimed Elsie, kissing her in a scramble. 'It's nothing, and anybody would—'

'I'll go back now and wait, then,' remarked her friend. 'I must not leave him for long.'

'Should Roy go on alone and I'll stay with you until the doctor comes?' suggested Elsie.

'No, thank you, dear. I am not in the least afraid of anything and I shall tell the servants now.'

Dr Page must have been immediately accessible, for in less than twenty minutes—he lived half a mile away—his cheerful, common-place mien and quiet confidence were diffusing a healthier feeling within Thornden Lodge. Miss Barrowford's face lost something of its unaccustomed greyness and the two maids no longer deemed it nec-essary to talk in whispers. No one ever thought of describing Page as a 'clever' doctor; 'good' was the word they used, and that meant that you generally got better soon.

'So it's Master Vernon's turn this time, eh?' he remarked, as he walked across to the unresponsive figure sitting huddled in the big easy-chair—he had dosed 'Master Vernon' through whooping cough and measles thirty years before. 'When I was last here on business it was your turn, I think, Miss Barrowford.'

'Oh, then!' she exclaimed disdainfully. 'That was nothing—a touch of 'flu.'

'Nothing when you were all right, again, was it?' he acquiesced tolerantly. 'That's the way with things, isn't it? No, he'll do very well where he is thanks. Now let us see.'

Miss Barrowford stood aside while the detailed examination went on, ready to do just as she was told, and too sensible a woman to in-terrupt with needless, anxious questions. When he had finished, Page walked thoughtfully to the window and looked out; she followed with her eyes, now definite in inquiry.

'The simple word "shock" covers a multitude of effects. "Shock", Miss Barrowford. Does that satisfy you?'

'I don't understand yet. It is all so very sudden—and—terrifying. Is he—is he dangerously ill?'

'Meaning "Will he die?" No, he is not. You have a convalescent on your hands. All the mischief has been done; the business is to bring him back to normal health.'

'But—doctor—what is it—what has happened?'

'Shock. That is what I crudely indicate. There is no external lesion of any kind: no blow has been experienced. Bellmark told me how he arrived. Whether there is any especial reason—business or personal, for instance—why Vernon should be likely to have any very violent mental disturbance just now, you would be in a better position to know than I should.'

'I know of nothing—nothing at all. And it's so dreadful, his never speaking.'

'You must not ask him. That is the chief thing now—perfect rest. If he begins to wake up don't encourage him to talk. If they send here from the business wanting to know anything they'll have to do without it. You understand that quite literally, don't you. Miss Barrowford? No matter what it is. If the office can't go on without him it must stop. Better the business than the man—he's our job.'

'Is it so serious then?' she whispered, the clutch at her heart tightening again.

'It might easily become so if we don't take care, In a few days we shall know more about it—whether, for instance, the loss of speech extends to true aphasia or is only the temporary reflex of the first excitement. I should like to get McFlynn here to have a look—it's his especial subject. Tomorrow or Monday, shall I?'

'Certainly,' she replied. 'Oh, doctor—anything—everything—you can do.'

'Yes, yes,' he nodded. 'I know. You'd better have a nurse in—for a week, at any rate. Miss Hodge is doing nothing just now and she is handy. Shall I ring her up when I get back?'

'If you think I'd better. Of course'—a little wistfully 'you know I *can* nurse fairly well; still—'

'For a week,' he said, smiling reassuringly. 'Then perhaps—'

'Very well. I will sit on the doorstep like a veritable dragoness and keep intruders off. But are we to do nothing to find out what has happened doctor?'

'Oh, yes; indeed we must. Everything short of asking him about it. It will be the first step towards repairing the damage to find out what has caused it. We know that he arrived at Stanthorpe in this condition, so we must try farther back. He may have had a terribly narrow squeak of some sort.'

'There's the warehouse. But everyone will have left long since.'

'Still, that's the place to begin from. Isn't there a manager I've heard of?'

'Yes—Mr Pridger. He lives at Croydon.'

'You have his address?'

'Oh, yes, Shall I—'

'Yes, wire him to come up and see you as soon as he can get—tonight or tomorrow. Find out all he can suggest, but'—with a warning finger—'don't take him in to your brother. No reminders of the past just yet.'

It was the capable manager's long-established custom to escort Mrs Pridger to a theatre once a week, and Saturday evening had come to be the occasion of this rite. It not being a matter of life and death—Miss Barrowford's telegram simply enjoined 'as soon as possible'—there seemed no pressing reason why Mr Pridger should set forth on an adventurous journey from Croydon to Stanthorpe after midnight, so that, as it developed, it was not until Sunday afternoon that he learned of his employer's condition.

Turning in at the gate of Thornden Lodge, on her mission 'to inquire', Elsie Bellmark came face to face with a departing stranger, and, preoccupied as she was, she wondered vaguely at the queer look his face wore in the momentary flash before he recognised that she was calling there. The front door stood open, and it seemed very quiet within. With a freedom born of the circumstances Elsie ventured to investigate unannounced. The door of the morning-room was slightly ajar and from beyond came a low, intermittent note. She tapped very gently.

'Come in,' said Miss Barrowford's voice, and the other sound stopped.

She was sitting on a couch—it was plain that a moment before she had been lying there, and her eyes and handkerchief betrayed the nature of her occupation. Mrs Bellmark was appalled.

'Oh, dear Louise!' she said, and began to back out again.

'Don't run away,' called out the occupant. 'That was the last of it anyway. Thank you for coming. I was expecting you some time to-day.'

'He isn't worse, is he?'

'Oh no; he is almost the same as you saw. It wasn't that.'

'You don't mean that there's something else?'

'Did you meet Mr Pridger as you came in? He has just gone.'

'I did meet a man—at the gate. Whatever is it?'

'It feels rather like the end of the world. We've had a fire.'

'Here?'

'No—at the office and warehouse. It's practically burnt out, he says.'

'Mr Pridger?'

'Yes; that's why he couldn't get here this morning. The police came across his address first and they sent for him. He found the place a wreck. Isn't it disastrous?'

'Had it—the fire—anything to do with Mr Barrowford being ill?'

'We don't see how it could. Mr Pridger knows practically nothing of Vernon's movements yesterday, as he himself had to go to another part of London to see a customer and he didn't think it worthwhile going back to Culver Street afterwards. The fire was not discovered until late on Saturday night, and long before that Vernon was here.'

'Yes,' agreed Mrs Bellmark; 'but it seems funny, all the same. I suppose it's insured anyway, being a business.'

'Oh, yes, I'm certain it will be. But it's bound to be unsettling to Vernon, don't you see. Just when he will be getting all right again and wanting to go back to work he will have to be told of this upset. It will take months to rebuild and straighten up.'

'It will be a good chance for him to take a long rest, I should say,' declared Mrs Bellmark. 'And, another thing, dear, from what you said yesterday I imagine that your brother might not be sorry to give up the business. We don't know, of course, but this might be an oppor-tunity—'

'Oh, don't think that,' exclaimed Miss Barrowford hastily. 'I am sure Vernon would never dream of taking advantage of such a way out.'

'Well, I don't know,' said Elsie. 'It isn't as if he had set it on fire himself. But what's the good of talking about that? You are no nearer getting at what happened then?'

'Not a bit. And I'm beginning to wonder what next to do if, as I expect, he left the office all right.'

'I've been thinking,' volunteered her friend. 'Did you ever hear of Mr Carrados?'

'I don't think so,' admitted Miss Barrowford vaguely. And then with the common frailty of mankind she added: 'But the name seems somehow familiar.'

'He finds out things. He's quite wonderful at it, considering that he's blind. It's a hobby of his, because he is quite rich.'

'But if he is blind, dear—'

'You hardly notice it. If you had lost something from here—stolen or disappeared, I mean—and he was helping you, he might come into this room and in a few minutes he would know all about it: the size and where the furniture was and the colour of the wall-paper and when you last had the chimney swept and why you had moved a picture from one place to another. All the time you would be talking about nothing in particular as you thought and then he would pick up an old nail that no one else had noticed or touch a scratch on the paint.'

'How could he see the nail to pick it up?' demanded the elder lady practically.

'He couldn't, of course, but he would pick it up all the same. And in a few days or a few weeks it would lead in some absurdly simple way straight to what you had lost.'

'It sounds very marvellous,' conceded Miss Barrowford dubiously, 'but in any case we do not know this Mr Carrados.'

'We know him pretty well—from the time when we used to live at Groats Heath,' said Elsie. 'An uncle of mine is his great friend. I am sure he would come if he thought that it would help us: we are under a very great obligation to him.'

'But, my dear,' corrected Louise Barrowford precisely, 'that's the wrong way about. It would be if he was under an obligation to you.'

'Oh, he doesn't do things like that,' responded Elsie from the heights. 'Besides, if he was I shouldn't like to ask him.'

When Max Carrados learned the particulars of the Barrowford case his first proceeding—before he decided whether it interested him or not—was an obvious one. He made inquiry at Scotland Yard and at certain divisional headquarters to find out if anything had been observed on the Saturday that would promise to bear on the mystery. It had not. No trace of Vernon was picked up until Baker Street Station was reached, where a porter who knew him as a 'first season' had noticed that he seemed 'groggy'. The blind man decided that the case offered enough obscurity to attract him.

It was not until the Wednesday after the tragic happening that Max Carrados found leisure to get across to Stanthorpe. Elsie took him on to Thornden Lodge, where Miss Barrowford, now almost accustomed to her silent charge, received him with some trepidation. It was clear that Mrs Bellmark's rather freely coloured portrait had sunk in, and the lady of the house expected curious things to materialize beneath her eyes. Carrados had never seemed more matter-of-fact in his procedure. He betrayed no startling knowledge of the surroundings (to his sponsor's despair) and merely encouraged Miss Barrowford to talk about her brother from every angle. She was nothing loath, but Elsie had heard most of it before. Nor were his inquiries less commonplace.

'You have looked through his pockets, I suppose?' he asked. 'You found nothing unusual?'

'Nothing that I had not seen a hundred times before—with one exception. There was a large enamelled badge or check with a number on.'

'Perhaps I might see it?' suggested the inquirer. 'Oh, yes'—when it was produced—'this is a cloak-room voucher from the reading-room at the British Museum.'

'He frequently went to the National Gallery, I know,' suggested Miss Barrowford. 'Might it not perhaps be from there?'

'No,' replied Carrados. 'A benevolent authority has arranged that you shall not procure your neighbour's new silk umbrella from one institution by depositing your own worn-out walking-stick at another, and so all the sets of tickets vary. Is your brother absent-minded in a general way, Miss Barrowford?'

'No, indeed; he is one of the most precise of people. Why?'

Carrados held up the numbered badge significantly.

'Whatever that stands for he omitted to reclaim,' he explained. 'It is generally a stick or umbrella.'

'Of course,' she acquiesced. 'Vernon invariably carried an umbrella, and on Saturday he returned without it. I took it for granted that he had left it in the train.'

'If this usually exact man forgot it after going specially to the reading-room—umbrella or whatever it may be—it is assumable that he may have learned something important there, isn't it?'

'Yes, yes,' exclaimed Elsie keenly. 'Can you find out what?'

'If it turns upon a book it is doubtful. You help yourself to the thousands of more general works of reference. I suppose'—to Miss Barrowford—'you did not come across a cancelled application slip for a book?'

'I know the sort of thing you mean,' she replied. 'No, he had none about him.'

'They are usually torn up,' agreed Mr Carrados.

'Apropos of papers now,' continued Miss Barrowford, Miss Hodge—the nurse, you know—found something rather curious this morning. Vernon was sitting by a table on which there happened to be some stationery—a few sheets of paper and a pen and ink. He wasn't looking at it, but Miss Hodge noticed that his hand was moving on the paper. When she went to him she found that he had actually been scribbling there—hardly words, perhaps, and quite unintelligible, but she thought it was encouraging.'

'Yes,' assented Carrados, speaking so quietly that one might have thought he was afraid of startling so wonderful a thing of promise away, 'I am sure it would be. What became of the paper?'

'I think it was left about—or she may have thrown it away. Do you want it?'

'It is not without interest,' admitted the blind man. 'I think we ought to see it.'

It had not been thrown away, though Miss Hodge hoped for much more coherent signs of intelligence ere long. Carrados accepted the sheet and grasped its details of shape, weight, and texture as readily as another would by sight, while the two ladies overlooked his movements curiously.

'I cannot make head or tail of it,' confessed Miss Barrowford, as the senseful fingers crossed and recrossed the scrawl, now following a vague spidery line, now drawn where no visible mark appeared to lead. 'Is there any meaning, do you think?'

'That little arrangement comes in more than once,' said Elsie, indicating a hieroglyphic twist. 'I'm sure it must mean something.'

'That little arrangement is the word "red", and it comes in seven times,' interpreted the patient seeker. 'It is the strongest impression that persists.'

'Red! But what—' conjectured the sister with a tremor in her voice.

'Oh, a lamp-post—a sunshade—a picture,' reassured Mr Carrados quickly. 'Even a lead pencil if it happened to be there at the right moment.'

'Or a fire, I suppose?' suggested Elsie unfortunately.

'Here is a test for ingenuity.' Carrados was anxious to repair his indiscretion. 'That is a single word manifestly, but what?'

'It doesn't make a word to me,' declared Miss Barrowford, after a minute's scrutiny.

'"Meou" or "miaow", if there was such a thing,' suggested Elsie.

'Well, isn't there? What does one call a cat noise?'

'But why not write "cat"?' Miss Barrowford objected. 'If that is it.'

'Because the noise is the most arresting thing about it,' he replied. 'A "miaowing" cat.'

'Shut in,' contributed Elsie. 'Now I wonder what that long scrawl may be?'

'I think I had better take this for detailed tests,' said Mr Carrados, coolly transferring the paper to his pocket. He was not anxious for the broken man's sister to discover that the 'long scrawl' (twice repeated) stood for 'horrible', or that the poignant exclamation 'Oh!' had been penned four times. Later search disclosed only one other word. 'This,' considered Max Carrados as he reviewed his slender clues that night, 'this is the flashlight on a man's brain at the moment of its extinction,' and he arranged the impressions according to their persistence:

Red Red Red Red Red Red Red
Oh Oh Oh Oh
Horrible Horrible Horrible
Miaow Door

But as yet Mr Carrados was still in Miss Barrowford's drawing-room, and at the moment he was there alone, for, on the question of certain rather delicate G.F.S. procedure, the lady of the house had sought an excuse to carry off her other visitor.

Why Mr Pridger, on being shown in a few minutes later, should have tacitly assumed that the gentleman who seemed so tolerably at home on the hearthrug must be his employer's doctor, does not appear. Possibly there was an ambiguous word in the simple-mannered girl's exclamation of surprise at finding another visitor still there; possibly Mr Carrados's bland air of perfect self-possession lent itself to the idea.

'Sad business, isn't it?' remarked the manager expansively. 'Patient any better today, sir?'

So far, although one might hazard a guess, the blind man had no knowledge of his new acquaintance. A wisely professional shake of the head committed him to nothing.

'Ah! Looks like being a long business, I'm afraid. I wonder if you could give me an idea—I'm his manager, by the way—any sort of an idea how long it might be before he would be fit again?'

'That is a difficult question to answer at all, and an impossible one to answer satisfactorily.'

'Yes, I guessed as much. But it makes it rather awkward for me, sir. And when he does come, as you may say, to himself—I suppose there have been plenty of other cases similar—what will he be like should you say?' There was a moment of hesitation in framing the crux of what he sought, an assumption of negligence that stood out like the postscript of a lady's letter, but it had to come: 'Will he remember what happened to him up to the last?'

'*Will he remember!*' What did Mr Pridger anticipate; what had he to fear? Carrados could not see the respectful, serious-eyed, decorously-attired manager who stood there. The whole of Mr Pridger's eminently respectable appearance went for nothing, but a hundred other indications that he had never taken into account were signalling their message through subtler mediums.

It was a question to which there could be no absolute reply, but it fell in with the investigator's impulse to lull the man's misgivings, and in his impromptu character Carrados spoke to that end of other curious cases. Mr Pridger seemed to breathe more freely.

'So far as the actual business is concerned, of course his being away wouldn't make a ha'p'orth of difference,' he confided. 'I'm the practical man and the governor looks on. But there isn't any business now; the fire has put the lid on that. And the latest is that the insurance company is going to be nasty.'

This was news, and Mr Carrados encouraged its recital by a sympathetic question.

'They don't say so yet, but the suggestion is incendiarism. They sent down a man at once in the ordinary way, and now we've had a notice to leave everything just as it is pending a further examination.'

'Why should they think anything wrong?'

'These insurances go a lot by the fire brigade report. I suppose the officer in charge has suggested something.'

'But surely he must be mistaken?'

'Well, it isn't for me to say. I'm an employee of the firm and bound to stand by it. Besides, I was away all the Saturday after ten o'clock, so I couldn't say what happened. But it's no secret that W. & S. have been getting short of the ready for more than a year now; it's claimed that the fire began in three or four places at once; and Mr Barrowford was the last to leave the premises. We've got to make the best of that whether we like it or not.'

'How gratuitously a rogue gives himself away; every clumsy insinuation is a window to his mind,' ran the hearer's thoughts, while his commiserating voice was saying, 'Dear, dear me! This is very surprising.'

'Of course'—implied the loyal manager, and 'Oh, of course; not a word,' assented his confidant. He had at that moment picked up the returning footsteps on the stairs and the *tête-à-tête* was at an end.

'I don't altogether trust that manager,' confessed Mrs Bellmark as she carried the blind man off a little later. 'I came suddenly face to face with him here a few days ago and he was grinning in a most sinister fashion. Why should he seem so taken aback that you were not a doctor?'

'People get such curious ideas, don't they?' agreed Mr Carrados. 'I thought that he seemed annoyed about something when your friend said who I was. And yet he had been talking quite confidentially to me just before.'

'You hadn't misled him about being the doctor, had you?' asked a rather startled Elsie.

'Misled? I! Good gracious no; I wouldn't mislead a tortoise.'

'No, of course I didn't actually mean that you would,' said the amiable girl almost penitently. 'But really and truly I don't always quite know what to say about you, Mr Carrados. I was trying to tell Miss Barrowford what you would do and I could think of nothing better than to say that you might pick up a pin or a needle and that would be sufficient clue for you, and, do you know, all the time we were there she was craning her neck to see if you picked one up!'

'I wish I'd known,' he chuckled. 'I certainly would have done.'

'I wonder,' mused Elsie artlessly, 'if you did pick anything up?'

'No needles,' he replied lightly. 'A few loose threads at the most.'

It was in pursuit of the other ends of those same threads that Mr Carrados motored up to Culver Street on the next day. It was a neighbourhood of small industries with their contiguous offices, almost deserted after business hours and a wilderness at week-ends. Such shops as appeared to exist there were those supported by a special and assured clientage, with here and there a modest establishment of the humbler catering class. Widdowson and Stubb, not being in need of even such publicity as that peaceful thoroughfare afforded, had been thrust into the background by more assertive neighbours and had to be reached along an inner passage. A back entrance with a trade approach was discoverable in a *cul-de-sac* that seemed to have no name.

Parkinson accompanied his master, and with the perfect understanding of long association he reproduced from time to time just those details of the surroundings that he knew to be required. So much was routine, for any special need a word was enough to direct his peculiar talent for observation into the desired channel.

Interest in No. 33 as the scene of the fire had passed away—indeed nothing of the premises involved could be seen from Culver Street. The door, the sole evidence on that side of the existence of Widdowson & Stubb, opened to a push and the visitors found themselves in a long, bare passage, where a notice painted on the wall directed the inquirer onward to the office.

'We will wait here a moment and consider the circumstances,' directed Mr Carrados.

'Very good, sir,' replied Parkinson. He knew that at those close quarters his descriptive powers were not required unless to some specific end, and the blind man's interest in the floor and walls did not concern him. He sauntered down the passage and then back again.

'I imagine that Mr Carlyle is in the room beyond, sir,' he remarked. 'I can hear what I apprehend to be his voice.'

'Yes,' assented Carrados. 'He is part of the circumstances.'

They found the inquiry agent dominating the ruin of what had been the principal's office, and with him Mr Pridger. The manager's greeting was not by any stretch of imagination cordial, but Mr Carlyle's triumphantly assertive cry of welcome drowned the other's formal inquiry as to how he could serve the visitor.

'You, of all men, by the immortal powers!' he proclaimed enthusiastically. 'What piece of luck brings you this way, Max?'

'I scarcely think that the Barrowfords would describe it as that,' replied Carrados, indicating their surroundings. 'Do you happen to know that Elsie is quite a friend of theirs?'

'What, my niece?' exclaimed Mr Carlyle, with a sudden drop in his elation. 'No, by gad, I didn't. To be sure, they all live at Stanthorpe, don't they? I shall get into hot water over this, Max; I'm here for the Business and Domestic Insurance people.'

'I may as well go on with my own work now, Mr Carlyle,' interposed the manager, with severe formality. 'For any other particulars you may require I'm entirely at your service.'

'Queer affair,' explained the professional investigator, with a gracious gesture of assent towards the departing Pridger. 'Shocking barefaced attempt, Max, if ever there was one. And now, I hear, this Barrowford is playing possum to avoid explaining things.'

'Oh, have you extracted that admission from the reluctant Pridger, Louis?'

'Egad, the fellow feels it, being connected with such a job; but he sees that there's nothing to be gained by piling perjury on the top of arson. Four separate fires, all starting about the same time, figure in this remarkable outbreak, and the first things to be consumed are the firm's books.'

'That was very unfortunate,' admitted Max Carrados.

'It was, when you consider. Books, Max, are about the most stubbornly uninflammable things that you find about an office. So long as it remains closed it is next to impossible to light a solidly-bound ledger; what happens is that it slowly chars for an inch or two inwards all round. These'—indicating the heap of soaked debris on the floor—'have been deliberately thrown open, drenched with some spirit, and set fire to.'

'Turpentine,' declared the blind man, picking up the relic of a volume. 'All this must have taken time, Louis.'

'Undoubtedly; the preparations were thorough enough for anything.'

'Vernon Barrowford—the last to leave as you very naturally insist—locked the Culver Street door after him at half-past twelve. The general office clerk was here certainly up to twelve-twenty. Ten minutes at the outside, Louis.'

'I haven't gone into that yet. He may have returned again. We learn that he did not reach home until rather late that day.'

'I think he very likely did return, and my interest lies in what he found here. He certainly went meanwhile to the reading-room of the British Museum—I have his umbrella in my car at this moment.'

'To pass the time until it was safe to return here? The brigade think half-past twelve too early to assume this fire which was not discovered until about ten at night.'

'The place is shut in all round and a moderate fire might go on for a long time unseen, but three or four o'clock would suit me better than half-past twelve,' agreed Carrados. 'What case of motive are you making against him, Louis?'

'The suggestion is that the stock has been going down ever since this Barrowford took on the business—five years ago—and the insurance has remained the same. The concern is practically bankrupt now, and the manager admits—'

'Don't say "admits", Louis; I have already conversed with that good, and faithful servant.'

'Well, I am only dealing with facts, whatever we call the source of our information. For months past Barrowford has been trying to get in capital. Lately he found some people who were not unwilling, but of course they stipulated for a proper stocktaking and an independent audit. Now that's just what—'

'I say,' came a plaintive voice from outside the door, 'I don't want to intrude, but—'

'Come in by all means,' called back Mr Carlyle. 'The formalities of office routine are suspended for the nonce. But if you want to see the manager—'

'No, I don't want to see good old Pridger,' said the visitor, disclosing himself as an elderly young man of rather languid aspect; 'I just drifted across, *en passant*, for a nod and a sympathetic word with dear old Vernon, but the bright young Frederick intimates that he hasn't arrived—'

'We are afraid he isn't likely to arrive,' volunteered Mr Carrados. 'Your friend is rather seriously ill at present.'

'You don't say so,' replied the caller, balancing himself against his walking-stick after looking vainly round for an unburnt piece of furniture to lean upon. 'Nervous breakdown and all that, I suppose? The fact is, dear old Vernon wasn't cut out for the turmoil of modern business competition. It was a fundamental error for him ever to have crept out of his cosy corner in Somerset House, where he really was integral. He didn't fit the wall space here.'

'I understand that his tastes were literary and artistic,' remarked Mr Carrados.

'Literary and artistic? Literary *and* artistic!' repeated the new acquaintance, with some play in emphatics. 'Certainly, the dear old somniloquist achieved an occasional letter to the *Moribund Review* on "Telepathy among Cab Horses", or something of that sort, but, my good Lord, artistic! And that reminds me—what has become of the Van Doop amid the cataclysm?'

'The Van Doop?'

'Yes; you've come across the atrocity, haven't you? He had it hung

571

up there when I was last in—Saturday. You don't mean to say—'

'If it was anywhere in this room on Saturday last it has certainly gone the way of all flesh,' declared Mr Carlyle briskly. 'A painting, I suppose? Those may be the remains of a frame where you are looking. Was it valuable?'

'If the dear old chap has had the mental acumen to insure it for what he claimed it to be worth I should say it was very valuable indeed,' was the sage reply. If not—'

'There is no picture of any sort in the schedule,' declared Mr Carlyle, after consulting his papers.

'Then I don't mind telling you that it was rotten. Under the impression that anything signed "Van Doop" was by Van Doop, and that anything by Van Doop was worth about the level thousand, the poor old haddock seems to have let a gang of Bond Street rooks put it across him to the tune of some three hundred. Of course it was easy, because he thought that he was a born judge, and that is the beginning of ignorance.'

'Was he likely to find this out on Saturday?' asked Mr Carrados.

'Well, I told him. I don't see that you could have anything more conclusive than that,' explained the gentleman with some complacency.

'"My dear old image," I said quite plainly. "Van Doop painted only one 'Portrait of a Father-in-Law' and that's in the Eremitage and has been for the last half century."'

'The where?' inquired Mr Carlyle with alert curiosity.

'Eremitage—the Hermitage Museum at St Petersburg, you would probably call it.'

'Yes, or course,' assented Mr Carlyle hastily. 'I didn't quite catch the word, that was all.'

'"As for this mutton-faced adventurer," I told him; "he is probably a worked-up piece by Jan Van Doop—an obscure relative of the man. As a matter of fact, I think Lenlau disposes of this canvas in his list of spurious Van Doops." "Lenlau?" he said helplessly, and I saw that the unfortunate oyster had never heard of the one man who wrote intelligently on the subject of Van Doop. "Good heavens, old thing!" I said, being really too overcome to rub it in, and then, as he asked me, I gave him the details of the work, and that's about all there is to it.'

'I think that explains why Barrowford came back,' said Carrados when the two were alone again. 'That egregious *poseur* knew what he was talking about, at all events. Our man went to the reading-room, got out "Lenlau", and then returned here to verify some point of description.'

'More desperate than ever,' remarked Mr Carlyle significantly.

'Not desperate enough to burn a picture that he hasn't had the prudence to insure, especially as there might be a chance of getting something back yet,' replied his friend. 'Did he find the place on fire when he got here? It is difficult to imagine anything particularly "horrible" about the redness of a burning room. Did he surprise Pridger, who attacked him? Then the cat? Of course it might—'

'One moment, Max, one moment,' cut in Mr Carlyle's assertive protest. 'It is very flattering of you to credit me with a supernatural intuition, but it makes your monologue unnecessarily cryptical. If this is a case of incendiarism—and, by Jupiter, on the evidence lying round I shall advise my clients to resist the claim tooth and nail—who is the perpetrator if not Barrowford?'

'Who?' said Max Carrados, and then his attention suddenly faded. With one of his disconcertingly exact movements he went direct to the mantelpiece, skirting a heap of debris in his progress, and picked up a few letters that were ranged there. 'Oh, Louis, Louis, and we two sleuths are asking, you "Who?" and I "How?" and here are Barrowford's neglected letters.'

'Pshaw!' fretted Carlyle impatiently. 'What business are they of ours, Max? Besides, the fellow is too ill to deal with them by your account.'

'And no letter-box to the door.'

'Well, what of that?'

'The letters fall upon the floor.' The blind man's inquiring fingers were touching off every word and sign accessible to them as he threw aside one packet after another. 'What do you make of this, Louis?'

'A post card. Not very confidential that, eh? "Thanks for your kind inquiry. At the moment we have not—" This is merely formal.'

'Try the other side.'

'Ah, the post mark, "London, E.G., 12.30 p.m., 25 May"—Saturday last. You mean that if this was picked up on Saturday it indicates that someone was about after—let me see, twelve-thirty, say two-thirty delivery, say three o'clock here—and if it wasn't picked up—I see.'

'Not exactly that. Isn't there a sort of a—' and he indicated the cancellation.

'A mere pinkish smudge from something. Do you mean that?'

'What one might perhaps describe as the faint impression of a cat's

573

paw transferred in red. Now, Louis, what was the office cat—'

'But, good heavens, Max, seriously, what have we to do with the peregrinations of this feline marauder? You are not suggesting that the abandoned quadruped deliberately set fire to the establishment, are you? My only concern is who—'

'Oh, who, of course,' apologised his friend. 'You asked that before, didn't you, and I got led away to something else? Naturally, Pridger set the place on fire—hasn't he told you that yet?'

'The manager?' Louis Carlyle stared hard and incredulously for a moment, and then swung half round to Carrados's lead with his usual mental agility. 'Do you know, Max, I always had an underlying instinct that there was something fishy—but so long as it *is* incendiarism I don't suppose it matters to my clients who the criminal is.'

'Oh, don't you, my friend?' retorted Max. 'It may considerably.'

'How so?'

'Barrowford is the sole proprietor of this concern. If he sets it on fire that naturally invalidates his insurance. But if someone else does—'

'His manager,' the other reminded him. 'His confidential employee, Max.'

'True. But you don't suggest that burning the place down is "in or arising out of" his duty, do you?—especially as it was after hours! If you are thinking of your clients, Louis, you had much better stick to Barrowford.'

'Well, after all, I shall keep an open mind on the subject yet. I have still to question some of the men—only Pridger and a boy come here now, and I must hunt the others up.'

'And I must hunt the cat up. We won't trouble Pridger about it, but the boy might be worth seeing.'

'Extraordinary fancies you sometimes get, Max,' said Mr Carlyle, regarding this whim with benevolent toleration. 'I believe half of them are to mystify the simple-minded. The curious thing is that now and then they seem to lead—indirectly, of course—to something we've been looking for.'

'You've noticed that?' responded Carrados. 'I thought that perhaps it was only my imagination.'

'If you really want the boy I'll call him,' preferred Mr Carlyle. 'But I should warn you that even as boys go, he doesn't seem to be a very intelligent member of his tribe.'

The blind man nodded a smiling assent, and Mr Carlyle, going to another door across the way, sent out his ample authoritative voice in a call for 'Fred'.

An undersized, weak-eyed lad of about fifteen emerged unwillingly from a secluded lair, and stuffing an untidy paper-backed book into a pocket as he came he greeted Mr Carlyle with a boorish 'Well?'

'This is the brilliant individual, Max,' said the inquiry agent with elegant disdain. 'Democratic education, egad!'

'Can you tell me where we are likely to find the cat, Fred?' asked Mr Carrados persuasively. 'Perhaps there is more than one kept here?'

'Cat?' repeated the unwholesome-looking boy stupidly. 'The cat isn't none of my business.'

'But you might perhaps know where it usually is,' suggested the inquirer mildly. 'Cats have habits, you know.' But Fred was not to be cajoled by mildness, and turning away he muttered something of which only the words 'if you use your eyes' emerged.

'You young ruffian!' exclaimed the irate Carlyle; 'is that the way to reply to a gentleman—and a blind man, too! If I were Mr Carrados I'd have you skinned, by Jupiter!'

Mr Carlyle was not unaccustomed to his impressive voice and forensic manner carrying effect, but he was hardly prepared for the dramatic change that his words produced.

'Mr Carrados, did you say—blind!' came from the boy in a wholly different tone. His doltish look was gone, his sulky bearing had given place to lively excitement, and his dull eyes were now charged with intelligence—almost with cunning. Coming nearer he laid a hand eagerly on the venerated sleeve, and dropping his voice to the tone appropriate to melodrama, 'Are you Max Carrados, the blind 'tec?' he demanded.

'Come, come; really!' protested Louis Carlyle, scandalized by his familiarity, but his friend only laughed understandingly.

'Was that "Jake Jackson, the Human Bloodhound" you were reading just now?' he asked. 'Pretty good, isn't it?'

'I'll tell you about the cat, sir,' whispered the boy. 'It was suffocated by the smoke on Saturday, and it's out at the back by the dust-bins now. Is it the fire or embezzlement you're on to now, sir?'

'Fred!' sounded the manager's voice not so far away. 'Fred, where are—'

'Look out, sir,' cautioned the boy, as he made for the door. 'Old Pridger half suspects it's not going smooth. Bins straight through warehouse—yellow jinny cat.' Then his former lethargy descended on him and he lounged into the passage muttering, 'Electric fuses? 'Ow'm I to know—'

'Oh, Fred,' said the manager sharply, 'why the devil can't you come when—Here, get your hat at once and take this note across to March-mont's and wait an answer. Well, gentlemen—'

Two minutes later, as the three walked towards the warehouse, they encountered Fred on his way out. The loutish youth, not dreaming of giving way, barged into Mr Carrados and earned a reprimand for clumsiness and a further word for the whistle of studied disrespect with which he artistically rounded off the affair. When the opportunity came the blind man smoothed out the screw of paper that the encounter had left in his hand and read as follows:

> If you want to know more about it meet me at twelve tonight (midnight) on Waterloo Bridge. Boss is all right, but old P. is a churlish swine. I've been dogging his footsteps for months and can put you on to two banks where he goes in different names. What ho!
>
> (Signed)   Frederick the Boy Detective."

'Frederick will probably be heard of again,' speculated Carrados as he slid the message into his wallet. 'All the same, I wish that his taste in appointments had not been quite so inconveniently dramatic.'

★★★★★★

Max Carrados wrote some time later:

Dear Louis, I will redeem the promise made when you were called away in the middle of the Barrowford affair. You complained that I did not seem to take much interest in that conflagration, and you were right, for a mere straightforward piece of incendiarism offers nothing new. But the mystery of Vernon Barrowford's condition struck quite another line. Whether we should ever have reached a true understanding of that curious case without the miraculous intervention of Frederick is beside the question. That boy, Louis, is in his way a masterpiece. Do you know, every article of clothing that he wears is reversible, so that he can present quite a different appearance at the shortest notice!

You will have seen that Pridger got five years. It might well have been more if Barrowford could have appeared, but that was out of the question, and so, much against the man had to be ignored. His is quite an ordinary case. His nature is not essentially criminal and he had no expensive tastes. For twenty years he had been an exemplary servant under the eye of old Conrad Stubb; but Stubb knew the business to his finger-nails, while Vernon never really touched it with a long pole. His coming was the beginning of Pridger's downfall. The man saw—it was, indeed, thrown at him—how easy peculation was. Everything was left to his unsupervised control. In five years, out of a salary of six or seven pounds a week, he had "saved" at least eight thousand pounds!

This wholesale success was the manager's undoing. The business grew poorer and poorer until it could no longer turn. Then Barrowford bestirred himself to get in outside capital. He found someone not unwilling to go into it, but that entailed a thorough audit. So far as Pridger was concerned the game was up. He had cooked the buying, he had cooked the selling, he had systematically pillaged the stock. He could, of course, have bolted—all his booty was conveniently arranged for that—but the man's conventional nature shrank from such a break with respectability. A fire was obviously the solution, and, as luck would have it, a fire just then might very easily be made to look like Vernon's expedient.

This brings us down to the Saturday of the deed. For some time Pridger had been waiting and watching for the occasion when his employer should be the last man to leave. In pursuance of this scheme it was his custom to announce that he was going and then secrete himself. This is what happened on the day in question, and when Barrowford saw all the others off and himself locked the outer door on his departure the manager decided that his chance had come.

He was in no hurry. There was the bare possibility at first that someone might return for something, while as the afternoon wore on the footstep of the occasional passer-by would get even rarer, and it was no part of the plan that the fire should be discovered by some premature busybody. Mr Pridger leisurely consumed his simple lunch and re-read through his morning paper. Then at about three o'clock he began work seriously.

We know now what had happened to Barrowford meanwhile. He had, I have since discovered, been the victim of a quite elaborate "plant" over the Dutch old master—thinking by his "connoisseurship" to improve his position—and he could not afford it. Whether the proof of the deception was quite such a simple affair as it pleased that debonair sprig to affect need not trouble us; at any rate, Barrowford found some reference so disconcerting at the British Museum that he hurried back to his office to verify the worst.

Three-thirty, let us say. Pridger had been burning books and other incriminating matter now for half an hour. Then on his startled ear there falls suddenly the sound of someone unlocking the outer front door. No need to think twice who. Only one man beside himself possessed the keys.

For this emergency the guilty knave had no plan ready. He had gone too far to make extrication possible; the evidence of his intention lay about in every room, and however slack a master Barrowford had been he would certainly read the plain riddle of the scene that met his eyes, and then Pridger was lost.

Flight was no longer possible; for even to reach the warehouse and the back he must have recourse to the long passage. It was then that Pridger's eye fell on the door of a small store closet—he was in the general office now—windowless and dark. I think that the man's impulse was simply to hide himself and gain a breath of time. But as he stumbled in there flashed to his mind the desperate expedient of this last chance. It was no sooner grasped than acted on.

A few months before a handy fellow among them had offered to paint the place and the materials were bought, but something intervened and the project hung. The tins of paint still stood there, already mixed, and it was to a lurid crimson that Pridger's mind had leapt. There was no subtlety—there was no time for it. He stooped, dipped both hands into the fluid, and simply laved his face with it. Then throwing completely round his form a sable cloth—one of those to be spread over the goods—he stepped out to meet his unsuspecting victim.

How they met—whether the dreadful apparition leapt out as the man drew near, whether it stood silently awaiting him, or whether it rushed shrieking down the passage threateningly—we shall perhaps never know. But reconstructing the scene among those silent walls in the precarious light, with the unforgotten ghosts of other crimes ready to emerge from every shadow, I can conceive that no more frightful spectre than this sombre being, dripping red from hands and face at every step, has ever walked. Its effect on a rather soft and just then greatly harassed mind was tragic. Vernon Barrowford has brought from that shuttered past just one vivid lightning flash—the ghastly, all-pervading redness of the Thing; his own paralysing sense of helpless terror; the panic-stricken howling of the flying cat; and the safety of the distant door that he must—must—reach. He did reach it, but he left something there behind.

The Strange Case of Cyril Bycourt

'I knew you in a moment, Mr Carrados. But I expect that you haven't the very faintest idea of who I am?'

'No,' admitted Max Carrados pleasantly; 'I am afraid that I must plead guilty. But,' he added, in his usual matter-of-fact, effective way, 'of course I know well enough who you were. Twenty years ago—at least, twenty to my account—we acted charades together and you were Gertie Hamilton.'

'I still am,' admitted the lady, with a suggestion of resignation in her voice. 'And it's every bit of twenty years as far as I'm concerned.'

That evening Mr Carrados (duly announced by an occasional small bill in the windows of dairies, fancy wool shops, and other refined establishments) had been delivering an address on 'Premonition, Hallucination, and Autosuggestion' at the Corn Market Hall in Overbury. It had amused the blind man to accept the invitation to give the annual Stalworthy lecture, as it frequently did amuse him to do unexpected things—sheerly to experience—but more than once before he was through the unentertaining business he cursed the moment of good-natured assent.

The last formal word of compliment was spoken and the audience dribbled away with a sense of having performed a duty only slightly less meritorious than that of going to church. Parkinson, at all events, in the glory of being seated on the platform, had thoroughly enjoyed himself. It was then that the lady, who had occupied a retired seat well down the hall, summoned up the resolution to approach the lecturer and to challenge his recollection.

'And you really do know me by my voice! How wonderful! I had been told—but you never know what to believe.'

'It does depend somewhat on the teller, doesn't it?' agreed Carrados.

'Well, it was chiefly Lydia Murgatroyd, I think. You remember her? Lydia married a drawing-master who had a pupil whose father—a wholesale druggist, you know—got into a case and employed a Mr Carlyle, who said—'

'Heavens!' interposed Carrados, 'that's five removes already. You can only believe a fifth of what you heard. Much better expect to find me as you found me in the past.'

'Well, we were always quite good friends, weren't we? You were Mr Max Wynn in those days, and you—you—'

'I had to trust my poor misleading eyes then? Yes; I wonder if I should have known *you*, Miss Hamilton, at sight.'

'Oh, I hope not!' she exclaimed ingenuously, and disclosing that train of thought she added, 'but my sister Mildred was the pretty one, you know.'

'Mildred; yes, I remember her very well indeed,' replied the blind man thoughtfully. 'We were all her devoted slaves. And she died?'

'You heard?'

'Not until now. Your voice told me that.'

Miss Hamilton's look expressed surprise, but she accepted what he said unquestioningly; it agreed with much that she had heard.

'Yes; she died five years ago. And, curiously enough, it has to do with that in a way that I am here now. I came'—she suddenly found her diffidence returning—'I came to see if the Mr Carrados I'd heard so much about really was the Max Wynn we used to know, and if so to ask your advice.'

At the back of the hall a sad man was already putting out the lights; in the neighbourhood of the platform another coughed hopefully from time to time. No one else remained; even the young lady who had played selections from Bach and Schumann before the lecture and 'God Save the King' after it had closed the hired piano, rolled up her music, and stolen silently away. At a suitable distance apart, exercising his unique gift of being profoundly impressed by a subject that he had no interest in whatever, Parkinson was deeply immersed in a chart illustrating a century of wheat averages of the British Isles.

'I suppose that I oughtn't to detain you here,' continued Miss Hamilton looking about. 'I wonder if you could spare the time to go back with me and tell me what you think. I live just outside Overbury—quite a short walk.'

'If you knew anything of life in the "Mitre" smoking-room you wouldn't sound so diffident about offering an alternative for an hour or two,' replied Carrados.

'That's just like you used to be,' she commented. Thanking me for asking you to do something.'

As they walked through the silent and deserted streets of the little market town, Carrados was reviewing his memories of the past. Twenty-five years ago (he had given the lady the benefit of five) he had been of very small account indeed—an unknown youth in a strange city, with the wealth that had afterwards suddenly descended on him as remote then as if it had been buried in the mountains of the moon. The Hamiltons had let him understand that he need not be solitary if he cared to accept the simple, kindly entertainment they dispensed. It had not lasted very long; promotion to another town had cut across his path, and the Hamiltons had never become more than an incident, but, a little tardily perhaps, he recognised that at the time their friendliness had meant much to him.

The now middle-aged Gertrude, padding rather heavily by his side as she guided his course, had been the elder of the sisters. The other—Mildred—had more than merited Gertie's claim and his own prosaic tribute. Her memory stirred no heartbeat now, but he could very well recall the shy wonder with which the adoring youth had watched her movements. Then there had been a brother of whom he was yet to hear. Both parents would be dead . . . .

'Here we are at last,' exclaimed Miss Hamilton with determined sprightliness, and Carrados heard the latch of a gate lifted. The garden they passed through was of the cottage order, but trimly kept; the blind man checked off one old English flower after another, and divined the care lavished on them before the door was reached.

'I wonder if Mr Parkinson would mind sitting in the kitchen with my old servant?' whispered Miss Hamilton. 'I am rather afraid of him, do you know!' The little grimace accompanying this indicated that the idea was to be regarded humorously, and Carrados understood that what she really doubted was the extent of Parkinson's discretion. 'Nothing would suit him better,' he replied. 'If he happens to approve of my address he will give your servant a selection of extracts from it, only in much superior language.'

'Then I will take him through, if you will excuse me.' She lingered at the door and laughed a little self-consciously. 'And generally—though of course you wouldn't remember a thing like that—we used to have just coffee and cakes as a sort of supper. But I hardly expect that now—'

'Do you still make the cake with pink icing and the orange flavour?' he inquired.

'Well, really, I wouldn't have believed!' she exclaimed, and bounced away like a delighted schoolgirl.

A little later, having successfully introduced Parkinson and arranged for the appearance of the celebrated cake, Miss Hamilton launched upon the subject of her trouble.

'It's really about Cyril I meant when I said Mildred,' she explained. 'Cyril is Mildred's son, the only child she had, and so, of course, my nephew, the only one *I* have.'

'Then Tom—'

'Tom went to South Africa ten—twelve—oh, fifteen years ago. We never heard from him after the war there; I think he must have been killed. You see, Mr Carrados, I'm quite alone except for Cyril now. Father—Mother—Tom—Mildred—all I had: all gone.'

'Your nephew lives with you here?' prompted Carrados. He was sorry for the poor lady, forlorn and rather unwieldy among the buffetry of circumstance, but he began to foresee that it might be necessary to keep her to the point.

'No; I'm coming to that. You must forgive me—I know I'm slow and tiresome. I can do nothing but think about things now, hour after hour: moping I suppose others would call it. It's so dreadful if it's true that I can hardly believe it possible; and yet, there it is. I must do something about it.'

'Yes,' said Carrados, smiling away the edge of his retort, 'you must really tell me about it.'

'There I go again!' confessed Miss Hamilton with a gesture of despair. 'How can I expect you to advise me? Well, Millie married a Mr Bycourt—Mark Bycourt—who still lives a few miles from here. He was quite a nice sort of man, but a little old for her, I thought, considering her looks and chances, and he really doesn't appear to be interested in any subject except water beetles. It seems a strange taste for a man. He might have taken up golf, or prize poultry, or politics, or lots of things, I mean, that would have seemed more—well, gentlemanly.'

'Quite a number of people are interested in water beetles,' observed Carrados mildly.

'So I am given to understand,' she admitted, 'and I suppose that I must be narrow-minded. But don't think that I have anything against Mr Bycourt; he made what I should call a good husband, though it must undoubtedly have been a little dull for Millie at times. When they had been married about three years Cyril came.... Did you ever hear of an Uncle Stace when you knew us at Midchester, Mr Carrados?'

'Stace? No, I have never heard the name before,' replied the blind man.

'I don't quite know where the relationship came in or if he really was any relation at all. I have heard that he had been very fond of mother years ago and wanted to marry her, but when we children knew him he seemed quite old and was said to be very rich. Well, all that he has to do with it is this: Millie was his favourite—as she was everyone's—and when he died it was found that he had left everything—almost everything—to her, and to Cyril afterwards.'

'To her and to her children generally afterwards?' suggested Carrados.

'No, just to Cyril by name. There were no other children, you see.'

'Quite so,' agreed the listener.

'Millie died when she had been married about eight years—it was appendicitis. Then Mark asked me if I would keep house for him and look after Cyril, and I did—for four years. Of course I got very fond of the child, especially after I had mothered him through his little troubles and illnesses; he was all that was left to me of the old days at Midchester. It was a great blow to me when Mark married again.'

Carrados contributed only a sympathetic nod; Miss Hamilton seemed fairly well set on her subject now.

'I should not have minded so much if the new Mrs Bycourt had been what I would call a suitable person, but really, one could hardly describe her as a lady. She was the very opposite of Mildred, and what Mark could have been thinking of I cannot imagine.'

'Some people are like that,' admitted Carrados diplomatically.

'Well, I suppose so; but it is a great pity. She was the widow of a sort of small country gentleman who owned one or two racehorses and came to grief, and she really seemed to have absorbed the atmosphere of the stable and the farmyard. Not that I mean there was anything definitely wrong about her—but the whiskies-and-sodas, the cigars, the slang (to call it nothing worse), the slap-dash of everything!—and Mark was such a refined man, whatever else he was. I really couldn't stand it for more than a week, although they both pressed me to remain until I could make my own arrangements; it was a sudden marriage, you know. That was about a year ago.

'It really was very terrible for me, Mr Carrados, to have to give little Cyril up. He was such an affectionate, dear little boy, and for four
years I had been neither more nor less than his mother. But there! I
took this cottage partly so that I could get across to Stacks—that's
their house—from time to time, and of course I have to consider ways
and means as well: Papa was unfortunate towards the last. In the meanwhile Cyril goes daily to a small school kept by a lady in the village; he
is delicate and rather too young to leave home yet. Mrs Bycourt has
two boys of her own, a few years older than Cyril and perfect young
ruffians. Fortunately, they are generally away at boarding-school.'

'And now?' prompted Carrados, for Miss Hamilton's silence was
becoming rather strained, and, after maintaining an admirable control
up to this point, the poor lady, brought face to face with her immediate distress, suddenly brimmed over.

'Oh, Mr Carrados,' she wailed appealingly, 'don't laugh at me, but
I'm sure the woman's murdering Cyril by degrees so that her own will
get his money. I know she is, and what am I to do?'

Now with regard to murder, experience had imbued the blind
man with two convictions: the first that it is a very easy thing to do,
and the second that it is a very difficult thing to do properly. If this
inauspicious Mrs Bycourt actually succeeded in removing her young
stepson, Max Carrados did not doubt that the chances were on the
side of justice overtaking her, but the more pressing need was to find
out if she had any such intention, and if so to frustrate it.

'Would the money go to her if your nephew died?' he asked.

'Oh, yes. I saw our old solicitor about that. As I said, it was left to
Millie and to Cyril after her. It is really Cyril's now, but held in trust
for him until he comes of age. Of course he can't make a will yet, so
that if he died the money would pass to his father, and he naturally
would leave it to his wife.'

'He probably would,' agreed Carrados. 'How much is there?'

'It was about thirty thousand pounds. I understand that by the time
Cyril could touch it there would be more than fifty thousand. That
seems a lot to people like ourselves. Mark is quite comfortably off, I
suppose, but by no means wealthy, and his new wife will have brought
him little. If she is determined to get rich or to provide well for her
own awful children, Cyril's fortune—'

It was quite clear that Miss Hamilton had definitely settled the offending Mrs Bycourt and Cyril in their respective roles of murderess
and victim, but when the patient investigator brought her up against

the test of concrete facts he felt that the most useful purpose he could serve would be to discount her fears.

'But I feel so absolutely convinced that something sinister is going on,' pleaded the distressed lady. 'Oh, Mr Carrados, the boy is growing thinner and more lifeless week by week, the woman is capable of any villainy, the inducement is plain before our faces—'

'Then why not persuade the father to get a doctor in?'

'The doctor has seen him already. I insisted on Dr Huntley being called in some time ago.'

Carrados passed the revealing word 'insisted'. 'And he said?' he inquired.

'Oh, he said that there was nothing really the matter. Of course he meant that Cyril hadn't measles or chickenpox, and we knew that well enough already. He recommended a little change. Cyril went with me to Eastbourne for two weeks. There he improved wonderfully. Then we came back and he went down again.'

'Could he not live with you here for some time?'

'I should love it. But Mrs Bycourt won't hear of such a thing— naturally. She says that the boy has been coddled enough already—me, of course—and that the sooner he gets over his morbid fancies the better, and that in any case if the air of Stacks doesn't suit him, it's hardly likely that this will as it's only five miles away. . . . Now whatever can that be at this hour? Did you hear a knock? I didn't, but Susan has gone to the door.'

'I heard a footstep outside and then a knock,' replied the blind man. 'It is a child who is uncertain.'

'Please, m'm,' said the elderly servant, opening the room door and standing there a little fluttered, 'here's Master Cyril from Stacks and in a pretty pickle.'

'Do you mean he's alone?' exclaimed Miss Hamilton, jumping up and making for the door. 'Oh, my poor lamb!' For the next half minute there was alternate rattle and murmur in the hall, while the staid Susan continued by the door, regarding Mr Carrados with a fascinated interest. Parkinson had undoubtedly been enlarging. Then Miss Hamilton returned, leading in a little boy who clung to her, his pale, over-refined young face not yet wholly reassured.

'This is Cyril, Mr Carrados,' she explained, patting the hand that gripped her protectively. 'He tells me that he has run away from home and walked all the way here, but I know nothing more because I thought that you had better hear it with me.'

'Well, he seems to have come just in time for some coffee and cake, unless the signs deceive me,' remarked Carrados with encouraging levity. 'Fond of cake with plenty of pink icing on it, Cyril?'

'Yes, thank you, sir,' replied the boy politely, as he took serious stock of this new grown-up.

'So am I,' confessed the friendly stranger. 'And I don't mind telling you, Cyril, that when I was ten—that's older than you perhaps—I ran away, because there was a very fat big boy who used to wait for me every morning and punch my head.'

'I *am* ten,' protested Cyril; 'and I am not much afraid of boys. But I am frightened of the man who comes to me in the night and is going to take me in his cart.' A look of pitiable terror came into his eyes and his voice rose almost to a scream. 'Don't let him; oh, don't let him take me, Auntie!'

With a croon of horror and affection Gertrude Hamilton flung her arms protectingly about her darling child and shot a meaning look of triumph at her unbelieving guest. '*Now* what do you think?' it seemed to say, and, for all the world as if he had met it, the blind man's scarcely-moving hand mutely signalled back, 'Quietly. Be careful now!'

'He shall not touch you,' he said reassuringly. 'You are going to stay here tonight. Now tell us what this man is like, so that we shall be able to prevent him from ever coming again.'

'He is a big man and very strong, so that he can carry people. He stands by my bed looking down; and there is a nasty smell comes with him.'

'What does he wear?'

'It is a long brown thing with a belt, and a queer high hat, not like men wear now. And he has a staff.'

'Can you tell us what his face is like? Have you ever seen another that reminds you of it?'

'It is only his eyes that you can see,' replied Cyril, in a voice low with the memory of his terror. 'There is something like a cloth over his face.'

'Oh, my precious!' was wrung from Miss Hamilton, but Carrados's insistent gesture cut shot her passionate outcry.

'It is a dream,' said the blind man quietly, taking up his patient again; 'a bad black dream. You are really asleep at the time, Cyril?'

'I am not quite awake,' admitted the boy consideringly, 'but I am not really asleep. It is very queer and—different. And he mutters.'

'Do you remember anything that he has ever said?'

'Only a little bit now and then. Last night he said, "He has the—the"—I forget the word; oh, yes—"the tokens on him, but he is not dead yet. I will come again tomorrow night". That was why I dare not stay any longer.'

Miss Hamilton left Cyril on the couch where they had been seated and crossed the room.

'Is it necessary to distress him any more with this?' she whispered. Her face was white and scared, but there was the ring of defiance in her voice. 'Whatever happens, he shall not go back while I'm alive.'

'It's extraordinarily fascinating,' replied Carrados in the same guarded tone, 'and we ought to get at the bottom of these things. On the face of it this is plainly nightmare—he has read it all. Do you ever,' he continued, turning to the boy again, 'do you ever hear a bell ringing while this goes on?'

'Yes,' was the reply, given without hesitation, 'it rings sometimes outside. That is before the man comes in or after he has gone.'

'You see,' explained Carrados aside; 'that bears it out. If this were someone got up to terrify the boy it's absurd that he should take the extra risk of having a bell rung outside, merely for a point of extra realism, but it is just the sort of detail that sticks in the imagination and reproduces in a very vivid nightmare.'

'But what is it?' demanded Miss Hamilton, beginning to be shaken in her high attitude. 'What is it that he is supposed to dream about?'

'What? Why the Plague to be sure; the Great Plague that furnished nightmares for many a generation in the past. Let me see, Cyril, you are fond of reading, aren't you?'

'Well, yes, sir,' said Cyril. 'If it's tales,' he added conscientiously.

'Oh, of course; we don't mean lessons, do we? Have you ever read *Robinson Crusoe*?'

'Rather! I've got it at home—with pictures.'

'Man Friday and the parrot and all? Do you remember who wrote it?'

'Yes; Daniel Defoe.'

'Bravo! Well, he wrote other books. Can you tell me any?'

Apparently not. Cyril considered, but remained dumb. 'Something about a "Journal" and a "Year", eh?' prompted the questioner. 'No? Well, never mind.'

'But why not ask him outright if you think it's that?' put in the lady. 'Shall I?'

'It is liable to suggest,' was his reply. 'But try.'

'Once upon a time a lot of people got very ill,' said Miss Hamilton coaxingly, 'and they called it a plague. Have you ever heard of it, my pet?'

'Yes, Auntie,' said Cyril, his large, considering eyes incapable of jest. 'It's what papa calls me when I ask him things.'

Miss Hamilton so to speak 'stood down' and Carrados resumed.

'Did you ever see a picture of a man in a long brown dress—'

'Like him?' interrupted the child with a shudder. 'No—and—please, sir—'

'My dear lad,' anticipated Carrados, going to the couch and laying his hand unfailingly on the boy's shoulder, 'we are going to help you. We intend that you shall never, never see the man again. But sometimes the doctor has to give you nasty medicine for your good. It isn't always pleasant to be left in the dark, even when you are ten, is it?'

'No, sir.'

'Well, when you feel like that, Cyril, you can think of me being in the darkness with you too. I am always in the dark because, you see, I am blind.'

'Oh, I didn't know, sir,' said the little boy with quick feeling. 'I am very sorry, but'—consolingly—'you look all right.'

'Thank you,' replied Mr Carrados gravely. 'Generally speaking, I feel all right. But we all have our moments in the dark.'

'Cyril has a little light always in his bedroom,' volunteered Miss Hamilton. 'Don't you, dear?'

'Quite right,' said Carrados idly. 'A nightlight?'

'Yes, but electric light, you know. A tiny bulb. It's new there. Mrs Bycourt said she couldn't stand lamps, and so Mark has recently put up an installation for the house.'

'Electric light, and recent?' mused Carrados. 'How long ago?'

'About, well—how long have you had the electric light, Cyril? A few months, isn't it?'

'At Christmas, Auntie. We had all the lights on at once on Christmas Day. Don't you remember; you were there?'

Miss Hamilton nodded assent, her eyes on her guest's impenetrable face. 'Yes, that is right,' she said.

'Let me see'—a most disarming unconcern had come into the blind man's voice—'was it before or after Christmas that the bad dream first came?'

'It was just after Christmas,' replied the boy.

'Quite sure?'—a little more insistent now.

'Oh, yes; I remember by my presents. And then he began to come oftener, and then he stayed away a bit, and—and I am frightened, but I'm glad I told you.'

'My treasure!' cried the fond lady, 'why didn't you tell Auntie sooner?' and for reply Cyril hung his head and whispered the fatal insuperable excuse of childhood:

'I didn't like to.'

'Another time you must,' she enjoined. 'And do you always sleep on your right side, as I told you?'

'Yes, Auntie.'

'And the bed is still pushed to the farther wall, away from the draught, where I arranged it?'

'Oh, yes Auntie. It is right up to the little pull-thing in the wall that does my light. I can send it in and out while I'm in bed.'

'And the best place for you to be now, young man,' said Carrados, taking out his watch and touching its fingers. 'Eleven-fifteen.'

'Yes, indeed,' chimed in Miss Hamilton. 'If you don't want another piece of cake Susan will take you up. I suppose'—turning to her visitor—'that I ought to let them know somehow at Stacks where Cyril is tonight?'

'I have been thinking of that. Are they on the telephone?'

'No—what a pity. You would have told them from your hotel, I'm sure.'

'Yes, but as they're not, so much the better. Just write them a line and I will take it round there now.'

'You, Mr Carrados? At this hour?'

'Why not? All hours are alike to me. Then we needn't disturb them if they know nothing of the escapade as yet. If I find the place in darkness I shall leave the note to be discovered with Master Cyril's absence in the morning. I have a fancy to "see" Stacks in my own particular way, Miss Hamilton, and, lo and behold! the Fates arrange it.'

Less than half an hour later a motorcar skated down the long, slight hill that ended in the village street of Irling and drew up before the cottages began. Mr Carrados and Parkinson got out, and leaving the hotel chauffeur to doze across his wheel they set out on the adventure of discovery.

'The turning to the left before the baker's shop,' directed the leader of the expedition. 'That must be it ahead, Parkinson, although the rural baker does not seem to bake by night. Edwards should be the name.'

'There is a shop, sir,' assented Parkinson, peering across the way. 'But I am unable to distinguish the name. If I may—' He was away a moment. 'Perfectly correct, sir, and there is the lane. The people hereabouts, sir, would seem to dispense with street illumination, and it is very dark tonight.'

'True,' replied Carrados, 'and fortunately there is no moon.'

'Yes, sir,' agreed the faithful servitor, catching his toe against the kerb and recovering by his master's guidance; 'I appreciate that it gives us the initial advantage.'

A short half mile, another turn, and presently a darker mass emerged lying back upon their left.

'That should be Stacks,' conjectured Carrados, when Parkinson gave him this information. 'Now is the murder out yet?'

'We are coming to the gates,' reported the proxy 'eyes'. 'There is a small lodge immediately inside. The gates, of open-work iron, are closed. The drive—'

'Wait,' interrupted Carrados. 'Any lights showing at the lodge?'

'No, sir; not on this side.'

'Have a look farther on.'

Parkinson walked fifty yards along the road and then returned.

'No lights anywhere,' he reported.

'Then the murder is probably not yet out. With so good an excuse for being on the premises, and every opportunity for losing ourselves if need be, I begin to despise the front way, Parkinson. Let us investigate.'

They continued along the road away from Stacks. Parkinson soon reported a small door in the garden fence, but this proved to be locked. A little farther on a lane gave promise on their left. A few stars had risen and the seeing eyes were more accustomed to the darkness. After a single futile cast a path was discovered through the fields that now separated them from Stacks, and with scarcely the tribute of a scratch they forced a likely hedge and fell through into what was unmistakably a private garden.

'Never mind the rhubarb plants,' said Carrados—his follower was standing rather aghast at the extent of their devastation. 'They made capital landing and usefully indicate that we are in an obscure part of the kitchen-garden. Can you see the house? Well, we will take a stroll round.'

Progress was slow and vicissitudinous. 'The advantage of beginning operations from here is obvious,' expounded the specialist. 'If we walk across a bed of onions—as we are, in fact, doing at this moment—we create an aromatic fixed point, so to speak, to which it is easy to return again whenever it becomes prudent. It is a line that holds.'

'I have always understood that onions possessed certain medicinal properties, sir,' replied Parkinson sagaciously, and heaven knows what profundities the ingenuous creature might not have advanced had not a parallelogram of emerging blackness disclosed the position of the house. Here also, ran the report, no lights were visible.

'Then the murder is certainly not out,' decided Carrados. 'We can resume out leisurely survey. But not, for preference, along their celery trench, Parkinson.'

'I am very sorry, sir. For the moment my attention was distracted. I have just observed another building, much nearer than the house, where a light is showing.'

'Make for it then. A light means someone, and we must put ourselves right by getting in the first word.'

But he was wrong. The place, a small, well-built shed standing in a remote corner of the grounds—half shrubbery, half waste, they judged—was deserted. Machinery, now idle, proclaimed its use; the light that had attracted them a single indicator lamp glowing above a switchboard.

'The dynamo house, of course, and now they're on the battery,' explained Carrados when they had investigated. 'I heard that they made their own light, but who would have expected to find the place down here.'

'I had some general conversation with the elderly person at Miss Hamilton's,' volunteered Parkinson tolerantly; 'and after the arrival of the young gentleman she expressed her opinions about the family living here. Mr Bycourt is a very nervous, irritable gentleman, it would appear, sir, and cannot put up with any noise or distraction. Perhaps on that account—'

'Aye, that will be it,' agreed Mr Carrados. 'The beat of the engine will scarcely be heard up there; but ssh! what the deuce is coming now?'

Someone was approaching at all events, and the two intruders shrank back into the readiest cover.

'A woman, sir,' whispered Parkinson.

'An old woman,' amplified his master. 'She carries something, and she's in a hurry. Also, she has no business here: which gives us a great advantage, because we have.'

At the threshold of the little house the burden was shot down. The watchers knew already that the door was fastened and looked for the unknown to produce a key. Instead, there was a sudden scrunch of iron, a splintering of wood, and the door swung loosely open.

'Forced, egad!' thought Carrados. 'Our lady is determined.' Then as she passed in, dragging along what now appeared to be a sack, he touched his attendant's arm and together they crept forward to the half-open door.

'It's shavings and wood she's brought,' conveyed Parkinson, his eye to a convenient chink. 'And, blow me, sir,' he added a second later, stirred to this deplorable lapse from his usual diction, 'but she's drenching the place with petrol! she means mischief!'

'Stop!' cried Carrados, disclosing himself in the doorway. 'Haven't you the sense to know that you'll blow yourself up too?'

The startled creature—never was there a meeker-looking *pétroleuse* than this tidy, grey-haired cottager—dropped the box of matches she was handling and literally fell upon her knees among the mess she had contrived.

'Oh, the dear Lord preserve us all!' she gasped in terror. 'Who are ye?'

'Never mind that. The question is who are you and what are you doing here?'

'Sure I'm only Mrs Laffey from the lodge just by, sir. Indeed I wasn't doing no harm at all, but you gave me a great turn—just a bit of arranging and tidying up, as you may say. I dhropped a spot of oil an'—'

'Parkinson,' threw out Carrados in a sufficient whisper, 'the police.'

'Oh, don't bring in the polis on me, kind gentleman,' implored Mrs Laffey with redoubled fluency; 'the dirty, thievin' sergeant that set the lie against me a short while back over Mister Johnson's sthrayin' pullets, it's little justice I should ever see. Be the good kind gentleman—'

'You have just one chance,' Carrados took out his watch and displayed it upon his outstretched hand. 'Get up and tell us the exact truth, no matter what it is. Come, out with it.'

'Indeed an' I will, sir an' your honour, for I'm sure ye'd not be after bethraying a poor old widder woman. 'Tis for me boy I'm doing of it, and that's the blessed truth this minnit, though nothing but black words and the lift of a hand maybe would be me thanks if he did know.'

'Your boy? Your son, you mean?'

'Me boy Jim, and he the only one I've got and me husband gone this seventeen years. Ever since he has left school he's worked in the garden, with a thing here and there maybe in the house beyond and a bit extry for it of a Saturday. Well—and it's the stark truth I'm telling ye the blessed knows—last back end the master calls him by and said, "Jim," he said, "the missis is determined on this electrey light and it's all arranged for. You'll have to learn to handle the dynamey an' what not, but 'tis no matter at all—an hour here and there maybe and a grand learning for you for to be an engineer". "Jim," I said when I hear of it, "don't do it. For 'twas handlin' of that stuff hoist your granda out of Donegal in the old days". "Oh, bother," he says, "how am I to say I an't when himself has said I am? 'Twould be the marching order I should likely get instead". "An' if you should," I up and said, "aren't there plenty other jobs as good in the long breadth of the land and you a handy thrifty chap?" "Have done," he says, souring on me, and—God forgive him!—well I knew the reason why he'd stay, eating the very dirt if need be and she little better than a pagan deity, as you may say.'

'He had charge of this place then?' said Carrados with a patience that Parkinson could not but disapprove of. 'Well, go on.'

'He had indeed, sir, and never a restful moment has he known since. First his bright pretty colour goes, and soon his appetite, and he that would eat me out of house and home now touching no more'n a sup of tay and fiddling with a little thin piece of currant cake maybe. And all the while he taking great store of the dynamey and that, and would spend long hours polishing and oiling up here alone. Then the sleep forsake him, or it'd be one sweaty terror of the livelong night the way he'd fetch likely a groan in his dreams or a curse at the long, still blackness stretching to the dawn, and me listening at the latch-hole of his door.'

'What did he dream?' asked Carrados.

'We made no talk about it, sir, him being that stubborn. But many's the queer word he's let out in his sleep, the same as if he'd claim that one was waiting there to fetch him in a cart. But give notice to himself he would not, as I am tellin' yous, and the very grip of death closing in upon him plain for eny to see, until I knew. 'Tis either Jim or that rampageous divil that's somehow desthroyin' him up there. And that's the sacred truth itself, God help me!'

For a full minute the blind man remained silent, prodding the loose earth with his walking-stick as he pondered. When he spoke, instead of any of the things that Mrs Laffey had hoped, or perhaps feared, it was to put an idle question.

'Did this part of the ground have any special name?' he asked. 'Before this place was built, I mean.'

'They did used to be calling it the Bone Mound, so I've heard,' she said, trying to catch his mood with surreptitious glances. 'There was a little hump, you'll understand, but they thrudged the top off ut for to make a level space.'

'Yes, of course they would. And now, Mrs Laffey, you'd better go on home again. Show this man the way to the front gate as you go. We'll leave that way, Parkinson, but don't come back to me for half an hour.'

'Very good, sir.' Parkinson knew of the times when his master would have no human eye upon him as he worked, and he had ceased—if, indeed, he had ever begun—to feel a trace of curiosity.

"Deed an' I will,' said Mrs Laffey cheerfully. 'The gentleman is welcome to me little front room too until your honour's ready. And, begging your pardon, sir, you'll overlook to mention what's passed tonight?'

'So far as I am concerned you can set your mind at rest,' was his reply; 'but you'll have to explain one or two things in the morning, it seems to me. I dare say you can put a very good face on it somehow.'

'I might contrive,' replied Mrs Laffey hopefully.

★★★★★★

Mrs Laffey did indeed contrive to put a very good face upon it, as Mr Carrados found when he visited Stacks openly the following day. It was not Mrs Laffey's fault that she missed seeing them, and doubtless dropping a word of timely preparation, but their own in discovering a wicket gate that saved the bend of the road and brought them upon Mrs Bycourt, who was exercising a pair of young hounds on the lawn.

'If ever there was a good Samaritan this side the Jordan it's surely you, Mr Carrados!' exclaimed that athletic lady when she had identified her caller. 'And'—she felt that she ought to indicate some concession to his infirmity—'in spite of your—'

'Or because of, perhaps,' he suggested, coming to her rescue. 'You got the note anyway?'

'Oh, yes. In fact, it was our first intimation that the bird had flown.

It really was a great kindness because my husband fidgets so over little things, and if he had found Cyril gone and no trace of him, heavens knows what! And then this other business coming on the top of it!'

'You mean the incident down the garden?' asked Carrados tentatively.

'Good gracious, yes! I hope there isn't anything else? Not that *I* mind a bit of a shindy any time, but I have my poor dear's nerves to consider. He is most tremendously indebted to you; it really was sporting in the circumstances. Mrs Laffey gave us a most glowing account of your exploit.'

'Oh, did she?' Carrados considered a little. 'I rather wondered what she would say.'

'Well, she said—as near as I can remember—"The way the sthranger gentleman, and he not seeing, put the shame of terror into the trapesin' interlopin' blackguards, who would wring the neck of their own father for a minted sixpence, is a walking masterpiece," only much faster and a great deal more of it. I am dying to hear all the details, but we concluded that you must have heard them down the garden as you came across to leave the note. Of course you could get no idea of what sort of men they were?'

'No,' admitted Carrados. 'I certainly could not.'

'Mrs Laffey says she arrived on the scene too late to be any use at all. Sometimes, do you know, I've been a wee bit sceptical of Mrs Laffey's romances, but in this case she is singularly modest about her own share in it. What gets me is why anyone should want to destroy our property.'

'Yes, that is the mystery, isn't it?'

'Of course we have enemies here and there I know. It seems strange that anyone who behaves in a perfectly simple, straightforward way, just saying exactly what you think of people, should be received with enmity, but there it is. We've found where they broke in—it's easy to see that they knew their way about—and they have deliberately trampled on the planted beds . . .'

'Disgraceful!'

'Yes, but unfortunately there's nothing positively to identify any of them by. Well, you'll come in, Mr Carrados, and—and meet my husband?'

'With pleasure, but can you guess what it is that chiefly brought me to Stacks today?'

'No. What?'

'Cyril's bedroom.'

'Oh,' pondered Mrs Bycourt, pausing in their progress.'I wondered what tale Cyril told.'

'You are not going to be angry with him for running away?'

'Angry? Good Lord, no! It's the best thing I've known him do yet. I'm delighted to find that he has that much spirit left in him. The fact is, Mr Carrados, ever since I've been here I've had to be a bit hard-cased towards Cyril, simply to counteract the "come-to-mammy-and-let-her-kiss-it-better" ways his dear Auntie Gertie had got him into. But I forgot—you are Miss Hamilton's friend.'

'All the same I want to understand just how matters are.'

'Then I'll tell you this. Do you know what was the deciding thing made me marry Mark Bycourt in the end? Yes: Cyril. I'm fond of boys, Mr Carrados, and I want them to have their chance in life. I have two dear little scrubby ragamuffins of my own—they're called Bob and Jack. Cyril was being brought up on *Eric*, *Misunderstood*, and *Little Lord Fauntleroy*, and Cyril will have more need of red stuffing than most people because when he is twenty-one he will come into a great deal too much money.You know that, perhaps?'

'I understood so much from Miss Hamilton.'

'Yes; and I dare say Miss Hamilton indicated that I was capable of dark designs on Cyril's fortune? No? Well, if she had, it wouldn't have been wonderful. The fact is, Mr Carrados, Gertrude is a misfire. It was the surprise of her life (if I said "disappointment" you'd think me catty) when Mark married me, and she didn't set out to be pleasant to the interloper.When I saw that, I—well, I certainly laid it on a bit thick for Gertrude's benefit. I'm not really a he-woman or a vamp, Mr Carrados. I'm watching Cyril very carefully, and—if I may confess it to you—rather affectionately. I hope that in the end I, with the un-conscious help of my two ragamuffins, may make a man of him. Now we have reached his room. Is there anything particular that you want to—to—'

'To see? To see in my own way? Well'—pointing—'the bed is there?'

'Yes. But how on earth do you know?'

'To make no mystery, by the familiar process of putting two and two together. And on the wall, quite near to the bed-head, is an elec-tric light plug?'

'Yes, there is.'

'So that Cyril, sleeping dutifully on his right side, as he has been taught to do, will be lying with his face quite near that plug?'

'Within a foot or so certainly. It seems to be a fad of Miss Hamilton's—sleeping on the right side. I suppose she was taught to as a child.'

'I was, too. But I've grown out of it. Now I will look into this fitting, if you don't mind.' He put his hand with baffling exactness on the rail of the bed and drew it from the wall so that he could approach the plug—approach it so closely indeed that to Mrs Bycourt's mystified curiosity his face appeared to touch it. 'Yes, there it is,' he remarked, as one who has brought a delicate experiment to a successful end.

'But what?' demanded the lady, not unreasonably. 'Why this hanky-panky, Mr Carrados? Nothing wrong, is there?'

'Forgive me, I really didn't intend to seem mysterious. There is nothing wrong, and if there had been we have got to the root of it at last. But there is something very curious, and there is something—I was, in fact, trying to break it to you mildly—something rather horrible.'

'But, my dear man, people don't break things to me—they throw them at me solid.'

'I'll be as brutal as you like then. You know that Cyril has been having nightmares lately?'

'Oh, yes. That is not unusual for a boy.'

'Not at all. Nor is the menace of a man standing by his bedside uncommon. What is significant is that it always takes the form of the Plague cart come to fetch him, and what is doubly significant is that your man James Laffey passes through exactly the same experience.'

'Cyril never told me what it was; but we all knew that Jim Laffey was pining for the blue eyes of my housemaid. But what a dreadful dream, and what a strange coincidence!'

'In my experience,' replied Carrados, 'coincidence—as we call it—is often merely a key I find that fits a lock I have. Laffey, spending long hours in the new building there, but not, I ascertain, with the electric light fitted in his cottage; Cyril, sleeping here with his face turned to that wall, but not, I learn, allowed to put his foot inside the dynamo-house. What is it, Mrs Bycourt, this strange coincidence?'

'I don't know,' she replied, awed in spite of her lavish spirit. 'What?'

'I will tell you. Over two centuries ago the Plague—the Great Plague of London as some histories call it—came to Irling, brought by a fleeing pedlar, and nearly wiped the village out. You have heard perhaps?'

'No, I don't think so. I don't remember anyway.'

'I find the tradition of it is almost lost here now. There are a few forgotten graves in the churchyard—but after the first weeks the dead were not buried there. It took too long to dig single graves and soon there was neither parson, clerk, nor sexton to perform the office of the Church. So a great pit was dug, well away from the houses of the living, in what was then an open field. But it is no longer that.'

'Oh!' exclaimed Mrs Bycourt, with the nameless horror beginning to take form before her eyes, 'do you mean—'

He nodded assent to the unspoken question.

'Yes; what was the distant grassland field is now your lower garden. The Bone Mound marks the hasty burial-pit, and right upon it they have built your power house.'

'But how does that—why does it—' she stammered.

'Who can say? It is easy enough to reply that you have stirred up the buried corruption of that dreadful place, but how is it that there have been awakened again the groans and the fears and the agonies of those heart-rending times?'

'Oh, how horrible—how horrible!' she cried. 'Is it true—can it be really true?'

'Is what true?' he asked. 'Do you mean—which detail?'

'I don't know,' she said. 'I mean any of it—all of it. It is like a nightmare in itself; it is so loathsome—so incredible. Why should it result in that?'

'That is the really interesting thing about it,' he replied. 'Your—'

'Interesting!' she retorted sharply. 'This!'

'To me,' he admitted mildly. 'I am merely an investigator, Mrs Bycourt. Your dynamo, designed to transform mechanical force into electrical energy, has here in some obscure way also changed physical effect into psychological experience. I dare say you know that in the house'—he indicated the wall plug—'the wires are carried through iron piping, and outside the cable is brought underground through drain-pipes. The lie being uniformly upwards, a warm room like this would create a slight but continuous current, so that, you see, Cyril has really been breathing direct—Yes, it is rather uncanny, isn't it? Laffey, of course, has been in more direct but shorter contact. Actually, we might have expected them both to contract the plague—there is record of that happening to some men who dug into a similar pit rather more than a hundred years after the interment. Instead, they caught the emotions of the victims. It will seem quite simple and obvious some day, but we know so lamentably little of that side of electrical energy yet. Even as it is I shall have to re-write my lecture.'

But Mrs Bycourt had no interest in his lecture. 'Oh, the dreadful, dreadful thing!' she moaned. 'What should one do? . . . I shall have that horrible place razed to the ground—I can't rest until it's gone—and then I shall have a great fire heaped on the spot and burned and burned for weeks until every trace of those poor creatures is reduced to decent ashes.'

'Yes,' assented Mr Carrados. 'That does seem to occur to one, does it not?'

The Missing Witness Sensation

In its earlier stages the Ayr Street Post Office robbery had attracted little notice. Afterwards, owing to causes with which this narrative has to do, it achieved the distinction of passing into the grade of what Detective Inspector Beedel was wont to refer to with quiet professional enthusiasm as 'First-class Crimes'. But so meagre was public interest in the initial proceedings that when Mr Carrados looked in at the magistrate's court purely for old acquaintance's sake one stifling afternoon, he found the place half empty.

'Post office hold-up—Ayr Street case, sir,' explained the officer on duty at the door. 'Party named Rank charged. Pretty nearly over now, I should say.'

'Philip Thaxted!' cried a voice across the court.

'New witness for the defence,' whispered the policeman. 'Like a seat, sir?'

'Don't trouble—I may only stay a minute. Who are conducting?'

'Mr Booker's for the Public Prosecutor. I don't know the defence—not one of our regular people here.'

'He is speaking now?'

'Yes, sir.'

A plainly dressed man with a firmly lined and rather artistic face, iron-grey hair, and a quiet, self-confident manner, had gone into the witness-box. The formal oath had been administered and the preliminaries were being rattled through. Yes, his name was Philip Thaxted and he lived at such an address at Kingston-on-Thames. Formerly in the lace business, both as manager and on his own account, but now retired.

'On the afternoon of Wednesday, the seventeenth inst, you were taking a walk in Richmond Park?' suggested the defending counsel.

'That is quite correct.'

'Tell us what occurred.'

The blind visitor leaned across and touched the attendant lightly on the arm.

'I should like to hear a little more of this evidence,' he remarked with lowered voice. 'Perhaps I had better have a seat.'

As he moved quietly to a place, piloted by the officer's unobtrusive hand, someone in making way dropped a stick with an exasperating clatter. The man in the witness-box glanced sharply across in the direction of the noise, and something almost as perceptible as a start touched him, and for a word or two his voice rang flat. The next moment the flicker, such as it was, had passed and he was continuing his story as evenly as before.

★★★★★★

'I suppose, inspector,' said Mr Carrados, 'it might seem rather unreasonable of me to ask you to come down here after being in court all day, eh?'

'Well, no, sir,' replied Inspector Beedel with his usual unpenetrable candour; 'I can't exactly say it did. You see, Mr Carrados, you've asked me to come and talk to you on one occasion or another a good dozen times now, and it's always been—as they say in the advertisement—"to hear of something to my advantage".'

Carrados laughed as he pointed to a chair and pushed the cigars across the table.

'Don't be too confident this time,' he advised. 'Can you give a guess what it's about?'

Beedel raised his slow, meditative eyes and wondered for the hundredth time at the strangely alive expression in the gaze that really seemed to meet his own.

'I may say that I noticed you in court today, sir, and putting one thing and another together—'

'Quite right,' assented Carrados. 'It is about today's case. These post office hold-ups are getting beyond a joke, inspector.'

'This one has certainly been beyond a joke for Lizzie Baxter, sir. We have it privately that the poor girl hasn't one chance in a thousand of pulling through. Then—'

'Aye. Then the case against Rank will not be one of Robbery with Violence, but Wilful Murder. That determined a special effort to get him off if possible before the graver charge came in.'

'The alibi, you mean, sir?'

'The alibi, yes. What did you think of that timely encounter at the exact minute that the job was taking place?'

A brightly-coloured band had adorned the cigar that Inspector Beedel was appreciatively considering. He smoothed out the pretty scrap and put it, carefully flattened, away in his notebook for the benefit of a stalwart young Beedel now rising five.

'It certainly staggered me more than a bit to hear that evidence this afternoon,' he replied. 'The man who comes forward and testifies that he was talking to Dennis Rank at half-past four that day isn't one of the sort that bob up after every assault or accident, prepared to swear anything for half a quid and a pot of beer. He has been in a good way of business, and so far from anything being known against him, inquiry goes to show that he has a creditable public record extending over twenty years. A police magistrate is a bit wary, and, as you know, Mr Lipscott committed, but if this chap sticks to his tale at the Old Bailey I doubt if any jury will convict.'

The blind man nodded weighty acquiescence. Plainly there could be no question about the importance of the Kingston evidence.

'He was walking in Richmond Park—quite a likely thing for a middle-aged gentleman who wants a little exercise to do—when this happened. A little dog coming out of a clump of bracken barked at him furiously, and he swished back with his walking-stick. Then it seized one of his trouser legs and tore it. The dog's master appeared on the scene and they fell to abusing one another, the owner accusing him of savaging the dog and he accusing the man of keeping a vicious animal. In the end he demanded this fellow's name and address, and there it is, written in his notebook with the date and the exact time of the occurrence.'

'That's it,' assented the inspector. 'All very reasonable and circumstantial.'

'Yes,' agreed Mr Carrados. 'More than that: almost providential one might say. Had it been one of Rank's friends the evidence might have been open to suspicion, but our Mr Thaxted appears as a total stranger. Had they met, say in Hyde Park, a very slight discrepancy of time might have made the alibi unconvincing, but Richmond is too far away to consider that. And then under how few circumstances are you likely to ask a total stranger for his name and address, to write them down, and to note the time and date of the occurrence?'

'There is no doubt that Rank had a small terrier that might have acted like that,' admitted Beedel.

'And certainly Mr Thaxted will be able to produce a pair of trousers that would prove to have been torn,' said Carrados dryly. 'Come; what is behind this business, Beedel?'

'Behind it, sir?' repeated the inspector with the utmost innocence.

'The Ayr Street Post Office hold-up wasn't an ordinary outrage at all. You know that as well as I do.'

'It's a funny thing,' remarked the visitor introspectively. 'Here for the last week I've been trying to persuade one or two up at the Yard to regard it in that light and almost your first words—'

'Of course I really know nothing about it,' qualified Mr Carrados.

'It's my belief,' declared Inspector Beedel with sombre relish, and repeating the expression of faith to emphasize it! 'it's my belief that there's a secret organisation at work in the background somewhere. I've never thought that Treasury notes were what those two fellows were after, though they certainly grabbed all they could as they went through it.'

'What then?' prompted Mr Carrados, for Beedel had relapsed into a keen professional abstraction.

'Something political, I'm pretty sure, sir. A lot of those Sinn Feiners are out to make trouble systematically just now. And you'd be surprised to find who are more or less in with them—all sorts of people.'

'The retired gentleman from Kingston, for instance?'

'I have no doubt he may be one. But people you'd never think of as, well, I mean—professional men and soldiers, civil servants, society ladies, dock labourers, skilled artisans. I dare say a good many of them wouldn't go very far for "The Cause", but some of them would, and then on the edge of it there are the usual crowd who are always keen to make something out of whatever's going on.'

'It's likely enough,' conceded the blind man. 'What were they after here?'

'There isn't a great deal of business generally at this Ayr Street Post Office, but it lies handy for certain public offices. Anything that had been registered would be lying beyond the counter, handy for collection, at the time of the raid. My idea is that they knew of something being posted that they were desperately anxious to secure or to stop. Lizzie Baxter wasn't shot holding on to the notes but because she got between Rank and the letters.'

'She hasn't spoken?'

'No; she probably never will. She is the only one who could identify the men, and without her the case against Rank is purely circumstantial; that's what makes it safe for Thaxted to come forward now.'

604

'Perhaps not entirely safe, after all, inspector,' remarked Mr Carrados with significance.

'How do you mean, sir?'

'I mean that as it happens on the seventeenth—the day concerned—Mr Thaxted and I sat on a retired seat in Kew Gardens from four to half-past and discussed carnation-growing and other impersonal topics. Afterwards we walked together as far as the Lion Gate and parted at about ten minutes to five.'

'Oho!' Inspector Beedel swung his shrewd but not very agile mind round to review the position created by this new factor. 'That's something of a facer for the defence, isn't it, sir? Do you mean that you know this Mr Thaxted?'

'Not at all. We were perfect strangers who just met and chatted a little and then went on our separate ways. I didn't know him from Adam until I recognised him in court today.'

'I see. Of course if he wasn't quarrelling with Rank in Richmond Park at half-past four he must have been somewhere else. But still, you would think—Well, he took a fairish risk.'

'Don't we all do that if we decide to commit perjury, inspector? After all, the man never mentioned his name, his business, any tangible personal detail; and he knew that it was a blind man who had sat by his side and talked with him. When—as we may assume—a volunteer was called for to save Rank by providing an alibi, it may have seemed to Mr Thaxted that the half hour or so that he must compromise himself over was pretty well secured.'

'Yes, yes,' agreed Beedel, rounding up the situation within his orderly mind as a rather slow but capable sheepdog brings in stragglers; 'it's all reasonable enough. . . . There's one weakness ahead—if you don't mind my mentioning it?'

'Let us examine the thin places, by all means,' encouraged Carrados.

'You are willing to give evidence, sir?'

'I suppose I must. I know nothing of Rank one way or the other, but I must either come forward or let an appalling perversion of justice go on. It may also help to clear off a trifle of my debt to you, inspector, eh?'

'Thank you, sir, but I think that's pretty good weight already. Still, I don't deny that it would do me a bit of good to produce evidence to upset that alibi. And that brings me to what I was saying.'

'Yes; only you seem rather reluctant to say it.'

'Well, it's like this, Mr Carrados. In the ordinary way you would give your evidence, and then the question would be put: "Do you see that man in court?" Now here—'

'When counsel says, "Have you heard that man in court?" and I reply, "Yes; when Mr Thaxted was speaking", you think it would fail to carry conviction?'

'I don't think the ordinary jury would see that it's as satisfactory to identify a man by his voice as by his face.'

'I am inclined to agree with you. If I said, "The man who sat with me bit his finger-nails, smoked Algerian cigars, and wore an elastic stocking", do you think it might impress the court?'

The inspector laughed rather contentedly.

'Why, yes, sir; I can't but suppose it might. We could challenge Mr Thaxted to show his finger-nails, produce his cigar-case, and pull up his trouser-leg. It ought to be a fair bombshell.'

'Then I must consider myself booked for Tuesday fortnight and as many days afterwards as the case lasts.'

'The fewer the better, sir,' replied Beedel cryptically. 'To tell you the truth, I shouldn't be sorry if tomorrow was Tuesday fortnight. It's a good thing that none of the lot know that you have anything to do with the case, and I hope you'll keep it close, up to the very last minute.'

'Oh!' Mr Carrados felt a trifle guilty, remembering that moment when the witness paused and faltered, but Beedel was-quite solicitous enough already. 'Any particular reason?'

'One of our witnesses has already had the misfortune to be rather badly run down while cycling, and I've had a natty-looking box of chocolates by post from an "unknown friend" myself,' replied the inspector. 'I imagine this Rank must be something of a top-hat among these people.'

★★★★★★

There was a form overlooking a deep expanse of country where Max Carrados often sat when he took a walk in that direction. Indeed, a mild pleasantry current at one time among park-keepers and their kind credited him with a weakness for pointing out the things of interest to any passing stranger who happened to share the seat with him, and the prospect threatened to become mysterious to posterity as 'Blind Man's View'.

One breathless July afternoon (the drought and languor of that summer have become a record) about a fortnight after Inspector

Beedel's visit, Carrados was sitting there alone when his ear picked up the footsteps of two men approaching. In a minute he knew that one man led the other, and with that came the intuition that the second man was blind. Then he found that they were making for the seat.

'This will do,' said the leader. 'You don't mind?'

'No, no; not at all. Only don't be long,' replied the other. 'I shall get anxious if you are and I—I feel so confoundedly helpless by myself.'

'There is a gentleman already on the seat,' dropped the voice warningly. 'That will be all right; I won't be long. I must have lost the damn thing within the last three minutes.'

His footsteps sounded on the turf, and then grew less along the gravelled road. The stranger turned to Mr Carrados.

'Could you give me the time, sir?' he asked, and at once enlarged the opening sociably. 'You'll have noticed that I'm blind. Helpless, of course. My friend dropped an important pocket-book some way back. Three minutes he said—say three minutes there, three back, and three looking about. Ten minutes at the outside.... I'll time him if you're staying so long. I don't mind being left in an ordinary way, but I get so confoundedly anxious if anything goes different. You see. . . . If anything happened and he didn't come back for a long time—or at all! Well—'

'That will be all right,' said Carrados. 'I shan't be going just yet. Ten minutes. . . .'

'I daresay it doesn't seem very long to you, but it's different when there isn't a single blessed thing for you to do. . . . Just to sit and smoke and think. . . . Oh, and talk, of course, when you're lucky enough to get anyone who will . . . . But it's a pretty dull outlook. You normal people have no idea—'

In all this there was, as it happened, an insidious temptation. 'You are as fond of showing off, Carrados, as a child with a recitation', had been the piqued barb flung across by a man at whose expense the 'showing off' had been effected and there was in the jibe just enough truth to twist the blind man's habitual suaveness for a moment. Max Carrados was admittedly prone to a certain vein of superiority, and his demonstrations were occasionally timed to achieve a theatrical effect, but all sprang from a not unworthy root—from a passionate insistence on being treated as an ordinary human being. To take in a seeing man—to outwit five senses by the use of four—was well enough, but might not the opportunity be at hand of demonstrating to another sufferer that his life need not be so empty as he pictured? He waited.

'The war?' he hazarded.

'Nothing so romantic. Cataract. I suppose I shall get used to it in time.... Surely it must be ten minutes now?'

'No—eight.' Carrados referred to the fingers of his watch. 'But don't think too much of the time. There may be a hundred things to cause delay. Ten minutes . . . that was altogether too fine a margin.'

'That's just it—a hundred things. Anything might happen to a man going along the road looking for a pocketbook. . . . . and then where should I be? I was a mug to let him go. . . . Suppose—'

'Don't suppose. I'll stay here till your friend comes back.. . . . At all events I'll see you through.'

'That's most confoundedly good of you. . . . I must strike you as a poor sort of wash-out. . . . .'

'No.' The situation was beginning to endear itself to Carrados's mind. 'I am interested in the blind. . . . Like faith, blindness moves in a peculiar way. . . .'

'Faith?' mused the stranger vaguely. 'Yes; I suppose so. . . . What's that—a car?'

'No,' replied Carrados. 'A plane going south. Queer how the sound varies, isn't it?'

'We left our taxi somewhere near—Heriot Lane the driver called it. I thought that perhaps—A flier, eh? . . . . Wings—"The wings of the morning", doesn't old Shakespeare or someone say? Suppose I shall never see a plane travelling again. Used to give me a funny touch sometimes, that. Just as if I was on the point of finding out what this old caboodle is all about anyway—only I never quite got it. Seemed as though I just needed that extra push through that I could never raise. Sounds mushy rot to you, I expect.'

'No,' admitted Carrados; 'most of us have been there. Seeing "through a glass, darkly", said the Jewish tent-maker of old.'

The other man gave a nod of ambiguous agreement. 'How's the time?' he asked. 'Confound Stringer; he ought to be here by now.'

'Going on for twenty minutes. But I don't suppose that it will have seemed like ten to your friend.'

They talked again and Carrados tried to interest his companion to make the time pass imperceptibly. Half an hour went by and still there was no sign of Mr Stringer. When three-quarters had been reached, Arnold—he had incidentally dropped his name—could stand it no longer.

'Look here. Something must have happened. I can't stay here for ever. And you—you've been most confoundedly decent, but you must want to be moving. Can you put me in the way of getting back to the taxi? Then I shall know where I am, whatever's gone wrong.'

'Certainly,' replied Carrados. 'I know Heriot Lane well enough. I'll take you there with pleasure. It isn't ten minutes' walk from here. What do you say to pinning a line here on the seat, so that your friend—'

'No, confound him! exclaimed Arnold with sudden warmth. 'He's left me in the lurch all right. Let him do a bit of guessing.'

It wasn't an outsider's affair either way. Carrados took the blind man's arm and led him from the seat. Out of consideration for his charge the pace was about half that at which the more experienced man usually walked. There was also still the chance that Stringer might appear. But he did not, and they reached Heriot Lane without incident.

'Is it far down?' asked Carrados. He knew that the lane was a winding little byway where even the humblest sort of traffic might not pass from one hour to another. He could take Arnold along it with a fair amount of confidence, but detection might come at any moment now. He had set himself to pilot the blind man right up to the door of the cab before he revealed the true situation—anything short of that failed to drive home the moral of his achievement. 'I don't see a taxi yet,' he added.

'A bit along, I suppose,' said Arnold. His eyes were open and he was looking sideways into his guide's face with an expression of peculiar and private amusement that did not carry into his voice. 'He may have drawn on....'

'Ah,' exclaimed the blind leader as they cleared a bend, 'there's something at last.' Ear and nose told him so much, and it would be an easy matter to bring his charge right up to the car. But—the chance of so inglorious a fiasco was small in that infrequent place—but how to be sure that this was indeed the taxi?

'Back again, sir?'

That settled it. Carrados moved on by the light of his own intuitive judgement. When he knew that he was three yards from the car the door was opened. He had reached the goal.

'Now!' said another voice in sharp command.

Before the word was spoken Carrados had had a flash of realization. It came with the nature-sense of overhanging danger, with the subtle change of intention in the arm that touched his own, with the slight chirrup of a stoppered phial being opened—but it came too

609

late. Arnold's light pressure on his right suddenly became a pinioning grip, another pair of arms closed on his left and a saturated cloth not unpleasantly odoured, was pressed against his face. . . .

'It worked? remarked one, rearranging himself after they had bundled the senseless form into the car.

'Like a charm,' replied the man called Arnold, smiling at a thought.

'Change that plate again, and move about it,' said the third of the gang shortly.

A minute later the renumbered car slipped out of Heriot Lane without any superfluous parade of warning, and taking on a pace much too moderate to suggest the remotest connexion with things sensational, it was soon swallowed up in the stream of evening traffic flowing eastward.

★★★★★★

'Ah. So ye're com'n' round now, aren't ye?' said a not unfriendly voice, as consciousness began to trickle at first and then rush into Max Carrados's perceptions. 'Feelin' just a thrifle sick, too, at first, I don't doubt.'

'Where am I?' asked the blind man mechanically. Sick he certainly did feel in more ways than one, for the stuff that had been used to drug him with was of an unholy texture that left nausea and headache in its wake, while to be drawn into so guileless a trap outraged his most vulnerable susceptibilities. 'Where am I and who are you?'

'Now don't be troublin' ye'self about things like those that don't really matter at all,' replied the other persuasively. 'Ye're right enough now, and so long as ye don't sthruggle, so to speak, ye can be as comfortable as a dormouse in a haystack.'

'I quite understand,' retorted the captive. 'And if I struggle, as you are pleased to call it, I may infer that I shall be treated as Lizzie Baxter was?'

''Tis a great mistake to dhrop from the exthract on to the conk-rate, as the man remarked whin he fell from the distillery window down into th' sthrate. Ye'll understand that whin there's a war goin' on there's likely to be cashoolties. Ye're a cashoolty just at the moment, Mr Carrados, but whether ye're ultimate destination is to be the reco-operation camp or the wayside simitry is a matter entirely awaitin' ye're own personal convenience.'

'I have an idea,' replied Carrados, 'that it will turn out to be the witness-box.'

'I shouldn't build on that now,' said the Irishman speculatively. 'With all due respect to the three classical females who arrange the destinies, I can see no indication of anything like that on the immed-jet horizon. Doubtless if ye were to consult the mysterious lady who prognosticates through the mejum of a chrystal sphere, or the obliging wizard who for the small consideration of haf a crown tells you what he sees in the smoke of an aromatic pastille, something in the nature of a witness-box might possibly be adumbrated; but for all practical purposes I should eliminate it from ye're calc'lations, Mr Carrados.'

'You appear to be a pleasant and ingenious gentleman, Mr—?'

'Murphy is a very handy name for the purpose of short refer-ence.'

'Mr Murphy, then. You appear also to have a general knowledge of me and my movements, while I, unfortunately, know practically noth-ing of you or my surroundings. As a guest, enjoying your hospitality, that naturally puts me in a very humiliating position. You see—'

'I appreciate the delicacies of the situation,' replied Mr Murphy in the same vein of guarded satire to which they had fallen. 'I should dearly love to act as a general *vade-mecum*, who's who, and illustrated gazetteer of the situation if it could be done. But ye'll understand there may be sthretegic reasons aginst lettin' on which end of Park Lane this mansion is situate in, or whether ye're host is a blue-blooded aristochrat or merely a Labour member.'

'Perhaps,' suggested the blind man, 'it would be permissible to say why I have been carried off in this outrageous manner and what you imagine you are going to do with me?'

'There's no harm at all in tellin' ye what ye know already,' replied Mr Murphy, with a sudden loss of geniality in his manner. 'Ye're here because ye intended giving evidence in a case that was no airthly concern of ye's, and ye'll stay here, or in some other suitable place of retirement, until that little matter's satisfactorily disposed of. What call had ye to go acting otherwise than sthrictly as a nootral if ye're not prepared to take the consequences?'

'A neutral!' repeated Carrados in amazement. 'Good heavens, man, neutral in what? This was simply a case of elementary justice. But per-haps,' he added pointedly, 'you have never heard of that?'

There was a movement of anger from more than one part of the room, and the man who had been carrying on the conversation strode across and stood over the captive. The taunt had served a useful pur-pose, for Carrados had learned a little more.

'I should advise ye to keep that sort of remark in ye're breeches po'k't while ye're here, Mr Carrados,' said Murphy. 'This once ye're blind eyes protect ye.'

'They often do,' replied Carrados imperturbably. 'I am confident that they often will.'

'Don't be too sure while ye are here, that's all.'

He heard the man turn sharply on his heel and walk across the room. The door banged and silence lengthened out, but the prisoner knew that unfriendly eyes still watched him and that he had not been left alone.

Nearly a week went by and nothing happened. Max Carrados was as completely cut off from the world as if he had been carried away to Mars. Food was put before him on a generous scale and his ordinary needs were attended to, but conversation with those who moved about was not encouraged. Mr Murphy seemed to have disappeared after the first evening.

From the moment of his recovering consciousness Carrados began to construct the details of his surroundings and to examine his prison. It was, he learned within a day, a spacious, old-fashioned house of three storeys and a basement, detached, and standing in some private ground. The rooms were generally large and lofty, but their former state was not kept up; several were empty and the furniture of the others was miscellaneous and haphazard. Gas was used, the telephone bell often rang, and a silent elderly woman did the cooking and attendance. The captive soon discovered that he was never left alone, and at night he slept in a room where the window was barred from top to bottom and the chimney blocked. The blind man smiled as he realized that an alarming reputation must have preceded him.

It was not until the second night that he could definitely locate his prison. How long the journey in the car had been he had no means of knowing, but the taste of the air, the touch of the water in which he washed, and the distant noises of the street were all unmistakably of London. It was a quiet and secluded back-water to which he had been brought, and at no great distance from the house he soon knew of a park-like space where thrushes sang at dawn and the owl proclaimed the night, but a great highway of traffic lay extended on the south and another, rather less busy, on the north. On the second night he heard Big Ben slowly booming out the hours on a line almost directly east, and applying to the sounds his own peculiar methods he found that he could assume the space between them as just about three miles. The next day he dropped a simple test.

'I suppose I can have a certain book I want? I think it could be got—'

'A book?' repeated the man who was then in charge of him, dubiously.

'Yes, from Mudie's in the High Street just below here'—nodding direction—'you know.'

The sharp breath of surprise confirmed what he had already guessed, even without the attendant's belated and rather hurt protestation that he 'could say nothing about that.' The matter of the book progressed no further.

For a couple of days Carrados had been speculating rather poignantly about his position. A crisis of some sort must, he conjectured, be at hand. Even if the trial of Rank lasted three days—a generous limit—the verdict was now due. He had, he assumed, been carried off purely to suppress his fatal evidence, but if the case went against the prisoner—how then? He had no illusions about the methods of the desperate little band of extremists into whose hands he had fallen, and, without flurry or visible concern, there were very few minutes of the day when he was not considering plans of escape. But so far the strength of his prison was unassailable, the guards not to be drawn by casual hints of gold.

It was on the evening of the sixth day of confinement that the expected crisis came. All that afternoon there had been less movement about the big house than was usual, but towards dusk men began to arrive by ones and twos until Carrados had accounted for at least a dozen above the usual company.

'They have all been to hear the verdict given,' surmised the blind man. 'Now for it.'

He was right. An hour later he was curtly summoned to another room—'the council chamber,' as he had always mentally described it from the meetings that obviously took place there—and found himself before an informal court.

'This is the man Carrados?' inquired someone, with brusque authority.

One of Carrados's regular custodians replied.

'He is blind, captain, though you mightn't notice it,' he added. 'Shall I give him a chair?'

'Was Dennis Rank given a chair once during the three days of his trial?' demanded the voice.

'He was not,' came the hearty response from half a dozen.

'Let the prisoner stand.'

'A prisoner,' remarked Carrados mildly, 'is usually charged with an offence. May I ask what mine is?'

'Conveying information to the enemy,' was the answer, rapped out with domineering harshness. 'It concerns you to learn, Carrados, that Dennis Rank was pronounced guilty this afternoon and sentenced to death.'

'That would be the very natural result of carrying me off, wouldn't it?' insinuated the blind man. 'You had surely thought of that.'

'What do you mean?'

Carrados was almost tempted to shrug his shoulders to underline the obviousness of what had happened.

'If I had appeared and given evidence it would have been perfectly easy to suggest that I was either mistaken or a liar—one man's word against another's. As it was, there was nothing on which to suggest that I was mistaken or lying. You simply advertised that my evidence was correct and true and that you daren't allow it to be given at any price.'

'There now, captain, what did I tell ye?' muttered a malcontent.

'Stow that,' commanded the man in authority. Then he turned to the prisoner again. 'You are not before us to express your own personal and private views on this or that, Carrados, but to hear the decision of this court. Needless to say an appeal is being lodged against the bloodthirsty tyranny of Dennis Rank's sentence. If you can suggest anything to help that along you'd do well to get busy right now and let us know.'

'Theoretically,' admitted Mr Carrados, 'I've never been in favour of capital punishment.'

'That's vurry opportune,' remarked the captain dryly. 'But there are exceptions, and possibly this may be one of them.'

'Oh, it may, you think?' roared the astonished inquisitor. 'Wall, let me tell you this: the hour the black flag goes up at Brixton Jail for Dennis Rank your family will have cause to go into mourning too.'

'What good will that do?'

'It will do this good, that you may as well begin to get a move on you to dodge it. We opine that you have a pull in more than one direction, Carrados, and pawsably your government may cawnsider your neck worth saving. Wall, you know the price, and you'd better make out the best case you can for the exchange when you let them know.

You can have pen and ink and paper and—under suitable examination, so don't try any of your slim tricks here—you can communicate with your own lawyer or anyone else you like.'

'Thank you,' replied Mr Carrados, 'but I won't trouble you.'

'Won't trouble! Hell! what d'ye mean?'

'Just what I say. I have no intention of writing. Of my own free will I might in ordinary circumstances sign a petition against Rank being hanged. As you put it, I am much more likely to sign one against his being reprieved. You'll have to do your own unpleasant work yourself.'

'The man's clean daft,' sighed one of the court in helpless bewilderment. 'What'll there be unpleasant in saving your nut?'

'Merely a point of view,' remarked Carrados, turning towards him quite courteously. 'There are things that we all stick at doing at any price. . . . Or, at all events'—his face was again in the direction of the president of the court 'most of us.'

For some reason, in the five minutes that they had been together there had sprung up between these two men a deep and corrosive antipathy. Towards all the others of his captors Carrados bore little beyond a philosophic tolerance, with an occasional lapse into mild annoyance. But here each felt the other's hatred, and recognised that between them there would be no accommodation, no compromise. The only difference was the way the motion showed—in the captain it produced a tendency to shout, in the captive an icy quietness.

'So you think you can ride the high horse here, do you?' exploded the leader, flashing out passionately. 'With ya blasted "point of view" and ya infernal five-cent style. Remember that ya're not dealing with any of ya're own shilly-shallying Dublin Castle trash, but with men that mean what they say. And show proper respect to the court ya're up before or, by heaven! the crack of a fist'll teach you.'

'I can't defend myself.' Carrados turned towards the others and held out his groping hands with a plaintive helplessness. 'Is there any man here who can strike me across my sightless eyes?'

'God know that's true!' murmured more than one.

'Then how are you going to hang me?'

The captain summed up his stalwarts with a cold, contemptuous glance.

'Leave that to me,' he said more quietly, 'when the time comes. There's a proverb about killin' a dog, Carrados, you'll maybe know. In the meanwhile you'll have a few days to think better of it. Bear in mind that it's not to hang you for preference that we're out, but to save Dennis Rank. Remove the prisoner.'

When Carrados was removed he guessed that the eventuality had plainly been foreseen, for he was not led back to his former quarters. Instead, he found himself traversing parts of the house where he had never been allowed before. Then came a downward flight of steps and a cooler atmosphere. He was to be imprisoned in a cellar.

His treatment, as he learned presently, was to be in keeping with the place. All the contents of his pockets were taken from him, but being now in close confinement he was left alone. Doubtless it was considered that forcible escape was impossible, and when he came to examine his surroundings he saw no reason to dissent. It was not so much a cellar as a blind passage to which a massive door had been fitted. Probably at the time of its conversion there had been some special use in view. Every quarter has its vague, half-forgotten legends of mystery and crime. The house was old, and who could say now why the remote, unwanted passage should have been so strongly turned into the semblance of a dungeon?

The prisoner paced it and examined its every corner with investigating hands. Five ordinary strides took him from one end to the other, and standing there he could without shifting his position touch its two long walls at the same time-with outstretched hands, and then the ceiling. Less than five yards in length it would seem to be, two yards across, and seven feet in height. The walls were stone, the floor was stone, and ceiling stone or concrete. Its most dreadful feature—the total absence of window or any source of light—did not trouble the man who now sat down to review his rather desperate plight. A single chair had been provided and a small pallet with a couple of rugs.

With the prison went prison fare—three very plain meals a day— enough, but far from lavish. It was perfectly indicated what this rigorous system meant: each day his jailer asked whether he wished for writing material, and each day he returned a negative. The odds were rather heavily balanced, but if it came to a test of mere obstinacy between the man they called 'Captain' and himself, Carrados was quite inclined to fancy his own chances. After the execution, or the reprieve, of Rank there would be no sane reason for detaining him. And somehow at the back of his mind the blind man could not abandon the feeling that even in the last extremity his star would see him through.

Three days passed. Carrados was not unendurably bored, for his mind was an inexhaustible storehouse, and with the unconcern for surroundings that was one of his assets he at once resumed the composition of a monograph on 'The Persian Archer on a Unique Tetradrachm of Corinth,' an entertainment that his capture had interrupted. But on the evening of the third day something occurred to make the Persian archer rather less interesting than he had been up to then. Night came, but no supper was brought, and as the hours went on and Carrados failed by the most delicate tests of hearing to discover any movement in the house above, a sudden misgiving shook him. What if.... He put the thought aside and went to bed as the simplest way of ignoring the situation.

But the next morning there was no breakfast. Again an unnatural silence lay upon the place. With his ear to the wall, the blind prisoner had been able to follow a footstep from his door up to the distant kitchen, but not the faintest echo now reached him. He took off a boot and beat a *crescendo* of remonstrance upon the door.... He might just as well have flicked it with his handkerchief for all the attention it provoked. Yet it could scarcely have failed to be heard, remote and subterranean as his prison was, if there had been anyone.—If there had been anyone!

The thought suddenly developed and spread in half a dozen directions like a flame among dry shavings: was it part of a plan to starve him to submission—had some been arrested and the remainder fled—was there some ghastly misunderstanding, everyone leaving his care or release to someone else—had they suddenly given up all hope of influencing Rank's disposal and in revenge had left him there to die? In less than five minutes he was speculating on the probable discoverer of his body and how long hence the event would be a month, a year, or so remote that he would be referred to as 'a shrivelled skeleton.'—He cursed his imagination and forced his mind back to the Persian archer and his significant appearance on a Greek *tetradrachm*.

But at noon there was no dinner. Hunger now began to make itself really felt, but more than that, a tormenting thirst had come over him. He raved a button off and kept it in his mouth to induce secretion, but it was a poor pretence. At measured intervals he beat upon the door as he had done before; to attempt to make himself heard by the outside world was, he knew, hopeless....

That night Carrados again went supperless to bed. He had been without food for a day and a half, but that was a small consideration beside the awful thirst that now possessed him. Those were the hottest days of an exceptional summer, and though the cellar was cooler than the house above it was also closer. A neglected drain somewhere near had given the prisoner 'a throat' which ticked and throbbed for relief in vain. His mind turned to innumerable tales of shipwrecked sailors dying of thirst, to accounts of men cut off and driven to frenzy through lack of water in the trenches, to the parable of the Rich Man and Lazarus, to a memory of a nauseous passage in Robinson Crusoe, to the awful case of. . . .Would it end in madness with him also? Before that . . . he had no weapon, but there were the blankets of his bed, and he had touched a substantial pipe running in the angle of the wall and ceiling of his cell that would surely bear his weight.

It was to escape these thoughts that he lay down and tried to sleep when his time-sense told him that it was something short of midnight. He still clung to the hope that morning would bring relief, and if so he was in the mood to write anything to avert another day of thirst and torment—even the ink, he reflected grimly, would be a godsend at that moment.

Thinking of the ink—the ink—ink—the door opened miraculously and Parkinson came in. 'What a horrible dream,' thought Carrados. 'I fancied that I was shut up in a cellar, and here I am sitting down to dinner at some nice restaurant. What soup have you got there, Parkinson?' 'I beg your pardon, sir,' replied his attendant, putting a large bowl before him, 'but I understand that the custom of this house is for a dish of water to be left at night on every table; otherwise, I am told, the rats will gnaw through the lead pipes in search of it.' 'Very well,' replied Mr Carrados. 'But this is ink that you have brought.' 'I'm extremely distressed,' stammered Parkinson, 'I will change—'

And as he spoke he changed into the magistrate at Lemon Square Police Court, and Carrados found himself listening to a case about a fountain-pen. 'Your worship,' pleaded the plaintiff, 'the pen was in perfect condition when I sold it. I would respectfully suggest that it was damaged by—' 'Rats!' interposed the defendant contemptuously as he proceeded to light a cigar. 'Silence in coort!' roared his worship. 'What this poor, honest man says is very true, belike. Sure, the craytures'll do anything for dhrink. Why, every morning don't I find the ink on me desk here lappit up and—' Again the court shook with laughter, and in the middle of it Carrados suddenly awoke—still in his cell and more thirst-racked than ever, but with a new hope to inspire. As he sat up he heard the rats outside scampering past his door.

'Idiot!' he apostrophised himself; 'not to think of that. You are certainly getting old and stupid. Dying of thirst with a water pipe—oh, my God, suppose it isn't! If it should be the gas!'

But it was not the gas. One tap with a finger-end set that at rest. In an old, rambling house it might have been anything, but an inch pipe giving the resonance of liquid contents could indicate nothing but the supply—an inexhaustible stream, of pure water was his for the taking. But how? His mind accounted for one useless article after another in a vain search for any kind of makeshift tool. Not a scrap of metal, not even a serviceable edge of broken stone or brick, had been left to suggest escape. Still, there must be something—must—Yes; the boot! His frequent poundings on the floor had already strained a heel; one sharp wrench against the other boot and the loose heel came away. In his hand he held a slab of leather bristling with rows of pointed nails: as effective a file as one could wish for.

In less than three minutes Carrados was drinking—drinking gloriously. He had rubbed through the soft metal of the pipe until the water began to jet, then he dropped the boot heel and used his hands to form a cup. He had no means of stopping the leak now; it might flood the cellar and ultimately drown him, but even if he had known that that must happen it would not have held him back—not at that moment.

When he had drunk sufficient for the time he took his handkerchief and held it to the stream, intending to sponge his face. On that slight incident—even on the hazard of the position he took up—depended all that happened after; for as he waited there—crouching rather on the uncertain chair and steadying himself with one hand upon the pipe a faint but distinct tremor passed beneath his hand. It was so trivial in itself, so barren of suggestion, that not one man in a thousand—even among desperate prisoners—would have given it a thought. But to Max Carrados his fingertips were eyes, and to him that slight vibration flashed a ray of hope. It told him little—definitely there was little it could tell—but he knew that somewhere someone was within reach of a signal in reply.

The supply pipe would lead to a cistern up above, and at that hour—about daybreak now he judged—it was unlikely that anyone should be moving there. But in the other direction—out, through the garden, and along the streets? For months past now no rain had fallen, and the air was full of the talk of great droughts and threatening water famine. Every wasted drop was grudged, and by day and night—especially by night when the streets were quiet—the company's inspectors made their rounds, tracing every suggestion of a leak, raising the little traps that give access to the mains, and stick to ear for the faintest distant sound, listening—oh, ray of hope, Max Carrados!—listening!

A second gone, perhaps. Still lightly touching the pipe to take up any response, the blind man dropped the unheeded handkerchief and with the strong bare knuckles of his other hand he began to spell out into the unknown the universal message of despair: short, short, short; long, long, long; short, short, short—S.O.S.; S.O.S.; S.O.S.

★★★★★★

About the time that Mr Carrados awoke and thought of a boot heel two men in the chaste blue attire favoured by the Metropolitan Water Board stopped at a small iron plate let into the road and prepared to enter upon the cabbalistic ritual of their tribe. The high priest, as it were, of the two carried a wand of office in his hand—a serviceable bamboo rod with a saucer-shaped top, and his ceremonial cap was dignified by the word *Inspector* blazoned on a neat oval badge above the peak. His acolyte differed from him only in the slight details of appearance, but instead of a rod he affected a dangerous-looking implement that could only be likened to a small—but not a very small—harpoon.

'When we've worked down to the High Street again we'll knock off for breakfast, 'Orras,' remarked the inspector, speaking as one who conveys encouragement.

"Bout as well,' commented 'Orras. 'My inwards are beginning to inquire audibly whether me throat's bin cut.'

'It's queer how young fellows are always thinking of their teeth nowadays,' mused his superior. 'They don't seem to have no endurance, somehow, 'Orras. Did I ever tell you how three of us signallers were up in a tower outside a place called Binchley for the better part of a week—'

'Often; yesterday for once,' retorted the younger generation. 'Contrive to forget those early days of crime, Father William. The war's over and done with, and we aren't going to have no more.'

The inspector sighed and, leaning against a convenient lamp-post, tactfully indicated to 'Orras a suggestion to get on with it, while he himself proceeded to write up current record in his book. Disdaining an offer of the listening stick the assistant impaled and raised the lid of the trap with his own sinister weapon, and probing the depths with the business end of it applied his ear to the other.

'Well?' inquired the inspector presently. 'All O.K.?'

'Nor yet in sight of it,' reported 'Orras gloomily. 'There's something going on somewhere that's beyond me.'

'That's queer.'The inspector meant nothing by it, but 'Orras twisted his neck to get a sight of his superior's face. 'What do you mean it's like?'

'Better have a look yourself,' suggested the junior, making way, while the other closed his book and took his place above the trap. 'Listening posts are more in your line than mine.'

A minute passed in silence as the more experienced man stooped with his ear upon the depression of his stick.

'It's rummy that we should be talking about signalling and what not just now,' he remarked, without raising his head. 'If such a thing was credible I should have said that someone was talking morse along the pipe.'

'Wha'd'z'e say?' inquired 'Orras with languid interest, as he rolled a cigarette.

'Nothing what you might call coherent—just a run of letters. Sos; sos; sos all the time. Half a minute though: isn't there something "S.O.S." stands for?'

'Yes,' agreed 'Orras with expression, 'there is. Sosagers. And very nice too for breakfast.'

'Tchk! Tchk!' clicked the inspector reproachfully. 'Can't you never leave off thinking of food for half a minute,'Orras? There! Now I've got it. S.O.S. It's the signal of distress a sinking ship sends out, of course.'

'Of course. Submarine must ha' come up the main, and now it can't neither turn nor reverse in the narrows. Why ever didn't we think of that at first?'

But the inspector was not to be put off by the cheap humour of irreverent youth. He had not lived five and forty years and gone through the war without discovering that very queer things do occasionally occur in real life. For a moment he twirled a pair of pliers absent-mindedly in his free hand; then kneeling on the pavement he struck the metal fittings down below a succession of measured taps—a score or so.

'What's that?' demanded 'Orras, intrigued in spite of his *blasé* outlook.

'I just sent "Who's there?"' explained the inspector, returning to the listening attitude again. 'They mayn't know the calls and general answer and such like.'

'Seems to me this isn't M.W.B. routine at all,' said the assistant flippantly. 'You must have got through to the cinema somehow, uncle. "Snatched from Death's Jaws" in seven snatches—'

The inspector's right hand shot out in a compelling gesture of warning and repression.

'Get this down, lad,' he said with sharp authority. 'You have a bit o' paper and pencil, haven't you? C-A-R-R—You have a bit o' paper and a pencil, haven't you? C-A-R-R....'

'Right-o,' responded the other, discovering an old Star in his pocket and turning to the 'Stop Press' space. 'C-A-R-R—Carry on, sergeant.'

'-A-D-O-S.'

'Carrados! Why, he's the bloke—'The boy dived into the paper until a head-line caught his eye. 'MISSING BLIND WITNESS. STILL NO TRACE OF MAX CARRADOS.' 'You don't mean to say—'

'Shut it!' snapped the inspector fiercely. 'Attend, can't you? T-R-A-P-P-E-D P-H-O-N-E N-E-A-R-E-S-T P-O-L-I-C-E S-T-A-T-I-O-N U-R-G-E-N-T L-I-F-E D-E-A-T-H-'

'Phew!' murmured 'Orras, perspiring ecstatically. 'That's the stuff to—'

'A-M O-P-E-N-I-N-G L-E-A-K G-U-I-D-E P-O-L-I-C-E R-E-W-A-R-D.'

'Orras drew his breath in sharply, almost overcome by the vista of gain and glory.

'That all?' he whispered meekly.

'S-E-N-D R-T I-F U-N-D-E-R-S-T-O-O-D—you needn't put that last bit in though.'

'Let's see you do it.' 'Orras, subdued by a technical efficiency that lay outside his range, shrewdly foresaw that for the next three weeks at least every word he might condescend to drop would be worth its weight in cigarettes.

The inspector bent down and gave the metal a few considered taps with the pliers.

'That's all. Now slip off into the High Street, boy, and get through on the nearest telephone. And for God's sake don't stop to have your breakfast anywhere on the way, and I shouldn't wonder if this doesn't mean a week's fishing at Southend for us.'

'Garn,' retorted 'Orras, now in a state of giggling bliss. 'A day at Barnes Reservoir more likely. What're *you* going to do?'

'Now hop it,' said the inspector firmly. 'And don't muck up your end of the job. I'm going to look into this leak.'

Ten minutes later he was still tapping the road at intervals when two quite unnoticeable gentlemen appeared in sight, walking that way. As they took in his occupation a few words passed hurriedly between them and instead of passing him they stopped.

"Morning, inspector,' said one affably—he had shot a glance at the official cap. 'Nothing wrong with the water supply up here, I hope?'

'Nothing that I know of, sir,' replied the inspector simply. 'Just our usual rounds.'

'Ah?' said the stranger. 'That so? But it's a hell of a summer, isn't it? Keeps you people busy, I bet. I thought you might be making a round to look at our taps and fittings to see there was no waste.'

'Everything O.K. so far as I have found,' was the reassuring answer. 'We don't like to give any more trouble than we need. As a matter of fact, I'm only waiting for my mate to knock off for breakfast.'

The two nodded pleasantly and passed on. The inspector threw his stick into the hollow of his arm and strolled idly along the road after them, whistling softly to himself, until they turned in at a distant gate. He had a particularly guileless face and mild, speculative eyes.

★★★★★★

As it turned out Mr Murphy and the captain could scarcely have timed their return better from one point of view. They had just entered, seen that everything was, as the genial Irishman took occasion to remark, 'Go'n' on schwimmin'' (there being then about six inches of water in the cellar), and brought up the prisoner to a higher and drier level for a little serious conversation (foreshadowed by certain references to necks and ropes and throats and knives on the captain's part) when a polite knock on the front door called one of them away for a moment. It chanced that the captain was the one who went and he did not immediately return. Noticing this, Mr Murphy was seized by a sudden desire to investigate the rear portion of the grounds, and he rather hurriedly opened a window and dropped down, with the evident intention of proceeding there. In his excitement, however, he had overlooked the presence of several policemen, standing in what he himself would have described as 'sthretgic attitoods', and he fell into their arms to be escorted ingloriously back again. . . .

'Do you know, Mr Murphy, I still have an idea that it will turn out to be the witness-box,' Mr Carrados observed when they all reassembled in the hall—an ignoble thrust admittedly, but much may be forgiven of a man who is carrying half a gallon of cold water after fasting for a couple of days.

LEONAUR

ALSO FROM LEONAUR
AVAILABLE IN SOFTCOVER OR HARDCOVER WITH DUST JACKET

THE EMPIRE OF THE AIR: 1 *by George Griffiths*—*The Angel of the Revolution*—a rich brew that calls to mind Verne's tales of futuristic wars while being original, visionary, exciting and technologically prescient.

THE EMPIRE OF THE AIR: 2 *by George Griffiths*—*Olga Romanoff or, The Syren of the Skies*—the sequel to *The Angel of the Revolution*—a future Earth in which nation states are given full self determination when the Aerians, the descendants of 'The Brotherhood of Freedom,' who have policed world peace for more than a century, decide they are mature enough to have outgrown war.

THE INTERPLANETARY ADVENTURES OF DR KINNEY *by Homer Eon Flint*—*The Lord of Death, The Queen of Life, The Devolutionist & The Emancipatrix.*

ARCOT, MOREY & WADE *by John W. Campbell, Jr.*—The Complete, Classic Space Opera Series—*The Black Star Passes, Islands of Space, Invaders from the Infinite.*

CHALLENGER & COMPANY *by Arthur Conan Doyle*—The Complete Adventures of Professor Challenger and His Intrepid Team-*The Lost World, The Poison Belt, The Land of Mists, The Disintegration Machine* and *When the World Screamed.*

GARRETT P. SERVISS' SCIENCE FICTION *by Garrett P. Serviss*—Three Interplanetary Adventures including the unauthorised sequel to H. G. Wells' *War of the Worlds-Edison's Conquest of Mars, A Columbus of Space, The Moon Metal.*

JUNK DAY *by Arthur Sellings*—". . . . his finest novel was his last, Junk Day, a post-holocaust tale set in the ruins of his native London and peopled with engrossing character types . . . . perhaps grimmer than his previous work but pointedly more energetic." *The Encyclopedia of Science Fiction*

KIPLING'S SCIENCE FICTION *by Rudyard Kipling*—Science Fiction & Fantasy stories by a Master Storyteller including 'As East As A,B,C' 'With The Night Mail'.

DARKNESS AND DAWN 1—THE VACANT WORLD *by George Allen England*—A Novel of a future New York.

DARKNESS AND DAWN 2—BEYOND THE GREAT OBLIVION *by George Allen England*—The last vestiges of humanity set out across America's devastated landscape in search of their dream.

DARKNESS AND DAWN 3—THE AFTER GLOW *by George Allen England*—Somewhere near the Great Lakes, 1000 years from now. Beneath our planet's surface tribes of near human albino warriors eke out an existence in a hostile environment.

www.ingramcontent.com/pod-product-compliance
Lightning Source LLC
Chambersburg PA
CBHW030739030726
47497CB00001B/43